PECHORIN

Alessandro del Guado

faktion

faktion

www.faktionbooks.com

First published by Faktion Books in 2025
Copyright © Faktion Books and Alessandro del Guado

Alessandro del Guado has asserted his right to be identified as the author of this Work in accordance with the Copyright, Designs and Patents Act 1988

Typeset in Goudy Old Style by Laura Kincaid
Cover design by Francesca Neri; cover image from a watercolour by Mikhail Vrubel
Graphic design by Cargo Creative
Printed and bound in Great Britain by Clays Ltd, Elcograf S.p.A.

A CIP catalogue record for this book is available from the British Library

ISBN 978-1-0683603-0-5

MIX
Paper | Supporting responsible forestry
FSC www.fsc.org
FSC® C018072

There remains in my possession another thick notebook, in which Pechorin recounts the events of his whole life. It too will one day be judged by society, but for the moment there are a number of important reasons why I do not dare take upon myself that responsibility.

— Mikhail Lermontov, A Hero of Our Time

CONTENTS

BOOK I

Chapter 1	A Bear in the Window	3
Chapter 2	Gilded Youth	11
Chapter 3	The Stolypins	19
Chapter 4	Vera and Katya	28
Chapter 5	The End of the Affair	38
Chapter 6	A Disappearance	51
Chapter 7	The Fate of Father and Son	60
Chapter 8	The Men of Honour I	71
Chapter 9	*Lèse-majesté*	84
Chapter 10	The Grey General	98

BOOK II

Chapter 11	Stavropol	113
Chapter 12	Taman	125
Chapter 13	Comrades-at-Arms	134
Chapter 14	The Mission of *The Thistle*	143
Chapter 15	His Imperial Majesty	155
Chapter 16	Pyatigorsk	165
Chapter 17	Grushnitsky	175
Chapter 18	Princess Mary	182
Chapter 19	The Eavesdroppers	196
Chapter 20	The Men of Honour II	209

BOOK III

Chapter 21	Maxim Maximych	225
Chapter 22	The Kidnappers	234
Chapter 23	Bela	244
Chapter 24	The Fatalist	252
Chapter 25	Fortress Sudden	262
Chapter 26	Shamyl	273
Chapter 27	The Hand of the Colonizer	284
Chapter 28	Surkhai's Tower	294
Chapter 29	The Siege of Akhulgó	304
Chapter 30	An Honourable Discharge	316

BOOK IV

Chapter 31	The Funeral	329
Chapter 32	The Brethren	338
Chapter 33	*Le Beau Monde*	348
Chapter 34	Sadovaya Street	359
Chapter 35	A Vision	370
Chapter 36	An Old Man's Fondest Wish	378
Chapter 37	A Young Man Looks to the Past	386
Chapter 38	Madame de Hell	394
Chapter 39	The Readiness is All	402
Chapter 40	The Men of Honour III	412
	Epilogue	423

PREFACE

IN ANY BOOK the preface is the first and, at the same time, the last thing; it serves either as an explanation of the aims of the work or as a justification and response to criticism. But readers will usually have no interest either in moral aims or attacks in the pages of literary journals and therefore do not read prefaces. This is a shame, especially in our country. Our public is still so immature and naive that it doesn't understand a fable unless there is a moral lesson at the end. It neither understands jokes nor senses irony; it has, simply, been badly educated. The public still doesn't understand that there is no place for outright abuse in a respectable society and in a respectable book; it doesn't understand that modern refinement has devised a sharper, almost invisible, but no less deadly weapon, which, disguised as flattery, will nonetheless deliver a telling and irresistible blow. Our public is like a provincial, who, overhearing a conversation between two diplomats from warring nations, would conclude that each was guilty of deceiving his own government for the sake of a most tender mutual friendship.

This book has itself suffered the misfortune of being taken literally by certain readers. Others are terribly and seriously offended that such an immoral person is offered to them as an example of a Hero of our Time. Others again have delicately suggested that the author has drawn his own portrait and the portraits of his acquaintances... An old and unfortunate joke! But it seems that Russia has been created in such a way that everything in it renews itself, with the exception of such absurdities. The most magical of magical fairytales would barely avoid the accusation that it is an attempt to slander an individual personality!

This book, my dear ladies and gentlemen, is indeed a portrait, but not just of a single person; it is a portrait composed of all the vices of an entire generation, in their fullest development. You will once again tell me that a person could not be so unpleasant and I will reply that, if you have believed in the existence of so many tragic and Romantic villains, why would you not believe in the reality of Pechorin? If you have admired much more terrible and monstrous inventions, why does this particular character provoke no mercy in you? Perhaps it is because there is more of the truth in him than you would have liked...?

You may say also that morality will not be the victor? Excuse me. People have fed upon sweet delights for long enough. Their stomachs are upset. Strong medicine is required, bitter truths. And do not think that the author of this book has ever harboured the proud dream of himself becoming a corrective to human vice. God save him from such ignorance! The author is simply amused by the idea of describing modern man as he understands him and, unfortunately for us all, as he has too often encountered him. The illness will merely be diagnosed; God only knows how it is to be treated.

Now I must somehow explain the reasons that have led me to make public the intimate secrets of a man I never knew. It would have been easier if I had been his friend: everyone understands the treacherous indiscretion of a true friend. Yet I saw Pechorin only once in my life, on the open road, and therefore cannot feel that inexplicable hatred towards him, which, in the guise of friendship, awaits only the death or misfortune of its object in order to bring down upon him a hail of reproach, advice, ridicule and regret.

On re-reading this book, I am convinced of the sincerity of a person who so mercilessly exposed his own weaknesses and vices. The history of a person's soul, even the least remarkable, is hardly less curious and instructive than the history of an entire people, especially when it is the result of the self-reflection of a mature mind and when it is written without the vainglorious desire to arouse sympathy or amazement. The chief deficiency of Rousseau's *Confessions* is that he read them to his friends.

And so only the desire to be of service has driven me to edit and publish a journal that came into my possession by chance. Although I have changed some personal names, those who are mentioned will doubtless recognise themselves and perhaps even find justifications for the actions of a person who has until now been the object only of accusation; we almost always forgive what we have understood.

Perhaps some readers will want to know my own opinion of Pechorin's character? My answer is that he genuinely was a Hero of Our Time. 'A cruel irony', they will say... I'm not so sure.

BOOK I

CHAPTER ONE

A BEAR IN THE WINDOW

IN THE BEGINNING, I didn't know who he was. He wore the uniform of the Hussars as if it was the first time he'd ever worn it and as if he'd worn it all his life. He came in alone and stood alone by an open window, partly concealed by a large woman in a dress too small for her, made, perhaps, in the last years of the reign of Alexander. His gaze kept returning to the same spot on the far side of the room, but I couldn't tell what drew it there.

At length, his comrades-at-arms revealed to me his name.

'Pechorin!' – cried an impossibly handsome young man in the same uniform – 'I knew you would come!'

The man who had been called Pechorin gave a look that seemed to me one of pain, but his companion, surrounded by a group of young men in an array of uniforms displaying the full glory of the Imperial army, had not noticed.

'I knew you would come, because I knew she would be here. And she is here'.

Pechorin's expression didn't change, but the shadow of the faintest of smiles appeared around one corner of his mouth.

'Come' – said the young man – 'I want to ask Natalya for the *mazurka*... and you must forget your idiotic pride and ask Katya'.

'I will' – Pechorin replied, the pain gone from his eyes.

The two young men moved through the crowd with all due delicacy, stepping aside with equal courtesy for *grand dames* and youthful beauties, their retinue of young officers bringing up the rear, peeling off one by one to engage their chosen or designated objective. As they approached a seating area to one side, the very same upon which Pechorin's gaze had earlier been fixed, they were greeted with a barricade of men's backs, some in military dress, others in the tail-coat of the civil servant.

'Listen here, Mungo' – said Pechorin – 'By the time we fight our way through this wall of masculine virtue, the *mazurka* will be long gone'.

'Nonsense' – replied Mungo, poised in the utter confidence of great beauty – 'Natalya likes nothing better than to disappoint the over-eager... and she has promised Katya that you will be here. Well... I have promised'.

'Pardon me' – he continued, easing himself between a Collegiate Assessor with silver-grey around the temples of his otherwise black hair and a fierce-looking Major, in whom the process of platinization was long ago complete.

Undeterred by their stiff grumbling, Mungo made straight for a young woman with glistening chestnut hair piled high above a face almost as handsome as his own. Her companion, who smiled as Mungo approached, but did not register the presence of Pechorin, still caught between the two older men, was the author of an instantaneous miracle: Mungo and Natalya, the very model of a beautiful couple, the pride or envy of St Petersburg society, depending on who you asked, paled in her presence into stereotype, became merely pleasing adornments, almost unremarkable in comparison with this pale and languorous Eurydice...

'Katya' - said Pechorin in an even voice as he stepped forward.

Pechorin had not laid eyes on Katya Yessentukhova - Princess Yekaterina Ivanovna Yessentukhova of Penza as she was known to the Imperial Court - for seven years. He had then been a boy of sixteen, an unwilling student of Moscow University, innocent in the ways of girls his own age, never mind those such as Katya, a year - and several worlds - older. Back then, he had pressed his lips innocently against those of only two girls. Unlike many young men of the lower nobility, whose apprenticeships in love took place among the hay-lofts of their fathers' - or, in Pechorin's case, his grandmother's - estates, he would have nothing to do with the servant girls, not because of any particular moral scruple, but rather because, in his estimation, they stank. Katya had appeared one summer with her aunt and grandmother, the latter an old friend of Pechorin's own grandmother, whose august and sprawling family was intertwined with every branch of the upper levels of Russian society. Katya had seemed to Pechorin a creature from another dimension, not a girl like those he had known, but a woman, a veteran of Paris and Venice, who might indeed have stepped out of one of the Titians or Michelangelos she had seen there. Grigorii Alexandrovich Pechorin, orphan and prodigy, was in love.

Katya, of course, had not seen Pechorin for those same seven years and now barely recognised the boy she had once disappointed in the assured, almost distant figure who stood before her in full military splendour, the two curt lines of a moustache and the daringly angled sideburns framing his confident face, arresting as it was mysterious. As in a myth reversed, Eurydice looked up into the face of Orpheus and was bedazzled.

'May I have the honour of the *mazurka* later this evening, Katya?' - Pechorin asked softly.

Katya's luminous black eyes became dimmed by a look of consternation.

'I am very sorry, Monsieur Pechorin, but I have already promised the *mazurka* to Monsieur Martynov, whom I believe you know'.

'A pity, but perhaps there will be another occasion' - Pechorin replied, yet more softly.

'I would very much like that' - said Katya, the light in her eyes restored.

'So much for my idiotic pride' - said Pechorin, not looking at Mungo.

They were once again surrounded by men of their own age, men in uniform, newly-minted officers of the Hussars, the Dragoons, and even one or two Engineers. Mungo's older brother Dmitrii, also a Hussar, but more sensible and not quite so handsome, was looking at Pechorin with amused pity.

'You wander back into the company of perhaps the most beautiful young woman in St Petersburg, who probably still thinks of you in short breeches, and imagine she'll melt at first glance!' – said Dmitrii.

'She did' – said Mungo.

'What on earth are you talking about? She refused him!' – exclaimed Dmitrii.

'The poor girl was devastated!' – replied Mungo – 'I was standing right next to her with Natalya... She almost swallowed her tongue when Pechorin stepped out of the crowd. I could see immediately that she was desperately hoping he wouldn't ask, so that she wouldn't have to decline...'.

'And Martynov!' – Dmitrii went on – 'That imbecile! The man thinks that if he cultivates his beard and moustaches and strides around like Don Juan no one will notice that he can barely ride a horse!'

'Come' – said Pechorin at last – 'What would we do for entertainment if we were to be denied the sight each morning of eight limbs moving in different directions...?'

'You mean you're not at all bothered?' – said Mungo.

'Not at all' – Pechorin replied.

'Not at all?' – Mungo asked again.

Some time later, as the ball reached that point when everyone had relaxed, but no one had begun to leave, the general ease was disturbed by shouts and commotion from the far side of the hall. Pechorin was dancing a *quadrille* with a pleasant young woman named Maria, one of his many second-cousins on his grandmother's side of the family.

'Pardon me' – he said with a short bow – 'I must go and see what is happening. I fear my uncle may be involved'.

Mungo, although he was eighteen months younger, was indeed Pechorin's uncle, although he was not, strictly speaking, his Uncle Mungo. His real name was Alexei Arkadevich Stolypin, son of Pechorin's grandmother's brother Arkadii, who had married a girl of twenty – Mungo's mother – at the venerable age of fifty-three. Pechorin had christened him Mungo because, at Military College, the impressionable Alexei's nose had never been out of a French translation of the Scots explorer Mungo Park's *Travels to the Interior Districts of Africa*. Park had known Sir Walter Scott and even spent the last night before embarking on his second, fatal journey to the upper reaches of the Niger at Scott's house at Ashesteil. This had greatly impressed Pechorin, but Mungo was more interested in the book's tales of Moorish prisons and the slaughter of natives as Park's canoe sped through the rapids of the newly discovered Niger. Mungo, like most young men of his age and class, had been reared on fantasies of the conquest of the Caucasus and had even looked upon their towering majesty from the spa towns of Pyatigorsk and Mineralnye Vody on childhood trips... But the Niger... Great Africa... here his youthful imagination took flight beyond even the confines of an Empire that had once seemed to him boundless.

As Pechorin approached he could see the glove of Mungo's left hand clasped perilously in his right, his back straight and chin raised as he glowered at an exceedingly tall, broad-shouldered and, it must be conceded, handsome man, with a mane of black hair flowing back from a tanned, almost muscular face. The effect was crowned, however, in the great dark beard and moustaches, shimmering with a cultivated sheen unmatched in the coiffure of even the most assiduous ladies.

'Monsieur Martynov' – said Mungo – 'The young lady has made it clear that she is indisposed. You have made it clear that you prefer the pleasure of wine to her company – to say nothing of her reputation. Look around you, sir; do you see any one of your comrades in a state of disrepair?'

'What? Half the men here are drunker than I am!' – Martynov replied.

'Yes, and not one of them in uniform' – said Mungo, looking at Martynov with an expression of condescension and pity.

'I won't have it!' – continued Martynov, now shouting – 'I requested the *mazurka* and the *mazurka* I will have!'

The glove twitched in Mungo's right hand.

'That really is too much!' – he cried – 'You are less than a gentleman!'

'And what' – Martynov replied – 'do you propose to do about it?'

'Gentlemen' – said Pechorin in a steady voice, once more stepping forward as if from nowhere – 'The young lady has left; we should follow her example. Mungo – shake hands with Monsieur Martynov. My carriage is waiting outside. I fear you have turned a virtue into a vice; you need a glass of wine. When you've caught up with Monsieur Martynov, we can return to the subject of decorum'.

Martynov looked at Pechorin with dumb suspicion. There were few men in St Petersburg below the rank of Colonel to whom Martynov would defer, but there was something in Pechorin's manner that both provoked and calmed him. He was never quite sure if Pechorin was silently mocking him, but, whenever he sought to explore that possibility, Pechorin would invariably say something to make him feel that his suspicions were entirely foolish. Still, this feeling of foolishness irritated him and he resented Pechorin for it, whether or not he was its cause.

'Where are we going?' – said Martynov.

'Need you ask?' – Pechorin replied.

It was a beautiful June evening, just past the longest day, the kind of evening on which dusk at some exquisite point of equilibrium gave way to dawn, night never managing to intervene. The company approached the house of Count Kuragin, a grand if slightly dilapidated three-storey building near the Imperial stables on Konyushennaya Square. The smell of stale wine caught at the back of Pechorin's throat as he picked his way through the hastily discarded shoes, coats, empty bottles, and sabres littering the floor of the entrance hall; the shouts and laughter from the inner rooms assaulted his ears.

In a doorway stood the Count's son, Anatolii, taller even than Martynov, but as thin as a reed; and swaying like a reed in the wind.

'Gentlemen!' - he cried - 'Gentlemen, welcome! We have dined, we have lost all our money at cards, but we have not run out of wine... and rum!'

Anatolii Kuragin, unique among Pechorin's acquaintances in St Petersburg, was neither officer nor civil servant. He was a man of no profession, living on the generous allowance provided by his father, who also had the good sense to spend the majority of his time at his estate in the countryside.

Kuragin pressed a glass into Pechorin's hand to loud cries of 'drink, drink!', but Pechorin merely passed it to Mungo.

'All in good time' - said Pechorin.

'Drink!' - cried Kuragin - 'Otherwise I won't let you in'.

'We're already in' - Pechorin replied, as Mungo drained the glass and threw it back over his shoulder into the chaos behind him.

The view to an inner room was blocked once again by a wall of gentlemen's backs, but Pechorin knew that the object of their attention could only be the current darling of Russian literature, Ivan Kizhanovsky, whose star had risen steadily since the dramatic emigration of Alexander Pushkin in 1829. Kizhanovsky was known to frequent Kuragin's gatherings and was currently the only person who might attract such a crowd. Where the scandalous nature of much of Pushkin's poetry had been eclipsed only by the scandalous colour of his skin, Kizhanovsky had led a revival of Neoclassicism and catalysed a literature that reflected more faithfully the order and the Imperial ambition of the Court of Tsar Nikolai. Poetry was of little interest to Pechorin these days, an affectation of his youth, no more; the unlikely story of Pushkin's dramatic escape through Arzrum, on the other hand, still exercised great power over his imagination.

Suddenly, from a room on the first floor, there came a roaring sound, which could hardly have been made by mortal man. Pechorin led Mungo, Dmitrii, and Martynov towards the bellowing din, which grew louder and more insistent as they approached. On turning right at the top of the stairs into a wide room with high windows onto the street below, they were greeted by the sight of a young officer of the Guards, holding a bear cub on a leash, playfully restraining it from molesting two of his comrades. In the corner, a French diplomat by the name of de Barante, son indeed of the Ambassador, looked on with faint disgust: these Russians, even the highest-born and most distinguished, were little more than savages.

'Not to your taste, my Gallic friend?' - growled Martynov, draining another glass of Burgundy.

'I see no reason to distress the beast for what you fellows imagine to be entertainment' - replied de Barante.

'What kind of entertainment would you prefer?' - asked Martynov.

'I regret that the entertainment, such as it is, may be over for the evening' - said de Barante.

'Oh-oh-oh!' - wailed Martynov, grabbing a bottle of rum from a side-table - 'This evening is far from over! Would you like to wager some of your ill-gotten gains from the card table that I can't down this bottle in one go?'

Savages, de Barante thought to himself.

'If it amuses you'.

'One hundred Imperial roubles would amuse me greatly!' - replied Martynov.

'A hundred? Are you out of your mind?' - said de Barante - 'I'll give you fifty if you can down it without the bottle leaving your lips... and another ten for your hospital bill'.

'Would it be worth a hundred if he were to perform this great feat sitting on the windowsill with his feet dangling over the edge?' - asked Pechorin.

Mungo and Dmitrii exchanged a resigned look amid shouts and gasps from the gathered throng. The bear cub gave another plaintive roar as the young officer allowed it to rear on its hind legs, its paws falling just short of his comrades, who amused themselves by making expressions of mock terror.

'Pechorin' - said Dmitrii reproachfully - 'He'll kill himself'.

'Hardly' - replied Pechorin - 'We're only a single floor up... and Martynov is made of strong stuff, aren't you my friend?'

'I'll down it in one go standing on my head on that windowsill!' - roared Martynov - 'And no French fop says I can't!'

de Barante looked intently at Pechorin, calculating how best to respond to the insult.

'Very well' - he said at last, to rousing cheers - 'One hundred roubles, sitting on the windowsill facing the street, legs over the edge, and the bottle must not leave your lips'.

The bear cub roared.

People came running in from the other rooms as news of Martynov's latest drunken exploit spread, including Kuragin himself, now drunk almost beyond comprehension. One or two voices were raised in protest, including that of Dmitrii, but Martynov nonetheless began to haul his enormous frame up into the windowsill. The lower part of the window-frame prevented his legs from resting flat, so he kicked it hard with the heel of his boot, smashing the frame and sending splinters falling down onto the street below. Pechorin handed him the bottle.

'On the count of three' - cried a diminutive civil servant, anxious to be involved - 'One-two-three...!'

Martynov, who had already been on the verge of drunkenness at the ball, was by now quite far gone. He swayed slightly in the windowsill, set his great torso, leaned back, and began to drink steadily from the neck of the bottle. The company, hushed for the first time that evening, looked on with every shade of fear, admiration, and disgust; one or two even secretly hoped that Martynov would fall. The expression on de Barante's face displayed every last shred of his loathing, not just for Martynov, but for the entire foul backwater into which his father's posting had dragged him. To think that these crude children had been masters of Paris in the year of his birth! Only Pechorin and the bear cub were indifferent, the bear still trying to paw at its tormentors, while Pechorin's cool gaze remained fixed not on Martynov, but on de Barante.

As the bottle slowly drained, so the angle of Martynov's back slowly approached the horizontal, until at last, with a great inrush of breath, he drained the last drop and crashed back into the room, coming to rest face down and near insensible amid a huddle of concerned faces. de Barante walked quietly over to the great prone hulk, scattered some banknotes on Martynov's back, and left.

An hour or so later, Pechorin was sitting in Kuragin's dining room with Mungo and Dmitrii, all three watching as Martynov gulped down great mouthfuls of dumplings and coffee. The bear cub lay sleeping peacefully in the corner, its leash tethered to a leg of the table. They were soon joined by Kuragin and an officer by the name of Dolokhov, who for reasons no one could fathom rented a room in Kuragin's house. The rest of the company had departed, some for home, others for the darker pleasures of the St Petersburg night.

'Let's go to Madame Lefortier's' - suggested Kuragin.

Dolokhov and Martynov, still chomping on his dumplings, nodded assent, while Mungo looked inquiringly at Dmitrii.

'Shall we?' - he said brightly.

'I'm not so sure, it's late' - replied Dmitrii.

'It's barely one o'clock' - said Mungo - 'Let's go'.

'What about you, Monsieur Pechorin?' - asked Kuragin with a tired, sly smile.

'Not for me' - Pechorin replied - 'I have business to attend to'.

'Business? At this hour?' - said Martynov, taking a last gulp of coffee and rising to leave - 'You're a strange fellow, Pechorin. Either that or you're lying'.

Pechorin arrived back at Tsarskoe Seló at around three. He dismissed the coachman and strode into his quarters, where old Gavril, the manservant his grandmother had insisted on, was asleep fully clothed on the divan Pechorin had installed at the far end of the kitchen.

'Wake up, old boy' - Pechorin said cheerfully - 'Are there any messages for me?'

Gavril got to his feet in an instant, with the automatic vigour of an old soldier, but his mind was slow to follow.

'Are there any messages for me?' - Pechorin said again, with just a hint of impatience in his voice.

'Yes, sir' - Gavril replied - 'There is a letter for your Honour, delivered by hand just before midnight... it's on the night-table by your bed'.

Pechorin rushed through to the bedroom, threw himself on the bed, and tore open the envelope.

My Darling Grigorii,
I know you will be angry that I am not there as I promised, but I know also that you will forgive me when you know the reason why. As I told you in my last letter, after we buried my poor father last week, I intended to remain here until all the relatives had departed and to return to St Petersburg this evening. I had assumed that my brother Alexei would remain on the estate to deal with my father's affairs; but Alexei now says he can't bear to stay here for a moment longer. I suspect he has other reasons to wish to be back in St Petersburg... he is suddenly a very rich young man, after all. We quarrelled for the entire day yesterday and I was eventually able to persuade him that he could not simply walk out without settling my father's affairs; we agreed that he would remain until the day after tomorrow. I wasn't able to get away today, partly because of our quarrelling, which has quite exhausted me. But I will come tomorrow, whatever Alexei says. We must wait just one more day. Say you will forgive me! I thought my heart would burst here without you, but the thought that you are angry with me... please, I beg you, say you will forgive me and that we will soon be together! Write to me at the St Petersburg address, tell me what you wish me to do... but please, my darling, forgive me!
Forever yours,
Vera

Pechorin threw the letter into the embers still glowing in the hearth, sat down at his desk, and scribbled a brief note in reply. He returned to the kitchen, where Gavril was fiddling with the *samovar*.

'Would your Honour like some tea before retiring?' - he asked, sensing Pechorin's agitation.

'No, that will be all... get yourself off to bed, old man. But make sure this goes with the boy who rides with the regimental post first thing in the morning; not the post itself, you understand, and give him twenty kopecks' - Pechorin replied, handing Gavril the note and a coin.

'Certainly, your Honour. Goodnight'.

'Goodnight, Gavril' - said Pechorin as he returned to the empty bedroom.

CHAPTER TWO

GILDED YOUTH

PECHORIN KNEW WHY Alexei Lopatkin had insisted on returning to St Petersburg with such unseemly haste after his father's funeral. Alexei was an official in the Ministry of War, a position chosen and secured for him by his father, who had insisted that war itself was no occupation for his beloved – and only – son. Alexei's position was respectable enough, head of an office in the department for military requisitions, soon to bring him the title of Collegiate Assessor. It was no position, however, from which to pursue Katya Yessentukhova. With the estate near Pskov, which guaranteed him 30,000 a year, the house on the Moika Canal in St Petersburg, and the pile of cash the old man was reputed – although Vera denied it – to have secreted in a locked drawer of his desk... well, this was the kind of eligibility that made an officer's uniform look like little more than a pantomime costume.

Alexei had worshipped Katya from afar, occasionally passing a brief remark at a recital or even, when he was feeling particularly bold, engaging her for a *quadrille* on the rare occasion he attended a ball. Pechorin knew this not because he had witnessed it, or because he had heard it from the lips of Alexei himself, but because he had been told by Sasha Vereschagina, a cousin of Vera and Alexei and a distant relative of Pechorin (Sasha was the niece of the second wife of one of Pechorin's great-uncles, Alexander Stolypin). Why Sasha had been so keen to provide Pechorin with the details of an event that had not happened – and, as far as Pechorin was concerned, never would – was a mystery to him, confounding his habitual confidence in his grasp of feminine psychology. Sasha may have harboured undeclared designs on Alexei herself, but this, too, seemed unlikely. She had nonetheless conceived the opinion that Katya, whose intelligence and constancy Sasha judged to be as lacking as her beauty was indisputable, would be a disastrous match for Alexei; and the more she convinced herself of the undesirability of such a match, the more vividly she conjured it into the realms of possibility. Pechorin had mockingly assured her that she had nothing to fear, and on two counts: first, he declared, Alexei Lopatkin would imagine himself deceased and gone to heaven if Katya were to return even a shred of his barely visible affections; further, and therefore, he was convinced that Alexei was in fact more likely to rise up to the heavens before their very eyes than to succeed in his undeclared pursuit. Convinced, that is, until now: Alexei's sudden inheritance had changed everything.

Sasha knew – in fact, everyone knew – of Pechorin's former affections for Katya. She had therefore decided that Pechorin, now a dashing figure in his Hussar's uniform and perhaps burning with unrequited love for Katya, might act as the force that would keep Alexei and Katya apart. What Sasha did not know was that Vera was hopelessly and secretly in love with Pechorin.

Pechorin slept until after mid-day and rose to find Gavril once more prone on the divan at the back of the kitchen.

'What are you doing there that's such hard work, old boy? Spitting at the ceiling and trying each time to hit the same spot?'

The old man was on his feet in an instant.

'Tea, your Honour?'

'Yes, Gavril, that would be very pleasant. Did my note go with the boy this morning?'

'Yes, sir, of course, your Honour'.

'Very well. Tell the coachman to prepare the horses... and remind the cook that I won't be dining at home this evening'.

On entering Military College two years previously, Pechorin had insisted on clear terms with his grandmother: she would provide him with an allowance of 250 a month while he lived in barracks, then rising to 500 when he passed out, which would allow him to rent quarters at Tsarskoe Seló, complete with manservant, cook, coachman and carriage. The old woman had agreed with surprising ease, throwing in an additional sum of 1000 roubles for the purchase of a sabre befitting his new status, uniform, tack for the horses, and other such sundries necessary for the life of a young officer in the Imperial capital.

The carriage for which his grandmother's money had paid came to a halt outside a once grand house on Sadovaya Street, the lower floor of which was now rented to a merchant and his family, leaving more than ample room for Sasha Vereschagina and her mother on the upper storey. Pechorin rang the bell and, hearing a woman's voice from above, entered the narrow hallway and mounted the stairs; the Vereschagins were long past the point where they were able to retain servants.

'We're in here' - came a clear bright voice from a room to the right.

From the doorway, Pechorin observed a most touching scene. Sasha was sitting in a high-backed armchair, her neatly trimmed hair, almost as short as a young gentleman's, framing quite the most intelligent face he could remember seeing on the body of a woman. She wore a pale grey dress with a high, round collar, which made her look taller than she in fact was. Her inquisitive green eyes were trained on the back of another young woman, seated at the piano.

'I really don't feel like playing' - said the woman at the piano without turning round.

'Then you must not' - said Sasha - 'Come and sit by me'.

'Play, Vera' - Pechorin said in a soft but commanding tone.

The young woman at the piano wheeled around on the stool, her look of surprise quickly replaced by a blushing smile. She had a quiet, almost mournful beauty, her fair hair held in a French *bandeau*, the dimple on her right check crowned by a perfect black beauty spot, so often imitated by less fortunate ladies of a bygone age. It therefore gave Vera a slightly old-fashioned air; she was only two years older than Pechorin, but seemed, even sitting here alongside Sasha, a woman of substance. Just as quickly as her surprise had given way to a blush and a smile, so now Vera was seized by a silent thought as both smile and blush gave way in turn to a demure but not uninterested outward demeanour.

'Monsieur Pechorin' – she said in an even voice – 'How very pleasant to see you'.

'I am delighted' – Pechorin replied – 'Charmed to see you both. I must say first of all, however, how very sorry I was to hear of your father's passing'.

'You are very kind, Monsieur Pechorin. My brother and I were touched by the many expressions of condolence we received'.

'Vera was just telling me that Alexei will be returning to St Petersburg tomorrow, much earlier than he had originally planned' – said Sasha.

'We must do what we can to help him overcome his grief' – Pechorin said cheerfully.

Sasha gave him a look of muted indignation.

'I hardly think he will be seeking public company so soon after recent events' – she said.

'Nonsense' – replied Pechorin – 'Why else would he have returned? Perhaps some of those beauties who barely knew who he was will find their interest piqued by his newly acquired position in society. I saw the lovely Princess Yessentukhova yesterday evening, for example; remarkable that such a woman has not yet acquired a husband'.

Pechorin could see that Sasha was struggling to disguise her annoyance.

'I must quickly have a word with my mother' – she said, rising from her chair – 'I won't be long'.

When Sasha had left, Pechorin turned to Vera, still sitting with her back to the piano.

'Listen, Vera, pay no attention to Sasha's "so soon after recent events" and so on... it will look all the more strange if you *don't* come this evening'.

'No, no' – Vera replied – 'I can't possibly come. I couldn't bear to have to disguise my feelings all evening. Come to me later, when the servants are asleep; enter through the little door from the rear courtyard... you know the one'.

'I will' – Pechorin replied – 'But don't you think it will look rather strange if you aren't here? Sasha will insist'.

'Sasha told me you asked Princess Yessentukhova for the *mazurka* last night? I couldn't bear to see you with her' – said Vera, her voice trembling

'You have nothing to fear in that respect' – replied Pechorin, his face downturned.

Pechorin spent the late afternoon strolling in the Summer Gardens, before calling on Mungo and Dmitrii at the house their late father had bequeathed to them near the Anichkov Bridge. Arkadii Stolypin, of whom Pechorin retained only the dimmest memories from childhood, was brother to his grandmother and his great-uncle Afanasii, and a now mythical symbol of the Stolypins' ambivalent position in St Petersburg society. Arkadii, like his brother Afanasii, had served with distinction at Borodinó alongside the then youthful General Velyaminov, before embarking, like Afanasii after him, on a career in the civil service. He was also, however, a close friend of the Decembrist poet Ryleyev; when that tragic figure was executed in July 1826, alongside Pestel, Bestuzhev-Riumin, Muravev-Apostol, and Kakhlovsky, their remaining comrades exiled to hard labour or transferred as privates to the Caucasus, Arkadii had come forward without a moment's hesitation to read the elegy at Ryleyev's funeral. Alexander Stolypin, Pechorin's grandmother's eldest brother, also decorated for valour during the campaign against Bonaparte, was a friend of Pestel, but had died in January of the same year, before the sweeping investigation into the Decembrist uprising could implicate him. 'Such breeding!', Pechorin thought to himself as he smoked a little cigar in the French style and limited himself to a single glass of Burgundy.

When they arrived at Sasha Vereschagina's *soirée*, the drawing room was already full, bustling with the usual mix of young officers, *littérateurs*, and young ladies of varying degrees of beauty and eligibility. Pechorin recognised Lieutenant Sinyukhaev and a couple of the other younger officers from the regiment, Gromov and Molnitsky. Sinyukhaev was a rather gloomy and unremarkable fellow; but at least he wasn't Martynov, whose imposing frame could not be mistaken in such a gathering. On the far side of the room Pechorin could see Sviatoslav Blagodatsky and his friend Afanasyev, both civil servants in the department that administered state property, deep in conversation with Sasha and Vera. Blagodatsky's mother had been orphaned during the Pugachev rebellion and subsequently brought up as a sister to Pechorin's grandmother, who later became the young Sviatoslav's godmother. Blagodatsky, like his father before him, was a graduate of Moscow University; he more than anyone – perhaps more even than Pechorin's grandmother – had been devastated by Pechorin's decision to leave the university and become an officer. Six years older than Pechorin, Blagodatsky was, in word and deed, if not by blood, the uncle that Mungo was not; his presence at such occasions was therefore, and notwithstanding Pechorin's deep affection for him, a source of slight discomfort.

Mungo filled Pechorin's glass with Burgundy and beckoned him towards a cold buffet that had been arranged on a table set against the far wall of the drawing room.

'Katya was very upset last night' – Mungo began – 'But that fool Martynov won't get in your way this evening'.

'Get in my way?' – Pechorin replied – 'What makes you think he's in my way?'

'I know he's not any kind of serious threat, but all the same... he did get in your way with his drunken foolery'.

'You misunderstand me, dear Mungo... What I mean to say is this: what makes you so sure that my way leads to M-elle Yessentuhkova? You overestimate my interest in her and, by the same token, her receptivity to me'.

'Nonsense!' - said Mungo - 'A beauty like that, for whom you fell at a very tender age, now quite dazzled by the man you have become. Natalya told me everything before she left: Katya could barely believe you were the same person'.

'We shall see' - said Pechorin, looking around the room - 'Now pull down your cuffs and unfasten that cravat, there's a good man'.

Pechorin moved steadily through the crowded room, Mungo following, towards a group of young women, resplendent in the fashion of the age. Mungo's handsome face brightened as he caught sight of Natalya among the group, laughing at something Katya Yessentukhova had said, grasping at the arm of a dark-haired, olive-skinned young woman neither he nor Pechorin had previously met. This was Nina Kireyeva, a cousin of Natalya who was visiting from Moscow, but whose ancestral home must have been Georgia or Armenia. Pechorin seized two glasses of champagne from a tray floating past and signalled Mungo to do the same. When they reached the spot where the ladies were standing, Mungo handed one glass to Natalya with a low bow and clinked the other against it. Pechorin handed one of his glasses to Nina and, after a moment's pause, the other to Katya. From across the room, Sasha rewarded him for this hesitation with a fleeting glance of reproach. Vera's face was turned towards the window.

'Ladies, it is an honour and a pleasure' - said Pechorin - 'But I must beg your indulgence for a few minutes; my coachman has not had his instructions'.

He gave a low bow, turned on his heels, and left the room.

As the evening progressed, little groups formed among the gathered throng, in ways that only the most obtuse observer would have failed to understand: Mungo managed to steer Natalya to a corner of the room next to a high window, where, in the warm light of the summer evening, they engaged in a silent mime-play, full of significant gesture; Dmitrii and Sinyukhaev chattered much less dramatically with Sasha; the Princess Yessentukhova found herself the object of the ardent and excitable attention of the two younger officers and many more besides; and Pechorin, restrained only by the presence of Blagodatsky and Afanasyev, loudly entertained the newcomer Nina Kireyeva with epigrams, witticisms and, of course, compliments. Vera flitted from the edge of one company to another, remaining for little more than a minute or two in any one place, seemingly distracted by something beyond the tall, light-filled windows.

After a while, the silent conversation between Mungo and Natalya became more animated. Mungo's contentment to be on the fringes of society, alone with the object of his affections, was suddenly in conflict with Natalya's insistence that he had a role to play beyond that of devoted suitor. Disguising his disappointment, he led Natalya to join Sasha, Dmitrii, and Sinyukhaev, still deep in apparently serious conversation, at which point Vera also came to join them. Mungo bowed with an imperceptible sigh and continued on to Pechorin's group, now swollen in number by many of the younger officers and ladies, who had happily become an audience for Pechorin's impromptu performance.

'Madame, I replied' - he heard Pechorin say as he approached - 'your daughter has many virtues, but virtue is assuredly not one of them'.

The company laughed; Pechorin merely made a curt bow, glancing up at Nina.

'Listen here, Pechorin' - said Mungo, drawing him to one side - 'You haven't said a word to Katya all evening... I thought you were intending to press your case?'

'I am' - Pechorin replied.

'Yes, with M-elle Kireyeva, but not with Katya. Have you seen the look on her face?'

'Quite' - said Pechorin - 'Watching me entertain M-elle Kireyeva will have more effect than a month of ardent pursuit'.

'Well, I hope you know what you're doing. You must at least speak to her before the end of the evening'.

'I will' - said Pechorin.

'You're quite the master of ceremonies, Grigorii Alexandrovich' - said Blagodatsky, coming to join them.

'I do my best' - Pechorin replied with a smile - 'What harm is there in entertaining ourselves if it involves entertaining others?'

'Quite so' - Blagodatsky replied - 'But I do hope they're still laughing in the final act. Light comedy is so much preferable to tragedy...'.

Pechorin and his grandmother had lived with Blagodatsky when they first arrived in St Petersburg in the tumultuous summer after he had left the university and set about gaining entry to Military College. Blagodatsky had known Pechorin since he was a child, recognizing in him great intellectual promise, but also a wilful and destructive tendency, which was just as frequently directed at himself as at others and society at large. Blagodatsky judged Pechorin's decision to leave university to be just such an act of self-destruction, a demonstration to his grandmother that his will would henceforth countermand her own, whatever the cost to either of them. Blagodatsky had not imagined, however - for he could not imagine - that Pechorin also intended quite specifically to reject learning: the young Pechorin had once resolved to give his life to study and thought, but realised quite suddenly that they would not even provide him with the basics of existence. He was not willing to wait for the old woman to die before becoming master of his own fate.

'I am very much in favour of comedy' - Pechorin replied, smiling again at

Blagodatsky and shaking him by the hand.
He then nodded to Mungo and set off across the room.

Katya's face was a study in composure as Pechorin approached, while Sasha struggled to suppress a smile of satisfaction; only Vera did not look in his direction.

'Good evening Princess Yessentukhova, good evening ladies' - he said, bowing and taking each of their hands in turn and grazing each in turn with a polite kiss, before turning solemnly to Dmitrii and Sinyukhaev - 'And good evening to you, too, gentlemen'.

'Good evening, Monsieur Pechorin' - Katya replied in a soft voice - 'You are, it would seem, a great success, with the young ladies as much as the young gentlemen'.

'Amusement' - as I was just saying to my dear friend Blagodatsky - 'is a coin with two perfectly smooth sides'.

'You like to be amused?' - Katya asked, with a daring that surprised even Pechorin.

'I am not against it' - Pechorin replied - 'But, as you have seen, I prefer to amuse. In any case, I wanted above all to apologise for yesterday evening; I believe I was, quite unintentionally, the cause of some distress'.

'Not at all' - Katya replied - 'You are not responsible for Monsieur Martynov. It is regrettable only that I had not received an invitation prior to his appearance, which might have saved us all what you call distress'.

'In future' - said Pechorin in an even tone - 'I will ensure that the opportunity for distress does not arise; although I can only aspire, not promise, to amuse you'.

Pechorin at last drew his gaze from Katya. Dmitrii and Sinyukhaev, models of courtesy, affected to be engaged in a conversation of their own; Sasha, on the other hand, had followed every word of his exchange with Katya without concealing her interest and now beamed as if she herself had been its object. When he looked for Vera, however, she was nowhere to be seen.

As Pechorin descended the stairs of the Vereschagin house, the silk glove Katya had pressed into his hand as she departed in the pocket of his tunic, he thought once again of that summer seven years past, when he had gathered his courage to bestow a single white lily upon the confused Katya, only to find it trampled into the dirt and straw in the courtyard after she and her grandmother had left. His carriage stood obediently in the dim, flickering light of a phosphorous lamp, which added a purely theatrical effect to the deep blue of the half-night. The lamplighter stood by the carriage, entertaining Pechorin's coachman with incredible tales of what he claimed to have seen from his vantage point atop the city's lamp-posts. In the distance, God only knows where, another light glimmered in the window of a watchman's box, which seemed to stand at the very edge of the world.

'Home, your Honour?' - asked the coachman.

'No' – Pechorin replied, glaring with undisguised menace at the lamplighter. The carriage made its way along the Moika Canal.

'Wait for me here' – said Pechorin.

He stepped down quietly and walked on for a hundred yards or so, before turning through an arch into the courtyard of the Lopatkin house. Pechorin pushed gently on a low door in the wall to the right, which he knew Vera had left open for him, and stooped slightly as he went through it. He moved quickly through the blue light of the deserted kitchen and found another door, which led to a hidden, narrow spiral staircase. Pechorin could not dispel from his mind the thought of how, fifty, sixty years ago, some fortunate young man, now rotting in his grave, might have ascended this very same staircase at this very same hour, his hair styled *à l'oiseau royal*, clutching his three-cornered hat to his beating heart, rushing to a secret assignation with some Countess, now also beyond the reach of earthly cares, troubled only by beetles and worms.

Pechorin stepped out into the hallway on the first floor. A servant lay asleep in an armchair under a standing lamp. Pechorin made his way past with a light, purposeful step. The drawing room was in almost total darkness, but for the weak light filtering through from the lamp in the hallway. A door on the right led to Alexei's office; Pechorin turned left and stepped into Vera's bedroom.

CHAPTER THREE

THE STOLYPINS

THE ROAD SOUTH from St Petersburg to Pechorin's grandmother's estate at Serednikovo to the north-west of Moscow was not quite as he remembered it. Two years had passed since he had made the journey in the opposite direction, then in the company of his grandmother, a woman apparently defeated by his decision to leave the university. Two years ago, Pechorin was exhilarated by the sudden consciousness of his own power: at a stroke, he had not only rejected learning in favour of a life of adventure, he had also finally exposed the weakness of his grandmother's authority over him, which had seemed an immovable fact of life for as long as he could remember. As he returned to the heart of that fallen Empire, however, he reflected that the power he thought he had seized was, if not quite illusory, at least extremely limited: authority, he had begun to understand, was not something that could be thrown over once and for all.

His grandmother's presence, mediated through her vast network of connections in the capital, but embodied in the seemingly eternal, impregnable actuality of Serednikovo, co-existed there with an equally unshakeable sense of absence. Pechorin's mother had died at Serednikovo when he was two years old; the child, of course, had no recollection of her death, or of her life, but he grew up in the space of her loss, for which he became, for his grandmother, the only compensation. He had no recollection, either, of his father leaving the estate and him in the care of his grandmother or, more properly, a stream of governesses and tutors. Besides his grandmother, Pechorin's recollection began with the first of these, a German governess by the name of Rhemer, to whom he owed his knowledge of that language and its literature: and perhaps also his tendency to seek reassurance in the company of women. His grandmother, eventually intuiting this unwelcome predilection, abruptly got rid of the unfortunate young woman after nearly three idyllic years. The boy was bereft, sullenly determined, even at the age of eight, to visit revenge on this old woman with the absolute power to obliterate the object of his childish affections.

Fraulein Rhemer was replaced by a certain James Swinson, an Englishman by birth, who introduced the precocious and impressionable boy to the Scots ballads: the tale of Thomas the Rhymer, in particular, who agreed to accompany the Faerie Queen to Elfland in return for the gift of prophecy, had conquered Pechorin's imagination. Thomas had disappeared without a word, later returning with supernatural powers, but with the proviso that he must return to the underworld whenever the Faerie Queen might choose to summon him. His grandmother's banishment of Fraulein Rhemer and the fate of his father seemed to merge in the figures of Thomas and the Faerie Queen.

It was Swinson, however, who would next suffer this fate. Pechorin woke one morning in summer to find him gone. He would never know that the learned Englishman did not share his own later aversion to the servant girls.

His grandmother then subjected the growing boy to a revolving cast of Englishmen and Frenchmen, which had broadened the range of his reading and prepared him impeccably for life in the *haut monde*, but had no doubt also sealed his fate with regard to institutions of learning. All the childish frustration with his powerlessness in the face of his grandmother – and his unconscious anger and despair at his father's absence – he poured into the daily battle with these hired pedants: if they insisted he read Byron, he would conspicuously walk through the gardens with a volume of Shelley in hand (reserving Byron for his clandestine, candle-lit bedside); if they insisted he read Racine, he would casually pick up a copy of Constant's *Adolphe* and declare that poetry was dead. Each time the conflict would come to a point of crisis; and each time *grandmaman*, repentant of her treatment of Fraulein Rhemer, would sacrifice discipline on the altar of her love for *grand-fils*, serially dispensing with the services of these most learned gentlemen. Only Swinson had managed to win Pechorin's favour and he, like his father, had disappeared quite without the exercise of the boy's will.

As Pechorin's carriage approached the gates of Serednikovo, he imagined himself slipping through the hedge at the far side of the little lake, like Thomas the Rhymer, never to be seen again. His daydream was interrupted by the shouts of the gateman, instructing a boy to run to the house and tell them the young gentleman had arrived, while himself hauling open the heavy gates. Pechorin's carriage rolled unevenly through the gates, skirted the ornamental French garden his late grandfather had planted in front of the main house, and came to rest in a courtyard by the stable block.

'Should I have the bags taken to your Honour's bedroom?' – asked Innokentii the valet, who seemed several times older than Pechorin's memory of him.

'No' – Pechorin replied – 'Put them in one of the guest rooms at the back of the house'.

Pechorin's grandmother was born Yelizaveta Alexeyevna Stolypina, daughter of Alexei Stolypin, a favourite of the Court of Catherine the Great. Alexei was one of the first beneficiaries of the granting of state licenses for the sale of vodka, which had the effect of increasing the quality of the product, while at the same time enriching the limited circle of the nobility to whom licenses were granted. By the time she reached the age of consent, Yelizaveta and her brothers and sister stood at the heart of a network of cousins, second cousins, aunts, uncles, nephews and nieces that reached into every corner of St Petersburg society. The young Yelizaveta, a prize for any man notwithstanding her lack of beauty, had married Mikhail Arsenyev, whose kindness and constancy were not equal to the sudden change in his social status. Mikhail had not, despite his many qualities, borne well the burden of such elevation and died in mysterious circumstances on New Year's Day at the not so ripe age of forty-one, leaving Yelizaveta a widow at the age – catastrophic for women in those times – of thirty-six. The circumstances surrounding Alexei's sudden death gave rise to the usual course of rumour in the surrounding area and one young man, while a fellow student at Moscow University, had been bold enough to relate to Pechorin the most intricate of the many myths that had grown up around his late grandfather. Pechorin's grandfather, the young man asserted, had played the role of Rosencrantz – or Guildenstern – in a family production of *Hamlet* at Serednikovo on New Year's Eve... and had hung himself from a beam in the hayloft in the early hours of the next morning. Pechorin had remained calm, pointing out that the performance was based on Sumarokov's translation of *Hamlet*, as opposed to Viskovatov's later, more complete translation: Sumarokov, Pechorin informed the mesmerized young man, had produced more of a free adaptation than a strict translation, not only significantly abridging the play, but excising Rosencrantz, Guildenstern, and the gravedigging scene in its entirety.

'Grandmaman' – said Pechorin, entering the drawing room – 'What a great pleasure it is to see you'.

Grandmaman was an imposing woman in her late fifties, dressed in a style that had seemed the very height of European sophistication during the reign of Alexander, but which now marked her as precisely what she was: an old woman, clinging to a past that would never return, her hopes and dreams tenuously invested in the young man – her only grandson – who now stood before her, resplendent in a uniform unaffected by changing fashion.

'Grigorii, my dear boy' – she said in a voice struggling to mask her emotion – 'How splendid you look... How well your new status suits you'.

'Thank you, *Grandmaman*' – Pechorin replied – 'I am glad you are happy'.

His grandmother's disappointment, her confusion, her fears, had been a constant, if distant, factor throughout his two years in St Petersburg, two years in which they had communicated only by letter. She had accompanied him to the city, half hoping he might change his mind and enrol instead at St Petersburg University. They lodged with Blagodatsky, who had nurtured Pechorin's extraordinary intellectual gifts since childhood and was also quietly devastated by his decision. While the grandmother petitioned Blagodatsky for support, appealing to what she knew to be his own convictions, that sophisticated soul had understood that Pechorin's actions were not directed at their persons, but rather were a necessary expression of his own autonomy – even maturity. Blagodatsky had also understood, therefore, that Pechorin's mind would not be changed and that the best course of action was to allow, even encourage, his self-determination; if only it could be channelled in a direction that might not lead to the dissolution his grandmother feared. Blagodatsky's tentative suggestion that the Officer Corps might be an appropriate environment for someone with Pechorin's temperament and capabilities was at first met with doubt: she had been surrounded by officers, including her late husband and her brothers, all her life, and therefore knew very well that an officer's epaulettes were no guarantee of respectability. Her doubts were eventually dispelled, however, by the intervention of her nephew, the son of her sister Natalya, who also bore the name Mungo had all but forgotten, Alexei Stolypin. Alexei had himself been a Hussar, before being appointed to a position of some responsibility at the Imperial Court. With the choral support of Blagodatsky, Alexei also pointed to the example of Dmitrii Stolypin, who had already enrolled at the Military College: after all, what finer exemplar of young Russian manhood could there be, particularly viewed through the *lorgnette* of a Russian grandmother? She had almost baulked at the price upon which Pechorin insisted – the allowance, the provision for his household once he had passed out – but here again his will prevailed: even in consenting to a course of action that had been far from her ideal, she could not refuse his demands.

Pechorin and his grandmother chatted amiably enough for an hour or so, she enquiring about his uncles, old and young, about cousins and acquaintances, he attempting to satisfy her curiosity without revealing anything significant about his personal life or habits. At length, the old woman became dissatisfied by his polite evasions.

'Irina Alexandrovna wrote to me last week' – she said, not looking directly at her grandson.

'Does she often write?' – asked Pechorin, affecting not to grasp the point of his grandmother's remark, leafing through an edition of the *Revue Étrangère* he had acquired just before leaving St Petersburg.

'No, not so often these days; and she hasn't visited in years. She clearly felt there was something important that she wished to convey to me'.

'Oh, and what was that?' – Pechorin replied, persisting in his feigned ignorance.

'She tells me that you saw Katya' – said the old woman in an even tone.

Pechorin continued to leaf casually through the pages of the journal, not lifting his eyes to his grandmother.

'It would hardly be possible not to see her in St Petersburg society' – he replied – 'And I might say the same of any number of young ladies, many of them also the nieces and grand-daughters of your unmatched circle of acquaintances'.

The old woman paused for a second, now looking straight at Pechorin's downturned head.

'I know how you suffered that summer' – she said.

'That summer was a lifetime ago' – Pechorin replied, still not looking directly at his grandmother – 'I must change for dinner. I bid you good afternoon, *Grandmaman*'.

He rose, kissed the old woman on her forehead, and made his way to the guest room at the back of the house.

Dinner that evening was entirely ruined by Pechorin's insistence that he would stay for only two days, although he suspected that the brevity of his visit was not as much of an issue as his intended destination, his late father's old estate at Kropotovo.

'What on earth will you do there?' – his grandmother asked – 'I have told you on a number of occasions that we should sell that dilapidated old ruin and every one of the creatures who populate it. You will inherit this place, after all'.

'Then I'll have two estates' - Pechorin replied - 'For the moment, I have only one'.

When Pechorin's father died and his grandmother was making the necessary arrangements for the management of the estate his father had left to him, the old woman also revealed that she had made him the sole beneficiary of her own estate many years before. At the time, the boy wasn't concerned to ask when this had been done, but he gradually came to associate it, quite naturally, with his mother's death and, for reasons that were less clear, with his father's departure.

'I like it there' - Pechorin continued - 'I'll ride the horses and read my books and rest'.

'You can do all that here' - said his grandmother - 'And besides, your great-uncle Afanasii will be here in three days; wouldn't you like to see him?'

'Grandmaman, I see him frequently in St Petersburg. He won't be in the least offended if I'm not here'.

'But I would like you to speak to him about Kropotovo. You'll listen to him, dear, even if I know you won't listen to me'.

Afanasii was Pechorin's grandmother's younger brother, who had, like his late brother Alexander, distinguished himself in combat, particularly in the glorious campaign of 1812. Afanasii had retired from military service at the grand old age of twenty-nine and entered the civil service, quickly rising through the ranks, just as he had done as a young officer. Now, approaching fifty, he was adviser to the Grand-Duke Mikhail, brother of Tsar Nikolai. Pechorin respected Afanasii for his military past, for his discretion, and for a certain understated manliness, which set him apart from the rather fey gentlemen of his age who moved in Court circles, as well as from the loud, bristling men of action who dominated the younger generation and had even risen to positions of some influence in certain government departments. At the same time, he maintained a respectful distance from Afanasii, suspecting that, his grandmother now rarely gracing the capital with her presence, it was he who formed the focal point of the Stolypin network, not quite doing the old woman's bidding, but ensuring that her influence had not entirely diminished.

'And what will he advise me about Kropotovo?'

'To sell'.

'Ah, but then there is no need for me to hear it from his lips. I am indebted to you, Grandmaman' - Pechorin said with a smile.

He rose the next morning before the household was awake, saddled one of the horses by himself, and set off around the perimeter of the sprawling estate. It, too, seemed to him much different than it had two summers ago, although in truth nothing at all had changed. He walked his horse past the little folly his great-grandfather had built towards the southern boundary, where he had spent all too fleeting moments with Katya Yessentukhova. He had been in love - the love of youth, naive, foolish love, but love all the same - whereas Katya had only indulged him, grateful for his attention, fearful of disturbing the ease between their two families. Pechorin recalled the moment he had understood that she was engaged in diplomacy, as opposed to courtship, and experienced again the pain of realization as if it had only just come to him. When Katya had given him one of her gloves on the eve of his recent departure from St Petersburg, a token of her willingness to erase the memory of the past, she had whispered: 'You were a child... We were both children'.

Pechorin took the glove from his waistcoat pocket. As he looked down at the slender fold of soft white silk, he tried to imagine the two of them, sitting together in some drawing room, the light streaming in from the tall windows as Katya played the piano or quietly took to her embroidery. He felt again the same pain of realization, the pain of a loss that could never be recovered. And suddenly into his mind's eye there came an image of Vera, not at the piano as he had seen her at Sasha Vereschagina's, but in her boudoir as he quietly closed the door behind him in the early hours of the morning he had left.

Pechorin woke at around mid-day, disturbed by the warmth of the sun, which had now risen high above the stately birch trees. The air was warm, the grass under his back deep and lush; his horse stood quietly by, nibbling at the grass, wise enough to have retreated into the shade.

At lunch, his grandmother's mood was no better than the evening before, but she at least managed, not without great effort, to maintain a conversation that involved neither Katya nor Kropotovo. By some impenetrable delicacy, only possible between people who had known one another all their lives and who were, although it might never be stated, deeply devoted to one another, they arrived at length at a kind of compromise. Afanasii Stolypin would be staying at Serednikovo for close on three weeks; Pechorin was intending to return to St Petersburg much before then; he would stay over for a night on his return journey. His grandmother would therefore not be denied the pleasure – although she felt it not as a pleasure, but as the satisfaction of a need – of pursuing the issues of both Katya and Kropotovo with all the delicacy she could muster, abetted, she hoped, by the judicious Afanasii, to whom Pechorin might listen, even if he would not listen to her.

The old woman was indisposed later that evening and Pechorin had the cook bring a cold supper to his room. He left the next morning before she was awake.

Pechorin's father, Alexander Iurevich, had not entirely disappeared when the boy was two years old. Like Thomas the Rhymer, he had initially returned, although, unlike Thomas, he did not appear to Pechorin to have acquired magical powers. He was nonetheless in the habit of disappearing once again, thus establishing an irregular cycle that continued throughout Pechorin's childhood until his father's death. At just short of seventeen years old, Pechorin was by no means mature enough to absorb the emotional impact of his father's demise, but he understood very well the finality with which the cycle of disappearance and return had been broken. His father had stepped behind a veil from which he would never return; he had gone not to the Faerie Queen, but into the soil on the estate at Kropotovo.

Pechorin had first seen Kropotovo at the age of five, when his father had suddenly appeared at Serednikovo and his grandmother reluctantly agreed that the boy might spend two summer weeks at his father's estate; she also insisted, however, that both she and Fraulein Rhemer would accompany him. At first, the sheltered child shared his grandmother's instinctive unease among the dirt and broken machinery, under the gaze of a breed of peasant he had never before encountered. He would much later recall how, acknowledging his own fear in the presence of these mute and shabby shadow-people, as far removed from the peasants of Serednikovo as they were from their masters, he began to acquire the habit of subduing and mastering his emotional response; what both friends and enemies correctly identified as Pechorin's quite extraordinary *sang-froid*, in the barrack-room and the ballroom alike, was born at Kropotovo. On later visits – initiated by the sudden appearance of his father, ritually resisted by his grandmother, before the latter would relent with some half-fabricated qualification – he came to love its shabbiness, the mysterious habits of the serfs who worked its land. Even a child could see that these people were given much greater freedom than at Serednikovo, which ran like a clockwork model of the ideal agrarian community; a child could not know, however, that this was more a consequence of their master's disinterest than a reflection of his enlightenment.

He had last seen Kropotovo a little under six years ago, on his seventeenth birthday, the day after his father's funeral. By that time, Pechorin's sense of his own being had grown sufficiently for him to begin to understand the peculiar relationship between his grandmother and his father. His father was by no means a poor man – otherwise Alexei and Yelizaveta Arsenyev (*née* Stolypina) would never have consented to his marriage to their daughter Maria. Neither was he rich, having come from a family of the lower provincial nobility, who were able to secure for him a commission but no property. Kropotovo, such as it was, had been purchased with the marriage bond provided by Alexei and Yelizaveta, who thought it generous while at the same time regretting the poverty of what it was able to buy.

Alexander and Maria Pechorin's life there together had been brief. Once the initial trauma of her delicate daughter's early death had receded, it was replaced in the old woman's heart by a hatred for both the place and for the man who had taken her there, accompanied by a conviction that she owed no obligation to Alexander, only to the boy, to her grandson. More than that, she became convinced that her obligation to the boy – and to the memory of her dead daughter – both required and justified that he be protected from a father who could do little for him.

Now, as Pechorin ambled through the overgrown meadows, nodding without a word to a family of serfs assembled in front of their *izbá*, each attempt to conjure the image of his father produced only a receding perspective on the dim outline of an upright figure, walking away. Just as the figure disappeared over the horizon, it was suddenly replaced by the image of his grandmother, stern but unmistakably pleased with herself.

Pechorin woke the next morning in a high fever. The only servant who remained in the house was an old woman by the name of Marfa, who fulfilled the role of sentry more than housekeeper, doubling as cook only on the rare occasions when there was anyone in the house to cook for. When she knocked gently at his bedroom door at around eight with a modest breakfast, Pechorin, imagining he was trundling through some desolate landscape in a poor carriage, saw no reason to reply. An hour later, the breakfast tray still untouched on the floor outside his bedroom door, Marfa was emboldened to follow her more brisk knock by opening the door by a couple of inches. Pechorin lay arched across a mountain of pillows, his saturated night-shirt open to the waist, his cheeks and brows grey-white under what appeared to be a coat of clear lacquer.

'Oh, my Lord!' - exclaimed the old woman, crossing herself - 'I'll send for the doctor right away'.

'Tell the driver to spare those poor horses. He'll kill them' - came Pechorin's reply, to an already empty room.

The doctor had immediately reassured the old woman that there was nothing to worry about; Pechorin - although she barely understood the words - was suffering from nothing more than nervous exhaustion. The doctor gave Pechorin a strong sleeping draught and left without ceremony.

'He'll sleep for twelve hours, perhaps more' - he said as he left - 'When he wakes, make sure he is accompanied for the next twelve... and try to get him to eat something'.

The afternoon sun was already high in the sky on the following day when Pechorin finally, gently opened his eyes. At the side of his bed sat a girl of seventeen or eighteen, her blond hair pulled into a tight knot at the back of her head, her dress plain under a linen smock in the peasant style. Pechorin closed his eyes once again and contemplated with all seriousness the possibility that something terrible had befallen him, that he had been despatched to what would be his final resting place, neither Heaven nor Hell, but some perverse Purgatory, in which, as it happened, he fully expected to spend all eternity. He opened his eyes a second time and studied the girl's face more closely. She did not, of course, possess the beauty of the ladies of Petersburg society, but neither did she resemble the peasant girls of this or any other estate, although, Pechorin acknowledged to himself, he had spent little time studying that particular class of our species. There was something plain but nonetheless appealing in the girl's strong cheekbones, her straight mouth and blond eyebrows, something faintly Ugrian about the whole. Pechorin for some reason recalled an old legend of the estate, about a peasant who had managed to escape and, as far as anyone in the immediate environs knew, avoid capture or death. He had returned almost ten years later, repentant before God and the master, unable, he claimed, to go on living in this world without expiating his sins before his own people. He had also, the rather incredible tale continued, brought with him a wife, but no money.

'Who are you? - Pechorin asked suddenly.

'I am Maria' - the girl replied, without a hint of fear or discomfort - 'Marfa told me to stay by your bedside until you woke up. She told me I should remain at your bedside for another twelve hours'.

'And what time is it now? - asked Pechorin.

'It's just after three o'clock, your Honour'.

Pechorin spent the next couple of hours in contemplation of this alien peasant girl through eyes barely open. The girl, for her part, bore this scrutiny without uttering a word or, much to Pechorin's surprise, without any outward sign of embarrassment. Her Ugrian features - or were they perhaps even Nordic? - steadily grew on him; he had certainly never encountered such features, or such a demeanour, in these or any other circumstances. At length, he noticed that he was hungry.

'Maria, my dear' - he said cheerfully - 'Could you ask Marfa to bring me something to eat?'

The girl rose and left the room without saying a word, returning in less than a minute.

'She'll be up in a moment' - said the girl, resuming her former position.

The old woman bustled into the room, beaming with pleasure and relief.

'Oh sir!' - she exclaimed - 'We were ever so worried about you... you looked like a wax figure... and what incredible things you were saying!'

'I feel much better now, Marfa' - Pechorin replied - 'There's no need to worry yourself'.

The old woman set down a tray with soup and black bread on a little table by Pechorin's bedside and asked if he wanted anything else.

'No, Marfa, thank you very much. I have everything I need'.

When he had eaten, Pechorin resumed his former pose, quietly contemplating this strange girl, who remained seated in her chair by the side of the bed. After a few hours, just as the light in the window began to fade, Pechorin turned to her with a playful smile, to which, once again, she made no visible response.

'Could you take my tray down to the kitchen, please, Maria?' - Pechorin asked.

'Why of course, your Honour'.

'And there's no need to return' - he continued - 'You have cured me'.

'But your Honour, the doctor said you should not be left alone for at least twelve hours' - the girl said, with the first signs of emotion - 'Marfa will scold me if I don't do as he asked'.

When he awoke the following morning, the dim light suggesting that sunrise was still half an hour away, the girl lay fast asleep in her chair, her features softened, strands of hair twining gently at her temples. Pechorin rose in silence, dressed, and left her there sleeping.

CHAPTER FOUR

VERA AND KATYA

A FANASII ALEXEYEVICH STOLYPIN had acquired the habit of rising early as a Captain of the Hussars and observed it in every circumstance, from the barracks in St Petersburg to the battlefields of Austerlitz and Borodinó; thus he had demonstrated his moral and physical superiority over his men by ensuring that he was already positioned in the Staff office or field-tent by the time they dragged themselves out of their bunks at five-thirty, a discipline they considered inhumane. Pechorin had risen before dawn, roused the coachman but not the cook, and set off for his grandmother's estate before the full circle of the sun had escaped the line of the horizon. By the time his carriage rolled through the gates of Serednikovo some four hours later, his Great-Uncle had walked the three miles or so to the post-station at Bryokhovo where he was able to pick up a copy of the twice-weekly *Moscow News*, returned, and was now finishing his breakfast of eggs and porridge oats, his spectacles perched on the end of his fine aristocratic nose, the newspaper covering most of the dining-room table.

At the sound of horse and carriage, Afanasii rose and came to the front door, where he found only an ornate woven bag sitting on the porch. He picked up the bag and deposited it in the hallway. By the time he returned to the dining room, Pechorin was sitting in his chair, chewing on a piece of egg-white, and scanning the obituaries on the back page of the newspaper.

'Uncle, how very pleasant to see you' – said Pechorin, looking up at the older man – 'I thought for a moment that you might still be in bed'.

Afanasii ignored this weak attempt at wit.

'And how very pleasant it is to see you, young man; we thought you might have got lost in the black hole of Kropotovo'.

Pechorin, in his turn, chose to ignore this immediate invitation to the most tedious of conversations.

'I would happily have remained there' – he said, affecting a distant air – 'had it not been for the pleasure of your company and, subsequently, the call of duty. But where is my grandmother?'

'Her young lady is attending to her toilette. She will no doubt join us for lunch'.

Pechorin spent the rest of the morning in the stables, sometimes helping the coachman and a serf boy from the estate groom the horses, sometimes lying back in the hay smoking a little cigar, oblivious to the peril of fire that seemed to have hypnotized the boy. Every time Pechorin took the cigar from his lips, the boy's eyes jerked from the cigar to the scrappy remains of last year's hay beneath Pechorin's cocked wrist.

'What's your name, boy?' - Pechorin asked.
'Fomá, your Honour' - the boy replied, his eyes fixed on the cigar.
'And what age are you?'
'I'll be twelve next month, your Honour'.
'And why would a stout lad like you, who'll be a man in no time, be so afeard of a little dot of fire'.
The boy looked at the ground, shifted on his feet, and said nothing. The coachman gave him a look of admonishment.
'Come now, don't be afraid of speaking out of turn; there's nothing you can say that will offend me' - Pechorin insisted.
The boy looked at the coachman, who gave an almost imperceptible nod.
'Well, your Honour' - the boy stumbled - 'There was a fire on an estate near Svetlye Gory last summer. The great house was burned to the ground, your Honour'.
'And you are concerned that my cigar might be the cause of a similar catastrophe?'
Fomá was once again silent. The coachman also now looked at the ground.
'Come on, my good fellow, out with it: what harm could possibly come from a little cigar?'
'It's just, your Honour' - the coachman interrupted - 'Well, it's just that some people said the serfs started the fire, that they were... dissatisfied with their treatment'.
'And what do other people say?' - asked Pechorin.
'Other people say that one of the young gentlemen accidentally started the fire by smoking' - the coachman replied after some hesitation.
'And what do you think seems more likely, Fomá?' - asked Pechorin, turning again to the boy - 'The carelessness of a gentleman? Or a peasant revolt?'
'I dunno, your Honour' - the boy replied, dimly understanding that there was no answer he could give that would not seem impertinent - 'P'raps there was some other reason'.
At lunch, Pechorin resolved that attack was the most effective form of defence and immediately set about interrogating his grandmother regarding events at Svetlye Gory in the summer of the previous year.
'It's just curious that you didn't mention it in any of your letters, *Grandmaman*. An event such as that must surely qualify as news in this or indeed any other locale'.
He knew, of course, that Blagodatsky's mother Irina had become a sister to his grandmother way back in 1775 in the most unpleasant of circumstances, when both her mother and father had been killed by their peasants during the Pugachev rebellion, and that his grandmother, more even than other ladies of her generation, had a mortal fear of such unpleasantness. The old woman was too young to remember the events themselves, having been born in 1773, when the first unrest broke out; and the environs of

Moscow had not been as badly affected as the deep provinces to the south and east; but she had nonetheless grown up with a living reminder of the savage potential of the peasantry in the form of this sister who resembled neither her nor her brothers.

'I hardly think it was an event' - said Afanasii, conscious of the old woman's disquiet - 'An accident, no more. And they have entirely rebuilt the house. Quite splendid, I'm told; much better than what was there before'.

'Yes, but at what cost?' - said the old woman - 'Renewing these old estates is even more ruinous than maintaining them and that is quite ruinous enough'.

'*Grandmaman*' - Pechorin said before she could go any further - 'I have no plans to sell Kropotovo, no intention of spending money - even yours - on its renovation, and absolutely no desire whatsoever to continue discussing the matter'.

'Is it costing you money?' - Afanasii asked quietly.

'It pays for itself' - Pechorin replied.

And, he thought to himself, it's worth ten times the sum I might get for it, or more; what price can a man place on a corner of the world in which he can be by himself?

The conversation turned to matters more mundane, the tribulations of relatives and acquaintances in both Serednikovo and, more to his grandmother's interest, St Petersburg. Pechorin replied dutifully to her enquiries, on occasion even in some detail or with a stray witticism, until the old woman asked about Sasha Vereschagina; here, Pechorin thought to himself, was the line of approach to her primary objective.

'Sasha is very well' - said Pechorin - 'As charming and intelligent as ever. She bears the burden of her mother's anxieties with the grace of a Penelope'.

'Ah, her poor mother' - said his grandmother - 'How fortune has deserted that noble woman. And yet Sasha, as you say, has made the best of a difficult situation and without entirely sacrificing herself to her mother's needs'.

'Sasha is perhaps too concerned with the affairs of others, *Grandmaman*'.

'She has every right to involve herself in the affairs of others if those affairs have the capacity to affect her own; a woman with a mind, but no discernible future, must do what she can'.

'You are very well informed, *Grandmaman*, but perhaps not quite well enough'.

'Then perhaps you might take the trouble to make good any deficit in my understanding' - the old woman replied.

Afanasii, who had not said a word since the matter of Kropotovo had been closed, affected disinterest in this new topic of conversation, but was nonetheless following it with quiet intent. Pechorin explained to his grandmother that, as far as he was aware, Sasha had decided that Katya Yessentukhova was a poor match for Alexei Lopatkin not because of any romantic ambition of her own - for how could she hope to compete with such a beauty? – but rather out of a sincerely held belief that Lopatkin required and deserved a wife with greater intellectual accomplishments in addition to Katya's undoubted beauty, which, in Sasha's view, could easily be found in any drawing-room in St Petersburg. She had, moreover, come to this conclusion long before Lopatkin's recent inheritance and elevation to the status of most eligible, which had, quite plainly, intensified the threat by bringing a beauty such as Katya into the realms of the possible; what had been a minor consideration for Sasha was now a matter of the gravest and most immediate importance.

'You *are* very well informed' – said the old woman – 'Has Sasha confided in you?'

'Sasha has not said a word to me about either the gentleman or the young lady involved' – Pechorin replied.

'Yet you have received encouragement from Mungo...'.

'I have received encouragement from no one, *Grandmaman*'.

'Grigorii, dear, if we cannot persuade you to dispose of an estate you do not need, then at least allow us to try to persuade you to acquire a wife befitting your breeding and status'.

The old woman looked at Afanasii for encouragement.

'She certainly is a beauty' – said Afanasii – 'And has many admirers'.

After lunch, Pechorin went to the stables, instructed the coachman to prepare his carriage and retrieve his luggage from the guest room, and went back into the house. He sat down at the desk in the drawing-room and wrote a note to his grandmother, explaining that he had decided to leave that afternoon. It would be three overnight stops before St. Petersburg, even if he left the next morning as planned; this way, he would arrive a day earlier. He gave the note to Afanasii, asking him to give it to his grandmother only after he had departed, and explaining that the drama of parting would be as distressing for his grandmother as it would be irritating for himself.

'Be careful, my boy' – said Afanasii – 'As I said earlier, Katya is a delightful and beautiful young woman; it will come as no surprise that she has many admirers, and I don't mean by that the Lopatkins of this world'.

Pechorin gave him a look designed to mask his curiosity.

'Thank you, Uncle. You are no doubt quite right' – he said as he leapt up into his carriage.

Pechorin arrived in the ancient city of Tver at dusk, dined poorly at the inn where he would spend the night, and, in his gloomy bed-chamber, wrote two brief letters, which he handed in person to the driver of the post-coach. The journey was dull and wearying, the monotonous bare countryside creating the illusion that Pechorin's carriage was not actually moving, its rattles and groans merely added for effect by some omniscient theatrical entrepreneur. He spent a hideous second night at a post-station near Lake Bologoe, bitten to the quick by bed-bugs, barely able to sleep. In those rare moments when he succeeded in drifting off, he dreamed of French roads, along which, he had been told, a man might travel from Paris to the Pas de Calais in six hours: from the boudoir of a mistress to the Dover ship before the unwitting husband had awakened to face the day.

Roused from intermittent sleep and once again confronted by the vast hollow emptiness of provincial Russia, Pechorin's mind retreated to a small, still point unaffected by the passage of time. When they reached Novgorod on the third evening, he remained in the carriage and instructed the coachman to change horses. They would continue through the night to Tsarskoe Seló; the roads from here on were much better, the sky clear and, Pechorin wagered, he would sleep better on the road, lulled by the rolling of the carriage, than in one more of these God-forsaken provincial inns in which Great Russia excelled, if that is the correct expression, like no other nation.

When they finally rolled into Tsarskoe Seló on the morning of the fourth day, Pechorin was exhausted and feared he had caught a cold on the road. He jumped down from the carriage and went straight through to his bedroom, shouting weakly to Gavril that he was not to be disturbed, lay down on his bed fully clothed, and slept the sleep of the dead until around six in the evening.

The warm late August sunlight still filled the room when he woke.

Pechorin lay there for some time, contemplating the evening ahead, weighing the fate that had placed the happiness of others in his reluctant hands. He recalled how the Scots adventurer from whom Mungo had taken his name had parted with Sir Walter Scott on the morning of his departure for Africa. Mungo Park's horse had stumbled as he and Scott reached the crossroads where they would go their separate ways, which Scott considered a bad omen. 'Omens follow those who look to them', Park replied, counting on Scott's familiarity with the ballad *Adam Gordon*, which Pechorin had read in the company of the unfortunate Swinson:

Wha looks to freits [omens], my master dear
It's freits will follow them

As a child, Pechorin had paid little attention to the lines that followed, which now seemed to contain the essence of the entire gory tale:

Let it ne'er be said that Adam Gordon
Was daunted by a dame

Adam Gordon's determination to be daunted by no dame had led in the end to his downfall; Pechorin would not be so foolish.

Later that evening, Sasha Vereschagina brightened, her spirits rising in a manner she could not conceal, when Pechorin, whose return to the capital had gone unannounced and unnoticed, slipped quietly into the room. Mungo was even moved to ask Pechorin if he had not perhaps acquired another admirer while the attention of those closest to him had been directed elsewhere.

'Nothing of the sort' - Pechorin replied - 'You really must learn, my dear Mungo, to pay attention'.

On the far side of Sasha's drawing-room, Katya was deep in conversation with Vera Lopatkina and her brother Alexei, who had acquired the outward manner of a gentleman of substance since Pechorin had last seen him, but nonetheless remained somewhat restrained in the art of conversation. He was not only in love with Katya, but now, contemplating the possibility that he might become her husband as something more than a forlorn hope, had become all the more tongue-tied in her presence. Pechorin watched for a moment or two, judging by the play of gesture that Vera, the dutiful sister, was doing everything she could to assist Alexei beyond the exchange of pleasantries.

'Alexei' - Pechorin said as he joined their company - 'I must offer you my sincerest condolences on the passing of your father. He was an honourable and admirable man'.

Pechorin gave a low bow.

'We are most grateful, Monsieur Pechorin' - Vera said before Alexei could speak

'Most grateful' - repeated Alexei.

'I'm sure the ladies will not object to me asking, but tell me, what are your plans? Do you intend to stay in St Petersburg?' - Pechorin continued.

'I intend to remain in St Petersburg for the foreseeable future' - Alexei replied - 'Beyond that, I'm not sure'.

'Well, a man of your considerable means has the prerogative of choice, of taking the time to choose and choose well'.

Katya, who had not spoken since Pechorin joined them, now looked at him with the outward appearance of implacable calm, beneath which Pechorin could discern only the merest flicker of dismay.

'Quite so' - said Vera, glancing at Katya - 'You are one of the most eligible young men in St Petersburg, Alexei. The doors of every house in the city are open to you'.

'Your sister is right, my dear fellow' - said Pechorin - 'I envy you'.

Pechorin found himself an hour or so later in his customary position at such gatherings, at the centre of a small crowd of young ladies and the younger officers, Mungo at his admiring side. For every three witticisms of a flattering nature, usually directed towards one of the young ladies, but occasionally in praise of some scandalous deed of one of the younger officers - who silently blushed their gratitude at being portrayed in such a favourable light - Pechorin allowed himself one scabrous dismissal of some figure of social prominence. Just as one ripple of laughter resolved itself into generous smiles, Pechorin, catching sight of the diplomat de Barante in conversation with Dmitrii Stolypin, glanced at Mungo and spoke in an unnecessarily loud voice.

'Mungo, my dear friend, your brother is in danger of forfeiting his reputation for impeccable judgement'.

The company, as if one body, turned their gaze towards the doorway where Dmitrii and the Frenchman stood. Dmitrii continued speaking in his quiet and respectful manner, not taking his eyes from de Barante. The Frenchman, however, who could not have heard Pechorin's remark, despite its theatrical volume, somehow became aware that he was being observed and began to strain his neck in such a way as to allow him to look towards Pechorin's company, without appearing to ignore Dmitrii. Pechorin told a fantastical joke about a French aristocrat, who, while travelling in some distant province in the interior, had mistaken a pig for a child and thus come to the conclusion that the peasants in this corner of his great country not only spoke a language other than French, but different in form and sound from any language on earth. The young men burst into uproarious laughter, while the young ladies, their laughter tinkling in accompaniment, glanced nervously in the direction of de Barante. When Dmitrii, who was praising some scandalous French novel, had finished speaking, de Barante, now struggling to maintain his composure on each occasion when laughter rang out from Pechorin's company, asked if Dmitrii would be so kind as to introduce him to his brother.

'Why certainly' - Dmitrii replied - 'Although I was under the impression that you had already met'.

'We have been in the same company, but I have not yet had the pleasure of an introduction' - said de Barante, as the two men moved off towards the middle of the room.

'Mungo' - said Dmitrii - 'I think you may know Monsieur de Barante, although I understand also that you have not been formally acquainted'.

'I am honoured, sir' - Mungo replied with a curt bow.

'And this is Monsieur Pechorin' - Dmitrii continued - 'Our esteemed nephew'.

The sound of light, indulgent laughter once again floated above the company.

'We have met' - said de Barante, giving a bow much slower and deeper than had Mungo.

Pechorin merely nodded and, just as he was about to speak, felt a hand gently squeeze his arm.

'Grigorii' - came the voice of Sasha Vereschagina, who had silently appeared at his side - 'I promised my dear mother you would call on her before it got too late. Gentlemen, please allow me to borrow Monsieur Pechorin for a few minutes. I promise to return him in one piece'.

Pechorin merely nodded once again in the direction of Dmitrii and de Barante, then gave a low bow to the young ladies.

'I beg your pardon, ladies' – he said – 'I must pay my respects to the household'.

The company watched as Pechorin walked towards the door, Sasha's arm locked in his.

'That I did not expect' – Dmitrii whispered to Mungo.

'You really must learn, my dear brother, to pay attention' – Mungo replied, breaking into a smile of glorious self-satisfaction.

The light seemed steadily to dim as Pechorin and Sasha made their way along the corridor that separated the living quarters from the slightly faded, but still mockingly opulent drawing-room in which the guests had gathered. In a room off to the left at the very far end, lit only by a small table lamp, Sasha's mother was sitting in a rather modest armchair, at her right hand a spinning-wheel. Pechorin looked upon her care-worn face in half-profile, but the woman in the chair, who passed as a contemporary of his own grandmother, despite being some ten years younger, had not noticed their entrance.

'*Maman*' – said Sasha in a quiet, cheerful voice – 'You have a visitor. Monsieur Pechorin has come to see you'.

Pechorin felt an unaccustomed tightness in his chest as the corner of Sasha's mother's mouth creased into a gentle smile, the light restored for one fleeting moment to her eyes. Yelizaveta Ivanovna Vereschagina, born Cheremushkina, had been perhaps the most remarkable young woman of her generation, possessed of a beauty lit by intelligence and even gravity, which distinguished her from her contemporaries in a manner that caused a certain type of man to find in her every gesture a perplexing combination of allure and reproach. She had become the hostess of a literary salon at her grandmother's St Petersburg residence at the age of twenty, confidante and enabler of many of the young men poised between military service and social engagement who would become the vanguard, if not the command, of the Northern Society. By the time of those fateful days in December 1825, Pechorin knew, the young Yelizaveta had become engaged to Alexei Vereschagin, an officer in the Hussars who was arrested on the evening following the bloodshed on Senate Square. Alexei, like hundreds of other young men, was tried and sentenced to internal exile. Yelizaveta's grandmother had appealed though some of her connections for the young couple to be allowed to marry in the chapel of the Petropavlovsk Fortress, where Alexei was being held. Her request had been granted on the expectation that Yelizaveta would then accompany Alexei into exile, as so many of the Decembrist wives did, following their disgraced husbands into a world entirely beyond their sheltered imaginations.

Yelizaveta looked up at Pechorin, her faint smile now transformed into a mask of desperate containment, tears beginning to well in her faltering eyes.

'It is so very kind of you to think of me, Monsieur Pechorin' – she said quietly, but with all the force she could muster.

'The pleasure is all mine, as ever' – Pechorin replied – 'You are a tonic to my jaded eyes. I am at your service'.

Pechorin imagined for a moment he could see the road to Kazan, along which the bereft Yelizaveta Vereschagina had returned after the physical death of her already dead young husband, alone but for the coachman her family had sent to retrieve her and the as yet unsuspected child growing in her womb. Young ladies of elevated birth did not, in those times, resort to the vulgarity of suicide – or, if they did, they at least contrived to make their demise appear the inevitable result of the unfortunate condition of feminine fragility – but in the days after Alexei's death from a fever contracted in prison, Yelizaveta had thought of nothing else. How could she return to a capital where all vestiges of freedom had been obliterated, where so many of Alexei's comrades had not been allowed the cruel privilege of a natural death, where no woman of her class and intellect could hope to forge anything resembling a future? Only the sudden spasm between her hips, which did not for even a fraction of a second conceal itself from her understanding as an effect of this poor carriage stumbling over these hellish roads, brought any thoughts of inevitability to a sudden, silent conclusion.

Yelizaveta raised her eyes as if to respond, but was halted by a discreet knock at the door. Pechorin sought her instruction by gently raising an eyebrow, but Yelizaveta only lowered her gaze.

'Come' – he said, after a moment's hesitation.

The door opened to reveal the rather flustered figure of Katya, her black eyes gleaming with a mixture of shame and determination.

'Madame Vereschagina' – said Katya quietly – 'I beg your pardon for the intrusion... your daughter Sasha assured me that I would not be unwelcome'.

Pechorin had on many occasions proclaimed the loss of the capacity to be surprised, but, although Katya could not have guessed from his exterior, it now cost him some effort to conceal his discomfort, glancing at the downturned head of Yelizaveta Vereschagina in an affectation of concern for decorum.

'I am sure Madame Vereschagina will not think too ill of me' – said Katya at last in a voice straining with the effort of false confidence – 'There was no other way I could speak to you'.

'And what do you wish to say to me in the presence of Madame Vereschagina that you would not wish to say in company?' – Pechorin asked evenly.

'I think you know very well' – Katya replied, turning down her head in apparent mimicry of the older woman.

When she raised it once again, a single crystalline tear paused for a moment on her cheek, deathly pale, before tracing a clean line through her otherwise perfectly intact *maquillage*.

Gavril, as instructed, had mounted two enormous blocks of sugar doused in rum on sabres that had been struck through from the underside of wooden boxes. These had been placed at either side of the hearth in what Pechorin affected to call his drawing room and now gave off a low blue flame, much prettier and more dramatic than the light of the fire, which it would, in any case, be impractical to light on such a fine evening in late August. The old man had retired, once again as instructed, leaving the front door open on the latch and a candle burning low in the hallway.

Pechorin set down two glasses alongside an already opened bottle of wine on a little table and set himself down on the divan. The shuttered doors to the bedroom beyond were closed. He looked around at his rather curious quarters, opulent in comparison to the barrack room from which he had so recently emerged, but decidedly poor, almost provincial, in comparison to the salons and drawing rooms to which not so young gentlemen of his class were accustomed. They certainly shrank alongside his still fresh memory of Serednikovo, decidedly provincial though it was; and they could not match the rooms in which he and his grandmother had first lodged on arrival in St Petersburg, nor even the faded splendour of the reception rooms at the Vereschagins. Pechorin was distracted by some inchoate disdain for the *haut monde* to which he would eventually, inevitably devolve, a feeling entirely unrelieved by any attachment to his immediate surroundings. He imagined himself on horseback in some faraway landscape, the Caucasus of youthful memory, his Hussar's tunic replaced by a streaming kaftan of local design, tearing along the floor of some deserted valley, his mount beginning to sweat up as it galloped through the sparse landscape, exulting in the exertions imposed on it by its impatient rider. He caught sight of a little church, impossibly perched at the top of one of the surrounding hills, dismounted, and began to climb towards its white walls set beneath a modest bell-tower.

Pechorin was disturbed by the faint sound of the latch sliding at the front door. He listened without moving as delicate footsteps traversed the dimly lit hall, as vivid in his imagination as the blazing sun in the Caucasian sky. He had still not moved when a light knock came at the door of the drawing room. Without waiting for a reply, the door opened to reveal a beautiful young woman still in evening dress, soft curls of hair beginning to unravel.

'Vera, my darling' – Pechorin said softly – 'Please, do come in'.

CHAPTER FIVE

THE END OF THE AFFAIR

Sofia Karamzina was the most dazzling young woman in St Petersburg society. Her salon, which she had conducted from the age of twenty-four, was frequented by the most brilliant writers and *philosophes* of the time. The cynics would mutter behind their hands that this was due only to the fact that she was the daughter of Nikolai Karamzin, author of society tales such as the celebrated 'A Knight of Our Time' and the monumental *History of the Russian State*, and Russia's leading literary figure until the emergence of Pushkin. Yet still they came, Zhukovsky, Viazemsky, later Turgenev, long after the death of her father in 1826; Pushkin himself had been a frequent visitor until his dramatic flight across the Black Sea in 1829.

They came, it must be said, not only because the Karamzina salon was one of the few places in St Petersburg where it was possible to conduct a serious conversation - in Russian! - about both literature and politics; they came also to be entertained. An evening at the Karamzins' under the direction of Sofia was not complete without a recital of one kind or another, sometimes verse, at others music. As the summer was drawing to a close, Sofia, in order to attract a younger generation to the salon, had conceived of the idea of mounting a dramatic performance; encouraged by Dmitrii Stolypin, and moreover afraid of arousing the interest of the censorship, Sofia had agreed to stage an unpublished play written by none other than Lieutenant Sinyukhaev, whose verse had begun to appear in the pages of albeit modest journals. Sinyukhaev had changed the title of his play on a number of occasions, eventually settling on the rather daring *Masquerade*, a comedy of manners that descended into tragedy, complete with the reckless gamblers and Napoleonic overtones so beloved of Romantic drama of the time.

'Why on earth would I become involved in such nonsense?' - Pechorin asked, the exasperation in his voice entirely unaffected - 'Sinyukhaev is a perfectly fine fellow, if a little reserved; but I would not have thought him capable of wasting his time on such waffle'.

'But Grigorii, my dear, you would not be attending for the play; Mademoiselle Karamzina has invited Katya' - said Sasha.

'And has she accepted?' - Pechorin asked, perplexed by the idea of Katya at the heart of St Petersburg's intellectual life, if not by the notion that she might harbour ambitions of acting, if only the stage were a respectable occupation for a beautiful and eligible young woman.

'Of course' - Sasha replied calmly - 'And not only that'.

Pechorin, determined not to rise, said nothing.

'Well I'll tell you' – Sasha continued – 'because I know you want to know: Alexei Lopatkin will also take part'.

'And?' – Pechorin said curtly, annoyed by Sasha's insinuation – 'Of what possible interest can that be to me?'

'Oh Grigorii, I know you too well'.

'I think perhaps that you do not know me at all, my dear Sasha: for one, I have no interest in Princess Yessentukhova; and, even if I had, I would consider it entirely unnecessary to lift a finger to frustrate the intentions of the estimable Monsieur Lopatkin'.

'As I said, my dear Grigorii, I know you too well'.

Later that afternoon, as was his custom when in St Petersburg without obligations, Pechorin took a stroll in the Summer Gardens, before calling on Mungo and Dmitrii at their father's old house near Anichkov Bridge, where he would smoke a little French cigar and sip a glass of Burgundy. Dmitrii, it seemed to Pechorin, was even more reserved than usual, while Mungo, by way of contrast, and if it were indeed possible, was more animated.

'You simply must ask Sinyukhaev' – Mungo exclaimed – 'He will be delighted to have you. In fact, I'll ask him to ask you myself'.

'You'll do nothing of the sort, my dear uncle' – Pechorin replied with a smile.

'But how on earth can you stand by and allow Alexei to go unopposed?' – asked Mungo – 'I'm sure she's in love with you; but they'll marry her off to his money if you let them, without a doubt'.

Pechorin paused to consider a response.

'I doubt very much that he'll be unopposed' – said Dmitrii before Pechorin could reply.

'What do you mean by that?' – asked Mungo, frowning.

'Well, you both pride yourselves on your great powers of observation' – Dmitrii replied with an ironic smile – 'Particularly you, my dear brother'.

Pechorin was seized by a quiet sense of awe, even exhilaration, as the words of his great-uncle at Serednikovo chimed in his mind with those just spoken by Dmitrii: Katya, he suddenly understood, was being pursued by some force more compelling than the unwitting Alexei Lopatkin.

'You have been paying attention, Dmitrii' – he said, hoping that Dmitrii might imagine he knew more than he in fact did – 'Are you able to share with your redoubtable brother the identity of the other party?'

'I'm surprised you think that either possible or desirable, Pechorin; unless of course you are no wiser on this account than my dear brother...'.

Pechorin gave his best impression of disinterest, all the while desperately trying to conjure a reply that would neither confirm nor dispel Dmitrii's suspicion. For a second time, he was spared, on this occasion by Mungo.

'What the devil do you mean by desirable, Dmitrii? Am I not to be trusted?'

Dmitrii and Pechorin exchanged wry glances.

'Calm yourself, my dear fellow' – Dmitrii replied gently – 'I merely wish not to say or do anything that might place you in jeopardy; or, for that matter, that might cause any difficulty between you and Natalya'.

'What on earth has Natalya got to do with it?' – replied Mungo, now raising his voice – 'I'll thank you to tell me this instant'.

'My dear Mungo' – Pechorin interrupted – 'Your brother is merely indicating, with all due delicacy, that, if the charming Katya has another admirer, then it is highly unlikely that your equally charming Natalya is unaware of his identity'.

'Whose identity?' – Mungo shouted – 'Who the devil would pursue Katya, knowing that the unfortunate – but suddenly rich! – Lopatkin is pressing his case, even if they were not aware of the girl's quite obvious feelings for Pechorin?'

'Who indeed?' – said Pechorin, almost under his breath.

Wishing to preserve in the mind of his uncles the illusion that he was already apprised of what Dmitrii knew and Mungo as yet did not, Pechorin left shortly after eight. He would not usually have allowed himself to arrive at the Kuragins so early – the sun still sailed, quite alone, in the sea-blue sky – when the most committed of card-players would be taking their seats, some hours before the more sociable majority had even arrived. He would, however, be compensated by the fact that no one, not even Anatolii Kuragin, could possibly be drunk at this hour.

Pechorin almost didn't recognise the orderly entrance hall, devoid of its customary trail of empty bottles, coats, shoes, and goodness what else. Kuragin, however, was well on the way to confounding Pechorin's expectation, seated in a room on the ground floor with a glass of Burgundy in his hand, cheerfully expounding to a young officer on the advantages, of all things, of agricultural reform: his father, it appeared, was in the grip of the most recent wave of modernisation, seeking at the same time to increase the yield from his estate and improve the lot of the bonded serfs who worked on it. On catching sight of the unexpected newcomer, he became faintly embarrassed by this topic of conversation, immediately switching to a register more in keeping, he felt, with Pechorin's sudden appearance.

'To what do we owe this great honour, Pechorin? Am I to understand that you may dine with us? Might there even be a possibility – *encroyable!* – that you may grace our humble card-table with your illustrious presence?'

'I wouldn't go quite that far, Kuragin' – replied Pechorin – 'Although I am rather hungry'.

Seated at an incongruously grand table in a room on the second floor, Kuragin and Pechorin resembled nothing other than imposters, two caricatures pressed onto boards, the officer and the dissolute gentleman. Kuragin was suddenly as sober as Pechorin had ever seen him, his blustering rhetoric toned down in preparation, Pechorin instinctively understood, for a discussion along somewhat more serious lines.

'It is always interesting to have a conversation with a clever man' - Kuragin began, not entirely to Pechorin's taste.

'I regret that we so rarely have the opportunity for conversation, Kuragin' - replied Pechorin - 'And what would you like to talk about?'

'About love' - said Kuragin in a voice that contained not a shred of mockery.

'I had no idea you were a philosopher of the affairs of the heart, my dear fellow' - said Pechorin - 'No idea at all'.

'Oh, I would not call myself a philosopher, Pechorin, but I do take an interest when affairs of the heart become entangled with the affairs of Court'.

Pechorin was struck by this apposition, but gave Kuragin no sign. He felt once again the distant echo of his great-uncle's remark at Serednikovo, somehow now yet more ominous in its association with Kuragin.

'How go your affairs of the heart, Pechorin?' - Kuragin asked.

'A gentleman, as you will understand, never speaks of such matters' - Pechorin replied.

'Then I will spare your sense of chivalry and speak for you. The Princess Yessentukhova is in love with you. You have encouraged her in such feelings, privately and publicly, stopping short of a proposal, as far as anyone can see, out of a sense of delicacy: our mutual acquaintance Monsieur Lopatkin, emboldened by his new-found wealth, entertains hopes of marriage; you are concerned not to compromise either the lady or the gentleman... at least in public'.

'You have a forensic imagination, my dear fellow' - replied Pechorin, disguising his relief that Kuragin's focus was exclusively on the fair Katya.

'Oh, I realise that your sense of honour demands that you say nothing at all, Pechorin, not even a denial. But I am not telling you this in order to add to what I already know'.

'Then why are you telling me?' - Pechorin asked.

'To warn you'.

Here again Pechorin heard the words of his great-uncle and of Dmitrii Stolypin, merging to form what was all but a premonition, complete only for the space into which Pechorin could not - or dared not - insert a name.

'What I am about to tell you could get us both arrested, so you should know beforehand that I will deny it in all circumstances. I'll say you were drunk... no, wait a second: I'll say that I was drunk' - continued Kuragin.

'You can be assured that I will tell no one' - Pechorin replied - 'Haven't I just demonstrated that, where affairs of the heart are concerned, I am the equal of Harpocrates'.

'My dear Pechorin, you are mistaken' - replied Kuragin, leaning across the table and lowering his voice to a whisper - 'We are not speaking of affairs of the heart'.

Pechorin's carriage made its way along the Moika Canal, the coats of the horses glimmering phosphorescent under the gas lamps, his mind in turmoil. Relief that Kuragin - and therefore, he reasoned, no one - knew anything of his relationship with Vera contended with horror at Kuragin's revelation, which, given the deadly seriousness of the circumstance, he had no reason to disbelieve. He had first set eyes on the Grand-Duke Mikhail on the same evening he had first set eyes on his elder brother, Tsar Nikolai, in the rather grand Pillar Hall of the Assembly of the Nobility in Moscow. The occasion was a recital given by the Irish pianist John Field, acquaintance of Haydn, Mendelssohn, and Beethoven, composer of the newly voguish *nocturne*, and, for the schoolboy Pechorin, a figure of almost unimaginable glamour. Field, beyond his impeccable pedigree as a composer and performer of European renown, had also famously refused the position of court pianist under Alexander I; now, between the faux marble pillars of the grand hall, Pechorin's ears were filled with Field's sublime melodies, his eyes fixed on Nikolai looking down on this curious Irishman who had refused his late brother.

The Grand-Duke Mikhail, seated to Nikolai's left, appeared to have no interest in either the music or the person of its performer, his rather bland countenance in marked counterpoint to the intensity of his brother the Tsar. Mikhail was the youngest of the ten children, and the four sons among them, of the unfortunate Tsar Pavel, assassinated while his eldest son Alexander was present in the Imperial Palace. Mikhail had lived with the unspoken and unspeakable knowledge of his eldest brother's complicity in their father's death; he had then watched as the rightful heir, his brother Konstantin, had been passed over for his brother Nikolai amid the bloodshed of December 1825. As if to confound some terrible inexorable fate, Mikhail and his wife Elena Pavlovna (born Princess Charlotte of Württemberg) had produced five children, all daughters. Pechorin did not attempt to resist the bitter recognition that, with Elena Pavlovna now approaching her thirtieth year, the last ten of which had been consumed by pregnancy and childbirth, the Grand-Duke's attentions might well have been captured by a beauty such as Katya.

As the carriage came to a halt some hundred yards short of the archway into the courtyard of the Lopatkin residence, Pechorin recalled how, some three days after the concert at the Assembly of the Nobility, he and his schoolmates had been roused at 4 a.m., instructed to dress quickly, stand to attention by their dormitory beds, and await inspection by an unannounced visitor, none other than Tsar Nikolai himself. The boy's heart seemed set to burst from his chest, his secret loathing of Nikolai's public surveillance of the estimable Field three nights before, he felt sure, now about to be exposed under the Tsar's suddenly intrusive gaze. By the time the cursory inspection was over, however, neither the clamouring of his heart nor the scandalous nature of his covert adolescent resentment had been revealed.

Pechorin stepped down from the carriage, made his way along the street to the archway, and disappeared into the courtyard and up the stairs to Vera's bedroom.

'Vera my darling, I assure you, there is no reason for you to be concerned'

– said Pechorin in an even tone – 'I have absolutely no designs on the Princess Yessentukhova'.

'Then why, tell me, is every person I know under the impression that you do?' – Vera replied, her eyes focused not on Pechorin, but on the dying embers in the fireplace behind him.

'The gossip of a society utterly bored with itself, nothing more' – said Pechorin – 'If I believed even a fraction of what is said about me, I would hand myself in to the *Gendarmerie*'.

'Then why do you encourage it?' – Vera continued – 'Why these public displays? And why, please tell me, are you of all people so keen to attend Mademoiselle Karamzina's. I wouldn't have thought that genteel dramatics were very much to your taste'.

Pechorin acknowledged with a barely perceptible smile the hand of the indefatigable Sasha, relentless in her desire to turn a wish into reality.

'I'm not' – said Pechorin – 'Whoever has furnished you with that piece of information is mistaken'.

Vera's gaze remained fixed on the glowing embers, a tear forming at the corner of her eye.

'Vera, my darling...' – he continued, resolving to counter emotion with reason – 'Have you heard even a word from these idle gossips about us? Consider: where there is... something – not a word; so, by the same logic, where there is nothing whatsoever – an avalanche of idle invention. Fact is accompanied by silence, fiction with abounding fiction. We should content ourselves with the hope that it will remain so'.

'Oh Grigorii, my darling!' – cried Vera, throwing her arms around Pechorin's neck, caught between desperate hope and inconstant fear – 'Do you really mean it?'

'Yes, my darling' – he said quietly – 'You must trust me'.

Pechorin entered the barracks the following morning to find Mungo and Dmitrii seated at a small card-table with Sinyukhaev, who was gently polishing a fine pair of leather top-boots. The focus of their attention, at this hour, was not cards, but the regimental parade scheduled for the following morning. Once a week this collection of young men, who at this stage in their military careers had few obligations beyond the riding, fencing, and shooting they all in any case enjoyed and keeping their uniforms in good order for all-too-frequent social engagements, were required to turn out on parade for their commanding officers. Once a month, however, these events, which had inevitably become somewhat routine and therefore lacking in military rigour, were conducted in the presence of a General from military headquarters.

'If only we could persuade Martynov to be ill' – said Mungo to the others as Pechorin approached.

'If only we could persuade him to retire' – Pechorin cut in, to snorts of knowing laughter.

'He may not be the only one about to embark on a change of career' – said Mungo, looking obliquely at Sinyukhaev – 'I hear we have an actor-manager in our midst'.

Pechorin gave Mungo a look of bitter reproach. Sasha, it would appear, was not the only one of his acquaintances possessed of a reckless energy.

'I think he'll do very well as the murderous husband' – continued Mungo, undeterred – 'Although it is little more than a crime against Aphrodite to cast the fair Princess Yessentukhova in the role of the unfortunate wife'.

'Don't listen to him, Pechorin' – Sinyukhaev said suddenly – 'I am honoured that you wish to be involved'.

Pechorin looked at Mungo once again, but said nothing.

'Drama is not my best suit' – Sinyukhaev continued – 'But Mademoiselle Karamzina is very persuasive'.

'Don't be so modest, my dear fellow' – said Dmitrii, before turning to Pechorin – 'Lieutenant Sinyukhaev has recently published some very fine verse in *The Contemporary*; we have great hopes for him'.

'I would be very much interested in reading it' – replied Pechorin, faintly nostalgic for a time when these words would have been true, but distracted also by the need to find a way out of the looming entanglement at Sofia Karamzina's without offending the reserved and self-effacing Sinyukhaev.

Before he could continue, the conversation was disturbed by a bustle in the hallway, followed by a loud clatter as the door flew open to reveal the stately figure of Martynov.

'*La scène est complète*' – muttered Pechorin.

'What was that?' – Martynov growled – 'I didn't quite catch you'.

'I was just telling Lieutenant Sinyukhaev how important it is to focus on staging' – Pechorin continued.

'Staging?' – Martynov spluttered – 'What on earth are you fellows talking about?'

'Sinyukhaev is to have a drama of his own composition performed at the salon of Mademoiselle Karamzina' – said Dmitrii – 'And it would appear that our dear Pechorin will play one of the leading roles'.

Martynov knit his brows in a look of utter confusion, shot a searching glance at Pechorin, before contenting himself with a vigorous sigh.

'Well' – he said, brightening somewhat, and with a rather sly look – 'We are all at some point required to perform, are we not? We must all at some point take to our very own stage'.

Pechorin had formed the habit of ignoring Martynov's crude attempts to be cryptic, but Mungo could not resist.

'And what on earth are *you* talking about, Martynov?' – he said with undisguised contempt.

'Oh' – Martynov continued – 'We are on parade tomorrow morning... we must prepare our costumes, rehearse our movements, and pull everything together on the day! Just like in the theatre, I suppose'.

'I hardly think it's the same' - said Mungo - 'Even when they send some Plautin or Fahrbender down from HQ once a month, we're quite literally going through the motions, old man; no one really cares'.

'Yes, it can be much more difficult when there are horses involved' - said Pechorin, but Martynov appeared not to have registered the jibe.

'Well, you may speak for yourselves, gentlemen' - Martynov went on - 'but we never know who may conduct the inspection... I, for one, would not be taking any chances'.

Pechorin felt once again the faintest sense of foreboding. He could not determine whether his affair with Vera had refined his intuitions to the point where he could sense in every remark an intimation of danger; or, on the contrary, whether he had simply become morbidly distrusting, seeing premonitions of peril in everything, even when there was none. He certainly would not give Martynov the satisfaction of revealing even the slightest hint of curiosity; but, all the same, he was loath to blunder into a situation he could not control if the contents of that fool's head might prevent it.

'Come now, Martynov' - said Pechorin - 'You're forever making a drama out of the utterly mundane; you must be very bored'.

Martynov bridled very slightly, but did not reply.

'Mungo is of course quite right' - Pechorin continued - 'Even if the Tsar himself were to make the inspection, I'm sure we could pull ourselves together given ten minutes notice'.

Martynov looked at Pechorin with his characteristic expression of uncertainty, never clear what Pechorin might actually know, never sure if there might be some insult concealed in his words.

'You're a queer fellow, Pechorin' - replied Martynov - 'I fancy you rarely know quite as much as you would like us to to think... but, well, the Tsar... not bad, not bad at all'.

Dmitrii and Mungo looked at Martynov with bristling unease; Sinyukhaev kept his eyes on the now gleaming boots in his lap. Pechorin felt again that uncanny sense of premonition, to which he was by now becoming accustomed.

'You boast of needing only ten minutes notice' - Martynov continued - 'Well, we are after all comrades at arms, so I'll give you rather more: we are to be inspected tomorrow morning by none other than the Grand-Duke Mikhail'.

Pechorin spent the night in a guest room at the house of Dmitrii and Mungo's father. He sent a brief note with one of the servants to Vera, apologizing that he had been unavoidably detained. He had briefly considered taking the carriage back to Tsarskoe Seló, but could not face the interminable journey back into the city in the early morning. Mungo had suggested, partly, no doubt, in an attempt to impress Pechorin, that they repair immediately to Kuragin's and, from there, prepare manoeuvres that would take them deep into the night. Dmitrii's suggestion that all three would be best served by spending the night in barracks with their comrades was met with undisguised derision. In the end, Pechorin shared a cold supper with his uncles, sipped a single glass of Burgundy, and bid them an early goodnight. He took a volume of Scott's earlier heroic verse from Mungo's bookshelf, but had barely read a stanza before settling into a deep, undisturbed sleep.

The next morning, Mungo found Pechorin sitting in the kitchen, alone but for the almost supernaturally old cook, who dragged herself back and forth as his imperturbable nephew busied himself with a plate of porridge oats and some black tea.

'Sleep well, Pechorin?' - Mungo asked, already in full possession of the answer.

'Like a baby, my dear uncle' - came the anticipated reply.

'Perhaps we should make a start' - said Mungo, unable to disguise his anxiety entirely - 'I'll see if Dmitrii is ready'.

'Oh, don't hurry him, Mungo' - Pechorin replied - 'Ten minutes to pull ourselves together and we'll be fine, eh?'

When the three officers - uncles and their nephew - arrived at the barracks on Mikhailovsky Square just after eight, almost an hour before the parade was due to begin, they were met with a scene of chaos. Martynov was bellowing at the younger officers, who raced around desperately trying to assemble belts, spurs, and epaulettes, while their Commanding Officer, Colonel Ignatiev, who they saw only on parade days, sat in a corner, fiddling with a rather ornate antique watch, and only occasionally barking an order at whoever was unfortunate enough to distract his attention. Amidst it all sat Sinyukhaev, ready for parade for some time now, resplendent in his impeccably turned out uniform and gleaming leather top-boots.

As the din gradually subsided, each officer busied himself with his final preparations, ensuring that no detail of his appearance might become the subject of reproach. Pechorin, a picture of young Russian manhood of which his grandmother would be justifiably proud, left Mungo and Dmitrii to their own last adjustments and strolled over to a large trunk against the far wall, in which officers such as himself, with the means to maintain private quarters, were permitted to store the everyday paraphernalia of the soldier's life. He lifted the lid of the trunk and felt for a rather modest, sheathed sabre, which he had been obliged to wear as a recruit, before his grandmother's allowance had allowed him to acquire the magnificent, gilt-handled sabre which now adorned his left hip. Next to it lay a sword of a quite different kind, a child's sabre in a brown leather sheath, more Caucasian than European in its curve, which he had been given as a present on one of the childhood trips he had made to Pyatigorsk and Kislovodsk with his grandmother.

'Come on, Pechorin' - came the cheerful voice of Martynov - 'The curtain is about to go up'.

Each rank presently took its place in little clusters in the ante-room adjoining the main barracks, which then led out onto the parade square.

Pechorin stood alongside Mungo and Dmitrii in the third wave, only the more senior officers at their back.

'Sixty seconds!' – shouted Colonel Ignatiev, looking up from his beloved watch.

Suddenly, Pechorin broke ranks, bustling through the line of senior officers behind him, and back into the barracks. He raced over to the far wall, unclipped his sabre from his belt, and reached into the trunk. In a moment, he had thrown down the lid of the trunk and returned, without so much as a 'pardon me', to the ranks before Dmitrii and Mungo had moved from their places. A second after he was through the line of senior officers behind them, the signal was given, and Pechorin stepped with his comrades out onto the parade ground, the toy Caucasian sabre bouncing at his left hip.

As the company formed ranks, Pechorin caught the gaze of a young Second-Lieutenant in the file immediately facing him, who had passed out of the Military College only a few weeks ago; this must be, Pechorin thought to himself, his first inspection conducted by anyone other than Colonel Ignatiev. The boy's features – he seemed no more than a boy to Pechorin, only perhaps two or three years his senior – were delicate but unremarkable, his complexion so pale that the freckles dotted across the bridge of his nose and cheeks looked more like a rather unfortunate birthmark. As the boy realised Pechorin was looking directly at him, he lowered his gaze in embarrassment, which quickly turned to confusion, even terror, at the sight of the child's sabre lying limp at Pechorin's side. Pechorin rewarded the boy with an enigmatic smile, noticing in the process that the boy's gaze was no longer fixed on him, but rather on Mungo, standing directly to Pechorin's right. Mungo, straining to keep his chin aloft and his shoulders straight, while desperately contorting his eyes to the left, could imagine only that Pechorin, wishing somehow to disrupt the parade in the presence of the Grand-Duke, was deliberately trying to unsettle the unfortunate boy. As his eyes strained downwards and left, however, he became dimly aware of some curious absence in Pechorin's profile; on peering down at his own regalia, chin still aloft, shoulders as straight as a ram-rod, he suddenly became aware of what it was – Pechorin, he concluded with horror, must have forgotten his sword. But then why the devil was he running back into the barracks at the very last second?

At that moment, Mungo caught out of the corner of his right eye the unlikely figure of the Grand-Duke Mikhail, proceeding slowly along the line towards them, making barely discernible noises designed to indicate satisfaction as he casually inspected each man in turn. The Grand-Duke was resplendent in the full military honours of a Field-Marshal of the Imperial Russian Army, gilded brocade caging his torso, elaborate moustache and side-burns concealing much of his face, a Prussian-style helmet topped with a pale grey cockade; yet nothing in his mode of dress could conceal the fact that he had never set foot on a battlefield and yearned instead for pleasant afternoons in the Summer Gardens and, perhaps, pleasant evenings in the arms of some young mistress. Mungo, of course, knew the Grand-Duke as well as any young officer of the Hussars could, his uncle (and Pechorin's great-uncle) Afanasii having for some years now occupied the office of chief adviser; he knew very well, therefore, his reputation for punctiliousness.

'Ah, young Stolypin' - came the voice of the Grand-Duke - 'Very good. How is life in the Hussars treating you, my boy?'

'Very well, your Majesty' - Mungo replied - 'We hope only to see active service at some point, now that the conflict in the Caucasus has escalated'.

'Don't concern yourself about that, my boy' - said the Grand-Duke. Then, in an undertone, just as he moved off to his right - 'And give my regards to your dear aunt'.

Pechorin had not moved an inch throughout this exchange, his head quite still and eyes forward, his gaze now filled with the moustaches and Prussian helmet of the Grand-Duke.

'Lieutenant Pechorin' - said the Grand-Duke - 'We have heard so much about your social successes; your great-uncle and your esteemed grandmother must be very proud'.

'I hope that I have not given them cause to think otherwise, your Majesty' - replied Pechorin evenly.

By now, every man in the ranks facing had become aware that Pechorin was standing before the Grand-Duke wearing a toy sword, including the unfortunate Colonel Ignatiev, whose complexion had gone from red to purple as he strained to remain still and face forward.

'And what is your view of the conflict in the Caucasus, Pechorin? Are you as keen to see action as young Stolypin here?'

'The forces of Shamyl can and will be defeated, your Majesty. I hope to be able to play my part in that great endeavour in due course'.

The Grand-Duke paused for a moment, then moved his face slightly closer to Pechorin's.

'In due course' - he said quietly, before moving off to his right.

Pechorin surveyed the massed ranks of astonished faces directly in front of him, Colonel Ignatiev silently incandescent to their right, and just about managed to suppress a smile.

Pechorin lay in the bunk, surveying a little wooden table and chair, the only other items of furniture in the roughly constructed cell that served as the Regiment's solitary confinement. He had spent a day here and faced two more, three days that prevented him entirely from participating in Sofia Karamzina's production of Sinyukhaev's little drama. He had not even been required to make his excuses. Colonel Ignatiev, over the course of a long, loud hour in the commanding officer's quarters, at the end of which the little man seemed near exhaustion, had assured Pechorin that it would have been three weeks had the Grand-Duke Mikhail noticed his indiscretion;

and, if there were any repeat, Pechorin should be assured that he would be expelled from the Regiment and transferred, with or without loss of rank, to a somewhat less eminent division, most likely one that was on active service. Disgraced officers, Ignatiev reminded him, were not simply permitted to return to the comforts of civilian life – the Imperial Army, after all, must not be seen to reward insubordination – but required to continue their military careers in a considerably more challenging environment. Above all, Ignatiev could not begin to make sense of why Pechorin had acted as he did; the latter's explanation that he realised he had forgotten to clean his sabre only moments before the parade was due to begin and, in a panic, had seized the toy sabre from his trunk instead of the spare he had intended, seemed only to infuriate Ignatiev all the more. Yet more mysterious, Ignatiev thought to himself once Pechorin had been dismissed, was what could possibly have distracted the Grand-Duke: how could he have failed even to notice what had transfixed every man on one half of the parade ground?

Pechorin heard a key rattle in the door of his little cell, which presently opened to reveal the figure of Staff-Sergeant Andriukhin, whose sole responsibility was the management of this miniature penal colony. Andriukhin was in his late fifties, almost unheard of in the lower ranks of the Imperial Army. He had served in the Caucasus under Yermolov before the Caucasus had become somewhat less heroic, somewhat more embroiled since Shamyl had united various groups of tribesmen in opposition to the sporadically occupying Russian forces. Now, with nowhere to retire to and no means of sustaining himself in retirement, he had secured this position, which he intended to occupy until death or infirmity intervened, whichever came sooner. The young officers of the Hussars were more or less an enigma to Andriukhin, although the contempt of the old soldier for such gilded youth, who had never faced a bullet in earnest, was tempered by the respect for rank that had become indistinguishable from the old man's consciousness over nearly forty years in occupation of the lower ranks. Pechorin he regarded with a kind of mute and inexplicable awe; he may never have faced a bullet or the *kinzhal* of the Caucasian mountaineer, but Andriukhin understood instinctively that, when the time came, this strange and proud young gentleman would not be found wanting.

'Andriukhin, old man' – Pechorin said with as much cheer as he could muster – 'Will you fetch me some paper, a pen, and ink'.

'Well, Sir, I would be honoured to oblige' – said the old man – 'but the Colonel has instructed that you are to be given nothing but bread and water'.

'Come now, I'm not going to eat them' – said Pechorin, warming to the comic possibilities.

'I'm sorry, Sir, but I can't. It's against orders'.

'And what if I ordered you to do so?' – asked Pechorin, playfully altering his tone.

'With respect, Sir, you're not in a position to give orders to anyone; confinement cancels rank and privilege'.

'I know that very well, Andriukhin, and I would not stoop to ordering you to do anything, even were I not in confinement' – Pechorin replied – 'You, too, know that very well'.

A little later, just as the sun was beginning to lose its battle with the faint odour of dusk, which penetrated even here, Pechorin sat down at the little table, took the pen so kindly provided by Andriukhin in his hand, and began to write:

> Respected Elena Andreyevna,
> I wish to assure you, first of all, that I write these lines out of the greatest respect for you and your family and I would apologise in advance for the discomfort they will inevitably cause, were it not for the unshakeable conviction that, in writing them, I am acting in the best interests of all parties concerned. Your grand-daughter the Princess Yekaterina Yessentukhova, as you may be aware, has received the attentions of a young Officer of the Hussars, a Lieutenant Pechorin. I consider it my duty to inform you that, in the absence of advice to the contrary, she has declared her love for him, but that he does not love her; indeed, I am in a position to know with certainty that the young gentleman harbours no intentions of marriage. You may also be aware that another young gentleman by the name of Alexei Lopatkin, son and heir of the late Ivan Lopatkin, has also pressed his suit in public. I consider it also my duty to inform you that, while Monsieur Lopatkin is undoubtedly sincere in his intentions, your grand-daughter is not in love with him. I would consider it most regrettable if the unfortunate girl, already bereft of dependable counsel, were to feel pressed into accepting the advances of Monsieur Lopatkin in the full spate of her grief with regard to Lieutenant Pechorin.
> I commend this information to you as true and reliable. Should you retain any doubts as to its veracity, even a brief conversation with your grand-daughter will be sufficient to dispel them.
> Regretfully, and with the greatest respect,
> Anon.

Pechorin laid down his pen, climbed into the bunk, and fell into a deep, peaceful sleep.

CHAPTER SIX

A DISAPPEARANCE

LIEUTENANT SINYUKHAEV HAD disappeared. The Deputy to the Tsar's own Physician had appeared at the barracks early in the morning, with the purpose, Pechorin would later learn, of establishing whether Sinyukhaev was in possession of all his faculties. The good doctor must have established sanity, for, little more than an hour later, two officers from the Third Department followed in his wake and escorted Sinyukhaev to a place of confinement, the Petropavlovsk Fortress on the northern bank of the Nevá.

Pechorin arrived at the barracks shortly before nine to find Mungo and Dmitrii in anguished conversation, which had continued for quite some time and was in fact now somewhat less heated than at its height. What struck Pechorin most forcefully, however, was the presence of Blagodatsky, as pale as a sickly child, and as out of place in this martial setting as a lady at a card-table. Blagodatsky, he was sure, had never once graced the barracks with his presence. Something of great import was afoot.

'Blagodatsky, my good fellow' – Pechorin said with a controlled cheerfulness – 'I'd say how very good it was to see you, but I rather fear that nothing good can have brought you into our rather unprepossessing domain'.

Blagodatsky did not reply, seeming only, if indeed it were possible, to turn a yet more distressing shade of pale. It was Dmitrii, interrupting just as Mungo opened his mouth to speak, who informed Pechorin of the morning's dramatic scenes.

'His poetic gift was not slow in bringing him to harm' – he concluded, as if offering Pechorin a curious comfort.

'Surely' – Pechorin said – 'the amateur dramatics in which I myself was so unfortunately prevented from participating cannot have caught the attention of the Third Department?'

'Hardly that' – agreed Mungo.

'Much less a few lines of tortured Romance in the pages of *The Contemporary*?' – Pechorin continued.

Mungo caught Dmitrii's disapproving glance and on this occasion did not reply. Blagodatsky, who had still not uttered a word, stared back at Pechorin, his face now a mask of worn alabaster.

Sinyukhaev, like Pechorin, had been a boy of fifteen when the news of Pushkin's dramatic flight had shocked every layer of educated Russian society and even, eventually, the vast illiterate masses. Pushkin had made his way to Paris at what appeared to be a most fortuitous time, days after the dissolution of the Chamber of Deputies by the embattled Charles X and his poisonously unpopular Prime-Minister, the half-mad, slave-owning Jules de Polignac. If Pushkin had not observed at first hand the Three Glorious Days of July 1830, as popular revolt and fighting on the barricades forced Charles into abdication and exile, his Russian imagination could not have conceived that such a thing was possible.

Pushkin flourished in the early days of France's new constitutional monarchy, living on the proceeds of modest editions produced for the equally modest Russian émigré population, hoping that editions in French translation might soon follow. Such hopes declined, however, as quickly as the popularity of the new civic King Louis Phillipe. By 1935, following a failed assassination attempt on Louis Phillipe, in which no fewer than eighteen innocent bystanders lost their lives on the end of the twenty-five barrels of Giuseppe Mario Fieschi's *machine infernale*, the political and cultural climate had deteriorated sufficiently to make Pushkin almost nostalgic for the gilded cage of St Petersburg he had so dramatically flown. No longer lauded as the heroic survivor of an authoritarian backwater, Pushkin now faced the bitter realities of life as a once-famous artist, restricted to the ever-diminishing circle of émigré society, a cage much smaller and with no gilt on its bars. In the febrile atmosphere of Paris in the late 1830s, deprived of fame and social status, Pushkin had even been inveigled into a duel on account of a calculated insult to his young French wife Natalie, but had been persuaded by friends that honour was not worth defending at the price of his own death and Natalie's impoverishment.

Sinyukhaev, in a display of temperament hitherto unsuspected by his comrades-at-arms, had been unable to bear this latest vicarious indignity; for him, as for much of the younger generation of the Russian lower nobility, Pushkin had come to stand for the principle of freedom, in their imaginations only temporarily banished until the reign of Nikolai could somehow be brought to an end. Too young to remember December 1825 – and therefore unable to learn its lessons or to resist the temptation to romanticize its causes and effects – poets of Sinyukhaev's generation had displaced their energies onto a heroic and romanticized past, an exoticised and no less heroic present in the image of the Caucasus, and, finally, onto a heroic and romanticized image of other poets.

'I tried to warn him' – said Blagodatsky, speaking for the first time since Pechorin had arrived – 'The first version was bad enough'.

'What do you mean, my good fellow?' – Pechorin asked, suddenly certain that Dmitrii also knew the full truth, but that Mungo, as ever, remained very much in the dark.

'Sinyukhaev had circulated a poem in manuscript, which the less careful among our delightful society had begun to refer to as "The Bitterness of Exile", lamenting our disgraceful treatment of Pushkin no less than his recent, and in some ways more disgraceful, treatment at the hands of the French' – said Dmitrii – 'I learned through Blagodatsky that it had fallen into the hands of the censor'.

'And was there much with which our esteemed censorship might take issue?' – asked Pechorin.

'Not at first' – came Blagodatsky's desolate reply.

Both Blagodatsky and Dmitrii had done all that they could to keep Sinyukhaev from harm. When Blagodatsky became aware that the first version of the poem had been passed to Count von Benckendorff, Chief of the Third Department, in person, he had also learned that von Benckendorff, although he would of course not allow the thing to be published, was untroubled, even ambivalent, in the face of Sinyukhaev's arraignment of slander and jealousy; Pushkin may truly have once been a 'slave to honour', even if he had disgraced himself by deserting his homeland. von Benckendorff's view was in fact not so far from that of Dmitrii Stolypin, who had asked Sinyukhaev to acknowledge that Pushkin's actions, whatever their cause, were hardly the actions of a patriot and a gentleman.

'You, Sir, are the antithesis of Pushkin', Sinyukhaev had replied, 'And I will not be answerable for my actions if you do not leave this very second'.

Blagodatsky had patiently remained with Sinyukhaev after Dmitrii's diplomatic retreat, impressing upon him how important it was to exercise caution; von Benckendorff, after all, would not countenance the publication of anything on the subject of Pushkin, unless it contained at least a flavour of condemnation. Sinyukhaev had sullenly agreed. The two had parted with Blagodatsky's cheerful and heartfelt recommendation that Sinyukhaev accept M-elle Karamzina's kind invitation that he offer something on a romantic theme for performance at her salon. The young officer-poet had done so; but he had also, in a fit of righteous anger, composed an additional twenty lines of verse, accusing the 'haughty sons of fathers famed for malice' and the 'greedy hordes around the throne' of murdering Freedom, Genius, and Glory. There would come a time, the poem foretold, when lies would no longer prevail... and when the 'black blood' of those greedy hordes would flow. Sinyukhaev had seemingly sealed his fate in the prophesy that:

The year shall come, the black year for Russia,
When the crown of the Tsars shall fall!
The rabble will forget its former love,
And the food of many will be death or blood.

The whole work was circulated under a different title, not of Sinyukhaev's composition, 'A Call to Revolution', and was in the course of the same day placed in the hands of von Benckendorff, whose ambivalence was now quite overcome. 'Shameless free-thinking', he had said to the Tsar. 'More than criminal'.

'Infantile blather' – said Pechorin, before asking impatiently – 'But to whom did Sinyukhaev entrust this foolishness, knowing that neither Dmitrii nor Blagodatsky would entertain him? And how did the wretched nonsense fall so quickly into the hands of von Benckendorff?'

Blagodatsky could only stare blankly back at Pechorin in response.

'But what are we going to do?' - asked Mungo, who had followed events with great difficulty - 'Pechorin?'

'Don't look at me, old man' - Pechorin replied - 'I have to see a man about a horse'.

And what a horse! So beautiful and lithe, indeed, was this creature by the name of Parader, that its current owner, General Mikhail Grigorevich Khomutov, commanding officer of the Hussars division at Tsarskoe Seló, insisted he wouldn't part with the beast for anything less than two thousand roubles.

'I've grown too old for him' - Khomutov confided to Pechorin, who was stroking the horse's shimmering neck as if it were already his own - 'But that doesn't mean I'm going to give him away for nothing'.

'If you insist on your price, Sir' - Pechorin replied - 'then the two of you will be growing old together'.

Pechorin understood very well that Khomutov's insistence on a price no one would pay was the old general's way of assuring himself he had taken the right and proper decision; but, if no one was prepared to take his Parader off his hands, then what could he possibly do about that? The trick was to manoeuvre him to a sum he would think worthy of the beast, while at the same time convincing him - or rather helping him convince himself - that the horse would be happier under Pechorin's hands.

'He once saved my life, you know' - the old man continued, his eyes drifting in memory - 'You can't put a price on a horse like that'.

'I daresay' - Pechorin continued - 'but I could buy two of the finest horses in St Petersburg for the same price and my life would be doubly insured. Besides, you wouldn't want him to end up in the hands of some Frenchman, interested only, if you'll pardon me, in parading the poor beast, but never riding him as such a horse was intended to be ridden'.

Later that afternoon, Pechorin wrote a brief note to his grandmother, requesting the sum of one thousand five-hundred and eighty roubles. He could hardly conceal the purpose for which such a sum was required, but made no particular attempt to persuade or justify. He handed the note to Gavril with the usual instructions, ordered his carriage to be prepared, and set off once again for the city.

Shortly after eleven, the carriage pulled up outside the Kuragin residence.

'We are honoured indeed!' - cried Anatolii Kuragin as Pechorin stepped into the entrance hall - 'But I must impress upon you that this is a house of pleasure, not at all equipped for the conduct of serious affairs'.

'I understand that very well, my dear Kuragin' - Pechorin replied - 'But I had a sudden fancy for a game of cards... I'm sure you'll be able to oblige'.

Kuragin fixed Pechorin with a gaze designed to signal knowingness, while at the same time retaining an air of mystery.

'And I am sure you will be able to find willing partners' – he said at last.

It was early and the Kuragin house was as quiet as Pechorin could remember it. He mounted the steps to the first floor, as yet free of the flotsam and jetsam the evening would surely bring, and stepped into the room where, not so long ago, Martynov had portrayed the true depths of the Russian soul. There was, thank goodness, no sign of Martynov and the room bore no resemblance to the chaos of that tumultuous evening. It was empty but for a round card-table to the left of the tall windows that opened onto the street, filled with the pale, ethereal light of the late summer evening. Two gentlemen Pechorin didn't recognise sat solemnly at the table, shuffling their cards and mechanically marking their points on little slates, facing a third gentleman, who appeared to be keeping score in his head. This gentleman Pechorin knew only too well. This was the man who had brought him to the deserted Kuragin house on a summer night better suited for other affairs.

'Ah, Monsieur Pechorin' – said de Barante, looking up from his cards – 'Always a pleasure'.

'A pleasure indeed' – replied Pechorin – 'May I join you?'

'Yes, of course... we were hoping that someone might make up a four for a round of Bridge?' – said de Barante.

The other two gentlemen looked dismayed at this prospect, although Pechorin could not tell if the cause of their displeasure was the game or merely the prospect of his participation.

'I had something less cerebral in mind' – said Pechorin – 'You have no doubt observed my countrymen in the grip of Faro, deep into the night, perhaps in this very room?'

'A game of pure chance, entirely without skill' – replied de Barante.

'*Bien sûr*' – Pechorin continued – '*mais c'est avant tout un jeu de nerf et d'intuition*'.

'*Il est préférable de jouer de tels jeux en tête-à-tête*' – said de Barante, handing Pechorin a pack of cards.

Pechorin shot a glance at the two increasingly discomfited gentlemen, who left without making their excuses.

'How are the great affairs of State, Monsieur de Barante?' – Pechorin asked as he shuffled his pack.

'I have very little to do with such matters, as I think you know' – replied de Barante – 'The influence of the German party at Court is as strong as it ever was and that is unlikely to change'.

'But your estimable father does what he can, no doubt?'

'That, Monsieur Pechorin, is the purpose for which he is employed... but anyway, which one of us will hold the bank?'

'We'll cut for it' – said Pechorin – 'Lowest wins'.

In those far off days cards were sometimes played with packs of fifty-two, but sometimes, in order to concentrate the range of probabilities, of only thirty-six, the Deuces, Threes, Fours, and Fives having been removed. More curious was the ranking, with the Ten having more value than the face cards. In Faro, however, the value of the cards, complicated matters of trumps and strategy, or even the more practical business of counting cards, had no place. The punter would simply shuffle his pack and lay down a card from the top, face up – or indeed from anywhere in the pack, if he preferred; the banker would then lay down two cards from the top of his pack, face down, one to the left of the punter's card, one to the right. When the cards were laid, the punter would place his bet, either by placing a coin on the card or chalking a sum on the reverse. The banker would then turn the card on his right; if it matched, the punter had won. He would then turn the card on the left; if it matched, the punter had lost; if neither matched, the bet fell and the cards were re-shuffled and the game continued.

de Barante had never played Faro, preferring the more sophisticated pleasures of Baccarat or Bridge, and felt himself at a great disadvantage as he nervously cut his pack. He could not know, however, that Pechorin, too, had never before played this game, although he had observed it on a hundred occasions and, moreover, had read about it in books.

'Jack of Clubs' – said de Barante.

Pechorin slowly shuffled his pack and cut.

'King of Hearts. Unlucky for me'.

Each man shuffled his pack once more, Pechorin slowly, de Barante in a state of some agitation.

'What is your opinion of our dear departed Pushkin? – Pechorin suddenly asked.

de Barante hesitated for a moment before replying, attempting to give the impression he was surprised by the question.

'I have no particular opinion, other than to say it is a shame such talent has met with such misfortune. But you must understand, Monsieur Pechorin, that relations between two great nations are more important than the fate of an individual'.

'And what harm would it have done to relations between our great nations to allow a man to live and publish without deprecation? A poet in exile poses no threat at all to your government and precious little to our own'.

'I quite agree, Monsieur Pechorin' – de Barante replied with a faint smile – 'But that, as you must understand, is not the view of his Imperial Majesty'.

Pechorin tapped his pack of cards on the table, laid it face down, took a card from the top, and placed it face up in the centre of the green baize. A Three (of Clubs, although the reader will understand by now that the suit is of no significance). Pechorin took a Half-Imperial, more platinum than gold, from his tunic pocket and placed it on the card. de Barante laid a card face down on either side, then slowly turned the card on the right to reveal a Seven.

'Unlucky for me' – said Pechorin.

de Barante then turned the card on the left to reveal an Ace.

'And unlucky for me, too'.

The cards were removed and Pechorin laid down another, a humble Eight of Diamonds, before placing another Half-Imperial on top of the first coin. de Barante turned over a Six to the right, hesitated for a moment, then turned over another Six to his left.

'It would appear that the cards have no desire to involve us in any kind of drama, Monsieur Pechorin'.

Pechorin gave no reply, once again removed the cards, and laid down a Jack of Diamonds. He placed another Half-Imperial on top of the two that already lay on the table and said without looking at de Barante:

'If what I suspect is true, it may already be too late for that'. .

'Oh' - de Barante replied - 'and what, as you put it, do you suspect, Monsieur Pechorin?'

Pechorin, although he had chosen his words with deliberation, had wanted to give de Barante the impression that he knew more than was in fact the case. Someone, he surmised, must have alerted von Benckendorff, or one of his many informants, to the fact that Pushkin's cause, in Russia and in France, had been taken up by a poet of the younger generation, and in terms that bordered on the scandalous, in Russia, at least, if not in France. And that someone must have had something quite concrete to gain, while at the same time remaining, officially at least, unconnected to the machinery of Court and government.

'I suspect' - Pechorin replied at last - 'that a modest and talented young officer in my regiment may have fallen under the wheels of the carriage of State, Monsieur de Barante... and that, notwithstanding his own rashness, someone may have pushed him into its path'.

de Barante turned over another Six to the right of Pechorin's Jack, paused for a second, then with great deliberation turned over the card to its left.

'Jack of Clubs' - said Pechorin drily - 'Once more at your service'.

'He has brought me some fortune, has he not?' - replied de Barante, sweeping away the cards and dropping the three coins into a pocket in his frock-coat - 'I bid you good evening, Monsieur Pechorin. May fortune be your guide and may your suspicions be unfounded'.

As de Barante pushed back his chair as if to leave the table, Pechorin rummaged in an inside pocket for a bundle of notes, part of the as yet incomplete sum he intended to lay out in acquisition of the fair Parader. He took out ten notes, each of the denomination of ten roubles, and laid them in the centre of the table.

'*Vous avez entendu, sans aucune doute, de la quatrième pari, Monsieur de Barante?*' - said Pechorin quietly.

'*J'avais l'impression que de telles choses n'étaient pas obligatoires*' - replied de Barante.

'*Seulement si on n'est pas un gentilhomme*' - said Pechorin.

de Barante hesitated for only a moment, then calmly sat back down in his chair, shuffled his pack, and waited for Pechorin to lay down his card.

'You Russians like to play for high stakes, Monsieur Pechorin' - he said, with an air of amusement.

'I have witnessed you playing - and losing - for stakes no lower' - Pechorin replied, recalling de Barante's anger and disgust on the evening the redoubtable Martynov failed to fall out of a window.

'It all depends on the game one is playing' - said de Barante.

'And on one's opponent', - Pechorin replied quickly, before the Frenchman could say another word.

'Play' - said de Barante.

Pechorin took a card from the top of his stack and laid it on the table. The Queen of Hearts. de Barante shot him a look of now barely disguised contempt, scribbled a note of assignation for one hundred roubles, placed it on top of the crumpled banknotes, and laid a card face up to the right of Pechorin's Queen.

'Unlucky for you' - said Pechorin, gathering up the notes and winking almost imperceptibly at the Queen of Spades, lying resplendent on the green baize alongside her fairer, younger cousin.

When Pechorin arrived at the house of Dmitrii and Mungo Stolypin later that evening, he found his youthful uncles in a condition far worse than that in which he had left them earlier in the day. Dmitrii was completely silent, his face a mask of perplexity, as if trying to solve some immensely complex puzzle, while Mungo's face wore a look of despairing bewilderment, his limbs carrying him from one end of the room to the other in an attempt to discharge the current of agitation which coursed through his body. More, however, than this display of temperament *ab reductio*, Pechorin was immediately struck by the conspicuous absence of Blagodatsky.

'What news?' - he asked at last.

Silence.

'Come, my dear uncles' - Pechorin continued - 'If we are to have any influence on the course of events, you must tell me everything, and quickly. I made what you might call enquiries of my own earlier this evening and I have a fairly clear picture of what may have happened. All is not lost'.

Dmitrii said nothing, but Mungo could no longer restrain himself.

'Pechorin' - he began with an unaccustomed and undisguised anger in his voice - 'Difficult as this may be for you to understand, there are circumstances in which you perhaps know nothing at all. The situation is very much worse than you imagine. Sinyukhaev is beyond help, and Blagodatsky along with him'.

'Blagodatsky?' - Pechorin replied, a dim suspicion rising through the fibres of his nervous system - 'What has Blagodatsky got to do with it? I would expect that he has been making representations on Sinyukhaev's behalf, but that in itself is not a crime'.

At this Dmitrii broke his silence.

'Blagodatsky tried to pass a note to Sinyukhaev in his cell at Petropavlovsk' – he said in a low monotone.

'And?' – Pechorin impatiently replied.

'And' – continued Dmitrii – 'the note was passed not to Sinyukhaev, but to an agent of the Third Department. Whoever has been supplying them with Sinyukhaev's verse is now acting, if you will, as agent for the prose of Blagodatsky'.

'And where is Blagodatsky?' – asked Pechorin.

Dmitrii did not reply.

'How clear is your picture now, Pechorin?' – Mungo interrupted, his indignation unabated.

'Clearer than it has ever been, my dear Mungo' – Pechorin replied – 'As clear as the nose on your handsome face'.

Pechorin emerged into the night, the calm exterior he had presented to Dmitrii and Mungo giving way to a rage that burned more fiercely than the phosphorous lamp that lit his solitary carriage. He bid his coachman make his way along the Moika Canal, a route with which the old man was by now very familiar.

'Get your head down, old boy' – said Pechorin – 'I may be late'.

Pechorin stepped down from the carriage and, as he had done a dozen times before, made his way quietly to the arch that led into the courtyard of the Lopatkin house. He entered through the familiar low door in the wall to the right and made his way through the deserted kitchen to the hidden spiral staircase. As he stepped lightly past the dependably unconscious servant in the hallway on the first floor, his mind was filled not with thoughts of romantic assignation, but of revenge. The image of de Barante, his half-smile and apparent hesitation as he sat at the card table concealing actions and intent of cold blood, loomed before him. He hesitated for a moment at Vera's bedroom door, gave a single gentle knock, and entered the room.

'Oh, my darling Grigorii!' – Vera exclaimed as he came in, throwing her arms around his neck – 'You are in great, great danger!'

CHAPTER SEVEN

THE FATE OF FATHER AND SON

VERA WAS AWAKENED by the thin grey light creeping through the shutters. The troubles of the previous night had left her and she lay for a moment in a state of perfect calm. Beside her, Pechorin lay sound asleep, his features softened in a way she had never before observed. She looked at him the way a mother might look at a sleeping child, softly willing him to remain in that realm where no earthly cares could reach him; and where he was hers and hers alone.

Pechorin at last awoke to be greeted by an image that would stay with him for the rest of his life. Vera had fallen asleep once more, her long blond hair flowing down in loose curls, free of its pins and the characteristic *bandeau*, her lips poised in a gentle smile. Pechorin felt again that unnameable mute force rising from the depths of his nervous system, diffusing through the blood vessels of his vital organs, clenching like a fist beneath his heart. He acknowledged wryly to himself that he feared this force far more than any de Barante or von Benckendorff, not only because of the universal human impulse to fear what one does not understand, but because he understood only too well that this force could not be tamed by the exercise of his wit – or at the barrel of a pistol. As he looked down at his sleeping Eurydice, he was suddenly overcome by a quite different emotion, to which he more willingly gave himself up: the merciless fury of the righteous would be the fate of any poor soul foolish enough to come between them. He would not, like Orpheus, sleep dead to the world while false gods laid it to ruin.

Vera woke for a second time to find him fully dressed, sitting leaning on the back of a chair at the bottom of the bed, his gaze fixed on her sleepy eyes, as the light began to gather beyond the shutters.

'Darling' – she said softly.

Pechorin smiled, but did not reply.

'It's getting late and you should go before the servants are up' – she continued – 'But you must promise me you will not involve yourself any further in this business with Blagodatsky... Oh, my darling Grigorii, promise me?'

'There is no need for such promises, Vera, my darling' – Pechorin replied – 'And even if there was, you know very well that I would not give them'.

'There is every need!' – Vera exclaimed in some distress – 'If it was simply a matter of honour, a disagreement between you and de Barante, or even just a matter of his cowardly machinations to gain favour at Court! But it is much more, and much worse, than that!'

Pechorin looked inquisitively at this orating vision, curious to learn what she might know without revealing what he himself knew, which might place her in that same jeopardy from which she sought to protect him.

'I fear your imagination may have deceived you, my darling' - he said at last - 'The politics of Court, however they might stand, are of no interest to me. My concern is for a young - and misguided - fellow officer; and, more than that, for the wellbeing of one of the few men in this city, of any generation, in whom one might place one's trust. The actions of de Barante have placed both in danger and that is for me a matter of personal honour'.

As he spoke, Pechorin held before him the image of de Barante's half-smile at the card table in the Kuragin house. Vera, he was certain, knew nothing of the 'machinations' of which she spoke, much less of how the Pushkin affair might be entangled in them. Such faint intimations of forces she could not possibly understand were not, he was sure, the root of her very palpable fear.

'Just promise me you will... be careful, my darling' - Vera persisted, faltering into tears.

Pechorin took her in his arms without saying a word.

'Don't you see, my darling?' - she continued - 'They hate you. I don't know why they hate you, but they do. Natalya told me - she is terrified of saying anything to Mungo that might further involve him - that the Grand-Duke Mikhail said some dreadful things about you on account of Katya. I don't know how or why, but de Barante has understood that the Grand-Duke's dislike for you is an opportunity to seek favour. They will use de Barante to harm you... And, if you should instead harm de Barante, they will use that to harm you... Oh, don't you see, my darling! Promise me you will take care!'

Pechorin looked at her with sincere compassion, tinged with admiration.

'I promise, my darling' - he said at last - 'I promise'.

Pechorin found his coachman wrapped in a rough thick blanket, still dozing contentedly from his slumbers. He decided to leave the old fellow for a minute or two longer and lit a small cigar. As he smoked, it occurred to him that leaving his carriage a hundred yards from the Lopatkin house might be sufficient to disguise his presence from the servants and other occupants of the house; but, in this city where no one paid very much to attention to anything, those who did, he knew, were invariably observers of the professional variety. Perhaps it was time to find a different station for his carriage and a different route, on foot, to Vera's warm embrace...

A few minutes later, the old coachman pulled the horses up in front of the house Dmitrii and Mungo's father had provided for them, a little way along the Fontanka Canal from Anichkov Bridge, marvellously convenient, as Pechorin frequently told them, for strolls in the Summer Gardens. Mungo was not at home, which Pechorin quickly concluded might be for the best; he loved his uncle, indeed, like a brother, but valued his assistance more in the theatre of action than in the cloister of deliberation. Dmitrii was as gloomy and silent as the previous day. He had convinced himself that nothing could be done for either Sinyukhaev or Blagodatsky: Sinyukhaev's words spoke for themselves; and Blagodatsky, whatever his intentions, had abetted, if not the circulation of the offending verse, then at least in its concealment. Pechorin began the conversation, as was his habit when there was something at stake, cautiously, seeking to establish what Dmitrii certainly knew.

'Such loudly radical verse will always find its way into the hands of the Third Department' - he said airily - 'But what remains unclear is how our good friend Blagodatsky can have been so thoroughly betrayed'.

'What does it matter?' - replied Dmitrii - 'If they have the note Blagodatsky attempted to pass to Sinyukhaev... well, what more do they need?'

'Perhaps some knowledge of the actions and intentions of whoever provided them with the note?' - said Pechorin, seeking to draw out of the extent of Dmitrii's knowledge.

'But how are we to find out?' - said Dmitrii - 'And, again, what does it matter?'

'What if the note - and the verses - were passed to von Benckendorff by a party who sought favour at Court in very specific circumstances and for very specific reasons?'

Dmitrii gave Pechorin a look of profound scepticism, before his quiet features leapt suddenly from the repose of gloom.

'You know, Pechorin!' - he cried - 'You know!'

Pechorin retained his air of studied calm.

'I do not know, my dear Dmitrii. But I suspect'.

'Who, then?' - asked Dmitrii.

'Answer your own question' - replied Pechorin - 'Whose interests might be served, here and abroad, by the suppression of this latest hymn to Pushkin? Whose countrymen have allowed that unfortunate exile to languish on the verge of poverty? Who is fighting a perfectly tedious losing battle against the influence of the German party at Court?'

Dmitrii though for a moment, but his mind could at first only produce answers of useless generality.

'Speak, my good fellow, speak' - said Pechorin - 'The answer is all but formed in your mind'.

Dmitrii, perplexed, hesitated for another second, before his features once again sprang into life.

'de Barante!' - he exclaimed at last.

Pechorin's revelation had on Dmitrii, however, an unintended and unsuspected effect. Much to his surprise, Dmitrii, like Vera, was suddenly more concerned for the safety of Pechorin, regardless of the fact that Pechorin stood amiably before him, while Sinyukhaev and Blagodatsky were making up their bunks in Petropavlovsk.

'Be careful, Pechorin' - said Dmitrii - 'You may not reckon much with Monsieur de Barante - although you should be careful even on that score; but he has, whether by accident or design, laid out a treacherous path for all of us, and none more so than you'.

Pechorin considered for a moment why fate seemed intent on placing him, in all circumstances, in the vanguard of danger, a lightning-rod for jealousy and resentment.

'Perhaps Martynov should fight him' - said Pechorin with a smile - 'It shouldn't be too difficult to arrange a *contretemps* between them. Short of that, however, I fail to see how at least exposing the role de Barante has played in this sorry affair cannot be to the benefit of both Sinyukhaev and Blagodatsky. It's true, Sinyukhaev will not escape punishment... and the fool will have deserved it, with or without de Barante. But Blagodatsky is too good and too honest a man to be punished for actions and intentions that have been nothing but virtuous'.

'That may be true' - Dmitrii replied - 'But there are others who are better placed to make such a case. No one at Court will be surprised if your great-uncle Afanasii makes sincere representations on Blagodatsky's behalf; indeed, they might be surprised - and suspicious - if he does not. Do you see, Pechorin, and begging your pardon, the Grand-Duke Mikhail will look more favourably on words of support from your great-uncle than from you, even if you were to find an acceptable way to deliver them'.

Pechorin recalled how the Grand-Duke had leaned menacingly towards him on the parade ground, alone unaware of the toy sword hanging at Pechorin's hip. He conceded to himself the force of Dmitrii's argument, but steadfastly refused to acknowledge his agreement in words.

'Care, Pechorin' - continued Dmitrii - 'Care above all else'.

'Care, indeed', Dmitrii thought to himself; he understood better than most the need for care in advising Pechorin, who, if he felt he was being manipulated or coerced, was apt to take precisely the opposite course to that which had been advised. Still, it was rare that Dmitrii had the better of Pechorin in any matter of will and, still smarting from the manner in which Pechorin had led him to de Barante, he could not deny himself a wry counter offensive.

'There is, incidentally, someone else you may wish to enlist to the cause, before leaping to the rescue of all and sundry yourself' - he said with a half-smile.

'Oh' - replied Pechorin casually - 'And who might that be?'

'Come, Pechorin' - said Dmitrii - 'Who else might easily and favourably influence the Grand-Duke, and even von Benckendorff himself? Who else holds Blagodatsky in as much regard as you, perhaps more so? Speak, Pechorin... the answer is all but formed in your mind!'

Pechorin looked blankly, trying to conceal the wisps of annoyance that had begun to rise in him.

'I am not at all interested in guessing what you are thinking, my dear uncle. There is no logic in it'.

'Why, my dear aunt, your esteemed grandmother' - said Dmitrii triumphantly - 'She is arriving in three days time'.

Pechorin acknowledged to himself the dull pain of regret as he walked past the Vereschagin house. He had not spoken to Sasha since the letter to Katya's grandmother. It was true that there had barely been an occasion for them to speak; but it was also true that neither had expended any particular effort in seeking one. He must do without Sasha's good offices until the present difficulties were behind him, he thought to himself; and, perhaps, that was all for the best.

He continued along Sadovaya Street until he came to the Shakhovskii house at number 61, in which his great-uncle Afanasii had rented rooms for his grandmother; for how long, he did not know. As he walked through the entrance hall and up the stairs to the first floor, regret for his necessary deceit of Sasha gave way to a familiar sense of resentment, which had accompanied the presence of his grandmother if not quite for as long as he could remember, then at least since those memories had come to seem like the memories of his present self. Resentment, in its turn, gave way to a mixture of concern and genuine affection at the sight of Yelizaveta Alexeyevna, as grand and self-possessed as ever, if showing some of the inevitable signs of age, seated by the window in a modest armchair, her concerns and her affections no less palpable than Pechorin's own.

'*Grandmaman*' - said Pechorin with mock reproach - 'I am of course delighted to see you, but most disturbed that you have put yourself to such trouble on my account'.

'My dear Grigorii' - replied his grandmother - 'It really is no trouble at all. I thought it much more sensible to deliver the sum you requested in person. I am only too happy to help, but the thought of such a sum of money in the hands of persons unknown... that would have been a trouble to me'.

She lifted an envelope from a little table by her armchair and handed it to Pechorin.

'I am very grateful, *Grandmaman*' - he said, quietly acknowledging defeat.

He had after all, he conceded to himself, provided her with a suitable pretext for visiting St Petersburg, without the slightest need to refer to the real reason for her sudden appearance.

It had ever been thus. Since the age of eleven or twelve, when the methods of total war appropriate to childhood had given way to a domestic great game of diplomacy, Pechorin had been able to establish for himself a degree of autonomy without ever loosening entirely the bonds of delicacy and affection. It was as if the old woman had an instinct for the precise point at which her authority approached its limits. She could not, she understood, command his actions; but she might provoke in him a self-reflection born of duty, be always that agency which might lead him to restraint, a counter to his own volition. She understood also that Pechorin did not regard his actions as reckless in any degree; and that, somewhere at the margin of his consciousness, he saw them also from his grandmother's perspective. She made him careful, at least to an extent, precisely by not seeking from him undertakings of restraint.

Pechorin bore this shadowplay of indirect influence with, for the most part, patient understanding. Both he and his grandmother understood also the processes by which this delicate balance was occasionally disturbed; they understood so well, in fact, that not a word was spoken by either one on the subject of his father, save for the rare exceptions on which the estate at Kropotovo served as a proxy, the name even sticking in the old woman's throat. On the last occasion he had seen his father, in Moscow a few months before his death, Pechorin had begun to piece together the events of his childhood, chiefly the settlement between his father and grandmother after his mother's untimely death. He had not, however, been able to reconcile the contradictory feelings his father's absence provoked. The impulse to identify with his father, whose low social standing had condemned him to a relationship of dependency Pechorin understood all too well, was joined in perpetual battle with the resentment the boy felt, not primarily because his father had abandoned him, but because he had lacked the wit or the courage to outmanoeuvre the old woman.

At that last meeting in Moscow, Pechorin's awareness of his own powerlessness, contending with a burgeoning adolescent will to power, combined to produce a blow no father could withstand, the shame of which still coursed in the subterranea of Pechorin's psyche. In response to Pechorin's mute reproaches, his father had attempted to explain that Pechorin's grandmother's wish to take responsibility for his upbringing and education had been in everyone's best interests, not least Pechorin's. 'How much did you get for me?' Pechorin had replied, his gaze fixed accusingly on his dumbfounded father.

Pechorin later learned from Blagodatsky that his father had taken a substantial loan from his grandmother shortly before his mother's death. Blagodatsky also hinted, but would not say outright, that the old woman had threatened not only to disinherit Alexander Iurevich, but also Pechorin, if his unfortunate – and bereaved – father did not accept her terms. Thus had this ageing Faerie Queen been able to persuade Thomas the Rhymer to remain on the margins of both their lives.

Yelizaveta Alexeyevna, sensing the turmoil in Pechorin's heart, looked out of the window at the pale grey sky, from which a haze of drizzling rain fell steadily.

'I can be of assistance' – she said firmly.

'Assistance, *Grandmaman*?' – replied Pechorin – 'You have been of great assistance to me on many occasions, for which I am sincerely grateful; but I am not currently in need of your help'.

'You may not be' – said the old woman – 'but Blagodatsky most certainly is'.

Pechorin surveyed his grandmother's implacable exterior with a studied calm, determined to display not the slightest hint of surprise at her sudden frankness. It was important, above all, to establish what she knew, without giving the impression that there was, perhaps, much more that she did not.

'We are both, no doubt, greatly indebted to Blagodatsky' – he began – 'And we both, no doubt, consider it our duty to do what we can to bring him aid'.

'The fulfillment of duty is not always to the benefit of those in whose service we enlist' – she replied – 'Or, for that matter, to the benefit of those by duty called'.

'*Grandmaman*' – said Pechorin softly – 'if your chief concern is for Blagodatsky, that is to say, frankly, if you fear my involvement will only worsen his plight, I am not offended. If on the other hand your concern is chiefly on my account, I would ask that you desist. I have no intention of placing myself in harm's way without good reason'.

'Reason you may have, my dear Grigorii' – the old woman replied – 'That is precisely what concerns me'.

Pechorin let the air escape slowly from the cavity of his chest, the calm he had a moment ago only affected now settling deep in his heart.

'I assure you, *Grandmaman*' – he said with mock gravity – 'I will do nothing that might bring dishonour on our family'.

General Khomutov stood leaning on the pristine white wooden fence which ran around the *manège* of the Hussars division at Tsarskoe Seló, a look of loss and admiration on his weather-beaten face as Pechorin emerged from the stables mounted upon Parader. The horse's brilliant black coat shimmered in the early evening sunshine, its mane more luxurious than the fur collars of even the most privileged of the ladies of St Petersburg. Pechorin sat easily in the saddle, like some Oriental princeling, his sheathed sabre glinting in golden response to the beast's deep black lustre.

'Look after him, Pechorin' – said Khomutov, manfully disguising his sadness.

'Oh, I will' – Pechorin replied – 'I intend this very evening to show him the sights of our Imperial capital, no less'.

Khomutov gave a look of incomprehension, but was too discomfited by his loss to reply.

'And besides' – Pechorin continued – 'I will stable him here, mainly, if you have no objection?'

Pechorin thought for a moment that the old man would burst into tears, but Khomutov once again recovered his martial poise.

'Of course' – he said, struggling to suppress a smile – 'Of course'.

Pechorin bid Khomutov farewell with a flick of his spurs into Parader's flank and cantered back to his own quarters, where he changed his shirt, disposed of his sword, and told Gavril not to expect him later that evening, before setting off for St Petersburg at a gentle trot. When horse and rider had cleared the limits of this strange little settlement, Pechorin once again paid his mount the compliment of a gentle spur, at which the creature accelerated into a smooth gallop. As Parader gathered speed, Pechorin gave him a sharp clip on his haunch; the horse responded by finding another gear, tearing through the blank countryside as if auditioning for the English Derby. Pechorin leaned forward onto his mount's glistening neck, the reins loose in his fingers, the wind rushing through his hair, sensing the power of the beast beneath him, the symmetry of control, the exhilarating freedom of headlong motion. The world flew past, invisible.

As the ramshackle buildings sparsely distributed on the southern approaches to the city came into view, Pechorin took a tighter grip on Parader's reins and gradually slowed him to a canter. Parader trotted on past the old cattle market and into the city over the Obvodny Canal, his regal head rearing impatiently, hungry still for the headlong rush of the open roads. Pechorin made his way to the Moika Canal, gestured to a boy in a rough cap and hemp trousers, and handed him a note and a coin.

'Do you see that house on the right?' - he said - 'The one with the archway? Take this and tell the servants it is to be delivered to the lady of the house. There's another coin for you when it's done'.

The boy set off eagerly without saying a word, ran to the main door of the Lopatkin house, knocked and waited. Pechorin watched as the door opened. A brief silent play ensued, culminating in the reluctant hand of the valet reaching out to take the note. The boy rushed back to where Parader stood to receive his reward, then strolled off along the canal, his work done for today and many, many days to come. Pechorin waited for a while, imagining Vera's downcast look as she read that he would not come that evening, perhaps giving way to relief that tomorrow he would send his carriage for her at nine. The note remained silent on the purpose of this request, asking only that she trust him. He knew without question that she did.

Parader set off once again at a gentle trot, past the Palace of the Grand-Duke Mikhail to the Tsaritsynsky Fields, and across the Troitsky Bridge into the Petropavlovsk Fortress. The sentry at the gates raised the barrier without a word at the sight of Pechorin's Hussar's tunic; it would not, he thought to himself as Parader carried him stealthily across the cobbles into the heart of the fortress, be quite so straightforward in the Staff HQ.

'You require written permission' - said the duty officer, a Second-Lieutenant ten years or more Pechorin's senior - 'No one can be admitted to see a prisoner without written permission'.

'That may take a day or two, comrade' - Pechorin replied calmly - 'And I fear that the prisoner may no longer be receiving visitors, at least not here, in a day or two'.

'I'm sorry' - said the Second-Lieutenant, his thin, worn features screwed in sullen determination under his over-sized cap - 'There is nothing to be done. I don't have the authority'.

Pechorin thought for a moment, took a chair from the corner of the Second-Lieutenant's chair, and sat down at the far end of the office.

'What are you doing?' - asked the little man.

'I'll wait' - Pechorin replied.

For the next hour or so, the Second-Lieutenant sat busying himself at his desk, looking up occasionally at Pechorin's blank, untroubled face. Eventually, able to contain himself no longer, he broke the silence, which had become much more uncomfortable for him than for Pechorin.

'You're wasting your time' – he said despairingly – 'It is impossible'.

Pechorin made no reply. A few minutes later, the Second-Lieutenant once again broke the silence.

'Look, I see from your uniform that the accused is a comrade-at-arms, I sympathise...' – he said rapidly – 'In your place, I might very well do the same. But there is nothing you can do for him. What purpose would be served by me allowing you to see him? And in any case, it's impossible...'.

'You are mistaken, comrade' – Pechorin said at last – 'I have no wish to see Lieutenant Sinyukhaev, for whom, as you rightly say, there is nothing I can do. I am here to see Sviatoslav Blagodatsky, who is more or less of my own blood, and who, as you will know, is accused of much lesser crimes'.

The little Second-Lieutenant stared back at Pechorin in confusion.

'You should have said' – he murmured – 'But there is someone with him'.

'I'll wait' – Pechorin said again, slouching down in his chair and pulling his cap down over his eyes.

An hour passed and then another. There was no window in the sparse little office, but night had long since fallen upon the city beyond the fortress walls when a slightly built man, young but already showing the signs of thinning hair, came quietly into the office. He was dressed in a manner that had of late become more common in the streets and salons of St Petersburg, somewhere between the frock-coat of the civil servant and the drab poverty of the lower classes. Pechorin, he was sure, recognised him, but could not say from where; perhaps from his time at Moscow University, but then that institution was teeming with slightly built young men destined soon to lose their hair. The newcomer gave Pechorin a curt nod, before turning to the Second-Lieutenant.

'I am most grateful' – he said – 'Lieutenant Sinyukhaev has asked that I deliver a letter to his mother. If you can make arrangements for its contents to be... um... approved, I will call for it at midday tomorrow'.

'Certainly' – replied the Second-Lieutenant – 'I'll ensure that everything is in order'.

The slightly-built stranger turned to Pechorin, without seeking to make introductions of any kind.

'It is hard to imagine how a mind such as this found its way into a military uniform' – he said, barely concealing his anger.

Pechorin hesitated from a moment, surveying the odd garb of this unknown stranger with an inquisitive eye.

'It is not his military uniform that has brought him to this place' – he replied – 'Perhaps he would have done better to save his valour for the battlefield'.

The stranger stared at Pechorin with undisguised contempt and left without a word.

The Second-Lieutenant led Pechorin along the dark stone corridors that ran deep into the heart of the fortress. It was almost midnight. They came at last to a heavy metal door, which led, presumably, to the cell in which Blagodatsky had been confined. The Second-Lieutenant turned his key in the lock and pushed it open for Pechorin to enter.

'I'll return in half-an-hour, no more' - he said, before pulling the door closed and locking it from the outside.

Blagodatsky sat on a low wooden bench, the only piece of furniture in the bare stone cell. His complexion had regained some of its colour since Pechorin had last seen him. He had an air Pechorin had never before observed, a mixture of resignation and a hitherto unremarked manly determination. Pechorin caught himself in the thought that he very much liked this new Blagodatsky, that he would happily have faced any enemy at his side.

'Why did that curious little man come to see you?' - asked Pechorin, concealing his new-found admiration.

'Belinsky?' - Blagodatsky replied - 'Courtesy, nothing more. He was really here to see Sinyukhaev. He believes, it would appear, that Russian Literature is about to suffer its latest tragic loss...'.

'You realise that there is nothing to be done for him?' - said Pechorin.

Blagodatsky paused for a moment, his eyes scanning the floor of his cell.

'I realise he will be punished' - he replied - 'Things have progressed too far. But I believe that it is not too late, if we deploy all of the resources at our disposal, to mitigate the punishment'.

'And you?' - asked Pechorin - 'Have things progressed too far for you?'

Blagodatsky looked at Pechorin with calm resolution.

'I am not important' - he replied - 'I will accept whatever punishment is handed down to me'.

'Even if you are not as guilty as others, who will perhaps not be punished at all?'

Blagodatsky looked at Pechorin with curiosity and resignation.

'It matters not what others may have done' - he replied - 'I have acted as I chose to act and must accept responsibility for that at least'.

'You are not a fool, Blagodatsky. You must have some sense of who betrayed you. And you are not, to my knowledge, a saint... have you no desire for retribution?'

'Pechorin, my dear fellow, you must know that Sinyukhaev's verse could have been passed to the authorities by any number of people, for any number of reasons'.

'And the note you wrote to Sinyukhaev?' - Pechorin asked quickly - 'How many pairs of hands can that have passed through?'

Blagodatsky once again looked at Pechorin steadily, curious and not a little afraid.

'I have no...' - he began, before his visitor interrupted.

'But I do' - Pechorin said curtly - 'I do'.

Pechorin stepped out alone onto the road, the stony path glistening through the mist, the wilderness listening only to God himself in the silent night, the stars in conversation. The pale-blue earth slept beneath the triumphant, miraculous heavens as he mounted Parader and set off for the city. His mount could not quell the insistent thoughts which assailed him as he rode. What was this pain in his heart? What troubled him? What was he waiting for and why this sense of regret? He knew only that life held no promise for him, but he could not regret the past. He sought only freedom and calm, forgetfulness and sleep. Not, he reproached himself, the cold sleep of the grave, but eternal sleep all the same, the force of life dozing in his breast, rising and falling with his gentle breath.

The Imperial Stables loomed suddenly out of the mist towards him. He had, quite insensibly, completed his journey. He dismounted and gave Parader to a sleepy youth who had been roused by his arrival and made his way on foot to the Stolypin house, where he crept through the darkened rooms without disturbing his sleeping uncles. He fell into a deep sleep the moment his head felt the embrace of the pillow and dreamt all night of a sweet voice soothing him with songs of love, above him, green through all eternity, the rustling of a dark oak tree.

CHAPTER EIGHT

THE MEN OF HONOUR I

A MODEST BUT RESPECTABLE carriage sailed along Obukhovsky Prospekt, its lacquered exterior glinting in the early morning sun. A young woman with long fair hair gathered into a black *bandeau* looked nervously from its windows. As the carriage approached the intersection with the Fontanka Canal, the driver slowed the horses and pulled over into an open space on the northern bank of the canal.

'Why are we stopping?' - asked the young woman.

'The master's orders' - replied the coachman.

Pechorin observed the carriage from the other bank of the canal, watching as the young woman sat in quiet reflection, no outward sign of pride in her beauty, waiting for she knew not what, only that she was waiting for him. He could only wonder at the source of such devotion, such selfless and unashamed love.

He remained on the far bank for a few minutes, with no thought of making her wait, but rather to fix this image of her in his mind, lest it become for some reason inaccessible to him. He then approached the carriage from the far side, walking around its rear to the window in which the young woman sat, her head slightly downturned, quite still.

'Vera!' - said Pechorin in a warm, affectionate tone - 'How very pleasant it is to see you!'

Vera made no reply, only turning her head towards the sound of his voice, a sudden light rising behind her soft features.

'Move over' - Pechorin said cheerfully - 'We had better get going or we'll be late'.

He hopped up into the seat Vera had vacated, signalled to the driver with a slap on the carriage door, and they set off across the little bridge over the canal, heading south along Tsarskoselsky Prospekt.

The carriage slowly picked its way through the now unrecognisable fringes of Tsarskoe Seló, congested with carts of every size and design, pedestrians from every stratum of Russian society, the poorest of whom had walked all the way from the city, and hawkers and charlatans of every type and trade. As they moved slowly in this stream of human curiosity, Vera gradually began to discern in the distance the outline of a gleaming, metallic object, around which people and carriages thronged in steadily increasing number.

'What on earth is that?' - she asked, still unable to identify the gleaming object, conscious only of its massive bulk as they came gradually closer.

Suddenly, a huge plume of steam rose from a kind of funnel emerging from the great beast's head, accompanied by a piercing blast of a whistle.

'My goodness!' – Vera exclaimed – 'What on earth is it? Grigorii, my darling, what are you trying to do to me?'

'Fear not, my darling' – Pechorin replied – 'That great smoking and whistling creature is nothing less than a steam locomotive. And you and I, along with a few dozen fortunate companions, are about to enter its belly and bid it transport us along the first railway tracks to be laid on our beloved Russian soil'.

'I'm really not sure if I want to, my darling' – Vera replied.

'Come now' – Pechorin said quietly – 'There is nothing to be afraid of'.

Pechorin took Vera gently by the hand as he made a path for them through the crowds swirling round the growling locomotive, its smooth curved flanks painted green and black, great plumes of steam periodically emerging from its black funnel. A little platform had been erected at the point where the rails suddenly began, complete with bunting in white, gold, and deep Imperial red. It was rumoured that the Grand-Duke Mikhail himself would cut the ribbon to inaugurate the railway and board the train for its maiden journey, but that august Royal personage was at this moment asleep in his chamber deep in the heart of the city.

A single carriage was attached to the rear of the locomotive, in which highbacked benches had been fixed in pairs facing one another. Most of these makeshift compartments were occupied by four people, most often two gentlemen and two ladies, but Pechorin led Vera to a pair of empty benches, reserved, it would seem, for them alone. As they sat down, Vera facing in the engine's direction of travel, Pechorin looking back, he tried to disentangle from her expression trepidation at this unexpected journey and the deeper fear he had seen in her eyes for almost a week now. As the engine slowly rumbled into motion, the grinding of its iron wheels on the wide-gauge track rising above the cheering and hurrahs of the crowd, Vera opened her lips to speak. Before a word could escape those charming lips, however, Pechorin placed a finger delicately across them and gave her a look of deep affection, such that she was unaccustomed to seeing in him, in private much less than in this curious public setting.

'Designed and built by serfs, would you believe?' – Pechorin said cheerfully – 'Can you imagine? I cannot tell whether it is to the shame or glory of our great Empire that it has taken the wit of unfree souls to drag us at last along the path opened by the Englishman Stephenson'.

'I cannot imagine the English suffer such discomfort' – Vera said, rolling with each jarring clank of wheel on rail – 'But I am not interested in the English, much less in their railways'.

Pechorin knew that he could forestall no longer, regretting only that there were perhaps a dozen miles until the locomotive reached its destination at Pavlovsk, but grateful that their conversation could not be heard above the noise of the engine and the wheels.

'Promise me you will play no role in this deplorable affair' – said Vera – 'It is bad enough that poor Blagodatsky has become embroiled... but they will not spare you as they will him'.

'What makes you so sure he will be spared?' - Pechorin asked, seeking at once to provoke and deflect.

'It does not matter' - she replied, refusing to be distracted - 'What matters is that they will seek any opportunity to punish you... and punish you severely. I have told you this, your friends have told you. I understand that you may not be disposed to adhere to my wishes, but you should place greater value on the advice of your friends'.

Vera broke off momentarily, a tremor of anger in her voice, vying with the urge, now so familiar to her, to break down in tears and throw herself into his arms.

'Don't you see, my darling?' - Vera continued - 'There is nothing to be gained. You must force your pride to concede that your grandmother, your great-uncle, by appealing to the Grand-Duke himself, are in a better position to exert some influence. But there is a great deal to be lost...'.

Pechorin looked past Vera out of the carriage window, determined neither to concede her point, nor to generate further anxiety.

'My darling' - he replied softly - 'I have no pretension of influence over the fate of Sinyukhaev and do not care enough to seek it'.

Vera could not disguise a look of disapproval.

'Blagodatsky' - Pechorin continued - 'is quite another matter. Whether or not I can act positively in his support, I am nonetheless duty bound to attempt to do so. You must understand that'.

Vera's expression confirmed that she did, but that his sense of duty could never be for her a source of any comfort. Pechorin shifted his gaze from the countryside sailing past the carriage window and fixed it on Vera, more beautiful in her pallor and concern than he had ever seen her.

'I assure you, my darling Vera' - he said with unmistakable sincerity - 'I will do nothing that will be the cause of your unhappiness'.

Vera looked past him out of the carriage window, a tear forming in her eye.

Countess Alexandra Grigorevna Lavalle, *née* Kozitskaya, God-daughter of Catherine the Great, was perhaps the most celebrated woman in all of St Petersburg, even as her mid-sixties approached, an age at which most women had long since retreated to the obscurity of their country estates. Countess Lavalle was married to Count Ivan Stepanovich Lavalle, Privy Councillor, First Class, in the Ministry of Foreign Affairs, but it was her fortune, inherited from her mother's family's mining interests in the Urals, that had built their exquisite *palazzo* on the English Embankment of the Nevá, which she had established as the unrivalled heart of polite St Petersburg society. Here Sofia Karamzina's famous father had first read his *History of the Russian State*; here Pushkin had first read his *Boris Godunov*; and here this very evening, as on half a dozen such evenings in every year, would Countess Lavalle host the most sought-after ball in the St Petersburg calendar.

Pechorin arrived, as was his habit, when all the other guests had already gathered and the conversation, amid the Lavalles' extensive collection of painting and sculpture and to the discreet accompaniment of a string quartet, had already risen to a feverish hum. The dancing was still some way off, little detachments of young, and not so young, gentlemen traversing between groups formed in conversation as discreetly as they could, seeking the promise of a waltz or a *mazurka* when the lights dimmed and the music struck up in earnest. Pechorin could see Vera perched on the edge of a group that also contained her brother Alexei; not to his surprise, there was no sign of the Princess Yessentukhova. On the other side of the large reception hall, Sasha Vereschagina stood in conversation with Dmitrii and Mungo. With them was a woman Pechorin did not recognise, a tall, imposing figure, with Germanic features and dressed, most certainly, in the German fashion. de Barante, he registered to his disappointment, was nowhere to be seen.

'Nephew!' - said Mungo with a genuine warmth as Pechorin approached the group - 'We had once again begun to imagine, as is so often the case on these occasions, that you had not come'.

'We are, however, very glad to see you' - said Dmitrii - 'Aren't we, Sasha?'

Sasha and Pechorin had not exchanged a word since Katya's sudden disappearance from St Petersburg, explained by her family as the result of an illness, not too serious, but nonetheless requiring rest and recuperation on her grandmother's estate. Sasha did not, of course, have any direct knowledge of Pechorin's role in Katya's departure - and, if she had known, might have been grateful that Pechorin had in effect achieved the aim she herself had sought, albeit by quite different means; but she could not put aside the idea that Katya's disappearance was in some way connected to Pechorin, an idea all the more vexing because she knew very well she would not hear the truth from him.

'You two are very rude' - Sasha said after a moment's pause - 'Do you mean to leave it to me to introduce your... your nephew to Madame von Bakherakht?'

Pechorin, glad that Sasha's reproach, on the surface at least, was directed elsewhere, gave a low bow and took the stranger's gloved right hand in his own.

'*Schön Sie zu treffen*' - he said - '*Ihr Ruf geht Ihnen natürlich voraus*'.

Theresa von Bakherakht was the daughter of the Russian Consul in Hamburg, had corresponded in her youth with both Pushkin and Viazemsky, and was, as Pechorin had heard and could not now deny, a strikingly beautiful woman, despite the approach of her thirty-fifth birthday. Her skin, pale but illuminated by a faint pink glow, was as smooth and soft as that of a girl of eighteen. Her clear intelligent eyes shone out from beneath a halo of luxurious deep brown hair, which framed her perfectly oval face.

'Madame von Bakherakht is visiting St Petersburg with her husband' - said Sasha - 'I must introduce you'.

Just at that moment, a commotion broke out on the far side of the room. Pechorin could see, to his amusement and to his dismay, the thick dark mane and moustaches of Martynov emerge above the crowd between them.

'What is that fool up to now?' - said Mungo, exasperated and, in the presence of Madame von Bakherakht, genuinely embarrassed.

As the crowd began to part, Pechorin could make out, still partly occluded by Martynov's hulking shoulders, the pinched features of de Barante. Dmitrii put his mouth discreetly to Pechorin's ear.

'Does Martynov know anything?' - he asked in a half-whisper.

Pechorin shook his head.

'Who is that man?' - asked Madame von Bakherakht?

'Which one?' - replied Pechorin.

'Why, the one in military uniform. Who appears to be coming to join us'.

All five heads turned towards the spectacle of Martynov, his dark hair flowing behind him as he cut through the astonished onlookers, his face confirmation that outrage and amusement might, in certain individuals, co-exist.

'Pechorin!' - cried Martynov as he drew alongside - 'You must introduce me!'

Pechorin gave Theresa von Bakherakht a brief, almost imperceptible look of apology.

'Madame von Bakherakht' - he said, his voice poised between ceremony and mockery - 'Lieutenant Martynov, of her Imperial Majesty's Hussars'.

'I am honoured indeed, Madame' - replied Martynov, rising from a theatrically low bow not only to take the startled Madame von Bakherakht's hand, but to place upon it a kiss.

'It is a pleasure' - she replied, elegantly concealing her embarrassment.

Martynov would not have left Madame von Bakherakht's side all evening if Sasha had not subtly promised to introduce him to as many ladies as he wished. As the two moved off, Martynov declaring ominously that he would return before the dancing began, Pechorin shot a glance across the room to where he had last seen de Barante. Nothing.

'Who was that other gentleman?' - asked Madame von Bakherakht when Martynov had gone - 'And why were they arguing?'

Pechorin looked at Dmitrii and Mungo in turn, before turning cheerfully to this beautiful new presence in their midst.

'Oh, our dear comrade has a habit of providing entertainment on social occasions, even where none has been requested'.

He paused for a moment, looked Dmitrii straight in the eye, and continued in an artificially raised voice.

'He has his faults, no doubt. But he is not, unlike some...' - he paused, drew breath, and continued with decisive force - 'a liar, a traitor, a disgrace to his homeland, or, perhaps most important of all, a coward'.

The colour drained from Dmitrii's face. Madame von Bakherakht looked at Pechorin with an exterior calm that concealed her inner astonishment.

Pechorin looked around to make sure that everyone within thirty feet had heard his words. Their openly astounded faces confirmed that they had.

Around half an hour later, as the hum of the gathering began to rise to a higher pitch in anticipation of the commencement of dancing, Pechorin was holding forth in a little group that had gathered around a grand piano. An elderly man in an impeccable frock-coat sat playing gentle melodies from another time, little more than a prop for the gathering of young officers and even younger ladies, Mungo and Natalya prominent among them. With each witticism, the laughter of Pechorin's audience became warmer and louder, partly in due acknowledgment of his skill and daring, partly a manifestation of the atmosphere that so often reigned at Countess Lavalle's balls. In the middle of an anecdote about the drinking habits of a notable civil servant Pechorin's audience could just about make out on the far side of the room, which Pechorin did not consider in any way scandalous, their demeanour suddenly changed; where once he had been confronted by a wall of amiability, he now, suddenly and without warning, detected something resembling fear. Did they imagine he might go too far and embarrass the more delicate of the young ladies, who had, he reflected, laughed with abandon at each of his scabrous sallies. Pechorin looked to Mungo for a clue, some sign of the cause of his loss of pitch. Mungo remained perfectly still, but for a faint gesture with his chin, which he raised momentarily, as if directing it over Pechorin's right shoulder. Beside him, Natalya stood as still and pale as a statue of white marble. Pechorin immediately understood that someone approached from his rear.

'Monsieur Pechorin' - said de Barante before Pechorin had turned round - 'Would you pay me the courtesy of a word in private?'

Pechorin looked once again at Mungo and turned slowly to face de Barante.

'Why of course, Monsieur de Barante' - he said, before turning once again to the ranks of concerned faces - 'Ladies, gentlemen... Please forgive me, I have business to attend to'.

He gave a bow, before turning sharply on his heels to face de Barante.

The two men moved off towards a carpeted area to the left of the marble staircase set into one wall of the reception hall. de Barante halted and turned towards Pechorin, his forced courtesy now replaced by a barely controlled rage.

'Is it true' - he began - 'that you allowed yourself to utter certain unflattering things on my account in conversation with Madame von Bakherakht?'

Pechorin was aware of his right eyebrow pulling gently towards the ceiling, paused for a moment while it settled into place, and smiled amiably back at de Barante.

'I have not said anything to anyone about you for which I might be reproached' - he replied.

'If the rumours that have reached me are true' - said de Barante - 'you have most certainly behaved very badly'.

Pechorin's outward expression remained perfectly amiable, but something stiffened in his shoulders, his jaw lifting as his teeth slowly clenched.

'I am not interested in your reprimands, much less your advice. In fact' – he continued, his tone rising imperceptibly – 'I find your conduct insolent and quite ridiculous'.

'If I were in my homeland' – said de Barante, his voice beginning to tremble – 'I would know how to conclude this affair'.

'In Russia' – Pechorin replied, his voice quickening as his moment of triumph approached – 'we obey the rules of honour as strictly as in any other country. In fact, we are less likely than others to allow ourselves to be insulted without punishment'.

de Barante's loathing of Russia was in that moment concentrated entirely in the person of Pechorin, his fear of consequences, or even injury, forgotten in a blur of rage.

'Then we will fight, Pechorin' – he spat through his teeth – 'We will fight. Do you accept?'

'It will be my pleasure' – replied Pechorin, already turning to rejoin the company.

Mungo was dispatched later that evening to discuss the terms of the duel with de Barante's second, Count Raul d'Anglais, with Pechorin's instructions still ringing like an alarm in his ears.

'Accept whatever terms he offers' – Pechorin had said, with monstrous calm – 'Do not negotiate on any point'.

d'Anglais proposed, to Mungo's surprise, that they would fight with swords; Mungo accepted without a word of a query, all too conscious of Pechorin's insistence. The duel would take place in an alley of elm trees on the Pargolovo road, just beyond the Black River, at five o'clock the following morning. d'Anglais also proposed that each man would be accompanied by not one, but two seconds. Here, Mungo's curiosity got the better of him; after all, he thought to himself, the fewer people who knew, the better.

'Why widen the circle of those involved? – he asked.

d'Anglais inwardly thanked Mungo for confirmation of what he strongly suspected, namely that this handsome, outwardly confident young Russian officer had never previously been involved in a duel.

'We must consider the practicalities of disposing of the body in the event that one of the participants is killed' – said d'Anglais with a pointed calm.

Mungo returned to the barracks to find Pechorin and Dmitrii in quite different modes of silent reflection, while Martynov careered around the room in periodic fits of anger and amusement.

'How dare the fellow!' – he bellowed – 'How dare he! I don't know what's worse, that he is a diplomat, or that he is a Frenchman! And in the presence of the beautiful Madame von Bakherakht... How dare he!'

Pechorin roused from his silence and shot a glance at Dmitrii.

'There may be just a touch more to it than that, my dear Martynov' – he said.

'Well' – Martynov replied – 'that is of no matter. The nerve to call you out in public! How dare he!'

Pechorin shook his head at Martynov's loud outrage and turned to Mungo.

'Has everything been agreed?' – he asked quietly.

'It has, Pechorin' – Mungo replied – 'and just as you asked. I agreed to all the terms proposed'.

'Then we are to fight with swords, this very morning, somewhere to the north of the city, and each man will be attended by two seconds' – Pechorin said with precise assurance.

Mungo looked back at him in astonishment, then at Dmitrii and Martynov in turn, as if seeking revelation of some trick that had been played upon him.

'You really must learn to pay attention, my dear uncle' – Pechorin said with his customary half-smile.

Dmitrii, who had said nothing since Mungo's return, remained locked in doleful silence. He saw now, as he had suspected all along, that Pechorin's concern for Blagodatsky, if not for the unfortunate Sinyukhaev, mattered little in comparison to his hatred of de Barante. Exposing de Barante's role in the affair was not calculated, as Pechorin had argued, to benefit Blagodatsky: it was calculated simply to damage de Barante. When Pechorin had accepted that de Barante would suffer no loss of reputation in the eyes of those who had benefited from his deceit – what did it matter to von Benckendorff that de Barante had lied? Wasn't that the name of the game they were playing? – he had resolved to find other opportunities to deliver the blow, without the need for intermediaries. What folly it was to presume to advise Pechorin! How foolish to imagine that the dynamics of cause and effect might withstand the perversity of his will! As he reached the terminal point in this chain of logic, Dmitrii looked up at Pechorin with melancholy resolve. But it was Pechorin who was first to speak.

'Martynov' – he said solemnly – 'Would you do me the honour of accompanying Mungo as my second?'

Martynov, as was his habit, studied Pechorin with a look of distrust for a few moments before speaking, searching for signs of mockery or deceit.

'It would be an honour' – he replied at last – 'An honour'.

Mungo and Martynov, conscious not only of their great responsibility, but of the quantity of Burgundy they had each consumed earlier in the evening, lay down for a few hours sleep, Martynov occupying Sinyukhaev's empty bunk. Pechorin remained with Dmitrii, the latter still burdened with melancholy.

'Will you sleep' – asked Dmitrii.

'Where on earth would I sleep, my dear uncle?' – Pechorin replied – 'But you should'.

Dmitrii hesitated for a moment, but then stood as if to obey. Pechorin lit a small cigar and settled back into his chair. As Dmitrii began to move off towards his own bunk, he stopped and turned his head back towards Pechorin.

'Have you no fear you might be killed?' – he asked, in a tone of restrained incredulity.

'None whatsoever' – Pechorin replied – 'I have no precise idea of the place and time of my death, my dear Dmitrii. I know only that it will not be this morning on the Pargolovo road at the hands of de Barante. Sleep well'.

When Mungo woke just before four o'clock, Pechorin was still sitting upright in his chair, fast asleep, the cigar extinguished in the ashtray by his side.

'Pechorin' – said Mungo gently – 'It's time'.

Pechorin's eyes opened mechanically, as if the night had passed in the moment of their closing. They roused Martynov and, a few moments later, three young officers of His Imperial Majesty's Hussars stepped out into the half-light of the St Petersburg morning. Pechorin felt the blood coursing through his veins, his senses attuned to the glow of the infant sun still dozing below the horizon, as they made their way on foot to the Imperial Stables, where he slipped a coin to the young Corporal on duty with no more than a barely perceptible nod. A moment later, he stood whispering into Parader's ear, affectionately stroking the beast's shimmering neck.

'What a fine morning' – he whispered – 'Let's you and I go for a ride'.

As they left the stables, Pechorin shouted to Mungo that he would ride in the rear. Mungo pulled alongside, a quizzical expression on his face.

'I know the road, of course' – he said – 'But don't you want to be at the front when we arrive?'

'Perhaps I will' – replied Pechorin – 'If I am to die on this fine morning, however, I can think of no more fitting way to spend my last moments on earth than watching Martynov commune with the natural world'.

Mungo followed Pechorin's gaze to where Martynov had already set off, his broad back rolling in the saddle as if he were indeed still drunk, the poor beast beneath him chopping and changing its stride in search of a steady rhythm. Pechorin gave Parader's rear a crack with his whip as he drew alongside and all three set off at a brisk canter for the Black River.

When they drew within sight of the appointed place, Pechorin pulled Parader to the front of the group, quickening to a gallop as they approached three men in civilian clothing standing in the shade of the trees, their horses tethered nearby. Parader sped past in a cloud of dust, before Pechorin halted and turned him, trotting gently back to face Mungo and Martynov as their horses pulled to a halt alongside de Barante, d'Anglais, and a third Frenchman, whose identity neither de Barante nor d'Anglais considered it necessary to reveal.

'A fine morning, gentlemen' – Pechorin said amiably, as Mungo and Martynov dismounted.

'Fine it may be' – replied d'Anglais – 'but we have business to conclude, and precious little time in which to do so. Monsieur Pechorin, it is my duty to ask you first if you will withdraw the remarks you made at a public gathering yesterday evening. You have both demonstrated your willingness to fight by your appearance this morning; we can therefore conclude that honour has been satisfied, if you will agree to remove the cause that first placed it under contention'.

Pechorin looked for the first time at de Barante, who stood alongside d'Anglais in a three-quarter-length coat of Delft blue cloth, stiff with pride.

'I will not' – Pechorin replied firmly, faintly conscious of an admiring smile breaking out under Martynov's moustaches.

de Barante leaned in and whispered something in the ear of d'Anglais.

'Very well' – said d'Anglais with a trace of weariness in his voice – 'Gentlemen, take your places'.

Pechorin removed his tunic, rolled up the sleeves of his flowing white shirt, took two steps into the middle of the alley and turned to face de Barante, perhaps six paces away. de Barante once again whispered something in the ear of d'Anglais, removed his coat, and handed it carefully to the unidentified third man. He then removed the links from the cuffs of his shirt and placed them in a front pocket; unlike Pechorin, however, he did not roll up the sleeves of his shirt, preferring to allow the cuffs to fall loose around his forearms. At this, d'Anglais stepped to one side and opened a long wooden case that lay on the ground between two elms. He returned with a pair of sabres, holding them by the guards with the blades pointing down under his arms. These he offered first to de Barante, who took one immediately and made two or three cutting movements through the air; the other he offered to Pechorin, who received it with a curt bow, weighing the sword in his right hand, but making no other movement.

'Gentlemen!' – cried d'Anglais – 'Obey my command! If one of you is wounded, I will offer him the opportunity to desist. Defend yourselves at all times... *En garde!*'

Pechorin remained perfectly still, surveying de Barante as the Frenchman raised his left hand behind his head and stepped forward onto his right foot. Pechorin then brought the tip of his sabre up to meet his opponent's, stamped hard with his lead foot and, with a circular flick of his blade, attempted to wrest the sword from de Barante's hand. de Barante held firm to the handle, his fist secure inside the ornate crescent-shaped guard, and stepped nimbly back, shifting the weight onto his rear foot. Pechorin flashed him an admiring smile, dropped his hand for a split-second, then tore forward, shifting his blade from outside to in and attempting a transverse cut from de Barante's right hip to his left shoulder. de Barante leaned back like a man hanging out of a first-floor window and, with a flick of the wrist, made a swift, short cut at Pechorin's right shoulder. Pechorin stepped back, motionless for a second or two, and looked down at the perfectly clean line of red that ran across the top of his arm.

As he paced slowly back and forward, he looked calmly towards Mungo, whose pale features floated between two elm trees.

'Monsieur Pechorin!' - cried d'Anglais - 'Do you wish to continue?'

Pechorin looked now at Martynov, then at de Barante, who stood quite still with his cuffs falling around his wrists, unable to disguise his satisfaction at the sight of Pechorin's blood.

'*Quand je ne pourrai pas continuer*' - Pechorin said with a half-smile - '*Vous n'entendrez pas de mes lèvres... en fait, vous n'aurez pas à demander*'.

It was now de Barante's turn to smile as he came charging in, the repeated blows of his sabre clashing against Pechorin's defences. Pechorin stood his ground under perhaps ten such blows, before taking one step back, then another, then three. Finally, as de Barante came rushing in pursuit, Pechorin leapt in a half pirouette to his right, his trailing left foot bringing de Barante crashing to the ground. Pechorin stepped slowly towards his opponent, brought his right hand across his chest, and swept his sabre down like the crack of whip, intent on burying the blade into the meat of de Barante's right shoulder. The stricken Frenchman somehow managed to bring his own sword across his chest a split-second before Pechorin's sabre clashed down against it like the pealing of church bells. A gleaming silver object fell in the dust at Martynov's feet. Pechorin stepped back, regarding with curiosity the stub of his broken sabre, only two-thirds of which now remained.

'Gentlemen!' - came the sound once again of the voice of d'Anglais - '*Ça suffit... l'honneur est satisfait*'.

'Non!' - cried de Barante - '*L'honneur ne sera satisfait lorsque Monsieur Pechorin retire son insulte*'.

'Monsieur Pechorin?' - said d'Anglais, his weariness masked by a tone of hopefulness.

'Mungo' - Pechorin replied - 'Bring out the pistols'.

'What is this?' - shouted d'Anglais - 'I won't allow it! We agreed that you would fight with swords; nothing was said about pistols. I won't allow it!'

'Monsieur d'Anglais' - Pechorin replied - 'My sword is broken. Monsieur de Barante has confirmed that honour will not be satisfied until I have withdrawn my "insult". I cannot withdraw an insult I have not made. I have spoken only the truth and will not withdraw a word of it'.

d'Anglais stepped towards de Barante, waving his arms, muttering in French that this could not continue, that he would have no part in it. de Barante did not look at him, or indeed at Pechorin. His gaze ran along the alley of trees and up to the sky, the sun somewhere low in the east, its light cast upwards in a blaze of blue, but still not penetrating the shade of the arena. That same sun lit the rooftops of Paris, thousands of miles to the west, the scene of another life, more real, more present, somehow, than this one. He would, he thought, recover his real life, or he would die.

'Eight paces' - he said directly to Pechorin, ignoring d'Anglais entirely - 'We'll draw lots to see who fires first'.

'*J'accepte volontiers*' - Pechorin replied, regretting only that he had not brought a pack of cards.

The combatants retired to their respective sides of the alleyway while Mungo and d'Anglais, still muttering, checked that the pistols were loaded. d'Anglais then whispered something in the ear of the third Frenchman, who had watched the entire proceedings without saying a word. He then called Pechorin and de Barante together, placed a pebble in one hand behind his back, and thrust both clenched fists towards them.

'Monsieur de Barante' – said Pechorin softly – 'You are a guest in our country; please, the honour is yours'.

de Barante clenched his teeth in renewed determination to ignore whatever barb this pestilent fellow threw at him and, when the moment came, not to miss. He lifted a hand to touch the right fist of d'Anglais, which opened to reveal a pebble the size of a pea.

'Unlucky for me' – said Pechorin, smiling directly at de Barante.

d'Anglais made a mark in the dirt in the dead centre of the alleway. Pechorin took his Hussar's tunic from Mungo, whispering something inaudible to the rest of the company as he did so. He then stepped to the mark, facing south in the direction of the city, and took four paces. As he paced, Pechorin fixed Martynov with a look the poor fellow had never been able to decipher, although he was certain that, in this instance, the joke was not on him. de Barante then took his place and the two combatants once again stood face to face, this time with loaded pistols in their hands.

On the command of d'Anglais, de Barante slowly raised his pistol, closed his left eye, and sighted on the same shoulder he had earlier cut with his sabre. He paused for a moment, then steadily shifted the barrel of his pistol towards Pechorin's breast-bone, raised his eyes to meet his opponent's, and slowly squeezed the trigger. A blaze of powder flared as the shot rang out. The smoke cleared to reveal Pechorin standing quite still, the epaulette on his right shoulder gone, beneath it the cloth of his tunic ripped through to reveal another steady stream of blood. de Barante faced him with a look of complete resignation, his impending fate, he assured himself, a mercy in comparison to the life he had lived these past two years.

Martynov, too, was transfixed, unable to take his eyes from this creature who had just a moment ago stared implacably into the face of death. Mungo had turned his back. d'Anglais and the third Frenchman looked on with astonished horror as Pechorin raised his pistol, a bitter smile playing on his lips, the barrel trained on de Barante's chest. Suddenly, Pechorin raised his hand above his head and discharged the pistol into the air.

'*L'honneur est satisfait*' – he said calmly and turned towards the unidentified third Frenchman – '*Vos services ne seront pas requis ce matin, docteur. Je vous souhaite une bonne journée*'.

The future Baron de Barante sat gloomily at the desk in his *cabinet*, shame still coursing through his veins, the regret that had been his constant companion throughout his time in this accursed backwater enveloping and consuming his entire being. Shame not only at his failure to get the better of this Russian upstart either with sabre or pistol, but, even more so, at having stood defenceless only for the accursed fellow, in the presence of four other men, Russian and French, to fire casually, contemptuously, into the air. How had he come to this miserable pit of fate? His father had once enjoyed the favour of Charles X, was a contemporary and close acquaintance of de Polignac, himself now languishing in exile in England, of all places. Service abroad had been the only available course of action after the accession of that other accursed upstart, Louis-Phillipe... but Russia? And a Russian Court in which, he had seen from the beginning, the interests of France must always cede their place to the influence of Germans of varying stripe, no matter how well the French ambassador sought to serve the interests of Russia. Even then, how had it come to this? How had he so fatally squandered the opportunity presented by Sinyukhaev's foolishness? And how, beyond all other considerations, had he allowed himself to be humiliated by savages...?

There was, however, a way out. The contours of an idea had been forming in his mind since the full horror of exile in this backwater had become apparent to him and had even, he now confessed to himself, conditioned his behaviour towards that fool Pechorin. Diplomatic immunity, he had come to understand, could in certain situations mean that to lose was in fact to win. His own involvement in anything untoward would either be silently tolerated or, if sufficiently serious, provoke the most welcome of all punishments... expulsion and a return to France. The code of honour of the duel, he acknowledged, required that no participant speak of his actions or involvement, under any circumstances. But Pechorin, he told himself, the black rage of shame once again rising in his breast, had not acted honourably; the honourable thing would have been to shoot him clean through the forehead. Pechorin had not spared his life, but only cast him further down into the pit of humiliation. If the authorities became aware of what happened, Pechorin – and his comrades-at-arms – would be punished, as they so richly deserved. He would return to France, as he so fervently wished. His father, once the initial embarrassment had subsided, would surely thank him.

de Barante took from a drawer in his desk a sheet of paper, an envelope, and a rough lump of sealing wax. He dipped the quill of his pen carefully into the inkwell and began to write.

CHAPTER NINE

LÈSE-MAJESTÉ

THE NEXT MORNING, as Pechorin lay sleeping in the regimental barracks, in the bunk vacated by the unfortunate Sinyukhaev, two officers of the Third Department informed the Duty Sergeant that they had important business with Lieutenant Pechorin. The poor man, still ashamed and alarmed by the arrest of Sinyukhaev only a few days earlier, had no choice but to admit them.

Pechorin awoke to find the two officers standing at either side of his bunk. He opened one eye, then the other, then once again closed them.

'Gentlemen' – he said, his eyes still closed – 'I had a very busy day yesterday, you can hardly imagine. Won't you allow an officer in his Imperial Majesty's Hussars a little rest? If you would be so kind as to inform me of a place and time at which I might help you with any enquiries you wish to make, I will be more than happy to oblige. Trust me, I'm not going anywhere'.

'I'm afraid that won't be possible' – said one of the officers – 'We have instructions to escort you to the military prison at the Haymarket immediately'.

Pechorin lay quite still in his bunk, eyes closed, his hands folded behind his head.

'In that case' – he said – 'I'm sure you can spare five minutes'.

Pechorin's good humour did not survive the desperate bleakness of the cell to which he was transported. The bare stone walls were relieved only by a tiny window behind iron bars, set above eye-level, through which he could occasionally see only the feet of passers-by. The sole item of furniture was the ancient wooden bench on which he sat. The officers had asked him no questions either en route or on arrival and had given him no indication of when he might expect to be interrogated; they had not even, if it were necessary, explained the cause of his detention. Pechorin began to search in his soul for any sign of concern or fear, but could find none; he was consumed instead by a terrible, familiar despondency.

As the light began to fade in the window above his head, he lay on his back on the bench, closed his eyes, and fell fast asleep. When he awoke, in precisely the same position, the thin grey light of the early autumn morning had seeped into his cell. He sat upright on the bench, fixed his eyes on the door, and waited. Hours passed. His gaze shifted between the door and the feet which occasionally hurried past the window. Every so often, he heard the sound of other feet, in the corridor beyond his cell door, and his attention quickened in expectation of the sound of a key turning in the lock. Each time, however, the footsteps receded and the door remained quite still. When the light in the little barred window once again began to fade, Pechorin again lay down on his back and fell asleep.

On the second morning, he was awakened before it was light. The two officers who had brought him here were standing in front of the door on either side of Colonel Ignatiev. Pechorin leapt immediately to his feet and saluted.

'Be seated, Lieutenant Pechorin' - said the Colonel - 'You are not on duty'.

Pechorin sat down.

'I have been asked to solicit from you an account of the events that have brought you here' - Colonel Ignatiev continued - 'You are in a great deal of trouble. In your own interests, I strongly advise that you omit nothing from your account and resist the temptation to protect others. We already know the roles played by young Stolypin and Martynov'.

Pechorin sought to conceal his surprise by replying immediately.

'I have nothing to hide, Sir. I would not insult you by attempting to conceal the truth. At Madame Lavalle's ball, I was approached by Monsieur de Barante, who accused me of insulting him in the presence of Madame von Bakherakht. I replied that I had not and declined to make any further explanation. He then informed me that, had we been in his homeland, he would know how to conclude the matter. I replied that in Russia we obey the rules of honour as strictly as in any other country and suggested that, in fact, we are less likely than others to allow ourselves to be insulted without punishment. He then challenged me to a duel. The next morning, we met on the Pargolovo road beyond the Black River. His seconds were Raul d'Anglais and another Frenchman whose name I don't know; I had never seen him before. Monsieur de Barante had elected to fight with swords, but, after he had wounded me in the shoulder, I somehow broke the tip of my sword. We then took pistols. Monsieur de Barante fired first, once again lightly wounding me in the shoulder. I then fired my pistol into the air and we parted. That, Sir, is a detailed and accurate account of everything that happened between us'.

Colonel Ignatiev looked at Pechorin with a trace of admiration he was nonetheless determined to conceal.

'I appreciate your honesty, Lieutenant Pechorin' - he said wearily - 'It would have been better, of course, to have brought this to my attention immediately'.

Pechorin hesitated for a moment, torn between acquiescence and a modest wager on Ignatiev's sense of honour.

'I apologise, Sir' - Pechorin began - 'I had no intention of bringing dishonour on the Regiment. But I did not expect that Monsieur de Barante would bring dishonour upon himself by revealing the nature of our dispute'.

'Perhaps let others determine where honour lies, Lieutenant Pechorin' - Ignatiev replied - 'But how did you know that de Barante...?'

Colonel Ignatiev shook his head in a display of exasperation, turned to the officers of the Third Department, neither of whom had said a word, and the three of them once again left Pechorin alone.

The next day, no one came to see Pechorin. He devised for himself a kind of routine, according to which he would stand for perhaps an hour - who knew? - beneath the barred window, studying the varieties of footwear and hose that passed by every so often; he then sat for a time on the bench, examining the immovable metal door; finally, he stood with his back against that same door, allowing himself to contemplate, if not quite the seriousness of his own situation, then at least, by the somewhat strained association so often produced by solitary confinement, the fate of his generation. How indifferent we have become, Pechorin thought, to good and evil alike; how miserably we respond to the presence of danger, cowering like contemptible slaves in the face of power. Life - his own and in general - seemed like a wide open, unremitting road to nowhere. He had, he acknowledged to himself, both loved and hated quite by chance, giving nothing to either; even as his rage at de Barante had boiled and overflowed, he had all the same felt a strange chill in his soul. He was nothing more than a stranger at someone else's feast.

Pechorin stirred from his reverie and noticed that the light in the little window had begun to fade. He lay down on the bench and went to sleep. When he awoke, the cell was already full of light, but he could not estimate how far the day had progressed. Just as he was preparing to embark once again upon his daily routine, he caught the sound of footsteps in the corridor, belonging, he immediately realised, to at least two men. He then heard the sound of a key turning in the lock and the heavy metal door creaking open on its rusty hinges.

'Pechorin' - said Dmitrii, standing a foot taller than the guard who accompanied him - 'Are you receiving guests?'

Pechorin's exterior shed the marks of solitary despondency in an instant and assumed once more its curious, half-declared, half-concealed confidence.

'I have been rather busy' - he replied without a hint of a smile - 'But please do come in'.

When they were alone, Pechorin's expression changed once again, now displaying insistent and impatient demand.

'What news of Mungo?' - he asked, before adding, after a brief pause - 'And Martynov?'

'Both are fine' - Dmitrii replied - 'Martynov is at the barracks and Mungo has spent the past few days at home with me'.

'So they haven't been arrested?' - Pechorin continued.

'Not yet. I have to tell you that Mungo took it upon himself to write a letter to no less a person than His Imperial Majesty the Tsar, confessing without reservation to his own involvement. He judged, perhaps correctly, that forthright confession, weighed against the machinations of de Barante, will be to the benefit of both of you. Between that and the information Monsieur de Barante has no doubt provided, we may assume that they know everything'.

Pechorin brightened, something like a smile returning to his lips.

'To His Imperial Majesty himself, eh?' - he said quietly, before continuing - 'I, too, have told them everything'.

'I didn't doubt that you would' - replied Dmitrii.

Uncle and nephew sat in silence for a few moments, bonds of kin and friendship requiring neither to say anything further on a matter so thoroughly understood by both. To Pechorin's surprise, Dmitrii became visibly uncomfortable as the silence was prolonged.

'My dear uncle' - Pechorin began - 'Your hesitation is already eloquent confirmation that matters have not gone so well for Sinyukhaev... and Blagodatsky?'

Dmitrii looked up, his perennial amazement at Pechorin's ability to read people and situations vying with the immense sadness of what he knew he must now convey.

'Sinyukhaev is in transit' - he said quietly - 'To the ends of the earth... the mines at Nerchinsk'.

'At least he'll be in good company' - replied Pechorin.

Dmitrii frowned but chose not to respond to his nephew's weak attempt at humour, which he had in any case expected.

'And Blagodatsky?' - Pechorin asked, his expression unchanged - 'I can't imagine he'll do quite so well in the company of ageing Decembrists'.

Dmitrii once again frowned.

'Discreet interventions by both your grandmother and your great-uncle Afanasii secured for him a rather less perilous fate: he has been transferred to the municipal authorities in Petrozavodsk, where he will continue his work as a civil servant'.

'At the same rank?' - Pechorin suddenly asked.

'Yes, I believe so' - replied Dmitrii.

'And, no doubt, without limit of time' - continued Pechorin, his gaze drifting once again to the immovable metal door.

In a small office in the Mikhailovsky Palace - hardly bigger, in fact, than Pechorin's cell - crowded with darkwood furniture, sat a small German man, with shoulders so rounded that another observer might have been tempted... well, I shall say no more. His name was Karl-Robert Nesselrode and, although he spoke no Russian, he had been Minister of Foreign Affairs of the Russian Empire since 1816. Nesselrode's birth on a British ship sailing for Lisbon and baptism into the Church of England was perhaps less strange than the tale of his progress through the Russian diplomatic service, aided by the influence of his father, the Russian ambassador to Prussia. He served under both Pavel and Alexander and, if he had not quite endeared himself to Nikolai, then he had at least gained his unquestioning trust. This he had achieved through a straightforward combination of suspicion and caution, which, he had instinctively understood without ever consciously reflecting on it, matched perfectly the tone and atmosphere of Nikolai's Court.

Nesselrode did not much care for Russians, but Russia - or its ruler - he served. Frenchmen, however, he despised, chiefly because he had never understood them and was therefore constantly confounded by the shifts and *volte-faces* of French foreign policy. He would not have given a passing thought to the tribulations of a Russian poet in exile in Paris, for he required no such bell-weather to inform him of the state of Franco-Russian relations. He was on the other hand obliged - for who at Court was not? - to pay due attention to the seditious license of Sinyukhaev. Yet Nesselrode alone had seen in the conjunction of these circumstances an opportunity to secure a small but important victory; and securing small victories, he told himself, was the only sensible way of conducting politics or diplomacy. He saw, moreover, that this objective could be achieved without placing his own ends in contradiction to the expectations and desires of the Tsar. 'Two birds, one stone', Nesselrode thought to himself, as the English were apt to say.

These somewhat self-satisfied reflections were disturbed by a not-unexpected knock at the door.

'Come', - said Nesselrode, as if someone had fired a pistol.

'Good evening, Your Excellency', - replied von Benckendorff as he entered and closed the door behind him.

General Konstantin Alexander Karl Wilhelm Christopher Count von Benckendorff, though he spoke the same language, was an entirely different breed of a man from Nesselrode. A Baltic German, whose father had been the military Governor of Livonia, von Benckendorff's career had in its own way matched the curious, elliptical contours of Nesselrode's. He had served with distinction during the Napoleonic Wars, routing French forces at Leipzig, before driving them entirely out of the Netherlands and Belgium; but his fate, like that of Nikolai, took its decisive turn in December 1825. von Benckendorff had attempted to warn Alexander as early as 1821 of the seeds of what would culminate in the Decembrist uprising, informing him that influential figures in the military were beginning to form societies dedicated to reform, by whatever means; but he was ignored. This furnished him with the credentials to form part of the committee of investigation that was set up after December, which, largely due to the efforts of von Benckendorff himself, give birth to a new *Gendarmerie* and secret police under the auspices of a new Third Department of the Imperial Chancellery. von Benckendorff, having helped create this body, became its first Chief in 1826, responsible not only for the surveillance of thousands of His Imperial Majesty's subjects, often in the highest places, but also for the apparatus of censorship. Like Nesselrode, his first loyalty was to Nikolai, to whom he reported directly on matters of sufficient importance; unlike Nesselrode, however, the ambit of his suspicion did not extend beyond Russia, nor for that matter much beyond St Petersburg. He was a policeman, whose second loyalty was to the network of agents and informants on whom the success of his endeavours depended. von Benckendorff had acquired, with good reason, the reputation of a ruthless, but logical servant of the Tsar; only those very close to him were aware that he was on certain occasions inexplicably unable to remember his own surname, which he on more than one occasion had to recall by reading aloud from his business card.

Nesselrode shifted slightly in his chair and peered up at von Benckendorff through his steel-rimmed *pince-nez*.

'Shall we conclude the details of this rather unfortunate affair, Count von Benckendorff?' – he asked, with just a hint of a sly smile.

'I don't imagine that will be too difficult, Count Nesselrode' – von Benckendorff replied – 'Pechorin must leave St Petersburg, of that there is no doubt. This nonsense about having deliberately fired into the air will not save him; and His Imperial Majesty would prefer that his departure is arranged on such terms that it will be difficult for him to return. As for the other two, Martynov and the young Stolypin, His Imperial Majesty wishes to exercise no punishment other than to remind them of their duties. I trust that all of this is satisfactory?'

Nesselrode paused for a moment and removed his *pince-nez*.

'And the Frenchman?' – he asked.

'Monsieur de Barante is not only the injured party in this matter, metaphorically speaking of course, but he has also been of great service to us, Count Nesselrode' – replied von Benckendorff – 'He may prove to be of further use'.

'I am certain there is no shortage of those who may be of use to you, Count von Benckendorff; but it is impossible for de Barante – and his father the ambassador – to remain in Russia in these circumstances. You too will have heard those voices who have sought, in furtherance of the wretched nonsense of the Pushkin affair, to turn this into a matter of patriotism. They are making a hero of this Pechorin, lauding him for defending the honour of a Russian officer and teaching the Frenchman a lesson. We can do very well without that kind of false idol, no doubt; but we can also do very well by gilding the necessary punishment of the Russian with the expulsion of the affront to Russian honour. Do you see, Count von Benckendorff? Now that word of the duel is out and despite – or precisely because of – the fantastical exaggeration in its re-telling, neither party can remain in St Petersburg'.

'Very well' – replied von Benckendorff with only marginal reluctance – 'But de Barante nonetheless remains the injured party, all the more so in fact because of the rumours that are circulating; permit me to recommend also to His Imperial Majesty that Pechorin write to de Barante, withdrawing and apologising for the claim that he fired intentionally into the air, which has done more damage to de Barante's reputation than any bullet might have done to his flesh'.

'Very well, indeed' – replied Nesselrode almost in a whisper – 'What passes between Pechorin and Monsieur de Barante is of no importance to me. Are we agreed?'

'Agreed' – replied von Benckendorff, silently anticipating the day he would no longer have to agree anything with this insufferable hunchback.

Colonel Ignatiev's weary expression, although by now familiar, conveyed in advance the news more eloquently than that gentleman's verbal capacity could ever have hoped to do. Pechorin was to be stripped of all privileges of the nobility and transferred to the Tenginsky Infantry Regiment in the Caucasus as a private soldier. He was to be deprived, in other words, of his social status, his right to reside in the capital, his rank, and his income. Pechorin understood very well – as he had done on that fateful morning, even as de Barante's pistol was aimed at his chest – that his punishment might have been yet more severe if he had shot or even killed de Barante; but this… this was scant vindication of his decision to fire in the air.

'Is that all?' – Pechorin asked curtly.

Colonel Ignatiev now looked back at Pechorin with a rather grave expression, which had replaced the look of genuine sadness he felt at the severity of the sentence.

'Count von Benckendorff also requires you to write to de Barante, withdrawing and apologising for your false testimony that you deliberately fired in the air, which de Barante considers a further insult to his reputation'.

Pechorin's eyes flashed with that same rage that had led him into this morass of deceit and dishonour.

'If I agree to write such a letter, Sir' – he replied as calmly as he could manage – 'will you ensure that it reaches Monsieur de Barante without the intercession of any third party? This is a matter of honour and, beyond the punishment I am to suffer, concerns no one but myself and Monsieur de Barante'.

Colonel Ignatiev fixed Pechorin with an inquisitive stare, paused for a moment, then agreed with some reluctance, his sympathy perhaps occluding his better judgement.

'Ask the guard to bring paper, pen and ink' – he gestured to one of the officers of the Third Department.

Later that same evening, de Barante was surprised to receive from his valet an envelope with only 'M. de Barante' on its face and a small clump of unstamped wax on its rear. As he absorbed its brief contents, his surprise gave way to astonishment, which in turn gave way to an all-too-familiar rage.

> Monsieur de Barante,
> It is my great pleasure to invite you to be my guest at His Imperial Majesty's military prison in the Haymarket tomorrow evening at 9 p.m. Please make yourself known to the duty Sergeant, upon which you will be escorted to my quarters.
> Faithfully,
> Grigorii Alexandrovich Pechorin

The following evening, at the first sign of the fading of the light and as the flow of feet and ankles past his window began to diminish to a trickle, Pechorin stood with his back to the metal door and gave it three clamorous kicks with the heel of his boot. The sound of footsteps was soon heard in the corridor, followed by the sound of a key in the lock.

'What is it?' – gasped the diminutive guard as he pushed open the heavy metal door – 'Are you alright?'

'Listen to me very carefully' – said Pechorin – 'In less than half an hour a foreign gentleman will present himself and ask to see me. Please inform the duty Sergeant that he is to be admitted without delay'.

The little man looked back at Pechorin with suspicion and disbelief.

'It's not possible, your Honour' – he said – 'It's against the rules. We'd be strung up...'.

Pechorin calmly slipped his hand into a pocket in his tunic and took out two banknotes of the denomination of ten Roubles. The little guard's mouth opened wider, his excitement now erasing any last trace of suspicion.

'One of these is for you' – said Pechorin – 'The other is for the duty Sergeant. Make sure my guest is escorted here as soon as he arrives. And leave us for no more than fifteen minutes'.

A little later, Pechorin remained seated on his bench as the metal door opened to reveal the figure of de Barante, who now barely corresponded to the image that persisted in Pechorin's imagination. de Barante turned nervously as the guard closed and locked the door behind him, before turning once more to face Pechorin.

'I'll be brief' – Pechorin began – 'Is it true that you are dissatisfied with my account of events?'

'I have no idea why you have insisted on saying you fired intentionally into the air' – replied de Barante.

'I did so for two reasons' – said Pechorin – 'First, because it is true; and second, because I see no reason to conceal something that will have no ill effect upon you, but may very well have been to my benefit. You know I am to be deprived of my social status and transferred to the Caucasus as a private soldier? Imagine what they would have done to me had I acted otherwise... and imagine, Monsieur de Barante, what might have become of you'.

'I did not know' – de Barante replied, his mind involuntarily conjuring a picture of a quiet Parisian alley on a warm summer's evening – 'The Caucasus... that is, indeed, a serious matter'.

Pechorin fixed him with a determined stare.

'If you are not satisfied with my explanation, then, when I am once again at liberty, I will be more than happy to face you a second time, if you consider it necessary'.

de Barante searched within himself for the remains of an ambition that had led him to betray Sinyukhaev and Blagodatsky, for even just a scrap of the rage that had driven him to kill this imperturbable demon who now sat quietly before him, or to be killed by him. He found only, as just a moment ago, Paris on a warm summer's evening.

'No, Monsieur Pechorin' – he replied – 'I am entirely satisfied by your explanation'.

They remained in silence, each contemplating the faint outline of the unknowable future, until at last the key turned once again in the heavy metal door.

When de Barante and the guard had left, Pechorin retrieved from the corner of the cell the paper, pen and ink he had retained on the previous evening, set himself awkwardly on the bench, and began to write:

Your Imperial Highness the Grand-Duke Mikhail!
While fully confessing my guilt and submitting with the deepest respect to the punishment handed down to me by His Imperial Majesty, I have until now been encouraged by the hope of being able to atone for my actions through committed service. I now understand from Count von Benckendorff, however, that I am also accused of giving false evidence, the most difficult accusation with which a person who values his honour can be faced. Count von Benckendorff has asked me to write a letter to Monsieur de Barante, in which I am to ask his forgiveness for having unjustly claimed to have fired into the air. I cannot agree to this demand, which is entirely against my conscience. Yet the thought that His Imperial Majesty and Your Imperial Highness might share this doubt as to the truth of my words is so intolerable that I have decided to appeal to Your Imperial Highness, knowing your generosity and sense of justice, for which I have on a number of occasions been indebted. I ask therefore that you defend and vindicate me in the opinion of His Imperial Majesty, otherwise I might unjustly and irretrievably lose the reputation of an honourable man.

I hope that Your Imperial Highness will allow me to speak openly: I sincerely regret that my evidence offended Monsieur de Barante; I did not expect that it would and had no intention of doing so; but I cannot now correct an error through a lie, a course of action to which I have never previously stooped. In saying that I fired into the air, I spoke the truth; I give my word of honour. This is confirmed by that fact that, when my second, Lieutenant Stolypin, handed me the pistol, I told him I intended to fire into the air. He will be able to confirm this.

While only too aware of my boldness, I dare also to hope that Your Imperial Highness will deign to consider my pitiful situation and, by intervening, restore my good name in the opinion of His Imperial Majesty and Your Imperial Highness.
I have the honour of remaining Your Imperial Highness' most respectful and devoted servant,
Grigorii Alexandrovich Pechorin
Tenginsky Infantry Regiment

A little less than two months later, Pechorin sat in a comfortable armchair in the house of Dmitrii and Mungo Stolypin near the Anichkov Bridge, smoking a little French cigar and sipping a glass of Burgundy.

'House arrest is tedious, my dear Dmitrii' - he said - 'but the accommodations and affordances are much superior to my previous place of confinement'.

'Enjoy it while you can, Pechorin' - Dmitrii replied - 'You will certainly find wine and cigars in the Caucasus, but I doubt your surroundings will be quite so pleasant'.

'More pleasant than they might have been' - said Pechorin - 'I'd much rather be a Lieutenant in the Nizhegorodsky Dragoons than a Private in the Tenginsky Infantry, wouldn't you?'

'I much prefer my current situation, Pechorin'.

'Oh, I'm not so sure' - Pechorin replied airily - 'I could do with a change'.

The Grand-Duke Mikhail had been very much surprised to receive Pechorin's letter, but it had nonetheless succeeded in having the desired effect. In any contest of honour between a Frenchman and a Russian, Pechorin had correctly surmised, there could be only one outcome in the eyes of the Grand-Duke, and even the Tsar himself. 'If he had fought with a Russian, I'd know exactly what to do', Nikolai had said in response to his brother's entreaties. As it was, Pechorin's transfer to the Caucasus at the same rank and with all the privileges of the nobility satisfied all parties: Nikolai was rid of this latest batch of insolent Sinyukhaevs, Blagodatskys, and Pechorins; Count Nesselrode had an iron pretext for the expulsion not only of d'Anglais and de Barante, but of de Barante's father the ambassador; de Barante would return to his mythical Paris; and Pechorin would encounter his own mythical Caucasus as an officer in His Majesty's Dragoons, a freedom for which his subconscious had been secretly yearning since childhood. The Grand-Duke himself, it may also be said, would no longer have to encounter Pechorin in his way, on the parade ground or in covert matters of the heart.

'When do you leave?' - asked Dmitrii.

'The day after tomorrow' - Pechorin replied - 'There are just one or two things I have to take care of'.

The next evening, an hour after the last light of the sun had faded entirely, Pechorin's carriage pulled up outside the Stolypins'. A gentleman in a Hussar's tunic and cap pulled down over his eyes hurried down the path and got in, before the carriage trundled into motion in the direction of Tsarskoe Seló. Half-an-hour later, Pechorin slipped out of the house by the back door, which led into an enclosed courtyard. From here, he was able to cut through between two little cottages and emerge into the street through an archway two doors down and set off on foot for Sadovaya Street.

When he arrived at the Vereschagin house, he rang the bell and entered without waiting for a reply, mounted the narrow stairs, and made his way to the drawing room. The door lay open, through which he could see Sasha and Vera sitting silently facing one another, Vera's hand resting in Sasha's.

'Good evening, ladies' - Pechorin said as he entered - 'It is indeed a pleasure to see you'.

Both faces turned to greet him, Vera's wearing an expression of childlike surprise, the grief in her eyes fading for just a second.

'Grigorii...' - she managed to say in a halting voice - 'but how on earth did you get here?'

'Never mind that' - Pechorin replied - 'You will understand that I can't stay long'.

Sasha let go of Vera's hand.

'I must see to my mother' - Sasha said quietly, rising to leave.

When they were alone, Vera placed her hands on the arms of her chair as if to get up.

'Don't, Vera' - said Pechorin - 'Stay exactly where you are and listen to me very carefully'.

Vera eased back into the chair and withdrew her hands to her lap, her face deathly pale beneath her blond hair and black *bandeau*, her eyes glistening with unformed tears.

'I'm leaving first thing tomorrow morning for the Caucasus' - he continued - 'We will not see each other again'.

She made as if to speak, but Pechorin raised his jaw slightly in a silent gesture of dissuasion.

'I do not know if I will return and, if I do, I hope to find that you are married and happy. You must not wait for me. I wanted you to know only that you have given me something for which I have been in desperate need, which no one has been able to give me before. For that, I am truly grateful. You know also, however, that our time has passed. I cannot return what you have given me and I cannot continue to accept it from you, knowing that I have nothing to give. So it is for the best that we must part, before time and circumstance can destroy what has passed between us'.

Tears now flowed in a pattern of silvered streamlets down Vera's pale cheeks. She withdrew her eyes from Pechorin and bowed her head.

'Leave me' - she said in a whisper through her tears.

As Pechorin reached the door, Sasha appeared at the far end of the dim corridor, a look of blank reproach on her face.

'Farewell, Sasha' - said Pechorin - 'Look after her'.

He turned and disappeared down the narrow staircase.

Pechorin threw open the shutters of the drawing-room window shortly after dawn, welcoming the rays of the new sun. Dmitrii was still asleep, but Mungo, who had very much enjoyed his role in the subterfuge of the previous evening, had already left the house, with orders from Pechorin to return, without fail, before his planned departure at nine. Pechorin's dismay at the prospect of the journey - no less than three weeks on the godforsaken roads of the provinces, night after night in dreadful inns at remote post-stations - was relieved only by the tantalising prospect of a different kind of existence in the Caucasus of his childhood recollection. Perhaps only there would he be free of both masters and slaves, of the pale-blue uniforms of the Gendarmerie, the all-seeing eye, the ear that hears everything.

At just after eight, Pechorin's carriage pulled up outside the house. Out of it stepped his grandmother, assisted by one of her young ladies. Pechorin, calm in the knowledge that whatever the conversation with his grandmother may hold, it would at least be brief, anticipated the knock by opening the front door to greet them.

'Grandmaman' - he said with an open smile - 'How pleasant, as ever, it is to see you'.

His grandmother merely nodded in response, brushed past him in the entrance hall, and made her way to a comfortable armchair in the drawing-room. The rather embarrassed young lady who accompanied her slipped through to the kitchen without a word.

'I'll be brief' - said Pechorin's grandmother curtly - 'I have three letters for you, which I would like you to deliver in person, ideally without submitting to the temptation to open and read them'.

'Grandmaman' - Pechorin replied, still with a smile - 'You do me a great dis-service; I have no interest in the content of your letters'.

'You don't yet know to whom they are addressed' - his grandmother replied with a withering stare - 'The first is for Lieutenant Martynov, from his mother...'.

'Martynov?' - said Pechorin, utterly confused.

'Ah' - the old woman replied - 'The news has not reached you. Lieutenant Martynov, no doubt expecting to be transferred to the Infantry as a result of his involvement in... in your affair, took it upon himself to request deployment to the Tenginsky Infantry Regiment. His request was granted and he is already, as far as I am aware, in Stavropol. He left without saying a word to his poor mother, who, as you know, has been a friend for more years than I care to remember'.

She handed Pechorin a sealed envelope, followed by another, unsealed.

'There is, I believe, three hundred roubles there' - she said - 'Make sure he gets it along with the letter'.

Pechorin took both envelopes and slipped them into an inside pocket, his confusion now supplanted by a burning resentment.

'The second' - his grandmother continued - 'is for General Yermolov, from your great-uncle Afanasii'.

Pechorin's face once again bore the marks of profound confusion.

'Grandmaman' - he began, with as much patience as he could summon - 'Where and how am I likely to come into contact with that esteemed gentleman, long retired from military service?'

'You will visit him at his house in Oryol. It is on your route, I believe' - she replied firmly, as if nothing could be more straightforward.

'Very well' - said Pechorin, slipping the envelope into his pocket alongside the others - 'And the third?'

'The third is for Pavel Ivanovich, to whom you will report in Stavropol' – his grandmother replied, an immense sadness flooding into her voice – 'It is from me'.

General Pavel Ivanovich Petrov was a widower. His wife Anna Akimovna Khastatova, daughter of Pechorin's grandmother's sister Yekaterina and cousin of his mother Maria, had died in 1836 at the age of twenty-four, leaving seven children in Pavel Ivanovich's care.

'We stayed with him at Shelkozavodskoe when you were a child; do you remember?' – asked his grandmother.

'I was four years old, *Grandmaman*' – Pechorin replied drily, taking the envelope and placing it alongside the others.

'He will remember you fondly, no doubt' – the old woman continued – 'You are very fortunate that fate has placed a member of the family in his position... I have no wish to dwell on the events that have sent you from us, but promise me one thing...'.

'And what is that, *Grandmaman*?' – Pechorin replied.

'Promise me you will listen to Pavel Ivanovich, that you will trust his integrity and his judgement in all things'.

'Oh, but I thought I was to promise not to read the letters... that's two things'.

The old woman let out a sigh Pechorin had heard on perhaps thousands of occasions, her face for a moment taking on an expression of anguish, before she recovered her equanimity.

'Promise me' – she said quietly – 'that you will entrust yourself to Pavel Ivanovich'.

Pechorin filled his lungs with air, regarded his grandmother with a wry, gentle affection, and exhaled.

'I promise'.

Before Pechorin's grandmother could speak another word, Dmitrii came cheerfully into the room and stepped over to the window.

'Mungo's here' – he said.

Pechorin joined his uncle in the window, from where he could see a young officer of His Imperial Majesty's Hussars mounted on quite the most beautiful black horse either of them had ever laid eyes upon. Parader snorted under the beaming Mungo and reared onto his hind legs, spinning in the dust as his hooves once again met the earth.

'Parting is such sweet sorrow, no doubt' – said his grandmother without rising from her chair.

'We're not parting quite yet, *Grandmaman*' – Pechorin replied.

A few minutes later, Pechorin sat astride Parader, while Mungo climbed in and took a seat in the carriage. Pechorin's grandmother stood by the side of the road, clinging to Dmitrii's arm.

'I'll ride him to the city limits – perhaps a little further, if you've no objection, Mungo?' – Pechorin explained – 'Then we'll change places and you will return him to the Imperial Stables. Make sure he's looked after, won't you?'

Pechorin turned to Dmitrii and his grandmother, only her long experience and profound sense of duty propping up the facade of dignity, while beneath the surface she wrestled with what she felt certain was the terminal loss of this strange, contradictory creature she had raised more or less as her own child. For a moment, she imagined herself by his graveside, the impulse to shed a tear having left her entirely.

'Farewell, *Grandmaman*' - said Pechorin with an eagerness designed to defuse the struggle he understood to be raging inside her - 'You would be doing us both the greatest of service by thinking little of me while I am in the south. Whatever must be, must be; neither you nor I can change that and it would be vain to imagine otherwise. I entrust myself to the mountains and to God; leave me to them'.

Yelizaveta Alexeyevna, now perfectly calm, looked up at Pechorin and imagined she was once again in the presence of a precocious twelve-year-old boy.

'If you will write to me, I will think of you only when I receive your letters' - she said firmly. - 'Promise me you will write'.

'More promises, *Grandmaman*?' - Pechorin replied with affectionate mockery - 'Of course I will write'.

He turned to Dmitrii, brought the forefingers of his right hand to his temple, then took Parader's reins firmly in both hands.

'Mungo, meet me at the Volkovskoe Cemetery' - he said in a voice that could not conceal his excitement - 'And take your time'.

Pechorin gave a light tap on Parader's right flank with his whip and they flew off through the rising dust, headed for the south.

CHAPTER TEN

THE GREY GENERAL

THE JOURNEY TO Serednikovo took two days longer than it had done in early summer, the gathering autumn slowly turning what passed for roads into rubble and mud. There, Pechorin dispensed with his carriage, which might not have survived the roads of the south and for which, in any case, he would have no further use. The Tsar's final decree had stipulated that he would not be permitted to stop for the night in Moscow, but it was necessary nonetheless for one of the serfs on the estate to convey him to the central post-station, whence he would continue his journey by coach. Pechorin thought for a moment about spending a last night at Kropotovo, but decided against it; that, too, was something for which he may have no further use.

Pechorin's strange procession through the streets of Moscow at mid morning confirmed in his mind the wisdom of his youthful departure. The Pension, the University, the Assembly of the Nobility all played with great effect the roles that fate had determined for them, little more than painted wooden set dressing, drifting past the windows of the coach. At the post-station, Pechorin enquired when the first coach would depart for the south and sat quietly smoking a cigar as the serf from his grandmother's estate, a thick-set man in his twenties Pechorin had never before set eyes on, set down the wooden trunk that constituted his luggage.

'Should I wait, master?' – the serf asked.

'Why would you?' – Pechorin replied, handing the fellow a coin and bidding him good-day.

Pechorin watched his carriage pull out of the station yard through the smoke from his cigar, seeking in himself even a scrap of regret; but there was none.

A few hours later, as he was thrown back and forth across the poorly upholstered seat of the post-coach, which rolled like a ship on the towering waves of an inconsolably angry sea, Pechorin would have given anything at all to be asleep in his own bed at Tsarskoe Seló. When at last reclining on what was little more than a bench at the post-station at Yasnogorsk, drifting fitfully in and out of sleep, he was assailed by images of de Barante, blood flowing from a bullet-hole in the middle of his forehead, his grandmother sitting quietly in the rear dealing cards. When the driver had changed horses and collected the mail, Pechorin found himself relieved to sit once again above the rolling of the waves, the sea that surrounded him invisible for the two hours until sunrise. At length, sleep conquered not only his body, but his fevered mind.

When he opened his eyes, the coach had pulled into the yard of the post-station at Mtsensk. The driver asked Pechorin if he wished to sleep at the station or perhaps seek lodgings in the town, but Pechorin replied with a dismissive wave of the hand, intended to communicate that he would sleep, if that were possible, precisely where he lay. As the bustle of the station yard slowly began to fade and the lamps, with the exception of the one that hung above the entrance archway, were at last extinguished, Pechorin opened his trunk and, after a moment's rummaging, brought out the letters his grandmother had given him on the morning of his departure, which now seemed like relics from some far-distant age. He examined the seal of the envelope addressed to Yermolov. After a few seconds, he returned all three letters to the trunk, closed it, and settled down to sleep in the quiet discomfort of the coach.

Not long after the coach had left Mtsensk the following morning, the driver pulled into the post-station at Oryol. Pechorin took his trunk from the coach, handed the fellow a silver coin, and bid him farewell.

'Will your Honour not be continuing?' - he asked, unable to mask his disappointment.

'All in good time' - Pechorin replied - 'But first, I have some business to attend to'.

Pechorin made his way into the Station-master's office with his trunk and asked the old man to look after them for a few hours, dispensing another coin as he left. He then haggled with one of the farriers in the yard for as serviceable a horse as could be found and a saddle, which turned out to be a difficult proposition for an undertaking set up to provide relay horses for the ever-increasing stream of coaches. At last a saddle was found for the beast Pechorin had secured and he set off at a canter, heading east towards the Yermolov family estate at Lukianchikovo.

As he passed through the gates of the modest estate, exhilarated by the gallop through open countryside, a blessed relief after the imprisonment of coaches and post-stations, a low building stretched out towards him into its surrounding gardens. Its windows were dark, the whole enveloped in a silence that seemed to Pechorin permanent, unbreakable. The door of near-black teak seemed designed to refuse entry to any visitor, to discourage them even from knocking. Pechorin knocked. An ageing servant appeared in the doorway and, without a word, escorted him to a small office, crammed with deep dark-green furniture, the walls covered with Circassian daggers and hunting horns, among them various portraits of none other than Napoleon Bonaparte, in each one his grey military uniform matching the clouds which hung above Oryol.

'The master is busy with his book-binding' - said the old servant, finally breaking the silence - 'He will be down presently'.

As he waited, Pechorin reflected on the mysterious forces that might transport a man from the position of master of the Caucasus - and perhaps more – to the gentle pleasures of book-binding. General Alexei Petrovich Yermolov had single-handedly transformed Russia's role in the Caucasus from a chaotic, costly adventure into an immutable fact of political reality. From 1819, his tactics in relation to the recalcitrant tribes of the mountains, from Circassia to Daghestan, had been brutal... and rational. Yermolov had understood that there could be no prohibition on the burning of crops and bloody reprisals, but also, and more important, that such measures were not an alternative to negotiation and diplomacy: they were in fact a necessary prelude. He had also understood, and had succeeded in persuading Tsar Alexander, that the building of roads and bridges was not some symbolic obligation of a civilizing power, but rather a matter of the most immediate practical necessity, the condition of possibility for any military success.

And then had come December. The Grand-Duke Konstantin, younger brother of Tsar Alexander, was serving as Governor of Poland when his brother died on 1st December 1825. Konstantin had secretly renounced succession to the throne in 1823, but had neglected to inform his own younger brother, Nikolai, who, on the death of Alexander, promptly proclaimed Konstantin Tsar of all the Russias. In the chaos that followed disclosure of Konstantin's proleptic abdication, a loose alliance of political reformers and army officers attempted to prevent the accession of Nikolai, which culminated in a public show of opposition on Senate square, followed by a massacre on the breaking ice of the Nevá. In the south, sympathisers with the political ambitions of the reformers had no knowledge of what was happening in the capital, but, when their leader Pavel Pestel was arrested and news of the defeated uprising filtered through, Lieutenant-Colonel Sergei Muravyov-Apostol led the Chernigov Regiment in a doomed insurgency against the throne. Throughout January, in an atmosphere in which the allegiance of the military could no longer be assumed, various rumours swept Moscow and St Petersburg: Yermolov was on the point of declaring an autonomous state in the Caucasus; worse, Yermolov was marching on the capital, gathering regiments and recruits as he progressed, with the aim of overthrowing the Romanovs once and for all. Pechorin had never believed in such nonsense; but others, whose opinion mattered, did. Regardless of the fantastical nature of some of the things that had been said about Yermolov, Nikolai's trust in him, already strained, never recovered and he was removed from his position in 1827. 'I trust him least of all', the Tsar had said of Yermolov. 'Quite', Pechorin thought quietly to himself.

'Don't get up' – said Yermolov as he came into the room, looking nothing at all like the rather pompous gentleman from the portrait made by the English artist George Dawe. His hair was no longer grey, but had turned almost white, cut short and spiky above his rather large head. Neither did he resemble Pushkin's description of the head of a tiger on the torso of Hercules; the years of inactivity, it would seem, had quelled all but the fire of curiosity still burning in his eyes of iron grey.

'Alexei Petrovich... Lieutenant Pechorin, at your service. I have a letter for you from my great-uncle Afanasii' – said Pechorin, reaching out a hand containing a sealed envelope.

'Ah, Afanasii Alexeyich' – Yermolov replied – 'A fine soldier and a fine man'.

Yermolov put the letter in the pocket of the curious grey jacket he wore, which made him look more like a tradesman or a merchant than a retired General. He then sat down in the armchair facing Pechorin, crossed one leg over the other, took a pinch of tobacco from a little wooden box which lay on the table next to him, and loudly snorted into each nostril in turn.

'So, Lieutenant Pechorin... what have you done?' – Yermolov asked suddenly, before blowing his nose loudly into an enormous white handkerchief.

Pechorin's customary ability to disguise surprise was pushed to the limit by the old man's frankness, but his features remained still, his tone even.

'I am sure my great-uncle will have provided you with all the necessary detail in his letter' – he replied.

'So you haven't read it?' – the old man asked quickly.

'I cannot imagine any circumstance in which I would read private correspondence between people for whom I have the utmost respect' – Pechorin replied after a slight pause – 'And, in any case, you will see that the seal is unbroken'.

'Very well' – Yermolov continued – 'But I'd like to hear it from you'.

Pechorin recounted how he had fought a duel with de Barante on a point of honour, how he had intentionally fired into the air, how the Tsar had initially bowed to the opinion of Nesselrode and von Benckendorff, before the intervention of the Grand-Duke Mikhail had at least secured his rank and privileges.

'A Frenchman, eh?' – said Yermolov, electing to ignore mention of Nesselrode – 'You should have killed him on the spot! Still, the Infantry is no place for a young man like you. They've just about done you a favour, despite themselves'.

'How do you mean, Alexei Petrovich? – asked Pechorin.

Yermolov fixed him with the kind of look one gives to a younger acquaintance who insists, contrary to all the evidence, that they are not in love.

'Do you honestly mean to tell me that you would rather spend the next couple of years of your life in that miniature prison, trying your best – and no doubt failing – to avoid fighting duels, than in the expanses of our Caucasus, drunk on the taste of freedom?'

'No, I do not' – Pechorin replied.

'I didn't think so' – Yermolov said with a smile.

The old servant brought them black tea and *khalva*. Yermolov settled back deeper into his chair and began to enquire after the health of Afanasii Stolypin and Pechorin's grandmother.

'I served with her eldest brother Alexander, you know' – he said with a warm smile – 'Another fine gentleman, who suffered only from the deficiency of being over-generous with his friendship'.

Pechorin gave Yermolov a restrained but still inquisitive look, anxious to hear more.

'You will learn in combat, my dear boy – although perhaps you already know? – that fools are easy to come by, men on whom you can rely – not so much. It matters not whether you're looking up, down, or to either side'.

'My great-uncle warned me, above all, that you do not suffer fools gladly' – said Pechorin.

'Why would I?' – spluttered the old man, reaching again for his handkerchief – 'Those fools who imagined that they could determine by whom they would be ruled! Look where their imaginations got them!'

Pechorin shifted in his armchair.

'And where did your loyalty get you, Alexei Petrovich?' – he asked in a low voice.

The old man stared back at Pechorin with a look of surprise, then let out a snorting laugh.

'Let me tell you a little tale, my bold young friend. You are clearly aware of the amusing rumours that attached themselves to me around the time of December; you should also be aware that there never was – there never could be – a shred of truth in any of them. Yes, I was personally acquainted with some of those who let their imagination overcome their better judgement; yes, I later intervened to help the unfortunate Griboyedov, and would do exactly the same again. But an officer – a General! – in the Imperial Army rebelling against the authority of the Commander-in-Chief, the Tsar himself? Impossible'.

Pechorin sat motionless, silently imploring the old man to continue.

'But the truth did not matter' – Yermolov went on – 'Even the Tsar came to believe in those rumours. Those rumours, impossible though it might seem, led to war with Persia! War! Every time we reported Persian incursions into Azerbaidzhan, every time we asked for reinforcements, His Imperial Majesty – and that German fool who does not deign even to speak our language – concluded that there was more to lose by strengthening our own forces, forces they feared they could not directly control, than by encouraging our enemy. Fools!'

Yermolov sat back in his chair and fell silent, anxious that he had said more than he had intended. Pechorin's inquisitiveness was now overcome by a proper respect for the old man's dignity and he resolved to allow him a few moments to recover his poise. After some minutes had passed, however, and Yermolov had said nothing further, Pechorin elected to break the increasingly awkward silence.

'I'm intrigued, Alexei Petrovich' – he began – 'by your interest in bookbinding'.

There was no reply. Pechorin leaned forward in his chair and saw that the old man, eyes still wide open, had fallen asleep. After fifteen minutes or so, Yermolov stirred and looked at Pechorin as if their conversation had continued uninterrupted.

'Excuse me for a few minutes' – he said abruptly, rising to his feet – 'I must read the letter you have so kindly delivered'.

Yermolov was gone for what Pechorin imagined was half-an-hour. When he returned, his indignation had disappeared entirely, replaced by a calm warmth, as if Pechorin were a solicitous grandchild enquiring after the health of his esteemed grandfather.

'I'll send a reply to Afanasii Alexeyich by post' – he said gently – 'But I would be most obliged if you could deliver these for me in person'.

He handed Pechorin two envelopes, one which bore the name 'General P. Kh. Grabbe', the other 'Lieutenant-General A. A. Velyaminov'.

'You will no doubt dine with General Grabbe in Stavropol' – he said – 'He is in the habit of entertaining the younger officers at HQ. If you don't have the opportunity to pass the letter to General Velyaminov in person, however, make sure it goes in the military post from Stavropol'.

Pechorin placed the letters in an inside pocket in his tunic and assured Yermolov that he would do everything in his power to deliver both by hand.

'Will you stay the night' – Yermolov asked.

'That is very kind of you, Alexei Petrovich' – replied Pechorin – 'but I have become accustomed to the delights of our post-stations and we will be able to make some considerable distance before nightfall'.

'As you wish' – said Yermolov with an ever brighter smile – 'They've done you a favour, my boy, remember that. They are fools, no doubt; but they've done you a favour... *Les grands noms ne se font qu'en Orient*' – he continued suddenly and unexpectedly in halting French, looking up at one of the portraits of Napoleon hanging on the walls – 'Oh, and Pechorin... watch out for the English; they're everywhere...'.

'I will, Alexei Petrovich' – Pechorin replied, once again disguising his surprise – 'I will'.

The journey from Oryol to Novocherkassk was more pleasant, not because the roads or, heaven forbid, the inns had improved, but because Pechorin knew where he would be staying in Novocherkassk and knew also that he had, by the speed with which he had travelled thus far, earned the right to spend two or perhaps even three nights there. Pechorin's first thought on leaving St Petersburg had been to return Parader, for only a very modest sum, to its original owner, General Khomutov. That gentleman, however, had been posted as Commander-in-Chief of the Preobrazhensky Regiment stationed at Novocherkassk, where Pechorin looked forward to renewing their acquaintance and to thanking him once again for his kindness in agreeing to sell his beloved horse. Pechorin had not known that Khomutov already knew he was about to be transferred when he agreed to sell; the old man had been determined not to weaken his bargaining position, which might have resulted in Parader being sold for a sum not befitting.

General Khomutov had been the most untypical commanding officer of all those under whom Pechorin had served in St Petersburg and Tsarskoe

Seló. On one occasion, informed by his adjutant that the majority of the younger officers had gone for the evening to St Petersburg to watch Maria Novitskaya in the lead role in Auber's *Fenella* at the Alexandrinsky Theatre, Khomutov promptly cancelled the following morning's drill and sent word that they should not concern themselves over too early a return to barracks. He was nonetheless happier when his officers remained at Tsarskoe Seló in the evenings, not from any desire to control their behaviour, but, on the contrary, because he was then able to enjoy the company of the brightest and most amusing among them at his dinner table: and Pechorin, for all his faults, Khomutov acknowledged, was probably the brightest of them all and certainly the most amusing.

'I am honoured, Pechorin, that you remember an old commander' – said Khomutov, smiling broadly across the dinner table, at which only he and Pechorin were seated.

'On the contrary, General Khomutov' – Pechorin replied – 'The pleasure is all mine... and not just, you understand, because you offer me refuge, however brief, from the road'.

'Please' – said Khomutov – 'Mikhail Grigorevich when we are not on duty... and we are very much not on duty'.

'Very well, Mikhail Grigorevich' – said Pechorin, raising a crystal glass full almost to the brim with a fine Burgundy – 'But informality makes me no less grateful for your hospitality'.

General Khomutov raised his own glass in response and they drank to renewed acquaintance.

'Tell me, Pechorin' – continued Khomutov – 'How is my... I mean how is your wonderful horse?'

'Oh, you can have no concerns on that score, Mikhail Grigorevich' – Pechorin replied – 'He will be well looked after at the Imperial Stables and neither Mungo nor Dmitrii Stolypin will miss an opportunity to exercise him'.

'Excellent' – replied General Khomutov – 'I never had any doubt I was placing him in the right hands, even though I should perhaps have anticipated that you might not be around to look after him in person'.

Pechorin gave General Khomutov a look of mock reproach, but judged that no reply was necessary. Khomutov refilled both glasses, a rather more grave expression settling upon his features.

'What was your impression of Yermolov?' – he asked.

Pechorin shifted slightly in his chair, concerned neither to give offence nor to be evasive in his response.

'He is old' – he replied at last – 'Not the agedness of long and exhausting service, but rather of inactivity. He was not what I expected at all and, I confess, I left his company in the grip of a profound sadness'.

Khomutov nodded his head gently in agreement and took another sip of Burgundy.

'I saw him in Moscow on my way here' - he said - 'Still full of plans for the Persians and the Turks, still in love with the Caucasus of twenty years ago. Quite out of touch'.

'How do you mean?' - asked Pechorin - 'Has so much really changed?'

'Yes, my dear boy' - replied Khomutov - 'Everything has changed. The spheres of influence of both the Persians and the Turks are now, if not quite distinct from our own, then at least very clearly defined. The key threat now resides within, as it were; Shamyl has managed - God alone knows how - to unite the various races scattered along our Left Flank under the banner of Allah. What once was conquest has become war'.

Khomutov paused for a second, noticing that his glass was once again empty.

'You are going to war, my boy' - he said, reaching for the bottle of Burgundy.

General Khomutov spent the next day at regimental HQ, signing off furloughs and requisitions, his heart never quite committing to the mundanity of military bureaucracy. Every time he came to the conclusion that someone could quite easily look after this kind of thing for him, he reminded himself that, should anything of any significance go wrong, he alone would bear the responsibility. At around four in the afternoon, satisfied that at least the appearance of order had been maintained, he climbed stiffly up into the saddle of his horse - a fine enough beast, but nothing in comparison to Parader - and set off for his private quarters.

There he found Pechorin, pen in hand, deep in the pages of a thick leather-bound notebook, a small cigar glowing in the ashtray on Khomutov's desk.

'I hope you're hungry, my boy' - said Khomutov with a hearty smile.

'It can't be much after four' - Pechorin replied.

'Indeed' - continued Khomutov - 'but I have arranged for us to eat early this evening. Have you ever had the pleasure of our provincial theatres, Pechorin?'

Pechorin suppressed a grimace, took a drag from his cigar, and fixed his gaze on the pages of his notebook.

'No' - he replied without looking up - 'but I have heard much about them'.

'Excellent' - said Khomutov - 'This very evening you will have the opportunity of testing the veracity of what you have been told'.

Pechorin made no reply, then, after scribbling a few more swift entries into his notebook, closed it and followed Khomutov through to the dining room.

Later, in the foyer of the modest little theatre, a sea of red carpet bounded by wood panelling and fixings of unapologetically ostentatious brass, Pechorin, glass in hand, was introduced in turn to a parade of local dignitaries and their wives.

'Charmed, I'm sure' – he said for the fourth or fifth time, on this occasion to the middle-aged wife of the Mayor, resplendent in a dress of shimmering turquoise, while her husband bowed nervously in response to Khomutov's description of Pechorin as a former comrade-at-arms, now on his way to active service in the Caucasus.

'How frightful it has all become' – said the Mayor's wife – 'We hear such tales... Is it true that they have taken to beheading our soldiers? And kidnapping our ladies?'

The Mayor frowned quickly at his wife, hoping that Pechorin and Khomutov had not noticed, but hoping also that his expression would be sufficient to arrest her rather colourful line of enquiry. Just at that moment, General Khomutov signalled to two young soldiers, both of whom were wearing the greatcoats of enlisted men, despite having the bearing and expressions of officers.

'Lieutenant Pechorin' – began Khomutov – 'May I introduce Private Golitsyn and Private Grushnitsky? Both of these fine young men, from two of Rostov's finest families, have enlisted as volunteers and will soon tread the same path as yourself to the Caucasus'.

Pechorin made a shallow bow and each of the two young men bowed in response.

'I couldn't help overhearing, madam' – said the one who had been introduced as Grushnitsky, turning to the Mayor's wife – 'your understandable fears about the worst excesses of these savages. But you must console yourself with the certain knowledge that the forces of rebellion will be vanquished, no matter how brutal their methods'.

Pechorin surveyed Grushnitsky and Khomutov in turn, surprised at the young man's rather brazen intervention into the conversation, but more surprised still by Khomutov's apparent tolerance of it.

'You are very certain' – Pechorin said after a moment's pause, looking directly at Grushnitsky.

'Are you not, Lieutenant Pechorin?' – Grushnitsky replied.

'I have no doubt that, in the long run, the Empire will prevail' – said Pechorin – 'But I will reserve judgment on how that happy circumstance might come to pass until I've seen with my own eyes the enemy on his home ground'.

Grushnitsky bridled slightly at the implication, but Khomutov intervened before the conversation could develop.

'Soon enough, for both of you' – he said gravely.

Grushnitsky once again seemed on the point of replying, but was interrupted by the sound of a little bell, signalling that the performance was about to begin and that the audience should take its seats in the auditorium.

General Khomutov guided Pechorin to his seat in the stalls, where, he explained, he much preferred to view the performance than in one of the rather tired boxes which flanked either side of the stage; one was a little too much on public display up there. They were seated so close to the front that, when Pechorin looked up, the wax candles that performed the function of stage lighting were right under his nose, their glow imprinting itself on his retina. When he looked around, he could see nothing behind him, because it was too dark. He looked to the right and once again saw nothing, because there was nothing there. Finally, he looked up to the left and there, ensconced in a box, sat the Chief of Police.

The orchestra consisted of four clarinets, two double-bass, and a violin. The lone violin was played by the Conductor, who was distinguished by the fact that he was deaf; when it was time to begin or to stop, the first clarinet would tug at the tail of the Conductor's coat, while the double-bass marked time on his shoulder with his bow. At one point, out of sheer personal hatred, the double-bass struck him so hard with his bow that the Conductor turned round to attack him with his violin; just at that moment, the first clarinet tugged hard at the tail of his coat and the Conductor fell flat on his face into the drums and cut himself. He skillfully leapt back to his feet to continue the battle, not realising that there was a drum on his head instead of his hat... The audience was in raptures, the curtain was raised, and the orchestra launched into tune.

'A hard act to follow' – said Khomutov, leaning into Pechorin's ear.

'I hardly know what to expect' – replied Pechorin.

The performance did not in the end live up to the promise of the impromptu opening act. General Khomutov and Pechorin travelled back to Khomutov's quarters in subdued silence and retired for the night, one resigned to the monotony of his new command, the other to resumed acquaintance with the accursed road, no longer quite so buoyed by the prospect of adventure to come.

Early the following morning, Pechorin gestured to the driver of the post-coach to load his trunk and turned to bid General Khomutov farewell.

'You don't have any letters you would like me to convey, Mikhail Grigorevich?' – he asked with a crooked half-smile.

Khomutov looked back in utter confusion.

'You are indeed a gentleman, Mikhail Grigorevich' – said Pechorin, before stepping up into the coach – 'Until we meet again'.

The driver swept up the reins, let out a sharp cry, and the coach pulled slowly out of the yard, Khomutov following its progress with a still mystified gaze.

As the coach approached the little town of Peschanokopskoye, on the road between Novocherkassk and Stavropol, Pechorin caught sight of a ramshackle sentry-post by the side of the road. The driver stopped to ask the old soldier asleep inside for directions. The old man woke with a start, gathered himself, and confirmed that yes, it was half a mile to the town, and that both horses and provisions might be had there.

Pechorin studied the old soldier's curious uniform with amusement.

'What are you doing here, old fellow?' – he asked.

'I'm on guard' – the old soldier replied.

'And what are you guarding?'

'Why, the road'.

Pechorin looked up out of the coach window at the driver, who responded with a bemused shrug.

'And who stationed you here to guard the road? – Pechorin continued.

'By Order of His Imperial Majesty Tsar Pavel' – the old man replied.

'Pavel?' – Pechorin asked with a wry smile.

'Thirty-five years I've been on guard' – said the old man – 'I went into town to ask and they told me that they had a ration ticket for me, but my orders were lost. And so I guard the road'.

'They left you here on guard?' – asked Pechorin.

'What can you do?' – the old man replied – 'My orders are lost. They made enquiries about five years ago, but there was no reply. And they feed me'.

Pechorin managed to buy excellent potatoes and some poor wine in the little town while the driver changed horses. He was silently glad when the driver told him there was no room at the post-station, but that an old man and his grand-daughter would lodge them a mile south of the town. They set off under the bright late-afternoon sun, wending their way through unenclosed fields, sparsely populated by badly fed oxen, none of which moved a step as the coach rolled past. As they approached a wooden house on the far side of the fields, backing into a little copse of birch trees, Pechorin caught the sound of a young girl singing.

A few minutes later, the horses stood nibbling at the grass, glad to be unhitched from the coach, the driver gently stroking one of their necks. The driver asked the young girl for some water, which she brought in two large buckets suspended on a pole across her shoulders and set down for the horses to drink. The girl lived with her grandfather, her father having died when she was an infant. Her husband, a Cossack, had disappeared more than a year ago. Pechorin ordered the driver to take the box with the potatoes and wine into the house and turned to the girl.

'What's your name, my dear? – he asked gently.

'Masha' – she replied with a smile.

When the sun had almost set, the driver sat on the porch with the old man, chewing on baked potatoes and pickled cucumbers, glad of the meagre wine. Inside, Masha set a rough tablecloth over the only table, at which Pechorin sat alone. She was broad in the shoulders and in the hips, but he noticed how lightly she moved around the room. Her face, too, was broad, her eyes wide and round, a snub nose above her full lips.

'Sit down, Masha' – said Pechorin, a half-mocking gleam in his eye – 'Let's have dinner together'.

'I've already eaten' – replied the girl.

When he had finished his meal, Pechorin took a glass of wine out onto the porch. The old man had retired for the evening and the driver was making a bed for himself in the coach.

'Masha, my dear' – said Pechorin – 'Is there somewhere to bathe nearby? How far is it to the river?'

'It's not far' – the girl replied – 'but it's very narrow; only children bathe in it. I can stoke up the *bania*, if you'd like?'

'Yes, I would like that very much'.

Pechorin sat in the hot, moist steam for over an hour, soaking in the smell of ancient oak and wet birch.

When he emerged at last from the humid little tomb, wrapped in a sheet, shorn of the dirt of the road and the cares of the world, Masha was sitting alone on the porch. Pechorin sat alongside her and pulled a blanket around his shoulders.

'Come closer' – he said quietly as he embraced her.

Pechorin woke the next morning to find the horses once again harnessed to the coach, the driver deep in conversation with the old man, who was leaning on the porch fence smoking a little wooden pipe. He stuck his head out of the window and whistled to the driver, who turned in the direction of the sound.

'Good morning, your Honour' – said the driver with a knowing smile – 'We had best be on the move if we're to reach Stavropol before nightfall. Everything is ready, with the exception of your good self'.

'Then I bid you farewell' – Pechorin replied – 'I bequeath to you whatever is left of the potatoes and that dreadful wine'.

The driver looked at him with blank incomprehension.

'I'll catch the next coach in a couple of days' – Pechorin continued – 'I'm staying here'.

BOOK II

CHAPTER ELEVEN

STAVROPOL

WHO HAS NOT heard upon a winter's morning, when the snow falls thick and soft, the red dawn peering hesitantly out onto the grey steppe, the bells ringing out from the monastery to do battle against the blustering wind? Who has not heard it, this herald of immortality or death? How Pechorin loved that sound, like a flower upon a burial mound, an eternal mausoleum, stronger than fate or petty misfortune! A sound forever alone, like the gloomy master of some high castle, at once the essence of all things, yet alien to both heaven and earth...

The snow fell thick and soft as Pechorin's carriage approached Stavropol, headquarters of Russian forces in the south, the bells of a church in that meagre city ringing out a faint welcome. Behind him, St Petersburg had receded to a point beyond the horizon of his memory, obscured finally by the image of a tear falling from the cheeks of a peasant girl standing alone on a deserted porch. Before him, beyond Stavropol, lay the springs of Pyatigorsk and Kislovodsk, and, finally, Yekaterinograd, gateway to the theatre of war. The snowflakes fell around the carriage as it slowly picked its way across the barren steppe. As he watched them fall, Pechorin was overcome by the certain thought that, once he had crossed this threshold, he would never return.

The streets of Stavropol were a blur of snow and mud, more difficult to navigate even than what passed for roads on the bleak outskirts. The coach ploughed on through the filthy snow, moving more and more slowly the closer it came to its destination. After what seemed like an eternity, it pulled into the yard of the military staff HQ, dispensed with Pechorin and his luggage, and continued its interminable journey to the post-station. Pechorin pulled the collar of his coat up around his ears and strode purposefully into HQ.

'Lieutenant Pechorin of the Nizhegorodsky Dragoons' - he began - 'Reporting to General Petrov'.

'Is he expecting you?' - asked the desk Sergeant.

Pechorin paused for a moment in the attempt to suppress a wry half-smile.

'General Petrov has been expecting me for some time' - he replied.

General Petrov was not as skilled as Pechorin in the art of disguising his feelings, nor did he have any particular reason to do so.

'Where on earth have you been?' - he asked with frank exasperation - 'You were expected three weeks ago'.

'I was unavoidably delayed between Novocherkassk and Stavropol' - Pechorin replied - 'A combination of the roads and ill health'.

'Ill health?' - continued General Petrov.

'Yes, Sir... I was overcome by a fever when we reached Peschanokopskoye.

I was fortunate enough to find lodgings with a local family and was gradually able to recover my strength'.

General Petrov looked up at Pechorin with weary suspicion. He had initially borne the responsibility for this unruly and not-so-distant relative with good grace, reasoning that the conventions of military command would not require to be stretched too far in order to ease the path of an inexperienced newcomer, relative or not. But here, before he had even arrived, Pechorin had already begun to cause him problems.

'I have a letter for you, Sir' - said Pechorin, before General Petrov could continue - 'From my esteemed grandmother'.

Pechorin took an envelope from his tunic pocket, a small daub of unbroken wax on its rear, and handed it to General Petrov. He hesitated for a moment, his mind's eye drifting to the letter Yermolov had given him for General Velyaminov, but some mute instinct prevented him at last from speaking.

'Ah, Yelizaveta Alexeyevna' - continued Petrov - 'It is quite some time since we last had the pleasure of her company. I trust she is well? Not too disturbed by... recent events?'

'She is as well as might be expected for a woman of her age and has, I think, borne... recent events with admirable resolve' - Pechorin replied - 'But she will no doubt speak for herself in her letter'.

General Petrov once again looked up at Pechorin, his suspicion, if not his weariness, beginning to recede, and placed the letter in the top drawer of his desk.

Pechorin was shown to his quarters by an adjutant. The cramped little room, its floor, walls, and ceiling made from the same dull wood, seemed to Pechorin a more fitting prison even than his cell at the Haymarket or the accursed coaches in which he had spent his time since Moscow. He lay down on the narrow bunk fully clothed, closed his eyes, and imagined himself in a coffin. Sleep on this occasion did not come, but his eyes, his racing mind, and his mortal soul found brief respite in this dark temporary grave.

Later that evening, as Yermolov had confidently foretold, a number of the younger officers gathered together by some unspoken principle of selection to join General Petrov at the dinner-table of General Pavel Khristoforovich Grabbe. Among them was Pechorin, as ever weighing his *ennui* against the countervailing force of his curiosity. General Grabbe was in his early fifties, perhaps two or three years older than Petrov. Pechorin knew, as indeed did all of Russia, that Grabbe had distinguished himself in the campaigns against Napoleon, in the war against the Turks, and in the suppression of the Polish uprising; but then, Pechorin mused to himself, hadn't they all? He knew also, however, what was whispered only by a select few, whether friend or foe: Grabbe had been arrested at the time of the December uprising as a former member of one of the secret societies from which the seeds of revolt had sprung and had been imprisoned for four months in the Petropavlovsk Fortress. It emerged that Grabbe had played no active role in anything that might have been classed as political dissent at least since 1821 and he was, like so many of his peers, given the opportunity to redeem himself in the Caucasus, in Turkey, and in Poland.

General Grabbe was not only possessed of a sophisticated intellect, he was also perhaps the bravest of all senior commanding officers in the Imperial Army. The most common story told about him, gleefully repeated by his many admirers, was of how, while still at Military College, when presented with a variety of tactical situations and asked to determine where the Commanding Officer should be positioned, Grabbe had answered in all cases, sincerely and naively, 'at the head of his troops'. And this unorthodox practice he had maintained throughout his career, provoking the loyalty, admiration, and even love of those he commanded; his enemies confined themselves to the insistence that, although undoubtedly a courageous and impressive individual, these very qualities nonetheless made him a very bad general.

'Lieutenant Pechorin' – Grabbe began, when the meal had been disposed of and only the Kakheti wine remained – 'I understand you are on your way to join the Nizhegorodsky Dragoons?'

'Yes, Sir' – Pechorin replied – 'I was intending to join the Regiment near Tiflis, but a number of battalions have already been deployed and are heading north into Daghestan. I'm awaiting orders as to where and when I should report'.

General Grabbe surveyed Pechorin with a relaxed smile, just a trace of confusion in his tone.

'It all sounds rather complicated' – he said quietly.

'Lieutenant Pechorin was unfortunately beset by illness on the road from Novocherkassk' – explained General Petrov – 'Unavoidably delayed'.

'I'm sorry to hear that' – continued Grabbe – 'I trust you're fully recovered?'

'Indeed, Sir, I am' – Pechorin replied – 'I very much appreciate your concern'.

'In any case' – Petrov once again cut in – 'Given that Lieutenant Pechorin has missed his original rendezvous, it isn't entirely clear if he will immediately join his own Regiment'.

Pechorin kept his gaze firmly on the glass in his hand.

'General Velyaminov has requested reinforcements on the Black Sea line' – continued Petrov – 'Work on the coastal fortifications is behind schedule and his limited forces have come under attack by Circassian mountain men from the rear'.

General Grabbe furrowed his brow, suppressed a sigh, and took a sip from his glass.

'You know my views on those so-called fortifications, Pavel Ivanovich' – he said impatiently, turning to Petrov – 'Completely unnecessary as a defence from attack from the sea... and entirely useless – in fact worse – as a defence from attack from the rear. Coastal defence is a naval matter and the harbours at Gelendzhik, Anapa, and further south on the Georgian coast are all the defences we require. The Turks are perfectly resigned to their naval inferiority and the Circassians are hardly likely to attack the sea from the land! All we've done is waste money, men, and time building targets for them...'.

General Petrov looked discreetly down at the table in front of him, then raised his gaze calmly to face General Grabbe.

'We are both aware, Pavel Khristoforovich, that His Imperial Majesty has personally insisted that the Black Sea coast is secured against the threat of Turkish invasion' - said Petrov.

'Turkish invasion!' - snorted Grabbe, before turning to Pechorin - 'And what do you think, Lieutenant Pechorin? Where do you think you're most needed? Digging trenches in the hills above the Black Sea coast, occasionally dodging a stray Circassian bullet? Or rooting out Shamyl and his pack of stray dogs in the mountain settlements to the east?'

Pechorin glanced calmly at General Petrov, then turned to face General Grabbe.

'I will, of course, be honoured to serve wherever I am commanded, Sir' - he replied - 'I am entirely at your service'.

At the end of the evening, as the company slowly and reluctantly dispersed, Pechorin approached General Grabbe, who was sitting alone at one end of the table smoking a large cigar.

'Will you join me in a cigar, Lieutenant Pechorin?' - Grabbe asked amiably.

'Thank you, Sir' - Pechorin replied - 'but I am tired from the road; perhaps there will be other occasions. I have a letter for you from General Yermolov, Sir, which he asked me to deliver in person'.

Grabbe took his cigar from his lips and looked intently at Pechorin, quite taken aback by these last words. Pechorin handed him the letter with a short bow.

'From Yermolov, eh?' - said Grabbe, his smile warming once again - 'And what does it say?'

'I have no idea, Sir' - Pechorin replied evenly - 'I bid you goodnight'.

The next morning, Pechorin was asked to report to the Staff HQ physician, Dr Werner, who was, despite his name, Russian. What's so surprising about that? I once knew a man called Ivanov who was German. Dr Werner was a remarkable man, for many reasons: a sceptic and a materialist, like almost all medics, but also a poet, and of the most genuine kind: a poet, always, in deed; and a poet sometimes also in words, although he has never written a line of poetry in his life. He has studied each living strand of the human heart no less than he has studied the veins and sinews of the human corpse, although he has never had the opportunity to put his knowledge of the former to good use; a fine anatomist may sometimes not know how to cure someone of fever...

Werner was in the habit of having a sly laugh at his patients' expense, although I once saw him weep over a dying soldier. He was poor, dreamed of having millions, but would never lift a finger in pursuit of money. He once told me he would rather do a favour for an enemy than for a friend, because the latter would mean selling his charity, while, in the former case, his generosity would make his enemy hate him all the more. He had a wicked tongue; more than a few perfectly good fellows have been written off as vulgar fools due to Werner's epigrams.

Pechorin arrived at the appointed time to find the door to Dr Werner's office lying wide open, with no one inside. His first thought was to return to his quarters and await further orders, but, recalling the dull interior of his latest place of confinement, he decided instead to step inside and wait there for the doctor. The office was no different from any of the others flanking the corridors of HQ, but for a stethoscope hanging on the back of the desk chair, three or four labelled bottles of fluids of varying colour sitting on the desk itself, and a human skeleton standing silent in the corner of the room. Pechorin surveyed the yellowed bones with an air of frank amusement, wondering at how this fully intact, entirely unharmed specimen had met his demise, wondering still further by what grisly process his skeleton had come to stand elegiacally in the corner of the office of a military doctor in Stavropol.

'And who might you be?' - said a voice, just as a small man came bustling into the room.

'Lieutenant Pechorin, Sir' - came the halting reply, as Pechorin drew his gaze from the skeleton.

Dr Werner had the kind of looks that at first made a poor impression, but which one would later come to like, when the eye had become accustomed to reading in his irregular features the signs of an enlightened and elevated soul. There have been cases where women have fallen madly in love with such men and would not exchange their unsightliness for the beauty of the freshest, rosy-cheeked Endymion. We must pay women their due: they have such an instinct for inner beauty; perhaps that is why men like Werner love them so much. He was short in height, thin, and as weak as a child; one of his legs was shorter than the other, like Byron. His head was disproportionately large for his body and his hair was cropped short, revealing the unevenness of his skull, in which a phrenologist would have identified a strange mix of contradictory tendencies.

'And why are you here?' - Werner continued with an ironic smile.

'General Petrov suggested I have a medical examination' - Pechorin replied - 'I'm awaiting orders'.

'You're as healthy as I am' - said Werner curtly - 'And besides, healthy lungs are just as likely to be pierced by a bullet as unhealthy ones'.

Pechorin glanced at this curious little creature, his small dark eyes never still, as if they were trying to penetrate to his inner thoughts.

'Thank you, doctor' - he said drily - 'Very reassuring'.

Werner took the stethoscope from the back of his desk chair, placed the tips into his ears and the bell on Pechorin's back, and settled into an expression of profound concentration. After a few seconds, he slipped the stethoscope around his neck and took Pechorin's left wrist in one hand, while glancing at a stopwatch in the other.

'You should find ways to relax more' - said Dr Werner with the same ironic smile, amused by the leisurely rhythm of Pechorin's pulse.

'I hardly think that's likely where I'm going' - Pechorin replied.

'And where are you going, Lieutenant Pechorin?' - said Dr Werner - 'Where are you going?'

Pechorin looked up at this unlikely fellow, whose eyes twinkled in open, almost affectionate challenge.

'You know, my good doctor' – he began – 'I don't actually know'.

'Well' – said Werner – 'Perhaps it might be best not to give too much thought to that for now and concentrate on what is immediately in front of you'.

Pechorin glanced once more at this diminutive jester, his curiosity rising.

'This evening, for example' – continued Werner – 'What are you doing this evening?'

'I have no plans whatsoever, as it happens' – Pechorin replied, amused by the question.

'Excellent' – said Werner – 'There are some people I would like you to meet. Come to my quarters at eight o'clock sharp'.

With that, Dr Werner swept out of the room, leaving Pechorin as speechless as his new acquaintance standing in the corner.

When Pechorin arrived at Dr Werner's quarters shortly after eight the same evening, the doctor was, to Pechorin's great surprise, alone.

'You're late' – said Dr Werner as Pechorin entered.

'I do beg your pardon, doctor' – Pechorin replied, looking around – 'But I appear in fact to be early, relative, that is, to the other guests'.

'The other guests will be here at eight-thirty' – said Dr Werner – 'I wanted to have a brief word with you beforehand... and to do it here, rather than at Staff HQ'.

Pechorin looked back at the doctor with renewed curiosity.

'One of the gentlemen who will shortly join us is no doubt very well known to you, at least by repute; the other, you may or may not have heard of. The first is Lev Pushkin, brother of the most unfortunately departed poet. The other is a gentleman who was once known throughout St Petersburg society, but whose name, if not forgotten, is no longer spoken in polite company'.

Pechorin opened his mouth to reply, but, before he could speak, there came a discreet knock at the door. Dr Werner put his finger to his lips.

The two gentlemen who appeared in the room moments later were, each in his own way, entirely unlike anything Pechorin had involuntarily conjured in his mind. The smaller of the two was Lev Sergeyevich Pushkin, a Major in the Nizhegorodsky Dragoons, younger brother of the once celebrated and now disgraced poet. Major Pushkin shared his brother's East African complexion, but was distinguished by a quite remarkable mane of light brown hair, his brows almost blond from the Caucasian sun. His companion was older and taller, although his humble air and slight stoop somewhat undermined the effect. His thinning hair, grey around the temples, framed unexpectedly soft, almost sensuous eyes, which gazed calmly out from the emaciated ruins of his features. Pechorin had observed the face of suffering on many occasions since his childhood, among the serfs on his father's estate and on the streets of St Petersburg, but he had never before encountered the marks of suffering at such odds with the nobility of the soul that bore them.

'Oleg Abramovich Lazarev, Sir' - said the older man - 'Private soldier in the Tenginsky Infantry Regiment'.

Pechorin's surprise at being addressed as a superior was betrayed by his uncharacteristically blank expression.

'There is no need for formalities here, gentlemen' - said Dr Werner - 'Is that not the case, Grigorii Alexandrovich?'

'Of course' - Pechorin replied, quickly recovering his poise - 'Lev Sergeyevich, Oleg Abramovich... I am delighted to make your acquaintance'.

Dr Werner had not had time to prepare Pechorin for the particular but by no means uncommon circumstances in which Lazarev found himself. Unlike the younger Pushkin, who was acquainted with virtually all the literary figures associated with December, but too young to have played any active role, Lazarev had served under Pestel and subsequently found himself at the heart of the southern organisational structure in the months following the uprising, for which he was arrested and summarily sentenced to twelve years of penal servitude. He had spent nine of those years at the infamous Petrovsky works on the Chita peninsula, followed on his release by three years of mandated exile in the Kazakh town of Kustanai. Lazarev had also spent time in St Petersburg, where his self-directed but expansive education had brought him into the orbit of progressive literary circles; it was in St Petersburg, in fact, that he had first met the young Lev Pushkin, who regarded Lazarev with quiet awe and had become accustomed, in these hitherto unimaginable circumstances, to cloaking his discomfort in cheerful irony.

'Private Lazarev and I are at your service, Lieutenant Pechorin' - said Pushkin, with a modest bow of the head - 'Welcome to the Siberia of the South'.

The evening passed in increasingly animated conversation. Dr Werner saw no contradiction between his role as a military doctor and the imperative to lay in as much Kakheti wine as he could wrest from the clutches of his superior officers. Lev Pushkin was a match for the good doctor's wit, in energy at least, if not in its bleak sophistication. Pechorin enjoyed their contest between gentle, relatively youthful irony and the mordant, deceptively double-voiced cynicism of advanced years, only occasionally offering up his own subtle coda to a particular remark or witticism, almost unfailingly echoing or modifying some intervention by Dr Werner. Lazarev restricted his contributions to a quiet word of agreement or a sigh of mock exasperation at Pushkin's occasional excesses, a gentle, restrained smile never leaving his face.

'So where are you headed, Lieutenant Pechorin... excuse me, Grigorii Alexandrovich?' - asked Pushkin, as the two cold roasted pheasant Dr Werner had generously provided lay before them in ruins and the conversation began to mellow.

'It isn't entirely clear where Grigorii Alexandrovich is, as you so aptly put it, headed' - said Dr Werner before Pechorin could reply.

Pechorin glanced across at Werner, conscious that this was the second time in twenty-four hours he had been interrupted before responding to this same question, and all the more curious that it was Dr Werner, with whom he had been acquainted for a matter of hours, who on this occasion intervened.

'I was originally intending to join my regiment, your own Nizhegorodsky Dragoons, outside Tiflis' - Pechorin said evenly - 'It would appear, however, that the Black Sea fortifications may instead be my destination, for reasons that are not entirely clear to me'.

'One or two of our battalions are already in Daghestan, sure enough' - replied Pushkin - 'Although I myself will be joining them in four days time, from Yekaterinograd... I'm leaving tomorrow; perhaps we might travel together?'

Dr Werner looked over at Pechorin, whose expression had not changed.

'That would indeed be splendid' - Werner began - 'It would give you two the time to get to know each other better. Although I am sure General Petrov will do what is best'.

'And what about you, Oleg Abramovich?' - asked Pechorin, turning to the silent Lazarev - 'What does fate have in store for you?'

'Oh' - Lazarev replied meekly - 'I am long accustomed to waiting for my orders before imagining even one foot stepping before the other. Whatever the good Lord decrees, I will humbly accept'.

On this occasion, it was Pechorin who looked in the direction of Dr Werner, seeking, but not finding, some clue to this subdued presence, whose ravaged features peered out from beneath a mask of beatific meekness.

'You must excuse my dear Private Lazarev, Grigorii Alexandrovich' - said Pushkin - 'Like many of his contemporaries, he acquired a certain unapologetic devoutness during the period of his servitude in the East. We may not be unbelievers, but there it was not uncommon - perhaps it was even necessary - for the habit of youth and society to devolve into a profound and active belief'.

'And you, Lev Sergeyevich?' - said Pechorin - 'In what in particular are you not an unbeliever?'

Pushkin's mercurial features absorbed and transformed his surprise at Pechorin's boldness in an instant.

'Oh, it's not that I don't believe, Grigorii Alexandrovich' - he replied with a smile - 'It's just that I cannot find it within myself to be... certain'.

'Is there nothing of which you are convinced?' - Pechorin continued.

'I myself am convinced of only one thing' - interrupted Dr Werner.

'And what is that?' - Pechorin asked, keen to discover the views of a man who had until now remained silent whenever the conversation had strayed from the quotidian.

'That one fine day, sooner or later, I will die' - Werner replied.

'I can go one better' - said Pechorin - 'I am sure of one more thing, namely that on one miserable evening I had the misfortune to be born'.

'Not much' - said Pushkin quickly - 'Not much at all. Although I'll be damned if I can find anything more intelligent or even amusing to say in response'.

Lazarev remained silent, his emaciated features still obscured by the veil of grace his will had summoned upon him many years ago and which would not be lifted until his mortal soul had no further need of it.

The strange company dispersed not long after. But from that evening, for the remainder of his time in Stavropol, Pechorin and the grizzled Dr Werner always picked one another out in the crowd. They met often and would discuss the most abstract subjects with great seriousness, until they realised that each was trying to make a fool of the other. Then, looking one another meaningfully in the eye, like the Roman augurs according to Cicero, they would burst out laughing. When their laughter had subsided, they would part, pleased with the way they had spent the evening.

Pechorin woke the following morning in his little wooden cell with a single thought orbiting around the still sleepy core of his consciousness. Why had General Petrov and Dr Werner – the former an old friend of the family he had not seen for some years, the latter, however amenable, a man he had met only the day before – both been so keen to cast doubt on his immediate destination? His regrettable lateness was, surely, only a secondary factor; he might very easily join the regiment from Yekaterinograd, as Pushkin had made clear. For a fleeting moment, this single thought was joined by another: why on earth had he not simply read the letter from his grandmother to General Petrov? We are all, no doubt, susceptible to such momentary lapses in our sense of what is right, distinguished only by the duration and frequency with which we are assailed. The thought passed and was swiftly replaced by another. General Petrov was clearly in possession of information which bore directly on his fate; he would, therefore, having declined to acquire it by nefarious means, simply ask him to divulge it.

General Petrov had been in his office for two full hours when Pechorin knocked, having informed his adjutant that he was not to be disturbed.

'Lieutenant Pechorin' – said Petrov in a voice that sought to balance civility with dissatisfaction – 'You'll forgive me, but I had asked not to be disturbed; how did you manage to get past the front office?'

'Forgive me' – Pechorin replied – 'I had no idea, because, well... there was no one there when I came in, so I took the liberty of knocking'.

'Come in, sit down' – continued Petrov, his expression softening just a little – 'How can I help you?'

Pechorin took a chair, placed it with its back facing General Petrov's desk, and sat down.

'I'm anxious to know why there has been a delay in my posting. I made the acquaintance of Major Pushkin yesterday evening and he informed me that he will be leaving for Yekaterinograd tomorrow, from there joining a battalion of the Nizhegorodsky Dragoons on its way into Daghestan'.

'Delay?' – replied General Petrov, one eyebrow gently arching towards his brow – 'I would remind you, Lieutenant Pechorin, that you were three weeks late in arriving. Whatever the cause, that is the reason for the delay'.

'All the more reason, Sir, if I may' – said Pechorin – 'to hasten my departure. Whatever the circumstances that have brought me to the Caucasus, you should know that I have no desire to evade active service. In fact, I wish nothing more than to face our enemy'.

'I don't doubt it' – replied Petrov.

'I request permission, Sir, to depart with Major Pushkin for Yekaterinograd' – said Pechorin with sudden conviction.

General Petrov sat back in his chair.

'I'm afraid I am unable to grant permission, Lieutenant Pechorin' – he said after a long pause – 'I was intending to inform you later today that you will join General Velyaminov's forces at the Mikhailovsky Pass above Gelendzhik. I'm afraid also that I am unable to disclose to you all the circumstances informing this decision, which has been approved, albeit with some reluctance, by General Grabbe'.

Pechorin stared quietly at General Petrov, his expression betraying neither resentment nor resignation.

'My grandmother' – he said quietly.

'Look, my boy' – General Petrov began to reply – 'I know you did not read the letter from your grandmother, for which I commend you; I'm not sure I would have done the same in your situation. I can say only that representations have been made in support of you being posted to the Black Sea, not, I hasten to add, out of any desire to protect you: God knows, you're as likely to perish from malaria in the hills above the Black Sea as you are from a bullet in Daghestan'.

General Petrov paused for a moment, then fixed Pechorin with a calm but steady gaze.

'More than that, however, I cannot tell you. You must trust me and, indeed, the instincts and goodwill of those who care about you'.

After a brief pause, Pechorin stood without a word and saluted. General Petrov returned the salute and made as if to continue, but was interrupted before he could speak.

'I will, of course, be honoured to serve wherever I am commanded, Sir' – said Pechorin – 'I am entirely at your service'.

Pechorin lowered his hand and turned to leave, before pausing in the doorway and turning once again to General Petrov.

'There is also the happy consequence' – he began – 'that I will be able to deliver a letter with which I was entrusted to General Velyaminov in person'.

General Petrov smiled quietly at the faint implication that he might enquire from whom the letter had been sent.

'Splendid' – he replied – 'You will also be able to deliver the other letter currently in your possession in person'.

The small scrap of solace Pechorin imagined he had found in revealing to General Petrov a detail of which his superior officer was not aware now gave way to a familiar mute suspicion.

'Oh?' – Pechorin replied with studied nonchalance – 'And who might be the recipient of this other letter?'

'Why Lieutenant Martynov, of course' – replied Petrov – 'Your grandmother is an extremely thorough woman, Pechorin. Lieutenant Martynov has been with the Tenginsky Infantry regiment for some weeks now. General Velyaminov speaks very highly of him'.

Pechorin left General Petrov's office without another word and without closing the door behind him.

By the time Pechorin joined Dr Werner and Lazarev in the yard of Staff HQ, Pushkin was already seated in his sturdy coach, one of a growing number that had been rebuilt from the wheels up for use on the rough pathways that served as roads the deeper one travelled into the Caucasus. Pushkin maintained his playful air, his mood diminished only by what was, for him, the impenetrable mystery of why Pechorin had not been allowed to accompany him. Dr Werner, on the other hand, was either entirely untroubled by such uncertainty; or perhaps, for him, it was not in fact a mystery.

'Farewell, then' - said Pushkin from the window of the coach - 'I hope to see all of you esteemed gentlemen very soon, although you will forgive me, Dr Werner, if I insist upon a social opportunity, as opposed to some occasion for the exercise of your professional responsibilities'.

'I forgive you' - replied Dr Werner drily - 'The less often I am required in the line of duty, the happier I am'.

'I expect I will see you soonest of all, Lieutenant Pechorin' - continued Pushkin - 'It won't take long for them to realise that your training was deficient in trench-digging and stone-masonry'.

Pechorin might have taken this as a not-so-guarded insult from another man with whom he was barely acquainted, but something in Pushkin's tone conveyed a hidden empathy, a genuine desire to prolong the acquaintance.

'I try not to wonder at what fate might hold in store for me, Major Pushkin' - he replied - 'And, whatever that may be, I hope to be able to bear it with all the equanimity fate demands'.

'Bravo' - said Dr Werner in an undertone.

Pushkin gave a short wave of farewell as the coach pulled noisily out of the yard. Dr Werner shot Pechorin an inquisitive glance, before bidding Pechorin and Lazarev, who had not uttered a word the entire time, good day and returning to his quarters. Pechorin was himself on the point of leaving, searching only for some polite word of farewell, when Lazarev turned to him and took from his tunic pocket a small notebook bound in weathered dark-brown leather.

'We may not meet again' - said Lazarev, the quietness of his voice at odds with the ripple of shock Pechorin felt at hearing him speak - 'There are battalions of the Tenginsky Infantry posted all across our Right Flank and I do not have the luxury of foreknowledge as to which one I may join at any given time'.

Lazarev reached out the hand in which he held the notebook, gesturing to Pechorin to take it from him.

'I hope you will accept a modest gift, Grigorii Alexandrovich' - he continued.

Pechorin raised his hand smoothly and quickly to take the notebook, anxious to conceal any hesitation or embarrassment at Lazarev's sudden and unexpected gesture.

'Why thank you, Oleg Abramovich' – he said in an even tone – 'I am very much obliged'.

Lazarev responded with the faintest of smiles, his ruined features for a second redeemed by the light of some inner covenant. As he turned to leave, he spoke again, yet more quietly than before.

'May God be with you, Grigorii Alexandrovich'.

Pechorin stood alone in the deserted yard of Staff HQ, the weak winter sun hazing his eyes without warming his skin. After a few minutes, he returned to his little wooden cell and placed the notebook Lazarev had given him in his trunk alongside the letters for General Velyaminov and Martynov and the envelope containing money for the latter.

Pechorin dined that evening alone with Dr Werner. At first, their conversation was animated, Werner slyly tempting the younger man into revealing what he knew about some circumstance or other, while Pechorin studiedly gave the impression that he knew much more than delicacy would allow him to say. As the days passed, each man began to reply more often with a look or a subtle modification of their facial expression than with words. Werner's enquiries about Yermolov or, more to the point, Pechorin's attempts to garner how much Werner knew about the mystery surrounding his posting, were met with knowing glances rather than explicit replies. Each man was content to imagine he knew what the other was thinking; and, if he didn't, to conclude that his companion was unfortunately somewhat less acute than he had at first taken him to be. Only when Werner dared, with great subtlety and artifice, to probe the circumstances of Pechorin's departure from St Petersburg, which was little more than a polite way of communicating that he perhaps knew everything, did the conversation conclude in a manner that would have appeared extremely curious to anyone observing these two unlikely companions. Werner would allude to some figure from St Petersburg life, some friend of an acquaintance of an acquaintance, whom he knew very well to have played some small role in Pechorin's disgrace, whereupon Pechorin would fix the doctor with a mockingly grave stare, which he would maintain for as long as he could, before the two men burst out laughing simultaneously.

On the evening before Pechorin's departure, neither man had much to say and was content to enjoy the company of the other without demanding anything in return. Werner told Pechorin that he would be at the military hospital from dawn the following morning, so would say his farewells now. In any case, Werner insisted, he was tired of saying farewell to one fellow or another, only to run into him on the street two days later! Such were our Caucasus: only death or dishonour might prevent you from running into someone at some point, even if you tried your damndest to avoid the fellow! Pechorin laughed in agreement and they raised their glasses to long encounters and brief farewells.

CHAPTER TWELVE

TAMAN

TAMAN IS THE vilest of all the coastal towns in Russia. Pechorin almost died there from hunger and someone even tried to drown him. He arrived late at night by coach. The coachman stopped the tired horses at the gates of the only stone building in the town, just at the entrance. When he heard the coach bell, the sentry, a Black Sea Cossack, shouted out in a wild voice, half-asleep: 'Who goes there?'

A Cossack Sergeant and Corporal came out to meet the coach. Pechorin explained to them that he was an officer on his way to his unit in the field on official business and asked for quarters. The Corporal took Pechorin through the town, but at every shack he got the same answer – full. It was cold and Pechorin hadn't slept for three nights; he'd had enough and was beginning to get angry.

'Take me anywhere, you robber! To the devil himself, but somewhere!' – he shouted.

'There is one more place' – said the Corporal, scratching his head – 'It's just that your Honour won't like it: it's unclean'.

Without really understanding the precise meaning of this last word, Pechorin ordered the Corporal to set off and, after a long journey through muddy backstreets, alongside which they could make out only ramshackle fences, they came to a small shack right on the seashore. The full moon shone on the thatched roof and white walls of Pechorin's new quarters. In the little courtyard, bounded by a stone wall, stood another crumbling hovel, smaller and older than the first. The sheer cliff plunged to the sea almost by the walls and dark blue waves crashed below with a ceaseless murmur. The moon looked quietly down at the restless elements it commanded, its light picking out two ships far out from shore, their black sails, like spiders' webs, quite still against the pale line of the horizon. 'Ships at anchor', Pechorin thought to himself. 'Tomorrow I'll sail for Gelendzhik'.

A Cossack from the front was travelling with Pechorin as his valet. Pechorin ordered him to take down his trunk and let the coachman go, then began to rouse the owner. Silence. He knocked again. Silence... and then... what was that? At last a boy of about fourteen crept out of the porch.

'Where's the owner?' – Pechorin asked.

'Nane' – answered the boy.

'What do you mean? None at all?'

'Nane'.

'What about his wife?'

'Gone to the village'.

'So who's going to open this door for me?' – Pechorin asked, kicking it as he spoke.

The door fell open. A damp smell came from the shack. Pechorin lit a match and raised it to the boy's nose, illuminating the two white circles of his eyes: he was blind, completely blind from birth. He stood motionlessly in front of Pechorin, who began to examine his face. I confess to a strong prejudice against the blind, the lame, the deaf, the dumb, amputees and hunchbacks. I've noticed that there is always some kind of strange relationship between a person's exterior and his soul, as if the loss of a limb or faculty is accompanied by a loss of feeling.

Pechorin began to examine the blind boy's face; but what can one read from a face with no eyes? Pechorin looked at him for a long time with some sympathy, when suddenly a barely discernible smile ran across the boy's thin lips, which, although he didn't know why, made the most unpleasant impression on Pechorin. It occurred to him that perhaps this blind boy was not quite as blind as he seemed. He tried in vain to convince himself that it was impossible to fake those white, pupil-less eyes; and in any case, why would he? But what is to be done, who among us is not frequently inclined to such prejudices...

'Are you the owner's son?' – Pechorin asked at last.

'Na' – the boy replied.

'Who are you then?'

'An orphan, a beggar'.

'Does the owner's wife have any children?'

'Na. She had a daughter, who went to sea with a Tatar'.

'What do you mean, with a Tatar?'

'Who knows! A Crimean Tatar, a boatman from Kerch' – said the boy.

Pechorin went into the shack. The only furniture was a table and two benches and a huge chest next to the stove. Not a single icon hung on the walls – a very bad sign. The sea breeze blew in through the broken window. Pechorin took the stub of a candle from his trunk, lit it, and began to unpack his things. He put his sword and rifle in the corner, laid his pistols on the table, and spread his cape out on one of the benches. The Cossack did the same on the other bench and ten minutes later began to snore, but Pechorin couldn't sleep. The blind boy with the white pupils still hovered before his eyes in the gloom.

An hour passed. The full moon shone through the window, its rays playing on the dirt floor of the shack. Suddenly a shadow passed across the bright strip of light that dissected the floor. Pechorin sat up and looked out of the window: someone passed by for a second time and hid God knows where. It simply wasn't possible that whatever it was had run down the sheer incline to the shore, but otherwise there was nowhere for it to go. Pechorin got up, threw on a hat, strapped on his dagger, and crept out of the shack as quietly as he could. The blind boy was coming towards him. Pechorin hid by the fence as the boy walked straight past, with a sure but cautious step. He was carrying some kind of knotted bundle under his arm and, turning towards the pier, went down a narrow, steep path. 'And on that day', Pechorin thought to himself, 'the mute will cry out and the blind will see'. He followed the boy at a distance, not letting him out of his sight.

The moon began to cloak itself in clouds and a mist rose on the sea, through which a lantern on the deck of the nearest boat faintly glimmered. The foam of the breakers glistened by the shore, threatening at any moment to sink the boat. Pechorin descended with great difficulty, struggling down the steep slope, and saw the boy stop before turning right at the foot of the cliff. He walked so close to the water that it seemed a wave would catch him and carry him away at any moment. It was clear, however, that this was not the first time he had walked this route, judging by the confidence with which he stepped from stone to stone, avoiding the ruts between them. At last he stopped, as if listening for something, sat down on the ground and laid the bundle by his side. Pechorin followed his movements from behind an outcrop in the cliff face. After a few minutes a white figure appeared from the opposite direction; it approached and sat down beside the boy. From time to time fragments of their conversation could be heard on the wind.

'So, blind boy?' – said a girl's voice – 'The storm is bad. Janko won't come'.
'Janko isn't afraid of storms' – the boy replied.
'The fog's getting thicker' – countered the girl, sadness in her voice.
'It's easier to get past the coast guard in the fog' – came the reply.
'And what if he drowns?'
'Well, you'll go to church on Sunday without a new ribbon in your hair'.
Silence. Pechorin was struck by the fact that the blind boy had spoken to him in the local dialect, but now spoke perfect Russian.
'You see, I was right' – said the boy, clapping his hands together – 'Janko isn't afraid of the sea, the wind, the fog or the coast guard. You can't fool me, that's not just the water splashing, that's Janko's long oars'.
The girl leapt to her feet and looked anxiously into the distance.
'You're raving, boy' – she said – 'I can't see anything'.
No matter how hard he tried, Pechorin couldn't make out anything resembling a boat in the distance. Ten minutes or so passed. And there among the mountainous waves appeared a black spot, which first grew in size, then receded. It slowly rose to the crests of the waves, before quickly falling back from them as it approached the shore. Brave was the sailor who would venture more than ten miles through the sound on a night like this and compelling the reason that made him! So thought Pechorin, his heart thumping involuntarily as he looked out at the poor vessel. Yet like a duck it dived down, before leaping back from the foaming abyss, its oars flapping like wings, sure to crash against the shore and be smashed to pieces; but once again it deftly rolled on its side and came up safely into a little bay.

A man of medium height in a Tatar sheepskin hat disembarked, waved his hand, and all three figures began to drag something from the boat. The cargo was so large that it must surely have sunk the boat. Each of them took a bundle across their shoulders and set off along the shore, disappearing from sight. Pechorin had to get back to his quarters, but he was so disturbed by these strange events that he could hardly wait for morning.

The Cossack woke astonished to find Pechorin fully dressed, although he didn't explain the reason. Pechorin lay for a while, looking admiringly through the window at the blue skies dotted with broken clouds above the distant Crimean coast, stretching out in a violet strip which ran to a craggy cliff topped by a lighthouse. He then set off for the fort at Phanagoria to ask the Commandant when he could leave for Gelendzhik.

The Commandant had nothing definite to say. The vessels at anchor in the bay were all either patrol ships or merchant vessels that had not even begun to load their cargo.

'Perhaps in three or four days there will be a packet ship' - said the Commandant - 'Then... we'll see'.

Pechorin returned angry and gloomy. The Cossack met him at the door with a look of fear on his face.

'It's bad, your Honour' - he said.

'Yes, brother, God knows when we'll be able to get out of here!'

At this the Cossack became even more agitated and, leaning towards Pechorin, said in a whisper.

'This is an evil place! Today I met a Black Sea Cossack officer who was in our division last year. I told him where we were staying and he replied: "An evil place, brother... bad people!" And what about that blind boy, who goes everywhere on his own, to the market, for bread, for water... they're obviously used to him here'.

'Yes, what about it? Has the owner's wife at least shown up?' - asked Pechorin.

'Today when you weren't here an old woman came with her daughter'.

'Daughter? She doesn't have a daughter'.

'God knows who she is if she's not her daughter; the old woman's there now, sitting in her hut'.

Pechorin went into the hovel. The stove was hot, with a meal cooking, and not bad fare for poor people. The old woman responded to all his questions by saying that she was deaf and couldn't hear. Pechorin turned to the blind boy, who sat in front of the stove putting brushwood into the flames.

'Now then you little blind devil' - he said, grabbing him by the ear - 'Tell me where you were going with your bundle last night, eh?'

The boy suddenly burst into tears, shouting and moaning.

'Where? Nowhere. Wi' a bundle? Whit bundle?'

This time the old woman heard well enough and grumbled:

'Making things up about the poor soul! What do you want with him? What has he done to you?'

Pechorin grew tired of this and left, resolving to get to the bottom of the mystery.

Wrapping himself in his cape, he sat down on a rock by the fence and looked into the distance; the sea, still wild from the previous night's storm, stretched out before him, its monotonous sound, like the low rumble of a city as it falls asleep, reminded him of days gone by, taking him back to the North, to our cold capital. He lost himself in troubled recollection...

An hour passed, or more, and suddenly something like a song caught Pechorin's ear. It was a song, sung by a fresh female voice – but where was it coming from? He listened... it was an ancient song, sometimes slow and mournful, sometimes brisk and lively. Pechorin looked around, but there was no one there. He listened again... it was as if the sounds were falling from the sky. He raised his eyes and saw a girl in a striped dress standing on the roof of the hut, her flowing hair falling loose, like a mermaid come to life. Shading her eyes from the light of the moon, she gazed intently into the distance, laughing and talking to herself, then returning to her song.

I know the song word for word:

Tall ships sail o'er the deep green ocean,
White sails set on the billowy wave.
My little boat sails there with the tall ships,
Sails has she none, just her two good oars.
Storm winds will blow and the old tall ships
Will lift their wings and fly over the sea.
Then I'll curtsey and beg so humbly:
'Have pity on my boat, oh wicked sea.
Precious are the goods that my boat carries,
Bold is the heart that steers her through the night.'

It occurred to Pechorin that he had heard that same voice in the night. He thought for a moment, but when he looked again at the roof, the girl was no longer there. She suddenly ran past humming a different tune and, clicking her fingers, ran inside to the old woman. They began to argue. The old woman was angry and laughed loudly. Pechorin then caught sight of his Undine once again, now running briskly: when she reached him, she stopped and once again looked intently into his eyes, as if amazed by his presence; then she casually turned and walked quietly to the pier.

It didn't end there. All day she hung around Pechorin's quarters, never ceasing for a moment her singing and skipping. Strange creature! There were no signs of madness on her face; on the contrary, she looked at him with a bold, penetrating gaze and it seemed that her eyes possessed some magnetic power, as if constantly expecting a question. But as soon as Pechorin began to speak, she would run away with a sly smile.

Pechorin had never seen a woman like her. She was far from beautiful, although I also have certain prejudices when it comes to beauty. She had great breeding... and breeding in women, just as in horses, is an important matter

– a fact discovered by Victor Hugo and *Les Jeunes-France*. This – breeding, that is, not *Les Jeunes-France* – is mainly visible in the manner of walking, in the hands and in the feet; the nose is also very important. In Russia, a well-formed nose is less common than a pretty little foot. The songstress looked no more than eighteen years old. The unusual flexibility in her movements, the particular way, unique in fact to her, in which she tilted her head, her long red hair, a certain golden shimmer in the lightly tanned skin on her neck and shoulders, and especially her perfect nose – all this was captivating. And although there was something wild and suspicious in her indirect glances, something elusive in her smile, such is the power of preconceptions: her perfect nose drove Pechorin out of his mind. He imagined that he had encountered Goethe's Mignon, that miraculous creation of the German imagination. And there really were similarities between them: the same sudden transitions from great agitation to complete stillness, the same mysterious words, the same little skips and strange songs.

Towards evening, Pechorin stopped the girl at the doors and began the following conversation.

'Tell me, beauty' – he asked – 'What were you doing earlier today on the roof?'

'I was looking to see which way the wind was blowing' – she replied.

'Why do you care?'

'Happiness comes from where the wind blows'.

'Really? And were you summoning happiness with your song?'

'Where there is singing there is happiness'.

'And what if you sing yourself into trouble?'

'What do you mean? Wherever isn't better, is worse. And from good to bad is not so far'.

'Who taught you that song?'

'No one taught me. It comes to me, and I sing. Whoever hears it, hears it. And whoever isn't meant to hear it, won't understand it'.

'And what's your name, my songstress?'

'Whoever christened me will know'.

'And who christened you?'

'How would I know?'

'Secretive, aren't we? I've found something out about you all the same'.

The expression on the girl's face didn't change, her lips didn't move, as if Pechorin was talking about someone else.

'I found out that you went down to the shore last night' – he said.

And here he told her everything he had seen in a very serious tone, hoping to upset her – but not at all!

'You've seen a lot, but know little. And what you do know, better keep to yourself' – the girl replied.

'And what if I decide to inform the Commandant, for example?' – said Pechorin, making a serious, even stern face.

She suddenly jumped up, began to sing, and disappeared, like a bird that had been scared out of a bush. Pechorin's last words had been the wrong ones. He didn't suspect then how significant they would be or that he would later have cause to regret them.

It was beginning to get dark and Pechorin told his Cossack to make tea, lit a candle, and sat down at the table smoking a cigar. He was just finishing his second cup of tea when the door creaked suddenly; there was a rustle of skirts and footsteps behind him. Pechorin gave a start, turned round, and there she was, Undine! She quietly sat down facing Pechorin and looked silently into his eyes. He didn't know why, but her gaze was incredibly tender. It reminded Pechorin of one of those looks that, in days past, had played such a powerful role in his life. It seemed as though she was expecting Pechorin to ask her something, but, inexplicably disconcerted, he said nothing. Her face was pale, suggesting some kind of deeply-felt emotion. Her hands wandered across the table without purpose and she was trembling very slightly. At one moment her chest would heave, at the next she seemingly held her breath. This comedy began to bore Pechorin, who was about to end the silence in the most prosaic manner by offering her some tea, when she suddenly jumped up, threw her arms around his neck, and planted a moist, passionate kiss on his lips. Pechorin's eyes grew dark, his head spun, and he pressed her to himself with all the force of youthful passion, but she slipped, like a snake, from his arms, whispering in his ear:

'Tonight when everyone is asleep, come down to the shore'.

She flew out of the room like a shot, knocking over the teapot and the candle on the floor in the hall.

'She-Devil!' – shouted the Cossack, lying in the hay and dreaming of warming himself with the left-over tea.

Only then did Pechorin recover his wits.

Two hours later, when everything was quiet at the pier, Pechorin woke his Cossack.

'If I fire my pistol' – he told him – 'come down to the shore right away'.

The Cossack opened his eyes wide and said mechanically:

'Certainly, your Honour'.

Pechorin thrust his pistol into his belt and left.

The girl was waiting for him at the edge of the cliff. Her clothes seemed somehow lighter, a small scarf around her supple waist.

'Follow me!' – she said, taking Pechorin by the hand, and they began to descend.

It's nothing short of a miracle that Pechorin didn't break his neck, but they eventually turned right at the bottom and took the same path along which he had followed the blind boy on the previous night. The full moon had not yet come up and only two little stars shone like warning beacons in the dark blue sky. The heavy waves followed one another in steady rhythm, barely lifting the only boat moored at the shore.

'Let's get in the boat' – said the girl.

Pechorin hesitated, not being one for sentimental trips out to sea, but this wasn't the moment to back off. She jumped into the boat and he followed her. He barely had time to think before he realised they were afloat.

'What does this mean? - Pechorin said angrily.

'It means' - she answered, putting her arms around his waist - 'it means that I love you...'.

The girl's cheek was pressed close to Pechorin's and he could feel her warm breath on his face.

Suddenly, something fell noisily into the sea. Pechorin grabbed at his belt - no pistol. A terrible suspicion crept into his soul, the blood surged in his head. He looked around and saw that they were a hundred yards from the shore; he couldn't swim. Pechorin tried to push her away, but she clung onto his clothes like a cat and suddenly a heavy blow almost threw him into the sea. The boat rocked, but he regained his balance and a desperate struggle began between them. Rage gave him strength, but he soon realised that he was no match for his opponent's dexterity...

'What do you want?' - Pechorin shouted, squeezing her small hands until her fingers cracked, although she didn't cry out; her serpent-like nature was able to withstand such torture.

'You saw' - she replied - 'You'll report us!' - and with supernatural strength tried to throw him overboard.

They were both hanging out of the boat from the waist, her hair touching the water. The decisive moment. Pechorin braced his knee against the hull, grabbed her by the hair with one hand and by the throat with the other, and she let go of his clothes. In the blink of an eye he threw her into the waves.

It was already quite dark. He twice glimpsed her head among the foam and then, nothing...

Pechorin found half of an old oar in the bottom of the boat and somehow, after great efforts, managed to get back to the mooring. Going along the shore back to his hut, he found himself looking in the same direction where, the night before, the blind boy had been waiting for the nocturnal sailor. The moon was up in the sky and he thought he could see someone dressed in white sitting by the shore. Pechorin hid, gripped by curiosity, and lay down in the grass above the cliff-edge. By raising his head a little he could see everything that was going on below. He wasn't surprised, but was even glad to recognise the mermaid. She was wringing the foam from her long hair, her wet blouse showing the outline of her lithe waist and her high bosom. A boat soon appeared in the distance and quickly drew near; as the night before, a man in a Tatar hat got out, although he was shaved in the Cossack style, and a large knife was sticking out of his belt.

'Janko!' - she said - 'All is lost!'

Their conversation was so quiet that almost nothing could be heard.

'Where's the blind boy?' - Janko said at last in a raised voice.

'I sent him back' - came the reply.

After a few minutes the blind boy appeared with a sack on his back, which they placed in the boat.

'Listen, blind boy!' – said Janko – 'You guard that place... you know the one? There's valuable stuff there. Tell (a name Pechorin couldn't make out) that I'm no longer his servant; things have gone wrong and he won't see me again. It's dangerous. I'm going to look for work somewhere else; he won't find another daredevil like me. Tell him that if he'd paid better, then Janko wouldn't have left him. I go where I please, where the wind blows and the sea roars!'

After a little silence, Janko continued.

'She's coming with me, she can't stay here. Tell the old woman it's time to die. She's lived too long and should do the honourable thing. She won't see us again'.

'But what about me?' – said the blind boy in a plaintive voice.

'What are you to me?' – came the reply.

While this was going on the mermaid climbed into the boat and waved to her companion, who put something in the blind boy's hand, murmuring:

'Here, buy yourself some biscuits'.

'Is that all?' – the blind boy said.

'Here's some more' – said Janko, and a coin fell and tinkled as it hit the stone.

The blind boy didn't pick it up.

Janko got into the boat, the wind blew from the shore, and they raised their little sail and quickly took off. The sail shone for a long time among the dark waves under the light of the full moon. The blind boy cried for a long, long time... Pechorin became melancholy. Why had fate cast him into the peaceful company of honest smugglers? Like a stone thrown into a quiet pool, he had disturbed their peace; and, like a stone, he had almost sunk to the bottom!

He returned to his lodgings. A burnt-out candle on a wooden plate flickered in the hallway and the Cossack, despite what he had been told, slept soundly, his rifle in both hands. Pechorin left him in peace, took the candle, and went into the hut. Alas, his sword with the silver sheath and his Daghestan sabre had disappeared, along with his money, with the exception of the three hundred roubles for Martynov, which had appeared to the thief as nothing more than another letter. He now realised what the accursed blind boy had been carrying in his bag.

Pechorin angrily woke the Cossack with an unfriendly push and swore at him; but there was nothing to be done! How ridiculous would it be to complain to the authorities that he had been robbed by a blind boy and very nearly drowned by an eighteen-year-old girl!

The next morning, thank God, there was a ship, and Pechorin left Taman. What became of the old woman and the poor blind boy, I don't know. But what are the joys and pains of mankind to me, or to Pechorin, a travelling officer on official business...

CHAPTER THIRTEEN

COMRADES-AT-ARMS

THE DARK SAILS of the brig that brought Pechorin at last to Gelendzhik were still visible on the horizon as the rather flimsy trap, pulled by a single horse, climbed slowly above the fortress, which from above looked more like a model village than a military fortification. Were it not for the stern grey stone walls that ran around its perimeter, the casual observer might have mistaken it for a creation of Prince Potemkin, who had managed to convince Catherine the Great that the provinces of the Russian south, even in the century past, were in no way inferior to her Prussian homeland.

Pechorin was convinced that a bullet, expertly dispatched between his eyes, must be preferable to what he imagined of the next weeks or months of his life, drifting among the network of fortifications along the Black Sea coast, most of which, unlike Gelendzhik, did not deserve to be called fortresses. He sought at first solace in the sentiments he had expressed as Lev Pushkin took his leave of Stavropol, trusting to equanimity in the face of whatever fate may bring. This he embellished with a pragmatism no less stoical: he would, after all, be able to discharge his debts to his grandmother and to Yermolov by delivering their conveyances to Martynov and General Velyaminov. Yet neither romantic nor pragmatic submission to the workings of fate could dispel the gloom that seemed to have settled like a fog on the hills above the coast as far as the eye could see in either direction.

Pechorin's mood was worsened by the sudden realisation that he was, to all intents and purposes, penniless. The only money remaining in his possession was the three hundred roubles sent, by a route most circuitous, by Martynov's mother; and these, he resolved, he would hand over immediately, without a word to Martynov about what had befallen him in Taman. For the first time since entering Military College, on terms he calculated would guarantee a degree of financial independence, then and in the future, he found himself without means; entirely dependent, in fact, on his officer's stipend... and God alone knew when that might be delivered unto him on these damp foothills, which God appeared quite conspicuously to have forsaken!

The rough track beneath the wheels of the trap began to level. Through the mist, Pechorin could make out the outline of wooden huts, built from the intact trunks of mature trees. Beyond the huts, there were huge piles of earth and rubble. He had never seen the work camps of Siberia and the Far East, but he could not dispel the thought that the scene before him must bear greater resemblance to those dolorous places than to a military settlement. The young Private in the box-seat brought the trap to a halt outside one of the huts and began to grapple with Pechorin's trunk, which had been perched perilously alongside him on the single passenger bench throughout the slow bumpy ride up the hillside. Pechorin nodded to the boy to leave the trunk by the door, rummaged through its contents for a moment, then stepped into the hut.

The room was cluttered with long, low benches sitting around a single enormous table, all hewn from the same timber as the walls. Greatcoats and galoshes hung on great hooks on the walls, the odd pair of boots on the rough wooden floor; but there was not a human soul. An unmarked door was set into a partition running down the left-hand side of the room. Pechorin knocked and waited. Hearing no reply, he knocked again. Silence. He knocked for a third time and, once again hearing no reply, gently opened the door. The walls and floor of the small partitioned room were no different from the room from which he had entered; but, at its centre, sat a large desk of dark, polished teak, with ornamental carvings at its corners, somewhat, Pechorin imagined, in the Japanese style. At the desk there was a high-backed chair of the same material, its padded seat and backing of an intricate woven silk, portraying scenes of a hunt in some Asiatic land, dominated along its upper diagonal by a long-necked bird of some kind, perhaps a crane, pearlescent white against the greens and blues of the landscape and the pink shade of a cherry-blossom tree. Pechorin smiled quietly to himself at the endeavours that must have brought these exquisite artefacts to this unlikely place, any sense of incongruity quickly replaced by a clear grasp of their owner's determination to furnish his bleak surroundings with an item of constant consolation. There was no other chair in the room. Pechorin settled into the lustrous woven silk upholstery and waited.

The strange peace was disturbed by the barking and yelping of what seemed an entire pack of dogs, followed by the scurrying of paws on the wooden floor and a sudden flood of seven or eight Caucasian hounds into the room. As the dogs milled excitedly around Pechorin's feet, taking turns to leap up into his lap, sniffing and licking, they were followed by a tall man in a General's uniform, a grave expression suspended beneath his dramatic widow's peak.

'Lieutenant Pechorin, I presume' - said the newcomer.

'Yes, Sir, General Velyaminov' - replied Pechorin, standing to salute.

'It's Lieutenant-General' - said Velyaminov - 'But no matter. Do you have something for me, Lieutenant Pechorin?'

Pechorin slipped a hand into the pocket of his tunic, took out the letter from General Yermolov, and handed it to Lieutenant-General Velyaminov.

'I am very much obliged' - continued Velyaminov, his solemn expression unchanged - 'And very glad to make your acquaintance'.

Pechorin had known the name Velyaminov since childhood and was now taken aback by its collocation with the curiously indeterminate rank of Lieutenant-General. Velyaminov had commanded a division of the artillery at Borodinó alongside the division commanded by Pechorin's great-uncle

Afanasii, who had often spoken of Velyaminov as an example of iron loyalty and brutal honesty. Velyaminov's ability to take difficult decisions without concern for what people might think of him had consistently led to a most desirable outcome: honest men thought highly of him, while the dishonest despised him. After the defeat of Napoleon, Velyaminov had risen to become second-in-command to Yermolov in the Caucasus; when Yermolov was eventually removed, Velyaminov was offered the position of Chief of Staff – and refused it out of loyalty to his erstwhile superior. Despite heroic victories over the Persians at Yelizavetopol and the Turks in the Balkans, his reputation – in government circles, at least – had never recovered. It was his fate now to oversee the project almost no one else in the military believed in, but from which the Tsar could not be dissuaded: the only Lieutenant-General serving in the Caucasus would spend his last years faithfully overseeing the fortification of the Black Sea coast, a task with which he had been entrusted by a Tsar who did not trust him, but who was nonetheless satisfied with an arrangement that would keep Velyaminov far from his former spheres of influence.

'You don't mind if I read this right away?' – asked Velyaminov, sitting down in the exquisitely upholstered chair.

'Not at all, Sir' – Pechorin replied, relieved that, at last, he might glean something of the contents from the expression on the face of one of the recipients of these letters, by which he had at first been intrigued, but which now provoked a species of resentment he had not experienced since wresting control of his destiny from the protective grasp of his grandmother.

Velyaminov, however, gave no indication whatsoever of the content or subject of Yermolov's letter and Pechorin silently reproached himself for the presumption that this communication between two old comrades might in any way concern him.

When he had finished reading, Velyaminov folded the letter and slipped it into his tunic, his expression as solemn and still as when he had entered the room. The dogs' excitement at the sound and smell of a newcomer had subsided and they had arranged themselves in a rough pile in the corner of the room, snouts and legs entangled in one another, like a litter of overgrown puppies.

'You will spend the night here, Lieutenant Pechorin' – Velyaminov began – 'then travel by horse to the Tenginsky Fortress above the Shapsukho River tomorrow. I believe you know Lieutenant Martynov?'

Pechorin nodded in confirmation, then shifted uneasily from one foot to the other. Suddenly, without any preparation or consideration, he felt compelled to broach a matter he had earlier resolved to mention to no one.

'Lieutenant-General Velyaminov, Sir' – Pechorin began – 'I also have a letter for Lieutenant Martynov, from his mother, along with a sum of money. Unfortunately, after a regrettable incident in Taman, this is the only money in my possession. I intend of course to hand it over to Lieutenant Martynov immediately, but...'.

'I understand, Lieutenant Pechorin' - interrupted Velyaminov - 'You won't be needing much in the way of money over the next couple of weeks' - he continued - 'but I'll send orders to the purser at Tenginsky to provide an advance on your stipend, enough to keep you in cigars'.

'I am very much obliged, indeed, Sir' - Pechorin replied, the solemnity in his expression now matching that of Velyaminov.

The following morning, Pechorin set off on horseback for the Tenginsky Fortress, with the young Private who had accompanied him from Gelendzhik as escort. He divided most of the contents of his trunk between two large saddle-bags, which were now strapped across the back of a fine chestnut Circassian horse. They took their leave of Lieutenant-General Velyaminov amid the mountains of earth and rubble that rose up behind the rough timber cabins. The sound of men working had been carried on the air for over two hours already, although the sun had only just come up. Velyaminov stood erect among the mud and noise, surrounded by his dogs, who performed an elaborate drill around his feet, their snouts hovering just above the earth.

'I'll join you at Tenginsky in two or three days, Lieutenant Pechorin' - said Velyaminov - 'Once I'm satisfied that the work on broadening the pass is progressing'.

'Very well, Sir' - replied Pechorin, saluting, before digging his heels into the flanks of his horse and setting off at a canter south above the line of the coast, the young Private following at his heels.

'What's your name, boy?' - Pechorin asked as the young Private's horse drew alongside.

'Shapovalov, your Honour' - came the reply.

'Well, Shapovalov' - said Pechorin - 'How long do you think it will take us to reach the fortress?'

'I dunno, Sir... the best part of the morning'.

Pechorin looked out over the tree-lined hills to his left, then down to the shimmering sea beyond the line of the shore to his right, before giving his horse a firm slap on its flank and breaking into a gallop along the unknown path that forged a perilous route between them.

The terrain was uneven, now falling towards the shore, now pulling once again uphill, but Pechorin managed to find a steady gallop which did not appear to trouble his mount. Poor Private Shapovalov, however, who knew the path very well, was nonetheless obliged to ride at the very limit of his not inconsiderable skills of horsemanship in order to keep up. After an hour or so, as the path turned decisively down towards the shore, Pechorin began to ease back to a canter and the boy once again drew alongside, his cheeks flushed and his breathing as short as that of his horse. Ahead lay the Dzhubga River, broad and deep as it fell into the sea. Pechorin was about to ask Shapovalov where they might ford the river when, just off his to left among the trees, he caught sight of an ancient stone structure, the like of which he had never seen before. A huge table of stone had been laid across two standing stones. The surface between them had been filled with another stone, into which a large circular hole had been carved; on either side, two more large stones lay like arms reaching down towards them.

'What on earth is that?' - asked Pechorin - 'Some kind of well?'

'No, your Honour' - Shapovalov replied - 'The locals call it *ispun*. There are hundreds of them all along the coast, some dating back to the second millennium B.C. when the Koban culture ranged across the Caucasus, from Daghestan in the east to Circassia in the west'.

Pechorin looked at the boy with renewed interest.

'You're a mine of information, my boy' - he said drily - 'Where did you learn this?'

'From my grandmother, your Honour, on my mothers's side' - replied Shapovalov - 'She was a Circassian'.

'Ah' - said Pechorin, his face lighting up - 'So I am in the hands of a native informant! How splendid!'

Shapovalov remained silent.

'Well, my boy?' - asked Pechorin - 'Out with it'.

Shapovalov hesitated for a moment, then raised his chin and spoke in a quiet, firm voice.

'It's just, your Honour... it's just that I am Russian'.

'Even better!' - Pechorin replied - 'A humble servant of His Imperial Majesty like myself, but with the blood of the mountains running through his veins... How splendid indeed! Anyway, what are they for these *ispun*, if not for drinking?'

Shapovalov hesitated once more.

'They are tombs, your Honour' - he said at last - 'This is a burial ground'.

Pechorin gave a little tug at the reins and pulled his mount off to the left. When he reached the curious structure, he stopped and dismounted, removed the saddle from his horse's back, and let the beast drink from the snowmelt in the pool that had formed at the base of the *ispun*, its flanks glistening in the weak winter sun. Shapovalov repeated the sequence of Pechorin's actions without a word and lay down on his back in the grass, relieved to have survived, for now at least, his trial of nerve and horsemanship.

'How long have you been here, my boy?' - Pechorin asked, as he also settled down in the grass.

'Six months, your Honour' - the boy replied.

'And how long have you been a soldier?'

'Six months, your Honour' - said Shapovalov after a brief hesitation.

Pechorin took a little cigar in the French style from a case in his hip pocket and offered one to Shapovalov.

'Go ahead' - said Pechorin gently, before lighting both cigars - 'And what do you do here?'

'I spend most of my time exactly as you saw, your Honour' - Shapovalov replied - 'Moving goods and people between the fortress and Gelendzhik.

Sometimes I go as far as the new harbour they're building at Sudzhuk-Kale, but not often'.

'And do you like it?'

'Well, it's better than labouring on the Mikhailovsky Pass... they've been at it for months, your Honour'.

'And what about the enemy?'

Shapovalov sat up in the grass and put a hand above his eyes to shade the sun.

'We rarely see the enemy, your Honour' – he said quietly – 'But we hear them and we sometimes hear their bullets, most often at night'.

'How do you mean?' – asked Pechorin.

'Well, your Honour' – Shapovalov replied – 'During the day – like today – you'd be forgiven for thinking there was no enemy. They come down out of the hills at night, stealing the little livestock we have or, if there's enough of them, attacking our sentry posts in the hills above the fortress'.

Pechorin suddenly imagined himself alone at dusk, high in the hills above the coast, peering out into the gloom, trying to distinguish the silhouettes of Circassian raiders from the shadows and the trees, only his rifle and the warning beacon standing between him and certain death. He glanced up into the sun.

'Come, my boy' – said Pechorin quietly – 'Let's get ourselves up that hill'.

Shapovalov led the way upstream to a point where the horses could walk with ease through the shallows of the Dzhubga and they set off at a gentle trot along the shore of the Black Sea, the path now even and in places littered with sand that had been washed up by the waves. When they reached the mouth of the Shapsukho, the path once again turned inland, rising gently toward the Tenginsky Fortress, the low outline of which was already visible in the distance. As they approached, Pechorin suddenly understood why Grabbe had been so dismissive of the Black Sea fortifications and, perhaps, the pall of gloom which hung permanently over the figure of Velyaminov. The fortress consisted of no more than a three-sided timber stockade, the fourth wall backing onto the muddy shores of the river, punctuated at its centre by a raised sentry-post. Within these walls stood a single stone building, surrounded by timber huts of the type Pechorin had seen at the Mikhailovsky Pass. Beyond the walls, the forest had been cleared in a rough semi-circle, bounded at its base by the wending course of the river. Two sentries sat perched on either side above the entrance gate, which swung open to reveal a makeshift yard; Pechorin could not help making unfavourable comparisons with the comparatively expansive and reassuring fortifications at Gelendzhik, which were as a bustling metropolis to this rustic improvisation, resembling more closely the dismal post-stations that had punctuated his journey south. The brief release of the headlong gallop through the foothills that morning now seemed as distant as the outskirts of St Petersburg as his weary horse walked mournfully through the gates.

Pechorin reported to the Commandant, Major Severyanin, who barely looked up as he entered the room.

'Major Severyanin, Sir' – said Pechorin, saluting – 'Lieutenant Pechorin, reporting for duty'.

'At ease, Lieutenant Pechorin' – replied Severyanin, without returning salute or rising from his chair – 'How can I help you?'

'I received orders from Lieutenant-General Velyaminov to report to you' – said Pechorin.

Major Severyanin put down the pen with which he had been scribbling and looked at Pechorin impatiently.

'Yes, I'm aware of that' – he rasped – 'And?'

'I wish to enquire as to my duties, Sir' – said Pechorin gently.

Major Severyanin's distracted air now gave way to a knowing weariness as he surveyed the curiosity standing above his desk: the mud and grime of the road did not in any measure obscure the stamp of a St Petersburg gentleman.

'Your duties' – Major Severyanin began – 'will be determined by the enemy, Lieutenant Pechorin'.

'I'm not sure I quite understand, Sir' – replied Pechorin, a faint crease running along his brows.

'When the enemy is quiet, your duty is to be watchful' – continued Severyanin – 'And when the enemy makes a noise, your duty is to make him quiet once again'.

'Has there been much noise of late?' – Pechorin asked with a half-smile.

Major Severyanin now granted weariness full sovereignty over his expression.

'Hardly a peep' – he replied with a long sigh – 'They have been very quiet indeed since we managed to cut off the supply of arms from the English'.

'Then I will remain watchful, Sir' – said Pechorin with a curt bow.

Major Severyanin searched Pechorin's face for some sign of insolence, but could find none.

'Report to Lieutenant Martynov' – he replied – 'I believe you know him?'

'Indeed' – said Pechorin, his expression unchanged – 'And where will I find Lieutenant Martynov?'

'I believe you'll currently find him swimming' – said Severyanin without looking up – 'Dismiss'.

Major Severyanin distractedly ordered a Cossack Sergeant to show Pechorin to his quarters. As he stepped into the tiny stone-walled room, the only furnishings a bunk and a night-table, Pechorin was once again overcome by a strange nostalgia for his cell at the Haymarket, which had at least allowed him to spectate upon the footwear of the inhabitants above through its little barred window and thus to imagine the life of the city beyond. Here, his imagination could find no such outlet. He reached into one of the saddlebags, slipped the letter and money for Martynov into his tunic pocket, and left the room less than a minute after entering it. In the yard, Pechorin caught sight of Private Shapovalov and gestured for him to approach.

'Tell me, my boy' – he began – 'Where do people swim around here?'

'At the waterfalls, your Honour' – replied Shapovalov breathlessly – 'It's not far, I can show you'.

After twenty minutes of steady climbing through dense forest, Pechorin and Shapovalov emerged from the shade of the trees into a rocky clearing, bounded at its farthest edge by a dramatic wall of green moss and shimmering jets of white water. The waterfall was the first – and largest – of an entire complex, which rose in a giant cascade almost to the highest sentry post above the fortress at Atsker. At the foot of the waterfall, a large pool of pale blue water, shot through with calciferous white from the sediment and the minerals in the rocks, stretched out invitingly towards them. To the left, a natural grotto in the shape of a dramatically obtuse triangle had formed in the layered rock face, a figure so perfect that for a moment Pechorin imagined himself studying a painting of the Pantheon in Rome. Above the waterfall and to the right, some adventurous soul had built a wooden platform with a rail, although here Pechorin's imagination failed him entirely: how on earth had this mysterious fellow got himself up there? And to what purpose?

'Isn't it good?' – said Shapovalov – 'When I first got here last summer, we'd come here every day to get some relief from the heat'.

'Yes, my boy' – Pechorin replied, distracted by thoughts of the icy waves in the bay at Taman – 'Not quite so appealing on a day like today...'.

As he spoke, Pechorin's gaze drifted towards a small dark pile to the right of the pool. He took a few paces towards it and soon realized that it consisted of a military tunic and shirt, roughly gathered on top of a pair of boots. He turned back towards Shapovalov with a beckoning gesture, when suddenly a deep baritone rang out, its cry reverberating around the rock faces.

'Pechorin!' – cried the voice – 'How marvellous to see you!'

Pechorin looked once again at Shapovalov, whose expression provided no answer to the implied question, before both looked up to see a dark-haired, broad-shouldered figure standing on the platform above the waterfall in nothing but a pair of officers' breeches. The figure climbed with purpose over the wooden rail, before suddenly throwing himself up into the air, tucking his knees up into his chest, and plunging with a great crash into the milky-blue water.

'Martynov' – said Pechorin, almost under his breath – 'How marvellous it is to see you, too...'.

Martynov hauled his frame from the pale blue lagoon, wrapped himself in a sheet he had hung in the lower branches of a tree, and sat down magisterially on a large smooth rock at the water's edge. Pechorin signalled to Shapovalov that he could return to the fortress and reached out a hand containing an open cigar-case to his newly restored acquaintance.

'Don't mind if I do' – said Martynov, pushing a corner of the sheet through his thick wet hair and leaning forward to accept a light.

Pechorin lit himself a cigar and blew a huge swirl of smoke up into the cool afternoon air.

'Are you keeping yourself busy, Martynov?' - he asked with a smile.

'Oh, I wouldn't say busy' - Martynov replied - 'because there's absolutely nothing to do here. But I keep myself entertained'.

'I have a letter for you from your mother' - Pechorin continued, reaching into his tunic for the two envelopes - 'And a sum of money'.

Martynov took the envelopes with a look of undisguised suspicion. Pechorin felt a dull anger rise in his chest, but maintained an air of outward calm.

'The letter will no doubt contain what is now very old news' - he said evenly - 'But money is money, don't you think?'

'I'm very much obliged, Pechorin' - replied Martynov with some effort, before stuffing both envelopes into a pocket of his tunic, which still lay on top of his boots - 'We should get back to the fortress so I can get properly dry'.

As they made their way back down through the forest, Pechorin sought from Martynov a more detailed picture of life at the fortress, but received only terse confirmations or denials; perhaps Martynov had been serious when he said there was absolutely nothing to do? The anger that had risen in him as he handed the letters to Martynov had not receded, caused not by Martynov's suspicion, but rather by the fool's inability to ask the question betrayed by his expression. Yermolov, in sharp contrast, had simply made a provocation and a joke out of it. The implication that he was in any way interested in what Martynov's mother might have to say to her beloved son infuriated him, but a more focused, cold anger was sustained also by his determination not to answer a question that had not been asked and, moreover, to remain silent about the price he had paid for discharging his obligations.

'It's good to see you, Pechorin' - said Martynov with slightly forced enthusiasm as they reached the fortress gates.

'You too' - Pechorin replied in an even tone - 'I imagine we'll be seeing quite a bit of one another'.

Martynov was about to reply when, just as they reached the stone building at the centre of the fortress, a handsome young fellow in the overcoat of an enlisted man overtook them from the left on his way into Staff HQ.

'Grushnitsky!' - called out Martynov - 'Let me introduce you to Lieutenant Pechorin!'

CHAPTER FOURTEEN

THE MISSION OF *THE THISTLE*

GRUSHNITSKY WAS WELL-BUILT, with a dark complexion and dark hair; he might have been taken for someone twenty-five years old, when in fact he had barely turned twenty-one. He had a habit of throwing back his head when he spoke and would constantly twirl his moustache with his left hand, traits Pechorin had observed even during their brief acquaintance in Novocherkassk.

'Why Lieutenant Pechorin' - Grushnitsky began with a slightly forced amiability - 'I had no idea you were joining us. What are the chances?'

Pechorin offered his hand with a similarly amiable smile.

'I had no idea myself...' - he replied, unsure of how to address Grushnitsky.

'Private Grushnitsky' - said Martynov - 'But we'll make an officer of him yet!'

'Delighted to renew our acquaintance, Private Grushnitsky' - continued Pechorin - 'Tell me, have you managed to put your certainty of the inevitability of our success to the test?'

'Let's just say I would much prefer to face the Circassian bullet than endure the provincial theatre' - replied Grushnitsky, quietly delighted by his own understated wit.

Martynov frowned in incomprehension.

'On that, Private Grushnitsky, I think we can agree' - replied Pechorin with a now unforced smile, before nodding in farewell - 'You must forgive me, gentlemen; I have an appointment with an extremely important fellow'.

Pechorin returned to his quarters after a brief and unsatisfactory conversation with the purser. The five silver roubles he had been given as an advance on his stipend cut more deeply than any insult from the likes of de Barante. He sat down on the bunk, took pen, ink, and notepaper from one of the saddle-bags and began to write, perched uncomfortably over the little night-table.

Chère Grandmaman!

Forgive me if I have been the occasion for concern in the absence of letters; I asked that you think of me only when I write for very good reason! The cause of my silence is that I have been posted, at the insistence of both General Grabbe and Ivan Petrovich, to the division of General Velyaminov on the Black Sea coast. So I won't, at least for the foreseeable future, be travelling to Georgia and Daghestan. The post this far south is slow and unreliable, so please address your replies to Pavel Ivanovich in Stavropol; he will make sure they reach me here.

> I expect you are already aware that I delivered the letter to Ivan Petrovich in person, as well as the letter my great-uncle Afanasii sent to General Yermolov. Today I also managed to deliver the letter from Martynov's mother, along with the sum of money. Due, however, to an unfortunate incident on the journey here, I myself am virtually without funds, and would be grateful if you could send me some money. I have almost nothing to live on and will have to make a number of purchases before finally joining my own regiment. Please send it also to Pavel Ivanovich, requesting that he forward a small portion of it to me here, while holding onto the remainder until I am once again in Stavropol.
>
> Rest assured, my dear grandmother, that I am as healthy as I've ever been. I have no idea how long I will remain in this God-forsaken corner of the Empire, although I hope it will be some consolation to you, if not to me, that I remain for the time being out of harm's way. Most important of all, please don't worry about me: God willing, we'll see each other very soon.
>
> Farewell, chère Grandmaman! I kiss your hand and bless you!
> I remain, your devoted grandson,
> Grigorii

When he had finished writing, he folded the letter and slipped it into an envelope, which he returned to the saddle-bag. As he did so, his eye fell upon the little leather-bound notebook Lazarev had given him in Stavropol. The pale yellow pages were blank, but two pieces of stiff card had been pasted into the front and back covers, each of which was covered to the very margins in a miniature, unimaginably precise handwritten script. The inside front was almost entirely covered in verses from the Gospel according to St John, beginning with words that Pechorin recognised from his uneven youthful exposure to the ways of the Church.

> *He was not that light, but was sent to bear witness of that light.* John 1:8

At the back, John gave way to the Epistles of St Paul. Pechorin read now with a sense not of vague recognition, but mild shock.

> *The just shall live by faith.* Romans 1:17

He closed the notebook, cursing Lazarev's living ghost under his breath, lay down and went to sleep.

Pechorin returned to the purser's office the next morning even before he had managed to drink some tea. The wretched fellow at first refused to speak to him, then insisted that he come back the next day. Torn between imposing his will and dispensing with the entire tawdry business, Pechorin was on the point of leaving when, without warning, Velyaminov stepped quietly into the room.

'Lieutenant-General, Sir...' – the purser began.

Velyaminov raised a hand in admonition before the purser could explain his plight and, as Velyaminov had immediately understood, add embarrassment to the insult Pechorin had no doubt already suffered.

'Lieutenant Pechorin will be leaving with a detachment for Gelendzhik this afternoon, Sergeant Kopeikin' - said Velyaminov calmly - 'Please ensure that he has sufficient resources to cover any unforeseen circumstance'.

'Yes, Sir, Lieutenant-General Velyaminov' - replied the purser, standing to attention and saluting.

'Lieutenant Pechorin' - continued Velyaminov, turning to leave - 'Join me in the Staff HQ as soon as Sergeant Kopeikin is finished with you'.

Pechorin remained expressionless as Kopeikin, barely looking up, fumbled in a metal box in the bottom drawer of his desk for a small canvas bag of coins, which he handed over with an unconcealed look of disdain.

Pechorin made his way along the corridor to Staff HQ, where he found Velyaminov alone, but for the pack of Caucasian hounds which had accompanied him at the Mikhailovsky Pass. Pechorin had been mystified as to how Velyaminov had arrived at Tenginsky before mid-morning, but even the rather splendid image of this unruly pack of dogs dragging themselves faithfully along at their master's heels could not entirely dispel the curiosity provoked by Velyaminov's sudden mention of a detachment... and that very afternoon.

'Sit down, Pechorin' - said Velyaminov - 'And listen very carefully'.

Pechorin obeyed immediately.

'You will take five men to the fortress at Gelendzhik and report to Major Lugin' - said Velyaminov.

'Yes, Sir' - Pechorin replied - 'And from there?'

'You will take your orders from Major Lugin'.

'Is that all, Sir?'

Velyaminov shifted uneasily in his chair and fixed Pechorin with a look of great seriousness and even compassion.

'There are two objectives, Pechorin' - he continued - 'The first concerns intelligence we have received that the English are about to launch some kind of provocation. I hope my men have explained to you already that there have been very few raids on any of our positions over the last few weeks, largely, we suspect, because the supply of arms to the Circassian tribes across the Black Sea has been curtailed. Commercial vessels may only dock at Anapa and Redoute-Kale, which the English and their blasted Lord Palmerston affect to think is some terrible affront to free trade. And we have been able, aided no doubt by the season, to suppress the petty smuggling along the coast that was previously the main - the only - supply of arms'.

For the second time since arriving at the Tenginsky Fortress, Pechorin was transported to the bay at Taman, once again observing strange and shadowy figures as they flitted across the dark shore.

'And what are we to expect, Sir?' - asked Pechorin - 'What action are we to take?'

'That's just it, Pechorin' - replied Velyaminov - 'We don't know. You are to report to Major Lugin and respond as and when the situation develops. Just bear in mind that there is no question of an attack; the English can be seeking only to provoke some kind of response, so it is imperative that we don't give them it'.

'Very well, Sir' - said Pechorin quietly, disguising his confusion at this most imprecise of instructions - 'And the second objective?'

Velyaminov lowered his head for a moment, then looked up directly into Pechorin's eyes.

'I'm afraid I can't tell you anything at all about the second objective' - he said firmly - 'We will speak again once this first matter has been dealt with'.

'Very well, Sir' - repeated Pechorin after a slight pause, with a renewed determination to conceal the resentment that now contended with his curiosity - 'Will that be all?'

Pechorin arrived at the fortress at Gelendzhik at dusk, accompanied by Martynov, Grushnitsky, Shapovalov, and two silent Cossacks in the shaggy brown hats known as *papakha*. Each man wore a sabre at his hip and a sidearm, with a rifle strapped across his back. Martynov, in particular, was like a man reborn, puffing out his chest and holding his great dark mane aloft as he rode; Pechorin could not help observe, however, that he had become no kinder to the poor beast beneath him since the parade ground in St Petersburg.

'I thought there was absolutely nothing to do here, Martynov' - said Pechorin with a half-smile as he leapt down from the saddle.

'There wasn't, Pechorin' - Martynov replied, a grudging admiration in his voice - 'You are, it would seem, a veritable magnet for drama of one kind or another'.

'I do my best' - replied Pechorin as he stepped out of the fading light.

Major Lugin was a rather small, stooped man, his doleful expression entirely consistent with the air of defeat that clung to him as persistently as the mists that clung to the hillsides above the fortress. The bare walls of the office in which he sat were as blank as his face, relieved only by a framed reproduction of Tsar Nikolai as a young Cavalier, painted by the same George Dawe who had immortalised Yermolov. Pechorin stepped forward to Major Lugin's desk and saluted.

'Lieutenant Pechorin, Sir, reporting with detachment from Lieutenant-General Velyaminov' - he rapped out, with all the rhythm and solemnity of gunfire.

'At ease, Lieutenant Pechorin' - Lugin replied - 'What are your orders?'

Pechorin paused for a second, suddenly conscious of the faint crease gathering at his brow.

'I'm awaiting your orders, Sir' - he said.

Major Lugin leaned forward in his chair and clasped the fingers of both hands together, before placing them under his chin.

'I'm afraid I have no further orders for you, Lieutenant Pechorin, beyond those given to you by Lieutenant-General Velyaminov' – said Lugin, with a weariness now familiar to Pechorin from his encounters with the middle-ranking officers of the south – 'All I can tell you is that naval reconnaissance has confirmed the presence of an English merchant ship, *The Thistle*, within a league of the coast on two consecutive days. We believe they may be carrying salt, but, if that is the case, there is no explanation as to why they haven't simply put in at Anapa'.

Martynov shifted his weight from one foot to the other and let out a snort of impatience, but Pechorin calmly raised a hand before he could speak.

'Is that all?' – Pechorin asked.

'The navy have been ordered by Lieutenant-General Velyaminov not to engage while *The Thistle* remains at sea' – Lugin explained, before breaking off in silence – 'There is one other thing' – he continued after a short pause – 'We also have reason to believe that the Englishman David Bell is aboard'.

'Aha!' – shouted Martynov, now unable to remain silent – 'Salt, indeed! Since when did salt have barrels and triggers? Guns, mark my words, and ammunition'.

Martynov turned triumphantly to Pechorin and laid a hand amiably on his shoulder.

'You're a magnet, Pechorin!' – he cried, breaking into a broad smile – 'A magnet!'

Pechorin was struck by the force of Martynov's recognition of the Englishman Bell. After all, he thought to himself, it was hardly Martynov's habit to inform himself of the intrigues of his immediate environment. When the detachment had quartered, the Cossacks laid out on bundles of hay smoking their long clay pipes, while Shapovalov boiled water for tea by the dim glow of a candle, Pechorin lit a cigar and turned casually to his erstwhile comrade-at-arms.

'Tell me, Martynov' – he began – 'Who on earth is this Bell?'

'Ah, Pechorin' – Martynov replied, delighted to be the bearer of knowledge at which Pechorin, for once, could not guess or obtain from other sources – 'Bell is a smuggler: in fact, he controls, in one way or another, everything that comes in away from Anapa and Redoute-Kale. That means everything from Turkish rugs and jewelry to salt; but it also means guns for the Circassian tribes'.

Pechorin was once again distracted by recollection of a full moon shining down on angry waves as an imperiled vessel fought its way to the shore.

'He is more than that' – said Grushnitsky suddenly.

'How do you mean?' – asked Martynov, annoyed that he had been usurped in the role of privileged informant.

'What kind of smuggler bothers to pass himself off as a journalist?' – asked Grushnitsky, turning his glance to Pechorin – 'What kind of smuggler sells rifles to the Circassians, who have no other supply of arms than those provided by the English and the Turks, for a price lower than that for which he bought them? What kind of a smuggler is addressed by the grateful natives not with the name with which he was born, but as Daoud Bey?'

Pechorin turned to the Cossacks lying in the hay, one of whom gave a curt nod of confirmation without removing his hands from behind his head.

'Those are excellent questions, my dear Private Grushnitsky' - said Pechorin - 'But I have another: what kind of smuggler sails back and forth along the coast for two days advertising his presence?'

'There's only one kind of smuggler' - said Martynov angrily before Grushnitsky could reply - 'I'll be damned if there aren't guns aboard that vessel! You two can sit up all night trying to convince yourselves otherwise, but I'm going to sleep'.

Martynov wrapped himself in his coat and lay down on one of the low bunks. Pechorin responded to Shapovalov's imploring gaze with a nod and the confused and frightened boy put down his tea and extinguished the candle.

The following morning, Pechorin woke before the sun had climbed over the tree-lined hills above the fortress, gently roused Shapovalov, and hurried out to the stone observation tower which stood at the left-hand corner of the fortress, right on the shoreline. The two ships permanently stationed in the bay to give artillery cover sat becalmed, the light breeze barely disturbing their sails. Pechorin took a telescope from Staff HQ, sent Shapovalov scurrying to the mess to scavenge whatever provisions he could find, and strode off towards the shore. As he approached the observation tower, two sentries who had just relieved the night-watch challenged him.

'Who goes there?' - said a perilously tall Cossack with emaciated features and dark eyes.

'Lieutenant Pechorin, on Lieutenant-General Velyaminov's orders' - Pechorin replied evenly.

Neither of the sentries had ever laid eyes on Pechorin and now looked at one another in confusion. Pechorin stood for a moment or two in silence, looking calmly into the sunken eyes of the Cossack, who seemed to be waiting for some sign that would reveal to him the true meaning of his duty.

'Who is on guard at the top of the tower?' - Pechorin asked at last.

'Ibrashkin' - replied the Cossack.

'Ibrashkin!' - shouted Pechorin to the heavens through cupped hands - 'This is Lieutenant Pechorin. You are relieved'.

A few seconds later, the bewildered Ibrashkin appeared at the bottom of the stairs, searching the faces of his comrades for some explanation.

'That will be all, Ibrashkin' - said Pechorin.

'And what about us, your Honour?' - asked the towering sentry.

'As you were' - replied Pechorin - 'Don't let anyone up unless they're with Private Shapovalov'.

The sentries once again exchanged bemused glances as Pechorin stepped into the tower and began to climb the steeply spiralling staircase.

The view as Pechorin emerged at the top of the tower was breathtaking. The bay of Gelendzhik stretched out before him, the High Cape at the southern end to his left, beyond it the open sea, shimmering white and blue in the morning sun. In 1831, General Berkhman, fulfilling the orders of Velyaminov and the Tsar himself, had wanted to build the fortress right on the High Cape, but had been defeated by the marshy, sulphurous land and the associated lack of fresh water supply. Its eventual location, tucked into the bay itself, had certain strategic advantages in terms of protection from attack from the sea; but it did not command the coastline in the manner desired by Nikolai and had therefore not been furnished with the heavy artillery positions his imagination so fervently craved. The rather sparse artillery emplacements by the shore and the two white-sailed brigs in the bay were a constant reminder of its peculiar limitations. Pechorin raised the telescope to his eye and looked out over the line of the Cape. Nothing. He sat down with his back against the low stone wall, still facing out to sea, and waited for Shapovalov to arrive with something for breakfast.

He was disturbed by the sound of voices at the foot of the tower, followed by quick footsteps on the stairs. Shapovalov emerged, beaming, with a small sack in one hand and a pot of tea in the other. He carefully took two glasses in ornate metal holders from the sack and poured the tea; boiled eggs and black bread soon followed.

'Bravo, Shapovalov' - said Pechorin, his own smile almost as broad as the boy's - 'We'll need something to occupy our time by the looks of it'.

Shapovalov sat down and poured himself some tea, determined to conceal how pleased he was to have been of service. Pechorin gulped down an egg and some bread, lit a cigar for himself and for Shapovalov, and rested his head on the low stone wall behind him.

'Tell me, my boy' - said Pechorin - 'What do you think the day has in store for us?'

'I wouldn't know, your Honour', - replied Shapovalov. - 'But I'd rather be up here with a glass of tea than hauling backwards and forwards like every other day'.

'You may not think the same tomorrow or the day after' - said Pechorin drily, handing Shapovalov the telescope - 'Point that thing out to sea every ten minutes or so, there's a good fellow'.

Pechorin stubbed out his cigar, pulled his cap down over his eyes, and fell silent.

An hour or more passed. Every so often - closer to five minutes than ten - Shapovalov raised the telescope and pointed it out to sea beyond the High Cape. Delighted with the novelty of this most solemn of duties, he surveyed the horizon in a slow sweep from left to right, each time amusing himself by allowing the telescope to come to rest on one of the brigs in the bay. At that short distance, he could see the braid on the tunic of the midshipman, the expressions on the faces of the sullen ratings as they came above and returned below deck, the intricate patterns of the rigging, even the texture of the blackened powder at the rims of the cannon. The brig was like a model ship, authentic in every detail, encased in the glass at the end of his telescope.

'Can you see anything?' - Pechorin asked suddenly.

'No, your Honour' - replied Shapovalov, wheeling quickly away from his model ship.

'Then what is that?' - Pechorin continued.

'What, your Honour?'

Pechorin took the telescope from Shapovalov's shaking hand and directed it just to the right of the High Cape. In the brilliant white strip of the sun as it fell upon the sea, no more than a league from the shore, ran a ship with tall masts at full sail.

'That' - said Pechorin - 'Get back to quarters as quickly as you can, tell Martynov and the others to saddle the horses. Saddle a horse for yourself and one for me and lead it back here. And tell him to inform Major Lugin en route'.

'Inform him of what, Sir?' - asked Shapovalov, his smile now replaced by an expression of near terror.

Pechorin paused for a moment, then fixed Shapovalov with a look of stern reassurance.

'Tell him we have guests' - he said calmly - 'Now go'.

As Shapovalov hurtled down the steps, Pechorin once again turned the telescope out to sea. A merchant ship at full sail was heading directly for the bay, a Union Jack fluttering at its bow. To his right, he could see the two brigs, resting peacefully as if unaware of the imminent intrusion. He followed the intruder as it continued on its course for a few short minutes, until he heard the sound of horses' hooves behind him, followed by Grushnitsky's voice rising up from the base of the tower.

'What is it, Pechorin?' - he cried - 'Can you see their flag?'

'English' - Pechorin shouted below - 'They clearly want our fleet to engage, but I'm damned if I know why'.

One of our brigs was now making its way to the mouth of the bay, where it slowed and turned broadside to the intruder. When the brig had completely come to rest, the English merchant suddenly shifted course, tacking north-east towards the Low Cape on the far side of the bay, then setting course due north parallel to the line of the shore.

'What in the name of God are they up to?' - Pechorin said aloud.

He could just about see through the telescope the point at which, a league to the north, the coast once again receded into the bay at Sudjuk-Kale. He looked down from the tower at the small band of Grushnitsky, Shapovalov, and the two Cossacks, mounted alongside his own riderless horse, Martynov galloping awkwardly to join them from Major Lugin.

'Mount up!' - cried Pechorin, throwing himself into the staircase - 'To Sudzhuk-Kale!'

The band of riders were soon hurtling through the gates of the fortress, Pechorin, Grushnitsky, and the Cossacks to the fore, Martynov and Shapovalov already labouring in the rear. Pechorin lost sight of the English ship for a moment as they made their way around the curve of the bay, its course momentarily obscured by Low Cape, but it hove once again into view as they rose onto the Sudjuk-Kale road. The ship hugged the line of the shore before making its way across the wide mouth of the bay towards the harbour at the Spit of Sudjuk, tucked in beneath the ruins of the old Turkish fortress. As Pechorin and his comrades came down onto the path that ran tight by the shore, they were close enough to see through the telescope figures moving around on the deck and to make out the name of the ship painted in silver letters at its bow. '*The Thistle*', Pechorin said to himself. 'How very quaint'.

'We've twice the distance to travel' - said Grushnitsky breathlessly, drawing alongside - 'We have to go all the way around the bay itself'.

'It's not a race, Grushnitsky' - Pechorin replied, laughing - 'I confess I have no idea what their intentions are, but they would not be heading for the harbour if the avoidance of capture was any part of it'.

By the time the riders had made their way around the bay, *The Thistle* had docked and its crew of diminutive Turks in hooped shirts were rolling great heavy barrels down a wooden gangway onto the shore. Pechorin eased his mount to a walk and raised his hand.

'Go quickly to the garrison and tell the Captain that Lieutenant Pechorin from the Tenginsky Regiment requires a dozen men at the harbour immediately' - he said to one of the Cossacks, who immediately set off at a brisk canter.

'What do you propose to do?' - asked Grushnitsky.

'I propose' - Pechorin replied - 'to seize this ship, search the hold, and impound its cargo. And I propose also to get to the bottom of whatever it is these bold fellows might be up to'.

Pechorin bid his mount walk forward to where the Turkish sailors were straining to turn the barrels upright as they came off the gangway. They looked up as he approached, but once again lowered their heads and continued with their task.

'Stop that' - said Pechorin in a firm, even voice.

The sailors did as he asked and turned towards him, now quite still, some of them shading their eyes with their hands from the low sun.

'Who is your Captain?' - Pechorin continued - 'Summon him'.

Some of the crew looked left and right at one another, their hands still above their brows, amid a hum of Turkic muttering. After a few moments, one of them walked along the gangway and disappeared into the ship through an open hatch.

A minute passed and then another. At last, a thin bearded man in his fifties wearing a naval cap with an anchor above its peak stuck his head through the hatch. He surveyed the scene on shore, the Turkish sailors standing stock still with rocks of salt littered around their feet, three Russian officers and a glowering Cossack looking on, before stepping gingerly out of the hatch onto the gangway.

'Identify yourself' - said Pechorin.

'Captain James Fitzwilliam of the merchant vessel *The Thistle*' - replied the grizzled Englishman.

'What is your purpose at Sudjuk-Kale?'

'We're carrying a cargo of salt' - replied Captain Fitzwilliam in a halting voice - 'but we navigated too far south to dock at Anapa, so were forced to come in at Sudjuk-Kale'.

Pechorin looked to Martynov, then Grushnitsky.

'How many men are aboard, Captain?' - he continued.

'Apart from myself, there's a crew of a dozen Turks and a midshipman and purser from the English merchant navy' - replied Fitzwilliam, who paused for a second then continued - 'And one private citizen, an English journalist'.

Grushnitsky broke out into a broad smile, which he turned in the direction of Martynov.

'I am impounding this vessel in the name of His Imperial Majesty Nikolai the First' - said Pechorin decisively - 'Captain, tell your crew to line up on the far side of the gangway. You, your midshipman, and your purser will place yourselves in the hands of Lieutenant Martynov. Inform the journalist travelling with you that I personally await the pleasure of his company'.

Captain Fitzwilliam cast his eyes over the forlorn sailors standing between the barrels, then above Pechorin's head, where he could see a dozen Cossacks on horseback trotting down towards his vessel. He turned and disappeared into the bowels of his ship.

The Turks were already ranged in two lines of six when Captain Fitzwilliam emerged once again through the hatch, his midshipman and purser at his back. Pechorin gestured to them to move towards Martynov.

'Lieutenant Martynov' - said Pechorin firmly - 'Take these gentlemen to the garrison and make sure they are made comfortable. Shapovalov will accompany you'.

He then turned to one of the Cossacks from the fortress at Gelendzhik, Yeremeyich, and ordered him to take six of the Cossacks from the garrison as an escort for the Turkish crew.

'What will I do with them, your Honour?' - asked Yeremeyich uncertainly.

'Just make sure they're under lock and key' - Pechorin replied - 'And make sure the poor creatures are at least fed and watered'.

'What are you going to do, Pechorin?' - asked Martynov, suddenly resentful that Velyaminov had placed such trust in someone who was, after all, the most recent arrival.

'I'm going to give Mr Bell a welcome befitting an English journalist' - Pechorin replied, oblivious to Martynov's annoyance - 'Then Grushnitsky and his little detachment are going to search the ship'.

The bewildered Englishmen set off in front of Martynov and Shapovalov on horseback, the band of Turks and their Cossack guard following in the rear. There was still no sign of the reluctant Bell. Pechorin was about to send two of the Cossacks aboard to hasten the mysterious passenger's disembarkation, when suddenly from the hatch in the side of the ship appeared a most elegant gentleman in a fine blue velvet coat, his blond hair combed back so meticulously he might have been wearing a wig from the century past. His fine woollen breeches to the knee ran down to exquisite silken hose and a pair of polished black leather shoes with a silver buckle at each instep. The effect was completed by the leather briefcase held under his arm and a cane of black ash with an ornate silver thistle at its top. He was of medium height, with a slim but supple frame, a slight bow in his legs as he walked languorously down the gangway.

'Mr Bell, I presume' – said Pechorin in a clear, almost theatrical English, before turning to Grushnitsky – 'Search the ship'.

Pechorin and Bell stood alone among the barrels and the rocks of salt littering the dock. Bell quietly surveyed Pechorin's uniform for a moment, his head slightly tilted to one side, before opening his mouth to speak.

'And who might you be?' – he asked, his engaging tone belying the impertinence of the question.

Pechorin returned Bell's amiable gaze, consciously mimicking the tilt of his head.

'I am Lieutenant Grigorii Pechorin' – he replied – 'Currently of the Tenginsky Infantry, more properly speaking of the Nizhegorodsky Dragoons. I have been ordered by Lieutenant-General Velyaminov, on behalf of His Imperial Majesty the Tsar, to impound and search this vessel, which, as you may know, merely by virtue of being docked at this harbour, is in breach of customs regulations'.

'That is no concern of mine, Lieutenant... Pechorin?' – replied Bell – 'I am a journalist with *The Times* of London, seeking to report on the lives and customs of the Circassian tribes. I bargained with Fitzwilliam to transport me from Constantinople. He assured me my destination would be the port of Anapa, from where I hoped to engage the services of amenable locals to travel into the interior'.

'Is there much call for tales of Circassia in the drawing rooms of England?' – asked Pechorin with the same amiable smile.

'It is all the rage, Lieutenant' – Bell replied without the slightest pause – 'Tales of the mountains and unfamiliar customs are universally popular'.

'Indeed' – said Pechorin with a wry smile – 'Nothing is more apt to excite the mind of the ladies of St Petersburg than travelogue. But don't you have mountains of your own?'

'Ah, my dear Lieutenant Pechorin, we do... but they are not nearly so interesting to our readers as your Caucasus, particularly since the fate of the Circassians passed from the hands of the Turks to the Russian Empire'.

Pechorin was about to reply when Grushnitsky stuck his head out of the hatch.

'Nothing but salt, Lieutenant'.

Bell stood almost majestically, one hand resting on his cane, and turned to look out across the shimmering waters of the Black Sea.

Pechorin ordered Grushnitsky to repeat the search before turning to the apparently unperturbed Bell.

'May I see your papers, Mr Bell?' – he asked in a relaxed, almost cheerful tone.

Bell drew his gaze from the open sea and calmly opened his briefcase, from which he produced a passport and an unsealed letter.

'You'll see that everything is in order, Lieutenant Pechorin' – he replied – 'There's also a letter from my editor in London, verifying the purpose of my visit'.

Pechorin took the letter, read it quickly, and handed it back to Bell, whose air of distraction now gave way to something approaching impatience.

'I wonder, Lieutenant Pechorin' – he continued – 'if you might arrange for me to be transported to Anapa, where I will be able to resume my journey?'

Pechorin hesitated for a moment, partly in order to suppress a now slightly less than amiable smile.

'I'm afraid that won't be possible, Mr Bell' – he said as gravely as he could manage – 'You see, I have no authority in this matter beyond the fulfillment of my orders. I am, if you will, merely the messenger'.

'And who does have authority?' – asked Bell, his studied calm beginning to desert him.

'Lieutenant-General Velyaminov, Commander-in-Chief of the Black Sea divisions' – Pechorin replied.

'May I request, then, that you ask Lieutenant-General Velyaminov to arrange for my conveyance to Anapa?' – continued Bell, now quite insistent.

'You can ask him yourself' – Pechorin replied – 'Come: the fortress at Gelendzhik will no doubt be of great interest to your readers'.

CHAPTER FIFTEEN

HIS IMPERIAL MAJESTY

THREATENING DARK CLOUDS had gathered above the bay of Gelendzhik and a ferocious wind blew from the north-east as morning broke. Pechorin woke to find Martynov, Grushnitsky, and his two Cossacks still fast asleep, but there was no sign of Shapovalov. An intuition told him to throw on his overcoat and battle through the howling wind and freezing rain to the mess, where he found Shapovalov cajoling the filthy cook into adding eggs and porridge to the tea and black bread he had already secured. Pechorin approached, placed a ten-kopeck coin in the soiled and greasy hand of the cook, and sat down at one of the wooden tables.

'We'll have it here' - he said to Shapovalov with a smile.

When they had finished eating, Major Lugin's adjutant came running into the mess, damp and windblown from the gathering storm outside.

'Lieutenant Pechorin, Sir' - he said breathlessly, almost forgetting to salute - 'You are to report to Lieutenant-General Velyaminov at Staff HQ'.

Pechorin took a sip of tea and pondered once again Velyaminov's apparent talent for overcoming the limitations of space and time.

'And in this weather...' - he said abstractedly to a confused Shapovalov - 'Still, let's see what else the esteemed General Velyaminov has in store for us, eh my boy?'

Sitting calmly behind a desk in the warm Staff HQ, Velyaminov appeared untouched by wind or by rain. There was no sign, however, of his dogs. What stamp of a man could turn artillery fire on a heaving mass of defenceless Turks as if he were lighting a candle, but would not expose his beloved dogs to a spot of bad weather? Pechorin looked for some sign in Velyaminov's eyes, before inwardly acknowledging his folly: he already understood that it made more sense to seek answers from the mountains above Gelendzhik than to hope to identify the subtle modulations in that gravest of expressions.

'I've spoken to Bell' - said Velyaminov suddenly - 'He affects to know nothing of the movements of *The Thistle*, insisting only that he was a passenger on its voyage from Constantinople and that he is...'.

'... a journalist for *The Times* of London' - Pechorin interrupted - 'And do you believe him, Sir?'

Velyaminov shifted uneasily in his chair, not, as it would turn out, due to annoyance at Pechorin's interruption.

'I believe' - he began - 'that *The Thistle* had two objectives: either to provoke our fleet into a response at sea, thus sparking a controversy that might strengthen the hands of the Russophobes in the English government; or, if that failed, to demonstrate to the world that the Turks have no interest in preventing English vessels from coming through the Dardanelles and, worse, that Russia's vaunted fortifications on the Black Sea are incapable of preventing even a merchant ship from going where it pleases'.

'And do you believe, Sir' - Pechorin continued - 'that the good Captain Fitzwilliam might alone be entrusted with command of such a mission?'

Velyaminov gave a snort and, to Pechorin's surprise, a half-smile spread across his lips.

'I would not have believed that even without the events of last night' - he replied bitterly

'Events, Sir?' - said Pechorin.

Velyaminov's saturnine features took on a solemn weariness that Pechorin would not have thought possible in a living being.

'We believe also' - he began - 'that a small vessel put ashore to the north of Sudjuk-Kale last night, just before the storm got up'.

'May I enquire as to the nature of its cargo, Sir?' - Pechorin asked.

'Let's just say it wasn't salt' - replied Velyaminov, his voice mimicking the weariness of his features.

Pechorin made his way between the workshops, stores, and dwelling houses that clustered within the walls of the fortress, the wind and rain assaulting him as he turned each corner. His curiosity about the Englishman Bell struggled for attention with a mute and unnameable intuition of a different kind: Velyaminov, for all he had been willing to share detail of *The Thistle* and its mission, had said nothing about the other reason Pechorin had been despatched to Gelendzhik. Might they be connected in some way? And why in God's name had Velyaminov been so insistent on his involvement? Pechorin could find no answer to these questions and abandoned the search entirely as streamlets of icy rain began to course down his back.

Bell was incarcerated in what Grushnitsky insisted on calling the *Lazaretto*... 'Why not just call the damn thing an infirmary and be done?' Pechorin thought to himself as he pushed through the driving rain. The wind tussled with the trees just as the cold water that had found its way under Pechorin's tunic battled with the misty veils of Velyaminov's dark expression. Suddenly, as if himself impelled by the wind and the rain, Pechorin turned away from the quarters where Martynov and the others were no doubt still sheltering from the elements and headed towards the infirmary. Perhaps it was, as Kuragin had once remarked to him - and particularly in weather such as this! - always nice to have a conversation with a clever man.

The two sentries at the entrance to the infirmary nodded as Pechorin swept past, relieved at last to be out of the wind and rain. Inside, the single sentry who stood at the door of the locked room in which Bell was detained did not replicate the *sang-froid* of his comrades. Eventually, however, under the matter-of-fact, unrelenting glare of Pechorin's gaze, he swallowed the objections of dutiful pedantry and slipped a key from a large, jangling bundle into the door.

'Lieutenant Pechorin, we meet again!' - said Bell, uncommonly cheerful for a man in his predicament.

Pechorin observed the still impeccable velvet coat and hose, the glossy hair pulled neatly back from the face, the air of a man who believes the world can do him no harm.

'Is there something I can do for you?' - Bell continued.

'Oh, I'm just sheltering from the rain, Mr Bell; it is quite foul outside' - replied Pechorin - 'And besides, I'm curious'.

'Curious about what?'

Pechorin paused.

'Curious about the circumstances that bring a man of your obvious sophistication and education to the damp shores of the Black Sea in the dead of winter'.

'My profession, Lieutenant Pechorin' - Bell replied, still smiling.

'Ah, but of course. You are an esteemed member of the Fourth Estate. But what is it that's so compelling about our Caucasus that you would drag yourself halfway across the earth simply to describe it?'

Bell gave Pechorin a look intended to convey disbelief more than surprise or disappointment.

'Lieutenant Pechorin' - he began, with the air of a schoolmaster who feels he should not have to explain - 'the notes of travellers are as much in vogue in London as they are, by your own testimony only yesterday, in St Petersburg. People wish to experience things they will themselves never see. I merely fulfill a demand'.

'You are quite right' - replied Pechorin, brightening - 'The Russian public cannot get enough of tales of derring-do in the mountains and misty valleys of the mind. Their taste for such exotic landscapes was prepared, in fact, by your own Walter Scott; are the English public no longer satisfied with what the bard has provided for them?'

'Ah' - Bell replied, warming to the theme - 'Scott painted on the canvas of the imaginary past; my own canvas is the all too real present. Your Russian public may not be quite so enamoured with tales of war on the frontiers of Empire, whereas the English public - not to mention our esteemed politicians - are only too keen to read of the realities of Russian misfortune.'

'I see' - Pechorin replied, now with genuine enthusiasm - 'You are a propagandist, Mr Bell'.

Whether because the conversation never came close to touching the real purpose of his voyage or because he was perversely flattered by Pechorin's attention, Bell displayed no sign of resentment at this presumption, which may have seemed to another man the very opposite of flattering. He surveyed Pechorin now with a cool gaze, while Pechorin disguised his inner determination to get to the bottom of the riddle of Daoud Bey with the same amiable smile.

'There is one thing you might do for me, Lieutenant Pechorin' - Bell continued - 'You wouldn't happen to have a cigar, would you?'

'My pleasure' – Pechorin replied, taking his cigar-case from his tunic pocket and noting with satisfaction how dry were its contents.

He offered Bell a cigar, then leaned forward slightly to light it. Bell took a long draw before blowing out a series of perfectly formed smoke rings. Pechorin lit a cigar for himself.

'Tell me, however' – he continued – 'What is it about the Caucasus? I'm sure your readers would be as beguiled by tales of China or India, where I'm sure no respectable Englishman need travel like a stowaway on a merchant vessel'.

'I am not an Englishman, Lieutenant Pechorin' – said Bell quietly – 'I was born in Cromarty in the Highlands of Scotland. The western Caucasus, if I am honest, remind me of my childhood'.

Pechorin was suddenly and immediately defenceless before great waves of romanticised memories of his own childhood, steeped in tales of Thomas the Rhymer and the Faerie Queen and the imagined landscapes of the Ballads so lovingly collected by Scott. He could find no place in that environment for the refined, almost synthetic figure who stood before him. He felt a sudden urge to ask Bell why it was so important that the Circassian Highlanders remain free of Russian rule, while he did not question why the Highlands of his youth were a part of the British Empire. Perhaps – perhaps! – Byron was right about the English understanding of the relationship between virtue and hypocrisy...

The rain had eased by the time Pechorin emerged and continued on his way back to his quarters, but the wind blew as if it might never cease until all traces of Russian presence had been blown into the sea. Pechorin thought involuntarily of artillery emplacements sinking under the waves, their gunners along with them, horses and cattle oblivious to the same fate, while only the detritus of life floated to the surface.

When he at last got out of the accursed wind, he found Martynov still in that state of gloom which had descended when no guns and ammunition had been found aboard *The Thistle*. His mood was matched only by Grushnitsky's cheerfulness. Shapovalov and the Cossacks were silent.

'There's a steamship just beyond the mouth of the bay, Pechorin' – said Grushnitsky, as if he were confirming that the weather was, indeed, inclement.

'Really?' – Pechorin replied – 'I can't say I've noticed, what with this incessant wind and rain. Are we to receive yet more guests?'

'I dare say' – replied Grushnitsky.

'Any idea who?' – asked Pechorin, keen not to display too much interest.

'None at all' – said Grushnitsky – 'They're flying no flag and I imagine there's no possibility of landing until the storm has passed'.

'Shall we investigate, my dear Grushnitsky?' – asked Pechorin, chiming with Grushnitsky's demeanour – 'Even it means going back out into that wind?'

'I dare say' - replied Grushnitsky.

'Are you coming, Martynov?' - said Pechorin.

Martynov only grumbled in response, but raised his great bulk from his bunk, threw on his overcoat and cap, and bundled through the door out once again into the merciless elements.

Little clumps of soldiers had gathered on the ramparts of the fortress on the shore side, clinging onto their caps in the wind, entranced by the unlikely vessel rolling uncomfortably on the waves at the mouth of the bay. Most, although they spent their days and nights by the shore of the Black Sea, had never laid eyes on a steamship. The great funnel, positioned to the rear of the main mast and flanked on each side by the arch of a wheelhouse, seemed to them almost demonic, pumping out plumes of thick black smoke, which streamed horizontally in the wind. As they looked on, the vessel began to turn its bow slowly towards the mouth of the bay and plough steadily towards land. Once in the bay itself, it tacked to the starboard side and sailed directly towards the spectators on the ramparts, whose numbers increased by the minute. The two brigs stationed in the bay remained at anchor, their sails lowered to protect them from the wind. Pechorin was gripped by the same curiosity as the men around him, which battled with a sense of unease to which he could not put a name. He watched as the steamship came as close to the shore as it dared. Suddenly, it raised a yellow flag with the symbol of the eagle and a great 'hurrah' rang out from the crowd, the force of which was lost on the wind.

'His Imperial Majesty' - said Pechorin in a whisper, unheard even by himself.

Martynov put a hand on his shoulder, but said nothing.

A band of Cossacks appeared at the shore, wrapped up in great sheepskins, but without their *papakhi*, which had been abandoned in deference to the elements. The Cossacks wrestled with two long wooden boats. To the amazement of the throng now gathered on the ramparts, they intended to row out to *The Northern Star* and bring the Royal party ashore. Eight men set off unsteadily in each boat. They rowed furiously, aided by the north-east wind at their rear, but obstructed by the furious waves, which from time to time crashed against the pushing prow of the boats, lifting them up to forty-five degrees or more, before leaving them to lash down once again onto the flat water behind.

'They'll be drowned!' - cried Martynov - 'And even if they make it to the ship, how on earth will they make it back to the shore into that wind?'

'The wind will be against them, it's true' - said Grushnitsky - 'but those damn waves will be behind. If they make it out, they'll surely make it back'.

The first of the boats had now made it almost to *The Northern Star*, which provided some small shelter from the wind as it approached. The Cossacks pulled their vessel alongside as the second boat followed into the pool of relative calm. Once the boats had been secured, a series of figures began, one by one, to descend a metal ladder down the side of the ship, at the foot of which they were helped into the boat by the Cossacks. When the first boat had received three passengers, it moved along the side of the ship to allow the other to take its place at the foot of the ladder. When a further four figures were securely in the second boat, they pulled around and began to make for the shore, their passengers sheltering between the two lines of oarsmen down each side.

'Enjoy the entertainment, gentlemen' – Pechorin said suddenly – 'I must get out of these wet clothes'.

Warm and renewed in a clean shirt, breeches, and tunic, wrapped in his overcoat with the collar turned up and a cap pulled down tight almost over his eyes, Pechorin made his way quickly to the Staff HQ. Velyaminov greeted him with a look of compassion, the meaning of which Pechorin could still not guess. Major Lugin looked on with the air of a man in shock, astonished by the Royal party's insistence not only that they should land in these conditions, but that the Tsar would proceed with an inspection of the troops on the parade ground adjacent to the fortress on the High Cape side.

'His Imperial Majesty has made it very clear how much he wishes to thank the men in person for their efforts' – said Velyaminov calmly – 'If he is not concerned by a little wind, why should we be? Assemble the troops Major Lugin'.

Lugin gave a petrified salute and hurried out towards the parade ground, barking orders as he went. Velyaminov turned to Pechorin with the same look of unfathomable compassion.

'His Imperial Majesty intended to make a tour of the forces of the south and the Black Sea fortifications last autumn' – he said in a matter-of-fact tone – 'He was prevailed upon, however, to delay on the basis that he might find matters more to his satisfaction if we had a few more months to progress with the work, even if it meant coming in winter'.

He paused for a moment, now seeking compassion in return from Pechorin.

'Look where that has got us' – Velyaminov said quietly.

'I expect, Sir' – Pechorin began – 'that it might have been reasonable to assume, once winter was upon us, that the tour would have been further postponed to spring or even summer of this year?'

Velyaminov gave Pechorin a look of resigned assent.

'The funny thing is, Pechorin' – said Velyaminov, brightening a little – 'that although I was only officially informed of His Majesty's arrival yesterday evening – for reasons of security, you understand? – I had in fact known, more or less, for a number of days'.

He looked up once again, this time inquisitive, even challenging, keen to gauge Pechorin's response.

'And how did you come into possession of that information, Sir, if I may ask?' – said Pechorin in an even tone.

'I was informed by none other than General Yermolov, Pechorin, in the letter you so kindly delivered' – said Velyaminov – 'Alexei Petrovich assured me that, notwithstanding the unorthodoxy of the communication, I should be in no doubt as to its veracity'.

He broke off for a second before continuing.

'He did not, of course, reveal the identity of his source, but insisted only upon the impeccable nature of the gentleman's credentials'.

Velyaminov paused once again.

'The thing is, Pechorin, Alexei Petrovich also for some reason led me to believe that you yourself are extremely well acquainted with his source... perhaps more than that'.

Pechorin maintained a studied calm, determined, as if by reflex, to disguise his inner response to the unfolding drama.

'I can assure you, Sir, I have no knowledge of General Yermolov's intentions or imputations' – he replied coolly – 'Although I am grateful to you for your confidence in my discretion'.

Pechorin once again emerged into the teeth of the wind, beneath a dark and tumultuous sky, his face a study in fierce concentration.

By the time he reached the parade ground, the infantry divisions were already lined up in formation, their backs to the bay, the vicious wind cutting into their faces. Grushnitsky and Shapovalov stood in the first row, Grushnitsky, Pechorin understood, more than willing to face the elements for the chance, however small, of a word from His Imperial Majesty; poor Shapovalov had simply fallen in line. In front of them at the edge of the parade ground was a marquee of rough canvas, in which the High Command would gather before and after inspections. The Royal party had been escorted here for shelter and Pechorin now watched as Velyaminov and Lugin rushed towards the great tent and disappeared inside. The single division of Cavalry Guards stationed at Gelendzhik trotted into position to the left of the infantry, as close to the wall of the fortress as they could without falling back into the moat, seeking whatever protection could be found for their frightened mounts. To the right, four divisions of Cossacks had formed in lines as orderly as the elements would allow, bundled up in sheepskins held in place by cross-belts of ammunition, their *papakhi* pulled down over their eyes. Pechorin took his place in the rank of officers that had now formed in front of Grushnitsky and Shapovalov, which partially shielded the lower ranks behind. Martynov stood to his left, his chest pushed out into the unrelenting wind. The lower ranks were still in their overcoats, but the officers, on Velyaminov's orders, had removed them to reveal the tunics below, the braid on their chests and cuffs glinting weakly in the failing light.

The storm continued to rage and had become so wild that the precise formations of both officers and recruits swayed back and forth under the force of its sudden, furious gusts. All the elements seemed to have armed themselves against the massed ranks, assembled on the shore of a foreign sea, about to burst over them and swallow up each mortal soul. It took three or four men to hold the banners in place; if the wind could not take our soldiers, it would surely take our flags.

Velyaminov emerged from the marquee at the far end of the parade ground, at his elbow Tsar Nikolai, behind them his eldest son and heir, the Tsarevich Alexander. They were followed by Prince Orlov, who had negotiated the peace of Adrianople with the Turks and was now Commander-in-Chief of the entire Black Sea fleet, Admiral Menshikov, and His Imperial Majesty's young aide-de-camp, Nikolai Adlerberg. Major Lugin, a picture of bedraggled obsequiousness, brought up the rear. Pechorin could barely bring himself to believe that the morale of the troops was of sufficient importance to anyone in this august company to justify the exposure of both Tsar and heir to the risk of drowning or pneumonia, but the words of General Grabbe once again resonated in his mind: perhaps nothing really was more important to His Imperial Majesty than the misplaced fear that the Turks might once again rise on the south-west frontier of the Empire.

The Royal party was greeted by a renewed burst of heavy rain. Major Lugin and young Adlerberg had emerged from the marquee carrying umbrellas, but quickly abandoned them to the merciless wind. His Imperial Majesty, led by Velyaminov, ploughed steadily through the driving rain towards the infantry. Pechorin stood to attention alongside Martynov, third from the left in the front rank, icy rain once again running down his back and seeping into every garment. His Imperial Majesty approached the line, then paused for a moment to shake hands with Martynov without saying a word. Pechorin understood in an instant the not so mysterious forces that had brought him to this place at this moment. The tireless network of the Stolypins, his grandmother at its private heart, his great-uncle Afanasii its public plenipotentiary, had once again stretched out its fibres in an attempt to protect him, activating The Grand-Duke Mikhail, Yermolov, Velyaminov, and every acquaintance and contact in the spaces between in order to place him in the path of a perhaps merciful Tsar. He now understood why Velyaminov had entrusted him with the arrest of *The Thistle*, which had become an occasion for conspicuous service to the Crown, without, of course, the inconvenience of any conspicuous danger. His Imperial Majesty stepped in front of him, rain coursing down his face and soaking into his beard and moustaches. Pechorin saw only the image of his grandmother.

'Lieutenant Pechorin' – said the Tsar with a somewhat rigid smile, lifting his head in acknowledgement of the rain – 'I did not expect to make your acquaintance in quite these circumstances. Lieutenant-General Velyaminov has apprised me of your endeavours in thwarting an agent of the English. I commend you'.

'Thank you, Your Imperial Majesty' – Pechorin replied – 'I am honoured to serve'.

'It's a pity, however, that the arms still made it through' – the Tsar continued.

'Indeed, Your Majesty' - Pechorin replied - 'We had no intelligence in that regard'.

'Very well, Lieutenant Pechorin. You will have many more opportunities to serve, you can be assured'.

Pechorin barely heard these last words. His Imperial Majesty saw that this confounded nuisance was no longer even looking at him, but had turned his gaze to the left towards the fortress.

'I trust that is not a disappointment to you, Lieutenant Pechorin' - continued Nikolai, faintly annoyed that even here, on a rain-soaked parade ground in the distant south of the Empire, he could not command the attention of recalcitrant youth.

'It's not that, Your Imperial Majesty' - Pechorin replied, gesturing with his head towards the fortress.

His Imperial Majesty turned slowly in the direction Pechorin had indicated. Flames blazed above the fortress. Velyaminov ran towards the fire, shouting orders all around. Not knowing what else to do, The Tsar and his bewildered party followed.

The flames and smoke carried over the artillery emplacements by the shoreline, which were filled with powder and live rounds. As His Imperial Majesty made his way through the flames, surrounded by loyal subjects running in panic, now oblivious to his presence, he saw soldiers pick up live rounds with extraordinary calm and stuff them into their overcoats. The provision store was ablaze, as were the barns containing hay for the animals; the air was filled with the pungent aroma of burning tobacco.

Pechorin, like Velyaminov, had understood immediately that the fortress was under attack; fire could not have broken out accidentally beneath these saturated heavens. He shouted to Martynov and Grushnitsky to head to the main gates, then, the smell of tobacco once more overwhelming his senses, ran with Shapovalov to the infirmary. The sentries at the entrance were nowhere to be seen. Inside, the sentry who had stood at the door to Bell's room lay dead on the floor, his throat cut. The door lay open and the room was empty.

By the time Pechorin reached the main gates, Grushnitsky had mustered a party of Cossacks and was adamant they should give chase. On the slopes above the fortress, stretching out towards the tree line, a band of Circassians, their emancipated Daoud Bey among them, rode steadily towards the forest. Pechorin knew that once the Englishman and his native confederates reached the cover of the forest, they would be entirely out of reach.

'What are we waiting for?' - cried Grushnitsky - 'They're getting away!'

'Do as you wish, Grushnitsky' - Pechorin said calmly - 'We'd be more use helping quench the last of the flames'.

Grushnitsky looked to Martynov, who was struggling with the knowledge that Pechorin was surely right.

'Forward!' - Grushnitsky cried to the band of Cossacks, raising his sword and spurring his mount into motion.

Only three or four of the Cossacks obeyed his command, the remainder fixing their troubled gaze on Pechorin.

Just at the moment, the crack of a rifle was heard, coming from the direction of the fleeing Circassians. Pechorin and Grushnitsky leapt for cover behind the pillared ramparts as the remainder of the Cossacks pulled their panicked horses back into the fortress. In the now empty space between the gates, alone in the mud and trampled hay, lay the body of Private Shapovalov, his chest almost entirely obscured by an enormous bullet wound. Pechorin felt the damp of his saturated clothing seep into his flesh, his nose and eyes burning from the acrid smoke of the fire. Before him still was the face of the Tsar, pale from the cold and wet from the rain, vying for attention with the devastated features of his grandmother, each of them looking down with calm regret at the figure of the slain Shapovalov. As the earth began to slide and consciousness leave him, he imagined he could see the ghostly features of Lazarev, running towards him through the flames and smoke.

Pechorin spent the next week in the infirmary at Gelendzhik without recovering consciousness. He was oblivious to the fever that gripped him and to the fears of those around him, not least Velyaminov, that he might never recover. It was another two weeks before Velyaminov could be persuaded that Pechorin was fit enough to be transported to Stavropol and even then agreed only on the understanding that he would remain there in the infirmary for a further two or three weeks in the care of Dr Werner. When he arrived in Stavropol, however, as weak as a child, Pechorin found not only that Dr Werner had been discharged from military service, but also that no one could explain to him the circumstances of his departure.

On the rare occasions when he saw General Petrov, Pechorin's curiosity was disarmed by the realization that Petrov had not only silently taken responsibility for the futility of Gelendzhik, but was too embarrassed even to acknowledge that he - and General Grabbe - had allowed themselves to be influenced by those voices who had thought it possible that Pechorin might be pardoned. Pechorin, whether out of respect or due simply to the delicate state of his health, made no reference to this unspoken failure. As soon as he had regained sufficient strength, he was rewarded for his delicacy with authorization to recuperate, without limit of time, at the spa town of Pyatigorsk.

CHAPTER SIXTEEN

PYATIGORSK

PECHORIN ARRIVED IN Pyatigorsk and rented quarters on the edge of town, at the very highest point, in the foothills of Mount Mashuk; during storms the clouds would come down right to the roof of the building. When he opened the window at five the next morning, the smell of flowers and plants growing in the modest front garden filled the room. The branches of flowering cherry trees looked in through the windows and the wind sometimes showered the desk with their little white flowers. The view on three sides was wonderful. To the west, the five peaks of Mount Beshtu shone blue like 'the last cloud of the scattered storm'; to the north, Mashuk rose up like a jagged Persian sabre, blotting out the entire horizon. The view to the east is more cheerful: directly below lay the mottled buildings of the bright new little town, full of the sounds of the healing springs and the chatter of many languages; and beyond it, like an enormous amphitheatre, bluer and darker mountains, at the edge of which, on the horizon, stretches out a silvery chain of snow-covered peaks, beginning with Mount Kazbek and ending with the twin peaks of Mount Elbrus. How pleasant to live in a land such as this! A certain joyful feeling coursed through Pechorin's veins. The air was pure and fresh, like a child's kiss. The sun bright and the sky blue – what more could a man want? There was no place here for passions, desires, or regrets.

It was, however, time to get moving. Pechorin was going to the Yelizavetinsky spring, where, I'm told, the spa society gathers every morning. As he was walking down into the town along the main boulevard, he encountered a few doleful groups of people heading in the other direction. Most of them were families of steppe landowners, which could be seen from the worn, old-fashioned coats of the men and from the elegant clothing of the wives and daughters. They were obviously familiar with all of the younger generation gathered at the spa, because they looked at Pechorin with gentle curiosity; the Petersburg cut of his overcoat fooled them at first, but, when they recognised the military epaulettes, they turned away with indignation.

The wives of the local dignitaries, the ladies of the waters, so to speak, were more favourably inclined; they carried with them *lorgnettes* and were less bothered by a military uniform. They had become accustomed in the Caucasus to the possibility that a passionate heart might lie beneath a row of buttons, that an educated mind might lurk beneath a white officer's cap. They were very sweet, these ladies, almost to a fault. Every year, their admirers would be exchanged for new ones, and perhaps this was the secret of their unstinting amiability. As Pechorin began to climb the narrow path to the Yelizavetinsky spring, he caught up with a crowd of men, military and civilian, who, as he would later discover, composed a very particular class among those awaiting the movement of the waters. They drink, but not the water; they do very little walking and are only half-heartedly interested in women; and they gamble and complain that they are bored. They are dandies, who strike serious poses as they lower their ornamented glass into the spring. The civil servants among them wear pale-blue ties, while the military men let their ruffs stick out from their collars. They profess a deep contempt for provincial households and sigh longingly for the aristocratic drawing rooms of the capital, to which they are not admitted.

And, at last, the spring itself... In the square, alongside the well, a little house with a red roof has been built over the baths and beyond it a terrace, where people walk when it is raining. A few wounded officers, pale and sad, were sitting on a bench, their crutches propped alongside them. Some of the ladies, with brisk little steps, were walking back and forward across the square, waiting for the waters to flow. Among them were two or three pretty faces. Above, in the vine-lined terraces covering the slopes of Mount Mashuk, the bright hats of those ladies who preferred to be together alone could occasionally be glimpsed. Alongside the ladies' hats, Pechorin could always see a military cap or some ugly round hat. At the top of the steep climb, where a pavilion called The Aeolian Harp had been built, those who liked to look at the views could be seen pointing their telescopes at Elbrus; among them were two governors with their pupils, who had come to be treated for scrofula.

Pechorin stopped, out of breath, at the foot of the mountain, leaned against a little house, and began to look at the surroundings, when suddenly he heard a familiar voice behind him.

'Pechorin! Have you been here long?'

He turned round to see Grushnitsky. They embraced. Pechorin had not seen Grushnitsky since the attack on the Tenginsky Fortress. He had later taken a bullet in the leg and had come to the waters just a week before. Grushnitsky had been serving for less than a year, but wore, in a very particular manner of showing off, the greatcoat of an enlisted man. He had been awarded the George Cross and had not outgrown the habit of throwing back his head when he spoke and constantly twirling his moustache with his left hand. His right rested on his crutch.

Grushnitsky spoke quickly and pretentiously, one of those people who was always ready with an elegant phrase for any of life's eventualities, who with great self-importance drape themselves in the most unusual feelings, exalted passions and exceptional sufferings, but who have no sense whatsoever of beauty. Provoking a reaction is their greatest pleasure. Romantic provincial girls love them to distraction. By the time they are old they have either become peaceful landowners or drunks – and sometimes both. They are often possessed of many fine qualities, but there is not a hint of poetry in their souls. Grushnitsky's passion was to declaim: as soon as the conversation moved beyond the circle of everyday ideas, he would bombard you with words. Pechorin could never bear to argue with him: he didn't respond to objections, didn't listen at all. As soon as you stopped speaking, he would embark on a long tirade, which appeared to have some link to what you had said, but was in fact merely an occasion for his own speech.

He was, however, fairly sharp. His epigrams were often amusing, but were never to the point or malign. He could never silence someone with a single word, because he knew nothing of people and their weaknesses, having spent his whole life occupied only with himself. His ambition was to become the hero of a novel. He would try so often to convince others that he was a creature not of this world, destined for some mysterious suffering, that he almost believed it himself. This is why he so proudly wore his Private's greatcoat. Pechorin understood all of this, for which Grushnitsky disliked him, although on the surface their relations were most friendly. Grushnitsky also had a reputation for outstanding bravery, but Pechorin had of course seen him in action: he would wave his sword, shout, and throw himself forward... not a very Russian kind of bravery...

The dislike was mutual; Pechorin had often thought that they would one day meet on a narrow path... and that one of them would come off worse.

Grushnitsky's arrival in the Caucasus was also a consequence of his Romantic fanaticism. I am convinced that, on the eve of departing his native village, he had told some pretty neighbour, with a solemn expression, that he was not simply enlisting... that it was death he sought, because – and here he would no doubt cover his eyes with one hand – 'No... you don't need to know! Your pure soul will tremble! And for what... what am I to you? Do you understand?'... and so on. He had told me himself that the reason he enlisted in the Kaluzhsky Infantry Regiment would remain a secret between himself and the heavens. In those moments when he took off his tragic mantle, however, Grushnitsky could be quite pleasant. Pechorin was curious to see him in the company of women: there, he was sure, Grushnitsky would really make the effort...

The two men greeted one another as if they were old friends. Pechorin began to ask about life at the spring and about certain notable people.

'We live a fairly prosaic life' – said Grushnitsky with a sigh – 'Those who drink the waters in the morning are dull, like all sick people; those who drink wine in the evening are unbearable, like all healthy people. There is female company, although it doesn't provide much in the way of solace: they play whist, dress badly, and speak appalling French. The only exception this year is Princess Ligovskaya, who is here from Moscow with her daughter, but I don't know them personally: my soldier's greatcoat is like the mark of an outcast. I find the sympathy it provokes difficult to accept, like charity'.

Just at that moment, two ladies walked past towards the well, one of them elderly, the other young with a good figure. Pechorin couldn't see their faces under their hats, but they were dressed according to the strict rules of the finest taste; nothing superfluous. The younger woman wore a pearl-grey high-necked dress, with a light silk scarf tied around her soft neck. Her dark tan boots fitted round her slender ankles so perfectly that even those uninitiated in the secrets of beauty would have gasped, and from astonishment. Her light, genteel step had a certain girlish quality, which almost eluded definition, but which was immediately obvious to the observer. As she passed, there was a hint of that indescribable fragrance that sometimes wafts from the letter of an intimate friend.

'Princess Ligovskaya and her daughter, Princess Mary' - said Grushnitsky - 'She named her in the English style. They've only been here for three days'.

'And you already know her first name?' - asked Pechorin.

'Yes, I just happened to hear it' - Grushnitsky replied, blushing - 'I must say I have no desire to make their acquaintance. The aloof nobility look at us soldiers as if we were savages. What is it to them if there is a mind under this numbered cap or a heart beneath this greatcoat?'

'Your poor overcoat!' - Pechorin said with a smile - 'And who is that fellow walking towards them and so obligingly offering them a glass?'

'Oh, that's Rayevich, a dandy from Moscow. He's a gambler, as you can immediately see from the huge gold chain across his pale-blue waistcoat. And what about that thick cane of his, like Robinson bloody Crusoe! Not to mention the beard, or the hairstyle *à la moujik...*'.

'You're disaffected with the entire human race' - said Pechorin.

'And with good reason'.

'Really?'

Just then, the ladies moved away from the well and walked alongside the two young men. Grushnitsky managed to adopt a dramatic pose with his crutch and answered Pechorin loudly in French:

'*Mon cher, je haïs les hommes pour ne pas les mépriser, car autrement la vie serait une farce trop dégoutante*'.

The pretty young Princess turned and gave the orator a long inquisitive look, ambivalent but certainly not mocking, for which Pechorin silently, and sincerely, congratulated him.

'This Princess Mary is exquisite' - said Pechorin - 'She has eyes like velvet... velvet. I would advise you to use that expression yourself when you tell her about her eyes; her lashes are so long, the rays of the sun don't reflect in her pupils. I like eyes like that, with no shine: they're so soft, as if they're stroking you... In fact, all her features are good... Were her teeth white? That's very important! It's a pity she didn't smile at your elegant remark'.

'You speak of a beautiful woman as if she were an English horse' - Grushnitsky said indignantly.

'*Mon cher*' - Pechorin replied, attempting to mimic Grushnitsky's tone - '*je méprise les femmes pour ne pas les aimer, car autrement la vie serait un mélodrame trop ridicule*'.

Pechorin turned and walked away. He walked for half an hour among the vines, by the limestone cliffs and the bushes between them. It grew hot and he hurried home. As he was walking past the sulphur spring, he stopped by the covered terrace to rest for a while in its shade; here he happened to witness a fairly curious scene. The *dramatis personae* were situated as follows: Princess Ligovskaya was sitting on a bench in the covered terrace with Rayevich the Moscow dandy, engaged, it would appear, in a serious conversation. Princess Mary, having presumably drunk her last glass of water, was walking near the well, deep in thought. Grushnitsky was standing at the well; there was no one else in the little square. Pechorin moved closer and hid by the corner of the terrace. Just then, Grushnitsky dropped his glass in the sand, tried to bend down to pick it up, but his injured leg meant that he was unable to. The poor soul... how cunning he was, leaning on his crutch, and all for nothing! His expressive face really did portray suffering...

Princess Mary saw this better than Pechorin. She skipped towards Grushnitsky, light as a bird, picked up the glass and handed it to him with a movement of inexpressible charm. She then blushed deeply, looked towards the terrace and, making sure that her mother had not seen, immediately became calm. By the time Grushnitsky had opened his mouth to thank her, she was already far away. A minute later she came out of the terrace with her mother and Rayevich and, as they passed, she adopted the most dutiful and solemn expression, not noticing the devoted gaze with which Grushnitsky followed her for quite some time, until they reached the bottom of the hill and disappeared among the lime trees on the boulevard. There was just a glimpse of her hat as she crossed the street, before running through the gates of one of the finest houses in Pyatigorsk; Princess Ligovskaya followed, bowing farewell to Rayevich at the gates.

Only then did poor Grushnitsky notice Pechorin's presence.

'Did you see?' - said Grushnitsky, firmly squeezing Pechorin's hand - 'She is an angel!'

'How so?' - Pechorin asked, with an air of complete innocence.

'Did you not see?'

'Oh, I saw' - said Pechorin - 'She picked up your glass. If the caretaker had been here, he would have done the same, only quicker, in the hope of getting a tip. Although I can see why she felt sorry for you: you made such a terrible face when you tried to stand on your wounded leg...'.

'And were you not touched at that moment, when her soul lit up her little face?'

'Not at all'.

Pechorin was lying. He wanted to make Grushnitsky angry. He had an inborn passion for contradiction, his entire life one long chain of sad and unfortunate contradictions of the head and of the heart. The presence of an enthusiast would turn him as cold as the grave; and I daresay that frequent contact with the dullest pragmatist would turn him - once more - into a passionate dreamer. He confessed to himself also, unpleasant though it was, that at that moment a familiar feeling ran faintly through his heart – the feeling of envy. He named this feeling 'envy' quite openly, because he had become accustomed to admitting everything to himself. You are, after all, unlikely to find any young man who, on meeting a beautiful woman who has captured his idle attention, would not take it badly when she suddenly and in his presence favours another (any young man, that is, who has lived in society and grown accustomed to indulging his own vanity).

Grushnitsky and Pechorin went down the hill in silence. They walked along the boulevard, past the windows of the house that concealed the beautiful object of their desires. She was sitting by the window. Grushnitsky, grabbing Pechorin by the arm, gave her one of those misty-eyed looks that have so little effect on women. Pechorin looked at her through his *lorgnette* and saw that, while Grushnitsky's look had made her smile, his own presumption only made her genuinely angry. After all, how dare a mere soldier from the Caucasian front turn his eye-glass on a Moscow Princess...

Pechorin bid Grushnitsky good day and began the climb out of town in the other direction, wending slowly up to his own quarters in the foothills of Mashuk. He arrived to find a short man in black frock-coat standing facing his front door. As Pechorin's footsteps gradually more insistently announced his arrival, the little man turned to face him, his face illuminated with a broad crooked smile.

'Lieutenant Pechorin!' – beamed Dr Werner – 'They told me I'd find you here!'

Dr Werner had been in Pyatigorsk almost since the time Pechorin left Stavropol. The persistent rumours about his former practice in Moscow, which seemed always to revolve around the wife of some dignitary, had initially been of little concern to the military authorities. Yet, when certain highly placed figures formed the indisputable impression that Werner seemed to be on close terms with every man in Stavropol who carried with him a somewhat tarnished reputation, these rumours became the pretext for complaints about his conduct, professional and otherwise. Werner was nothing if not a realist and required no instruction as to the likely course of events; he had therefore sought and been granted permission to retire from military service. A return to Moscow was out of the question. Where else, he had asked himself, might he find an agreeable confluence of the affluent and the sick? He already knew in advance that he would find no better answer than the springs of Pyatigorsk.

Pechorin surveyed his curious and unexpected visitor with his own characteristic half-smile. Werner's clothes revealed both taste and orderliness: his small, scrawny, sinewy hands were resplendent in pale yellow gloves; his coat, waistcoat and tie were invariably black. No wonder the younger men referred to him as Mephistopheles. Outwardly, Werner pretended to be angered by this, but he was in fact secretly flattered. Werner had already managed to make new enemies in Pyatigorsk to replace those he had left behind in Stavropol and Moscow: the envious doctors of the spa spread rumours that he drew caricatures of his patients, which resulted in almost all of them furiously dispensing with his services. His friends, who seemed to comprise every genuinely honest man serving in the Caucasus, tried in vain to restore his twice-ruined reputation.

Pechorin and Werner had quickly understood one another, although Pechorin was entirely incapable of friendship as such. With any two friends one will always be the slave of the other, although neither will admit it to himself: a slave Pechorin could not be; and to be the dominant partner in such circumstances is an exhausting business, because it requires, along with everything else, pretence... and, in any case, he was accustomed to both servants and money.

'Come in, my good doctor!' – he said, his smile now as warm as the afternoon sun – 'Make yourself at home!'

Pechorin lay down on the divan and stared at the ceiling with his hands behind his head. Werner sat down in the armchair, laid his cane in the corner, yawned, and declared that it was very warm outside. Pechorin replied that the flies had been bothering him and they both fell silent for a while.

'My dear doctor' – Pechorin said at last – 'Wouldn't the world be a dull place without idiots? Here we are, two intelligent men, who know in advance that we could argue eternally about just about anything and who therefore choose not to argue. We know just about all of each other's hidden thoughts. For us, a single word speaks volumes; we see through the triple outer layer to the very core of each of our emotions. Sad things make us laugh, the ridiculous makes us sad. Although, in truth, we are more or less indifferent to anything but ourselves. Exchange of ideas and feelings between us is therefore impossible; we know everything we need to know about one another and have no desire to know any more. All that remains is to pass on news... do you have any news for me?'

Exhausted by this long speech, he closed his eyes and yawned...

Werner thought for a moment and then replied.

'In among all that rubbish you talk there is, I assume, a point of some kind?'

'There are two!' – Pechorin replied.

'You tell me one and I'll tell you the other'.

'Okay, you begin...' – said Pechorin, continuing to look at the ceiling but smiling inwardly.

'You wish to know some detail or other about some person or other who has come to the spa; and I've already guessed who it is, because they have already been asking about you...'.

'Doctor! It really is impossible to have a conversation with you... we read each other's minds'.

'Now tell me the other thing'.

'The other thing is simply this: I wanted to get you to talk. First of all, because listening is less exhausting than speaking; second, because there's no danger of me saying more than I want to; third, because I might then find out another's secret; and fourth, because intelligent men such as yourself prefer those who listen to those who talk. Now, to business... What did Princess Ligovskaya say about me?'

'You're quite sure it was the old Princess and not her daughter Mary?'

'I'm entirely certain'.

'Why so?'

'Because Princess Mary asked about Grushnitsky'.

'You have great powers of insight. She told me she's certain the young man in the greatcoat has been reduced to the ranks because of a duel...'.

'I hope you didn't disabuse her of that pleasant misunderstanding'.

'Of course not'.

'The plot thickens!' – Pechorin exclaimed with delight – 'We must have a think about the *dénouement* of this comedy. Fate has clearly decreed that I should not be bored'.

'I sense already that poor Grushnitsky will be your victim...'.

'Keep going with your story, doctor...'.

'Princess Ligovskaya said that your face seemed familiar. I replied that you had probably met at some point in St Petersburg society. I told her your name... she recognised it. It would appear that your adventures there caused quite a stir... She began to tell me about your escapades, no doubt adding something of her own to the society gossip. Her daughter listened with interest; she imagines you as the hero of a novel in the modern style. I didn't contradict the old Princess, although I knew she was talking nonsense'.

'You are a friend indeed!' – said Pechorin, offering his hand.

Werner shook it warmly and went on.

'I can introduce you if you wish?'

'Really, Doctor' – said Pechorin, throwing up his hands – 'Heroes require no introduction; the only proper way for a hero to meet his beloved is in the act of saving her from certain death...'.

'So do you really mean to pursue Princess Mary?'

'Quite the contrary! I've won at last, Doctor... you've misunderstood me!'

'Although I am a little disappointed in you, Doctor' – Pechorin continued after a moment's silence – 'I never tell you my secrets, but love it when you manage to uncover them, because then I can always deny them when it suits me. However, you must describe for me both mother and daughter... what kind of people are they?'

'Princess Ligovskaya, first of all, is around forty-five' – Werner replied – 'Her stomach is in good order, but she has a problem with her blood; she has red blotches on her face. She has spent the latter part of her life in Moscow and there she has quietly become fat. She loves to be told slightly *risqué* jokes and sometimes even says impolite things herself when her daughter is not in the room. She told me her daughter is as pure as a dove... what has that got to do with me? I wanted to reply that she shouldn't worry, I won't tell anyone! She's here for her rheumatism, although goodness knows why Princess Mary is here; I advised them both to drink two glasses of mineral water a day and to bathe twice a week. Princess Ligovskaya, it would appear, isn't terribly accustomed to being in charge and is somewhat in awe of her daughter's intellect and knowledge... she has read Byron in the English original and knows algebra... the young ladies of Moscow appear to have taken to learning; good for them! The men down here are such brutes that flirting with them would appear to be quite unbearable for any intelligent woman. Princess Ligovskaya very much likes young people, while her daughter holds them in contempt; such is the Moscow habit! Forty-something wits are all the rage there...'.

'Have you ever been in Moscow, Doctor?' - asked Pechorin.

'Yes, I practiced there for a while'.

'Do go on'.

'That's it, I think... Oh, there is one more thing: Princess Mary seems fond of discussing feelings, passions, that kind of thing... and she spent a winter in St Petersburg, which she didn't like, particularly the society; she no doubt received a cold welcome'.

'You didn't see anyone with them today?'

'On the contrary, there was an adjutant and a rather prim officer of the Guards... and a woman who has just arrived, a relative of Princess Ligovskaya on her husband's side; very pretty, but also, it would seem, very ill. But perhaps you saw her at the well? She's blonde, medium height, with fine features... and a hint of consumption in her complexion. She also has a beauty spot on her right cheek. I was really quite struck by the expressiveness of her face'.

'A beauty spot!' - Pechorin murmured through his teeth - 'Really?'

Werner looked at him, placed a hand over Pechorin's heart, and said triumphantly:

'You know her!'

Pechorin's heart beat faster than usual.

'Now it's your turn to crow' - he said - 'Although I know I can count on you; you won't betray me. I haven't seen her yet, but I recognise from your description a woman I once loved. Say nothing to her about me... and if she asks, speak badly about me'.

'Whatever you say!' - said Werner, shrugging his shoulders.

A terrible sadness gripped Pechorin's heart when Werner had left. Had fate brought them together again here in the Caucasus... or had she come here on purpose, knowing that she would find him? How would they meet... and was it really her? Pechorin's intuition had never let him down before. There was no man in the world over whom the past had more power; every recollection of every passing sorrow or joy beat painfully upon his soul and struck the same old chords... It was the way he was made: he could forget nothing... nothing.

After tea, at around six, Pechorin went out onto the crowded Boulevard. Princess Ligovskaya and Princess Mary were sitting on a bench, surrounded by young men who constantly paid them compliments. He positioned himself on a different bench some distance away, stopped two officers he happened to know from the Dneprovsky Regiment, and began to tell them some tale or other; it must have been very funny, because they laughed like madmen. This provoked the curiosity of one or two of those gathered around Princess Mary, who gradually moved away from her and joined Pechorin's little circle. He kept talking: his stories were the height of cleverness, the way he made fun of the original creatures passing by was furiously vicious. Thus he continued to entertain the public until the sun went down. Princess Mary walked past several times, hand in hand with her mother, accompanied by an older man with a limp; on each occasion, she looked at Pechorin with annoyance, all the while trying to appear indifferent.

'What was he telling you?' – she asked one of the young men who had returned to her circle out of politeness – 'An engaging story about his exploits in battle, perhaps?'

She said this quite loudly, no doubt in an attempt to give offence.

'Well, well', Pechorin thought to himself, 'You really are angry, my dear Princess; but wait awhile... there's more to come!'

All this time, Grushnitsky followed her movements like a wild beast, not once letting her out of his sight. Tomorrow he will surely ask someone to introduce him. And she will be very glad; for she is quite bored.

CHAPTER SEVENTEEN

GRUSHNITSKY

IN ONLY TWO short days Pechorin's affairs developed rather quickly. Princess Mary positively hated him; he had already learned of two or three epigrams she had composed about him, barbed but at the same time rather flattering. It seemed very strange to her that a man so accustomed to the best society and on good terms with her cousins and aunts in St Petersburg should make no attempt to make her acquaintance. People gathered every day at the well or in the Boulevard; and every day Pechorin would do whatever he could to distract her admirers, the brilliant adjutants, the pale Muscovites, and the rest; and he almost always succeeded. He always hated having guests, but now had a full house every day, for lunch, for dinner, and for cards; his champagne, alas, had triumphed over the power of her magnetic eyes!

Pechorin ran into her yesterday in Chekhalov's emporium, where she was haggling over a magnificent Persian rug. She was imploring her mother not to be mean: this rug would look so good in her study! Pechorin bought it for forty roubles more than the asking price, for which he was rewarded by a look of the most delightful fury. Around lunchtime he arranged for his Circassian horse to be led past her window with the rug on its back. Dr Werner was with her at the time and he later told Pechorin that the scene had the most dramatic effect: Princess Mary wants to set the militia on him. He even noticed that two of the adjutants bow very stiffly to him when they're with her, although they dine at Pechorin's place every day.

Grushnitsky has adopted a mysterious manner: he walks with his hands behind his back and acknowledges no one; and his leg has suddenly healed, so that he barely has a limp. He has managed to find a way to begin a conversation with Princess Ligovskaya and to pay some kind of compliment to Princess Mary: the latter is apparently not very discerning, because she now responds to his bows with a most charming smile.

'Are you sure you don't want to meet the Princesses?' – he asked Pechorin yesterday.

'Quite sure'.

'Forgive me, but it's the best house at the spa! All the best people here...'.

'My friend, I've had quite enough of the best people anywhere. But have you visited them?'

'Not yet. I've spoken to Princess Mary a couple of times, but beyond that... well, you know, trying to engineer an invitation is a touch crude, although that sort of thing does happen here... It would be a different matter if there were an officer's epaulettes on my shoulders...'.

'Forgive me...' – Pechorin replied – 'You're much more interesting as you are! You just don't know how to take advantage of a favourable situation... a soldier's greatcoat makes you a hero and martyr in the eyes of a sensitive young lady'.

Grushnitsky gave a self-satisfied smile.

'What rubbish!' – he said.

'I'm convinced' – Pechorin continued – 'that Princess Mary is quite in love with you!'

Grushnitsky blushed deeply and puffed out his chest.

Oh, vanity! You are the lever with which Archimedes would lift the globe...

'It's all a joke to you!' – said Grushnitsky, trying to look angry – 'In the first place, she doesn't even know much about me...'.

'Women love only those they do not know'.

'I have no pretensions whatsoever to her affections; I simply want to make the acquaintance of a good house. It would be quite ridiculous for me to have any hopes... You, on the other hand, are quite a different matter! One look from one of you lions of St Petersburg and women melt... Although, do you know what Princess Mary said about you, Pechorin?'

'What? She said something about me...?'

'Don't be too pleased... I happened to fall into conversation with her at the well, quite by chance; almost the first thing she said was "Who is that unpleasant, severe looking gentleman? He was with you when...". At this she blushed and didn't want to mention the day, recalling her charming little trick. "You don't need to mention that day" – I replied – "It will live in my memory forever...". Pechorin, my friend! I must congratulate you; you really are in her bad books. What a pity! Mary really is very sweet'.

It should be said that Grushnitsky is one of those people who, when speaking about a woman he barely knows, calls her 'my Mary' or 'my Sophie', provided she has the good fortune to be liked by him. Pechorin adopted a serious expression and replied.

'Yes, she's not bad at all... but be careful, Grushnitsky: most Russian young ladies live for Platonic love, without any thought of marriage; and Platonic love is the most troublesome kind. Princess Mary would appear to be one of those women who want to be entertained; two minutes of boredom when she's with you and you're finished for good. Your silence must provoke her curiosity and your conversation must never entirely satisfy her; you must discompose her at every turn. She'll confound public opinion a dozen times for your sake and call it a sacrifice; then, to reward herself, she'll begin to torment you... and then simply say that she cannot bear you. If you don't get the upper hand, even the first kiss will give you no right to a second; she'll mess you around to her heart's content and in a couple of years marry some monster out of loyalty to *Maman*. She'll then persuade herself she's unhappy and that she's only ever really loved one man (you, that is), but the heavens have chosen not to unite her with him because of his soldier's greatcoat, although beneath that thick grey coat beats an ardent and noble heart...'.

Grushnitsky brought his fist down on the table and began to walk back and forth around the room. Pechorin laughed inwardly and even allowed himself a smile or two, although fortunately Grushnitsky didn't notice. He was clearly in love, because he became even more trusting: he even brought out a silver ring inlaid with *niello*, made locally; it looked a little suspicious and, when Pechorin looked closer, he could see that the letters 'M-a-r-y' had been engraved in small letters on the inside – and alongside them the date on which Mary had picked up the famed glass. Pechorin didn't show that he had noticed because he didn't want to force any confessions from him. He wanted Grushnitsky to choose him as his confidante by himself... then Pechorin would have his fun.

Pechorin got up late the next morning. When he got to the well, everyone had already left. It was getting warm; thick white clouds raced in from the snowy peaks, threatening a storm. The summit of Mashuk smoked like an extinguished torch, surrounded by grey wisps of cloud, crawling and twisting around it like a snake, halted in their movement as if clinging to the sparse scrub on its slopes. The air was filled with electricity.

He went deeper into the vine-lined alleyway that leads to the grotto. He thought of the young woman with the beauty spot on her cheek the doctor had told him about and he felt sad... 'Why is she here? Is it really her? Why do I think it's her... why in fact am I certain? There are plenty of women with a beauty spot on their cheek...'. So ran Pechorin's thoughts as he came to the grotto itself, where he could see, in the cool shade of its dome, a woman in a straw hat sitting on a stone bench; she was covered in a black shawl, her head resting on her chest. The hat covered her face. He was about to turn back so as not to disturb her daydreaming when she looked up.

'Vera!' – Pechorin cried without meaning to.

She gave a start and turned pale.

'I knew you were here' – she said.

Pechorin sat down beside her and took her by the hand. A long-forgotten thrill coursed through his veins at the sound of that sweet voice. Her deep, calm eyes looked into his; they spoke of distrust and something like reproach.

'It's been a long time' – said Pechorin.

'A long time... and we've both changed so much'.

'You don't love me any more...?'

'I'm married' – said Vera.

She pulled her hand away; her cheeks were ablaze.

'Perhaps you love your husband?'

She turned away without replying.

'Or perhaps he is very jealous?'

Silence.

'What then? Perhaps he's young, handsome, no doubt rich, and you're afraid to...'.

Pechorin looked at her and was afraid; there was a look of profound despair on her face and tears glimmered in her eyes.

'Tell me' – she whispered at last – 'Do you take great pleasure in tormenting me? I should hate you. Ever since we've known one another you've caused me nothing but suffering'.

Her voice wavered as she leaned towards him and laid her head on his chest. Perhaps that's why you loved me, he thought to himself: joys may be forgotten, but sorrows – never.

He held her tight and they sat there for a long time. Finally, their lips moved towards each other and merged in a warm, entrancing kiss; her hands were as cold as ice, her head was burning. They began one of those conversations which makes no sense when written down, which should never be retold or even remembered; one in which the meaning of sounds replaces or enriches the meaning of words, like in an Italian opera.

Vera on no account wished Pechorin to meet her husband – the lame old man he had seen briefly on the boulevard. The husband is rich and suffers from rheumatism. Pechorin didn't allow himself a single joke at his expense: she respects him as a protector – and will no doubt deceive him as a husband... The human heart is a very strange thing, especially the heart of a woman.

Vera's husband, Semyon Vasilevich Gorbunov, is a distant relative of Princess Ligovskaya. They're neighbours. Vera often visits Princess Ligovskaya; Pechorin gave his word that he would make her acquaintance and pursue Princess Mary in order to distract attention from Vera. And so his plans were in no way disturbed; and he would enjoy himself...

Enjoy himself! Well, he was already past that stage in life when a person seeks only happiness, when the heart feels the need to love someone powerfully and passionately – now all he wanted was to be loved, and only by a very few. Even a single permanent attachment would be enough: oh, pitiful habit of the heart!

Although, strange as it may seem, he had never become a slave to the woman he loved; on the contrary, he had always managed to acquire an irresistible power over their hearts and their will without even trying to. Why is that? Perhaps it's because he had never really valued anything very much, while they were constantly afraid he would slip through their fingers? Or perhaps the magnetic attraction of a strong organism? Perhaps he had just never met a woman with a strong enough character? Although I must confess I really don't like strong-willed women; that's not their place...

It's true, however, that Pechorin had once – and only once – fallen for a woman with a strong will and couldn't conquer her... They parted as enemies – although perhaps if he'd met her five years later things might have been different...

Vera was in fact ill, very ill, although she wouldn't admit it; Pechorin was afraid she had consumption or the not at all Russian illness they call *fievre lente*, for which there is no name in our language.

The storm broke while they were still in the grotto and kept them there for half an hour. Vera didn't insist that Pechorin promise to be faithful, didn't ask if he had loved others since they had parted... She trusted him without question, just as she had before – and he resolved not to deceive her. She was perhaps the only woman in the world he was incapable of deceiving. He knew they would soon part once again, this time perhaps forever; that each would take their separate path to the grave... but her memory would remain untouched in his soul. He had always told her that and, although she denied it, she believed him.

At last they parted. Pechorin watched for a long time until her hat had disappeared among the bushes and cliffs. His heart was gripped with pain, as if they had parted for the first time. And how he rejoiced in that feeling! Did youth, with all her beneficent passions, mean to return to him? Or was this merely her farewell glance, a parting gift? It's absurd to think that he still looked like a boy: his face, although pale, was still fresh; his limbs were supple and strong; his locks were thick and curly, his eyes still shone and his blood was hot...

On arriving home, Pechorin mounted his horse and galloped off into the steppe; he loved to gallop through the long grass on a spirited horse, the desert wind on his face. He greedily gulped the scented air and fixed his gaze on the blue distance, trying to make out the hazy outlines of things as they gradually became clearer and clearer. No matter what grief is in your heart, no matter what anxiety weighs on your mind, everything instantly falls away; the soul can breathe more easily, the tiredness of the body overcomes the worry of the mind. At the sight of the twisting mountains beneath a clear blue sky, lit by the southern sun, the sound of a stream cascading down the cliffs... he could forget the gaze of any woman.

The Cossacks yawning in their watchtowers must have been long troubled by the mystery of Pechorin galloping past without reason or purpose, or perhaps they mistook his clothes for those of a Circassian. He had in fact been told that he looked more like a Kabardinian than many Kabardinians when on horseback in Circassian dress. He was quite the dandy in this noble warrior dress: just the right amount of braid, expensive weapons plainly decorated, the fur-trim on his hat neither too long nor too short, breeches and boots perfectly fitted, with a white *beshmet* and a maroon *cherkeska*. He had carefully studied the way in which the highlanders mount their horses and nothing flattered his vanity more than to be told that he had great skill in riding in the Caucasian style. He kept four horses, one for himself, the others for his companions, so that he would never be bored riding through the fields; people never turned down the opportunity to ride with him.

It was already six in the evening when Pechorin remembered that it was time to eat. His horse was exhausted as he joined the road between

Pyatigorsk and the German colony, where the spa society would often go *en pique-nique*. The road twists its way between the bushes, then drops down into little ravines, through which streams run noisily beneath the tall grass. The great blue mass of Beshtu, Zmeinaya, Zheleznaya and Lysaya rises up all around like an amphitheatre. Pechorin dropped down into one of these little ravines, which the locals call *balki*, and stopped to water his horse. Just at that moment, a noisy and brilliant cavalcade appeared on the road: the ladies in black and pale-blue riding-habits, their suitors in a mixture of Circassian and regimental dress. At the front rode Grushnitsky and Princess Mary.

The ladies of the spa still believed that Circassians might attack in broad daylight, which was probably why Grushnitsky wore a sword and a pair of pistols on the outside of his greatcoat; he looked quite ridiculous in this heroic display. A tall bush concealed Pechorin from view, but he could see everything through its leaves and could guess from the expressions on their faces that the conversation was of a sentimental nature. As they at last came to the slope, Grushnitsky took the bridle of Princess Mary's horse and Pechorin caught the end of their conversation:

'And do you intend to stay in the Caucasus for the rest of your life?' – said the Princess.

'What is Russia to me!' – replied her suitor – 'A country where thousands will look at me with contempt just because they are richer than I am... Whereas here... Here this thick greatcoat did not prevent me from meeting you...'.

'Quite the opposite...' – said the Princess, blushing.

There was a look of pleasure on Grushnitsky's face as he continued.

'Here my life will pass noisily, but swiftly and unnoticed among the bullets of savages... and if God were to send me each year just one radiant glance from a woman as radiant as...'.

Just at that moment, they came level with Pechorin and he struck his horse with the whip and came charging out from behind the bush...

'*Mon Dieu, un Circassien!*' – cried the Princess in terror.

To reassure her completely, Pechorin replied in French, with a slight bow.

'*Ne craignez rien, madame... Je ne suis pas plus dangereux que votre cavalier*'.

She was embarrassed... but why? Because of her mistake? Or because Pechorin's reply had seemed insolent? He hoped the latter supposition was correct. Grushnitsky gave him a look of displeasure.

Late that evening, at around 11 o'clock, Pechorin went out for a stroll through the lime trees along the Boulevard. The town was asleep, but for the lights that burned in one or two windows. The view was enclosed on three sides by the dark peaks above the slopes of Mashuk, an ominous cloud at its summit. The full moon rose in the east; in the distance, a gleaming silvery fringe of snow-capped mountains. The shouts of sentries merged with the noise of the hot springs, which were left running for the night. From time to time the clatter of horses' hooves rang out through the street, accompanied by the creak of a Nogai cart and a plaintive Tatar song. Pechorin sat on a bench and thought for a while. He felt the need to pour out his thoughts in intimate conversation, but with whom? 'What is Vera doing now?' he thought... He would have paid dearly to hold her hand at that very moment...

Suddenly, he heard quick, uneven steps... Grushnitsky, no doubt... and it was!

'Where have you been?' - asked Pechorin.

'At Princess Ligovskaya's' - Grushnitsky replied importantly - 'How well Mary sings!'

'Do you know what?' - said Pechorin - 'I'll bet you she thinks you've been reduced to the ranks'.

'Perhaps... But what do I care?' - Grushnitsky said casually.

'I say this only because...' - Pechorin went on.

'Do you know you've made her very angry?' - Grushnitsky cut in - 'She found your behaviour incredibly insolent. I managed with some difficulty to convince her that you are sufficiently well bred and know society so well that you couldn't have meant to offend her. She said that you have a quite brazen look about you and, in all likelihood, a very high opinion of yourself'.

'She is not mistaken. But do you intend to take her part?'

'I'm only sorry that I don't have that right...'.

'Aha', Pechorin thought to himself, 'it seems he already has hopes...'.

'Although it is all the worse for you' - Grushnitsky continued - 'It will be very difficult now for you to make their acquaintance... A pity! It's one of the most pleasant houses I know'.

Pechorin smiled inwardly.

'The most pleasant house for me at this moment is my own' - said Pechorin, yawning and getting up to leave.

'You regret it, don't you... admit it?' - said Grushnitsky.

'What rubbish!' - said Pechorin - 'If I want to, I'll be at Princess Ligovskaya's tomorrow evening'.

'Let's see'.

'I might even, if it pleases you, make advances to Princess Mary...'.

'If she even wants to talk to you...'.

'I'll wait until she's bored with your conversation... Farewell!'

'I'm staying out for a while' - said Grushnitsky - 'There's no way I'll get to sleep just now... Listen, why don't we go to the restaurant? They'll be playing cards... and I need strong sensations just now'.

'I hope you lose' - Pechorin said as he left.

CHAPTER EIGHTEEN

PRINCESS MARY

Almost a week had passed and Pechorin still hadn't made the acquaintance of the Ligovskayas. He was waiting for a convenient opportunity. Grushnitsky followed Princess Mary everywhere she went, like a shadow; their conversations were endless. How soon, though, would she get bored of him? Her mother paid no attention, simply because he was not a husband in waiting... a mother's logic! Pechorin had cast her – the daughter, not the mother – two or three tender glances; he must now, he thought, bring it to a conclusion.

On the previous day, Vera had appeared at the well for the first time. She hadn't left the house since the day they had met at the grotto. They happened to dip their glasses at the same time and, as they leaned forward, she whispered to Pechorin.

'Don't you want to get to know the Ligovskayas? That's the only place we can meet...'.

Reproach. How dull. Although he had deserved it... On the following day, however, a ball was planned at the restaurant and there he would dance a *mazurka* with Princess Mary...

The restaurant had been transformed into a hall suitable for an assembly of nobility. At nine, everyone began to gather. Princess Ligovskaya and her daughter arrived with the last of the guests. Many of the ladies regarded them with envy and ill-will, because Princess Mary was dressed with great taste. Those who consider themselves aristocrats in this locality, full of concealed envy, now attached it to Princess Mary. But what can one do? Wherever there is the society of women, two circles will appear, the upper and the lower. In the window, in a crowd of people, stood Grushnitsky, his face pressed to the glass, his eyes fixed upon his goddess. She, as she passed, gave him a barely perceptible nod. He beamed like the sun. The dancing had begun with a *polka*; a waltz followed, accompanied by the clink of spurs and the whirling of tail-coats.

Pechorin stood behind a plump lady with pink feathers in her hair. The splendour of her dress was reminiscent of the age of crinoline, while her mottled, uneven skin evoked those happy times when women's faces were adorned with false beauty spots. The largest of the moles on her neck was concealed by a jewelled clasp. She said to her suitor, a Captain in the Dragoons:

'This Princess Mary is quite insufferable! Can you imagine, she not only bumped into me without apologising, she then turned and peered at me through her opera glass... *C'est impayable!*... And what does she have to be so proud of? She needs to be taught a lesson...'.

'Shouldn't be too difficult!' - replied the dutiful Captain as he went into the next room.

Just at that moment, Pechorin approached Princess Mary and invited her to a waltz, taking advantage of the freedom of local custom, which permitted one to dance with ladies with whom one was not acquainted. She could barely suppress a smile or conceal her triumph, although she managed fairly quickly to adopt an entirely indifferent, even severe disposition. She casually laid her hand on Pechorin's shoulder, tilted her head slightly to one side, and off they went. Pechorin had never known a waist more voluptuous and supple! Her fresh breath glanced his face; from time to time a lock of her hair came loose in the whirl of the waltz and brushed against his burning cheek. They completed three turns (she waltzed unbelievably well). She was slightly short of breath, a distant look in her eyes, her half-opened lips barely able to whisper the obligatory '*Merci, monsieur*'.

After a few moments of silence Pechorin adopted the most humble look and said to her:

'I have heard, Princess, that although we are not acquainted, I have already had the misfortune to earn your displeasure, that you think me impertinent... is that true?'

'And you now intend to confirm my opinion of you?' - Mary replied with an ironic expression, which, incidentally, suited her mobile features very well.

'If I have been so bold as to offend you in any way, please allow me to be bolder in seeking your forgiveness. I would like very much to prove to you that your opinion of me is mistaken...'.

'You will find that rather difficult'.

'Why might that be?'

'Because you do not visit us and these balls are not likely to be repeated terribly often'.

That means, Pechorin thought to himself, that their doors are forever closed to me.

'You know, Princess...' - he said with a certain sadness - 'it's never right to turn away a penitent sinner, for he may, from despair, become doubly a sinner... and then...'.

Laughter and whispers of the people around them made Pechorin turn and break off mid-speech. A group of men, among them the Captain of the Dragoons who had declared his hostile intentions towards the charming Princess, stood a few paces from Pechorin. The Captain was extremely pleased with himself about something as he rubbed his hands together, laughing and winking at his companions. Suddenly from their midst stepped a gentleman in a tail-coat with long whiskers and a red face, heading with uneven steps toward the Princess; he was drunk. Coming to rest in front of the embarrassed Princess and crossing his hands behind his back, he fixed his dull grey eyes on her and pronounced in a wavering high voice:

'*Permettez*... well, anyway... I'm asking you for the *mazurka*'.

'May I help you?' – she said in a quivering voice, casting an imploring glance all around her. Alas, her mother was some distance away and none of her accustomed suitors were nearby; one of the adjutants had seen everything, but hid himself in the crowd in order to avoid a scene.

'What?' – said the drunken gentleman, winking at the Captain, who was making signs of encouragement – 'Does that not suit you?... I once again have the honour of requesting you *pour mazure*... perhaps you think I'm drunk? Don't worry! It makes me dance more fluently, I can assure you...'.

She was on the point of fainting from fear and indignation. Pechorin approached the drunk gentleman, took him fairly firmly by the hand and, looking intently into his eyes, asked him to withdraw – because, Pechorin added, the Princess had some time ago promised to dance the *mazurka* with him.

'Well, that's a shame!... Perhaps another time!' – the drunk said laughing and went off to his abashed companions, who immediately took him into the next room.

Pechorin was rewarded with the most profound, miraculous look.

Princess Mary went off to her mother and told her everything. Princess Ligovskaya sought Pechorin out in the crowd and thanked him. She told him that she had known his mother and was friendly with a clutch of his aunts.

'I don't quite know how it has happened that we haven't yet made your acquaintance' – she added – 'although, you must confess, you alone are to blame: you are so unsociable with everyone, like nothing I've ever known. I hope, however, that the air in my drawing room will drive out your spleen... might it?'

Pechorin replied with one of those phrases that all of us must have prepared for such an occasion. The *quadrilles* continued for a terribly long time. At last, the orchestra struck up the *mazurka* and Princess Mary and Pechorin took their places.

Pechorin made no mention of the drunk, of his own earlier conduct, or of Grushnitsky. The impression the unpleasant scene had made on her gradually began to fade, her face recovered its bloom, and she began to make charming little jokes; her conversation was witty without any pretension of wit, lively, and free; her remarks were sometimes profound... He gave her the impression, with one tangled phrase, that he had admired her for some time. She lowered her head and blushed slightly.

'What a strange person you are!' – she said with a forced laugh, raising her velvet eyes to him.

'I didn't want to meet you' – Pechorin continued – 'because you're surrounded by so many admirers I feared I'd get lost in the crowd'.

'You had no reason to fear! They're all so boring...'.

'All of them? Really?'

She looked intently at him, as if trying to remember something, then once again blushed slightly and, finally, declared decisively: all of them!

'Even my friend Grushnitsky?'

'Is he your friend? – she said, with a look of doubt.

'Yes'.

'He, of course, doesn't belong in the ranks of the boring...'.

'But in the ranks of the unfortunate' - said Pechorin, laughing.

'Of course! Do you think that's funny? I'd like to see you in his position...'.

'What do you mean? I was without rank myself and, truly, it was the best time of my life!'

'Is he really a Private?' - she said quickly, then added - 'I thought he was...'.

'What did you think?' - asked Pechorin.

'Oh, nothing... Who is that woman?'

At this the conversation changed direction and did not return to its earlier subject.

The *mazurka* finished and they took their farewell - *au revoir*. The ladies went home. Pechorin went for dinner and met Werner.

'Well, well!' - said Werner - 'What about that? I thought you wanted to make the acquaintance of the Princess in no other manner than by saving her from certain death'.

'I did better than that' - Pechorin replied - 'I saved her from fainting at a ball...'.

'How so? Tell me all about it'.

'No... work it out for yourself; you who know everything under the sun'.

At around seven the next evening Pechorin was walking alone on the Boulevard. Grushnitsky saw him from a distance and approached, with a certain amusing delight shining in his eyes. He shook Pechorin's hand firmly and said in a tragic voice:

'I thank you, Pechorin... Do you understand?'

'No, I don't; and in any case there's no reason for thanks' - Pechorin replied, absolutely without any good deed on his conscience.

'What? But yesterday, have you forgotten?... Mary told me everything...'.

'Told you what? Do you now share everything in common, even thanks?'

'Listen' - Grushnitsky replied importantly - 'Please, if you wish to remain my friend, do not poke fun at my beloved... Do you see, I love her madly... and I think - I hope - she loves me too. I want to ask you a favour: You will now be visiting them in the evenings... promise me you'll observe everything; I know you have experience in these matters, you know women better than I do... Women!... Who really understands them? Their smile contradicts their glance, their words promise and deceive, the sound of their voice spurns... One moment they guess at our most secret thoughts, the next they misunderstand the clearest signal. Take Mary, for example: yesterday her eyes burned with passion when she looked at me, today they are cold and dull'.

'Perhaps it's the effect of the waters' - Pechorin replied.

'You see the worst in everything... materialist!' - said Grushnitsky with contempt - 'However, let's deal with the matter at hand'.

Pleased with his bad pun, Grushnitsky cheered up.

The two men went together to Princess Ligovskaya's after eight. As they passed Vera's window, Pechorin caught sight of her standing there and they exchanged a fleeting glance. Soon after they entered, Vera joined them in the drawing room. Princess Ligovskaya introduced her to Pechorin as a relative. They drank tea. There were many guests and the conversation was of the most general kind. Pechorin tried to ingratiate himself with Princess Ligovskaya with jokes and on a few occasions made her laugh heartily. Princess Mary also wanted to laugh on more than one occasion, but she held herself back, not wanting to deviate from the role she had decided to play; she was of the opinion that languor suited her – and she was perhaps not mistaken. Grushnitsky seemed very glad that Pechorin's cheerfulness had no effect on her.

After tea, everyone went through to the hall.

'Are you pleased with my obedience, Vera?' – Pechorin asked as he passed by.

She gave him a look of love and gratitude. He was used to such looks, although once they had been a source of bliss. Princess Ligovskaya sat her daughter at the piano and everyone asked her to sing something. Pechorin remained silent and, taking advantage of the general hubbub, moved over to the window with Vera, who apparently wanted to tell him something very important for both of them... although that turned out to be nonsense. Princess Mary was dismayed by Pechorin's indifference, as was clear from one angry, flashing look... Oh, how astonishingly clearly he understood this silent yet expressive, brief yet powerful conversation...

She began to sing. She had a good voice, although she sang badly... not that Pechorin was really listening. Besides, Grushnitsky was resting his elbows on the piano facing her, devouring her with his eyes and constantly murmuring '*Charmant! Delicieux!*'

'Listen' – said Vera – 'although I don't want you to meet my husband, you must without fail ingratiate yourself with Princess Ligovskaya; that shouldn't be too difficult for you... you can do anything you wish. We'll see each other only here...'.

'Only...?'

She blushed and went on.

'You know I am your slave; I was never able to resist you... for which I will no doubt be punished: you will stop loving me. But I must at least protect my reputation... not for my own sake, you know that very well!... Oh, I beg you, don't torment me with empty doubt and false indifference like you did before. I may die soon, I feel myself weaken with every passing day; yet I still can't think about what lies ahead, I think only of you. You men don't understand the pleasure of a look, the touch of a hand; and, I swear, the sound of your voice brings me a strange, profound bliss that not even the most passionate of kisses could replace'.

Princess Mary had stopped singing. There was a ripple of applause; Pechorin approached last of all and somewhat casually complimented her voice.

'All the more flattering' – she said – 'considering you weren't even listening. But perhaps you don't like music?'

'On the contrary... especially after dinner'.

'Grushnitsky was right to say you have the most prosaic of tastes; I see you like music purely from a gastronomic perspective...'.

'You're once again mistaken. I'm no gourmand; in fact, I have a terrible stomach. But music after dinner helps me sleep and it's good to sleep after dinner: so, you see, I like music from a medical point of view. Earlier in the evening, on the contrary, music affects my nerves: it either makes me too sad or too happy. And both are quite exhausting when there is no good reason to be happy or sad; moreover, sadness in public is ridiculous, too great a happiness impolite'.

Before Pechorin had finished, Princess Mary wandered off and sat down beside Grushnitsky. They struck up a sentimental conversation; she replied to his words of wisdom rather vaguely and inappropriately, although she tried to give the impression that she was listening attentively. Grushnitsky looked at her from time to time in amazement, trying to work out what might be causing the inner agitation that occasionally showed on her face.

'But I understand you, dear Princess', thought Pechorin! 'You want to repay me in kind, to prick my vanity – but you won't succeed! And if you declare war on me, I will be merciless...'.

As the evening progressed, Pechorin tried on a few occasions to involve himself in their conversation, but she met his remarks coldly and he eventually retired, pretending to be annoyed. Princess Mary – and Grushnitsky – were triumphant. 'Enjoy your triumph while you can, my friends', he thought to himself, 'for it will not last long... How so? I have the power of premonition. When I meet a woman, I am always able to guess whether or not she will love me...'.

Pechorin spent the rest of the evening with Vera and they talked for a long time about the past... Why she loved him, he really didn't know. She was the only woman who had ever understood him completely, with all his little weaknesses and idiotic passions... Can wickedness really be so attractive?

He left at the same time as Grushnitsky. On the street, he took Pechorin by the hand and said after a long silence:

'Well?'

'You're a fool', Pechorin wanted to say, but restrained himself and simply shrugged his shoulders.

For almost a week Pechorin stuck to his plan. Princess Mary was beginning to warm to his conversation: he told her about certain strange events of his life and she had begun to see him as an unusual person. She no longer dared to engage in sentimental conversations with Grushnitsky in Pechorin's presence and, on a few occasions, even responded to Grushnitsky's attempts at humour with a mocking smile. Pechorin, whenever Grushnitsky approached, would adopt a modest demeanour and leave them to themselves. The first time he did this, she was pleased, or at least tried to pretend that she was; the second time, she became angry with him; and the third time... with Grushnitsky.

'You think so little of yourself!' - she had said to Pechorin the day before - 'Why do you imagine that I enjoy Grushnitsky's company more than yours?'

Pechorin replied that he was sacrificing his own pleasure for the happiness of a friend...

'And mine' - she added.

He looked intently at her and adopted a serious expression. Then, for the rest of the day, he didn't say a word to her. By evening, she was deep in thought; this morning at the well, even more so. When Pechorin came up to her, she was absently listening to Grushnitsky as he rhapsodized about nature or some such subject; when she caught sight of Pechorin, she began to laugh inappropriately, at the same time pretending she hadn't noticed his presence. He stepped to one side and began to observe her surreptitiously as she turned away from Grushnitsky and twice yawned. There was no doubt about it, she was bored with him. Pechorin would give it another couple of days without speaking to her.

Pechorin often asked himself why he so determinedly pursued the love of a young girl he had no intention of wooing and to whom he would never be married. Why such feminine coquetry on his part? Vera loved him more than Princess Mary will ever love anyone. Perhaps if he had thought Mary was an unconquerable beauty, then the difficulty of the task alone might have consumed him... but nothing of the sort. It couldn't even be explained by that restless need for love which torments us in our youth, which drives us from one woman to the next until we find one who cannot bear us... and there begins our faithfulness, a sincere and limitless passion, which can be mathematically expressed by a line stretching from a point in space. The secret of this limitlessness lies in the impossibility of achieving our goal, the impossibility of an ending.

Why then did he bother? Out of envy for Grushnitsky? The poor fellow was not even worthy of such envy. Or perhaps it was a result of that vile but irresistible impulse to destroy the sweetest illusions of those close to us, to have the petty pleasure, when a fellow asks us in despair whom he can trust, of saying 'My friend, quite the same thing happened to me and, as you can see, I am able to eat and sleep without trouble... and I hope to be able to die without cries and tears!'

There is, however, an inconceivable pleasure in possessing a young soul, barely even in bloom. It's like a flower giving off its finest scent to the first ray of the sun: you have to pluck it at that very moment and, having breathed it in until you can breathe it in no more, throw it in the road... someone will pick it up. Pechorin sensed in himself an insatiable hunger, which consumed everything in its path; he looked upon the joys and sufferings of others only insofar as they concerned him, like sustenance for the powers of his soul. He was no longer capable of losing his mind to passion; his ambition had been suppressed by circumstance, but now took on a different form, because ambition is nothing more than the thirst for power and his chief pleasure was to bend to his will everything that surrounded him. Is not the arousal of love, devotion and fear the most obvious sign and greatest triumph of the will? To be the cause of joy and suffering for someone over whom you have no rights – is that not the sweetest sustenance for our pride? For what is happiness but satiated pride?

If Pechorin considered himself to be better, more powerful than everyone in the world, he would have been happy; if everyone loved him, he would have found in himself endless resources of love. Evil begets evil. The first suffering begets an understanding of how pleasurable it is to torment another. The idea of evil cannot enter someone's mind without him wishing to bring that idea into being. Ideas are organic phenomena, someone once said: the moment of their creation gives them form and this form is action. He who gives birth to more ideas will act more readily than others; from this it follows that genius, bound to the desk of the civil servant, must perish or go out of its mind, just as the man of powerful physique who lives a sedentary and respectable life will die of apoplectic fit. Passions are nothing more than ideas in their early development; they are the property of the young at heart, but only a fool would think to be moved by them for a lifetime... many quiet rivers begin as noisy waterfalls, but none of them leaps and foams all the way to the sea. Such calm is often, however, a sign of great, albeit hidden strength: completeness and depth of thought and feeling does not permit wild outbursts; the soul, taking pleasure in its own suffering, accounts in full to itself and is convinced that it must be so. It knows that, without the occasional storm, the constant heat of the sun would dry it out entirely; it lives its own life, indulging and punishing itself like a favourite child. Only in this heightened state of self-knowledge can a man appreciate divine justice.

Grushnitsky went to see Pechorin and threw his arms around him: he had been granted his commission as an officer. They drank champagne. Dr Werner came in shortly after.

'I won't congratulate you' – Werner said to Grushnitsky.

'Why not?'

'Because a soldier's greatcoat suits you very well and, you must confess, the uniform of a line officer, made here at the springs, will do nothing much for you... Do you see, you have until now been an exception, whereas now you will be the general rule'.

'Talk, talk, Doctor! You won't spoil my joy' – said Grushnitsky, adding in a whisper to Pechorin – 'He doesn't know what hopes these epaulettes have given me... Oh, epaulettes, epaulettes, with your stars, your guiding stars... At last, I am utterly happy'.

'Are you coming with us to the gorge' – Pechorin asked him.

'Me? No, I absolutely don't want Princess Mary to see me until my uniform is ready'.

'Should we tell her your good news?'

'No, please don't... I want to surprise her with it myself'.

'Tell me, how are things going with her?'

Grushnitsky became thoughtful and a little embarrassed; he wanted to boast and lie and was at the same time ashamed to confess the truth.

'What do you think, does she love you?' - asked Pechorin.

'Love me? My dear Pechorin, what strange ideas you have! How could she be in love with me so soon? And even if she is, a respectable woman will not say so...'.

'Good! And no doubt according to you a respectable man should remain silent about his passion?'

'My dear friend... there is a certain way to go about things; some things can't be said, they have to be guessed at'.

'True... But the love you may see in a woman's eyes in no way obliges her, whereas words... Be careful, Grushnitsky, she is playing with you...'.

'Is she?' - replied Grushnitsky, raising his eyes to the heavens with a self-satisfied smile - 'I feel sorry for you, Pechorin'.

He left.

Towards evening a large company left on foot for the gorge. According to local scholars, this gorge was nothing less than the crater of an extinct volcano on the lower slopes of Mashuk, less than a mile from town. It was reached by a narrow path between the bushes and the crags. As they climbed the hill, Pechorin offered his hand to Princess Mary and she didn't let it go for the entire journey.

Their conversation began scabrously. Pechorin went through their mutual acquaintances, both present and absent, pointing out their amusing features, followed by their less attractive ones. His scorn rose: he had begun in jest, but ended with genuine spite. This amused Princess Mary at first, then frightened her.

'You're a dangerous man!' - she said - 'I would rather find myself in the forest at the point of a murderer's knife than on the end of your tongue. I ask you, quite seriously: if you ever think to speak ill of me, just take a knife and kill me. I don't think you'll find that so hard to do...'.

'Do I really look like a murderer?'

'Worse...'.

Pechorin thought for a moment, looked as though he had been deeply touched, and said:

'Yes, that has been my fate since childhood. People would read on my face the signs of unpleasant feelings that didn't in fact exist; but they thought they saw them - and so they appeared. If I was modest, I was accused of deceit; so I kept to myself. I had a profound sense of right and wrong, but instead of kindness, received only insults; and so I became resentful. I was gloomy, whereas the other children were happy and outgoing. I felt that I was better than them, but they placed me beneath them; and so I became envious. I was ready to love the entire world, but no one understood me;

and so I learned to hate. My bleak childhood passed in conflict with myself and with society. In fear of ridicule, I buried my finer feelings in the depths of my heart; and there they would die. If I spoke the truth, no one believed me; and so I practiced to deceive. I learned well the ways of the world and became skilled in the art of living; yet I noticed how others, less skilful, were nonetheless happy, enjoying for free the advantages for which I had worked so hard. And so my soul was gripped by despair; not the kind of despair that can be cured at the barrel of a gun, but a cold, impotent despair, hidden beneath amiability and a good-natured smile. I became a moral cripple. One half of my soul no longer existed, it had withered, evaporated, died; so I cut it out and threw it away. Yet the other half still moved, living at the service of others, although no one noticed it, because no one knew that the better half had ever existed... You have reminded me of it and I have read you its epitaph. Many might think all epitaphs ridiculous, but not me, especially when I recall what lies at rest beneath it. I don't, however, expect you to share my opinion; if what I have said seems ridiculous to you, please, just laugh... I won't be at all offended'.

He met her glance just at that moment. Tears welled in her eyes. Her hand, still resting in his, was shaking; her cheeks were aflame. She felt sorry for him. Compassion, which so easily conquers all women, had sunk its claws into her inexperienced heart. For the rest of the day she was distracted and didn't flirt with anyone – a sure sign.

When they reached the gorge, the ladies parted with their suitors, but Princess Mary didn't let go of Pechorin's hand. The witticisms of the local dandies did not amuse her, the sheer cliff above which she stood did not frighten her, although the other ladies squealed and closed their eyes.

On the way back Pechorin didn't resume their sad conversation and she replied to his banal questions and jokes curtly and absently.

'Have you ever been in love?' – he asked at last.

She looked at him intently and shook her head, before once more becoming lost in her own thoughts. It was clear that she wanted to say something, but didn't know where to begin. Her bosom heaved, and no wonder... A muslin sleeve is poor defence against the electric spark that flowed between them. Almost all passions begin in this way and we often deceive ourselves into thinking that a woman loves us for our physical or personal qualities. Such qualities only prepare her heart to receive the sacred flame; but it is the first touch that determines everything.

When they had finished their walk, Princess Mary gave him a forced smile and said:

'I've been very nice today, don't you think?'

They parted.

She was displeased with herself. She reproached herself for being unresponsive. The first and most important triumph! Tomorrow she would want to reward Pechorin somehow; he knew this as if by heart... how dull!

Later the same day, Pechorin went to visit Vera. She tormented him with her jealousy. Princess Mary, it would seem, had decided to trust Vera with the secrets of her heart: a fine choice, I must say!

'I can see where all this is leading' - Vera said - 'It would be better to tell me right now that you're in love with her'.

'And what if I'm not in love with her?'

'Then why pursue her, upset her, arouse her imagination? Oh, I know you so well! If you want me to believe you, come to Kislovodsk next week; we're going the day after tomorrow. Princess Mary will stay here longer. You can rent quarters nearby: we'll be living in a large house near the well, on the mezzanine, with Princess Ligovskaya downstairs; the same landlord has another house next door which has not yet been taken... will you come?'

Pechorin promised he would and on the very same day sent ahead to Kislovodsk to rent the house.

Grushnitsky came to see him at six and said that his uniform would be ready the next day, just in time for the ball.

'At last I'll be able to dance with her the whole evening... and talk!' - he said.

'When is the ball?'

'Why tomorrow, of course! Didn't you know? It's a holiday and the local authorities have decided to have a ball'.

'Let's go for a walk'.

'What, in this awful coat?' - said Grushnitsky.

'Not so fond of it now, are we?'

Pechorin went out alone and, running into Princess Mary, invited her to dance the *mazurka* the following evening. She was pleased and surprised.

'I thought you only danced when you had to, like last time' - she said with a charming smile.

She didn't seem to have noticed Grushnitsky's absence at all.

'Well, tomorrow you will be pleasantly surprised' - Pechorin replied.

'How so?'

'It's a secret... you'll see for yourself at the ball'.

He finished the evening at Princess Ligovskaya's. There were no guests, other than Vera and a rather entertaining old man. Pechorin was in a good mood and improvised for them various unlikely stories. Princess Mary was sitting right across from him and listened to his nonsense with such deep, intense, even tender attention that he began to feel a pang of conscience. What had happened to her liveliness, her coquetry, her caprice, her bold manner, her contemptuous smile, her absent glance...? Vera watched all this with a profound sadness on her sallow face. She sat by the window, sunk in a great armchair. Pechorin felt sorry for her... so began telling the dramatic story of how they had met, of their love - concealing the truth under fictitious names. He described his most tender feelings, his fears, his joys so vividly, portrayed her actions and character in such a favourable light, that she must surely, he thought, forgive his flirtation with Princess Mary. Vera got up, came to sit with the rest of the company, her mood lifted... It was only at two in the morning they remembered that Werner insisted they go to sleep at eleven.

Grushnitsky appeared half an hour before the ball resplendent in the uniform of an infantry officer. A bronze chain with a *lorgnette* hung from the third button of his tunic; the incredibly large epaulettes were turned upwards, like the wings of Cupid; his boots squeaked. He held a pair of brown kid-leather gloves and a cap in his left hand, his right hand constantly rising to tease the curls of his carefully arranged hair. A mixture of self-satisfaction and uncertainty showed on his face. His festive appearance and proud bearing would have made Pechorin laugh out loud, if indeed that had been consistent with his purpose.

Grushnitsky threw his cap and gloves on the table and began to pull down the tails of his tunic and attend to his appearance in the mirror. He wore an enormous black scarf, fastened at the neck by a comb which supported his chin; only a couple of inches of the scarf were visible above the neck of his tunic, so he pulled it up at the sides as far as his ears. This difficult task - the neck of the tunic was uncomfortably tight - made him turn bright red.

'I hear you have been chasing after my Princess' - he said casually, without looking at Pechorin.

'Where else might fools such as you and I get something to drink?' - replied Pechorin, borrowing a favourite saying of one of the most artful rogues of recent times, whose praises were sung by Pushkin himself.

'Tell me, how does the uniform sit on me? Ach, that accursed Jew tailor... it's too tight under the arms! Do you have any scent on you?'

'Why, pray, do you need more? You already smell of roses...'.

'Never mind. Give it to me...'.

Grushnitsky sprinkled about half a bottle on his neck-tie, his handkerchief, his sleeve.

'Will you dance?' - he asked.

'I don't think so' - replied Pechorin.

'I fear that I might have to begin the *mazurka* with Princess Mary... and I hardly know any of the steps' - Grushnitsky went on.

'Have you asked her for the *mazurka*?'

'No, not yet...'.

'Watch someone else doesn't get there before you...'.

'Of course!' - he said, striking himself on the forehead - 'Goodbye... I'll wait for her at the entrance'.

He picked up his cap and ran.

After half an hour, Pechorin followed. It was dark and the streets were empty. There was a little crowd of people outside a tavern and the sound of a *polka* carried on the evening breeze. He walked slowly and sadly. Was the ruination of other people's hopes, he thought to himself, really his only purpose on earth? For as long as he had lived and breathed, fate had always somehow involved him in the denouement of other people's dramas, as if no one could possibly die or fall into despair without him. He had been an essential character of the fifth act, unwillingly playing the role of the hangman or the traitor. What purpose did fate have in mind? Perhaps he was meant to be an author of bourgeois tragedies or domestic novels, or perhaps a contributor of stories to *Reader's Library*? How was he to know? There are many people who begin life thinking they might be an Alexander the Great or a Lord Byron... but spend their whole lives as minor civil servants.

He entered the ballroom and hid in a crowd of gentlemen so that he could observe the situation. Grushnitsky was standing beside Princess Mary, talking with great excitement. She listened passively, looking from side to side, her fan pressed to her lips. Her face bore a look of impatience, her eyes sought someone out in the crowd. Pechorin quietly moved behind them so that he could hear their conversation.

'You are tormenting me, Princess!' - said Grushnitsky - 'You have changed terribly since I last saw you...'.

'You have changed, too' - she replied, casting him a quick glance, the hidden mockery of which he didn't catch.

'Me? I have changed...? Never! You know that isn't possible! He who has once laid eyes on you will never forget your divine image...'.

'Enough...' - said Princess Mary.

'Why do you no longer wish to hear what not so long ago, and so frequently, you paid such favourable attention?'

'Because I don't like repetition'.

'Oh, how badly I was mistaken! I thought, fool that I am, that these epaulettes might give me the right to hope... But no, better I had remained forever in that contemptible greatcoat... although perhaps that was what attracted your attention...'.

'As a matter of fact, the coat did suit your face very much...'.

Just then, Pechorin approached and bowed to Princess Mary. She blushed a little and said quickly:

'Monsieur Pechorin, didn't Monsieur Grushnitsky's grey overcoat suit him much better?'

'I don't agree' - Pechorin replied - 'He looks more boyish in his uniform'.

Grushnitsky could not endure such a blow. Like all boys, he had pretensions of being an old man; he thought the deep marks of passion on his face would replace the stamp of age. He gave Pechorin a wild look, stamped his foot, and left.

'Confess' - Pechorin said to Princess Mary - 'that, although he has always been quite ridiculous, not so long ago he seemed interesting to you... in his grey overcoat?'

She lowered her eyes and didn't reply.

Grushnitsky pursued Princess Mary for the entire evening, dancing with her or *vis-à-vis*; he devoured her with his eyes, sighed, wore her out with his pleas and reproaches. By the end of the third *quadrille*, she hated him.

'I didn't expect this from you' – he said, coming up and taking Pechorin by the arm.

'Expect what?' – replied Pechorin.

'Have you asked her for the *mazurka*?' – said Grushnitsky in a triumphant voice – 'She told me...'.

'And? Is it a secret?'

'Of course not... I should have expected as much from a girl... from a coquette... But I will have my revenge!'

'Blame it on your greatcoat or your epaulettes, but why blame it on her? Is it her fault that she no longer likes you?'

'Then why give me hope?'

'Hope? Wanting something and getting it, that I can understand... but what does hope have to do with it?'

'You've won your bet' – Grushnitsky said with a spiteful smile – 'Only not quite...'.

The *mazurka* began. Grushnitsky chose only Princess Mary, the others chose her in his absence; there was clearly a plot against Pechorin. So much the better, he thought: she wants to talk to him, they are preventing her; she will want it twice as much.

Pechorin squeezed her hand on a couple of occasions; the second time, she drew her hand away without saying a word. When the *mazurka* had finished, she said:

'I won't sleep well tonight'.

'Because of Grushnitsky?' – Pechorin asked.

'Oh, no!' – she said and became so pensive and sad that he promised himself he would kiss her before the evening was over.

The company began to disperse. As Pechorin was helping Princess Mary into her carriage, he quickly pressed her little hand against his lips. It was dark and no one could have seen.

He went back into the ballroom very pleased with himself. The younger people were eating at a large dining table, Grushnitsky among them. Everyone fell silent as Pechorin came in; they were obviously talking about him. Many of them still bore a grudge from the last ball, especially the Captain of the Dragoons; now, it would seem, they were forming against him a hostile gang under Grushnitsky's command. Grushnitsky looked so brave and proud... Pechorin was glad: he liked to have enemies, only not in the Christian sense. Enemies entertained him, stirred his blood. To be constantly on guard, to catch every glance, the meaning of every word, to guess at intentions, break up conspiracies, pretend to be deceived, and, with a single push, bring down the entire, elaborate structure of their cunning plans – that was living.

Grushnitsky whispered and winked at the Captain of the Dragoons all the way through supper.

CHAPTER NINETEEN

THE EAVESDROPPERS

THE NEXT MORNING Vera left with her husband for Kislovodsk. Their carriage passed as Pechorin was on his way to Princess Ligovskaya's. Vera nodded to him, but in her eyes there was reproach. Who is to blame? Why would she not allow him to see her alone? Love is like a flame: without oxygen, it dies. But perhaps jealousy would succeed where his pleas had failed...

He sat with Princess Ligovskaya for a whole hour. Princess Mary didn't join them; she was ill. In the evening, she didn't appear on the Boulevard. The newly formed gang, armed with *lorgnettes*, adopted a genuinely threatening manner. Pechorin was glad Princess Mary was ill; otherwise, they would surely have attempted some impertinence. Grushnitsky wore a rather dishevelled hairstyle and a desperate air. He seemed genuinely hurt; his vanity, in particular, had been wounded... but there are people who continue to be amusing, even in a state of despair...

When Pechorin returned home, he noticed something was missing... he hadn't seen her! She was ill! Had he really fallen in love? What nonsense!

At eleven the next morning, at an hour when Princess Ligovskaya was usually sweating it out in the Yermolov baths, Pechorin walked past her window. Princess Mary was sitting there deep in thought. When she saw him, she jumped to her feet. He stepped into the entrance; there was absolutely no one there, so, without invitation and taking advantage of the casual manners of those parts, he went straight through to the drawing room. Princess Mary stood by the piano, her face dull and pale, one hand perched on the back of an armchair. Her hand was shaking very faintly. He approached quietly and said:

'Are you angry with me?'

She gave him a languid, impenetrable look and shook her head. Her lips wanted to say something, but could not. Her eyes filled with tears and she sank into the armchair, covering her face with her hands.

'You don't respect me! Leave me alone!'

Pechorin took a few steps towards the door... She sat up in the chair, her eyes ablaze. He stopped with his hand on the door handle and said:

'Forgive me, Princess! I've behaved like a madman... it won't happen again, I'll make sure of that. How could you know what my soul has been through? You will never know, and all the better for you. Farewell'.

As he left, he thought he could hear her crying.

He wandered until evening on the foothills of Mashuk. He was incredibly tired and, when he got home, he threw himself on the bed in a state of complete exhaustion. Werner called to see him.

'Is it true' – he asked – 'that you are to marry Princess Mary?'

'What?'

'The whole town is talking about it; all my patients are full of this important news and you know what kind of people the sick are: they know everything!'

'Grushnitsky's idea of a joke', Pechorin thought to himself.

'In order to prove to you the falsity of these rumours, Doctor, I should inform you, in the strictest confidence, that I am leaving tomorrow for Kislovodsk'.

'And Princess Ligovskaya?'

'She will be staying here for another week...'.

'So you're not getting married...?'

'Doctor, Doctor... Look at me. Do I look very much like a groom or anything of the kind?'

'I'm not saying you do... but there are circumstances' – Werner added with a sly smile – 'in which a man of good breeding is obliged to get married; and there are mothers who may not be inclined to prevent such circumstances arising... So I would advise you, as a friend, to be very careful. The air here at the springs is most dangerous: I've lost count of the fine young people I've known who deserve the very best in life, but who have left here beneath a wedding garland... Believe it or not, someone even tried to marry me off! One of those provincial mothers, whose daughter was very pale. I had the misfortune to tell her that the colour would return to her cheeks after she was married.... At which, through tears of gratitude, she offered me her daughter's hand and all of her estate – fifty souls, apparently. But I told her I couldn't possibly oblige...'.

Werner left, convinced that Pechorin was forewarned. It was clear that various foolish rumours about Pechorin and Princess Mary were circulating around town. Grushnitsky would not get away with this!

Pechorin had been in Kislovodsk for three days. He saw Vera each day at the well and out walking. When he woke in the morning he would sit at his window and train his *lorgnette* on her balcony; she would already have been dressed for some time and waiting for his signal. They meet, as if by chance, in the gardens which run down from the houses towards the well. The healthy mountain air has returned the colour to her cheeks and restored her strength. Not for nothing do they call Narzan the 'Water of Heroes'. The locals insist that the air in Kislovodsk inclines people towards love, that here all those romances that have begun at the foot of Mashuk must come to their conclusions...

There really is an all-enveloping air of solitude. Everything here is mysterious: the thick shade of the alleys of lime trees bending over the stream that foams noisily over the stones, forging a path between the verdant hills; the ravines, full of mist and silence, which branch out in all directions; the fresh aromatic air, infused with the scent of tall southern grasses and white acacia; and the constant, sweet, lulling hum of the glacial streams, which meet at the foot of the valley and good-naturedly race one another until they at last fall into the Podkumok River.

The gorge is wider from this side and eventually opens out into a green hollow, through which winds a dusty road. Each time Pechorin looked along the road, he imagined he could see a carriage, with a rose-pink little face looking out of the window. Many carriages travelled along the road, but not that one. The little settlement beyond the fortress was now full of people. In the restaurant on the hill, just a few steps from his quarters, lights twinkled in the evening among two rows of poplars; the sound of glasses rang out until the early hours. Nowhere in the world is more Kakheti wine and mineral water drunk.

Many are fond of combining the two
But I am not one of their number.

Grushnitsky spent each day raucously in the tavern and barely acknowledged Pechorin. He arrived only yesterday and had already managed to fall out with three elderly men who wanted to go into the baths before him. There's no doubt: misfortune has made him belligerent.

They've come at last. Pechorin was sitting at his window when he heard the rattle of a carriage. His heart leapt... What's this? Was he really in love? He should have expected nothing less from someone so foolish...

That evening, Pechorin dined with the Ligovskayas and Vera. Princess Ligovskaya looked at him tenderly and never left her daughter's side... a bad sign! And Vera was jealous; Pechorin had at least managed that. What won't a woman do to upset her rival? I recall one woman who fell in love with me simply because I was in love with someone else. There is nothing more paradoxical than the mind of a woman. It's impossible to convince a woman of anything; you have to lead them to the point where they convince themselves. The order of proofs through which they destroy their earlier convictions is most original; in order to understand the feminine dialectic, you must forget every rule of logic learned at school. In normal circumstances: 'this man loves me, but I'm married; it follows that I should not love him'. But according to feminine logic: 'I must not love him, because I'm married; but he loves *me*... therefore...'. I can say no more, because reason here plays no part; what matters is the tongue, the eyes, and – if she has one – the heart. And what if this book should fall into the hands of a woman? 'Slander!', they will indignantly cry.

For as long as poets have written and women have read their words (for which my deepest gratitude), women have been called angels so often that, bless their simple hearts, they have believed it, forgetting that these same poets – and for money – hailed Nero as a demigod! It is not for nothing that I speak of women with such malice... I, who have loved nothing else in the world but women, who have always been prepared to sacrifice for them my peace, my ambition, my life... It is not from some attack of annoyance or wounded vanity that I attempt to lift that magic veil through which only the practised eye can see. No, everything I have to say about women is the result only of

> The cold observation of the mind
> The heart's filthy lesson

In fact, women should wish that all men understood them as well as I do, because I have loved them a hundred times more since I stopped fearing them and began to understand their little weaknesses. Even Werner, the other day in conversation with Pechorin, compared women to the enchanted forest in Tasso's *Jerusalem Delivered*.

'As soon as you step inside' – he said – 'you are assailed from all sides by such terrors – duty, pride, respectability... God forbid! You must therefore pay no attention, but walk straight ahead; the monsters gradually disappear and there opens before you a peaceful, sunny glade, bursting with green myrtle. But if your heart quakes at those first steps and you turn back – you are lost'.

The evening turned out to be quite eventful. A couple of miles out of Kislovodsk there is a cliff above the ravine of the Podkumok called the Ring. It is a natural gateway, rising up on the hillside, through which the setting sun casts its last fiery gaze at the world. A bustling cavalcade set off to watch the sunset through this window of rock, although no one, to be truthful, was thinking about the sun. Pechorin rode alongside Princess Mary. On the return journey, they had to ford the Podkumok. Even the smallest mountain rivers are dangerous, especially because their beds are like a veritable kaleidoscope: the current changes them from one day to the next; where yesterday there was a rock, today there is a hole. Pechorin took Princess Mary's horse by the bridle and led it into the water, which didn't quite come up to his knees. They began to move slowly across against the current. It's well known that you shouldn't look at the water when crossing a fast-flowing river, which makes your head spin. Pechorin had forgotten to warn Princess Mary about this.

They were in the middle of the river, at its quickest point, when she suddenly slouched in the saddle.

'I don't feel well!' – she said in a weak voice.

Pechorin quickly reached over and wound his arm around her supple waist.

'Look up!' – he whispered – 'There's nothing to be afraid of... I'm here'.

She began to feel better and wanted him to let go, but he held on more tightly to her tender, soft body. His face almost touched hers. She was aflame.

'What are you doing to me?' – she cried – 'Oh God...!'

He paid no attention to her trembling or her embarrassment. His lips brushed her cheek. She quivered, but said nothing. They had fallen behind the others; no one saw.

When they reached the far bank, the others broke into a trot. The Princess restrained her horse and Pechorin stayed alongside her. It was clear that his silence disturbed her, but he resolved not to say a word – out of curiosity. He wanted to see how she would get herself out of this difficult situation.

'Either you despise me or you love me very much!' – she said, in a voice filled with tears – 'Perhaps you wish to make fun of me, torment my soul, then leave me... That would be so vile, so base... the very thought!'

She went on in a tender, trusting voice.

'Is it not true that there is nothing in my character that would deny me your respect? Your bold actions... I must... I must forgive them, because I allowed them. Answer me, say something... I want to hear your voice!'

There was such womanly impatience in these last words that Pechorin smiled involuntarily; fortunately, it had begun to get dark. He didn't reply.

'Are you going to say anything?' – she continued – 'Perhaps you want me to say that I love you first...?'

Pechorin said nothing.

'Is that what you want?' – she went on, turning quickly towards him.

There was something genuinely frightening in her look and her voice...

'For what?' – Pechorin replied, shrugging his shoulders.

Princess Mary whipped her horse and set off at a gallop along the narrow, dangerous path. This happened so quickly that Pechorin only managed to catch up with her as she rejoined the rest of the company. For the rest of the journey home she talked and laughed incessantly. There was something feverish in her movements. She didn't look at Pechorin once. Everyone else noticed her unusual cheerfulness. Princess Ligovskaya was inwardly happy as she looked at her daughter, not realising that she was having a nervous attack. She will not sleep tonight, she will weep. This thought gave Pechorin boundless pleasure... There were moments when he understood the vampire... but for now he would play the fine young man and try to deserve the name...

The ladies dismounted and went into Princess Ligovskaya's. Pechorin was in a state of agitation and galloped off into the hills to try and clear the thoughts that crowded into his mind. A nourishing freshness was carried on the dew-filled breeze. Every stride of his fiery steed resounded in the silence of the ravine. He let her drink at the waterfall, greedily sucked in the fresh air of the southern night, and set off for home. As he rode through the settlement on the outskirts, lights began to go out in the windows. The watchmen on the ramparts of the fortress and the Cossacks at surrounding outposts exchanged long shouts...

One of the houses, built right at the edge of the cliff, was extraordinarily brightly lit. From time to time there came the broken conversation and shouts of an officers' drinking party. Pechorin dismounted and crept up to the window. A shutter that hadn't been closed properly allowed him to see the drinkers and hear their conversation. They were talking about him.

The Captain of the Dragoons, emboldened by wine, beat his fist on the table and called them to attention.

'Gentlemen!' – he said – 'What are we to make of this? Pechorin must be taught a lesson! These Petersburg dogs in the manger can get a bit uppity if you don't give them a good punch on the nose! He seems to think he's the only one who has lived in society, with his clean gloves and his polished boots!'

'And what about that arrogant smile!' – someone shouted – 'I'm convinced he's a coward... yes, a coward!'

'I agree' – said Grushnitsky– 'He likes to pass everything off as a joke. I once said such things to him for which anyone else would have slaughtered me on the spot, but Pechorin made a joke of it. I of course didn't call him out; that's for him to do. I didn't want anything to do with him'.

'Grushnitsky is only angry with him because he nabbed Princess Mary' – someone said.

'A likely story!' – said Grushnitsky – 'It's true I pursued the Princess a little, but I immediately backed off because I have no wish to marry... and I'm not the type to compromise a young woman'.

'I assure you he is a coward of the first order' – said the Captain – 'Pechorin, that is, not Grushnitsky... Gentlemen! Will no one here defend him? No one? All the better! Shall we test his courage? It will be good sport...'.

'Yes, but how?'

'Listen... Grushnitsky is particularly angry with him, so he will have a leading role... He will take offence at some nonsense and challenge Pechorin to a duel! But listen... this is the whole point: he will challenge him to a duel – marvellous! – and everything – the challenge, the preparation, the conditions – will be done as triumphantly and fearsomely as possible... I'll make sure of that: I'll be your second, my poor friend... Marvellous! But here is the twist: we won't load the pistols! I guarantee that Pechorin will flunk it! I'll have them at no more than at six paces, God help me! Are we agreed, gentlemen?'

'A wonderful idea! Agreed! Why ever not?' – rang out on all sides.

'And what about you, Grushnitsky?'

Pechorin waited in trepidation for the answer. A cold spite took hold of him at the thought that, but for chance, he might have become the butt of these fools' joke. If Grushnitsky did not agree, he would throw himself at him. But, after a brief silence, Grushnitsky got up, offered his hand to the Captain and said with great importance:

'Yes, I agree'.

It is difficult to describe the joy that took hold of that honest company of men.

Pechorin returned home in the grip of two contending emotions. The first was sadness. 'Why do they all hate me so much?' he thought. Why? Had he offended someone? No. Did he belong to that class of people, the very sight of whom provokes only hostility? But he also felt a poisonous spite gradually overcoming his soul: 'Take care, Monsieur Grushnitsky!' he said out loud. 'You don't play those games with me... You may pay dearly for the favour of your idiotic comrades. I am not your plaything...!'.

He didn't sleep all night. By morning he was as yellow as a grapefruit. He met Princess Mary at the well.

'Are you ill?' - she asked, looking intently at him.

'I haven't slept'.

'Nor have I... and I blamed you... perhaps wrongly? Please explain... I can forgive everything...'.

'Everything?'

'Everything... Only tell me the truth, and quickly. Can't you see, I've thought about this a lot, tried to explain it to myself, to justify your behaviour... Perhaps you're worried about objections from my parents? Don't: when they find out...' - her voice shook - 'I'll persuade them. Or perhaps it's your own position? Well, I am ready to sacrifice everything for the man I love... Oh, please say something, have pity on me...! Say you don't despise me!'

She seized Pechorin's hand.

Princess Ligovskaya was walking in front with Vera's husband and hadn't seen anything. But some of the patients at the well, the nosiest of all gossips, could see them, so Pechorin quickly pulled his hand from her passionate grasp.

'I'll tell you the whole truth' - he said - 'I won't justify or explain my actions... but I'm not in love with you'.

Her lips turned slightly pale.

'Leave me' - she said, almost inaudibly.

Pechorin shrugged his shoulders, turned, and walked away.

Sometimes Pechorin despised himself... perhaps, he thought, that's why he also despised other people? He had lost his capacity for noble impulse. He was afraid to seem absurd even to himself. Anyone else in his position would have laid down before Princess Mary *son couer et sa fortune*, but the word 'marriage' had a mystical power over Pechorin: no matter how much he was in love with a woman, the moment she gave him the slightest hint that he should marry her - well, so much for love! His heart turns to stone and nothing can bring back the flame. He was ready to sacrifice everything, except that. He would risk his life, his honour, twenty times on the turn of a card... but his freedom was not for sale. Why did he value it so much? What use was it to him? What was he preparing for? What did he expect from the future? Precisely nothing. It was nothing more than a kind of inherent fear, an inexplicable foreboding... There are people, after all, who have an irrational fear of spiders, cockroaches, mice...

If Pechorin had been more honest with himself, he would have acknowledged the real explanation. When he was still a child, an old woman told his fortune for his grandmother: she foresaw that he would die at the hand of an evil woman. This affected Pechorin deeply. An indefinable aversion to marriage grew in his soul. And something told him that this premonition would come true... all he could do was try to delay it for as long as possible...

The magician Apfelbaum came to town yesterday. A large poster appeared on the doors of the restaurant, informing the esteemed public that the above-mentioned astounding magician, acrobat, alchemist and illusionist would have the honour of putting on a wonderful performance today at eight in the evening in the Assembly Rooms (in other words, the restaurant). Two roubles fifty kopecks a ticket. Everyone in town would gather to see the amazing magician, even Princess Ligovskaya had bought a ticket, despite the fact that her daughter was ill.

After lunch Pechorin walked past Vera's windows. She was sitting alone on the balcony. A note fell at Pechorin's feet.

> *Come this evening at eight; use the main staircase. My husband is in Pyatigorsk and won't get back until tomorrow morning. Everyone else, including the servants, will be out: I've given them all tickets for the show, Princess Ligovskaya's servants, too. I'll be waiting for you; come without fail.*

'So', he thought, 'things are finally beginning to go my way'.

At eight o'clock he went to see the magician. The audience was seated shortly after eight and the performance began. Pechorin could see Vera's and Princess Ligovskaya's valets and servants sitting in the back rows; all present and correct. Grushnitsky was sitting in the front row with his *lorgnette*. The magician turned to him every time he needed a handkerchief, a watch, a ring. For some time now, Grushnitsky had not bowed when he and Pechorin met; and he now cast Pechorin a couple of bold glances. Pechorin would remind him of this when the time came to settle their account.

Just after nine, Pechorin got up and left. It was pitch black outside. Cold, heavy clouds lay on the peaks of the surrounding mountains; occasionally, the dying wind rustled the tops of the poplars around the restaurant. The crowd was visible through the windows. He went down the hill and quickened his pace as he went through the gates. He had a sudden feeling that someone was following him. He stopped and looked around. He could make nothing out in the darkness, but, to be safe, walked around the house, as if out for stroll. As he passed under the window of Princess Mary, he once again heard steps behind him and a man wrapped in a greatcoat ran past. Pechorin was troubled, but nonetheless crept to the porch and quickly ran up the dark staircase. The door opened and a small hand seized his.

'Did anyone see you?' - Vera asked in a whisper, pressing herself to him.

'No one!'

'Now do you believe that I love you? Oh, I've hesitated for so long, tormenting myself... But you will do with me as you please'.

Her heart was thumping, her hands as cold as ice. The reproaches, jealousies, complaints began. She demanded Pechorin tell her everything, saying that she would bear his unfaithfulness with humility, because she wanted nothing else but his happiness. Pechorin didn't entirely believe this, but calmed her with vows and promises...

'So you are not going to marry Princess Mary? You don't love her? But she thinks... do you realise she's out of her mind in love with you, the poor girl?'

At around two in the morning Pechorin opened the window and, with two shawls knotted together, let himself down from the upper balcony to the lower, steadying himself against the pillar. Princess Mary's light still burned. Something drew Pechorin to her window. The curtains weren't quite closed and he looked inside with some curiosity. Princess Mary was sitting on her bed with her hands clasped in her lap. Her thick hair was gathered up into a lace-trimmed nightcap, a large crimson shawl over her pale shoulders, her little feet in brightly coloured Persian slippers. She sat quite still, her head lowered. In front of her on a little table lay an open book, but her eyes, unmoving and full of an indescribable sadness, scanned the same page for the hundredth time, while her thoughts were far away...

Just at that moment, something moved in the bushes. Pechorin jumped down from the balcony onto the turf. An unseen hand grabbed him by the shoulder.

'Aha!' - said a coarse voice - 'Got you! I'll teach you to go visiting princesses after dark!'

'Hold him tight!' - shouted a second voice, jumping out from round the corner.

It was Grushnitsky and the Captain of the Dragoons.

Pechorin punched the Captain in the face, knocking him to the ground, and threw himself into the bushes. He knew each one of the little paths on the slope in front of the house.

'Thief! Sound the alarm!' - they shouted.

A rifle shot rang out. The shell, still smoking, fell right at Pechorin's feet.

In less than a minute he was back in his room, undressed, and in bed. No sooner had his valet locked the outside door, than Grushnitsky and the Captain began knocking loudly.

'Pechorin! Are you asleep? Are you here?' - the Captain shouted - 'Get up! There are thieves abroad... Circassians...'.

'I have a cold' - Pechorin replied - 'I don't want to catch a chill'.

They left. Perhaps he shouldn't have answered: they would have spent an hour or more looking for him in the gardens.

There was a terrible commotion outside. Cossacks came galloping out of the fortress. The whole town was in uproar, searching for Circassians under every bush. Nothing, of course, was found, although many were convinced that a couple of dozen of the beasts would have been taken, if only the garrison had shown greater courage and initiative...

The next morning at the well, the only topic of conversation was the night-time raid of the Circassians. When Pechorin had drunk the prescribed number of glasses of Narzan and walked ten times through the long alley of limes trees, he ran into Vera's husband, who had only just returned from Pyatigorsk. He took Pechorin by the arm and they went into the restaurant for some breakfast; he was terribly concerned about his wife.

'How frightened she was last night!' - he said - 'It would happen when I was away, wouldn't it?'

They sat down by a door that led through into a side-room, where a number of the younger folk sat, Grushnitsky among them. For a second time, Pechorin was destined to overhear a conversation that would seal Grushnitsky's fate. Grushnitsky couldn't see him, so Pechorin couldn't tell if the fool was doing it on purpose; but that only made Grushnitsky more guilty in his eyes.

'Was it really Circassians?' - someone said - 'Did anyone actually see them?'

'I'll tell you the whole story' - said Grushnitsky - 'But keep it to yourselves. This is what happened. Last night a certain person, who I won't name, came up to me and said that, some time between nine and ten, he had seen someone sneaking into the Ligovskaya house. I should emphasize that Princess Ligovskaya herself was here at the performance, while Princess Mary was at home. This person and I set off to wait for the lucky fellow beneath the windows'.

Pechorin was a little afraid. Although Vera's husband was busy with his breakfast, he might hear certain unpleasant details if Grushnitsky really had guessed the truth. Grushnitsky, however, was blinded by jealousy and had no idea what had really happened.

'So you see' - he continued - 'we set off with our rifles, loaded with blanks so as to frighten whoever it was. We waited in the gardens until two. At last he appeared, although God only knows where he came from: it couldn't have been from the window, which was closed; he must have come through the little glass door by the pillar... But at last, as I said, we saw someone coming down from the balcony... What about that for a Princess, eh? These young ladies from Moscow, I really don't know! I can believe anything after this... Anyway, we tried to grab him, but he got away and ran into the bushes. That's when I fired at him'.

There was a ripple of disbelief.

'You don't believe me?' - he continued - 'I swear on my honour, it's the absolute truth; and, to prove it, I'll tell you who it was...'.

'Tell us, tell us, who was it!' - they shouted on all sides.

'It was Pechorin' - Grushnitsky replied.

Just at the moment he lifted his eyes and Pechorin was standing in the doorway in front of him. Grushnitsky turned bright red. Pechorin approached and said, slowly but clearly:

'I am extremely sorry that I came in only after you had given your word of honour in support of the most disgusting slander. My presence might have saved you from such an unnecessarily despicable act'.

Grushnitsky sprang up as if angry.

'I ask you' – Pechorin continued in the same tone – 'to withdraw your remarks. You know very well that it isn't true. I don't think a woman's indifference to your dazzling qualities deserves such terrible revenge. Think very carefully: if you insist on what you have said, you lose the right to call yourself a man of honour... and you put your life at risk'.

Grushnitsky stood in front of him, his eyes lowered, extremely agitated. But the struggle between his conscience and his vanity didn't last for long. The Captain, who was sitting next to Grushnitsky, dug him with an elbow. Grushnitsky took a breath and replied quickly, without lifting his eyes:

'My dear sir, when I say something, I mean it... and am prepared to repeat it. I'm not afraid of your threats; I'm ready for anything...'.

'You've made the last point very clear' – Pechorin replied coldly.

Taking the Captain of the Dragoons by the arm, he left the room.

'How can I be of service?' – the Captain asked.

'You are a friend of Grushnitsky and will no doubt act as his second?'

The Captain gave a solemn bow.

'You're quite right' – he replied – 'In fact, I'm obliged to act as his second, because the insult you have just delivered also applies to me; I was with him last night' – he went on, pulling his slouching figure erect.

'Ah, so it was you I hit with that poor punch?'

The Captain turned a little yellow, then a little blue; his face burned with repressed malice.

'I will have the honour of sending you my second later today' – Pechorin added, bowing courteously and giving the impression that he hadn't noticed the Captain's anger.

At the entrance to the restaurant Pechorin met Vera's husband. He was waiting for him.

'Noble young man!' – he said, with tears in his eyes – 'I heard everything. What a scoundrel! How ignoble! No one will have him in any respectable house after this... Thank God I don't have daughters! The woman for whom you are risking your life will reward you. And be assured of my discretion at all times' – he continued – 'I was young myself once and saw military service; I know it's best not to interfere in these matters. Goodbye'.

The poor fellow! Glad that he doesn't have daughters...

Pechorin went straight to Dr Werner's, found him at home, and told him everything: the relationship with Vera, with Princess Mary, and the conversation Pechorin had overheard, from which he had learned of these gentlemen's intention to make a fool of him by making him fire blank rounds. But the whole thing had now gone beyond a joke; they had perhaps not expected quite such an outcome. Werner agreed to act as second and Pechorin gave him some instructions about the conduct of the duel: he must ensure that the whole thing is conducted in secret, because, although Pechorin was ready at any moment to risk death, he was not prepared to ruin forever his prospects in this world.

Pechorin went home and, in an hour, Werner returned from his expedition.

'There is definitely a plot against you' - he said - 'I found Grushnitsky with the Captain and another man, whose name I can't remember. I was taking off my boots in the hallway... there was a loud and terrible argument in the other room: "In no circumstances!" shouted Grushnitsky. "He has publicly insulted me; it was entirely different before...". "What does it matter to you?" the Captain replied. "I'll see to everything. I've acted as second in five duels and I know how to organise it. I've thought of everything. So please, don't interfere. It would be no bad thing to give him a fright, but why put yourself in danger when there's no need...?"'

'I came into the room at that moment' - said Werner - 'They fell silent. Negotiations went on for quite some time, but in the end we agreed the following: about three miles from here there is a deep ravine; they will set off at four tomorrow morning and we will follow half an hour later; you will shoot at six paces... Grushnitsky asked for that. And if one of you is killed, we'll put it down to Circassians. But here are my suspicions: I think that they, the seconds, may have changed their initial plan and now intend to load only Grushnitsky's pistol with a live round. That would be very close to murder, but in time of war, and particularly war in the Caucasus, it would appear that a certain amount of cunning is permitted. Although Grushnitsky is, I think, a little more honourable than his comrades... What do you think? Should we let them know we've guessed their plan?'

'Not for anything on earth, Doctor!' - said Pechorin - 'Don't worry, they won't get the better of me'.

'What are you going to do?'

'That's my secret'.

'Be careful... it's only six paces!'

'I'll expect you tomorrow at four; the horses will be ready. Farewell'.

Pechorin remained at home until evening, locked in his room. His valet came to tell him he had been invited to Princess Ligovskaya's. Pechorin told him to say he was ill.

Two in the morning. Pechorin could not sleep. And he would need to get some sleep, so that his hand would be steady in the morning. Although it's quite hard to miss at six paces.

'Oh, Monsieur Grushnitsky!' Pechorin thought to himself, 'Your little ruse won't work! The tables will turn: it'll be my turn to search your pale face for signs of hidden fear. But why have you insisted on these fatal six paces. Do you imagine I'll offer myself without a fight? Oh no, we'll draw lots to see who fires first, and then... then...'.

But what if Grushnitsky's luck holds? What if Pechorin's star betrays him at last? And why not? It has for so long obeyed his whims, but there is no more constancy in the heavens than there is on earth... 'And what of it?' asked his fevered mind, 'If I die, I die! It will be no great loss to the world. I've had quite enough... Like a man yawning at a ball, who doesn't go home to bed only because his carriage hasn't arrived... But the carriage awaits! Farewell!'

Pechorin's mind raced through his past life, stumbling reluctantly over the 'eternal questions': why had he lived? For what purpose was he born? There must have been a purpose, he must have been intended for something great, because he could feel in the depths of his soul an immeasurable strength... But he had never found it, he had been lured by empty and unworthy distractions. He emerged from the furnace as hard and cold as steel, but had lost forever the passion for noble deeds - the finest flower of life. And how many times since then had he played the role of the axe in the hands of fate! Like an instrument of punishment, he came down on the heads of the condemned, often without malice, always without mercy... His love had never made anyone happy, because he had sacrificed nothing for those he loved. He loved only for himself, for his own pleasure: he satisfied only the strange demands of his heart, greedily devouring the feelings, joys, and sufferings of others - and he could never be satisfied. Like a man exhausted by hunger who falls asleep and sees before his eyes a luxurious feast and sparkling wines, who gorges himself on the ethereal gifts of his imagination and feels better - only to awake and find that the dream has died... that only greater hunger and despair remain...

So, perhaps, tomorrow he would die! And there will no longer be a single being on earth who might have understood him entirely. Some will say he was a fine fellow, others - a scoundrel. Neither is true. Is life really worth the candle? To go on living out of curiosity, hoping for something different? How absurd... how shameful.

CHAPTER TWENTY

THE MEN OF HONOUR II

ON THAT NIGHT before the duel, Pechorin didn't sleep a wink. He tried to continue his journal, but couldn't write for long; a strange unease had taken hold of him. He paced around the room for an hour or so, then picked up a novel that was lying on his desk: it was Walter Scott's *Old Mortality*. He read with difficulty at first, but was gradually carried away by its magical story... the Scots bard must surely have been rewarded in heaven for every joyful moment his book has given us...

Dawn broke at last. Pechorin's nerves were calmed. He looked in the mirror: the tortuous sleepless night had left a dull pallor on his face, although his eyes, despite the dark rings beneath them, shone proudly and implacably. He was quite pleased with himself. He ordered the horses to be saddled, got dressed, and ran down to the baths. He felt his physical and spiritual strength return as he plunged into the icy, foaming Narzan water. He left the baths feeling cheerful and revived, as if he was going to a ball. Don't tell me the soul doesn't depend on the body...

When Pechorin got back, Werner was in his room. He wore grey jodhpurs, a striped kaftan, and a Circassian hat... Pechorin laughed out loud at the sight of his slight figure beneath the huge shaggy hat, his face, not at all warlike, even longer than usual.

'Why so gloomy, Doctor?' - Pechorin asked him - 'You've no doubt seen people off to the other world a hundred times and with complete indifference? Imagine I have jaundice, from which I might die or I might recover; nothing out of the ordinary. Or try to think of me as a patient who is suffering from a disease you've never encountered before; then your curiosity really would be aroused... you could make any number of physiological observations about me. Is not the expectation of violent death a genuine illness?'

This idea made an impression on Werner and he cheered up.

They mounted up. Werner clung to the reins with both hands as they set off, galloping quickly past the fortress and through the settlement. They were soon in the gorge, through which twisted a road, half-overgrown with tall grass and criss-crossed by rushing streams; they had to ford each one, much to the dismay of Werner, whose horse insisted on stopping in the water each time.

Pechorin could not recall a brighter, fresher morning. The sun had barely crept above the verdant peaks and the combination of its warm rays and the vanishing chill of the night filled his senses with a comforting ease. The joyful rays of the new day had not penetrated all the way into the gorge, but painted in gold the tops of the crags that hung above them on both sides.

The thick leafy bushes that grew out of cracks in the cliff-face showered them with silvery dew at the least breath of wind. Pechorin thought how much he loved nature, now more than ever. He studied in fascination every dew-drop as it trembled on its broad vine leaf, reflecting the sun in a million tiny rainbows. How greedily he gazed into the darkening distance where the road came to an end, as the crags became darker and more threatening, before finally coming together in what looked like an impenetrable wall. They rode in silence.

'Have you written a will?' – Werner suddenly asked.

'No' – Pechorin replied.

'And what if you are killed?'

'My heirs will no doubt come forward...'.

'Is there really no friend to whom you would like to send your last wishes?'

Pechorin shook his head.

'Is there really no woman on earth to whom you would like to leave something, as a keepsake...?'

'Perhaps you'd like me to open my heart to you, Doctor? – Pechorin replied – 'You see, I'm past the age when a man dies with the name of his beloved on his lips, when he might bequeath a lock of his hair – with pomade or without! – to his best friend. When I think about the possibility of imminent death, I think only of myself. Some people don't even manage that. To hell with friends who will have forgotten me by tomorrow or, worse, who will invent God knows what kind of fairytales about me! To hell with women who, in the arms of another, will ridicule me, so as not to make him jealous of the deceased...! I've managed to salvage only a few ideas from the storm of life, but not one emotion... I have for a long time lived not by the heart, but by the head. I sort and weigh my own actions and feelings with a severe, detached interest. There are two people inside me: one lives in the fullest sense of the word, while the other thinks and judges him; one of them might bid you and the world farewell in the next hour... but what about the other?... Look, Doctor... Can you see those three figures on the cliff to the right? Our opponents, no doubt...'.

They broke into a trot.

Three horses were tethered to the bushes at the foot of the cliff. Pechorin and Dr Werner tethered their own horses and set off along the narrow pathway to the ledge where Grushnitsky, the Captain, and another second were waiting; they called this last fellow Ivan Ignatevich, but I never knew his last name.

'We've been waiting a while' – the Captain said with an ironic smile.

Pechorin took out his watch and showed it to him. The Captain apologised, saying that his watch must be fast.

There was an awkward silence, which was broken at last by Dr Werner, who turned to Grushnitsky and said:

'It seems to me that, having shown your willingness to fight and thereby satisfied your debt of honour, you gentlemen might end this matter amicably'.

'I'm willing' – said Pechorin.

The Captain winked at Grushnitsky, who, although his face had been deathly pale until that moment, adopted a proud look; he thought Pechorin was afraid. Grushnitsky looked at him for the first time since they arrived; but his troubled face betrayed an inner turmoil.

'What are your terms?' – said Grushnitsky – 'Rest assured, I will do all that I can to...'.

'These are my terms' – Pechorin replied – 'You will publicly withdraw your slanderous remarks and apologise to me...'.

'My dear sir, you amaze me! How dare you propose such things!'

'What else could I propose?'

'So we fight...'.

Pechorin shrugged his soldiers.

'If you wish' – he continued – 'But think carefully: one of us will certainly be killed'.

'I hope it will be you...'.

'And I am quite sure it won't be...'.

Grushnitsky blushed in confusion and gave a forced laugh. The Captain took him by the arm and led him to one side; they talked in whispers for some time. Pechorin had arrived in a relatively peaceful state of mind, but this was beginning to make him angry.

Dr Werner walked over to Pechorin.

'Listen to me' – he said with obvious agitation – 'Have you forgotten their plot? I don't even know how to load a pistol, but in this case... Oh, you're a strange man! Tell them you know their intentions and they will not dare... Otherwise...! They'll shoot you down like a little bird...'.

'Please keep calm, Doctor, and wait... I'll make sure they don't profit by this. Let them whisper...'.

'Gentlemen, this is getting boring' – Pechorin said loudly – 'If we're going to fight, let's fight. The time for talking has passed...'.

'We're ready' – said the Captain – 'Take your places, gentlemen! Dr Werner, could you please measure out six paces?'

'Places!' – echoed Ivan Ignatevich in a squeaky voice.

'Wait a moment!' – said Pechorin – 'I have one more condition... As we are to fight to the death, we're obliged also to do whatever we can to ensure that this remains a secret and that our seconds are not held responsible. Agreed?'

'Agreed'.

'So here's what I propose: do you see the narrow little ledge at the top of that sheer cliff, to the right? The drop from there must be two hundred feet or more and there are jagged rocks below. Each of us will stand at the very edge of the ledge; that way, even a light wound will be fatal... this is no doubt in accordance with your wishes, as you yourself agreed to six paces. Whoever is wounded will certainly fall and be smashed to pieces; the Doctor will remove the bullet. The sudden death can be put down to an unfortunate fall... We'll draw lots to see who will fire first... And let me finish by saying I won't fight on any other terms...'.

'As you please!' – said the Captain, with a meaningful look at Grushnitsky, who nodded in agreement.

The expression on Grushnitsky's face changed from moment to moment. Pechorin had placed him in a difficult position: if they had fought on the usual terms, Grushnitsky might aim at Pechorin's leg and wound him, thus satisfying his revenge without over-burdening his conscience; but now he must either fire into the air or become a murderer... or at last relinquish his despicable plan and expose himself to danger on equal terms. I would not like to have been in his shoes at that moment. He took the Captain off to one side and began to speak to him in a heated voice; Pechorin could see his bluish lips trembling. The Captain turned away with a spiteful smile.

'You're a fool!' – he said, loud enough that everyone could hear – 'You don't understand a thing! Gentlemen, let's go!'

A narrow path led up the steep slope through the bushes; fallen rocks formed a rickety natural stairway. They began to scramble up the slope, grabbing on to the bushes. Grushnitsky led the way, followed by his seconds, then by Pechorin and Dr Werner.

'You astonish me' – said Dr Werner, taking Pechorin firmly by the hand – 'Let me take your pulse... Aha! It's racing... although there is no sign at all on your face... but your eyes are shining more brightly than usual'.

Suddenly, small rocks began to roll about their feet... what was that? Grushnitsky had tripped and the branch he was holding onto had broken; he would have slid down on his back had the seconds not caught him.

'Be careful!' – Pechorin shouted to him – 'Don't fall too soon... Remember Julius Caesar!'

At last they reached the top of the overhanging cliff. The ledge was covered with fine sand, as if especially for a duel. The mountain tops crowded in all around, like a numberless herd, disappearing in the golden morning mist. The white mass of Elbrus rose in the south, locked in a chain of icy peaks, through which wispy clouds drifted in from the east. Pechorin walked over to the edge of the ledge and looked down. His head almost began to spin. Beneath him was as cold and dark as the grave. The mossy, jagged rocks, thrown down by storms and time, awaited their prey.

The ledge on which they were to fight was almost perfectly triangular. Six paces were measured out from the corner projecting out into space. It was agreed that the first to face enemy fire would stand right at the brink, his back to the precipice; in the event that he wasn't killed, the combatants would change places.

Pechorin decided to give Grushnitsky every advantage. He wanted to test him. Some spark of goodness might ignite in Grushnitsky's soul and then everything would turn out for the best; or perhaps vanity and weakness of character would triumph... Pechorin wanted to give himself every right to be merciless should fate smile upon him. Who among us has not made such a bargain with their conscience?

'Toss a coin, Doctor!' - said the Captain.

Dr Werner took a silver coin from his pocket and threw it in the air.

'Tails!' - Grushnitsky shouted quickly, like a man suddenly awakened by a friendly nudge.

'Heads!' - said Pechorin.

The coin spun in the air and fell with a clang; everyone rushed forward.

'Lucky for you' - Pechorin said to Grushnitsky - 'You'll shoot first... But remember, if you don't kill me, I won't miss - I give you my word of honour...'.

Grushnitsky blushed. He was ashamed to kill an unarmed man. Pechorin looked at him intently; for a moment, he looked as though he would throw himself at Pechorin's feet and beg forgiveness... but how could he confess to such a despicable plan? Only one option remained: he could fire into the air. Pechorin was certain he would fire into the air. Only the thought that Pechorin might demand a second duel might prevent him from doing so...

'It's time!' - Dr Werner whispered to Pechorin, tugging at his sleeve - 'If you don't tell them we know their intentions, all is lost. See... he's loading. If you don't say something, I...'.

'Not for anything in the world, Doctor!' - Pechorin replied, restraining him - 'You'll ruin everything.... You gave me your word. And what business is it of yours? Perhaps I want to be killed...'.

Werner looked at him in astonishment.

'Oh, that's another matter altogether... Only, when you reach the other side, don't blame me...'.

The Captain loaded the pistols and gave one to Grushnitsky, whispering something to him and smiling. The other he gave to Pechorin.

Pechorin stood on the corner of the ledge, firmly bracing his left leg against the rock and leaning slightly forward, so that he wouldn't fall backwards if he only got a slight wound. Grushnitsky stood facing him and at the given signal began to raise his pistol. Grushnitsky's knees were shaking. He aimed right at Pechorin's head... An indescribable rage burned in Pechorin's breast. Suddenly Grushnitsky lowered the pistol and turned to his second, his face as white as a sheet.

'I can't' - he said in a dull voice.

'Coward!' - said the Captain.

A shot rang out. The bullet grazed Pechorin's knee. He involuntarily took a few steps forward to get away from the edge of the cliff.

'Well, Grushnitsky old boy!' - said the Captain - 'It's a pity you missed! Now it's your turn... take your place! But first, let's embrace: we won't see each other again!'

They embraced. The Captain could barely stop himself from laughing.

'Have no fear' - he added, giving Grushnitsky a sly look - 'This world is a nonsense! Nature is a fool, fate an imposter, and life's not worth the candle...'.

With these tragic words, spoken with all due seriousness, he withdrew to his place. A tearful Ivan Ignatevich also embraced Grushnitsky. And then he stood alone, facing Pechorin. Who will ever know what kind of feeling raged in Pechorin: a combination of injured pride, contempt, and a malice born of the realisation that this person, who now looked at him with such certainty, with such calm effrontery, only two minutes ago, and without exposing himself to the slightest danger, was prepared to kill him like a dog, or at least wound him badly enough that he would certainly have fallen from the cliff. For a minute or two, Pechorin looked intently into his face, searching for even the slightest trace of regret. But it seemed to Pechorin that Grushnitsky was smiling.

'I advise that you pray to God before you die' – Pechorin said to him.

'Do not be more concerned for my soul than you are for your own' – replied Grushnitsky – 'I ask only one thing: shoot quickly'.

'So you will not renounce your slander? You will not ask my forgiveness? Think very carefully: has your conscience nothing to say?'

'Monsieur Pechorin!' – shouted the Captain – 'Let me remind you, you are not here to take confession. Finish it quickly, or someone will come through the gorge and see us'.

'Very well... Doctor, can I have a word?' – said Pechorin.

Dr Werner approached. The poor Doctor! He was paler even than Grushnitsky had been ten minutes ago.

Pechorin spoke his next words loudly and clearly, purposely drawing them out, as if pronouncing a death sentence.

'Doctor, these gentlemen, no doubt in haste, have forgotten to put a bullet in my pistol; can I ask you to reload it... and do it well!'

'Impossible!' – shouted the Captain – 'Impossible! I loaded both pistols! If the bullet has fallen out of yours, it's no fault of mine...! And you have no right to reload... no right whatsoever... it's quite against the rules, I won't allow it...'.

'Very well!' – Pechorin said to the Captain – 'In that case you and I will fight on the same terms...'.

The Captain was silent.

Grushnitsky stood with his head lowered, gloomy and embarrassed.

'Leave them!' – he said to the Captain, who was about to grab Pechorin's pistol out of the Doctor's hand – 'You know they're right'.

The Captain tried without success to make various signs at Grushnitsky, who refused to look at him. Meanwhile, Dr Werner had loaded the pistol and handed it to Pechorin. On seeing this, the Captain spat and stamped his foot.

'You're a fool!' – he said – 'Nothing but a fool! If you had only done what I told you... serves you right! Die like a fly...'.

He turned to leave, murmuring as he went.

'And it's quite against the rules...'.

'Grushnitsky!' – said Pechorin – 'There is still time: retract your slander and I will forgive you. You haven't managed to make a fool of me and my pride is satisfied... Remember, we were once friends...'.

Grushnitsky's face flared and his eyes burned.

'Shoot!' – he replied – 'I despise myself... and you I hate. If you don't kill me, I'll slip round a corner one night and cut your throat. There's no place on this earth for both of us...'.

Pechorin fired.

When the smoke had cleared, Grushnitsky was no longer on the ledge. There was only a fine column of dust swirling at the edge of the cliff.

Everyone shouted in a single voice.

'*Finita la commedia*' – Pechorin said to Dr Werner.

Werner didn't reply and turned away in horror.

Pechorin shrugged his shoulders and bowed farewell to Grushnitsky's seconds. As he went back down the little path, he saw Grushnitsky's bloodied body among the clefts of the rocks. He involuntarily closed his eyes...

Pechorin untied his horse and slowly set off for home. A stone weighed down his heart. The sun seemed to have dimmed, its rays no longer warmed him. Before he reached the settlement, he turned right and continued along the gorge. The sight of a living person would have been too painful for him. He dropped the reins, lowered his head, and rode for a long time. When he eventually recovered his senses, he was in a place he didn't recognise at all. He turned his horse and tried to find the road. The sun was already setting when he reached Kislovodsk, exhausted on an exhausted horse.

His valet told him that Werner had called and left two letters, one from Werner himself, the other... from Vera. He unsealed the first, which had the following contents:

Everything has been arranged as well as it could be. The body has been recovered, badly disfigured, the bullet removed from the chest. Everyone believes the cause of death was an unfortunate accident. Only the Commandant, who was probably aware of your quarrel, shook his head, but said nothing. There is no evidence against you and you can sleep easily... if you are able to. Farewell.

It was a long time before he opened the second letter. What could she write to him? A heavy sense of foreboding troubled his soul. Here it is, this letter, each word of which is indelibly etched in Pechorin's memory:

I am writing to you in full certainty that we will never see each other again. A few months ago, when we parted, I thought the same thing; but the heavens took it upon themselves to test me a second time. And I have failed that test. My feeble heart has once more been conquered by a familiar voice... You won't despise me for that, will you? This letter is both a farewell and a confession: I have to tell you everything that has built up in my heart ever since I've loved you. I won't accuse you. You've behaved towards me as any other man would: you loved me like a possession, like a source of joy or worry or sadness, constantly changing places, without which life would be dull and monotonous. I understood this from the very beginning... But you were unhappy and I sacrificed myself in the hope that someday you would recognise my sacrifice, that you would understand my tender feelings for you, which sought to impose no conditions. A lot of time has passed since then. I have seen through to all the secrets of your soul... and I know now that my hope was in vain. How cruel! But my love for you was a part of my very soul: it has dimmed, but it could not die.

We part now forever, although you can be sure that I will never love another; my soul has given you all it had to give, all its hopes and tears. A woman who has loved you can only feel a certain contempt for other men, not because you are better than them – far from it! – but because there is something in your nature that is yours and yours alone, something proud and mysterious. There is in your voice, regardless of what you are saying, an irresistible power; no one else wants so much to be loved; in no other is evil so attractive; no other glance promises so much bliss; no one else knows how to make the most of their advantages and no one can be so profoundly unhappy, because no one tries so hard to convince themselves that they are.

Now I must explain the reason for my hurried departure, which will seem unimportant to you, because it concerns only me. This morning my husband came to me and told me about your quarrel with Grushnitsky. My expression must have changed quite noticeably, because for a long time he looked right into my eyes; I almost fainted at the thought of you fighting a duel because of me... I thought I'd go out of my mind. But now that I am able to think straight, I'm convinced that you will live; it's simply impossible that you will die without me... impossible! My husband walked around the room for some time; I don't know what he said to me, I don't remember what I answered... I must have said I loved you. All I can remember is that he ended the conversation by calling me a terrible name and left. I've been sitting at the window for three hours now waiting for you to return... But you are alive, you cannot be dead!

The carriage is almost ready... Farewell, farewell... I am ruined, but what does it matter? If I could only be sure that you would always remember me – I say nothing of love... no, only remember me... Farewell... They are coming and I must hide this letter...

Tell me you don't love Princess Mary? Tell me you won't be married to her? You must make this sacrifice for me, do you hear? I have sacrificed everything for you...

Pechorin sprang out into the hallway like a madman, leapt onto his Circassian horse as he was led around the courtyard, and galloped off towards Pyatigorsk as fast it would carry him. He drove the exhausted beast on mercilessly, as it snorted and foamed, sweeping him along the stony road.

The sun had already hid itself behind a black cloud resting on the ridge of the mountains in the west; the valley had become dark and damp. The Podkumok raced across the rocks with a dull, monotonous roar. Pechorin galloped on, breathless with impatience. The thought of not finding her in Pyatigorsk was like a hammer to his heart! Just one minute, one more minute, to see her, to make their farewells, to squeeze her hand... no, nothing could express his anxiety, his despair! The thought of losing her forever made Vera seem more dear to him than anything else in the world, more than honour, fortune, life itself! God only knows what strange, wild thoughts swarmed through his mind as he galloped on, mercilessly driving on his horse. Pechorin noticed then that the horse was breathing with difficulty; twice she almost stumbled on level ground. It was another three miles to Yessentukhi, a Cossack village where he could change horses. All would be saved if his horse had only the strength for ten more minutes!

But suddenly, as they came up out of a little gully just as they were clearing the mountains, the horse crashed to the ground. Pechorin managed to jump clear and tried to raise her, tugging at the reins, but to no avail. A barely audible moan escaped through the horse's clenched teeth. A few minutes later, it died. Pechorin was alone on the steppe, his last hope gone. He tried to continue on foot, but his legs gave way beneath him: exhausted by the day's fears and the sleeplessness of the night before, he fell into the wet grass and began to weep like a child.

He lay there for some time and wept bitterly, without trying to stem the tears and sobs. He thought his chest would burst; all his steeliness, his self-control had vanished like smoke. He had lost heart; reason had deserted him. If anyone had seen Pechorin at that moment, he would have turned away in contempt.

When the evening dew and the mountain breeze had cooled Pechorin's burning head and he was able to gather his thoughts, he understood how futile and irrational it was to pursue a happiness that had died. What more did he want? To see her? For what? Wasn't everything over between them? One bitter parting kiss would not enrich his memories... and would only make it harder to part.

It felt good, however, to be able to weep! Although that was no doubt due to his strained nerves, a night without sleep, two minutes staring down the barrel of a pistol, and an empty stomach... But so much the better! This new suffering, to use the military jargon, had been a 'welcome diversion'. It's good to weep. And if he had not been riding all day, had not been forced to walk another ten miles home, he might not have closed his eyes that night, either. As it was, he got back to Kislovodsk at five in the morning, threw himself on the bed, and slept like Napoleon after Waterloo.

It was already dark outside when he woke. He sat down at the open window and unbuttoned his kaftan; the mountain breeze cooled his breast, which had not been stilled even by the deep sleep of exhaustion. In the distance beyond the river, the lights of the fortress and the settlement below glimmered, illuminating the tops of the thick lime trees. It was quiet in the courtyard and Princess Ligovskaya's house was in darkness.

Dr Werner came in. He was frowning and, contrary to his habit, didn't offer Pechorin his hand.

'Where have you come from, Doctor?' - Pechorin asked.

'From Princess Ligovskaya's. Her daughter is ill: a nervous disorder... But that's not what I've come about: the authorities have an idea of what has happened and, although they won't be able to prove anything for certain, I would advise you to be careful. Princess Ligovskaya has just told me she knows you fought a duel for her daughter; that old fellow who saw your spat with Grushnitsky at the restaurant - what's his name? - told her, so I've come to warn you. Farewell: we will perhaps not see one another again... they'll no doubt send you away somewhere'.

Werner stopped in the doorway: he wanted to shake Pechorin's hand... and if Pechorin had given him the slightest encouragement, he would have thrown his arms around him. But Pechorin remained stone cold... and Werner left.

That's people for you! They're all the same: they know the disadvantages of a particular action from the beginning, but nonetheless help, advise, even encourage it, seeing that there is no alternative... and then they wash their hands and turn indignantly away from the person who has had the courage to take upon himself the full weight of responsibility. They're all the same, even the kindest and most intelligent among them...

The next morning, having received orders from high command to transfer to the Nalchik Fortress, Pechorin called on Princess Ligovskaya to say goodbye. She was astonished when, in response to her question as to whether he had something particularly important to tell her, he replied simply that he wished her all the very best and suchlike.

'Well, I must tell you something of great importance' - she said.

Pechorin sat in silence.

She clearly didn't know where to begin. Her face turned purple, her chubby fingers drummed on the table. At last she began in an uneven voice.

'Listen, Monsieur Pechorin! I think you are an honourable man'.

Pechorin bowed.

'I'm even convinced of it' - she continued - 'Although your conduct is somewhat dubious. Perhaps there are reasons of which I am unaware... and which you must now entrust to me. You have defended my daughter from slander, fought a duel for her... and therefore risked your life. There's no need to reply, I know you won't admit it, because Grushnitsky is dead (she crossed herself). God forgive him... and, I hope, you also! But that does not concern me and I would not dare to judge you, because my daughter was the cause, albeit innocently. She told me everything... at least I think it was everything: how you declared your love for her, how she confessed her love for you (at this the Princess gave a heavy sigh). But she is ill and I'm convinced it's no ordinary illness! Some secret sorrow is killing her; she won't tell me, but I'm convinced that you are the cause. Listen to me: you perhaps think I seek rank or great wealth... but you're wrong! I wish only that my daughter is happy. Your current position is unenviable, but it may improve; you have a certain status, my daughter loves you, and she has been brought up in such a way as to make a husband happy... and I am wealthy, she's my only daughter. Speak, why don't you? What's holding you back? I should not have told you all of this, but I rely on your good heart, on your honour: remember, I have only one daughter... one...'.

She began to weep.

'Princess' - said Pechorin - 'it's impossible for me to answer you; allow me to speak to your daughter alone...'.

'Never!' - she exclaimed, getting up from her chair in a state of great agitation.

'As you wish' - he replied, preparing to leave.

She thought for a moment, signalled for him to wait, and went out. Five minutes passed. Pechorin's heart beat fast, but his thoughts were calm, his head cool. No matter how he tried to find in his heart a spark of love for the charming Princess Mary, the attempt was in vain.

Just then the doors opened and she came in... God, how she had changed since he last saw her... had it really been so long? She swayed slightly as she reached the middle of the room; Pechorin leapt up, offered her his hand, and led her to a chair. He stood facing her. There was a long silence. Her large eyes, filled with an indescribable sadness, seemed to be searching in his for something akin to hope. Her pale lips made a vain effort to smile. Her delicate hands, folded in her lap, were so thin and translucent that he felt sorry for her.

'Princess' - Pechorin said - 'you know that I have been making fun of you? You must despise me'.

A sickly flush spread across her cheeks.

'It therefore follows' - he continued - 'that you cannot love me...'.

She turned away, her elbows resting on the table, her face covered by her hands; tears shone from her eyes.

'My God!' - she said in a barely audible voice.

It was becoming unbearable. Another minute and he would have thrown himself at her feet.

'And so, as you can see for yourself' - Pechorin said in as firm a voice as he could and with a forced sneer - 'you can see for yourself, I cannot marry you; even if you wished to do so now, you would soon regret it. My conversation with your mother forces me to explain things so openly and crudely; I hope she is mistaken... you can easily disabuse her. You see, in your eyes I have played the most pitiful and despicable role... and I confess to it; that is all I can do for you. Whatever bad opinion you have of me, I submit to it... You see, I abase myself before you. Is it not true that, even if you did love me, you would from this moment despise me?'

She turned towards him, pale as marble, only her eyes blazed with a miraculous fervour.

'I hate you' – she said.

Pechorin thanked her, bowed respectfully, and left.

An hour later the post-coach whisked him away from Kislovodsk. A few miles from Yessentukhi, Pechorin recognised the corpse of his fiery steed by the roadside; the saddle had been taken, no doubt by a passing Cossack, and two ravens sat in its place. He sighed and turned away...

BOOK III

CHAPTER TWENTY-ONE

MAXIM MAXIMYCH

WHAT BECAME OF Pechorin after he left the spa towns of the Caucasus and returned to active service would have been lost forever had I not, some years later, out there on the open road of our wild and deathless South, made the acquaintance of a singular and remarkable man.

I was travelling on the post-coach from Tiflis. My luggage consisted entirely of a single trunk, half-filled with travel notes on Georgia. The greater part of them, fortunately for you, dear reader, has been lost; although the suitcase itself and the rest of my things, fortunately for me, have not. The sun was just disappearing behind a snow-covered ridge when I entered the Koishaur Valley. The Ossetian coachman relentlessly drove the horses on so that we would make it over Mount Koishaur before nightfall, singing at the top of his voice.

What a glorious place was this valley! On all sides there were inaccessible peaks, cliffs in shades of red hung with green ivy, crowned with clusters of sycamore trees, yellow precipices streaked with little gullies, and there, on the highest peak, a golden fringe of snow... and below the silver thread of the Aragva, stretching out like the shimmering skin of a serpent, locked in the embrace of another, nameless river, which roared out of a dark, misty gorge.

When we reached the foothills of Koishaur, we stopped at the inn, noisy and crowded with a couple of dozen Georgians and mountain men; a caravan of camels had halted nearby for the night. I had to hire some oxen to pull my cart over this accursed mountain; it was autumn and the two-mile long climb was already covered in ice. There was nothing else to be done. I hired half-a-dozen oxen and some Ossetians.

One of the Ossetians threw my trunk up onto his shoulders, while the others helped the oxen along by doing no more than shouting. Behind us, to my amazement, a team of four oxen were pulling another cart, loaded to the gunnels, without any difficulty at all. Its owner walked behind smoking a little silver Kabardinian pipe. He wore an officer's tunic without epaulettes and a shaggy Circassian hat. He looked around fifty, his dark complexion confirming that he had long been acquainted with the Caucasian sun; the premature grey of his beard was at odds with his firm stride and cheerful appearance. I walked over to him and bowed; he silently returned my bow and blew out an enormous puff of smoke.

'We're heading the same way, it would seem' – I said.

He once again bowed silently.

'You're no doubt going to Stavropol?' – I went on.

'Yes, Sir... on government business' – he replied.

'Perhaps you can tell me why four oxen can pull your heavy cart as if it's nothing, while six of the beasts and these Ossetians can barely move mine, which is empty?'

He gave a crafty smile and looked at me knowingly.

'You've not been long in the Caucasus, have you?'

'About a year' – I replied.

He smiled again.

'And what of it?' – I asked.

'Well! These Asiatics are dreadful savages! Do you really think that shouting is doing any good? And the Devil alone knows what they're saying! Although the beasts seem to understand; you could harness twenty of them, if you like, but they shout something in that language of theirs... and they won't move an inch. Dreadful crooks, but what can you do? We've been too soft on the scoundrels! Just you wait and see, they'll be after a tip as well. I know their game... they don't fool me!'

'Have you served here long?'

'Yes, since Yermolov's time' – he replied with pronounced dignity – 'I was a Second-Lieutenant when Alexei Petrovich arrived at the front' – he added – 'and I was promoted twice under him for service against the mountain men'.

'And now?'

'Now I'm a Captain in the Third Battalion. And you, if I may ask?'

I told him.

Our conversation came to an end and we walked side by side in silence. There was snow at the top of the mountain. The sun set and night followed day without any interval, as is usual in the south. Thanks to the reflection from the snow, however, we could still quite easily make out the road, which continued to rise, although less steep than before. I ordered the Ossetians to put my trunk in the cart and switch the oxen for horses. I looked for the last time down into the valley, but it was completely covered by a thick fog which had surged in waves from the surrounding gorges. Not a single sound from the valley reached our ears. The Ossetians crowded noisily around me demanding a tip; but the Captain shouted at them so fiercely that they immediately scattered.

'These people!' – he said – 'They don't even know the Russian word for "bread", but they've learned how to ask an officer for a tip... I prefer the Tatars... at least they don't drink'.

It was less than a mile to the post-station. All around was quiet, so quiet you could follow the flight of a mosquito by the sound of its buzzing. To the left was a deep, dark gorge, beyond it the outline of the dark blue peaks of the mountains against the skyline, creased with wrinkles and covered in layers of snow, still lit by the last gleam of the sunset. Stars began to glimmer in the dark sky; they seemed, strangely, much higher than in our northern skies. Bare, dark rocks rose up on both sides of the road; in places, little bushes peeped out from beneath the snow, but not a single dead leaf rustled, and it was good to hear the snort of tired post-horses and the occasional jingle of Russian harness bells amid this deathly sleep of nature.

'Tomorrow will be a beautiful day!' – I said.

The Captain didn't say a word in reply, but merely pointed at the high mountain rising immediately before us.

'What's that?' – I asked.

'Gud-Gorá' – he replied.

'And?'

'Look at the way it's smoking'.

And, in fact, Gud-Gorá was smoking: thin trails rose from its sides and a great black cloud sat at the top, so black that it looked like a stain even against the dark sky.

We could already make out the roofs of the huts surrounding the post-station, its welcoming lights twinkling, when a bitterly cold wind began to howl through the gorge, bringing with it some light rain. I had barely managed to throw on my cape when it began to snow heavily. I looked at the Captain with awe...

'We'll have to stop for the night' – he said with annoyance – 'There's no way we can cross the mountain in a blizzard like this... Hey, you!' – he asked the driver – 'Have there been any avalanches on Mount Krestovaya?'

'No sir' – replied the Ossetian driver – 'But much snow hanging...'.

There were no rooms for travellers at the station, so we were put up for the night in a smoky hut. I invited my travelling companion to drink some tea; I had an iron kettle with me, my one pleasure on my Caucasian travels. One side of the hut was built into the cliff-face; three wet, slippery steps led to its door. I bumped into a cow as I groped in the darkness; these people have cowsheds instead of servants' quarters... I didn't know what to do with myself amid the bleating of sheep and the barking of dogs, but fortunately a dim light, glimmering to one side, led me to another opening which served as a door. Here an engaging scene unfolded: the large hut, its roof supported by two smoke-blackened pillars, was full of people. A little fire crackled in the middle of the floor, its smoke blown back by the wind coming in through the opening in the roof and spreading all around like a thick shroud, so that at first I couldn't see around me.

Two old women sat by the fire with some children and a thin Georgian, all of them dressed in rags. There was nothing else for it but to settle in by the fire, light our pipes and wait for the kettle to give its welcoming whistle.

'These poor people!' – I said to the Captain, indicating our filthy hosts, who looked at us in dumb silence.

'Stupid people, you mean!' – he replied – 'They can't do a thing, would you believe it? You can't teach them anything! Our fine Kabardinians or Chechens may be tramps and thieves, but they're as brave as they come; this lot have no interest in weapons, you'll never see one of them with a decent dagger on him. That's Ossetians for you!'

'Have you spent much time in Chechnya?'

'Yes, I was stationed with my company at a fort near Kamennyi Brod for about ten years... have you heard of it?'

'Yes, I have'.

'Those cut-throats made it hard for us, my friend... they're more peaceful now, thank God! At one time, if you went more than a hundred yards from the ramparts, there'd be some shaggy devil on the lookout... drop your guard for a moment and you'd have a rope around your neck or a bullet in your head... But what fine fellows, eh!'

'You must have had quite a few adventures in your time?' - I asked with genuine curiosity.

'How could I not? I certainly have...!' - the Captain replied.

He began to tug at the whiskers on the left side of his face and lowered his head in thought. I was desperate to drag a story of some kind out of him, a desire common among writers of travel notes.

When the tea was ready, I took two travel glasses from my trunk, poured, and placed one of them in front of him. He took a sip and said again, almost as if to himself:

'I certainly have...!'

I was greatly encouraged by this. I knew that these old veterans of the Caucasus loved to talk, to tell stories, perhaps because they so rarely got the chance to do so... They might spend five years in some God-forsaken outpost without anyone saying so much as a proper 'Hello' (for the Sergeant-Major will only salute). And they have much to talk about: curious, savage people all around; danger every day; marvellous events... it's just a pity more of it isn't written about.

'Would you like some rum in your tea?' - I asked my companion - 'I have some white rum from Tiflis... It's turned cold...'.

'Thank you, but no... I don't drink'.

'How so?'

'I just don't. I made a vow. Once, when I was a Second-Lieutenant, you know, some of us had too much to drink and the alarm sounded at night... We went out onto the parade ground in a very jolly condition and didn't half catch it when Alexei Petrovich found out! God, he was angry! He almost had us court-martialed. That's the way of it: you might go a whole year without seeing anyone... vodka on top of that and you've had it!'

On hearing this, I almost gave up hope.

'Or take the Circassians' - he continued - 'They get drunk on *buza* at a wedding or a funeral... and out come the knives. I had a lucky escape myself once and that was with one of the friendly Chiefs...'.

'What happened?'

'Well' - he filled his pipe, took a long drag, and began to tell his tale - 'It was like this...'

I was stationed at a fortress beyond the river Terek... about five years ago... One autumn a convoy arrived with supplies; a young officer of around twenty-five came with it. He came to see me in full uniform and informed me that he had orders to remain at the fortress. He was very slim, very pale and his uniform looked so new that I guessed he had not been in the Caucasus long. "You've no doubt been posted here from Russia", I asked. "Quite so, Captain, Sir", he replied. I shook his hand and said "Very pleased to meet you, very pleased. You will be a little bored here... but you and I will be on friendly terms: please just call me Maxim Maximych... and, please, there's no need for full uniform... a cap will be fine when you come in to see me". Quarters were found for him and he settled in at the fortress'.

'What was his name?' - I asked Maxim Maximych.

'His name...? His name was Grigorii Alexandrovich Pechorin...'.

'He was a grand fellow, take it from me' - continued Maxim Maximych - 'Only a little strange... For instance, we could spend the whole day out hunting in the cold and rain, everyone else would be tired, chilled to the bone, but not him; another time he'd stay in his room at the slightest puff of wind, convinced he'd caught a cold; or a shutter would rattle and he'd shiver and turn pale... Yet I've seen him go face to face with a wild boar. Sometimes you couldn't get a word out of him for hours on end; at others he'd have you in stitches at his stories. Yes sir, he had many a strange way, although he must have been quite rich... All those expensive little things he had!'

'Was he with you long?' - I went on.

'About a year. But what a memorable year it was! He caused me a lot of trouble, I'm sorry to say! There are just certain people who are destined to have unusual things happen to them!'

'How unusual?' - I exclaimed with curiosity as I poured him some tea.

'I'll tell you... About four miles or so from the fortress there lived a peaceful Chief. He had a son of around fifteen, Azamat, who used to come over to see us; every day he'd come for one thing or another. And Grigorii Alexandrovich and I really spoiled him. The boy was a real cut-throat, ready for anything: he could pick a hat up off the ground at full gallop, he was a great shot with a rifle. There was only one thing wrong with him: he had a terrible weakness for money. Once, as a joke, Grigorii Alexandrovich promised him ten roubles if he'd steal the best goat from his father's herd. And what do you know? The next night the boy came, dragging it along by the horns... Sometimes we'd tease him and he'd see red and reach for his dagger: "Mind you don't cut your own head off, Azamat", I'd say to him. "It'll be *yaman* for you!"

'One day the old Chief himself came to invite us to a wedding. He was marrying off his eldest daughter and, as he and I were *kunaki*, it was impossible to decline, even though he was a Tatar, you know... So we set off. In the mountain village we were met by a pack of barking dogs. The women covered themselves up when they saw us; those whose faces we could see were far from beautiful. "I had a much better opinion of the Circassian women", said Grigorii Alexandrovich. "Just wait!" I replied, grinning. I knew what I was talking about...

'The Chief's hut was already crowded with people. These Asiatics are in the habit of inviting just about anyone to their weddings, you know... They welcomed us with all due ceremony and showed us into the room for guests of honour. I didn't forget to check where they'd put our horses, however, just in case of unforeseen circumstances...'.

'And how do they celebrate a wedding?' – I asked the Captain.

'Oh, in the usual way. First the *Mullah* reads out something from the Koran; then the couple and all their relatives are given presents, they eat, they drink *buza*; then begins the *dzhigitovka*, their trick-riding and knife-play... there's usually some greasy ragamuffin on some poor, lame horse, who takes it all too far, playing the fool to entertain the company. Then, when it gets dark, what we call a "ball" begins in the guest-of-honour room: some poor old man starts to strum a three-stringed... I've forgotten what they call it, but it's like our *balalaika*. The girls and the young men line up in two rows facing one another and clap their hands and sing. Then a girl and a boy go into the middle and sing verses to one another, whatever comes to mind, while the others join in the chorus. Pechorin and I were sitting in the place of honour and the host's younger daughter, a girl of about sixteen, comes up to us and begins to sing to him some kind of... what would you call it?... a compliment'.

'What did she sing, can you remember?'

'Yes, something along the lines of "Fine are our young horsemen, silver threads in their kaftans, but finer is the young Russian officer with his braids of gold. He's like a poplar tree among them... but he will not flourish in our garden". Pechorin got up, bowed to her, and placed his hand first on his brow, then on his heart. He asked me to reply to her; I know their language well, so I translated for him.

'When she had left us, I whispered to Grigorii Alexandrovich: "Well, what do you think?" "Delightful!" he replied. "What's her name?" "They call her Bela", I said. And she really was beautiful: tall, slim, with dark eyes like a mountain chamois, which, it seemed, looked right into our souls. Pechorin was lost in thought and couldn't take his eyes off her; and she frequently shot surreptitious glances at him. But Pechorin was not the only one to admire the beautiful Princess; two other eyes, blazing intently, were looking at her from a corner of the room. I glanced over and recognised my old acquaintance Kazbich. He was one of those, you know, who couldn't quite be called peace-ful, couldn't quite be called an enemy. Many suspected him, although he had never been caught in any mischief. He would sometimes bring sheep to the fortress and sell them cheap; but he would never bargain... you had to pay the price he asked; he wouldn't relent for anything. They say he liked to ride with the mountain guerillas on raids into the Kuban and, to be honest, he did look like a real brigand: he was small, quiet, broad-shouldered... and sharp, as sharp as a tack! His tunic was always tattered and patched-up, but his weapons were mounted in silver... and his horse was famous throughout Kabardinia. You really couldn't imagine anything better than this horse... Every horseman envied him, with good reason, and there were many attempts to steal the horse, but without success. I can still almost see the horse now: black as pitch, legs like wire... and eyes no less beautiful than Bela's. And such strength! He could gallop for thirty or forty miles and still, exhausted, come running to his owner like a dog... Even recognised his voice! Kazbich would never even tie him up... the perfect horse for a brigand!

'That evening Kazbich was gloomier than I had ever seen him and I noticed he was wearing a coat of mail beneath his tunic. "There's a reason for that chain-mail", I thought to myself... "He's up to something". It became rather stuffy in the hut, so I went outside for some fresh air. Night had already fallen on the mountain-tops and the mist was beginning to roll in through the valleys. It occurred to me to look in on the stall where our horses were to see if they had been fed... and you can never be too careful: I myself had a beautiful horse and more than one Kabardinian had looked longingly at her, saying "*Yakshi tkhe, chek yakshi!*"... that is, "Good horse, very good...". As I made my way along the fence I suddenly heard voices. One of them I recognised immediately: that scoundrel Azamat, the son of our host. The other spoke more sharply and more quietly. "What are they talking about?" I thought, "Not my horse, I hope...". I crouched down by the fence and began to listen, trying my best not to miss a word. The sound of singing and talking coming from the hut occasionally drowned out this highly interesting conversation...

"You have a wonderful horse!" - said Azamat - "If I was master of the house and owned three hundred mares, I'd give half of them for your mount, Kazbich!"

"Ah, Kazbich", I thought to myself, recalling the chain-mail.

"Karagyoz?" - replied Kazbich - "You won't find another one like him in the whole of Kabardinia. Once, on the other side of the Terek, I was riding with the mountain guerrillas, going to steal Russian horses; we had no luck and went our separate ways. Four Cossacks came after me; I could hear the infidels shouting behind me and there was a thick forest ahead. I lay down in the saddle, entrusted myself to Allah, and, for the first time in my life, insulted my horse with a crack of the whip. He flew like a bird between the branches; sharp needles tore at my clothes, branches of dead elm trees hitting my face. My steed jumped through the tree stumps, charged through bushes. It would have made more sense to leave him at the edge of the forest and hide, but I couldn't part with him... and the Prophet rewarded me! A few bullets whistled over my head; I could hear the Cossacks running after me... Suddenly a deep ravine opened up in front of me; my horse thought for a moment... and jumped! His hind hooves slid off the far bank of the ravine and he was left hanging there by his forelegs... I let go of the reins and fell into the ravine; this saved my steed and he leapt up onto the bank. The Cossacks saw all this, but they didn't go down into the ravine to look for me: they probably thought I'd been killed. I could hear them trying to catch my steed. My heart bled. I crawled through the thick grass at the edge of the ravine and looked out: the forest came to an end and the Cossacks came riding out onto a meadow. Just then, my Karagyoz came galloping out of the forest straight towards them. They all went after him, shouting, chasing him for a long time; one of them almost managed once or twice to throw a rope around his neck... I trembled, lowered my eyes, and began to pray. A few moments later, I raised my eyes... and there was my Karagyoz, flying across the ground, his tail in the air, as free as the wind... while the Infidels trailed in the distance, one after the other, on their exhausted horses! Allah be my witness, that's the truth, the absolute truth! I sat in my ravine until late at night. Suddenly, what do you think, Azamat, what do I hear in the gloom? I hear my steed running along the edge of the ravine, neighing, snorting, and stamping his hooves on the ground; I recognised the voice of my Karagyoz... it was him, my dear comrade! We've never parted since that day...".

'I could hear him running his hand along the smooth neck of his horse, calling him various affectionate names.

"If I had a thousand mares" – said Azamat – "I'd give them all for your Karagyoz!"

"*Yok*, I don't want them" – Kazbich replied, unmoved.

"Listen, Kazbich" – said Azamat, trying to endear himself – "You're a good man, a brave horseman, but my father is afraid of the Russians and won't let me out into the hills; give me your horse and I'll do anything you want me to... I'll steal my father's best weapons for you, his rifle or his sabre, whatever you want... his sabre is a genuine *gurda*: just lay it on your arm and it will cut into the flesh by itself... your chain-mail would be no use at all".

Kazbich said nothing.

"The first time I saw your steed" – Azamat went on – "As he pranced and spun beneath you, flaring his nostrils, flinty sparks flying out from his hooves, something inexplicable happened in my soul... and everything has disgusted me ever since. I look at my father's best horses with contempt and am ashamed to be seen riding them. Melancholy has taken hold of me; I've spent days sitting on the cliff-top, melancholy, your black horse constantly in my mind, his graceful step, his smooth back, straight as an arrow. He'd look at me with his eager eyes as if he wanted to tell me something... Kazbich, I'll die if you won't sell him to me!" – said Azamat, his voice shaking.

'I heard him begin to cry, although, I must tell you, Azamat was a tough boy and nothing could make him cry, even when he was younger. In reply to his tears I could hear something close to laughter.

"Listen!" – said Azamat in a firm voice – "I'll do anything... If you want, I'll steal my own sister for you? How she dances! How she sings! And her wonderful gold embroidery! Even the Turkish Sultan never had such a wife...! If you want, wait for me in the gorge by the stream tomorrow night: I'll bring her past on the way to the next village... and she'll be yours! Surely Bela is worth giving your horse for?"

Kazbich was silent for a long, long time. At last, instead of replying, he began to sing an old song in a quiet voice:

Our villages are filled with beauties,
Eyes shining like stars in the gloom,
To love them sweet envious fate,
But freedom is sweeter than doom.
Gold may buy many wives,
But a fiery steed has no price,
Of the storm and the steppe unafraid,
Faithful and true, without vice.

Azamat tried to persuade him, but to no avail. He wept, he cajoled, he made promises, until at last Kazbich lost patience and interrupted him.

"Get away from me, you crazy boy! Where would you go on my horse? He'd throw you off after three strides and you'd smash your head on a rock".

"Me?" – Azamat shouted in a frenzy, as the metal of his dagger rang out against Kazbich's chain-mail. A strong arm pushed him away and the fence shook as he crashed into it. "Now there'll be some fun", I thought to myself as I slipped into the stable, harnessed the horses, and led them out into the back courtyard.

'Two minutes later all hell broke loose in the hut. This is what happened: Azamat ran in with his tunic torn and said that Kazbich had tried to kill him. Everyone jumped up and grabbed their rifles... and the fun began! Shouts, noise, gunfire... But Kazbich was already on horseback, weaving his way through the crowd and waving his sabre like a demon.

"This is none of our business" – I said to Pechorin, grabbing him by the arm – "Perhaps we'd better get out of here?"

"Let's wait and see how it ends" – he replied.

"It will end badly: these Asiatics are all the same... first the *buza*, then out come the knives...".

We mounted up and galloped off home'.

'But what about Kazbich?' – I asked the Captain impatiently.

'What about him?' – he replied, finishing his tea – 'He got away'.

'Not even wounded?' – I asked.

'God knows! They take some killing, these brigands! I've seen them in action... as many holes in them as a sieve, sabre still swinging...'.

The Captain was silent for a moment, stamped his foot, and went on.

'I'll never forgive myself one thing: the devil alone knows why, but when we got back to the fortress, I told Pechorin everything I'd heard sitting behind that fence... He just laughed, the sly fox... He was up to something'.

CHAPTER TWENTY-TWO

THE KIDNAPPERS

MAXIM MAXIMYCH DRAINED his glass of tea, long since cold, and stared into the dwindling embers. He looked older than when I had first seen him only a few hours ago, the expression on his face torn between an obscure sense of guilt that he had perhaps already said too much and a pitiful admiration for his departed friend.

'And what was he up to?' – I asked, fearing that he would say no more – 'Tell me, please'.

'Well, there's nothing else for it' – he said quietly – 'I've started my story, so I may as well go on...

'Four days later Azamat came to the fortress. As usual, he came in to see Pechorin, who always had something good for him to eat. I was in the room. A conversation began about horses and Pechorin began to praise Kazbich's mount: such a beauty, frisky as a mountain goat; there was, according to him, simply nothing like it in the entire world. The little Tatar's eyes gleamed, although Pechorin seemed not to notice. When I began to talk about something else, he would immediately bring the conversation back to Kazbich's horse. This continued every time Azamat came. After about three weeks I began to notice that Azamat was growing pale and thin, like they do in those novels when in love... Astonishing!

'Well, you see, I later learned the whole story: Grigorii Alexandrovich had teased him to the point where he was ready to drown himself. Once he said to him:

"I see you're mad about that horse, Azamat... but you've as much chance of getting it as you have of seeing the back of your own head! Tell me, what would you give someone in exchange for that horse?"

"Everything he wanted" – replied Azamat.

"In that case, I'll get it for you, but on one condition... Swear that you'll fulfil it".

"I swear... but you must swear, too!"

"Very well! I swear that you will own that horse... but you must bring me your sister Bela in exchange. Karagyoz will be her dowry. I hope the bargain suits you".

Azamat was silent.

"Don't you want to?" – Pechorin asked – "Well, as you wish! I thought you were a man, but you're still a child... still too young to be in the saddle...".

Azamat exploded.

"But what about my father?"

"Is he never away from home?"

"Yes...".

"So you agree?"

"Agreed" - whispered Azamat, pale as death - "But when?"

"The next time Kazbich is here; he's promised to bring a dozen rams... leave the rest to me. And Azamat... don't let me down!"

'And so they arranged it between them... a bad business, to be sure! I told Pechorin this later, but he just replied that a savage Circassian girl should be glad to have such a pleasant husband; because, according to their custom, he would in fact be her husband; and that Kazbich was a brigand who must be punished. Judge for yourself: what could I say in response to that! At that time, however, I didn't know anything about their plan. And so Kazbich duly came and asked if we needed rams or honey; I told him to bring them the next day.

"Azamat!" - cried Grigorii Alexandrovich - "Tomorrow Karagyoz will be in my hands; but you'll never see him unless Bela is here this very night...".

"Very well!" - said Azamat and galloped off to the village.

'In the evening, Grigorii Alexandrovich armed himself and left the fortress. How they managed it, I don't know, but that night both Pechorin and Azamat returned and the sentry could see a woman lying across Azamat's saddle, her hands and feet bound and her head covered by a *yashmak*'.

'But what about the horse?' - I asked the Captain.

'Soon enough...

'Early next morning Kazbich came in with a dozen rams for sale. He tethered his horse to the fence and came in to see me. I treated him to some tea; although he was a brigand, we were *kunaki* all the same. We talked about this and that, until suddenly Kazbich shuddered, the expression on his face changed. He rushed to the window, which, unfortunately for him, opened onto the rear courtyard.

"What's wrong?" - I asked.

"My horse! My horse!" - he shouted, shaking all over.

And in fact I did hear the clatter of hooves.

"No doubt some Cossack" - I said.

"No! *Urus yaman, yaman!*" - he roared as he leapt out the door like a panther.

In two strides he was in the courtyard. The sentry at the fortress gates tried to bar his way with his rifle, but Kazbich leapt over it and set off running along the road... In the distance there was a cloud of dust as Azamat galloped off on the prancing Karagyoz. Kazbich whipped his rifle from its case as he ran and fired, then stood stock still for a moment until he was certain he had missed. He then let out a shriek, dashed his rifle against a rock, smashing it to pieces, and fell to the ground weeping like a child. A crowd of people from the fortress gathered around him, but he didn't notice them at all; they stood there for a while, talking about what had happened, then went back into the fortress. I ordered someone to place the money for the rams alongside him, but he didn't touch it, and lay there face-down as if he was dead. And would you believe it, he lay there like that all night long? It was only the next day that he came into the fortress, asking the name of the thief. The sentry, who had seen Azamat untie the horse and gallop off on it, saw no reason to conceal that fact. On hearing the name, Kazbich's eyes flashed and he set off for the village where Azamat's father lived'.

'And what did the father do?' – I asked.

'Well, that's the whole point... Kazbich didn't find him. The father was away somewhere for a few days; how else could Azamat have managed to carry off his sister? When the father returned, both daughter and son were gone. Azamat was no fool: he knew they'd cut off his head if he were caught. And he hasn't been seen since: he no doubt fell in with a band of mountain guerrillas and is probably lying dead somewhere beyond the Terek or the Kuban... Good riddance!

'I must say, this business caused me no little trouble. As soon as I found out that the Circassian girl was with Pechorin, I put on my epaulettes and sword and went in to see him. He was lying on the bed in the front room, one hand behind his head, the other holding a pipe that had gone out. I noticed immediately that the door to the back room was locked and there was no key in the lock. I coughed and stamped the heels of my boots in the doorway, but he pretended not to hear.

"Lieutenant Pechorin!" – I said in as severe a voice as I could – "Have you not noticed that I've come to see you?"

"Ah, Maxim Maximych, hello!" – he replied – "Would you like to smoke a pipe?"

"Excuse me!" – I went on – "I am not Maxim Maximych... I am 'Sir' to you".

"All the same... would you like some tea? If only you knew how troubled I am".

"I know all about it" – I replied as I approached the bed.

"So much the better; I'm not in the mood to explain".

"Lieutenant Pechorin! You have committed an act for which I may be held responsible...".

"Enough! Why all the fuss? We've always shared everything equally...".

"You think it's funny? Your sword, please!"

"Mitka" – Pechorin called to his servant – "My sword".

Mitka brought in the sword.

'Having fulfilled my duty, I sat down on the edge of the bed and said:

"Listen, Grigorii Alexandrovich, admit it... this is not good...".

"What's not good?" – he replied.

"Why, carrying off Bela like that! That savage Azamat! Come on, admit it..." – I said.

"And what if I like her?" – he insisted.

Well, what can you say to that? I was speechless. Although, after a little silence, I told him that he must hand her over if the father asked for her.

"Not at all!" – said Pechorin.

"And what happens when he finds out she's here?"

"How will he find out?"

I was once again speechless.

"Listen, Maxim Maximych!" - he said, sitting up - "You are a kind man... and if we give that old savage back his daughter, he will only cut her throat or sell her. What's done is done; let's not spoil the party. Leave her with me... and you can hold on to my sword".

"Show her to me" - I said

"She's behind that door. Only I've just tried in vain to see her: she's sitting in the corner, wrapped in a shawl, won't speak and won't look at you. She's as frightened as a wild chamois. I've hired the woman from the tavern: she speaks Tatar and will look after her and get her used to the idea that she's mine... For she will belong to no one but me!" - he added, banging his fist on the table.

Once again I agreed. What else would you have me do? There are certain people with whom you just have to agree...'.

'And what then?' - I asked Maxim Maximych - 'Did he really manage to get her used to the idea? Or did she fade away from homesickness and captivity?'

'But why in mercy's name would she be homesick?' - he replied - 'She could see the very same mountains from the fortress as she could from her village... and these savages need nothing more. And Grigorii Alexandrovich gave her a present every day. At first she would silently refuse them... the woman from the tavern got them and praised them to the heavens! Ach, presents? What won't a woman do for a brightly coloured scrap of rag? But that's another story...

'Grigorii Alexandrovich had a long struggle with her. He even learned to speak Tatar and she began to understand our language. She gradually began looking at him, at first surreptitiously, out of the corner of her eye; but she was still sad and would sing her little songs in a low voice, so that sometimes even I felt sad as I listened in the next room. I'll never forget one scene. I was walking past, glanced in the window, and there was Bela sitting on the ledge by the stove with her head lowered, Grigorii Alexandrovich standing in front of her.

"Listen, my angel" - he said - "You must know that, sooner or later, you will be mine... so why torture me? Do you love some Chechen? If so, I'll let you go home right now".

She made a barely perceptible movement and shook her head.

"Or perhaps" - he continued - "Perhaps I'm completely repellant to you?"

She sighed.

"Or perhaps your religion forbids you from loving me?"

She turned pale, but remained silent.

"Believe me, Allah is the same for all races and, if he allows me to love you, why would he forbid you from repaying my love?"

She looked at him intently as if struck by this new thought; in her eyes there was both distrust and a desire to be convinced. And those eyes! Blazing like hot coals!

"Listen to me, dear, kind Bela" - Pechorin went on - "You see how much I love you; I would give anything to cheer you up; I only want you to be happy. If you go on being sad, I will die... tell me you'll cheer up".

She thought for a moment, her black eyes still looking at him, then smiled tenderly and nodded her head in agreement. He took her hand and tried to persuade her to kiss him. She feebly resisted, repeating "Please, please... No, no".

Pechorin insisted and she trembled and started to cry.

"I am your prisoner" - said Bela - "Your slave. You can force me".

More tears.

'Pechorin struck his fist against his forehead and ran into the other room. I went in to see him. He was pacing grimly back and forth with his arms crossed.

"What is it, old man?" - I asked.

"She's a devil, not a woman!" - he replied - "But I give you my word of honour... she will be mine...".

I shook my head.

"Would you like to bet?" - he said - "This time next week!"

"If you wish" - I replied.

We shook hands and parted.

'First thing next day Pechorin sent a courier to Kizlyar to make various purchases; many and varied Persian cloths were brought, too many to count.

"What do you think, Maxim Maximych?" - he asked as he showed me the presents - "Will the Asiatic beauty be able to resist such an onslaught?"

"You don't know Circassian women" - I replied - "They're quite different from Georgians or Caucasian Tatars, quite different. They have their own rules; they're brought up quite differently".

Pechorin just smiled and began to whistle a march.

'It turned out, however, that I was right: the presents had only half the intended effect. Bela became more affectionate, more trusting... but no more than that. And so Pechorin took the last resort. One morning he ordered his horse to be saddled, dressed in the Circassian style, armed himself, and went in to see her.

"Bela!" - he said - "You know how much I love you. I decided to carry you off because I thought once you got to know me, that you would love me too. I was mistaken... so farewell! Everything I own is yours. If you wish, you can return to your father... You are free. I have wronged you and I must punish myself... Farewell! I am leaving... where to, I do not know... Not for long will I seek a bullet or the blow of a sabre... and then... remember me, forgive me...".

He turned away and offered her his hand in farewell. She didn't take it and remained silent. From where I stood on the other side of the door I could see her face through a crack... and I felt sorry for her. A deathly pallor now covered her beautiful little face. Hearing no answer, Pechorin took a few steps towards the door. He was trembling and, do you know what, I think he really was now capable of doing what he had at first spoken of in jest. God knows, he was that kind of man! But just as he reached the door, Bela leapt up, began to sob, and threw her arms around his neck. And, would you believe it, as I stood on the other side of the door, I too wept? Well, not quite wept, but... well you know what I mean... How stupid!'

The Captain fell silent.

'Yes, I have to admit' – he said after a moment, tugging at his whiskers – 'I was sorry that no woman had ever loved me like that...'.

'And did their happiness last long?' – I asked.

'Yes, she admitted to us that she had dreamt about Pechorin from the day she had first seen him and that no man had ever made such an impression on her... Yes, they were happy!'

'How boring!' – I said without meaning to.

I had in fact expected a tragic end and my hopes had been so suddenly deceived.

'And did the father really not guess she was at the fortress?' – I continued.

'Well, it seems he did suspect... A few days later we found out that the old man had been killed... This is what happened...'.

I was once again rapt with attention.

'I should tell you that Kazbich imagined that Azamat had stolen the horse with the agreement of his father... or at least I think he did. So one day he waited by the roadside a couple of miles from the village. The old man was returning from a fruitless search for his daughter. It was dusk and his men had fallen behind him; he rode slowly, deep in thought. Suddenly, Kazbich leaps out of the bushes like a cat, jumps on the back of the old man's horse, and fells him with a blow of his dagger. Then he grabbed the reins and was gone. Some of the men saw all of this from a hill above and set off in pursuit; but they couldn't catch Kazbich'.

'He made good the loss of his horse and revenged himself in the process?' – I said, trying to elicit the opinion of my companion.

'Of course: according to their ways, he was entirely right' – said the Captain.

I was struck by the capacity of we Russians to adapt ourselves to the customs of the peoples we live among. I don't know if this capacity is deserving of praise or contempt, but it certainly proves an incredible flexibility and the presence of that clear common sense that is able to forgive evil wherever it is seen to be necessary, or wherever its eradication is impossible.

In the meantime, we had finished our tea. The horses, which had been harnessed for some time now, were chilled to the bone. A pale full moon shone in the west, but was about to dive into the black clouds that hung on the farthest peaks like shreds of tattered curtains. We came out of the hut. Contrary to my companion's prediction, the weather had cleared and there was promise of a calm morning. The stars danced in a circle, making wondrous patterns on the distant horizon, before fading one by one as the pale light from the east poured into the vault of the heavens, turning it a deep shade of violet and gradually illuminating the mountain slopes covered in virgin snow. There were great chasms to left and right, black, gloomy, and mysterious, while the fog, coiling and twisting like a snake, climbed down into them along the folds of neighbouring cliffs, as if sensing and fearing the approach of day. All was as quiet in heaven and on earth as in the heart of man during morning prayers. Only the occasional cool easterly wind ruffled the horses' manes, still covered in frost.

We set off on our way. Five feeble nags toiled with our carts up the winding road towards Gud-Gorá, while we walked alongside, placing stones beneath the wheels when the horses no longer had the strength to pull. The road seemed to lead right up to the sky; it continued to rise for as far as the eye could see, eventually disappearing into a cloud that had been resting on the peak of Gud-Gorá since the previous evening, like a black-winged kite awaiting its prey. The snow crunched beneath our feet; the air became so thin that it was painful to breathe; blood kept rushing to our heads. Yet for all this I felt great joy in every fibre of my being. I was strangely happy to be so high above the world... a childish feeling, no doubt, but we can't help becoming like children as we leave the conventions of society behind and come closer to nature. Everything we have accumulated falls away from the soul, which becomes once again what it once was... and will no doubt be again. Anyone who has, like me, wandered through the deserted mountains, intently studying their miraculous outline, greedily drinking in the invigorating air that fills every ravine, will understand my desire to convey, to narrate, to describe these magical scenes...

At last we reached the summit of Gud-Gorá, stopped, and looked around us. A grey cloud hung on the mountain top, its cold breath threatening the coming storm; but in the east, all was so clear and golden that we forgot all about it... even Maxim Maximych. After all, the feeling for the beauty and majesty of nature is a hundred times stronger in the heart of a simple man than it is in rhapsodes such as us, tellers of tales in words and on paper...

'You're no doubt accustomed to these marvellous views?' – I asked him.

'Yes, Sir... you can even get used to the whistle of bullets, that is, you can get used to hiding the pounding of your heart'.

'I've heard, on the contrary, that for certain old soldiers it's music to the ears'.

'Well, yes, if you will, it can even be pleasant... but only because it does make the heart beat faster... Look' – he added, pointing to the east – 'What a place this is!'

And, truly, I am unlikely ever to see such a panorama again: beneath, us lay the Koishaur valley, crossed by the silver threads of the Aragva and another, nameless river, the pale blue mist that drifted through the valley sheltering in the neighbouring gorges from the warming rays of the morning sun. To left and right stretched a range of interlocking mountain peaks, one higher than the next, covered in snow and scrub. In the distance were yet more mountains, no two peaks alike, the snow ablaze with a reddish glow so bright, so cheering, that you felt like you could stay and live here forever. The sun barely showed above a dark blue mountain that only a practiced eye could distinguish from a storm cloud; but my companion paid particular attention to a blood-red streak that lay across the sun.

'I told you!' – he exclaimed – 'Now we'll see some weather; we must hurry, or it will catch up with us on the Krestovaya. Move out!' – he shouted to the drivers.

We put chains on the wheels as a kind of brake to stop them rolling too fast, took the horses by the bridle, and began to descend. There was a sheer cliff to the right and, to the left, a chasm so deep that the entire village of Ossetians who lived at its bottom looked no bigger than a swallow's nest. I shuddered at the thought of some courier, passing this way ten times a year in the dead of night, not enough room for two carts to pass one another, not even bothering to get out of his jolting carriage...

One of our drivers was a Russian peasant from Yaroslavl, the other Ossetian. The Ossetian unharnessed the front pair of horses and was leading them by the bridle as carefully as possible, while our carefree Russian hadn't even got down from his seat. When I suggested to him that he might at least trouble to look after my trunk, because I wasn't too keen on climbing down into the abyss after it, he replied:

'Ach, Master! If God wills, we'll make it, like the others have... We've done this before, you know...'.

And he was right. It's true that we might never have made it, but make it we did; if people would only think about it a little more, they'd realise that life isn't worth worrying about so much...

But perhaps you'd like to hear how Bela's story ended? Well, I cannot make the good Captain tell his story sooner than he did in actual fact. So you must wait or, if you like, turn over a few pages... although I don't advise you to do so, because the crossing of the Krestovaya – or, as the learned Gamba calls it, *le mont St. Christophe* – is worthy of your attention...

And so we descended from Gud-Gorá into the Chertova valley... what a romantic name! You imagine the lair of the evil spirit among inaccessible peaks... but you are wrong: the name doesn't come from the word *chert*, 'devil', but from *chertá*, 'line' or 'boundary' – this was once the border with Georgia. The valley was filled with snowdrifts, which vividly reminded me of Saratov or Tambov and other such delightful parts of our homeland.

'There's the Krestovaya!' – said Maxim Maximych when we reached the valley, pointing at a hill shrouded in snow.

A stone cross glowered on its peak alongside a barely visible track, which is only used when the main road that skirts the mountain is blocked with snow. Our drivers declared that there had not yet been any avalanches and took the lower road in order to spare the horses. At a turn in the road we met five Ossetians who offered us their services. They grabbed hold of the wheels and, with a shout, began to pull and steady our carts. The road was certainly dangerous: above us to the right were great piles of overhanging snow, which looked as though the first gust of wind would bring them crashing down into the pass; the narrow road was also partly covered in snow, which in places gave way beneath our feet, but in others had been turned to ice by a combination of the sun's rays and the night frosts. We progressed with difficulty; the horses stumbled. To the left opened a deep gulch with a stream rushing through it, which sometimes disappeared beneath a crust of ice, then foamed and leapt over the black rocks.

It took us almost two hours to get round the Krestovaya: just over a mile in two hours! In the meantime, the clouds came down and it began to rain, then snow; the wind howled through the pass, whistling like Nightingale the Robber in the old folk-tale, and the stone cross at the top of the hill was soon lost in the fog that rolled in from the east in great banks, each one thicker and more dense than the last...

There is by the way a strange, though widespread story about this cross: it's said that Peter the Great put it there when he was travelling through the Caucasus... but, in the first place, Peter was only ever in Daghestan; and, second, it's inscribed on the cross in large letters that it was erected by order of Yermolov, in the year 1824 to be precise... But the story has become so established, despite the inscription, that it's difficult to know what to believe... particularly when we are so unaccustomed to believe inscriptions...

About three miles of icy cliffs and slushy snow remained down to the station at Kobi. The horses were exhausted and we were chilled to the bone. The blizzard howled more and more furiously, like one of our own, northern storms, only its wild refrain more sad and plaintive. 'You, too, are an exile', I thought to myself. 'You weep for the wide expanse of the steppe, where you might spread your icy wings! Here you're stifled, closed in, like an eagle, crying and beating its wings against the bars of its cage'.

'I don't like it!' - said Maxim Maximych - 'Look... Can't see a thing; nothing but snow and fog. We'll end up over the edge or down some gully if we're not careful; and, lower down, the Baidara is flowing so strong we won't get across... Ach, Asia! Its rivers, its people... you can't rely on any of them!'

The drivers shouted and swore as they whipped the horses, which baulked and snorted, not wanting to take another step for anything on earth, regardless of the eloquence of the whip.

'Your Excellency' - said one of the drivers at last - 'We won't make it to Kobi. Permission to turn off to the left, while we still can; I can make out something on the hillside... some huts, I think. Travellers always stop there in bad weather. They say they'll get us there if you give them a tip' - he added, pointing to the Ossetians.

'I know, brother... I don't need you to tell me!' - said Maxim Maximych - 'Savages! Always on the lookout for the chance of a tip...'.

'Although admit it' - I said - 'we'd be much worse off without them...'.

'Yes, I know' - he murmured - 'but all the same, these guides! They seem to sense where the advantage lies, as if we couldn't find the way without them...'.

So we turned left and somehow, with great difficulty, reached our humble shelter, two huts made of rubble and flat stones, enclosed by a wall of the same materials. The tattered hosts gave us a joyfully warm welcome; I learned later that the government pays their keep on condition that they take in travellers caught in the storm...

'So much the better!' - I said, sitting down by the fire - 'Now you can finish your story about Bela... I'm sure it didn't end there...'.

'And why are you so sure?' - replied Maxim Maximych, with a wink and a sly smile.

'Because it's not in the nature of things: what begins in unusual circumstances must also end unusually...'.

'Well, you're right'.

'I'm glad'.

'It's all very well for you to be glad...' - he said - 'But it makes me sad to recall it...'.

CHAPTER TWENTY-THREE

BELA

'SHE WAS A wonderful girl, Bela! In the end she was like a daughter to me; and she loved me, too. I should say that I have no family of my own: I've heard nothing from my father and mother for a dozen years now and I should have thought to take a wife sooner... it wouldn't be right now. So I was glad to have found someone to spoil...

'She would sing us songs or dance the *lezginka*... and how she danced! I've seen our provincial young ladies, I was even once at the Assembly Rooms in Moscow, some twenty years ago now... but they weren't in the same class. Nothing of the sort! Grigorii Alexandrovich dressed her up like a doll, cherished and pampered her; and it was amazing how much more beautiful she became living with us... the sunburn faded from her face and arms and her cheeks flushed pink. And what a rascal she was, always happy, always teasing me... God forgive her!'

'But what happened when you told her about the death of her father?' - I asked.

'We kept that from her for a long time, until she'd got used to her situation; when we told her, she cried for two days, then forgot about it...

'About four months passed like never before. Grigorii Alexandrovich, as I think I've already said, loved to go hunting; he was always out in the forest after wild boar or goats. Now, however, he rarely went beyond the fortress walls. Soon, though, I could see he was distracted, as he paced around the room, hands behind his back. Then one day he went out hunting without telling anyone; he was gone the whole morning. This happened once, twice, then more and more often... "Not good", I thought to myself. "Something must have happened between them...".

'One morning I went in to see them; I can see it now... Bela was sitting on the bed in a black silk kaftan, so pale and sad that it frightened me.

"Where's Pechorin?" - I asked.

"Out hunting".

"Did he leave this morning?"

She was silent, as if it was difficult for her to speak.

"No, he left yesterday" - she said at last with a heavy sigh.

"You don't think anything's happened to him, do you?"

"I thought about that all day yesterday" - she said through her tears - "I imagined all kinds of horrible things: perhaps he'd been injured by a wild boar, or carried off into the mountains by some Chechen... Now I just think he doesn't love me anymore".

"Oh, my dear, you really couldn't imagine anything worse than that...".

She began to cry, then proudly raised her head, wiped away her tears and went on.

"If he doesn't love me, no one is preventing him from sending me home. I'm not forcing him. If this goes on, I'll leave by myself. I'm not his slave – I'm a princess!"

I tried to talk her round.

"Listen, Bela... You can't expect him to sit around here all day tied to your apron strings; he's a young man, he loves the hunt... let him come and go. Because if you're unhappy, he'll soon get tired of you".

"True, true! I'll be cheerful" – she replied and took up her tambourine and began to sing and dance and leap around me. But not for long; she soon lay down once again on the bed and buried her face in her hands. What could I do with her? I've never had much to do with women, you know... I thought and thought about how to comfort her, but couldn't come up with anything. For a few minutes we both sat in silence... a very unpleasant situation!

At last I said to her:

"We could go for a walk on the ramparts, if you like? The weather is beautiful".

It was September and a really marvellous day, bright and warm; the mountains seemed so very close, right in front of our eyes. We went out and walked back and forth along the ramparts in silence. At last she sat down on the grass and I beside her; it's amusing to recall how I ran after her like a nursemaid.

'Our fortress stood on high ground and the view from the ramparts was beautiful. To one side there was meadowland, broken up by little gullies and leading into a forest, which stretched all the way to the mountain ridge; here and there you could make out smoke and livestock from the mountain villages. To the other, there was a little stream, surrounded by the thick scrub of the stony mountains that lead to the main Caucasus range. We sat there in the corner of a bastion so that we could see in both directions. And then I saw someone on a grey horse riding out of the forest, coming closer and closer, until at last he stopped on the far side of the stream, no more than two hundred yards from us, and began to spin round on his horse like a madman.

"Look, Bela" – I said – "Your eyes are younger than mine... Who's that on horseback? Who's he trying to impress?"

"It's Kazbich!" – she shouted.

"That brigand! Come to make fun of us, has he?"

I looked out and saw that it really was Kazbich, with his dark face, dirty and tattered as always.

"That's my father's horse" – said Bela, seizing me by the arm.

She was shaking like a leaf, her eyes ablaze. "So," I thought to myself, "the brigand blood flows in your veins, too, my darling".

"Come here" – I told the sentry – "Inspect your rifle and take down that fine fellow... there's a silver rouble in it for you".

"Yes, your Honour... only he won't stay still".

"Then order him to..." – I said, laughing.

"Hey, my good man" - the sentry shouted, waving to Kazbich - "Hold still a minute, why are you spinning like a top?"

Kazbich did actually stop and began to listen; he no doubt thought we wanted to parley with him... but nothing of the sort! My grenadier took aim and... crack!... he missed... The moment the powder flashed in the pan, Kazbich had spurred his horse and it took a jump to one side. He now stood up in the stirrups, shouted something in his own language, threatened us with his whip... and was gone.

"You ought to be ashamed of yourself" - I said to the sentry.

"But your Honour! He's gone off to die" - he replied - "You can't kill these damned people in one go!"

Fifteen minutes later, Pechorin got back from the hunt. Bela threw her arms around his neck without a word of complaint or reproach that he had been away so long... Even I was angry with him.

"Now look here" - I said - "Kazbich has just appeared on the other side of the stream and we fired at him. You could easily have run into him... They're a vengeful people, these mountain men: do you really think he hasn't guessed you helped Azamat? And I swear to God he recognised Bela just now. I know he was mad about her a year or so ago, he told me himself; if he'd been able to put together a respectable bride-price, I'm sure he'd have asked for her hand...".

Pechorin thought to himself for a moment.

"Yes" - he said - "We must be more careful... Bela, from now on, you mustn't go out walking on the ramparts".

'That evening, I had a long talk with him. I was sorry his feelings for the poor girl had changed. Not only did he spend half the day hunting, he was cold towards her and rarely showed any affection. I could see she had begun to sicken: her face was drawn, her big eyes had lost their sparkle. Sometimes I would ask her "Why do you sigh, Bela? Are you sad?"... "No!" "Can I get you anything?"... "No!" "Are you missing your family?"... "I have no family". There were days when you couldn't get anything out of her except "yes" and "no".

I began to tell him this.

"Listen, Maxim Maximych" - he replied - "I have an unfortunate character. I don't know if it's my upbringing or if it's just the way God made me; all I know is that, though I may be the cause of unhappiness in others, I'm no less unhappy myself. This may be no comfort to them, but it's a fact. When I was very young, as soon as I left the care of my family, I threw myself into all the pleasures money could buy, but, needless to say, I soon grew tired of such pleasures. I then entered society... and soon became bored of it. I fell in love with society beauties and was loved in return, but their love merely aroused my imagination and my vanity and my heart remained empty. I read and studied, but learning also bored me. I saw that neither fame nor happiness depended on learning in any way, because the happiest people are those who are ignorant; fame is fortune and you have to be crafty in order to get it. So I became bored... Then they sent me to the Caucasus. This has been the happiest time of my life. I hoped that boredom could not survive for long among Chechen bullets, but in vain. After a month, I was so used to the hum of bullets and the proximity of death that I took more notice of the mosquitoes. I became even more bored than before and all but lost hope. When I saw Bela in my quarters for the first time, when I sat her on my lap and kissed her dark curls, I, like a fool, thought she was an angel sent to me by merciful fate. But I was wrong. The love of a native girl is little better than the love of a society lady. The ignorance and simplicity of one are as dull as the coquetry of the other. If you wish, I am still in love with her; I'm grateful to her for certain sweet moments, I'll give my life for her... But she bores me. I don't know if I'm a fool or a scoundrel; but I know that I'm as deserving of pity as she is, perhaps more so... My soul has been ruined by society, my imagination is unquiet, my heart rapacious. Nothing means anything to me. I can just as easily accustom myself to sorrow as to pleasure, my life grows more empty with every passing day. There is one thing left to me: to travel. I'm leaving as soon as I can... but not, God help me, for Europe! I'll go to America, or Arabia, or India... and perhaps I'll die somewhere out on the open road... I'm certain, at least, that this final solace, through storms and on bad roads, will not soon run its course...".

'He spoke like this for a long time and his words are etched in my memory: this was the first time I had heard such things from a man of twenty-five and, God grant, I hope it will be the last. What on earth!

'Tell me, please' - the Captain went on - 'You've spent time in the capital, and recently: do the young people there really all talk like that?'

I replied that were many people who did talk in precisely the same way; and that some of them may even speak the truth; but disenchantment, like all fashions, began in the upper echelons of society, then passed down to the lower orders, until it wore itself out; and that now those who are really disenchanted try to conceal their misfortune at all costs... The Captain didn't grasp these subtleties, shook his head, and said with a sly smile:

'All the same, it was probably the French who introduced the fashion of being bored?'

'No, the English...' - I replied.

'Ah!' - said the Captain - 'So that's it... they always were notorious drunkards!'

At this I recalled a certain Moscow lady who insisted that Byron was nothing more than a drunk. The Captain's remarks were more forgivable, however: in order to stay away from wine, he had naturally convinced himself that all the misfortunes of the world were caused by drunkenness...

Maxim Maximych continued his story.

'Kazbich didn't appear again. But, although I didn't know why, I couldn't get the idea out of my head that he had shown up for a reason and that he was up to something. On one occasion Pechorin tried to persuade me to go hunting with him, but I managed to put him off for a while... what did I care for wild boar! Eventually, though, he managed to drag me along. We took five soldiers and set off early in the morning. We chased around the woods and the bulrushes until about ten... no beasts.

"Hey, let's go back?' – I said – 'Why go on? It's clearly not our day".

But Grigorii Alexandrovich, despite the heat and the fatigue, didn't want to go home empty-handed, that's what he was like: if he wanted something, he had to have it... he was no doubt spoiled by his mother as a child. At last, around mid-day, we came upon an accursed wild boar... Bang! Bang! But no, it got away into the bulrushes. It really wasn't our day! So we rested for a while and then set off for home.

'We rode alongside one another in silence, the reins loose, and had almost reached the fortress, which was just out of sight beyond some bushes. Suddenly, we heard a shot. We looked at one another with the identical thought in mind... We galloped off at full tilt towards where the shot had come from and saw a group of soldiers gathered on the ramparts, pointing out onto the plain below. A horseman flew across the plain at full gallop with something white across his saddle. Pechorin let out a cry as good as any Chechen, took his rifle from its holster, and took off in pursuit... with me after him.

'Luckily, because the hunt had been unsuccessful, our horses weren't exhausted; they tore across the ground beneath us as we came closer and closer with each passing second... At last I recognised Kazbich, but I couldn't make out what he had across the saddle. I came level with Pechorin and said "It's Kazbich!" He looked at me, nodded, and gave his horse a crack of the whip.

'At last we came within a rifle shot of him. Either Kazbich's horse was exhausted or it wasn't as good as ours and, despite all his efforts, was making painful progress. I thought about how, at that moment, Kazbich must have remembered his Karagyoz... I watched as Pechorin took aim with his rifle on the gallop...

"Don't shoot!" – I shouted at him – "Save your ammunition, we can still run him down".

But what can you do with the young? Always losing their heads at the wrong moment... A shot rang out and the bullet caught Kazbich's horse in the hind leg. It managed another ten desperate steps or so, before stumbling and falling to its knees. Kazbich leapt off and we saw that he was carrying in his arms a woman wrapped in a *yashmak*... It was Bela... poor Bela! He shouted something at us in his own language and raised his dagger above her... There was no time to waste: it was my turn to fire without taking aim and I must have got him in the shoulder, because he suddenly dropped his arm... When the smoke had cleared, the wounded horse was lying on the ground with Bela beside her; Kazbich had thrown away his rifle and was scrambling up the cliff face like a cat. I wanted to bring him down but had to reload!

'We leapt down from our horses and ran to Bela. The poor girl was lying quite still, blood pouring from her wound... the villain couldn't even stab her in the heart and be done with, but in the back... the most villainous of blows! She was unconscious. We tore up her *yashmak* and bound the wound as tightly as we could. Pechorin kissed her cold lips, but in vain; nothing could bring her round.

'Pechorin mounted up and I lifted Bela from the ground and sat her in front of him on the saddle; he held her with one arm and we set off for home. After a few minutes of silence, Grigorii Alexandrovich said to me:

"Listen, Maxim Maximych... We'll never get her home alive like this".

"True!" – I replied and we began to drive the horses as fast as we could.

A crowd of people was waiting for us at the fortress gates. We carried Bela carefully to Pechorin's quarters and sent for the doctor, who came despite being drunk. He examined the wound and declared that she wouldn't live for more than a day; but he was wrong...'

'Did she recover?' – I asked the Captain, seizing him by the arm joyfully, despite myself.

'No' – he said – 'The doctor's mistake was that she lived another two days...'.

'But explain to me how Kazbich managed to get hold of her'.

'It was like this: despite Pechorin forbidding her, she left the fortress and went down to the stream. It was very hot, you know, and she sat down on a rock and put her feet in the water. Then Kazbich crept up on her, grabbed her, put his hand over her mouth, and dragged her off into the bushes, where he jumped on his horse... and was gone. Bela managed to shout out, the sentries heard the alarm, fired, but missed... and that's when we arrived'.

'But why did Kazbich want to carry her off?'

'My good fellow, these Circassians are renowned thieves: if it's not tied down, they'll have it... even if they don't need it, they'll still take it... It's not really their fault. And anyway, he had liked her for quite some time...'.

'And did Bela die?'

'Yes, she died. Only she suffered for a long time, and us with her. She recovered consciousness at around ten in the evening. We were sitting by her bed. The moment she opened her eyes, she began to call for Pechorin.

"I'm right here by your side, *dzhanechka* (darling, that is, in our language)" – he replied, holding her hand.

"I'm going to die!" – she said.

We tried to comfort her, told her the doctor had promised absolutely to make her better. She just shook her head and turned her face to the wall... she didn't want to die!

'She became delirious in the night: her head was burning, feverish convulsions sometimes ran through her body; she said unconnected things about her father, her brother. She wanted to go home to the mountains. She also spoke about Pechorin, calling him all sorts of affectionate names, and reproaching him for falling out of love with his *dzhanechka*... He listened in silence, his head in his hands. But all this time I hadn't noticed a single tear in his eyes. Whether he was incapable of crying or he had managed to control himself, I don't know. For myself, I've never seen anything more pitiful in my entire life.

'Towards morning the fever passed. For an hour or so she lay still and pale, so weak you could hardly tell if she was breathing. Then she got a little better and began to speak... and can you imagine about what? Such thoughts can only occur to someone who is dying! She began to regret that she wasn't a Christian and that her soul would never meet Grigorii Alexandrovich's soul on the other side: another woman would be his partner in paradise. It occurred to me that I might christen her before she died. I suggested this to her and she looked at me uncertainly, unable for some time to say a word; then at last she replied that she would die in the same faith in which she had been born.

'The entire day passed like this. And what a change came over her in the course of that day! Her cheeks became sunken and pale; her eyes grew larger; her lips burned. She felt a great heat inside, as if a hot iron lay on her breast.

'The second night came. We didn't close our eyes or leave her bedside. She suffered terribly, groaning, and, when the pain subsided, trying to convince Grigorii Alexandrovich that she was better, that he should go to bed, all the while kissing his hand and never letting it out of her own. Just before dawn she began to feel the call of death, tossing and turning so that her bandages came loose and the blood once again began to flow. When we had re-dressed the wound, she became calm for a minute or so and asked Pechorin to kiss her. He got down on his knees at the side of the bed, lifted her head from the pillow, and pressed his mouth to her cold lips. Her shaking arms held him tight around the neck, as if with this kiss she was trying to pass her soul to him...

'No, she was right to die... What would have become of her if Grigorii Alexandrovich had left her? And that's what would have happened, sooner or later...

'For the first half of the next day she was calm, silent, and obedient, no matter how much the doctor tormented her with his poultices and potions.

"Look here" – I said to him – "You yourself say that she won't survive, so why all the medications?"

"It's better this way, Maxim Maximych" – he replied – "So that my conscience is clear".

Conscience!

'In the afternoon she was seized by a terrible thirst. We opened the windows, but it was hotter outside than in the room. We brought ice in by the bedside, but nothing helped. I knew that this unquenchable thirst was a sign that the end was near and said this to Pechorin.

"Water, water!" – she said in a breaking voice, sitting up in bed.

Pechorin was as white as a sheet. He picked up a glass, poured, and gave it to her. I covered my eyes with my hands and began to say a prayer, although I don't remember which one... Yes sir, I've seen a lot, watched people die in hospitals and on the battlefield, but not this... not this! I should also confess that something else makes me sad: she never once remembered me before she died, although I loved her like a father... Well, God forgive her! And, if I'm honest, who am I that anyone should think of me on their deathbed?

'As soon as she drank the water she felt better, but two or three minutes later she passed. We put a mirror to her lips - nothing! I took Pechorin out of the room and we went out onto the ramparts. We walked back and forth for some time without saying a word, hands behind our backs. There was no particular expression on his face, which annoyed me; in his place, I would have died of grief. At last, he sat down on the ground in the shade and began to draw something in the sand with a stick. I wanted to console him, you know, more out of decency than anything else, and began to say something; but he just raised his head and started to laugh... That laughter sent cold shivers down my spine... I left to arrange a coffin.

'I confess I did this partly to distract myself. I had a piece of Persian silk which I used to line the coffin. I decorated it with some silver Circassian lace that Grigorii Alexandrovich had bought for her.

'We buried her early the next day beyond the fortress walls, by the stream, at the place where she had last sat. White acacia and elder have grown around her grave. I wanted to put a cross on it, but, well, it wasn't quite right... she wasn't a Christian, after all...'.

'But what about Pechorin?' - I asked.

'Pechorin was ill for some time, lost weight, the poor fellow. But we never once spoke about Bela. I saw that it would be unpleasant for him... and what would be the point? About three months later he was posted to the Nizhegorodsky Regiment and he set off for Georgia; I haven't seen him since, but I seem to recall that someone told me recently he'd returned to Russia... although there's no mention of it in divisional orders. But the likes of us are always the last to know'.

Here he launched into a lengthy disquisition on how unpleasant it is to hear news a year late... no doubt in order to subdue his sad memories. I didn't interrupt him, but nor did I listen.

An hour later we were able to leave. The storm had passed, the sky had cleared, and we set off. When we were on the road, I couldn't resist returning to the story of Bela and Pechorin.

'Did you ever hear what became of Kazbich?' - I asked.

'Kazbich? No, I don't know... I've heard there's a desperado in a red *beshmet* by the name of Kazbich among the Shapsugs on our western front, who rides slowly under our rifle fire, bowing courteously whenever one of our bullets whistles close by him... but it can hardly be the same one'.

Maxim Maximovych and I parted ways at Kobi. I left on the post-coach, but he couldn't come with me because of his heavy baggage. We had no thought of ever meeting again; but in fact we did meet again and, if you like, I'll tell you the whole story...

But don't you think Maxim Maximych is deserving of respect? If you do, then I will have been amply rewarded for my perhaps too lengthy tale.

CHAPTER TWENTY-FOUR

THE FATALIST

THE LAST FEW weeks at the fortress were for Pechorin a kind of living death. Apart from the hunt, in which he progressively lost interest, there was little to be done but sit on the ramparts taking pot-shots at unsuspecting passing riders. After a few weeks there were no targets at which to aim, the news of Pechorin's erratic behaviour having circulated widely among the local population.

Pechorin and Maxim Maximych barely spoke. The old man gave no outward sign of reproach for what had happened, but Pechorin knew in his heart that he blamed him for the loss of the girl he had come to regard as a daughter. And Maxim Maximych, to be sure, would have no other daughters.

His target practice curtailed, Pechorin lost the habit of dressing and emerging from his quarters. He had brought with him from Pyatigorsk a copy of Henry Brunton's Tatar-Turkish Bible, which he had acquired at Karras, better known as *Shotlandka* for the rattle-taggle band of Presbyterian missionaries who had founded it in the seventeenth century. Pechorin found it darkly amusing that the text he now used to improve his Tatar, sometimes translating the verses from St John and St Paul scribbled into the notebook Lazarev had given him, like a schoolboy cloistering in preparation for an examination, was reviled by those for whom it was intended. The book itself, however, was pleasingly handsome, bound in dark leather, an intended object of reverence and desire for the heathen population. What, Pechorin wondered to himself, could have become of the remaining two thousand nine hundred and ninety-nine copies of Brunton's ambitious print run? He tried to imagine them in the hands of now pious mountain men, their heads bowed, surrounded by their wives and children at Sunday prayers; but such scenes soon gave way to the image of a burning book, women and children fleeing the chaos of a settlement razed to the ground.

One morning, some six weeks after the death of Bela, Maxim Maximych, his reproach slowly giving way to concern that Pechorin himself might follow his departed daughter, tried to persuade his gloomy young companion to go out hunting for wild boar. Pechorin declined and Maxim Maximych departed with a company of men.

'We'll be gone for two days' – said the old man – 'In other circumstances, I'd leave a sentry on the ramparts, but... well, you've seen to that, I suppose...'.

Pechorin was alone. He sat by the window. The grey clouds came right down to the foothills of the mountains. The sun looked like a yellow stain through the mist. It was cold; the wind whistled and shook the shutters. And he was bored. He decided to continue his journal, which had been curtailed by so many strange events...

As he re-read the last page he had written, he could only laugh... On that ledge, facing Grushnitsky, he had thought he was going to die. But that wasn't possible; he had not yet drained the cup of suffering. He now felt as though he would live for a very long time... Everything that happened was clearly and precisely inscribed in his memory. Not a single detail or nuance had been erased by time...

Pechorin wrote through the day and night, recounting, indeed, every detail and nuance of his last few days in the magnificent foothills of Mashuk, his latest encounter with death, his doleful conversations with Princess Mary and her mother, and his silent departure at dawn. As his recollection approached his present circumstances, however, he grew suddenly tired and put down his pen. The story of Bela he would not tell. He would submit for judgement his actions in St Petersburg, in Kislovodsk, in Taman and Gelendzhik... even in Peschanokopskoye; but for his actions towards Bela he would submit only to the judgement of God.

He thought of Vera, of how to love for a time was not worth the trouble and cares it brought... but to love eternally was impossible. An empty, ridiculous joke. He was the author of his own suffering. Fate had twice offered him the joys of mutual love, twice he had refused them. To repudiate fate was one thing, but to provoke the love of a pure and untouched soul, only then to destroy it, was a sin for which no expiation could be sought. And now, here in this dull fortress, as he ran through thoughts of the past, he asked himself: why had he not wanted to go down the path fate had opened for him, a path to quiet joys and spiritual peace? No, he could not have settled for such a fate! He was like a sailor, born and raised on the deck of a pirate brig, his soul forged by battles and storms, so that if he is cast ashore, he languishes, bored, no matter how tempting the shaded glade, no matter how bright the peaceful sunshine. He walks alone all day on the sandy shore, listening to the constant murmur of the breaking waves, staring into the foggy distance, hoping, somewhere on that blank space between the blue depths and the grey clouds, to catch a glimpse of a sail, which at first looks like a seagull's wing, but gradually becomes distinct from the foaming breakers, steadily making its way to the deserted pier...

When sleep came at last, Pechorin dreamed of an encounter not with God, but with some entity who appeared to him as the Mother of God. She asked him to offer his confession or to plead for his salvation. Pechorin replied calmly, as if speaking to the mother of some lovelorn girl, that he had no need of either.

'I will not pray for the empty soul of a wanderer in an alien land' - he heard himself say - 'But I entrust to you the beautiful soul of an innocent girl. Send down your finest angel to receive it'.

He awoke before the Mother of God could reply. Instead, he imagined he heard Bela's clear and tender voice, like the song of a captive bird. The burden of all doubt had been lifted from his soul, replaced by the certainty of self knowledge and a strange desire to weep. In that instant, all was light and ease.

When Maxim Maximych returned, Pechorin surprised him with a hearty greeting.

'Good hunting?' – he asked.

The old man, although taken aback and still harbouring some unspoken resentment towards Pechorin, was nonetheless keen to embrace this apparent change of heart.

'Oh, so-so' – he replied coolly – 'But perhaps you'll see for yourself next time, eh?'

'Perhaps I will' – Pechorin replied – 'Perhaps I will'.

As it turned out, Pechorin and Maxim Maximych would not again share the pleasures of the hunt. Within a few days, Pechorin received orders to report to Vladikavkaz, whence he would join the forces of General Grabbe in Daghestan. They did, however, resume their habit of dining together in the evenings, when Maxim Maximych, despite Pechorin's sincere efforts, would carry the burden of the conversation. On one or two occasions, the old man was on the point of saying something admiringly about Bela, but he caught himself in time, eager not to disturb the balance that had been restored between himself and Pechorin.

Shortly before joining the Nizhegorodsky Regiment, Pechorin spent two weeks in a Cossack outpost on our left flank, where an infantry battalion was stationed, and where, in the evenings, the officers would gather together to play cards. One evening, bored with their game of Boston and having thrown the cards under the table, they sat up late in the quarters of Major Svistonov. The conversation was, unusually, very engaging. They discussed the fact that there were, even in this Christian company, many sympathisers with the Mussulman belief that a man's fate was written in the heavens. Each man told various unusual stories *pro et contra*.

'All of that, gentlemen, proves nothing' – said the old Major – 'Were any of you witness to the strange events with which you support your opinions?'

'No, of course not' – said more than one voice – 'but we heard these stories from reliable sources'.

'What rubbish' – someone said – 'Where are these reliable sources who have seen the list on which the time of our death is written? And if there really is such a thing as predestination, why have we been given the powers of will and reason? Why do we have to account for our actions?'

At that moment one of the officers who had been sitting in a corner got up and slowly walked towards the table, surveying the company with an untroubled gaze. He was, as will be clear from his name, a Serb. The exterior of Lieutenant Vulich corresponded perfectly to his character. He was tall, with a dark complexion, black hair, dark, penetrating eyes, and the large, straight nose that is characteristic of his nation. A sad, cold smile eternally played on his lips. The overall picture was of a very particular creature, someone who was unable to share his thoughts with those fate had determined would be his comrades. He was brave and said very little, but what he did say was to the point. He trusted his spiritual and intimate secrets to no one, hardly drank at all, and never chased after the young Cossack women, whose beauty it is difficult to convey to those who have never seen them. It was said, however, that the Commandant's wife was not indifferent to his expressive eyes, but Vulich would become genuinely angry if anyone mentioned this.

There was only one passion he didn't hide: the passion for gambling. At the green baize Vulich would forget about everything; and usually he would lose. But these persistent misfortunes only made him more determined. Once, on a night mission, he was dealing out the cards on his pillow, and losing badly; shots suddenly rang out, the alarm sounded, and everyone leapt up and ran for their weapons.

'All in!' - shouted Vulich at one of the keenest punters, without getting up.

'A Seven' - came the reply, as the soldier ran away.

Despite the general chaos, Vulich played out the hand, the card was dealt. There was already heavy fire when he appeared in the line, but Vulich was untroubled by bullets and Chechen sabres alike; he was looking for the fortunate punter.

'It was a Seven!' - he shouted when he caught sight of the soldier in the line of riflemen, which had begun to force the enemy out of the forest.

Vulich approached, took out his purse and wallet, and handed them to the fortunate soldier, ignoring his protestations that there was no need to pay. Having fulfilled this unpleasant obligation, Vulich threw himself into the battle, gathering around him a group of soldiers, and to the very end fought ruthlessly against the Chechens.

Now, as Vulich approached the table, the company fell silent in expectation of some original antic.

'Gentlemen!' - said Vulich, his voice quiet, but deeper than the average - 'Gentlemen! Why the pointless arguments? You want proof? I propose that we ourselves test whether a man freely commands his own life, or whether the fatal minute is fixed in advance for all of us... Who's interested?'

'Not me, not me!' - rang out from all sides - 'What a character! What will he think of next?'

Pechorin looked calmly at Major Svistonov, an indefinable smile playing on his lips.

'I propose a bet' - said Pechorin, half in jest.

'On what?' - asked the Major.

'I contend that there is no such thing as predestination' - said Pechorin, throwing twenty gold coins on the table, everything he had in his pocket.

'I'll take the bet' - Vulich replied in a muffled voice - 'Major, you hold the stakes; here's fifteen... would you be so kind as to add the five you owe me?'

'Very well' - said the Major - 'although I confess I don't really understand what's at stake or how you intend to settle the argument...'.

Without saying a word, Vulich went into the Major's quarters; the company followed. He went to the wall on which hung a range of weapons and randomly took down one of the pistols of different calibre. The Major, like everyone else in the room with the exception of Pechorin, still didn't understand, but, when Vulich cocked the pistol and sprinkled some powder into the chamber, people began to shout and grab him by the arm.

'What are you doing? Listen, this is madness!' - they shouted at him.

'Gentlemen' - Vulich said slowly, freeing his hands - 'will any of you put up twenty gold coins in my place?'

Everyone silently stepped away.

He went back into the other room and sat down at the table; again everyone followed him. He signalled for them to sit and they silently obeyed; he had for the moment acquired a mysterious power over them. Pechorin stared intently into his eyes, but Vulich met his inquiring gaze with a calm, still look of his own and his pale lips smiled. Despite his indifference, Pechorin imagined he could see the mark of death on Vulich's pale face. I have noticed, and many old soldiers have confirmed, that often on the face of a man who must die in a few hours there is a kind of strange mark of his inescapable fate, unmistakable to the accustomed eye.

'You are about to die!' - Pechorin said to him.

Vulich turned quickly towards him, but replied slowly and calmly.

'Perhaps so... perhaps not...'.

Then, turning to the Major, he asked:

'Is the pistol loaded?'

The Major, in his confusion, could not properly recall.

'Enough, Vulich!' - someone shouted - 'Of course it's loaded, it was hanging right above the bed, stop joking around!'

'A pretty stupid joke!' - put in another.

'Fifty roubles to five the pistol isn't loaded!' - shouted a third.

New bets were made.

Pechorin was impatient with the long ceremony.

'Listen' - he said - 'either shoot yourself or put the pistol back where you got it and we can all go to bed'.

'Yes' - exclaimed others - 'let's go to bed'.

'Gentlemen, I ask that you stay where you are' - said Vulich, putting the barrel of the pistol to his head.

Everyone turned to stone.

'Pechorin' - Vulich continued - 'Take a card and throw it in the air'.

Pechorin took from the table, as he would later recall, the Ace of Hearts and threw it in the air. Everyone had stopped breathing. With a mixture of fear and an indefinable curiosity, all eyes flitted between the pistol and the fateful Ace, fluttering as it fell slowly through the air. At the precise moment it hit the table, Vulich pulled the trigger... The pistol misfired!

'Thank God!' - they shouted - 'It wasn't loaded...'.

'Let's see, shall we' – said Vulich, and once more cocked the pistol, aiming at a cap hanging above the window. A shot rang out and smoke filled the room. When the smoke had cleared, someone took down the cap; there was a hole right through the middle and the bullet had buried itself deep in the wall. For a few minutes no one could utter a word. Vulich tipped Pechorin's gold coins into his purse.

The company discussed the reasons the pistol hadn't fired the first time; some insisted the chamber had been dirty, others said in a whisper that at first the powder had been damp and that Vulich had added fresh powder between shots. Pechorin insisted, however, that this last suggestion was untrue, because he had not taken his eyes off the pistol the entire time.

'Lucky for you' – he said to Vulich.

'For the first time in my life' – Vulich replied, with a self-satisfied smile – 'That was much better than Bank or Faro'.

'Only a touch more dangerous'.

'So, now do you believe in predestination?'

'I do. Only I can't understand why it seemed to me that you would certainly die just now'.

The same man who had only just calmly aimed a gun at his own head now flared up and became suddenly discomposed.

'That's enough!' – he said, getting up – 'Our bet is over and your remarks are now, it seems to me, quite inappropriate'.

He took his hat and left, which struck Pechorin as strange, and for good reason.

Soon everyone returned to their quarters, giving various accounts of Vulich's extravagance and, no doubt, to a man declaring Pechorin an egoist who would bet against someone who wanted to shoot himself; as if Vulich could not have found a suitable opportunity without him!

Pechorin walked back to his quarters through the empty alleyways of the village. The moon, full and red, as if from the glow of a fire, was coming up from behind the jagged outline of the houses; the stars shone quietly in the dark blue vault of the sky. Pechorin recalled with a smile how ridiculous it was that wise people had once thought that heavenly bodies played a role in our miserable arguments over a scrap of land or for some imaginary rights! And for what? These lights, which they thought had been lit to illuminate their battles and their triumphs, burn as brilliantly as ever, while their hopes and passions have, like them, long ago been extinguished, like a fire lit at the edge of the forest by a carefree wanderer. Yet what strength of will came with this certainty that the entire heavens, with all its countless inhabitants, looked down on them with sympathy, silent but immutable! And we, their pitiful descendants, wandering the earth without conviction or pride, without pleasure or terror, save for the unbidden fear that grips the heart at the thought of our inevitable demise... We are no longer capable of great sacrifices, for the good of mankind or for our own personal happiness, because we know the impossibility of both and move indifferently from one doubt to the next, just as our ancestors lurched from one error to the next; but we, unlike them, are without hope or even that indistinct but no less sincere satisfaction the soul encounters in each battle, with people or with fate...

Many such thoughts coursed through Pechorin's mind, although he tried not to dwell on them; he didn't like to brood on abstract thoughts. Where does that get you? Pechorin had been, in his early youth, a dreamer, who loved to dwell fondly on the sometimes gloomy, sometimes radiant images produced for him by his restless, greedy imagination. But what did that get him? Nothing but the fatigue that follows the battle with an apparition that comes in the night, nothing but vague recollections, filled with regret. In this senseless battle he had expended all the fire in his soul and the persistence of his will, both necessary for an authentic life. He had embarked on this life having already lived it in thought and had therefore become bored and repelled, like someone reading a poor imitation of a long familiar book.

The events of the evening had made a profound impression on Pechorin, setting his nerves quite on edge. I don't know even today if I believe in predestination or not, but on that evening Pechorin believed in it entirely: the proof was clear and, despite having ridiculed our ancestors and their obliging astrology, he had unwittingly fallen into that way of thinking. But Pechorin managed to stop himself on this dangerous path just in time and, holding to the rule that one should deny nothing outright nor believe blindly in anything, he cast metaphysics to one side and began to look at the ground beneath his feet. Such precaution was timely, as he almost fell over something soft and thick, although not, it would appear, alive. He leaned over – the full moon was shining right on the road – and... what was that? Before him lay a pig that had been chopped in two by a sword...

Pechorin had barely time to take a closer look when he heard the sound of footsteps. Two Cossacks came running out of an alleyway and one of them asked if he had seen a drunken Cossack chasing after a pig. Pechorin declared that he hadn't seen the Cossack and pointed to the unfortunate victim of his fierce courage.

'Brigand!' – said the other Cossack – 'Gets drunk on *chikhir* and wants to slaughter anything that crosses his path. We had better go after him, Yeremeyich, we'll have to tie him up, otherwise...'.

They moved off and Pechorin continued on his way with greater caution, eventually making it back safely to his quarters.

He was lodging with an old Cossack sergeant, whom he liked for his kindness and, especially, for his pretty daughter, Nastya. She was waiting for Pechorin by the gate as usual, wrapped in a fur coat, her sweet lips, slightly blue in the evening cold, lit up by the moon. She smiled when she saw him, but Pechorin wasn't in the mood.

'Goodnight, Nastya' – he said as he walked past.

Nastya wanted to say something in reply, but could only sigh. Pechorin locked the door of the room behind him, lit a candle, and threw himself on the bed; but sleep on this occasion made him wait longer than usual. It was already growing light in the east when he fell asleep. But it was clearly written in the stars that Pechorin was not destined to get much sleep that night.

At four in the morning two fists knocked on his window.

'Get up! Get dressed!' – shouted a number of voices.

Pechorin dressed quickly and went out.

'Do you know what has happened?' – three officers asked in a single voice. They were as pale as death.

'What?'

'Vulich is dead'.

Pechorin was thunderstruck.

'Dead' – they continued – 'Let's go'.

'Where to?'

'You'll find out on the way'.

They set off and the officers told Pechorin everything that had happened, mixed with remarks about the strange predestination that had saved Vulich from certain death only a half hour before death finally came.

Vulich had been walking alone on a dark street. The drunken Cossack who had slaughtered the pig had run into him and might have walked straight past without noticing, had Vulich, stopping suddenly, not asked:

'Who are you looking for, brother?'

'For you!' – the Cossack replied, and struck Vulich with the sword, cleaving him from the shoulder almost down to his heart.

At that moment, the two Cossacks who were looking for the murderer appeared and lifted up the wounded Vulich, but he was already breathing his last and could utter only three words:

'He was right!'

Pechorin alone understood the dark significance of these words. They were about him. He had unwittingly foretold the poor man's fate. Pechorin's instinct had not deceived him: he had accurately read in Vulich's altered face the mark of his impending death.

The murderer had locked himself into an empty hut at the edge of the village, to which they now headed. A crowd of weeping women were running in the same direction. From time to time a Cossack would run into the street, hurriedly strap on his sabre, and run on ahead. The confusion was terrible. When they eventually arrived, Pechorin saw that the crowd had surrounded the hut, the doors and shutters locked from the inside. The officers and Cossacks were deep in heated conversation; the women howled and wailed their condemnation. Among them was the expressive face of an old woman, lost in frantic despair. She was sitting on a thick log, her elbows on her knees and her head in her hands; this was the murderer's mother. Every so often her lips moved, but it was not clear if they whispered a prayer or a curse.

Meanwhile, they had to decide how best to seize the criminal, although no one could pluck up the courage to go first. Pechorin approached the window and looked through a crack in the shutter. The murderer lay on the floor, pale-faced, with a pistol in his right hand; beside him lay the bloody sword. His expressive eyes darted around the room in terror as he shuddered and clasped his head, as if dimly recalling the events of the night before. There was no great resolve in his troubled gaze and Pechorin assured Major Svistonov there was no reason to delay the command to break down the door and send in the Cossacks; it was better to act right away than to wait until he had fully recovered his senses.

At that moment an old Cossack Captain went up to the door and called to the murderer by name; he answered.

'You have sinned, Yefimych' - said the Captain - 'You have no choice but to surrender'.

'I won't surrender!' - shouted the murderer.

'Fear God. You're not some godless Chechen, you're an honest Christian. If you've been misled by sin, then there is nothing to be done; you can't escape your fate'.

'I won't surrender!' - shouted the murderer in a threatening voice.

The sound of a pistol being cocked could be heard.

'Mother' - the Captain said to the old woman - 'speak to your son, he might listen to you... He is only angering God; and these gentlemen have been waiting for two hours now'.

The old woman stared back at him and shook her head.

'Vasilii Petrovich' - said the Captain, approaching the Major - 'he won't give himself up; I know him. And if we break down the door, he'll kill many of our own. Why not just give the order to shoot? There's a wide crack in one of the shutters'.

At this a strange thought flickered in Pechorin's mind; like Vulich, he decided to test his fate.

'Wait' - he said to the Major - 'I'll take him alive'.

Pechorin ordered the Captain to talk to the murderer, positioned three Cossacks by the door, ready to break it in and come to his aid at an arranged signal, circled the hut, and at last approached the fatal window. His heart pounded in his chest.

'Curse you!' - the Captain shouted to the murderer - 'Do you think you can make fools of us? Do you think we won't get the better of you?'

He began to bang on the door as hard as he could, while Pechorin, his eye to the crack in the shutter, observed the movements of the murderer, who was not expecting an attack to come from this side. Suddenly, Pechorin tore off the shutter and threw himself head first through the window. A shot flew right past his ear, the bullet ripping the epaulette from his shoulder. The smoke filling the room prevented his opponent from finding the sword that had lain by his side. Pechorin was able to grab him by the arms, the

Cossacks burst in, and in three minutes the criminal had been bound and taken away in convoy. The people dispersed. The officers excitedly congratulated Pechorin – as well they might.

Who, after all this, would not become a fatalist? Who, indeed, knows for certain if he believes in something or not? And how often do we mistake for conviction mere illusion or a failure of reason? I prefer to doubt everything. This attitude does not detract from decisiveness of character; on the contrary, I for myself am more inclined to step forward boldly when I don't know what awaits me. The worst that can happen is death; and death is inescapable.

When Pechorin got back to the fortress, he told Maxim Maximych everything that had happened and to which he had been witness and asked his opinion on predestination. At first, Maxim Maximych didn't recognise the word, but Pechorin explained as best as he could, at which Maxim Maximych said, with a meaningful shake of the head:

'Well of course! An interesting business... These Asiatic triggers quite often misfire if they haven't been oiled properly or if you don't press hard enough. I don't like these Circassian rifles, either, they're somehow just not right for us: the butt is so short you'll get your nose burnt if you're not careful... Their swords, though... they really are something!'

He thought for a moment, then added:

'It's a shame for that poor fellow, all the same... Only the Devil himself can have made him talk to drunks after dark! Still, if that is what fate had in store for him...'.

Pechorin couldn't get another word out of Maxim Maximych, who really did not care for such metaphysical conversations.

CHAPTER TWENTY-FIVE

FORTRESS SUDDEN

PECHORIN SPENT A few brief days in Vladikavkaz before at last joining the Nizhegorodsky Regiment at the fortress Yermolov had named 'Vnezapnaya', although Fortress 'Sudden' seemed to Pechorin, as he dismounted in the gathering dusk, little more than an ill-advised provocation of fate. He left his exhausted horse with the farrier and was about to make his way to Staff HQ when his gloomy reverie was disturbed by a clear, familiar voice.

'Bow down thy snowy head, O Caucasus!' - the voice rang out - 'Submit: Pechorin comes'.

Pechorin turned in the direction from which the voice had come to see the neat figure of Lev Pushkin beaming through the gloom, accompanied by two officers Pechorin didn't recognise; and by a third he very much did.

'My dear uncle Mungo' - Pechorin said brightly - 'It's about time'.

When Pechorin had quartered and washed away the dirt of the road, he joined Mungo and Pushkin in the quarters of Lieutenant Trubetskoi, who, along with Captain Voronin, he had seen, but not recognised, in the yard. Mungo had known Sergei Vasilevich Trubetskoi in St Petersburg, where the slightly younger man had acquired a scabrous reputation for juvenile, if nonetheless daring, escapades at the expense, most commonly, of the ladies of our capital: on one occasion, learning that Countess Bobrinskaya and guests from the Imperial Court would be spending an afternoon boating on the Black River, Trubetskoi and his comrades from the Cavalry Guards had approached from the opposite direction, all dressed in black, on a punt replete with flaming torches and an empty teak coffin. The renowned life and soul of every company had then astonished St Petersburg society by marrying, at the tender age of twenty-two, one of the young ladies who attended the Empress; society was no less astonished when that doomed union ended in divorce after only three months and Trubetskoi, through boredom or shame, volunteered for service in the Caucasus. Trubetskoi was no less striking than Mungo, with glistening chestnut hair and refined, intelligent features, which yet did not detract at all from his unobtrusive masculinity; and, true to the letters of recommendation from General Grabbe and none other than Yermolov himself, his youthful reputation was soon eclipsed by the bravery with which he threw himself into every encounter with the enemy.

Trubetskoi was rarely to be seen at Vnezapnaya without the company of both Mungo and Lev Pushkin; but no one could recall a single instance when he was seen without Voronin, his constant companion and, in all but uniform, his opposite in every way. No one knew or much cared how old was Vladimir Nikolaevich Voronin; but all knew as certainly as they knew their own fingers that he was old enough to have already entered military service in the fateful year of 1825, disgraced and reduced to the ranks for his albeit inconsequential role in the Decembrist uprising. Pechorin imagined he could see in him a trace of the haunted features of Lazarev, although Voronin otherwise bore no resemblance. The ghost of a ghost, Pechorin thought to himself; or perhaps the ghost of what may come to pass. Voronin was slightly built, exuded a scholarly air, particularly when he donned his spectacles to read whatever book was in his hands, and permanently wore an immobile, gently uncommitted smile, which had the fortunate – if occasionally highly unfortunate – effect of signifying whatever those who beheld it wished it to signify. Even more so than Trubetskoi, he had acquired the reputation not only for astonishing valour in the face of the enemy, but also an unsurpassable ingenuity in the face of danger. Mungo would later recount to Pechorin the story of how the young Voronin, at the rank of Private, had nonetheless rescued the failing siege of Yerevan in 1826 by repositioning the artillery after the death of his commanding officer, all the while under heavy fire from the Turks above. Witnesses to the events swore that Voronin must have been protected by some invisible force as he manoeuvred his slight frame amid the swarming, buzzing hail of bullets. Mungo's excitement in the telling of the tale came to a crescendo as he told, with magnificent indignation, of how Voronin was rewarded only with promotion to Corporal; and his disgust was complete in all its glory as he recounted how the Tsar himself had refused to grant Voronin the Cross of St George after a similar feat during the siege of Kars two years later. For Nikolai, it would seem, political crimes were never to be forgiven or forgotten, no matter the heroism with which they were expiated on the battlefield.

The conversation was amiable, ironic in the manner Pechorin had expected from his previous encounter with Pushkin, but once again, as in Stavropol, curiously diffuse. Whenever Pechorin enquired as to the mood of General Grabbe, who had assumed command at Vnezapnaya a month or so earlier, or asked what lay in store over the coming weeks, Pushkin or Voronin would interject with some witticism about the wisdom of generals or the imprecations of fate. Pechorin looked to Mungo on one or two occasions for some sign of the key that might unlock this playful evasion, but Mungo only flashed a beneficent smile in return.

'So tell me' – Pechorin said at last, his mild impatience cloaked in amiability – 'Have I come all this way to dine in the officers' mess, smoke cigars, and lie in the hay polishing my boots?'

'And what could be so objectionable about that, Grigorii Alexandrovich?' – replied Pushkin, his fair hair burnished in hues of copper from the Caucasian sun – 'I can think of worse ways to pass the time'.

'And I can think of better' – said Pechorin – 'And better locations in which to do it'.

'I can hardly imagine more beautiful surroundings' – said Voronin casually – 'The problem is, the more beautiful they are, the more dangerous they become. I wouldn't be in such a hurry to see the sights, if I were you'.

Pechorin was painfully aware that he was in the company of men who had served, even if only for a year like Mungo, on the Left Front, whereas fate had somehow limited him to the futilities of the Black Sea coast, the absurd comedy of Pyatigorsk and Kislovodsk, and, finally, to the role of hero in a bad exotic novella. He felt for the first time a rising shame at his collapse at the fortress at Gelendzhik, then, in contemplation of the events that had brought him at last within touching distance of an enemy deserving of the name – nothing.

'But we must fight' – Pechorin said at last – 'Mustn't we?'

'Oh, we will fight, my dear Lieutenant Pechorin' – said Trubetskoi – 'But as my dear Captain Voronin has put it so delicately, there is no need here to seek battle. In fact, if I may say, you will very quickly learn to cherish those moments when you are free to smoke a cigar or polish your boots. Battle will find you – and all of us – quite soon enough'.

Pechorin returned to his quarters before eleven, suddenly exhausted from the road. On this occasion, Mungo responded to his glance by taking his leave of his comrades-at-arms and following Pechorin out into the moonless night. Only the bright stars in the deep vault of the heavens lit their way to Pechorin's quarters, suddenly augmented by the flash of a match as Pechorin lit a cigar for himself and Mungo.

'They are fine fellows, Pechorin, are they not?' – said Mungo cheerfully.

Pechorin had noticed that his youthful uncle now wore his hair somewhat longer than he had done in St Petersburg, his sideburns now trimmed almost to nothing, the sharp line of a moustache above his lip emphasizing features that, while no less pleasing, had become more stern to a degree that might have been imperceptible to anyone who had not know Mungo, as Pechorin had, since they were children.

'Indeed they are' – Pechorin replied – 'But tell me, Mungo, why were they so reluctant to say anything about the enemy?'

'Oh, don't be concerned about that' – Mungo replied – 'They were precisely the same with me. Voronin has been in Persia, Turkey, and the Caucasus for longer than he can remember; it is an authentic miracle the man is still alive. And Trubetskoi, although he has been in the Caucasus for only a little longer than I have, appears to be engaged in some lunatic race to catch up with him'.

Pechorin took a draw from his cigar, glanced up at the twinkling heavens, and continued.

'And do you have any notion of why that might be?'

'It's very simple, Pechorin' – said Mungo – 'They have reached the conclusion that valour is not a choice, but a necessity; that a man is more likely to lose his life in these circumstances by seeking to protect it than by exposing it to the vicissitudes of fate; or, at the very least, that if a man's life is to be lost, it must be lost in glory, not in ignominy and cowardice'.

Pechorin took another draw from his cigar but said nothing.

'Therefore' – Mungo continued – 'when the demands of the battlefield are not immediately present, they have acquired the habit of putting them entirely out of their minds'.

'And what about you, my dear Mungo?' – asked Pechorin – 'Have you also managed to acquire this habit in the time since I last saw you?'

Pechorin could see the white of Mungo's smile even in the gathering darkness.

'I have' – he replied – 'But we must always be careful that such demands do not re-assert themselves without warning, while we are busily engaged in their forgetting... don't you think?'

The next morning, after he had reported to a sullen and unresponsive General Grabbe, Pechorin dragged Mungo to the stables, where he hoped, with or without deployment of his remaining funds, to secure for himself a better horse than the clumsy beast upon which he had arrived. The farrier would let him have only a poor Circassian Bay the wrong side of twelve, but Pechorin's gaze was drawn again and again to a sleek black mare perhaps no more than half that age. Pechorin knew she was not Circassian or Arabian and imagined he could detect in the line of her crest something of the English stock occasionally found in St Petersburg. But here, deep in Daghestan, idling in what passed for regimental stables?

'You haven't lost your taste, Pechorin' – said Mungo, smiling knowingly at the silent farrier.

'How much?' – Pechorin asked the farrier.

The shaggy and dishevelled fellow shifted from one foot to the other, but did not reply.

'How much?' – Pechorin repeated.

'You're asking the wrong person, Pechorin' – replied Mungo, relieving the farrier of his misery – 'Perhaps you should ask General Grabbe'.

An hour later, Pechorin and Mungo galloped along the banks of the Aktash River, Mungo astride his fine Circassian Chestnut, Pechorin exulting in the deft poise of his newly acquired black beauty. General Grabbe, yet more sullen than he had been in the early morning, was at first dumbfounded by Pechorin's intrusion, but quickly relented, only too pleased to be allowed to return to his affairs. He had half a dozen horses and cared little for which of them trotted beneath him, even on the rare occasion he was able to ride at all; and he understood that the three hundred and fifty-seven roubles Pechorin had insisted on was not a figure plucked from nowhere: it was all the money the deranged fellow had left. Now, penniless once more, Pechorin dug his heels into the mare's glistening flanks and she accelerated smoothly towards the peaks towering in the distance, the spring sunshine now flooding in above their heads.

The officers were under strict orders to venture no further than the second bend in the river when unaccompanied. When they reached it, Mungo made a circling gesture with his right hand and both riders turned and sped back towards the fortress, before slowing to a trot and stopping under an ancient elm tree almost by the riverbank.

'Does she have a name?' - Mungo asked, gesturing towards the elegant black mare, now drinking at the water's edge.

'I'm going to call her Ballad' - Pechorin replied - 'Much better than the insult she had previously been given...'.

Mungo made no reply, but Pechorin felt again what he had rarely felt since leaving St Petersburg: he knew precisely what Mungo was thinking.

'I'm not surprised Grabbe let you have her' - Mungo said after a long pause.

'Why is that?' - Pechorin asked.

'Well, you will have seen already how preoccupied the man is. In normal circumstances, he would have sent you packing'.

'No doubt' - Pechorin replied - 'Now tell me, my dear uncle: why, apart from the vagaries of war, is our esteemed General Grabbe so preoccupied? He's barely recognisable from the fellow I encountered in Stavropol'.

Mungo looked out over the gently flowing river, picking its narrow course through the exposed white stones within its raised banks.

'This may sound quite foolish, Pechorin' - he replied - 'He is trying to transform the vagaries of war into a slightly more manageable number of variables.'

Pechorin sat up in the warm grass.

'I'm not sure I understand, my dear Mungo' - said Pechorin - 'Are there really so many variables in play? Trubetskoi seemed in no doubt yesterday evening that we will fight...'.

It was Mungo's turn now to feel what he had not felt since the moment they had parted at the Volkovskoe Cemetery: the unutterable pleasure of possessing knowledge at which his nephew could not possibly guess.

'Last night, while you no doubt slept like a baby' - he began - 'we received two scouts from Hadji Murad'.

Pechorin waited for a moment in the expectation that Mungo would continue, then, acknowledging and accepting his uncle's right to take pleasure in the telling of the tale, lay back in the grass with a satisfied smile and closed his eyes.

'Well, go on' - he said in an even tone - 'I'm listening'.

Mungo explained with quiet relish how Hadji Murad had quarrelled with Shamyl. He explained also that the Tsar, frustrated by the limited success of the policy of careful and gradual incursion, cutting down forests and bribing and flattering villages into acquiescence as we go, had been persuaded that bringing Hadji Murad over to our side, arming him and those loyal to him, might prove more expedient in the war with Shamyl. General Grabbe had been entrusted with execution of this plan; his frustration at the detail and delicacy necessary for success – and his agonised uncertainty as to whether Hadji Murad could be trusted – were the causes of his current temper.

'And how did it go?' – Pechorin asked, with a deliberate cheerfulness.

'Oh, well, I think' – Mungo replied, disguising his faint annoyance.

'Come, my dear Mungo' – said Pechorin – 'We know one another too well to play games. I understand that this may be a matter of great importance; but didn't you tell me only last night, in so many words, that there is a time and a place to take matters as seriously as they require?'

Mungo smiled in acknowledgement of the fact that to be understood by someone who had known you long enough to make such understanding possible was indeed a greater pleasure than the flimsy delights of a surplus of knowledge.

'I think Grabbe entertains genuine hopes' – he said, now smiling – 'Shamyl has come closer to unifying the scattered tribes of the Caucasus than anyone before him. Why should we fight, whatever Trubestkoi might have to say about it, if there are those who might fight on our behalf?'

'*Divide et impera*' – said Pechorin in a sonorous, mocking voice, pushing out his chest towards the sunlit heavens.

Pechorin and Mungo joined Pushkin, Trubetskoi, Voronin and a number of other officers in the mess at around seven. Some enterprising fellow at Vnezapnaya had fashioned a still out of an old iron bathtub and something that passed for vodka had been in production almost since the fortress had been built. Trubetskoi handed a filthy glass half full of the clear liquid to Pechorin, followed by a hunk of black bread.

'Don't worry, there will be wine with dinner' – said Trubetskoi, amused at Pechorin's disgust – 'At least, if General Grabbe joins us'.

Pechorin glanced at Mungo, who also had glass and bread in hand, and they threw back the vodka in perfect synchrony, before raising the black bread to their noses, then chewing off a bite to pursue the rough liquid down into their grateful stomachs. Another glass followed after an indecent interval. Yet another would have followed, had not the doors to the mess suddenly flown open to reveal the figure of General Grabbe, resplendent in full uniform, complete with epaulettes and sash, almost filling the doorway in which he stood.

'Gentlemen!' – he cried, with a beaming smile that suggested he too had enjoyed the benefits of a pre-dinner drink – 'Dinner is served!'

Grabbe seated himself at a table long enough for eight or so and gestured to Pushkin and Voronin to join him. Mungo and Trubetskoi followed their comrades, when Grabbe suddenly called out to Pechorin, to whom he had said barely a word that morning.

'Lieutenant Pechorin!' – he cried – 'What are you waiting for? Don't worry, no one's going to send you off digging trenches on the Black Sea coast! We have other plans for you, don't we, Major Pushkin? And bring that vodka with you, eh?'

Pushkin only smiled in response as Pechorin took a seat at the table and poured another half-glass for everyone. Grabbe took up his glass and a piece of black bread and rose to his feet at the head of the table.

'Gentlemen!' – he began – 'A toast! ... To diplomacy!'

With that, he threw back his head, drained his glass, and threw the bread down his throat without bothering to take a sniff. Pechorin once again sought the gaze of Mungo in search of some clue to Grabbe's sudden change in demeanour, but Mungo, like the others, only followed Grabbe's example and drained his own glass.

'Might we assume that the business of the day has gone well?' – Pushkin asked with the same bright smile.

'Indeed it has' – Grabbe replied – 'And not before time'.

'And might we assume therefore that we will soon once again be roaming in the mountains and sleeping under the stars?' – said Trubetskoi, himself now displaying the effects of the vodka.

'That may very well be the case, Lieutenant Trubetskoi' – Grabbe replied – 'But, if things go as I hope they might, you will find you have more time to enjoy the view'.

Pechorin once more shot a glance at Mungo.

'We have lost too many men, too many guns, spent too long cutting down those blasted trees' – Grabbe continued – 'The policy of slow, incremental advance is all very well, but it was predicated entirely on limiting our losses in the process'.

'And what is the alternative? – Pechorin asked suddenly.

Grabbe looked down the length of the table to where Pechorin sat, still toying with his half-full glass.

'Allies' – Grabbe replied – 'We need allies. The northern slopes of the main range of the Caucasus are almost entirely peaceable, inhabited by all manner of peoples who have accepted the authority of His Imperial Majesty and a duty to provision his forces in return for possession of their lands. We must extend this kingdom of pacification throughout Daghestan and Chechnya until we meet again the peaceable tribes beyond the southern slopes'.

'And are allies to be found?' – asked Voronin.

'My dear Captain Voronin' – replied Grabbe – 'You of all men, who has dodged a thousand bullets in the Pashaliks of Turkey and the Khanates of Persia, should know that there are always allies... They just have to be, shall we say, persuaded'.

Before anyone could press Grabbe any further, the door to the mess opened to reveal a dishevelled cook holding a tray laden with whole-roasted chickens, which he thumped down unceremoniously in the middle of the table. He disappeared and immediately returned with another tray of baked potatoes.

'Dinner, at last, is served' – said Grabbe, reaching down for two bottles of Kakheti concealed by the leg of his chair.

When nothing remained of the chicken, the potatoes, and the wine, Grabbe rose unsteadily to his feet.

'Gentlemen' - he began - 'I must bid you goodnight. Tomorrow is not only another day; it may very well be a particularly busy one'.

Grabbe made his way to the door through the scattering of other tables, greeting the men seated at them with studied poise, and slipped unsteadily out into the night. Mungo and Pechorin once more exchanged glances filled with impenetrable significance, but it was Pushkin who broke the silence.

'As I'm sure you understand, Grigorii Alexandrovich' - he said, turning to Pechorin, his smile now extinguished - 'The success of the undertaking to which General Grabbe refers is entirely dependent on discretion. If any word of it were to find its way beyond the fortress walls, we would surely frighten off the bird we seek to catch'.

'I quite understand' - Pechorin replied - 'There's no need to explain. I am not offended by the need for secrecy. There is, however, one thing I don't understand'.

'And what might that be?' - asked Pushkin calmly, intrigued by what Pechorin might wish to know or, more properly, intrigued by what he might admit had eluded him.

'Well, if we are facing an enemy united by their faith, how are we to find among them allies? Surely they will remain our allies only until their huts have been rebuilt and their crops replanted?' - said Pechorin.

'Ah, that depends, my dear Grigorii Alexandrovich' - interrupted Voronin.

'Depends on what?' - replied Pechorin with an open, almost affectionate smile.

'It depends' - continued Voronin - 'upon whether you believe we are fighting a people driven by religious devotion or whether appeal to faith is no more than a means to an end'.

'That end being?' - said Pechorin.

'Why, deliverance from an enemy who could never be accused of religious intolerance' - replied Voronin - 'We have never sought to interfere with the practice of their faith'.

'That may be true, Voronin' - said Pushkin - 'But you must concede that, for us too, such tolerance is no more than a means to an end; and one which, to date, has not been successful'.

'True' - replied Voronin - 'But neither point of view has any bearing on the central fact of the matter'.

'And what is that?' - said Pechorin, now unsmiling.

Voronin took a long draw from the little cigar he had been nursing and extinguished it on the sole of his boot.

'That Shamyl will not be discouraged, with or without his faith' - Voronin replied - 'And that we will find ourselves bogged down in these mountains and valleys for time without end unless he is killed or captured. Neither his faith nor mine will change that'.

Pechorin looked across the table to confirm that not a drop of wine remained, then reached for his still half-full glass of vodka.

'And if he is killed?' - he asked - 'What's to prevent another *Imam* being elected in his place, as has happened twice already?'

Here Trubetskoi, who had been silent throughout, roused himself and answered with a passion that took Pechorin somewhat by surprise.

'If Shamyl is killed' - he said - 'things will return to the way they have always been in these regions. Blood loyalty was always the law. Blood loyalty ensured that different tribes and peoples, though they need not be at war with their neighbour, could not be mobilised in his defence. The Mussulmans have introduced a law higher than blood. He who is *Murshid*, adept in the way of the *Tarikat*, gathers to himself *Murid*, the followers he will lead to enlightenment. The *Imam* stands at the head of the pyramid, invested with the ultimate authority of Allah himself'.

Pechorin was aware as Trubetskoi spoke of a constant communication in glance and gesture between Pushkin and Voronin, neither of whom, however, was disposed to halt the flow of Trubetskoi's speech.

'Our religious tolerance in this context, however Christian we may believe it to be' - Trubetskoi continued - 'is an absurdity. War cannot be waged on Christian principles. We must not only capture or kill Shamyl, we must ensure that the Mussulman faith is entirely eradicated and that no *Imam* arises in succession'.

At this, Pushkin broke off his silent communication with Voronin.

'We have wandered far from our topic of discussion, gentleman' - he said softly - 'Shall we find something more to drink?'

It was almost two in the morning when Pechorin and Mungo returned to their quarters, Pechorin sensing a pleasure in his usually sober mind he only imperfectly recognised, but admitted nonetheless as a pleasure. Mungo, on the contrary, was quite drunk and Pechorin surmised that such a condition was not unknown to him since he had arrived in the Caucasus. Mungo had thrown an arm around Pechorin's shoulder as they made uneven progress across the yard, now illuminated by a brilliant full moon, which had only just made it above the crest of the mountains to the south.

'Let's have a smoke before bed' - Mungo insisted in an amused drawl.

Pechorin took out a pair of small French cigars, lit both, and handed one to Mungo without saying a word.

'What do you think of all that rubbish, Pechorin?' - asked Mungo, the smoke from his cigar billowing from his mouth as he spoke.

'What rubbish, my dear uncle?' - said Pechorin indulgently.

'All that religious nonsense!' - said Mungo - 'What does it matter who we're fighting?'

'Quite so' - Pechorin replied, conscious of the futility of discussing theology or military strategy with someone in Mungo's condition - 'Nevertheless, don't you find it all quite interesting?'

'Interesting?' - cried Mungo, before realising that he had spoken too loudly for the hour of night and placed a mocking finger over his own lips - 'What could you possibly find interesting about it?' - he continued in a whisper.

'Oh, I don't know' - Pechorin replied - 'How one man can follow another, even into the jaws of certain and bloody death. I suppose that's where Allah comes in'.

At that moment, Lev Pushkin, who had come out into the yard for a breath of the cool night air before retiring, caught sight of the two red dots of the cigars and came walking amiably towards them, his features glowing under the full moon.

'Still up?' - he asked with a tired smile.

'Yes' - replied Pechorin - 'I was just asking my dear uncle how one man becomes *Murshid*, while another becomes *Murid*'.

'And I was just asking why anyone would care' - said Mungo with mock indignation.

'You do know what those words mean, my dear Lieutenant Stolypin?' - asked Pushkin.

At this, Mungo's indignation became quite real, matched only by his embarrassment.

'I have no idea' - he said at last, recovering his poise - 'Why would I?'

'*Murshid* means "one who shows"' - said Pushkin, now enjoying himself - '*Murid* means "one who desires"'.

'And what of it?' - replied Mungo, now genuinely annoyed.

'No matter' - Pechorin interrupted, glancing at Pushkin - 'Let's get you to bed, my dear uncle'.

Mungo only grumbled, but did not resist, fatigue now enveloping his drunkenness. Pushkin took his leave and set off across the yard, before stopping after ten paces or so and turning once again to Pechorin.

'Which one are you, Grigorii Alexandrovich?' - he asked, an amiable smile just discernible on his lips.

'How do you mean?' - replied Pechorin.

'Well, are you "one who shows"? Or "one who desires"?'

'Goodnight, Lev Sergeyevich' - said Pechorin, before disappearing through the doorway with Mungo across his shoulders.

Such conversations are not typical of my countrymen, even the most educated and enlightened among them. On the rare occasions on which I have been party to them, I must concede that the views expressed by Trubetskoi have, almost without exception, met with little contradiction; in fact, it is rare even for there to be a place for the kind of ambivalence expressed by Voronin or Pushkin. It may appear paradoxical to a reader who has never had the misfortune to face an enemy whose motivations are quite different from our own that such ambivalence, even on the rare occasions it is heard, tends to come from the mouths of men who have witnessed the ferocity of native resistance over many years. I will not go as far as to commend the view of the English that the *Ghazavat* - the proper term for Holy War - would never have been preached in the Caucasus had we Russians been peaceful and friendly neighbours. I will say, however, that the only good thing I can find to say for war, if the reader will excuse me, is that it leads, if sufficiently prolonged, to an understanding of our enemy that would certainly have prevented us from making him our enemy in the first place.

I had been in the Caucasus for two years before I would entertain any notion that religious conviction was anything more than a tactical means of uniting, however imperfectly, such a variety of races and tribes, each with its own territorial interests. How could I have held any other view? We had laughed in Military College at stories of how the first man to preach the *Ghazavat* in the Caucasus had not been any kind of *Mullah* or *Imam*, but an Italian adventurer named Giovanni Battista Boetti, who had preferred the great adventure of travelling through Cyprus, Turkey, and Palestine as a Dominican missionary to the legal career his father had prepared for him, before appearing transformed as Shaykh-Mansour in Aldy in Chechnya in 1785 to utter that fateful word. Who knows whether Shaykh-Mansour - or Boetti, if you prefer - was a fake? The association of religious devotion and military ardour he bequeathed to the tribes of the Caucasus, we must now concede, was not.

During the time of the first *Imam*, Kazi Mullá, and the second, Hamzad Bek, the *Ghazavat*, if indeed it were taken at all seriously, derived its legitimacy from its association with what the Mussulmans call *Tarikat*, the 'path' that will lead the seeker after Faith from the earthly teachings of the Prophet to the Truth of Allah himself. It was only with the emergence of Shamyl, the third *Imam*, that the peoples of the Caucasus began to accept that, in times of subjugation by the Infidel invader, the *Tarikat* and the *Ghazavat* must be understood as one. For how could a man tread the path to enlightenment with his head bowed under the Infidel yoke? Political and military resistance were necessary preconditions for the practice of religious freedom and indeed for salvation itself. For a time, our certainty that religious devotion was no more than a powerful and convenient call to arms held sway; we believed that our tolerance in matters of religion, which even our enemies do not contest, would clear the path to political and economic mastery. That time came to an end, however, with the emergence of Shamyl, the warrior *Imam*.

CHAPTER TWENTY-SIX

SHAMYL

SHAMYL WAS BORN, like Hamzad Bek before him, in the village of Gimry in Daghestan in the distant year of 1797. An ethnic Avar – the Avars were the most populous of the many tribes of Daghestan – he was given the name Ali at birth; after six years as a sickly and weak child, whose parents feared he might not grow to adulthood, he was renamed Shamyl, 'all-encompassing', one of the hundred and one names of Allah. The lore of the Caucasus holds that from this point the boy grew healthy and strong, by his teenage years a gymnastic prodigy standing over six feet tall, who braved all four seasons alike barefoot and bare-chested, honing his resilience for whatever fate might bring. No man among those serving in the Caucasus, quite apart from the daring and savagery of Shamyl's military exploits they had witnessed at first hand, could fail to be impressed by the tale of how, at the age of fourteen, he had sought to correct the ways of his alcoholic father. Seven times, as the local legend has it, he made his father swear on the Koran to renounce the scourge of vodka; after the seventh relapse, he calmly informed the old man that, at the next insult from one of the villagers on account of his father's drinking, he would stab himself to death before his very eyes. From that moment, the old man, it is said, never had another drink and lived in piety until the end of his days.

This marks the beginning of Shamyl's fanatical – and often brutally unforgiving – insistence on temperance among the *Murid* who would follow him. When Kazi Mullá was *Imam*, he asked Shamyl to deliver forty blows of the rod in public because Kazi Mullá had tasted wine before he understood it to be a sin. Shamyl calmly administered the decreed punishment in front of a crowd of villagers at Gimry, then handed the rod to Kazi Mullá with the request that he subject Shamyl to the same punishment. Just as *Tarikat* and *Ghazavat* were one, so too were moral and physical fortitude.

Shamyl had fought at the Battle of Gimry in 1832 when Kazi Mullá was killed under the relentless attack of none other than Velyaminov. In fact, he was one of only two *Murid* who managed to escape. Eye-witnesses to this day are not believed, although this has not stopped them from recounting the tale of how Shamyl, trapped in a doorway by a line of rifleman, executed a standing leap clean over their heads, cut down three of them with his *kinzhal* as they turned to face him, before the fourth stuck a bayonet in his chest. Undeterred, Shamyl grasped the barrel of the rifle, clove the rifleman almost in two with his *kinzhal*, and pulled the bayonet out of his chest, before escaping half-alive into the forest. Friends and enemies alike exult in tales of how Shamyl was wounded on fifty occasions and left for dead ten times! His followers, because his many dramatic escapes seemed to mark him out as one predestined to carry out the work of Allah upon earth; his enemies, consequently, because this apparent anointment from the heavens marked him out as the prize above all other prizes. The upper echelons of our government and our military, from General Grabbe to Tsar Nikolai himself, fervently hoped that to kill or capture Shamyl would mean an end to resistance in the Caucasus.

After Gimry, Shamyl dragged himself to the mountain *aul* of Untsukul, where he lay for a month near death, the bayonet having passed through one of his lungs. His father-in-law, who practiced medicine insofar as medicine was practiced at all, applied to the wound a balm of wax, tar, and butter, which miraculously restored the fallen warrior to life. When his sister Fatima arrived at Untsukul, carrying with her jewels and silver and gold rescued from Gimry, Shamyl mysteriously relapsed and for two months once more hovered between life and death; he never doubted that the cause was the presence of precious stones and metals, which, according to the superstition of the Avars of Daghestan, exert a maleficent influence on wounds and disease and must never be admitted to the dwelling of the sick.

When he had at last recovered, saved by the practice and knowledge of his people, Shamyl learned that the corpse of Kazi Mullá had been discovered in an attitude of prayer, one hand clutching his beard, while the other pointed to heaven. We had sought quite understandably to make capital of the fact that the *Imam*, the chosen of Allah, had perished at the sword of the Infidel invader. The disbelieving natives were convinced only by the gruesome display of the corpse for four days in the blistering sun, until the signs of decomposition became visible, after which it was taken for burial to Makhachkala. When Shamyl had fully regained his strength, he sent two hundred horsemen under cover of night to exhume the body and return it to Gimry.

The death of Hamzad Bek was no less dramatic for the absence of Shamyl; and it was destined to have far greater influence on the course of future events. From his youth, Hamzad had demonstrated little of the moral fortitude so amply displayed by both Kazi Mullá and Shamyl. When Kazi Mullá's forces failed to overcome the last pocket of resistance to *Murid* rule at Khunzakh in 1829, repelled by the matriarch-Regent Pakhu-Bikhé, Hamzad had harried our forces in desultory fashion, before surrendering on condition of receiving a pension from the Russian Empire. He later failed to relieve Kazi Mullá at Gimry and became *Imam* while Shamyl was recovering from his wounds, presumed by many - and we unfortunate Russian officers chief among them! - to have perished. Hamzad now set about the task of finally bringing Khunzakh, capital of the Avars, under the control of his *Murid* forces.

The mountain stronghold of Khunzakh - built above a precipice almost twice the height of Mount Mashuk! - was ruled by the widow Pakhu-Bikhé, none of her three sons – the last surviving Avar Khans – having yet reached the age of maturity. Hamzad's father had served under Akhmet Khan, Pahku-Bikhé's departed husband, and she had taken the child Hamzad into her own house in honour of his father's service. Pakhu-Bikhé now accepted that resistance to the rise of Muridism was futile and, agreeing to negotiations with Hamzad, sent her eight-year-old son Bulach Khan as a guarantee of her sincerity; such practice was common among the tribes of Daghestan, although I have never been able to persuade a single inhabitant of our capital that the practice itself must not be regarded as a marker of savagery. Pakhu-Bikhé herself understood the importance of this practice so well that she immediately acceded to Hamzad's request that her two remaining sons, Abu-Nutsal Khan and Umma Khan, sixteen and fifteen years old, also join him as an act of trust. Abu-Nutsal was received by Hamzad with all the honours befitting an audience between *Imam* and heir to the Avar Khanate. We may never know whether Hamzad was sincere in his welcome or it was from the outset part of a deliberately planned deception. Whatever his intentions, he was surrounded on all sides by those who insisted that the line of the Avar Khans must be destroyed for all time. As *Imam*, Hamzad's duty to the *Ghazavat* must outweigh his ancient debt to those who dared stand in its way.

That night, struggling with some remnant of filial loyalty, Hamzad was eventually persuaded by the imprecations of none other than Shamyl, who dispassionately insisted that their great cause required the removal of any pretender to authority among the peoples of Daghestan. Hamzad gave the fatal order to shoot the attendants who had escorted Abu-Nutsal and Umma Khan. On hearing the shots, Umma Khan came rushing out of his tent into a hail of bullets. As Hamzad's *Murid* hurried to reload, his elder brother drew his *kinzhal* and, if the legends of the mountains are to be believed, killed as many as twenty of the executioners, before collapsing under blows from the swords of those who remained. Hamzad and his *Murid* forces now took possession of Khunzakh without meeting any resistance, beheaded the unfortunate Pakhu-Bikhé, and declared himself Khan. All resistance to the authority of the *Ghazavat* had been destroyed; the tribes of the Eastern Caucasus, if not united under Hamzad, were at least powerless to refuse his will. The full force of the *Murid* could now be directed towards the Infidel invader.

There was, however, a flaw in Hamzad's treacherous manoeuvrings, which may seem obscure to the inhabitants of our northern cities, but would have been immediately clear to any man born and raised in that wild territory, including Hamzad. Local custom allowed – and, as Trubetskoi had insisted, had once required – the operation of an elaborate system of blood-feud and vengeance. In his early preaching, Shamyl had often emphasized the superiority of the *Sharia* over local custom in that it both allowed just vengeance – and limited its worst effects. He regaled anyone who would listen with extravagant tales of how the theft of a hen three hundred years ago had eventually resulted in the deaths of thousands, most of them entirely innocent. 'And whomsoever shall be slain unjustly', he had thundered in the market square at Aldy, quoting from the Koran, 'we have given his heir power to demand satisfaction, but let him not exceed the bounds of moderation in putting to death the murderer in too cruel a manner, or by revenging his friend's blood on any other than the person who killed him!' I have on occasion offered this in conversation with my fellow countrymen as evidence of the civilizing influence of the Mussulmans in the Caucasus – even on occasion comparing our own less than merciful habits at the inevitably bloody conclusion of some siege! – but I have never once persuaded a single one of them that our own violence oftentimes exceeds even that of those we so comfortably deem savages.

Hadji Murad had fought on the side of the Avar Khans at Khunzakh in 1829, but had long been a follower of Kazi Mullá and, subsequently, Hamzad. Many years before, Hadji Murad's father had been entrusted for a time with the welfare of Abu-Nutsal Khan and Umma Khan, after the death of their own father; Hadji Murad's mother had in fact nursed both children (although she later refused to do the same for the much younger Bulach Khan). According to custom, this made Hadji Murad and his brother Osman half-brothers to the young Khans. Hadji Murad, whose cheerfulness and wide-eyed good nature belied uncommon strength and bravery, had always been suspicious of what he saw as the ruthless fanaticism of Shamyl; he was convinced, perhaps rightly, that a different accommodation with Pakhu-Bikhé and her sons would have been arrived at, were it not for the influence of Shamyl. He also understood, however, that it was not Shamyl who had ordered their execution. An uncle, their father's brother, now approaching the end of a long life, reproached Hadji Murad and Osman not only for having stood by while the Khans perished, but for allowing the death of their half-brothers to go unavenged. It was Osman, whose fiery temper matched the calm of his brother, who resolved that vengeance was not only necessary, but just.

The brothers waited until Shamyl was away from Khunzakh and laid their plans. Osman insisted that, because the avenger must certainly perish in the act, he would strike the blow in the company of a handful of accomplices; Hadji Murad should position himself in such as way as to make the escape of Hamzad and his *Murid* impossible in the event the attempt should fail. Hadji Murad, marvelling at his brother's courage, agreed; on the following day, when Hamzad answered the mid-day call to prayer, the deed would be done. Hamzad was in fact warned that same evening that a plot on his life was afoot, but turned angrily on the informant.

'Can you stop the Angels of Death when they come for my soul? If not, go home and leave me in peace. What is decreed by Allah cannot be avoided: if I am to die tomorrow, tomorrow I shall die'.

The next day, the *Murid* once again insisted that Hamzad take precautions, but he would agree only that no one should be allowed into the mosque wearing a *burka*, in order that weapons could not be concealed. When the *Muezzin* called the Faithful to prayer at mid-day, Hamzad entered the unlit mosque with a dozen *Murid* and knelt to pray. Just at that moment, he noticed to his left a group of worshippers kneeling at prayer dressed, contrary to the prohibition, in *burka*. One of their number, Osman, rose to face the *Imam* and said to his companions:

'Why do you not rise when your great *Imam* comes to pray with you?'

Hamzad looked at Osman and felt a bullet thud into his chest. The *Murid* opened fire as the *Imam* fell dead, killing Osman and many of his accomplices. Hadji Murad rushed into the mosque with a band of loyal men and put the remainder of the *Murid* to death, before pursuing the wretch who had almost ruined their plan to a tower at the edge of the *aul*, where he was locked in and burned alive.

When Shamyl learned of what had happened at Khunzakh, he rode with a band of *Murid* to the *aul* of Gotsatl, where the treasury of the Khanate was located for reasons of security. The young Bulach Khan was also secreted at Gotsatl, in the care of Hamzad's uncle. Shamyl, suspended between the demands of the custom into which he was born, the Faith he had entered, and his ruthless understanding of the political realities of war against a vastly superior invader, ordered the boy to be thrown from a cliff into the Koisu River. From Gotsatl, he rode in cavalcade to Ashiltá and was proclaimed *Imam*.

General Grabbe sat alone in the small room at the entrance to his quarters which served as his office. The despondency and frustration that marked the four weeks since he had arrived at Vnezapnaya had begun to lift with the news that Hadji Murad was prepared to come over to the Russian side. He now impatiently awaited authority from St Petersburg - from the Tsar himself - to grant the forces and munitions Hadji Murad had requested. It remained also, he mused, to make one last attempt to parley with Shamyl himself.

Despite his many successes, harrying and sometimes routing Russian forces when they least expected it, Shamyl had been driven from Khunzakh and had witnessed the total destruction of Ashiltá, including the mosque in which he had been proclaimed *Imam*. Dismayed and enraged by the transformation of the beautiful orchards and vineyards of that fruitful place into a wilderness, he set about the work of making Akhulgó, perched above Ashiltá on two imposing rocks and protected on three sides by the Koisu, a redoubt for his wives and children, his gold and his silver; and an impregnable base from which to continue to take the fight to the Infidel invader.

Grabbe had recruited a father and son from one of the neighbouring villages, who, this very day, he would despatch as scouts to invite Shamyl to a negotiation; to entrust such a task to any of our own men or even to our Cossacks would have been to sentence them to certain death. Even then, Grabbe's plan was to send the men first to the *aul* of Karanai, located on the high plateau on the far bank of the Sulak River, with orders - and payment

– to entrust direct contact with Shamyl to the elders of the village.

When the scouts returned all of five days later, they brought news that the elders of Karanai had made contact with Shamyl, but the *Imam* had declined to make an immediate reply. Grabbe barely managed to contain the urge to take his frustration out on the scouts, brusquely ordering his adjutant to make sure they were fed and rested for the repeat journey that would follow. When they returned a second time, their exhaustion was redeemed by their excitement at bringing their Commander the news he had sought: Shamyl had agreed to a parley by the spring near Karanai in ten days time.

Grabbe's attention was now consumed by two concerns: first, to mobilise a modest expeditionary force to within touching distance of Karanai, a force small enough to move quickly through the forests and over the mountain passes, but large enough to provide security in the event that Shamyl was laying a trap. A second expeditionary force would take the more direct route from north to south, positioning itself above Ashiltá against the eventuality, the likelihood of which Grabbe admitted to himself without distress, that Shamyl could not be persuaded. Grabbe was concerned above all that, in agreeing to the parley, Shamyl was procuring for himself certain knowledge of precisely where Grabbe and his forces would be ten days hence and reasonable certainty as to his movements in the intervening days. Second, he must maintain communication with Hadji Murad throughout, giving the impression that negotiations – and the business of receiving authority from St Petersburg – were inevitably taking some time. At least, he reassured himself, Hadji Murad was not liable to impute anything too concerning to the mobilisation of Grabbe's expeditionary force, knowledge of which could not be kept from him; he would no doubt conclude that Grabbe, quite understandably, was himself already moving against Shamyl.

At around midday, Mungo rushed to the stables with his accustomed enthusiasm to relay the news given to him by Lev Pushkin that Pechorin would ride with the advance expeditionary force. Pechorin, consistent with his own custom, received it with an outward calm that belied the anticipation that now rose within him.

'And what about you, my dear uncle?' – Pechorin asked, stroking the neck of his now beloved Ballad.

'Why, I will be with you, of course!' – Mungo replied.

'Excellent' – said Pechorin, looking around the stables at the thin Cossack horses, their heads hung in sadness.

In the yard, in the midday heat of this valley in Daghestan, two Tatars conscripted into the artillery fiddled with a heavy bronze gun.

'Let duty commence', Pechorin thought to himself as he watched in silence.

General Grabbe's expeditionary focus set out from Vnezapnaya on the most beautiful morning in early summer, the warm but still benevolent sun illuminating the cavalcade of around one thousand bayonets, two hundred

Cossacks with the infantry, another forty on horseback, and a dozen of the lighter artillery, which would allow the party to cover the ground as quickly as the circumstances required. The heavy guns would follow with another battalion taking the same route as Grabbe, a third marching due south towards the *aul* of Chirkata.

Pechorin and the remaining two dozen officers rode in groups of four between divisions of the main column, which was protected at the front and rear by sharpshooters and light, mobile artillery, on the flanks by two long chains of sharpshooters operating in pairs. The old hands of the infantry referred to this formation as 'carrying the column in a box', but, as Pechorin would soon learn, if it was a box at all, it was a box of maximal flexibility. When moving across open ground, the flanking chains would remain a rifle shot from the main column; but when entering a forest, more common – and more deadly – in Chechnya than here in Daghestan, they were required to perform the counter-intuitive manoeuvre of spreading further out, in order to prevent the enemy from directing gunfire from concealed positions directly into the main body of troops. As the column moved, the point of maximum opportunity for the enemy was in front when advancing, at the rear in retreat; but always on the flanks, at which the *Murid* forces would launch sporadic and unexpected attacks. The greatest danger, apart from moving through forest, came when a force of any substantial magnitude was required to negotiate a mountain pass, when the column might be reduced to two abreast or even single file; on such occasions, the flanking chains removed, cover was dependant on establishing parties of sharpshooters and, if possible, light artillery in positions of strategic importance prior to commencement of the traverse.

Pechorin rode at a gentle walk astride Ballad, with Mungo to his right and Trubetskoi to his left. A division of Cossack infantry marched before them across the broad plain of the left bank of the Aktash; in front of them, at the head of the column, Pechorin could see the figure of General Grabbe alongside Voronin and Lev Pushkin, the mountains in the distance looming above their heads. The plan was to follow the course of the Aktash until it met the Terengultar, where the column would turn east towards the ford at Miatli. This route would add a day to the march, but would almost completely obviate the need to traverse forest; moreover, Grabbe was far from being certain enough of Shamyl's good intentions to march by the most predictable route.

Pechorin's enjoyment of the wide-open valley under the morning sun was constrained only by the desire to fly ahead of the column on his Ballad along the bank of the river as he had done on his first morning at Vnezapnaya.

'Isn't it marvellous, Pechorin?' – said Trubetskoi, who had followed this path a dozen times.

'It is' – replied Pechorin – 'And Captain Voronin, as you may recall, has assured me that it will become more beautiful still, with all that may involve'.

'It will, Pechorin' - said Trubetskoi with a smile full of anticipation - 'You can be assured of that'.

By the time the column reached the *aul* of Dylym in the late evening, just at the point where the Terengultar River takes a dramatic turn to the south, Pechorin could not deny the persistent inner voice that informed him he was bored. He had stopped himself on a number of occasions from remarking to Mungo or Trubetskoi on the superfluous nature of the mechanics of the column or the seemingly unnecessary complication of Grabbe's preferred - and circuitous - route. When Grabbe signalled for the column to halt and make camp for the night on the far side of Dylym, however, Pechorin felt a sudden and enveloping fatigue. The camp was for one night only, so the company was ordered to make fires, but not to erect tents, with the single exception of the modest structure where General Grabbe would consult his staff - and later sleep. By the time Pechorin had wrapped himself in his coat and found a comfortable spot not too far from the embers of one of the many fires, Mungo, sitting on a log alongside, leaned over to offer him a cigar. Pechorin was sound asleep.

Late on the second morning, as the column approached the *aul* of Inchkha and Pechorin exchanged a few words with Mungo and Trubetskoi in a desultory attempt to assuage his boredom, the order came down the line to halt. The Cossacks to front and rear gratefully took off their hats and sat down in the warming sunshine; Pechorin, Mungo, and Trubetskoi dismounted and followed their lead. At the front of the column, Grabbe was assembling a reconnaissance party, which would go ahead to Inchkha and provide intelligence as to how best to proceed. Less than half an hour later, the little party returned with quite unexpected news: they had proceeded with caution to within a hundred yards or so without encountering a soul; they had proceeded with even greater caution to the outlying huts; and then, to their bewilderment, they had quickly moved through the *aul* and established that it was entirely deserted.

'What do you say to that, Captain Voronin?' - asked Grabbe with an easy smile, only half-seriously testing Voronin's understanding of the situation.

'Not good, Sir' - began Voronin - 'If they were peaceable, like the natives at Dylym, they would have stayed where they were'.

'Quite so' - said Grabbe - 'So where the devil are they?'

'I can only imagine the women and children are in the forest and the men have retreated to Miatli to reinforce the crossing' -Voronin replied, as if he were dictating a list of provisions.

'Quite so' - repeated Grabbe - 'Shamyl is hedging his bets... and who can blame him?'

Voronin remained silent, Pushkin at his side gazing towards the barren, rocky higher ground they would cross before the descent into Miatli.

'And if he stands in our way' - continued Grabbe - 'who can blame us for clearing our path?'

The column once more rumbled into motion. As they approached a lightly wooded area to the right, Voronin ordered the chain on that flank to move closer to the line of the trees, so sparse that he could see deep into them even from the column. Suddenly, just as the rear came level with the trees, Pechorin's boredom was dispelled by the crack of a rifle. He could see a group of infantry break off in the direction from which the shot had come and heard the return of fire from a pair of sharpshooters. In an instant, Trubetskoi had pulled his mount out of the column and galloped to join them. Pechorin glanced at Mungo and, without a word, they both set off in pursuit. As Trubetskoi caught up with the infantry, only a few yards from the line of trees, a burst of fire coincided with the fall of first one sharpshooter, then another. The infantry, scurrying along on foot, paused as they watched their comrades fall, before Trubetskoi rushed past into the trees, Pechorin and Mungo after him.

Pechorin slowed Ballad to a walk, zig-zagging between the sparse trees, wary of the lower branches but glad of the broken shade. He could hear Trubetskoi just ahead, then the sound of a pistol discharging; Trubetskoi was close enough to have at least one of the Tatars in his sights. Pechorin ploughed on ahead of Mungo, deeper and deeper into the thickening wood, following the sounds of Trubetskoi's mount as it pushed through the undergrowth. At last, he caught up with Trubetskoi, stationary in a little glade, on the near side of a stream his horse could easily have crossed, were it not for the steep rocks rising on its far bank. He heard again the sound of rifle fire, then watched as Trubetskoi returned one last pistol shot. By the time he drew alongside, all was silent. The Tatars had withdrawn into the deeper, elevated part of the forest, where they knew no Russian soldier would follow.

When they had returned by the same route, escorting the infantry back to the still-advancing column, it had almost reached the highest point of the barren rocks above Miatli. Voronin ordered the flanking chains to pull back to within a rifle shot of the column, advanced to a position two hundred yards above the *aul*, and once again gave the command to halt. Pechorin watched from his position amid a sea of Cossack infantry as the light artillery were wheeled to the front and lined up in a neat row as their gunners swarmed around them like giant worker bees. Soon, the artillery was in place and loaded, each gun attended by two gunners, neat little piles of live rounds to their right.

'Would it be superfluous to ask what happens now?' - said Pechorin, turning to Trubetskoi with a wretched smile.

For an hour or more the shabby collection of stone buildings and wooden huts perched on the bank of the Sulak below them was bombarded, steadily dwindling to rubble and tangled destruction, smoke rising from the charred remains of those structures that had taken direct hits. As the bombardment intensified and the *aul* steadily disappeared, Pechorin could see small groups of men, at first in twos and threes, then in dozens, escape to the right, not crossing the river, but following its course upstream, presumably to a point where they could merge into the forest. When this stream of refugees had dwindled to nothing, Grabbe gave the order for the bombardment to cease. The column once more slumbered into motion, this time more slowly as it descended over the last of the barren rocks, the flanking chain to its right quadrupled in force to protect from any counter-offensive.

At the edge of the *aul* itself, the infantry began to spread out, cautiously moving from building to building – or ruin to ruin. Pechorin followed on horseback in a small company including Grabbe, Voronin, Pushkin, and Trubetskoi. The only building to have survived was a low stone mosque, complete with minaret, right by the riverbank and just out of the range of the guns. Voronin positioned covering fire to the left and right and gave orders for a handful of infantry to approach. As they came within a few yards of the mosque, a shot rang out, taking down one of the infantry, wounded in the shoulder. Two of his comrades scrambled quickly to his aid and carried him away as the remainder of the party retreated.

'What are your orders, Sir?' – said Voronin calmly.

Grabbe thought for no more than a second.

'Well, we came to parley' – Grabbe replied – 'We may as well begin as we mean to go on'.

Voronin ordered two infantrymen who were Ossetian by birth to take off their caps and lay down their weapons. He then removed his own cap and tunic, took a makeshift white flag from one of the gunners, and walked forward towards the mosque, the two Ossetians at his side. When they had come as close to the mosque as he dared – a rifle-shot might kill him, a pistol perhaps not – Voronin called out in Tatar to whoever remained.

'Brothers!' – he cried – 'You have no choice but to surrender or burn! Lay down your arms'.

No sound or movement came from the mosque.

'If you surrender' – Voronin continued – 'we guarantee, in the name of the Emperor, not only that you will live, but that you will have the right of exchange with Russian prisoners. One day, you might return to your families... do you understand?'

Once again no sound or movement followed.

'Take a few minutes to consider' – said Voronin – 'But soon we must have your answer'.

After what seemed to Pechorin an age, but was in fact no more than the five minutes Voronin had insisted upon, the door to the mosque swung open. A short figure emerged, black with smoke, half-naked but still in his shaggy brown *papakha*, bound at the top into the white wrappings of a kind of turban the Mussulmans called *chalma*.

'We want no quarter' – he said at last – 'The only grace we ask of the Russians is that you tell our families we died as we lived, refusing submission to the Infidel yoke'.

He turned and once more disappeared into the mosque before Voronin could reply.

Orders were given to launch grenade and mortar fire from three sides, a further detachment of infantry having forded the river to the rear to confront anyone escaping by that route. Pechorin watched in silent awe as the mosque was illuminated by fire, the red glow replacing the sun that had set behind the mountains to the west. He listened as the low murmur of a death-song rose in the still air, loud at first, but sinking lower and lower as the numbers inside diminished through fire and smoke. Suddenly, the door of the mosque flew open once again and one of the *Murid*, unable to bear the death by fire to which he had resigned himself, came flying towards the infantry, brandishing his *kinzhal* and commending himself to Allah. Before anyone could move, Trubetskoi sank a bullet into his naked breast. Moments later, another appeared, black from head to toe, and burst off to his right towards the line of infantry. He took two bullets in the shoulder and thigh, before cutting down a man in the front line, only halting on a bayonet from the row behind. Pechorin watched, breathless, waiting for another apparition. None appeared. Soon there was silence, but for the low hiss of smoke from the charred remains. The last act of the drama was played out. Night covered the scene. The main actors had gone their way into eternity. Those spectators who remained soon sought the refuge of their tents, pitched in silence on the far bank of the Sulak.

As Pechorin lay in his tent, fighting with sleep that would not come, his mind was assailed by a small plaintive voice, which repeated, over and over, 'Why must such things be?' Is there no room for all on this earth, without distinction of speech or faith?

CHAPTER TWENTY-SEVEN

THE HAND OF THE COLONIZER

On the ninth day after setting off from Vnezapnaya, the bedraggled and exhausted force came to a halt on the high plateau above the Sulak. General Grabbe and Captain Voronin rode with a party of Cossacks to break bread with the elders of Karanai, while Pechorin bore witness to a scene as pitiful, in its own peculiar way, as the scene he had witnessed at Miatli a week before. Earlier that morning he had thought little of Mungo's silence as they covered the last few miles of a march that, although it had passed without further drama, had nonetheless depressed the spirits of all, officers and men alike. By the afternoon, however, a sheen of cold sweat glistening on his sallow complexion, it was clear that Mungo was ill. When they reached the point at which camp would be made, Pechorin sat with his uncle resting in his lap, a cloth pressed to his burning forehead, watching as a little city of orderly white tents slowly emerged from the chaotic activity of hundreds of exhausted men. When at last in the tent where they would sleep, Pechorin replaced the water he had been feeding to Mungo, like a bird to its young, with a few sips of tea, then, finally, a shot of the rough vodka they had become accustomed to at Vnezapnaya.

While Mungo slept, destined now to play no part in the events of the coming days, Pechorin was called to a briefing in the tent of General Grabbe, returned from Karanai. Grabbe was in expansive mood, keen to imprint each detail on the minds of his listeners, who were evidently confused as to why he sought to belabour what seemed to them an entirely uncomplicated process.

'We must proceed with a company large enough to protect against sudden betrayal' – said Grabbe – 'But smaller than the force with which Shamyl will present'.

'And how are we to know how large his force will be?' – asked Trubetskoi, as a proxy for his bemusement that Grabbe would propose to engage in the minority.

'Shamyl travels at all times with one hundred and thirty-two *Murid*' – said Pushkin – 'His Imperial Guard, if you will. I expect him to appear tomorrow with no more, no less'.

'Then we will present in half that number' – said Grabbe decisively – 'Furthermore, we will halt a good distance from the meeting place and I will go forward accompanied by Captain Voronin and one of the elders from the *aul*'.

Trubetskoi once again furrowed his brow in incomprehension, but said nothing.

'Major Pushkin will at that point assume command of the remainder of the company' - continued Grabbe - 'Our objective is peace. This is not, I repeat, not a military engagement'.

'And what role do you require me to play, Sir?' - asked Trubetskoi, sullen and uncomprehending.

Grabbe paused for a moment, surveying the faces of everyone in the tent but Trubetskoi.

'This is not an undertaking for which your particular skills are suited, Lieutenant Trubetskoi' - he said at last in an even tone - 'You will remain in camp'.

Pechorin alone met Trubetskoi's now furious gaze.

At first light on the following morning, General Grabbe set off from the camp outside Karanai accompanied by Pushkin, Voronin, Pechorin, thirty infantrymen, a dozen Cossacks, and a handful of natives from the *aul*. The sun rose unencumbered above the high plateau. The Sulak, suddenly brilliant pale azure, lay far below them, wending its way through bare mountain sides to the distant Caspian, a vast wall of sheer rock rising up to the heavens on its far bank.

As they rode steadily towards the appointed place, by the spring above the *aul* of Gimry, birthplace of Shamyl, Pechorin caught sight of a band of horseman over one hundred strong, which had taken up a position where the path from the *aul* reaches the edge of the plateau. As they came closer, he could make out the detail of their robes of many colours, topped by the pristine white of their *chalma*. Then, as the wind dropped and Grabbe's party came to within a quarter of a mile of the *Murid* horde, Pechorin caught the sound of a low, insistent chanting, which, although he could not make out the words, he assumed to be verses from the Koran.

Grabbe gave the signal for his party to stop when they were some hundred yards from a mound of grass near the edge of the plateau, beyond which an outcrop of rock rose up as if offering an entirely natural stage set for the drama that was to follow. He turned his horse to face his men.

'Brothers!' - he cried out - 'Maintain your position in all circumstances'.

His mind's eye was suddenly accosted by the distant memory of General Tsitsianov before the gates of Baku, riding out to parley with emissaries of the Khan, before he and his men were cut to pieces by fire from all sides.

'Well, almost all circumstances' - he continued - 'Major Pushkin, you will take command. Break rank only in the event that the *Murid* themselves break rank. Do not, on any account, react to anything that happens between myself and Shamyl. Is that clear?'

'Yes, Sir' - replied Pushkin with all the decisiveness required by the situation.

'Voronin, you will accompany me' - continued Grabbe - 'along with the elder Mahomá, who will act as translator'.

Voronin nodded his assent, clear in his understanding that his role, as a fluent speaker of Tatar, was to monitor the words of the unwitting Mahomá.

Grabbe turned his horse and Voronin and Mahomá moved to fall in behind him. Pechorin was captivated by the spectacle of this odd triumvirate, the two Russian officers in full uniform astride their powerful horses alongside this supernaturally thin creature of indeterminate age, wizened and bearded, in tattered *beshmet* and *chalma*, perched unsteadily astride a horse almost as thin as himself.

'Sir' – said Pechorin suddenly, as if waking from a dream.

'Yes, Lieutenant Pechorin? – replied Grabbe without any sign of displeasure.

'May I accompany you, Sir?' – said Pechorin.

Grabbe paused for a moment or two, looked back over his shoulder at Pushkin, then turned his gaze once more towards Shamyl and his horde.

'Fall in alongside Captain Voronin and the old man' – he said, still facing the horizon.

The four horsemen, Grabbe at their head, set off at a trot towards the sunlit mound at the edge of the plateau.

When they had reached the little mound of grass, a tall figure on horseback, bearded and crowned by the characteristic combination of *papakha* and *chalma*, emerged from the horde at the head of around twenty of his *Murid*. The two horsemen immediately behind him carried brightly coloured pennants on their lances, the remainder wore *kinzhal* at their hips, rifles strapped across their backs. As they approached, Pechorin was conscious that the only sounds in all the world were the gentle thud of hooves on grass and the murmur of water from the spring as it flowed over the coloured stones that had fallen from the cliff above. When the horseman at last reached the mound and stood face to face with the three Russian officers and the ancient Avar, the only sound that remained was the murmur of water.

General Grabbe could at first barely comprehend that he had to lift his eyes slightly to meet those of Shamyl; he had never encountered an Avar, a Chechen, a Circassian, or even a Georgian who was taller than him. Pechorin, however, was immediately transfixed by the head and features of the warrior *Imam*, his skin stretched like kid-leather over his cheekbones, or perhaps like waxed vellum over a painter's frame; the dark grey-blue eyes buried beneath black brows, two perfectly symmetrical creases of stern displeasure rising like inverted commas above them; and, above all, the tapered beard of deep, dark, incongruous red. For a moment, Pechorin imagined the *Imam* with head uncovered, hair flowing down to his shoulders, in kilt and plaid like some Highland warrior, a stout Claymore across his lithe, broad back instead of the rather prosaic rifle that in fact protruded above his shoulder. While Pechorin stared in wonder, Grabbe, who had not for a second broken eye-contact with the *Imam*, was suddenly conscious once again that war or a form of peace depended on what would pass between them over the next few minutes. He dismounted with almost regal grace, took a *burka* from the elder Mahomá, laid it on the ground, and gestured to the *Imam* to join him.

Shamyl dismounted, bowed almost imperceptibly, and sat down facing Grabbe with his heels crossed over onto the inside of his thighs. His confidante Surkhai Khan, not quite as tall, but broader in the back and shoulders, his complexion dark and his gaze yet more fierce, sat down alongside him in the same pose. Grabbe gestured to Mahomá to sit alongside him, while Pechorin and Voronin remained standing in the rear, facing the band of *Murid* over the heads of Shamyl and Surkhai Khan.

Grabbe began by instructing Mahomá to inform the *Imam* of His Imperial Majesty's respect for the peoples of Daghestan, the Avars chief among them; of His Imperial Majesty's solemn regard for the Faith by which the people lived; and of the respect in which Shamyl was held by all regiments and ranks of Russian forces in the Caucasus, on account of his unfailing valour in combat. As the old man translated these words, Pechorin noticed that Voronin was listening as carefully as Shamyl. At their conclusion, Shamyl lifted his head with an indescribably measured control and began to speak. Pechorin had to wait for Mahomá to begin to translate to confirm how much of Shamyl's words he had accurately understood.

'Your Great Emperor rules your lands by the Will of the Almighty' – Shamyl began – 'But the Almighty cannot allow the Faithful to bow to the will of the unbeliever'.

At this, Voronin glanced at the wizened figure of Mahomá, consumed by admiration for the skill of the translator.

'Neither we nor His Imperial Majesty seek to interfere with your Faith' – Grabbe replied – 'We guarantee freedom of worship across the Caucasus. Indeed, should we succeed in agreeing the terms of peace, we will offer aid in the rebuilding of your mosques'.

Pechorin immediately understood the boldness of Grabbe's forthright appeal to faith, but he saw too from the expression on Surkhai Khan's face the dangers involved in such an approach. The mosque at Ashiltá, at Miatli, and dozens of others across Daghestan, lay in ruins at the hands of our forces.

'Neither does His Imperial Majesty seek to take possession of your lands or interfere with your laws' – continued Grabbe.

Shamyl exchanged a few words in a hurried whisper with Surkhai Khan, before turning his grave expression once more to Grabbe.

'Then you must explain to me, *Komandir*, what is it that your Great Emperor desires?'

Grabbe composed himself for a moment, conscious that the success or failure of the day – and of the entire war – might rest on his next utterance.

'His Imperial Majesty desires only peace' – he began – 'I am authorised to guarantee you autonomy in all matters of faith, government, and commerce in return for accepting the authority of the Empire and withdrawing, if not laying down, your arms'.

Shamyl gave the impression of receiving these words with complete seriousness. He sat for a moment in silence, his head once again slightly bowed, before raising it once more to the benevolent figure before him in full Russian military uniform.

'And what arrangements does your Great Emperor propose in relation to taxation?' – he asked at last.

Pechorin and Voronin remained standing quite still behind Grabbe, their customary half-smiles replaced by firm, non-committal lines, etched across the lower part of their faces, each silently impressed by the simplicity and focus of Shamyl's responses.

'War is more costly than peace, *Imam*' – said Grabbe – 'His Imperial Majesty does not wish to impose an unnecessarily onerous burden. Further, in demonstration of good faith regarding autonomy, His Imperial Majesty proposes to leave collection in your hands'.

Shamyl explained to Mahomá that he and Surkhai Khan wished to speak in private, raised himself from the *burka*, and turned towards the *Murid* ranged behind him.

After a few minutes, both men returned to their positions and resumed the discussion.

'We are impressed by the *Komandir*'s honesty' – said Shamyl – 'And we are moved by the prospect of peace. But I cannot give a final answer until I have consulted with Kibit of Tilitl, Hadji Tashov, and Abdou Rahman of Karakhi. The fate of the peoples of Daghestan rests not only in my hands'.

Grabbe gave no sign of the disappointment that gripped his heart on hearing these words, pulled back his shoulders, and uttered words that took Pechorin as long to process as those uttered in a foreign tongue.

'If it will aid you in the making of your decision' – said Grabbe – 'I am also authorised to extend an invitation to an audience with His Imperial Majesty himself, at Tiflis, on a date I am not yet at liberty to confirm'.

Here for the first time in the course of the discussion Shamyl's expression betrayed the traces of surprise, although nothing in comparison to the frank astonishment etched on the faces of Voronin and Pechorin, who struggled to recover the inscrutability appropriate to the occasion. Shamyl sat in silence for a few seconds, head bowed, then raised his head once more.

'I am honoured and moved by the determination of your Great Emperor in the pursuit of peace' – he said – 'But I have given my answer'.

Grabbe had now reconciled himself to the failure of his mission, at least for today, and accepted with good grace this end to the negotiation. He rose to his feet, bowed gravely to Shamyl and Surkhai Khan, then extended his hand to the *Imam*. Unaccustomed to European manners and discomfited for a moment by Grabbe's apparent sincerity, Shamyl raised his hand towards the hand of his opponent. Before he could take it, however, Surkhai Khan struck the arm of Shamyl and shouted, as Voronin would later explain, that 'the Leader of the Faithful should not take the hand of the colonizer'. Grabbe turned angrily towards Surkhai Khan, seizing him by the collar of his *beshmet*, shouting in a manner that did not require knowledge of our language for comprehension. Pechorin watched as Surkhai Khan's hand moved in an instant to the heft of his *kinzhal*, the *Murid* behind him moving in perfect synchrony, before stepping forward and placing a hand on Grabbe's shoulder.

'General Grabbe, Sir' – he said evenly, in a tone that Voronin would later recount with marvellous incredulity – 'This gentleman cannot be reproached for his lack of familiarity with our customs. We have advanced the cause of peace and achieved, for now, as much as we might hope to achieve'.

Shamyl surveyed this new presence, who had not to this point uttered a word, held him in his gaze for no more than a few seconds, then placed a hand on the shoulder of Surkhai Khan, who let his *kinzhal* fall back into its sheath and turned towards his waiting horse. Shamyl bowed once more to Grabbe, then to Pechorin, whose hand remained on the General's shoulder, before leaping onto his horse and leading his *Murid* back down the perilous slopes to Gimry.

Two days passed without a word from Shamyl. General Grabbe returned to the state of permanent agitation in which Pechorin had encountered him at Vnezapnaya. Scouts were sent out to press Hadji Murad for a decision. Mungo lay still in the grip of the fever that had overtaken him on the day of their arrival, nursed according to a rota manned by Pechorin and Trubetskoi.

On the morning of the third day, the second division hove into view along the same road by which Grabbe's advance guard had come. News came, too, of the battalions preceding south as the crow flies, which had made camp below Chirkata, on the other side of the ridge from Ashiltá. Further south, the supply line to Khunzakh had been secured. Grabbe's downcast reticence should have been lifted by this confirmation that Shamyl, should he choose to decline the offer of peace, had no means of escape; the mountain stronghold of Akhulgó was his last and only redoubt. Yet Grabbe understood very well that the movements of his forces would be known to Shamyl and Hadji Murad alike, while he had no way of knowing what, if any, contact had been established between the two. His mind returned again and again to the irrepressible certainty that, although he had acted precisely as he should, the incalculable variable retained its sovereignty over all military orthodoxies.

Pechorin spent the time when he was not attending to the stricken Mungo riding Ballad across the expanses of the plateau beyond the camp. He had, without acknowledging it to himself, selected Pushkin as his companion for these excursions, for reasons he chose to keep at the margins of his consciousness. On the surface, at least, such preference made perfect sense: Trubetskoi now exuded a thirst for combat Pechorin found as unwelcome as it was unnecessary; and Voronin was consumed with the detail of preparation, intuitively compensating for the energy General Grabbe expended in morbid contemplation.

'You chose well' – said Pushkin, as they trotted gently towards the jagged horizon, the evening sun floating above it like an imperilled balloon.

'Yes' – Pechorin replied, smiling – 'It's important to have a good horse'.

'In general?' – Pushkin asked, returning the smile – 'Or is that sentiment particular to your current circumstances?'

Pechorin smiled now in recognition, only too pleased, beneath this deep blue sky, that his thoughts were entirely visible to his companion.

'Both' – he replied at last – 'I'd always thought so... but here... well, what other pleasures are left to us?'

'Do you have any regrets?' – Pushkin asked suddenly.

Pechorin thought for a moment, now once more solicitous of his own privacy.

'Regrets are of course an absurdity' – he said quietly – 'I would ask only that events take their course. This waiting is intolerable'.

'I quite agree' – replied Pushkin – 'Although I confess to having become accustomed to it, of necessity. But tell me, Pechorin, which course would you have events take?'

'As if that matters' – said Pechorin with a snort.

'Really?' – asked Pushkin – 'Is there no difference at all between an imperfect peace and brutal war?'

'In the long run' – said Pechorin – 'None whatsoever. The peace, if indeed it is possible, will not hold and will therefore only delay the brutalities of war. And both are preferable to waiting'.

'The flame of desire still burns in your blood, Pechorin' – said Pushkin – 'Although I can only guess at what may have wounded your soul'.

'Oh, don't be concerned for my soul' – Pechorin replied – 'It's in good hands'.

'Ha!' – said Pushkin, unable now to conceal his mockery and his delight in equal measure – 'Our good friend Lazarev was right!'

The sun had sunk below the jagged line of the mountains to the west as they rode back to the camp in silence. The sky above was still blue, relieved by a single star shining faintly. Behind them, it was slowly turning the deepest red; ahead, above the camp, hung a pale half-moon.

When Pechorin returned to his tent, Mungo was awake. He lay propped up on a stuffed canvas bag, covered in a blanket and his overcoat, his features pale and drawn, still coated with the faintest sheen of sweat, his curls damp and limp, clinging to his brow.

'What have I missed?' – he asked as Pechorin stepped into the tent.

'Nothing whatsoever, my dear uncle' – replied Pechorin – 'Your timing is impeccable. And how are you feeling?'

'Weak' – said Mungo – 'But the fever – and the delirium! – have gone'.

'And what did you see in your delirium?'

'Well, it's all a bit vague, as you might imagine. But we were in a room covered with the most opulent rugs. I was wrapped in a silken dressing-gown, my slippers velvet'.

'Nothing but fabric?' – asked Pechorin in mock indignation.

'That's it, more or less' – continued Mungo in wonder – 'The divan was luxurious, the curtains even more so. Like the inside of a woven cocoon'.

'I wonder, my dear uncle' – said Pechorin – 'if this vision is a premonition of your future or a buried remnant of your past?'

Mungo thought for a moment, the life restored to his eyes, if not his damp, pale complexion.

'I have no idea' – he said quietly – 'It was like nothing else I've ever imagined'.

Pechorin brought Mungo some tea and black bread and a cloth for his brow. They talked for an hour or so in the low light. When he had made Mungo as comfortable as he could, Pechorin began to make a bed for himself on the ground alongside. Just as he was about to take off his boots, he heard the sound of footsteps scurrying between the tents and broken, muffled whispers. He paused for a moment, contemplating whether to continue undressing and lie down to sleep, then, with a disgruntled sigh, pulled on his tunic and stepped outside to see what was happening. The half-moon was now directly overhead, so bright that the grass beneath his feet looked almost as it might under the full light of day. He could hear voices coming from the tent of General Grabbe, more distinct than the muffled whispers that had disturbed him, but not so much that he could make out what they were saying. Unsettled by some curious intuition, or perhaps by some obscure play of the light, Pechorin turned away from the voices coming from Grabbe's tent towards the jagged horizon, still imprinted on his retina from the afternoon. There out on the plateau, perhaps two rifle-shots from the camp, was a blazing beacon, its flames leaping up towards the moon. He stood transfixed for thirty seconds or so, before turning once again and hurrying towards the voices and shadows of Grabbe's brightly illuminated tent.

Before Pechorin had reached the tent, Grabbe himself came barrelling out into the stage-lit night, hauling on his tunic and issuing peremptory commands to the men straggling behind him. Grabbe looked up to see Pechorin standing ten paces in front of him.

'Mount up, Lieutenant Pechorin' – he said – 'We are about to learn whether the tree of diplomacy has borne fruit'.

Grabbe gave orders for two infantry detachments, numbering one hundred men each, to advance along the right and left flanks towards the beacon and position themselves within a rifle shot on either side. A larger force of some two hundred men was quickly assembled and given orders to remain at the edge of the camp until the signal was given. There was no time to fetch the elder Mahomá from the *aul*, so Voronin would on this occasion, if necessary, interpret in the front line. Pushkin was given command of the party on the right flank, Trubetskoi the left.

'And where would you like me?' – Pechorin asked, returning to the company astride Ballad.

'With me, Lieutenant Pechorin' – said Grabbe – 'You will ride with me'.

When the flanking divisions were in place, Grabbe set off on horseback at a steady walk, Pechorin and Voronin at his side. Pechorin noticed once again how vividly he could see the texture of the grass, each blade illuminated by the cold white light of the half-moon, softened by the warm glare from the beacon. As they approached, a series of whistles from either flank confirmed that no *Murid* forces remained on the plateau.

'If this isn't a trap' – Pechorin said in a low voice to Voronin – 'what in the name of God is it?'

'I have no idea, Pechorin' – Voronin replied – 'Perhaps the *Imam* has conceived a taste for the dramatic?'

Pechorin was about to reply when Grabbe raised his right hand to signal a halt. They were now no more than fifty or sixty yards from the beacon, standing as tall as a man, flaming its full length from a foot above the ground. Its light cast a rough circle, at the front edge of which a wooden casket lay on the ground.

'Lieutenant Pechorin' – he began – 'ride out to the right flank and ask Major Pushkin to send a pair of sappers in to inspect that object. I don't think it likely, but we have to ensure it's not booby-trapped'.

'Yes, Sir' – replied Pechorin, turning Ballad and galloping off into the other-worldly darkness.

A few minutes after he had returned, the General and his Lieutenants watched as two figures entered the circle of light from stage left, each holding a long stake. The shadows cast forward by the light of the beacon were extinguished as they lay down on the ground on their stomachs, arms stretched out towards the casket, their visible aspect in muffled darkness, protected from the light behind. Pechorin watched with intense concentration as each figure began to extend his stake, feeding it in handfuls along the ground. Then each man raised himself slightly on his elbows and, in unison, lifted the point of their stake under the lid of the casket. In a second, they had flipped the lid up and off, the silence accompanying this manoeuvre deafening in the absence of the explosion Pechorin had convinced himself must surely follow. The two figures then began to move slowly towards the casket, their stomachs still planted firmly in the grass. The first figure raised a hand in signal to his comrade, then began slowly to raise himself into a crouching position. This unlikely descendant of Pantomimus unfurled itself in slow motion into a standing position, leaning over the casket like a reluctant willow tree. Suddenly, the figure jerked itself erect and staggered back two or three paces. Pechorin could not see the expression on the face turned now towards them, obscured still by the light of the beacon from behind. The other figure now stood erect and exchanged words with his comrade. It approached the casket, still with stake in hand, and began delicately to rummage among its four corners. At last, it turned towards Grabbe, Pechorin and Voronin and waved them forward.

As they dismounted in front of the casket, Grabbe once again raised his right hand to signal that Pechorin and Voronin should remain where they stood. He stepped forward and looked down. The casket contained a severed head, clean-shaven, the skull protruding above the eyes, a neatly trimmed black beard and moustache, one eye opened and the other half-closed. The shaven skull had been hacked and beaten, the nose covered in clouts of blackened blood, the neck wrapped in a bloody cloth. Despite the wounds to the severed head, its blue lips retained a kindly, almost child-like expression. Wedged into the casket in front of the severed head were a pair of severed hands, any jewelry having been stripped from the black and bloodied fingers. Between them lay the pocket-watch Grabbe had sent as a gift to Hadji Murad, but Grabbe barely noticed it. He could not take his eyes from the terrible severed head, from the serene and friendly expression frozen upon its face, in which he had invested so much of his hopes.

Mahomá and two natives from Karanai arrived at camp the next day with a letter from Shamyl. Grabbe thanked them, asked them to wait, although he had no plans to send a reply, and retired alone to his tent to read it.

> From the poor writer of this letter, Shamyl, who leaves all things in the hands of Allah.
> This to inform you that I have decided not to go to Tiflis, even though I have oftentimes experienced the treachery of the Infidel.
> And this all men know.

Mahomá then informed Grabbe that Shamyl, on learning of the movement of Russian forces south, had captured Hadji Murad's mother, his two wives, his eighteen-year-old son Iosif, and his five younger children and was holding them at the *aul* of Vedeno. Hadji Murad had resolved either to free his family or to die in the attempt. Neither General Grabbe, nor indeed His Imperial Majesty, would ever know whether he had then intended to flee with his family into Chechnya or to come over to the Russian side once and for all.

CHAPTER TWENTY-EIGHT

SURKHAI'S TOWER

PECHORIN CANTERED LIGHTLY across the lush grass of the high plateau astride Ballad, basking in the gentle warmth of the morning sun, which glinted from the barrels of the heavy bronze cannon being hauled into position all around. By mid-morning, a line of eight of these beasts stood in precise formation at the edge of the plateau above Gimry. A scouting party had returned in the early hours with news that the *aul* was entirely deserted, but General Grabbe had resolved to take no chances.

Beyond Gimry, the bare rock rose up once again on the far side of the parched bed of the Sulak. In the distance, no more than two miles away, the mountain stronghold of Akhulgó rose still higher, overlooked and protected to its south by a stone tower built atop a pillar of rock, which the natives had named Surkhai's Tower after Surkhai Khan.

By the middle of the afternoon, the blistering sun at its zenith and the artillerymen beginning to wilt beneath it, Gimry lay in shattered ruins. No structure in the *aul* had been spared, including the mosque which had once sat at its heart. The walls of one or two of the rare stone buildings remained standing, the roof and facade gone, so that observers from the plateau, with the aid of an eyeglass, could see right into where the departed families had once lived out their modest lives.

Pechorin lay in the shade of his tent with Mungo, now almost completely recovered, listening to the incessant thundering of the guns. On each occasion when more than thirty seconds passed between the sound of one booming explosion and the next, they imagined the bombardment at an end, on each occasion suddenly jolted by disappointment as another great thunderous round rained down on Gimry. When the guns eventually ceased around four o'clock, the extended silence was more profound even than the shock that had accompanied the first explosion. Mungo allowed some minutes to pass before turning to Pechorin, who lay flat on his back with his tunic folded across his face.

'Do you think they'll march us down that hill this evening, Pechorin?' - said Mungo in a thin voice.

'Oh, I wouldn't be too concerned about that, my dear uncle' - Pechorin replied.

'How can you be so sure?' - asked Mungo, now gripped with a familiar indignation.

'Come, my dear Mungo' - Pechorin continued, his face still covered by his tunic - 'Shamyl has nowhere to go but Akhulgó, which has no doubt been prepared for this very eventuality. We will make no attempt on Akhulgó until the rather conspicuous Tower that looms over it has been destroyed. And we will make no attempt on the Tower until the divisions coming through Chirkata are in place'.

'When did you become the great military strategist?' - said Mungo, his indignation undimmed.

'Military strategy has nothing to do with it' - Pechorin replied, sitting up and pulling his tunic around his shoulders - 'You really must learn to pay attention'.

This was too much for Mungo, who threw his cap at Pechorin.

'Good to see you're feeling better' - said Pechorin, laughing - 'Come on, let's see if we can find something to eat'.

Uncle and nephew were obliged to content themselves, at least for the time being, with the meanest of rations. General Grabbe had ordered something of a feast for later in the evening, a sure sign that battle lay ahead. Little collections of infantrymen scurried about widening the stone circles around some of the campfires, loading them up with freshly chopped logs and suspending spits above them. The sound of hacking could be heard from the rear of the mess tent, as sheep, pigs, pheasant, and chickens acquired from the villagers of Karanai were prepared for roasting. The elder Mahomá had even been persuaded to provide *chikhir*, that strange Caucasian fluid which seemed to balance on the unnameable margin between wine and spirit; the inhabitants of Karanai were expressly forbidden from drinking alcohol, but Mahomá had nonetheless been able to procure it, at some considerable profit, from a neighbouring *aul*. There would be a feast, not quite in a time of plague, but rather before the gates of hell itself.

When Pechorin later sat by the dwindling camp-fire, his belly full of mutton and *chikhir*, the depredations of hell seemed infinitely remote, vanquished by the martial *bravura* that had taken hold of the intoxicated company.

'It will be over in a matter of days' - said Trubetskoi loudly - 'They have no way out and General Grabbe will make sure that any reinforcements Shamyl may be relying on will not find a way back in'.

Voronin sat facing him, his eyes fixed upon the embers, in silence.

'What do you say, Vladimir Nikolaevich?' - asked Pechorin.

Voronin raised his eyes in the direction of Pushkin, then returned his gaze to the fire.

'Weeks' - he replied in a low voice - 'Perhaps even months'.

'Nonsense!' - said Trubetskoi, sitting up and taking a long swig of *chikhir* - 'Shamyl will regret his decision and negotiate for peace within days, you mark my words'.

'He will not even turn his mind to that possibility until we have made preparations for a siege' - Voronin replied - 'That alone will take days. And General Grabbe will be obliged to take seriously the possibility that we have been lured into a trap. We won't even begin the process of laying the siege until the second column has fought its way through Chirkata and has taken up position on the terraces of Ashiltá on the other side of Surkhai's Tower'.

'And what about that Tower?' - asked Pechorin, his curiosity rising.

'What about it?' – said Voronin – 'Nothing at all will happen until the Tower has been taken or destroyed'.

Pechorin shot a glance at Mungo, whose annoyance remained subdued only by the fact that Pechorin had not, on this occasion, delivered it with his characteristic half-smile.

'Patience, gentlemen' – said Pushkin quietly – 'We have come here not for gold nor clamorous honour. We are here to subdue the enemy, at whatever cost, and however long it may take'.

Trubetskoi on this occasion made no reply, but took another long swig from the earthen *kuvshin* of *chikhir*, before passing it to Mungo.

Later, as the company began to disperse, the sober and the intoxicated alike dragging themselves off to their tents, conscious that sleep might become as prized as tea or tobacco in the days and weeks to come, Pechorin made a point of remaining by the embers of the fire until only he and Voronin remained.

'You are very confident', Vladimir Nikolaevich' – Pechorin began – 'How can you be so sure that events will proceed as you expect?'

'Ah, Pechorin' – replied Voronin – 'I can't. The future is open. It leads nowhere that can be determined with any certainty'.

Pechorin obeyed his custom of concealing his surprise, but his mind started at this entirely unexpected philosophical sortie on Voronin's part.

'But you nonetheless outline with great precision the sequence of events for which we must prepare?' – said Pechorin.

Voronin took a last drag from the stub of a small cigar and threw it into the embers.

'Of course' – he replied – 'The greater the detail with which we prepare, the more chance there is we will bring into being the objectives we pursue'.

'And if events suddenly take a quite different course?' – Pechorin continued.

'Then we adapt to our new circumstances as they unfold' – said Voronin – 'secure in the knowledge that we could not conceivably have prepared for them, but grounded still by the preparations we have in fact made'.

Pechorin looked again at this slight figure, softly lit by the faint red light of the dying embers.

'And how are we to reckon with what befalls us in the end?' – Pechorin asked suddenly.

'That depends' – Voronin replied, rising to leave.

'Depends on what?' – asked Pechorin, still more insistently.

'On whether you favour Kant or Hegel' – said Voronin softly – 'Goodnight, Lieutenant Pechorin'.

Pechorin remained alone by the light of the pale fire, lost in contemplation of the forces that had brought a man such as Voronin to this high plateau in service of the territorial ambitions of the Empire.

When his thoughts had returned to his own present circumstances, Pechorin gently kicked the loose earth over the last of the fire and rose to leave. When he reached his tent, however, he walked straight past to the rail where the horses were tethered. He mounted Ballad and set off at a trot across the bare plateau, now softly lit by the steadily waxing moon, but unrecognisable from the night when it had been illuminated by Shamyl's flaming beacon. Ballad trotted past the charred remains of the beacon towards the edge of the plateau, where Pechorin began to guide her steadily down the uneven path towards the remains of Gimry.

As he approached the edge of the shattered village, the devastation starkly lit by the light of the moon, Ballad came to an abrupt halt and could be persuaded to proceed into the ruins only by a series of sharp digs of Pechorin's heel into her flanks. The paths between what had been houses were strewn with broken stones, timber, and the mundane remnants of day-to-day life: items of clothing, smashed clay pots, the odd wooden toy. In the midst of the ruins, the moon picked out the three walls of what had once been a sleeping chamber, still intact amid the wreckage of the remainder of the house on either side. Pechorin dismounted and stepped through the absent fourth wall into the room, which, but for a few dusty stones that had come to rest on the bed, remained almost as it had been before the murderous onslaught had begun. A woven blanket covered the bed, at its foot a little carved wooden trunk. On the opposite side of the bed from the wall sat a modest cabinet, carved from the same wood, upon which Pechorin could see a short brass candle holder containing the stub of a candle, intact but long extinguished. By the side of the candleholder lay a heavy, thick book in a dark leather binding. Pechorin approached and picked up the book. A jolt of electricity seemed to pass through his spine and shoulders as he recognised, by the caressing light of the moon, Henry Brunton's Tatar-Turkish Bible. Pechorin felt an inexplicable tightness in his chest and was momentarily unable to breathe as he slowly opened this most unlikely of discoveries. As he did so, the leather binding came gently loose from the pages within. He realised in an instant, with an immense yet indecipherable relief, that the pages of Brunton's book had been torn from its binding and replaced with a tattered copy of the Koran. How many of the remaining copies of Brunton's translation had met this same fate, its luxurious binding coupled with a sacred text for which it had not been intended?

Almost two weeks passed, entirely as Voronin had foretold, before the news came that the second column, not without significant losses, had fought its way through Shamyl's rearguard at Chirkata, rebuilt the bridge over the Koisu the retreating Mussulman forces had destroyed, and taken their places on the blackened terraces of Ashiltá. General Grabbe now gave the order for the infantry to descend through Gimry, the cavalry proceeding with delicate care at their backs. The heavy artillery, which was of limited use in attacks on elevated objectives like Surkhai's Tower, would for now remain in place on the high plateau, closing off from that side any means of escape, just as the guns at Ashiltá, soon to be augmented by cavalry, would remove the possibility of escape through Chirkata. Grabbe had also determined that neither infantry nor artillery would be positioned on the lower ground on the far bank of the Koisu to the rear of Akhulgó, reasoning that such forces would be perilously exposed from the heights and, moreover, that the sheer cliffs which rose above the river, while offering natural protection to Akhulgó, also prevented escape from that side.

Intelligence from spies who had managed to penetrate Akhulgó - and had moreover succeeded in the more difficult task of making their way back out - reported that some four thousand natives had taken refuge in the settlement, but that only around one thousand of these were fighting men. The remainder were women, children, and hostages from many of the surrounding tribes who had vacillated in their commitment to Shamyl. These wretched souls huddled in makeshift shelters, partly underground, or even in caves etched into the cliffs on the far side of Akhulgó above the river. All had to be fed, even as the impending siege progressed and provisions inevitably declined. Worse, from the point of view of Shamyl, the only supply of water was from the river itself; this had to be obtained on a daily basis by sending fearless and agile boys down the vertiginous pathways of the cliffs, then hauling water up hundreds of feet in wooden buckets attached to ropes fashioned from vines.

Akhulgó in fact consisted of two separate rocks, bounded to the rear by the three sides of an almost perfect square traced by the course of the river. To the right, directly facing Surkhai's Tower, New Akhulgó rose higher than Old Akhulgó on its left. Between them ran a deep ravine, towards the foot of which a wooden bridge had been constructed, with the purpose of allowing the inhabitants to evacuate from one of the settlement's twin peaks to the other, in the event that the enemy succeeded in penetrating from either side. Grabbe's plan was simple: to prepare for a siege and give every indication that starving Shamyl into submission was preferable to any action that might incur losses on our side; but then, once the rhythm and dynamic of the siege had been established, to mount a surprise two-pronged attack after nightfall. Crucially, when the initial twin attack on New and Old Akhulgó was underway, a third column would attack the bridge between the two and bring weight of numbers to the battle on both fronts. Grabbe had calculated that Shamyl, even under attack, would hesitate to destroy the bridge that might offer a rearguard escape from his own position at New Akhulgó. Voronin, in whom Grabbe was accustomed to investing great trust in matters of strategy and tactical preparation, was in full agreement with this plan. He entertained doubts only as to the decision to trust that the cliffs and the river were adequate obstructions at Shamyl's rear, as opposed to at least some artillery presence. These doubts remained, however, unarticulated: Voronin understood from long experience that the committal of troops to danger marked the natural point of limitation of any authority he might have, regardless of how much Grabbe trusted his advice.

Voronin also understood very well that, although it was necessary to attend to such planning in advance, the time for its deployment remained distant; before the siege could be laid, Surkhai's Tower must be occupied or destroyed. General Grabbe's spies had provided no information as to the size of the force sequestered in the Tower, but, as Pechorin rode carefully down the slopes above Gimry alongside Pushkin and Voronin, he understood that even a dozen men might successfully defend such a position. The rock upon which the Tower had been built itself rose higher than Akhulgó, even without the slender white Tower that rose still higher, reaching towards the heavens like a carelessly placed minaret. The base of the Tower was connected to Akhulgó by a narrow ridge, which could be traversed by only one or two men at a time. Pechorin's mind's eye, entirely unbidden, conjured the image of some fearless *Murid* scurrying along the ridge in the darkness, cursing the moonlight, returning to his fellows in the Tower with priceless provisions.

'Accident or design?' - exclaimed Pushkin, puncturing Pechorin's strangely comforting reverie.

'How do you mean?' - Pechorin replied blankly.

'I mean, my dear Lieutenant Pechorin' - Pushkin continued - 'Have this fortress and its admirable fortifications been placed here by some Divine intelligence? Or has our all-too-mortal enemy been forced by events into a trap from which he will not escape?'

Pechorin surveyed the implausibly slender redoubt of Surkhai's Tower, descending to the ridge connecting it to the no less implausible brute mass of Akhulgó, uneven lines of infantrymen and Cossacks on horseback scrambling beneath them towards the foot of the hill.

'What does it matter?' - he replied - 'There is surely no way out. What do you say, Voronin?'

'There is, surely, no way out' - Voronin repeated slowly - 'None at all'.

When the assembled force had made a rough camp on the lower ground on the far side of Gimry, General Grabbe summoned the two dozen officers in his company. Pechorin filed in with Trubetskoi and Mungo and stood to the rear of the gathering, from where he could observe the only partially suppressed conflict assailing the usually imperturbable features of Voronin, unable even to communicate with Pushkin, who stood in silence on the other side of General Grabbe.

'Tonight, Sir?' - said Voronin in a neutral tone.

'Indeed, Captain Voronin' - Grabbe replied - 'This very night and no other'.

'Of course, Sir' - Voronin continued - 'I had thought that we might first prepare our positions for the assault on Akhulgó. We'll require some lines of light infantry, if only to provide cover for any advance'.

'We will indeed' - replied Grabbe - 'But there is plenty of time for that. Preparations for an assault on the Tower, on the contrary, will take you five minutes. And an assault on the Tower has the greatest chance of success if launched immediately, when the enemy will not be expecting it'.

'Very well, Sir' - said Voronin, any last trace of conflict beneath his calm exterior now erased - 'How would you like me to proceed?'

'I need half a dozen volunteers from among the officers' - said Grabbe firmly, turning to address the gathering - 'Captain Voronin will then assemble a force of two hundred volunteers from among the infantry and the

Cossacks and take responsibility, as soon as the sun has set, for deployment of whatever light artillery he thinks...'.

'I volunteer' - said Trubetskoi before Grabbe could finish his sentence, stepping forward from the crowd.

Mungo now shot a glance at Pechorin, which was met with a barely perceptible shake of the head. Two more officers stepped forward behind Trubetskoi, then another. Pushkin gestured as if he was about to speak, but Grabbe stopped him with a curt motion of his hand. After a silence that lasted only a few seconds, but seemed to Mungo as if it might never end, a fifth officer, a Captain in his late forties, stepped forward to join Trubetskoi and the others. Mungo began to turn his head once more towards Pechorin, but was interrupted by the sound of a resonant, familiar voice, suddenly made strange by the content of its utterance.

'I volunteer' - said Pechorin.

Only then did Pechorin consent once again to engage Mungo's confounded gaze.

'What were you thinking?' - asked Mungo when they had emerged into the half-light.

'Perhaps I wasn't thinking at all, my dear uncle' - Pechorin replied.

'Listen, Pechorin' - said Mungo in exasperation - 'We know each other too well. I perfectly understood that little shake of the head, which perhaps no one else will have noticed. Why discourage me, only then to volunteer yourself?'

'I had no intention of volunteering' - Pechorin replied.

'Then why did you?' - Mungo almost shouted, his exasperation now drawing the attention of a group of enlisted men smoking nearby.

Pechorin paused for a moment, then fixed Mungo with a familiar half-smile, designed, he hoped, to disarm his uncle's anger.

'Do you see, my dear Mungo' - he said warmly - 'I don't know! One moment I had no intention of volunteering... the next moment I volunteered! Perhaps I was afraid I might miss out? Perhaps I had some intimation of fate? But I'm now entirely certain that what must be, must be: you will enjoy the company of Pushkin and, once he has completed his preparations, Voronin; while Trubetskoi and I will lead a couple of hundred men up a rock face under cover of night, beneath a hail of God only knows what hurled down upon us by the savages above. That is what must be'.

Pechorin turned lightly on his heels and asked one of the nearby soldiers for a match for his cigar.

By midnight, Voronin had positioned two batteries of light mountain guns, one trained on the ridge between Surkhai's Tower and Akhulgó, the other, to the south, trained on the Tower itself. Grabbe's plan was to begin the assault at 2 a.m. by firing from this second position onto the breastworks the natives had constructed at the foot of the Tower where the rock naturally overhung, and thereby to test whether the defenders, in their surprise, might attempt to retreat along the ridge. The main assault, up the steep and perilous slopes of the rock, would commence from a position to the south-east where the gradient, although still vertiginous, was slightly less daunting. A second unit would attempt to take possession of the ridge. Both lines of assault would be afforded at least some cover by Voronin's batteries.

'Well, Pechorin' - said Trubetskoi - 'We have waited long enough. Let battle commence'.

Pechorin looked up towards Surkhai's Tower, grey under a moonless sky, then let his gaze drop to the slopes of the rock below it.

'A strange kind of battle, wouldn't you say?' - Pechorin replied.

'What kind of battle did you have in mind?' - asked Trubetskoi.

'Oh, I don't know' - said Pechorin - 'Perhaps I had fancied myself on horseback, dashing across verdant fields under the warming Daghestani sun?'

Trubetskoi allowed himself an almost conspiratorial smile.

'It never quite happens as you imagine it' - he said - 'Never'.

Voronin had met no difficulty in assembling his two hundred volunteers, the majority of them Cossacks. They assembled in two detachments, the smaller of which would be led by Captain Kozlov, who had volunteered immediately before Pechorin, with orders to break towards the ridge at the appropriate moment. The larger company, which would attempt to scale the Tower itself, would be led by Trubetskoi.

'We're a little more than a mile from the Tower' - said Voronin, addressing the company in General Grabbe's place - 'Commence the attack at the sound of the first gun. Captain Kozlov, you and your men must remain with the main detachment until the bombardment ends; only then break right towards the ridge'.

The company stood in silence, thankful for the clouds which stubbornly clad the vault of the heavens. Pechorin gazed calmly at Surkhai's Tower, narrowed his eyes for a moment, attempting to imagine in its place a peaceful church. He then closed his eyes completely and summoned the piercing light of sunrise, the first rays of the sun illuminating the brilliant white walls, a monk sweeping the dust from the courtyard. The first great crash of artillery fire resounded through the surrounding hillsides.

'Company!' - shouted Captain Kozlov - 'Forward, march!'

The crash of artillery became deafening as the company approached the foot of the rock. Then, as suddenly as they had begun, the guns fell silent. Captain Kozlov gestured towards Trubetskoi before barking an order to his men and wheeling to the right. Trubetskoi in turn ordered his detachment to fall into two columns and strode forward at the head of one of them, a dozen Cossacks immediately to his rear. Pechorin watched as the advancing party was met with a cannonade of broken rocks and wooden beams, hurled down by the defenders above. Three Cossacks fell dead, but Trubetskoi continued his ascent undeterred. With a great shout to the men around him, Pechorin rushed forwards to join Trubetskoi's group, stones and splinters of wood swirling like a ferocious rainstorm around his head. As they progressed inch by inch up the rock, the defenders opened fire with rifles, from a position above the ridge. Infantrymen and Cossacks fell under fire all around; as he moved forward, Pechorin on more than one occasion had to avoid a corpse rolling down the slope towards him like some grotesque boulder. Some of the infantrymen in Trubetskoi's group returned fire as they scrambled forward, shooting indiscriminately upwards, with little sense of a target. Pechorin could hear the sound of sustained fire coming from his right; he pondered for a moment as he crawled forward up the slope how absurd, how wonderful it was that Kozlov's detachment, with better perspective on the defenders' position, but none whatsoever on the current situation of Grigorii Alexandrovich Pechorin, were all that stood between him and certain death.

Ahead and to the left, Trubetskoi had led a band of men beneath a slight outcrop in the rock, protecting them from rifle fire, but also from the renewed bombardment of rocks and wooden beams, which launched out into the night sky in a murderous cascade, arcing above the heads of the grateful soldiers. As if in continuation of some telepathic choreography, after the surviving men had remained still beneath the outcrop for a few minutes, the artillery from the south once again struck up, like an orchestra comprising only timpani, hurling its fire in great percussive waves as far as it could towards the breastworks at the foot of the Tower.

'There's another outcrop a little further ahead' - Trubetskoi shouted to Pechorin - 'If we can make it, the Tower will be in range of our mortars'.

Pechorin glanced up and to the left. Trubetskoi's intended destination was only partly visible through clouds of smoke and dust, great lumps of broken stone and rubble raining down upon it as the artillery fire ravaged the breastworks above.

'That will take us into the line of fire of our own artillery' - said Pechorin.

'Yes, I know' - Trubetskoi replied - 'But they're hardly going to fire at their own side, are they?'

Pechorin silently acknowledged the insuperable logic by which Trubetskoi pretended to be guided, but also his total, unassailable capacity to believe what he required to believe in such circumstances.

'Let's hope you're right' - he said evenly.

When the sound of the guns had once again fallen silent, it was immediately replaced by the more modest crack of mortar fire from the right flank.

'Kozlov!' - cried Trubetskoi - 'They're on the ridge, close enough to launch their mortars! Come on, it's now or never!'

Before Pechorin could respond, Trubetskoi had leapt out from cover and was once again scrambling up the rock, a stream of infantrymen and now hatless Cossacks in his train. Pechorin flew after them, not bothering to take his rifle from his back. The hail of rocks and beams resumed, occasionally interspersed with the corpse of a fallen comrade. Just as he was approaching the sanctuary of the outcrop, a huge slab of masonry came tumbling towards him out of the smoke and dust. At the last moment, he hurled himself to his left. He felt a sudden, piercing shot of pain as the great slab caught him a glancing blow on the top of his right shoulder and flew out into the darkness. When he at last reached safety, he asked one of the soldiers to remove his right arm from the sleeve of his tunic, then bind it to his side by re-buttoning the tunic, wincing in pain until the arm was once again motionless. His rifle, now useless to him, was gratefully received by an infantryman who had lost his own on the ascent, in exchange for a pistol, which Pechorin now thrust into his belt with his left hand. There was, he understood, no way back down the hill. One-armed, and with a single round in the chamber, he would go forward to meet whatever fate had in store for him.

Trubetskoi instructed two of the infantrymen to establish mortar emplacements on either side of the outcrop, trained on the foot of the Tower at its extremities to left and right.

'As soon as mortar fire is underway' – he addressed the surviving troops, exulting now in the approach of the final assault – 'We storm the Tower. Keep straight ahead. If you must fall, be sure to fall under enemy fire'.

He glanced towards Pechorin at the rear of the huddled group, the only other survivor of the four officers who had stepped onto the rock with him, now awkwardly hunched with his right arm bound to his side under his tunic.

'How are we, Lieutenant Pechorin?' – Trubetskoi asked with a broad smile – 'Are you still with us?'

'I am' – Pechorin replied steadily – 'Three of my four limbs remain entirely functional. I do hope that will suffice'.

Trubetskoi laughed despite himself, abashed at any display of admiration for his strangely sanguine comrade.

'Ready?' – he asked, turning to the infantrymen grappling with their mortars.

'Ready' – came the choral reply.

Trubetskoi turned towards the Tower, its base obscured by clouds of smoke and dust, the scene accompanied by incessant rifle fire from above in counterpoint to the mortar fire from Kozlov's troops below. For a fleeting moment, the chaotic scene was displaced in his mind by the image of a punt on some mystic river, aboard it black-clad figures carrying torches, arranged around a coffin of black teak. The mortars fired. Trubetskoi leapt forward without a word, a long stream of bedraggled and bruised men flowing behind him, Pechorin scrambling one-armed at its rear.

Pechorin watched as Trubetskoi and a handful of Cossacks reached the base of the Tower, only for two of them to be cut down by rifle fire from the *Murid* above, who had now abandoned the outworks and retreated into the Tower itself. Trubetskoi lunged to the left and signalled for those pouring over the top to follow him. Three infantrymen positioned themselves against the wall of the Tower, the third man supported by the other two. Trubetskoi climbed onto the clasped hands of the men at the base, then onto the shoulders of the man above, before hurling a grenade flush between the narrow gap of an observation slit on the first floor of the Tower. All four fell back as the muffled explosion inside momentarily silenced the rifles. To the right of the Tower, a little wooden door some twenty feet above the ground, to which no staircase led, suddenly flew open and, one by one, a stream of blackened, shrieking Murid leapt from it down onto the ridge. As each man rolled to break his fall, then scrambled once again to his feet in an unbroken movement, he was cut down by rifle fire from Kozlov's company, who had held their position on the near side of the ridge, rather than attempting an assault on the Tower. In a few seconds, a dozen bodies lay dead or dying, strewn along the ridge, their arms reaching out towards Akhulgó.

Pechorin was struck by the sudden realisation that there was no way of knowing how many Murid remained in the Tower, nor how many remained alive. As he reached the base of the Tower, Trubetskoi called for ladders to be brought up from Kozlov's company and the infantry quickly positioned them against the wall beneath the door from which the last survivors had thrown themselves in their despairing attempts to escape.

'Wait!' - cried Pechorin, as Trubetskoi stepped towards the base of the ladder.

Trubetskoi turned in Pechorin's direction with a questioning frown.

'Can we be sure there are no survivors?' - said Pechorin.

Trubetskoi made no reply, but stepped back from the ladder, and called forward three infantrymen. Each in turn positioned himself a few paces from the Tower, directly beneath the little door, then hurled a grenade through it, one after another. Three thunderous cracks spat in their turn from the opening, accompanied by three flashes of flame and clouds of billowing black smoke, which then began to seep from the observation slits, higher and higher in the Tower walls until smoke streamed from its every aperture.

When at last the smoke had cleared, Trubetskoi stepped once again to the ladder and began to climb towards the opening. As he reached the top of the ladder, Pechorin's eye was suddenly drawn upwards, to what looked like a dark bundle of rags or a huge dead bird, swooping down from the heavens. In an instant, the indeterminate mass crashed into Trubetskoi, wrenching him from his unsteady perch. As Trubetskoi hit the ground, seemingly wrapped in some infernal cloak, from which emerged the incongruous white spot of a *chalma*, Pechorin drew his pistol with his left hand and fired into the indistinguishable dark mass. When the smoke from his pistol had cleared, Trubetskoi lay on his back, blood seeping from a deep wound in his throat. Beside him lay Surkhai Khan, his eyes bulging towards the heavens, the ferocity of his stare undimmed, his *burka* soaked in his own blood and the blood of the Infidel, the dagger that had ripped open Trubetskoi's throat still clutched tight in his bloodied fist.

CHAPTER TWENTY-NINE

THE SIEGE OF AKHULGÓ

PECHORIN AND MUNGO stood in silence at the grave of Trubetskoi, unmarked but for a rough wooden cross at the head of a patch of disturbed soil, their eyes fixed upon the earth. Trubetskoi had insisted to Voronin on a number of occasions that no attempt should be made to return his body to Russia; he would be buried, without ostentation, wherever he fell. The somewhat muted conversation was intermittently disturbed by the clatter of chains and the frustrated shouts of artillerymen, who had been ordered by General Grabbe to haul two of the heavy brass cannon down from the ridge above Gimry, then, with great difficulty, hoist them up the perilous slopes to the ridge between Surkhai's Tower and New Akhulgó. Voronin had left the graveside as soon as Trubetskoi's corpse had been lowered into the ground and was already overseeing the establishment of advanced artillery lines on the lower ground on either side of the ridge and beneath the terraces of Ashiltá. The final preparations for bombardment and, if necessary, siege were underway.

'He did insist it would be over in a matter of days' - said Pechorin quietly in a lull between the cries of soldiers and the clang of metal on rock further along the ridge.

Mungo looked back in open astonishment, unable to find words in response.

'And I did tell you, my dear Mungo, that what must be, must be' - Pechorin continued - 'I suggest you get used to it'.

The youthful uncle, his features ravaged by the contradictions of guilt and indignation, at first bridled at the implication embedded in the words of his ageless nephew, but nevertheless managed to collect himself before speaking.

'Oh, I'm used to it, Pechorin' - he said calmly, raising his chin slightly in a show of resolve - 'And next time, I'm sure, there will be no question of volunteering'.

'I expect not' - Pechorin replied.

The main camp had now been established in the ruins of Ashiltá and was awash with rumours emanating from the native spies who had once again accomplished the hazardous feat of entering - and subsequently leaving - Akhulgó. Shamyl's forces had been reduced in number by a steady flow of deserters, discouraged by the scarcity of fuel, food, and water. Some of the refugees who had come over to our side told of an atmosphere contaminated by the stench of decaying corpses, of hunger and disease taking hold of a dispirited people, encouraging Grabbe in the belief that Shamyl may be prepared to surrender.

'The bombardment will commence when we have secured the artillery' – Grabbe told Voronin with conviction – 'Then, and only then, we will once again test the *Imam*'s appetite for negotiation'.

Voronin paused, barely perceptibly, before saluting and taking his leave.

In a matter of three days, preparations were complete. At dawn on the fourth day, the guns once agains struck up their hellish percussion, raining heavy lead down upon the outworks of New Akhulgó. Pechorin lay in his tent, sheltering from the sun as it made its way steadily up into the arc of the heavens, his battered right arm in a sling, his tunic wrapped around his head to muffle the deafening noise. Mungo had taken up position with Voronin at the battery on the ridge below Surkhai's Tower, which afforded the most complete view of the scene.

By the middle of the afternoon, when the cannon fire had ceased, General Grabbe received the elder Mahomá, who had once again agreed to act as intermediary. When the fierce heat of the sun had begun to subside, Grabbe watched expectantly as the old man made his way to the bridge across the chasm between the two halves of Akhulgó, mounted alongside a younger man from the *aul* of Karanai. Mahomá's instructions were to secure Shamyl's submission to the Russian government, failing which no negotiations for peace were possible: the siege would continue until such undertakings had been received – or until no man remained alive in Akhulgó.

Pechorin emerged from his tent at dusk, just as the elder Mahomá was toiling slowly up the terraces of Ashiltá, his grim-faced young companion at his rear. He understood without a word, as they passed wearily on their way to report to General Grabbe, that the assault would begin that very evening and returned to his tent to make ready.

When darkness had fallen, disturbed only by the weak, gently twinkling lights atop the great dark mass in front of them, General Grabbe once again assembled his forces. On this occasion, as Mungo had anticipated, every man and every officer would take part in the attack, with the exception of a small group who would remain behind to coordinate communications and a division of cavalry, unsuited to attack in such circumstances, but able to provide swift redress in the event of any attempt to escape from Akhulgó. The main column, led by Captain Kozlov and consisting of three entire battalions, would advance on New Akhulgó, attempting to scale the rock and fight their way over the outworks that now lay ravaged by the afternoon's artillery fire. A second column, roughly one third in size, would attack Old Akhulgó from the left flank, led by Pushkin. A third, similar in size, would make its way into the ravine between them to the bridge Mahomá had crossed earlier that same day; their objective was to prevent any juncture of the enemy's forces – and, if the other columns had met with any success, to take the bridge, scale the cliffs, and seize possession of Shamyl's stronghold. On this occasion, General Grabbe, persuaded that all tactical preparations were complete – and in defiance of Voronin's unspoken reproach – would take it upon himself to lead this third and potentially decisive column. Grabbe had suggested that Pechorin remain with the cavalry on account of his arm, but Pechorin swiftly and politely explained that, precisely on account of his arm, he was currently incapable of riding a horse. Both Mungo and Pechorin would follow Grabbe into battle.

Pechorin stood quite still in the little valley facing the ravine between New and Old Akhulgó, his eyes adjusting to the deep darkness, faintly conscious of the enveloping silence. Suddenly, the silence was shattered by the loud crack of rifle fire from the heights above. It took two or three seconds to register that the fire was not trained on him and the men gathered around him – they were too far from the rock, he reasoned, unless a party of *Murid* had made its way out in the darkness to mount a daring and unexpected counter-offensive. He would only later learn from a surviving infantryman what had befallen Kozlov's column.

Kozlov's men had begun to make their way along the ridge, almost in single file, coming under immediate fire from the rock above them as they attempted to storm the enemy's outworks with scaling ladders. As they pressed on, they encountered a hitherto unidentified deep cut in the ridge, which blocked their forward movement. Then, as the men began to cluster on a small scrap of level ground just before the cut, they came under cross-fire from two concealed blockhouses on either side. Their position was desperate. Some six hundred men came under sustained fire from above and from both sides, an impassable cut in front of them, a precipice on either side, behind them a passage so narrow that retreat was only possible in tortuous single file, made worse by the obstacle of fallen and wounded men. Only the darkness prevented a total slaughter. By the time the scattered force eventually made it back along the ridge, almost two hundred men had fallen under fire or fallen from the rocks to their deaths; the majority of the survivors were wounded; no officer remained alive.

Pechorin's column was able to judge the course of events only by the sustained rifle fire and, judging therefore that battle had been joined, advanced towards the chasm between the rocks, General Grabbe himself at the head of his troops. No sooner had the bridge come into view than Pechorin once again found himself listening intently as he ran to the sound of rocks hurtling down the cliffs to his right.

'Keep moving!' – he called to Mungo, who had paused for a moment on Pechorin's left-hand side.

As they progressed deeper into the ravine, men falling all around under a hail of rocks and stones, rifle fire broke out from above and to the left. The men running in front gave no sign of arresting their motion. Pechorin urged Mungo once again to quicken his pace, until the two of them came abreast of General Grabbe, still to the fore of the column, Voronin at his right hand. The rifle fire from the left ceased as suddenly as it had begun. Pechorin became aware in that strange half-silence, despite the continuing fall of rocks, that something was missing, but he could not identify what it was, his mind estranged from the body that carried him relentlessly forward.

'Sir!' – Voronin cried out suddenly, reaching for General Grabbe's arm – 'Sir! The rifle fire on our right flank has ceased! Kozlov's men have turned back!'

Grabbe stopped in the midst of the surrounding chaos and fixed Voronin with an uncomprehending stare.

'What do you mean?' – he asked in a mechanical voice – 'How do you know?'

'There's no...' – Voronin began, his words drowned out by a renewed cannonade from Old Akhulgó.

Grabbe stood for a moment as if frozen, looked wildly up to his left, then back in the direction from which they had come.

'Retreat!' – he cried at last, as a wave of faltering bodies came pressing in, foundering as if against an invisible wall, before rebounding once again out into the torrid seas behind towards safety.

For almost a week, neither Pechorin nor any of the other officers saw much of General Grabbe, Lev Pushkin, or Voronin, who spent their days cloistered in the General's tent. Only the sound of raised voices occasionally reminded the company of their presence. Losses amounted to some three hundred men, including every officer who had followed Kozlov along the ridge. The wounded, many seriously, exceeded seven hundred. Pechorin could only reflect with a wry smile that his own wound, from which he had now almost recovered, he had taken into the field; beyond that, he had returned without a scratch.

Grabbe's initial response had been to consider abandoning any attempt to take Akhulgó by force, instead calling in medical and logistical reinforcements, prolonging the siege into the winter months if necessary, until Shamyl was left with no option but surrender or starvation. Not for one moment did he entertain the possibility of withdrawal, which would not only have been an acknowledgement of his own failure, but, worse, a herald of the power and influence of Shamyl, confirmation of the near supernatural mystique he had already acquired in the eyes of the peoples of Daghestan and Chechnya.

Voronin chose his moment carefully, anxious not to inflame further the wounded pride of his Commander-in-Chief. Four days after the catastrophe of the assault, as Grabbe paced around the tent in a rage of frustration, beseeching the heavens for some clue as to how best to proceed, Voronin shot a glance in the direction of Pushkin and at last voiced the concern to which he had until now silently accommodated himself.

'We have underestimated one aspect of Shamyl's position, Sir' – he said tentatively.

Grabbe merely stopped pacing to look back at him, but said nothing.

'We have assumed that because the cliffs to his rear are an insurmountable natural defence, they are also a barrier both to retreat and to the maintenance of supplies' – Voronin continued – 'The evidence suggests, however, that this is not the case. Hazardous though it may be, they are managing to pull water up from the river; they are even managing to bring in supplies of food from the far bank... and to remove the bodies of the dead. The smouldering remains of funeral pyres have been seen floating down the river. The same spies who told us of the desertions after the fall of Surkhai's Tower now tell us that, since the assault on Akhulgó, more than a hundred fighters from surrounding *aul* have rallied to Shamyl'.

The deep frown on General Grabbe's still muscular face had softened very slightly, his pacing now less furious.

'Major Pushkin' – he barked – 'Do you share Captain Voronin's view?'

Pushkin paused only for a moment.

'I do, Sir' – he said, the richness and compassion in his voice carrying in the silence.

Voronin's reappearance among the troops was, Pechorin understood, a sure sign that the future course of events had been determined. Every man searched his unassuming features for some indication, the boldest of the officers making some oblique remark designed to elicit an equally oblique, but perhaps revelatory response. Beyond the normal course of comradely chatter, however, Voronin remained silent, diligently going about the business of making preparations, including the construction of a mysterious covered gallery on the right-hand side of the ridge where so many had fallen. Pechorin restricted himself with Voronin to no more than customary greetings, until, on the morning of the eleventh day since the failed assault, he noticed a small detachment trudge past the camp, hauling two more of the great brass cannon from the plateau above Gimry in the direction of the bridge over the Koisu below Chirkata. Pechorin signalled to Mungo, who immediately fell in behind him as they set off for Voronin's tent.

'Very observant, Lieutenant Pechorin' – said Voronin drily, happy to conceal his admiration that anyone among the increasingly exhausted company had the energy for wit or observation, as opposed to gossip and complaint.

'So what does it mean?' – Pechorin asked in a tone more insistent than he had intended – 'Are we preparing another assault?'

'You'll be informed in good time' – Voronin replied with his customary indecipherable smile – 'General Grabbe has given orders that no details are to be shared until all preparations are complete. We're not the only ones with spies in the field'.

Pechorin quelled a fleeting spark of anger and met Voronin's smile with his own.

'Come, Vladimir Nikolaevich' – he replied calmly – 'Who are we going to tell?'

Mungo forced a little snort of laughter in acknowledgement of the point, but Pechorin discouraged him from any further intervention with a flashing glance, the meaning of which could bear no misinterpretation.

'Very well, Grigorii Alexandrovich' – Voronin replied – 'The next phase of the plan is very simple. We will position an artillery battery and a small force on the far bank of the Koisu, not primarily with the purpose of preventing escape, but rather to prevent anything else getting into the damned place'.

'And what about that strange wooden construction on the far side of the ridge?' – Pechorin continued.

'Ah, you really have been paying attention' – Voronin replied, with a broad, open smile neither Pechorin nor Mungo had previously witnessed – 'An invention of my own. If we do have to attack, we must ensure, above all, that the column on the right flank does not once again find itself unable to retreat'.

'If?' – said Mungo suddenly – 'If we attack?'

'Quite so, my dear Lieutenant Stolypin' – said Voronin – 'We plan to resume bombardment the day after tomorrow. The intention is to demonstrate to Shamyl that his rear is now cut off and that, sooner or later, he will run out of food, water, and ammunition'.

'And then?' – said Pechorin.

'And then' – Voronin replied – 'We will offer terms of surrender'.

Mungo searched Pechorin's features in vain for some trace of the response he knew his nephew would not utter.

On the morning of the next day, the infantry on the far bank of the Koisu cut down a party of four boys of no more than fifteen who had descended the cliffs to fill great wooden buckets with water, which would never find its way into Akhulgó. On the following day, the crash of cannon fire once again resounded through the valley, now hailing down not only on the outworks facing the camp, but also into the caves in the cliffs above the river, in which those among Shamyl's people not fit for fighting had sought – and, until now, found – refuge. When it had ceased, General Grabbe once again summoned the elder Mahomá, who had somewhat reluctantly agreed to repeat his mission. On this occasion, Pechorin did not emerge from his tent to witness the return of Mahomá and his young countryman, preferring to finish reading a battered copy of Alfred de Musset's *La Confession d'un enfant du siècle* he had borrowed from Pushkin.

Pechorin's instincts had once again not betrayed him. The camp settled down for the night in the knowledge that, tomorrow at dusk, the assault on Akhulgó would resume. Shamyl, as Pushkin and Voronin had surely understood, would prefer death to surrender. Pechorin completed his book by the light of a candle, satisfied himself that Mungo was already asleep, and slipped out into the warm night to smoke a little cigar. The moon was obscured behind a blanket of cloud, the air close and humid. He could just about make out the lines of the terraces of what had once been Ashiltá, the wall of the ridge leading to Surkhai's Tower, and there, in the middle distance, the dark mass of Akhulgó, rising to meet the cover of the clouds. Pechorin lit his cigar and leaned back onto the trunk of an ancient, dying sycamore tree. There was not a breath of wind beneath the still, dark grey sky, no sound could be heard from the camp or from the sentry-posts at the foot of the terraces or on the ridge below the Tower. His thoughts turned for some reason to St Petersburg, asleep beneath these same miraculous heavens. He recalled that evening, now seemingly so long ago, when he and Parader had slipped through the fog from Petropavlovsk to the Imperial Stables, the longing for eternal sleep wrestling in his soul with the force of life itself.

Pechorin stepped away from the dying sycamore, dropped the stub of his cigar to the ground, and extinguished it with his boot. As he turned back in the direction of the camp, he imagined he heard a strangled, muffled cry. He stopped, listening to the silence, peering down into the darkness towards Akhulgó. After a few moments, he turned again and began to make his way back to his tent. When he reached the edge of the camp, however, some mute instinct told him to conceal himself behind a flat-bed cart used for the transportation of supplies. Pechorin gazed down the slope towards Akhulgó, his eyes once again adjusting to the darkness. At first, he was convinced the indistinct clumps yet darker than the near black background were real only in that place where the retina generates images for the mind. Then, suddenly, without a doubt, there was movement, the pattern of greys and blacks shifting in a manner the mind's eye could not produce for itself. Pechorin moved swiftly and silently away from the cart, roused Mungo with a soft, insistent word, and hurried to the tent of Voronin.

'Wake up!' - he forced through his teeth - 'Wake up and listen very carefully'.

Voronin was alert in an instant.

'Gather a dozen men at the edge of the camp' - Pechorin continued, as if in a fever - 'Then, and only then, sound the alarm. We're under attack'.

Voronin, asleep as was his custom in his breeches, flew headlong out of his tent as Pechorin turned again towards Akhulgó, collecting Mungo and a pair of rifles on the way. When they reached the supply cart, there was no question that the indistinct shapes that had at first deceived Pechorin's senses were men, moving slowly across the ground - unless the earth itself was afoot like Dunsinane wood, carrying itself up the terraces of Ashiltá towards the camp. Pechorin was for a moment confounded by the question of how anyone or anything could have got past the sentries, but the thought departed as swiftly as it had arrived, extinguished entirely by the discreet scuffling behind him as Voronin and his advance guard hurried between the tents to join him. Mungo gave Pechorin a look of grim determination, then turned his rifle out towards the darkness, his elbow propped on the bed of the cart. Voronin drew alongside Pechorin, his confederates spread out on either side, flat on their stomachs with rifles cocked.

'What do you say, Lieutenant Pechorin?' - said Voronin calmly - 'Shall we sound the alarm?'

Pechorin gazed back through the enveloping darkness, no expression on his face.

'If we must, we must' – he said in a blank voice.

Voronin stepped back from the cart, let off a flare, which arced out into the dull grey sky towards Akhulgó, illuminating in shades of red the terraces below.

'Sound the alarm!' – he bellowed – 'Sound the alarm!'

The crack of rifles resounded in the night air, the dark indistinct shapes below rose into the fading red light to meet fire with fire, behind in the camp the sound of drums beat out to rouse the remainder of the slumbering troops. As the *Murid* came hurtling towards them up the last terrace, Pechorin followed Mungo's example and took aim at the front rank. As the horde approached, coursing over the fallen bodies at their front, Pechorin guessed that Shamyl had put some four hundred men into the field. Behind him, he could hear the sound of men running to join them, ahead the *Murid* horde drew closer.

When the first rank of the natives was some thirty feet from our line, Voronin gave the order for a bayonet charge, whereupon fifty or so men rose as one and stepped out to meet the advance. The *Murid* now dispensed with their rifles, drawing their *kinzhal* and cutting down half a dozen of our own, before falling under rifle fire from our second rank, who then joined the next wave of *Murid* in hand-to-hand combat, sabre against *kinzhal*. Pechorin stepped forward in the next rank, his sabre weighing in his still weak right arm, leapt suddenly to the left, and felled one of the *Murid* attackers with a cutting blow across his midriff. As two more came lunging towards him, he drew his pistol with his left hand and placed a bullet into the forehead of one, before hacking his sabre into the back of the other's neck. Hundreds of bleary-eyed soldiers now rushed into the field, some with bayonets, others preferring their sabre from the first. Pechorin glanced to the right, where Mungo swivelled first left, then right to face yet another attacker. Above Mungo's head, beyond the fray on the far right-hand side, he suddenly caught sight of the shadowy figure of a tall man on horseback, the white of his *chalma* hazily distinct against the black night. Another figure on horseback let out a piercing, guttural cry, the meaning of which Pechorin, in the surrounding chaos, could not guess. Suddenly, he realized that the weight of numbers had shifted in our favour. The cry must signal retreat.

As the *Murid* began to turn in retreat, the foremost of our troops giving chase in anger and relief, a band of horseman came surging in from the right flank between the lines of the fleeing *Murid* and their pursuers, hacking down with their *kinzhal* as they flew past. When they had cleared the field, they turned and repeated the manoeuvre from left to right. Voronin shouted an order to the advance guard to halt, whereupon they and the rank behind dropped to their knees. The third rank then stepped forward with rifles and opened fire on the horsemen, who flew out once again to the right.

Suddenly, from out of the darkness, a burst of rifle fire from the rear-guard of the retreating *Murid* came thudding into the line of our rifles, taking down a dozen men or more.

'Halt!' – cried Voronin, as the thud of horses' hooves resounded down the terraced slopes, gradually receding into the distance – 'Cease fire!'

Pechorin watched as the retreating horde poured like some dark, sentient, organic fluid, down and across the low valley to Akhulgó, relieved only by the dim glimmer of three or four specks of grey-white.

The thin light of dawn slowly seeped through the clouds to reveal a bloody ledger of some seventy of our men, fifty or so *Murid* corpses strewn among them. At the foot of the terrace, another dozen lay dead amid the silent sentry-post, their throats cut. Mungo had been taken to a hospital tent, his right thigh torn open by a blow from a *kinzhal*. Pechorin, who once again greeted the light of day entirely intact, stood at the back of General Grabbe's tent, listening to the delicately coded discussion between Grabbe, Pushkin, and Voronin.

'Immediately, Sir?' – said Voronin in a tone that consumed every measure of control available to him.

'Immediately' – Grabbe replied.

'And how shall we proceed, Sir?' – asked Voronin.

'As before' – said Grabbe. – 'The batteries are in place, aren't they? The covered gallery complete?'

'Yes, Sir' – Voronin said quietly.

'Then there is no reason to delay. Why give those dogs time to lick their wounds and recover? The time has come to bring this matter to its close, Captain Voronin. Dismiss'.

Pechorin stood once again in the little valley facing the ravine between New and Old Akhulgó, now in full daylight, the clouds above beginning to part to allow the downward rays of the sun to illuminate the scene. The reigning silence of the previous nights, he now reasoned, must have been linked in some unfathomable manner to the material properties of darkness; now, in the merciless light of day, numberless sources of sound competed for the attention of his senses, combining at last in an indecipherable cacophony akin, he imagined, to blindness. He knew only that he must step forward, as if indeed blind, into the blizzard of noise.

Up ahead he caught sight of General Grabbe, striding forward amid a guard of Cossacks, who whooped and shouted wildly in anticipation of blood. He glanced to his left, where Voronin walked calmly, as if shrouded in a cloak of silence from the hellish din, and thought of Mungo, in the arms of Morpheus, oblivious to the fate he had evaded.

The rifle fire from both sides had not abated even for a second by the time they came to the opening of the ravine, where rocks and timber once again began to rain from the skies, thudding into the earth or crushing men beneath their weight in a display of the indiscriminate, inexorable logic of space and time. Pechorin quickened his pace in automatic response to the example of those in front of him. Suddenly, as if waking from a dream, he looked up towards the bridge. A band of *Murid* came tumbling down the slopes from either side in anticipation of this third point of our assault and now opened fire into the body of the advancing force. Pechorin lowered his head to the blast of the rifles, stepping forward with renewed and desperate purpose over bodies as they fell beneath his feet. The Cossacks in front of him returned fire in desperate fashion, sufficient, however, to allow our forces to come within a few paces of the bridge before the *Murid* could reload. A last burst of rifle fire echoed from the walls of the ravine as the first of our men scrambled up onto the bridge and engaged in hand-to-hand combat, the vanquished falling to the bed of the ravine below. Seeing that the weight of *Murid* numbers lay to the right, descending from New Akhulgó, Pechorin made his way to the other side of the ravine and leapt up to join a clutch of infantrymen and Cossacks on the left-hand side. A wave of men followed in his wake, until one side of the bridge was secured, although still coming under fire from above. The front-line of the entire battle now stretched for no more than the width of the bridge, soldiers and *Murid* fighters cramming forward into one another at its middle, the dead and wounded falling to be replaced from the crush behind them.

Suddenly, above the far side of the bridge, Pechorin caught sight of a tall figure in a torn *chalma* and red *beshmet*, scrambling across the bare rocks, his hand reaching back to guide the incongruous figure of a woman, and with a bundle wrapped tight across his back. The figure made its way in a daring diagonal away from the bridge towards the point where the ravine met the river behind Akhulgó, clinging to the rock like a mountain lion. In obedience to some obscure conviction, Pechorin turned and began to press his way back through the inrushing crowd of soldiers on the bridge, eventually emerging on the far side and sliding down the bank of the ravine, coming to a shuddering rest in a shallow trickle of water at its foot. He began to make his way towards the river, his boots sloshing out water, stricken with a sudden panic that he would not regain sight of the fleeing figures. He scrambled up the right-hand bank of the ravine as it curved towards the river beyond, bathed in sunlight that could not penetrate the rock-bound confines of the ravine. Suddenly, in the shadow of a rock at the water's edge, Pechorin saw again a red *beshmet*, crouched over a raft, an indeterminate bundle still wrapped to its back. The woman was nowhere to be seen.

Pechorin slipped behind the trunk of a stout elm tree and watched as the figure arranged two bundles of rags on the raft, before gently pushing it out from the shadows into the sun-dappled current of the river. After an interlude of no more than ten seconds, rifle fire broke out from the far bank of the Koisu, shredding into the raft and its brightly-coloured cargo. The figure in the *chalma* and red *beshmet* turned and disappeared behind the rock. Pechorin set off in pursuit. When he had reached the rock from which the decoy raft had been sent out to draw fire from our troops, Pechorin saw that the woman had rejoined the figure in the red *beshmet*, scurrying along in his wake as they clung tightly to the base of Akhulgó, shielded from the rifles on the far bank by the tall bushes which overhung the water's edge. Realising that they could only intend to follow the river until out of the range of the sharpshooters, hoping at some point to find a place at which it could be crossed, Pechorin once again followed, keeping at a sufficient distance to conceal himself.

At certain points the path disappeared entirely, leaving Pechorin to scramble through the bushes, each time losing sight of his prey, each time some nameless panic subsiding as the white *chalma* and red *beshmet* once again bobbed into view. After what could have been no more than a mile, his hands and cheeks scratched by branches, his boots oozing dirty water, Pechorin saw the couple come to rest on a bare, flat rock which protruded slightly into the flow of the river. As he once again concealed himself, the figure in the red *beshmet* looked around in all directions, the woman now clinging to his side. Pechorin could still not make out what was in the bundle on his back; but now, as the tall figure stared back towards him, he confirmed what he had known on some obscure instinctive level since he had climbed down from the bridge between New and Old Akhulgó – it had fallen to him to arrest the flight of the warrior *Imam*.

Pechorin took his pistol from his belt and stepped out from his place of concealment. Shamyl placed an arm across the breast of the woman by his side as he registered the approach of a Russian uniform, but made no attempt to reach for a weapon of his own. As the uniform drew closer, a pistol cleaving a path before it, Shamyl recognised Pechorin as the officer who had interceded between the Russian *Komandir* and the departed Surkhai Khan. The woman's gaze now turned also in Pechorin's direction, the terror in her expression in dramatic contrast to her husband's silent concentration. Pechorin opened his mouth to speak, but was interrupted by a sudden, inconceivable cry, like the cry of an infant, which Pechorin imagined had emanated from the interior of his own mind, for what other source could there be? While Pechorin stood motionless, entirely consumed by this impenetrable riddle of cause and effect, the woman stepped in front of Shamyl, turning her breast to Pechorin's pistol in a gesture of terminal defiance. As Pechorin hesitated once more, Shamyl suddenly placed his arm round the woman's throat, drew her to his chest, and hurled them as one backwards into the river. Pechorin was jolted back to consciousness by another piercing infant cry, which ceased as the figures before him disappeared from view. Without lowering his pistol, he leapt up onto the now empty rock and looked down into the fast-flowing river. Shamyl, his wife, and the infant child strapped to his back had disappeared beneath the surface without trace.

CHAPTER THIRTY

AN HONOURABLE DISCHARGE

Pechorin and Voronin wandered through the shattered ruins of New Akhulgó. The previous day, while Pechorin was engaged in his ultimately futile attempt to prevent the escape of Shamyl, had ended in chaos. Though the *Murid* position was lost from the moment our forces had ended the struggle on the bridge, streaming up the hillsides both left and right into now sparsely defended strongholds, every hut, every cave still had to be taken by force of arms. Some of the women and old men, although recognising the inevitability of defeat, refused to surrender, preferring to throw themselves on the bayonets of advancing soldiers. Voronin had even witnessed a mother, infant child on her back like Shamyl, hurl herself over the cliffs above the Koisu and into the arms of Allah, rather than fall into the hands of the Russians. Those who had taken refuge in the caves dug into the cliffs above the river had to be prised out by soldiers lowered on ropes, who were on occasion obliged to open fire blindly into the caves.

The stench of numberless corpses filled the air. More than a thousand bodies were recovered; yet more had been carried away down the river. Over the course of the day, some nine hundred prisoners were taken, mostly women, children, and older men. Even here, and notwithstanding their wounds and their exhaustion, some did not refrain from desperate deeds, gathering up their last droplets of strength to snatch the bayonets from their guards, preferring death to a degrading captivity. In the valley below, some of the natives who had come over to our side and the exultant Cossacks had tied the severed heads of the vanquished to the saddles of their horses.

'A pitiful scene' - said Voronin, no trace of a smile now discernible on his lips.

'A little scrap of the future that is, decidedly, no longer open' - Pechorin replied, neither smiling nor giving any particular indication of dismay.

Voronin merely looked at him, stranded between admiration and some unnameable disquiet, grappling with some barely formed notion that he would never quite understand the forces that distributed themselves through the sinews, veins, and synapses of this unlikely officer in His Imperial Majesty's Nizhegorodsky Dragoons.

'And what about another little scrap of the future, Pechorin?' - he asked - 'Yours, that is...'.

'My dear Vladimir Nikolaevich' - Pechorin replied, brightening - 'Are you, of all people, suggesting that the future leads somewhere that can be determined with any certainty?'

'Not exactly' - said Voronin - 'Merely that - as I believe I may have told you on a prior occasion – we must nonetheless prepare for it, otherwise the objectives we pursue may never be realised'.

Pechorin looked out over the blasted, battered remains of New Akhulgó, the stench of corpses once again assaulting his nostrils.

'Objectives' – he said quietly – 'I'm not entirely sure we have understood one another, Vladimir Nikol...'.

Suddenly, a native boy of no more than fourteen years old burst forth from one of the huts, a rifle in his quaking hands, careering towards Voronin and shrieking at the top of his voice. Pechorin threw himself onto Voronin and they crashed to the floor as the sound of a single rifle shot resounded around the ruins. The bullet flew over the heads of the fallen officers and out into the bright blue of the sky, whereupon Pechorin grabbed the desperate boy by the ankle and brought him crashing down on top of them.

'Arjouk!' – the boy cried in terror – '*Arjouk la takolni!*'

'We're not going to kill you' – said Pechorin – 'We're going to put you in a uniform and train you to kill other people'.

General Grabbe spent his days grappling with the contradictions of victory and defeat. On one hand, he had successfully routed the stronghold of Akhulgó; on the other, Shamyl had managed to escape and the symbol of *Murid* resistance in the Caucasus remained unvanquished. The Tsar himself would later write in his own hand on Grabbe's official report of the campaign: 'Very good, but it's a pity that Shamyl has escaped and I confess to fearing fresh intrigues on his part, notwithstanding that, without a doubt, he has lost the greater part of his means and his influence. We must see what happens next'. Grabbe's response to such ambivalence, in himself and in others, was to set the niggardly price of only three hundred roubles for Shamyl's capture, dead or alive. Before the end of the year, Grabbe's successor, General Golovin, had increased the price ten-fold, reasoning that the harm caused by 'this troublesome man' justified any means that might be used to destroy him. Golovin actively promoted this bounty among the tribes of Daghestan and Chechnya he considered the most courageous and enterprising, reasoning that three thousand roubles was a small price to pay for curtailing the conflict, particularly when measured against the potential loss of three thousand men – or indeed more.

In the event, even Golovin's price was too low. By the spring of the following year, Shamyl, escaped into Chechnya, had recovered his strength and even extended his authority – which would persist for nigh on two decades to come.

Pechorin found General Grabbe in just such a mood of conflicted reflection. Not the best moment to raise the question that had suddenly entered his mind weeks before as he wandered alone through the moonlit ruins of Gimry; but there was, he resolved, nothing else to be done.

'I wish to be discharged, Sir' – said Pechorin in a firm voice, which did not however exceed the bounds of propriety.

Grabbe gathered himself, his seated frame progressing through a series of subtle yet lugubrious movements which spoke of immense weariness.

'As do we all, Lieutenant Pechorin' – he replied. – 'As do we all. In your case, however – and there is no reason for us to be anything other than frank with one another – discharge means also pardon'.

Pechorin felt the first stirrings of a bitter, contemptuous smile at the corner of his lips, but managed to repress it.

'I am very well aware of that, Sir' – he said calmly. – 'I understand that my request may not be granted. But that is no reason not to make the request'.

Grabbe considered for a moment, then continued.

'Very well, Pechorin. You have, as I understand, those who are willing to speak and act in your support?'

'I believe I do, Sir' – Pechorin replied.

'Then I would advise you to write first to them when we return to Vnezapnaya' – said Grabbe – 'And then submit your formal request for discharge'.

'Very well, Sir' – said Pechorin, turning to leave – 'I am grateful for your advice'.

'Wait a moment, Pechorin' – said Grabbe – 'You should know also that I have recommended you for the Order of St Stanislav for outstanding valour at Surkhai's Tower and Akhulgó'.

Pechorin paused in the doorway, momentarily unable to process Grabbe's words.

'I'm grateful, Sir' – he said at last.

'There is no need' – said Grabbe, whose turn it now was to flash a smile of mischievous irony – 'It might help. One never quite knows'.

Pechorin arrived at Vnezapnaya exhausted, but nonetheless encouraged by what had occurred on the return march. He had confided first in Mungo, then in Voronin his intention to request discharge from military service; whereupon each of his comrades in turn, not without pleasure at this rare occasion when Pechorin had not somehow divined their own thoughts, calmly informed him that they had also come to the same conclusion. In the case of Mungo, in hindsight, this should have come as no surprise. Pechorin had observed at first hand that his uncle's many qualities were perhaps not those required to survive, much less thrive in, the great feast of war. He now understood that Mungo had in fact negotiated his time in the Caucasus by means of a complex combination of outward enthusiasm, inward cold calculation, and a felicitous relationship with the circumstance of fate. He had placed himself in danger only when there was no choice but to do so, as on the night when the *Murid* had almost taken the camp at Ashiltá by surprise. Moreover, his indiscretions, such as they were, paled into insignificance alongside the real reason he had found himself manoeuvred into voluntary exile: namely, his association with Pechorin. This, Pechorin was convinced, was surely not sufficient cause to stand in the way of discharge.

The case of Voronin was from one perspective more complex, yet from another, Pechorin reasoned, entirely straightforward. It remained the case that Voronin belonged to a dark and disreputable caste, his name forever associated with the events of December 1825; he would carry that stain, perhaps, for as long as Tsar Nikolai remained on the throne. Yet it was also true that Voronin was now approaching twenty years in the military, all of it spent in Turkey, Persia, and the Caucasus, each year adding new lustre to his legendary status among men and officers alike. Pechorin himself had witnessed Grabbe's reliance on Voronin's vanishingly rare combination of unerring strategic imagination and scrupulous attention to detail, his performance of the role of General without any thought of the glory of its title. What more, Pechorin asked himself, did a man like Voronin have to do in order to expiate his trifling sins?

Lev Pushkin, alone among these unlikely comrades-at-arms, had given no thought to the possibility of discharge, having long ago accepted that his place was and would continue to be in the Caucasus for as long as his unfortunate brother lived out his pitiful life in Paris. For who among us would wish death upon our brother as the price for our own release?

'The raven to the raven flies' - said Pushkin cheerfully, his smooth complexion restored beneath sun-burnished curls - 'Such as I was before, so I will be once again - alone!'

'Come, Lev Sergeyevich' - Pechorin replied - 'The odds are three to one in your favour'.

'He's quite right' - said Mungo - 'Just because we all three have petitioned for discharge, that doesn't mean that all three - or indeed any - of us will be granted it'.

Only Voronin, sunk deep in thought, did not speak.

'Well, if you put it like that, my dear Stolypin' - Pushkin replied, his cheerfulness undimmed, now augmented by the light of some wry opportunism in his eyes - 'I'll lay a hundred roubles - in silver, mind - that each of you will be discharged. If I am to be alone, I may as well have the means to amuse myself'.

'Done' - said Pechorin in a flash - 'If I'm to remain here with you, I'll need something to stake in order to take these fools' money from you'.

'Mungo? Voronin?' - Pushkin insisted - 'Are we agreed?'

'Indeed we are!' - Mungo replied, brightening - 'That's a hundred roubles I'll be more than happy to lose!'

Voronin remained silent, signalling his agreement only with a curt nod.

Pechorin could not be persuaded, by Mungo or by General Grabbe, to write to his grandmother or to his great-uncle Afanasii, requesting their assistance - and the assistance of their impeccable and complementary connections - in the matter of his discharge. His reasons, although he did not give expression to them, were in no way related to a reluctance to put them to any trouble or indeed to place himself in their debt; on the contrary, he knew that both would do whatever they could, entirely without the need to ask. He was not mistaken. Yelizaveta Alexeyevna composed a letter to no less a personage than the Empress Alexandra Fedorovna, which she arranged to be delivered by hand through a certain lady of her acquaintance. Afanasii Alexeyevich raised the matter in person with the Grand-Duke Mikhail, in the hope that his earlier forbearance of Pechorin's behaviour might now, when he had distinguished himself in the service of the Empire, be parlayed into outright forgiveness.

Three weeks passed almost entirely without incident, Pechorin passing his days in reading, relieved only by an afternoon gallop astride Ballad along the banks of the Aktash. One morning after breakfast, as Pechorin lay in his bunk reading a book by an author of whom Mungo had never heard, Mungo was summoned to the office of General Grabbe. Mungo shot a glance of consternation at Pechorin as he left. When Mungo returned, Pechorin had not moved.

'Congratulations' - Pechorin said drily, before Mungo could speak.

Mungo had indeed been granted discharge. Of Pechorin and Voronin, on the contrary, there was no word.

'You should speak to him, Pechorin' - said Mungo with a forced decisiveness, occasioned, no doubt, by embarrassment and discomfort.

'I will do no such thing' - Pechorin replied quietly - 'What good would it do?'

Voronin remained in the doorway, his customary indecipherable smile now replaced by an expression of grim sincerity.

'What will you do?' - Voronin asked at last.

'I'll wait' - Pechorin replied, returning to his book.

Two days later, it was Voronin's turn to be summoned by General Grabbe. As he left his quarters, Mungo made as if to utter what would no doubt be words of encouragement, but stopped himself before anything came out, restrained, perhaps, by the unreadable smile which still played on Voronin's lips. No more than five minutes had passed when Voronin returned, his expression quite unchanged. All eyes were upon him, but he made no attempt to satisfy the thirst of enquiry, quietly sitting down at the table used for cards.

'You owe me one hundred roubles, Lev Sergeyevich' - he said quietly to Pushkin - 'In silver, mind'.

Pechorin was conscious that the image of Pushkin now before him would remain with him for the rest of his life, his sincere devastation at this confirmation that no service to the Empire was sufficient to erase the stain of December relieved only by an overwhelming, almost childlike gratitude that he would not, after all, remain here alone. For Voronin, as for Pushkin himself, the price of release from Caucasian service had been irrevocably set at death or failing health.

'That makes it even' - said Pushkin drily, attempting to mask the thunderous beating of his heart, unable to resist a glance in the direction of Pechorin.

'But not for long, one way or another' - continued Voronin - 'General Grabbe is expecting you, Pechorin'.

Pechorin unconsciously and imperfectly mimicked the indecipherable smile on Voronin's face, unable to disguise a certain steely glint in his eyes as he left the room.

The steel in Pechorin's gaze had colonised every contour of his face and every movement of his body as he sat down before Grabbe, who, by way of stark contrast, exuded the kind of mournful compassion that rarely finds expression among men, much less among men inured to the demands of the martial environment.

'I'm afraid I have bad news for you, Grigorii Alexandrovich' - said Grabbe, his voice in perfect accord with his funereal expression.

Pechorin made no reply, his mask of ironic fortitude inviting Grabbe to confirm what he felt, as certainly as Trubetskoi lay beneath the soil at Surkhai's Tower, he already knew.

'Your esteemed grandmother has passed away' - Grabbe continued - 'I am sincerely sorry for your loss'.

Lev Pushkin made great play of his delight at becoming one hundred silver roubles richer, inventing fantastical tales of what he would spend it on; but even his considerable fabulistic talents could not extend themselves to the matter of where and when such opportunities might present themselves. Mungo and Pechorin understood very well that Pushkin's words were a mask for his true feelings: he would certainly mourn their loss, but a mere hundred in silver weighed nothing against his profound relief that Voronin would remain - and provided also a pretext for an emotion he could not decently display. Mungo, for his part, had greeted the news of his aunt's death and the apparently consequent confirmation of Pechorin's discharge with the confusion of feelings that might have been expected in such circumstances; but this conflict was as nothing to the brutal contradictions with which Pechorin himself was obliged to wrestle. He would never seek nor receive confirmation of his suspicion that his petition for discharge had been rejected, only for the decision, in some bleak corridor of the Ministry of War, to be reversed at the news of his grandmother's death. Yet he remained as certain on the point as he had been in General Grabbe's office: what the old woman had failed to achieve in life, she had eventually secured in the act of death. He had for his own part become quite unafraid of the vicissitudes of fate; but this reminder that his assiduously cultivated *sang-froid* was no impediment to the effects of fate on those he could not protect was at once sudden and, at the same time, struck with the terrible force of the long expected. He had been convinced for some time that he had earned the right to entrust himself to fate; but who among us has the right to vouch for the fate of others?

Pechorin's determination to part with Pushkin and Voronin with the minimum of ceremony had met with only limited success. When the time came to say farewell to Vnezapnaya, he hoped forever, Pushkin had insisted that they sit on their trunks and drink a last toast for the road.

'It's time, my friends, it's time' – he said in a voice that sought for magnanimity and enthusiasm, but yet still betrayed his undeclared relief that Voronin would remain – 'Let fate prepare us for the hardest roads'.

'Not too hard, I hope' – replied Mungo cheerfully.

Voronin said nothing, but raised his glass and drained it, smiling impenetrably to the last.

Now, as Pechorin rode steadily astride Ballad, the little detachment of Cossack cavalry and covered wagons in front, the jagged outline of the Caucasus a constant presence to his left, he thought not of the comrades he had left behind, but of the world to which he must now return. When they came at last to within twenty miles or so of Vladikavkaz, the road skirting the forest before turning once again towards the south, Pechorin was struck by a sudden desire to obey the apparent command of topography and plunge once more into the heart of the mountains that rose up in front of him, on this occasion never to return. By two o'clock in the morning, however, dragging himself into a bunk in the fortress at Vladikavkaz, the dream of escape had been extinguished.

From Vladikavkaz, Pechorin and Mungo would continue with a military detachment as far as Stavropol, from there taking the post-coach through the endless steppe between Novocherkassk, Voronezh, and Moscow. All memory of Peschanokopskoye had been erased from his mind. Yelizaveta Alexeyevna, in line with the practice of her forebears, but in a manner that remained deeply controversial in the Orthodox Church, had expressed a desire to be embalmed before burial in the family tomb. Afanasii Alexeyevich had therefore been at liberty to arrange for the funeral to take place all of four weeks after her death, thereby ensuring that his great-nephew, the old woman's only surviving progeny, was able to attend. She had not stipulated such detail in her will, but Afanasii Alexeyevich had instinctively understood it to be her purpose.

Pechorin's only concern on arrival at Vladikavkaz, apart from the execrable roads upon which he would spend the next three weeks – the occasion for Pushkin's not so subtle joke as they had left Vnezapnaya – was what to do with his beloved Ballad. He could not bring himself simply to sell her to the farrier, a bad-tempered fellow Pechorin was amused to realise he could not distinguish from the farrier at Vnezapnaya.

'Perhaps I'll have her transported to St Petersburg?' – he said to Mungo as they lay on the sun-kissed banks of the Terek, its parched bed praying for the day the warm southern autumn would at last give way to winter.

'You have a much finer horse in St Petersburg' – Mungo replied from under his hat – 'If only you could find a way to become as attached to a woman as you do to these damned horses'.

Pechorin absorbed the careless blow with some ease.

'There speaks a man with his priorities entirely in order' - he replied - 'I imagine the fair Natalya has grown more beautiful with each passing day'.

Mungo sat up in the grass and removed the hat covering his face, which he placed by his side in the warm grass.

'There is no fair Natalya' - said Mungo in a dull voice.

'Whatever do you mean, my dear uncle?' - Pechorin replied.

'She wrote to me every month without fail for the first six months' - Mungo continued - 'Then, nothing. I haven't had a word from her for over a year'.

'But perhaps...' - Pechorin began.

'Please, Pechorin' - Mungo interrupted - 'We both know what that means. And we both know that an... that a former officer and a gentleman would rather perish in battle than stoop to any further enquiry'.

Pechorin's silence indicated that he did.

Pechorin spent the remainder of the morning making inquiries about how his beloved Ballad might be transported to join his beloved Parader in the Imperial Stables in St Petersburg. At first, he took the farrier's insistence that no such thing had ever been attempted and that the poor beast would certainly perish or come up lame on the journey as no more than an attempt to inveigle Pechorin into selling for a terrible price. The farrier, for his part, refused to take Pechorin's questions about means of transport seriously, equally convinced that Pechorin had conceived of an unnecessarily complex pretext upon which to haggle: these gentlemen officers - and, in particular, those who bore the manner of St Petersburg - would stop at nothing to cheat an honest man of his living. As this dialogue of mutual incomprehension proceeded to its comical - and, for Pechorin, infuriating - conclusion, he suddenly caught a fragment of another conversation, carried on the wind from the entrance to the stables. After a few moments of silence, which the disgruntled farrier told himself was merely Pechorin's next move in the game, the old fellow decided to bring the matter to a head.

'Well, will you sell?' - he asked insistently.

'No, I don't believe I will' - Pechorin replied calmly.

The old man took off his cap and scratched his balding scalp, his face a picture of bewilderment.

'So what will you do?' - he said - 'Do you really intend to box her up and send her to her death?'

'No, I don't believe I do' - Pechorin continued, before bowing curtly to the bewildered farrier, turning on his heels, and striding out of the stables.

When Pechorin returned to his quarters, he found Mungo packing a small wooden trunk in solemn silence.

'You're very organised, my dear uncle' - said Pechorin cheerfully - 'We don't leave until tomorrow'.

Mungo made no reply, continuing his task with measured movements.

'Well, I suppose there's no harm in being prepared' - continued Pechorin - 'And I can't say I'm looking forward to nearly three weeks on dreadful roads, in dreadful coaches, sleeping – as if! – in dreadful inns. You will keep me entertained, won't you?'

Mungo once again remained silent, not even looking up from his trunk. Pechorin looked closely at his youthful uncle, his soft curls, which shone softly in the weak afternoon light, falling across his cheeks as he leant forward. For a moment, he struggle to recall the effervescent, guileless youth of St Petersburg; and even at Karanai and Ashiltá, when inwardly wrestling with the demands of honour, Mungo had never fallen entirely silent. Perhaps, Pechorin reasoned, he was now enduring an assault upon his honour no less grave, and somehow more complex, than anything he had faced in combat, embarrassed at having confessed his loss to Pechorin – or mortified in anticipation of the questions and knowing glances that no doubt awaited in St Petersburg.

'Look here, my dear uncle' – said Pechorin, not entirely successfully concealing the effort of maintaining a lightness of tone – 'I'm not sure I want to spend three weeks on the road with you if I'm going to have to make all the conversation myself'.

Mungo now looked up from his trunk, a faint ironic smile all that stood between him and complete abjection.

'I'm not coming' – he said quietly.

Pechorin spent all of five minutes interrogating the reasons for Mungo's sudden and quite unexpected decision, before realising not only that changing his mind was impossible, but that persisting would only make things worse. The immediate change in his uncle's demeanour confirmed the wisdom of Pechorin's retreat.

'I'll happily live out my time in the south' – said Mungo, brightening – 'If only I can be assured that my time is not apt to be cut short'.

'Where will you go?' – asked Pechorin.

'To Tiflis' – Mungo replied – 'If anyone wants to shoot at me there, they'll no doubt be kind enough to observe the formalities'.

An hour later, Pechorin stood in the yard of the Vladikavkaz Fortress, shading his eyes from the wintery sun, still not quite able to process the image before him. Mungo looked down from his mount, his smile bursting with gratitude that Pechorin had neither judged him nor sought to change his mind. Pechorin had thought for a fleeting moment that he might perhaps offer Ballad to Mungo, but had just as quickly resolved to hold to his original plan.

'I must say, my dear Mungo' – Pechorin began – 'You seem quite disgracefully pleased to be taking leave of my company'.

'Ah' – Mungo replied, warming to the game – 'Let's not pretend that this is farewell'.

'How so?' – Pechorin replied – 'Are you planning to join us in the capital when the weather is more favourable?'

Mungo smiled, now more in recognition of Pechorin's subtle wit than from gratitude or excitement at the adventure which lay before him.

'I'll lay one hundred silver roubles to twenty kopecks that you will come to me before I to you' – he said.

'My dear Mungo' – Pechorin replied – 'You should know by now that I only wager when I am certain of the outcome'.

'Certain?' – said Mungo, regretting only that this most enjoyable exchange was approaching its end – 'You do surprise me, Pechorin'.

The little detachment began to make its way through the gates of the fortress before Pechorin could reply. Mungo fell in at its rear, raised his right hand to the brim of his cap in a cheerful parody of salute, and rode off, still smiling, into the afternoon sunshine.

Later that evening, having completed his preparations for the journey ahead, Pechorin leapt up into the saddle astride Ballad and began to make his way to the edge of the settlement that fanned unevenly out from the fortress. He soon came to a modest little house, almost at the outskirts, with a neatly fenced veranda and white acacia rising up and over the door. There was no light in the windows, but Pechorin nonetheless dismounted and knocked quietly at the front door. On hearing no reply, he tethered Ballad to the little fence, and kissed her on the nose.

'Farewell, my beauty' – he said quietly, before turning and making his way back to the fortress.

The following morning at six, before the sun had made its way to the line of the horizon in the east, a harassed little man came through the door beneath the white acacia, a doctor's bag in one hand, pulling his tunic around him with the other. He was about to rush down the steps of the little veranda and make his way to a patient he had left at the very portals of death on the previous afternoon, when he suddenly became aware, through the dense morning gloom, of a fine black horse tethered to his fence. He stopped for a moment in complete incomprehension, then broke into a smile poised perilously between exasperation and a sudden unburdening gratitude, which for one fleeting moment provoked the beginnings of a tear somewhere behind his eyes. Recovered, he took a deep breath of the fresh morning air as his shoulders relaxed and a weight lifted from his soul.

'What shall we call you, my beauty?' – said Dr Werner softly – 'And what adventures have you seen?'

BOOK IV

CHAPTER THIRTY-ONE

THE FUNERAL

A WEAK SUN PROGRESSED towards its modest zenith, barely disturbing the harsh, bracing St Petersburg winter, the still air resonant with frost, the sound of sledges on the broad, frozen Nevá competing with the laughter of rosy-cheeked girls; in the evenings, ballrooms – noisy, scintillating – resounding to the sound of champagne glasses, killing fields for bands of gloomy single men.

Pechorin pushed such thoughts out of his mind as he entered the precincts of the Smolny Convent, where the last respects were to be paid to the mortal remains of his grandmother. He felt no remorse, though he could not entirely quell the soft voice that insisted he had contributed in some way to her demise. In the place in his soul that might have been reserved for a desire for forgiveness, there rose instead an insistent, unquenchable anger: the passing of the flesh seemed a poor return for the faith that had once sustained it.

The chapel of the Convent was so full of people it was difficult to make his way through the entrance. An open coffin had been placed on a rich catafalque, beneath a canopy of velvet. His grandmother lay with her hands crossed on her breast, in a robe of white satin and head-dress of lace. Her closest family – his own closest family – was assembled around the catafalque, his great-uncle Afanasii prominent among them. Sasha Vereschagina and her mother sat in silence on a front pew, heads bowed. Towards the back of the chapel, unseen by Pechorin, Blagodatsky sat alone. Only Dmitrii Stolypin sought Pechorin's gaze as he took his place.

The servants stood on either side in black kaftans with a knot of ribbons on their shoulders, exhibiting the colours of the Stolypin coat of arms, each with a wax candle in hand. No one wept, their irrational souls fearing still the reproach of the old woman for their vulgar affectations.

The funeral sermon was delivered by a celebrated preacher. In a few simple, touching phrases he painted a picture of the triumphant departure of the just, of a woman who had passed the long years of her widowhood in contrite preparation for a Christian end. The service concluded in respectful silence. The relatives, led by Afanasii Alexeyevich, moved towards the deceased to take a last farewell. As Pechorin advanced towards the coffin, he knelt down for a moment on the flagstones, which were strewn with branches of fir. Then he rose, as pale as death, and walked up the steps of the catafalque. He bowed his head as he approached the coffin. When he raised his eyes to meet the extinguished gaze of his grandmother for the last time, he was suddenly overcome, reached out for the side of the coffin to steady himself, missed and fell backwards into a faint. As Dmitrii and two of Yelizaveta Alexeyevna's many nieces attended to Pechorin on the steps, the remainder of the congregation came forward in a long procession to bow for the last time. Finally, the gathered servants joined the procession, at the rear of which an ancient woman, supported by two younger servants, painfully made her way up the steps to the coffin. She had been Yelizaveta Alexeyevna's governess. Pechorin, recovering his senses, watched as the tears flowed from the old woman's eyes as she bent to kiss the hand of her departed mistress, inseparable in her mind's eye from the image of the seven-year-old girl she had once been.

A few minutes later, Pechorin took his place to the left of Afanasii Alexeyevich at the entrance to the chapel in order to receive the guests as they made their exit. Each mourner in turn - some Pechorin had known since childhood, others he did not recognise at all - bowed as they took Afanasii's hand, expressing in the same moment their profound condolences. Each then appeared in front of Pechorin to repeat the same ritual, before passing silently to his left, in the vast majority of cases, he was certain, never to be seen by him again.

At length, Yelizaveta Vereschagina stood before him, her head bowed, her lips murmuring a barely audible catechism. She stood for perhaps a minute or more until at last her murmurs devolved into silence. As she looked up into Pechorin's eyes, tears beginning to well in her own as they had done on a summer evening long ago, he thought not of his grandmother, but of Alexei Vereschagin, who had been lowered into the frozen earth of Irkutsk almost twenty years previously. The tears in Madame Vereschagina's eyes receded.

'I am so glad you have returned to us' - she said softly, some of the light returning to her faded eyes.

Pechorin merely bowed in response, looking for some clue in the expression of Sasha, who now glided into view as her mother slipped quietly from it, her head high and a gentle smile playing on her lips.

'Don't speak' - said Pechorin before Sasha could utter the obligatory words of condolence - 'There will be time enough for that'.

As the last of the mourners took the hand of Afanasii Alexeyevich, Pechorin cast a glance towards the gates of the Convent, anxiously seeking the features of a person he was now certain had not been present in the chapel, but who might, he conjectured, have wished to pay her respects from a discreet distance. But she had not come.

Throughout the day Pechorin suffered from a strange indisposition. He repelled all the imprecations of Afanasii Alexeyevich and Dmitrii to join them for lunch, preferring to walk alone among the bare trees in the Summer Gardens. He now consoled himself that it was for the best that Vera had not appeared. Her marriage, he reasoned, had therefore survived. And the ridiculous drama of their parting had at least presaged the final curtain.

He reproached himself for the yet more ridiculous thought that in his newly acquired condition - the estate at Serednikovo would yield perhaps 20,000 a year and he had not yet been apprised of the capital sum of his inheritance – he was at last in a position to overcome the obstacles economy and society had placed in the path of romantic legitimacy. Such thoughts were relieved only by the grim pleasures of irony: his grandmother's death had removed any last obstacle to the marriage she had so fervently wished for him; but it had also removed the only force that might conceivably have compelled him to embrace it. He had attained that state for which he had fought so unremittingly since the age of sixteen. He was – with regard to his private affairs, if not quite his public standing – a free man.

As the Embankment of the Nevá came into view beyond the boundary of the Summer Gardens, Pechorin was struck once again by the absence of remorse, or indeed any of the emotions associated with mourning. His attention was consumed instead by a curious sense of absence: the battles that had compelled him since childhood were over, their only casualty the innocence he would never recover. Perhaps, he mused, he would employ an estate manager for Serednikovo and retreat to Kropotovo, where there would indeed be nothing else to do but read his books and ride the horses. For a brief moment, he imagined himself as a breeder of horses, but this was soon extinguished by a more insistent and at the same time more practical thought. He turned on his heels before the grey swell of the Nevá had appeared beyond the Embankment wall and set off at a brisk walk towards the Imperial Stables.

Dmitrii had assured Pechorin that his beloved Parader had wanted for nothing in his absence, but only now, beholding once again this miracle of geometry and living matter, did he accept the truth of his uncle's word. Even this weak winter sunshine was enough to ignite a blaze of shimmering light on Parader's sleek coat as he skipped around the *ménage*, a stable boy in a scruffy cap and waistcoat offering only nominal instruction. Pechorin stepped quietly towards the surrounding fence without saying a word or seeking to attract the boy's attention and simply watched for a few minutes as Parader frisked and stamped. Eventually, the creature came to a halt in the near left-hand corner of the *ménage*, then walked gracefully along the fence towards him, where he lowered his strong, smooth neck almost to the ground and gave a snort of recognition and, Pechorin fancied, admonition. Pechorin reached out a hand towards Parader's glistening neck, whereupon the creature raised his head to its fullest height and let out a louder snort, now devoid of any reproach.

As Parader made his way at a walk along Sadovaya Street, Pechorin took in the buildings ranged on either side as if he had never before laid eyes upon them: the house in which Sasha Vereschagina and her mother still lived; the Shahkovsky house in which his grandmother had lived the last year of her life, declining to return to Serednikovo until, he suspected, she had secured his discharge from military service; and there in the distance, its blue dome gleaming in the sunshine, the Izmailovsky Trinity Cathedral, where the old woman had perhaps said her final prayers.

Pechorin brought Parader to a brief halt at the intersection of Obukhovsky Prospekt and the Fontanka Canal, where a lifetime ago he had collected Vera on their way to the grand opening of the steam railway at Tsarskoe Seló. For one brief moment, he thought of turning back towards the Lopatkin house, but then urged Parader into a canter across the bridge over the canal and south along Tsarskoselsky Prospekt. When horse and rider had cleared the Obvodny Canal, Pechorin pulled hard to his left and Parader broke into a gallop towards the Volkovskoe Cemetery. Pechorin beamed in admiration and relief that Parader had lost none of his smooth power as he accelerated effortlessly, the world around horse and rider disappearing in a blur. A year and a half ago, this glimpse of exhilarating freedom had seemed to presage a life that might be lived in such a permanent state. Pechorin now understood not only that this was impossible, but also, and therefore, that it must be savoured at any and every opportunity. The world would not remain invisible for long.

Pechorin returned to the city at dusk, his mood returned to an unobtrusively bitter melancholy. He made his way once again along Sadovaya Street, his thoughts only of rest and supper at Dmitrii's father's old house by the Anichkov Bridge. As he emerged alone from the Imperial stables, however, a sudden and inscrutable whim drew him to the other side of Nevsky Prospekt and into the warren of little streets behind the Kazan Cathedral. Hungry and increasingly aware of the cold that had settled upon the city with the departure of the sun, he pulled the collar of his coat up around his ears and quickened his step, now suddenly determined towards his destination. He made his way along the Yekaterina Canal, then turned into a narrow, filthy lane with no more than ten tall buildings on either side. He examined the plaques mounted above each doorway as he passed, some of them metal, others wooden, but each displaying the same signs of age and disrepair as the buildings. He came at last to an unlit archway, above which a new metal plaque had been mounted, but which as yet bore no inscription.

'What building is this?' – he barked at a boy of around eleven loitering in the doorway.

'The Kifeikin house, your Honour' – the boy replied, hopeful of a coin.

Pechorin did not disappoint, then swiftly made his way across the inner courtyard and up two flights of stairs on its far side. The stairway was broad, but the darkness could not disguise the thick layer of grime that clung to the walls. Pechorin struck a match in order to confirm that he was indeed standing in front of number twenty-seven, extinguished the match, and took a step back from the door.

Pechorin had not laid eyes upon Blagodatsky since he had slipped out of the Petropavlovsk Fortress into the concealing mists of the St Petersburg night. Blagodatsky's features now confirmed that a lifetime had passed since that night, that ineffable balance of the freshness of youth and the sagacity of experience having tipped over, in the abyss of Petrozavodsk, into grey middle-age. A weak smile of recognition and gratitude spread across Blagodatsky's face.

'How did you find me?' – he asked quietly when both were seated.

Pechorin returned Blagodatsky's smile, anxious to communicate warmth in response to his old friend's now seemingly habitual suspicion.

'Oh, when I learned that you had left the funeral without a word, I made discreet enquiries' – Pechorin replied – 'But don't be concerned. Both Dmitrii and my great-uncle no doubt imagine I am alone or in search of quite different company'.

'Were you followed?' – Blagodatsky asked suddenly.

Pechorin studied his erstwhile mentor with calm deliberation, concealing in the process his surprise at the implication of Blagodatsky's question.

'Why do you ask?' – said Pechorin.

'I was permitted to return to St Petersburg only on strict conditions' – Blagodatsky replied – 'I am forbidden from associating with anyone involved in the Sinyukhaev affair'.

'And me?' – asked Pechorin – 'Was I involved in the Sinyukhaev affair? Or was I involved in an affair of my own?'

Blagodatsky's smile remained, now tinged with a trace of indignation.

'You know very well how it works, Pechorin' – he said firmly – 'The rules are never clear. The crime may always be designed to fit whatever charges may please the estimable Count von Benckendorff; and who is to say what may please that gentleman from one day to the next?'

Pechorin smiled more broadly, partly in recognition of Blagodatsky's bitter logic, but partly also to convey his own disregard for any potential consequences. von Benckendorff had insisted in his case only that he be disbarred from attending public gatherings – with the exception of his grandmother's funeral – for a period of six months or until further notice. He could not conceal from himself the relish with which he anticipated the moment when his own resolve would be tested.

Pechorin's apparently blithe disregard had the opposite effect on Blagodatsky to the reassurance Pechorin had intended.

'Please, Pechorin' – Blagodatsky said gloomily – 'Enough of this. Have you learned nothing? They may very well have allowed you the grace of attending your grandmother's funeral without a pale-blue uniform to despoil the scene; but your movements will remain of at least as much interest to our friends in the Third Department as mine'.

Pechorin paused for a moment, torn between conciliation and frank confrontation of the new reality that pertained between them.

'I hardly think you're in a position to give advice' – said Pechorin at last, his smile once again blooming – 'Take a look at yourself, my dear Blagodatsky: you of all people enjoyed the trust of my dear grandmother, God rest her soul; your allotted role was to shepherd her errant grandson along the path of righteousness, to curb his excesses, and lead him at last to respectability, if not quite salvation. And what did you do?' – he continued, now laughing as he spoke – 'Why, you managed to get yourself arrested for sedition!'

Blagodatsky looked back at Pechorin in ambivalent silence. Then, as Pechorin's expression resolved into that characteristic half-smile Blagodatsky had known for as long as he could remember, his features softened, a shadow of his youthful complaisance returned, and he burst into grateful laughter.

'Do you see how things have turned out, my dear Blagodatsky?' – said Pechorin, triumphant – 'I was, after all, only following your example'.

When Blagodatsky had returned with a half bottle of Burgundy and poured a glass for each of them, Pechorin, relieved now to have shifted the conversation away from himself, began to interrogate him on the events of the past eighteen months. Blagodatsky recounted in a calm voice, though not without discomfort, how the family of his then *fiancée* had insisted that marriage was now out of the question: the daughter of a respectable family would neither follow him into disgrace, nor await his exculpation. While he had been allowed to retain his rank during his time in Petrozavodsk and the modest salary that went with it, the suspicious and timid officials in the municipal authority had asked him to do little more than attend his desk, never entrusting him with any kind of meaningful work. He had, for over a year, spent his weekdays sitting in a bare and silent office, pretending to cast his eye over an endless stream of meaningless documents. His weekends he had spent reading whatever books the local booksellers could provide, at inflated prices he never bothered to query. On hearing of Yelizaveta Alexeyevna's death, he explained quietly, he had initially requested only permission to return to St Petersburg to attend the funeral: then, on what he obscurely recalled as little more than a whim, he had written formally to request a pardon. His astonishment at its conferral was matched only by his horror at returning to a life which was no longer his own. The apartments he had once rented at a favourable price from a Titular Councillor in his former Department were now inhabited by someone else. He occupied a desk in a shared office in the Ministry of Foreign Affairs, his duties numerous, but none commensurate with his rank. As he drew to the conclusion of his sorry tale, he looked wistfully around the dank room in which they sat.

'And here I live' – he said quietly.

Pechorin searched for a moment for a way to revive the contradictory, ironic cheerfulness with which he had successfully countered Blagodatsky's initial gloomy suspicion. He then came quite suddenly to the realisation that to resist was futile, until such time as the store of Blagodatsky's despond had been exhausted once and for all.

'Tell me, Blagodatsky' – said Pechorin calmly – 'What news of Sinyukhaev?'

Blagodatsky had been anticipating this question since overcoming his surprise that it was indeed Pechorin who stood on the dark stairwell of his new lodgings, but was still somehow taken aback by its utterance. He fought for a moment against the incipient tightening of his throat and the muscles around his mouth, leaned forward to pick up his glass, and took the merest sip of wine.

'Dead' – he said, the monosyllable dropping with a faint thud into the space between them – 'He died six months after arriving at Nerchinsk. They buried him there, in a grave marked only with a wooden cross. There was no question of returning the body to St Petersburg or to his birthplace'.

Pechorin received these words as if Blagodatsky was speaking from a script Pechorin had written for him, so familiar was he with each nuance. He mimicked Blagodatsky's actions, raising his glass and taking a sip of wine.

'To the living' – Pechorin said in an even tone, raising his glass once more and draining its contents.

Blagodatsky's indignation was now, for the briefest of moments, shaded with anger, his features devoid of any trace of an ironizing smile. He fixed Pechorin with a gaze designed to communicate reproach, which nevertheless transformed in a matter of seconds into some barely describable combination of grief and defiance. At length, he too raised his glass and drank the last of the bitter wine.

'To the living'.

Pechorin's desire to curtail the conversation was soon accompanied by a sudden wave of fatigue. The depredations of the accursed road, the unwanted public spectacle of the funeral, with the attendant emotional cost of deflecting albeit sincere expressions of condolence and, worse, invitations to social distraction of one kind or another, had combined with the exhilarations of the afternoon and a lack of material sustenance to exhaust him completely. The thought of the exertions involved in making his way back to Dmitrii's house by the Anichkov Bridge, not to mention the exertions of the conversations that no doubt awaited him there, were relieved only by the thought of the cold evening air. He imagined himself, collar pulled up around his ears, walking by the banks of the Yekaterina Canal in the enveloping darkness for all eternity, walking and walking but, by some unfathomable trick of space and time, never arriving at his destination. He rose weakly to take his leave of Blagodatsky, throwing on his coat as he moved towards the door, where he turned once again to face his host.

'Goodnight, Blagodatsky' – he said, mustering what cheer he could.

'Goodnight, Pechorin' – Blagodatsky replied – 'Need I say it?'

Pechorin's features were once again enlivened by some pleasure he could not name, some comforting recognition of at least a part of himself in the mind of another.

'No, my dearest Blagodatsky' – he replied with a smile – 'There is no need to say it'.

Pechorin followed the path by the Yekaterina Canal, so convinced that it would never end that he was for a moment confounded entirely by the sudden appearance of a still bustling Nevsky Prospekt. He stopped for a moment, glanced across Nevsky to confirm that the canal did indeed continue on its mysterious way, then turned right along the Prospekt, suddenly aware of the cold that had until now relieved his slightly feverish state. For a few steps, he registered the expressions on the faces of the stream of passers-by against which he steadily moved; by the time he reached the Gostiny Dvor, however, he pulled the collar of his coat still higher, lowered his gaze to the flagstones, and hurried home without looking at a soul.

Dmitrii's entreaties and reproaches on Pechorin's arrival were easily repelled by the simple and sincere expedient of asking for something to eat. Pechorin was by now quite famished, unsure as to whether the feverish state of his mind was more an effect of causes psychological or physiological. The old cook Aglaya had been given the evening off to visit a niece in Sosnovka, too distant for her to return until the morning, but had prepared some roast chicken before her departure, which Dmitrii now embellished with bread, butter, and the obligatory glass of Burgundy. As Pechorin began to eat, with a conspicuous relish Dmitrii had rarely observed in him, uncle resolved to allow nephew a few minutes to satisfy his hunger, before launching the salvo of questions he had been accumulating for more than a year. Pechorin finished his meal and began coddling his wine glass, easing himself back into the deep armchair by the warming fireside.

Just as Dmitrii was about to make his first sally, however, there came a knock at the door. There being no servants in the house, Dmitrii, as annoyed as he was surprised by an intrusion at this late hour, rose to answer it himself. Pechorin could only hear a muffled and indistinct exchange of words at the open door, then the footsteps of two men along the parquet in the hall. He sat up in his chair and turned slightly towards the door, glass still in hand. Dmitrii appeared in the doorway, his features a knot of perplexion.

'There's a gentleman to see you, Pechorin' – he said curtly.

Pechorin now turned fully in his armchair and began to rise as a tall, emaciated figure stepped into the room, his wiry hands clutching a battered hat in a display of quiet modesty, his thin grey hair framing his large, expressive, although sunken eyes.

'Why, Private Lazarev' – said Pechorin politely, with the briefest glance of reassurance towards Dmitrii, his smile once again concealing his surprise – 'Do come in. Sit down and make yourself comfortable'.

Lazarev declined Dmitrii's offer of a glass of Burgundy, settled into an armchair at the other side of the fireplace from Pechorin, and clasped his hands across his knees.

'I'll leave you, gentlemen' – said Dmitrii quietly, retreating to his study at the rear of the house.

When Dmitrii had gone, Pechorin turned to Lazarev with an open and inviting expression.

'It is no longer Private Lazarev' – the visitor began – 'I am once again Oleg Abramovich, at your service. His Imperial Majesty was kind enough to release me from service, on account of the many years I had spent in the south and, moreover, their effect upon my health'.

Pechorin gave a nod of polite approval.

'I understand also that you are no longer Lieutenant Pechorin' – Lazarev continued – 'But first, Grigorii Alexandrovich, let me offer my condolences on the passing of your grandmother. "He that heareth my word and believeth in him who sent me, hath everlasting life and shall not come into condemnation; but is passed from death into life"'.

'St Peter or St John?' - Pechorin asked in a cheerful voice - 'You must forgive me, Oleg Abramovich, I was very grateful for your kind gift, but I was so rarely able to devote the time it rightfully deserved'.

Lazarev neither knew nor much cared whether Pechorin's response was sincere or delivered with the intention to mock.

'The Gospel according to St John' - he replied quietly - 'St Peter speaks not of the passing of the flesh'.

'He is wise indeed' - Pechorin continued - 'For what is there to say?'

Lazarev once again ignored the levity in Pechorin's response, smiling back at him with calm indulgence.

'You are quite right, Grigorii Alexandrovich. What we might have to say about the inevitability of our passing is as nought to what we so rarely say about the needlessness of suffering on earth'.

Pechorin now returned Lazarev's calm smile without any flicker of irony, intrigued by the direction of this strange creature's mind, although determined, as always, to disguise his interest.

'And what do you say about the needlessness of suffering on earth, Oleg Abramovich?' - said Pechorin in a studied, even tone.

'Only that it is needless' - Lazarev replied - 'And therefore, because it is needless, that it might be eradicated'.

Lazarev sensed Pechorin's surprise at the directness of his words, even as Pechorin strove to maintain an appearance of polite forbearance.

'Tell me, Oleg Abramovich' - said Pechorin after a brief pause - 'Do you have occasion to discuss such matters with your fellows?'

Lazarev thought for a moment, as if grappling with some terrible conundrum, then continued in a low whisper, his voice cracking with unspoken fear or exhilaration.

'That is what I have come to talk to you about, Grigorii Alexandrovich. There are places where such matters might be discussed and I have, since returning to St Petersburg, fallen into the company of those who are determined to discuss them'.

'I don't suppose these places are called churches?' - Pechorin replied, now anxious to counter the tone of conspiratorial solemnity Lazarev had somehow managed to impose on their conversation.

'No, Grigorii Alexandrovich. The church is not the place for such discussions' - Lazarev replied, his eyes glistening above his sunken cheeks and grey complexion - '"Thy will be done on earth, as it is in heaven"'.

Pechorin made no reply, but held Lazarev's exultant gaze for what seemed an eternity.

'It is late, Grigorii Alexandrovich' - Lazarev said at last - 'I have taken up enough of your time'.

CHAPTER THIRTY-TWO

THE BRETHREN

A RAW DECEMBER MORNING lay upon St Petersburg. The wet snow fell in thick clumps, the buildings seemed dirty and dark, the faces of passers-by green. The coachmen at the cab-ranks dozed under faded rugs in their carriages, the long wet coats of their poor horses gathered in plaits. Distant objects took on a lilac-grey tinge in the mist. The pavements only rarely resounded with the clatter of the galoshes of the civil servant, now accompanied by noise and laughter from a basement inn as a drunk young man in a rough overcoat was thrown out. Pechorin hurried past, his head down over his lacquered boots, covered in snow and mud, hands thrust deep into the pockets of his coat, with the uncertain steps of a man afraid to reach his destination – or who did not in fact have one. He stopped on Kokushkin Bridge, raised his head and looked around. His face bore the signs of mental fatigue, a strange disquiet in his eyes as he realised how far he had strayed into the depths of the city. As he stepped off the bridge into the adjoining lane, he suddenly recognised the Kifeikin house in which Blagodatsky lived, transformed in the bleak half-light. He was about to step through the archway beneath the blank metal plaque, but was halted by the realisation that Blagodatsky would no doubt at this moment be seated at his desk in the Ministry of Foreign Affairs. He continued his way along the filthy lane towards the crossroads, where, suddenly, a young man of no more than twenty in a ragged overcoat and a student's cap came hurtling out of a doorway, catching Pechorin in the midriff as he took off down the lane towards the canal. Pechorin made as if to shout his reproach, but the words dissolved into the freezing grey fog.

When at last he returned to the Stolypin house, his great-uncle Afanasii was seated by the fire in the drawing room, deep in amiable conversation with Dmitrii.

'My dear Grigorii!' – Afanasii Alexeyevich exclaimed as Pechorin came into the room – 'I am pleased to see that military service has had the desired effect on your habits'.

'I am a man after your own heart, my dear uncle' – Pechorin replied, shaking the morning gloom from his voice.

'I'm not entirely sure things have progressed to that stage' – replied Afanasii Alexeyevich, the cheerfulness now gone from his voice – 'But we live in hope'.

Dmitrii returned Pechorin's smile, relieved that the events of the previous day did not appear to have left their mark. Pechorin had, with some justification, pled fatigue after Lazarev's departure; and he had slipped out of the house that morning before Dmitrii was awake, determined to shake off his strange mood before submitting to conversations he knew to be inevitable.

'Afanasii Alexeyevich has some good news for you, Pechorin' - said Dmitrii quietly.

'Indeed I do, my boy' - said Afanasii - 'As I'm sure you will have anticipated, I was appointed executor of your late grandmother's estate. And, as you also know, she has left everything to you... with the exception of some minor provisions for some of her more favoured nieces and nephews'.

Afanasii Alexeyevich glanced discreetly in Dmitrii's direction, but Dmitrii made no sign of acknowledgement.

'The details are all in there' - continued Afanasii Alexeyevich, handing Pechorin a large manilla envelope, sealed at the top with an extravagant daub of red wax, which bore the imprint of the seal of the Imperial Chancellery - 'I congratulate you, my dear Grigorii. You are a man of property'.

Pechorin casually laid the envelope on a table by the window in a not so casual display that he had no wish to discuss the details of his inheritance. He had known the general outline from his grandmother for a number of years - as had Afanasii Alexeyevich - and the particularities now seemed of little significance. He resolved inwardly to ensure that both Dmitrii - if not already provided for - and Blagodatsky would be indirect beneficiaries of his newly acquired wealth.

'Have you given any thought to the matter?' - continued Afanasii Alexeyevich, undeterred - 'Where do you intend to live?'

Pechorin reasoned that his great-uncle's appetite for reassurance might more readily be satisfied with albeit limited candour, as opposed to outright resistance.

'Indeed I have' - Pechorin replied - 'Insofar as thought is required'.

Afanasii Alexeyevich frowned indulgently.

'I will live here' - Pechorin continued - 'For the moment at least, I have no intention of selling Serednikovo or Kropotovo; at the same time, I have no intention whatsoever of involving myself in their administration'.

'I'm not entirely sure I understand' - said Afanasii Alexeyevich, his frown now one of concern.

'My intention is to employ an estate manager for Serednikovo, who will no doubt make a better fist of the affair than I would myself. Kropotovo, as you know, has survived without a master or a manager since the death of my father; I see no reason for that to change'.

Afanasii Alexeyevich shifted in his chair, anxious not to over-play his concern at Pechorin's cavalier attitude to the business of wealth, knowing from long experience that any such display was apt further to entrench his great-nephew's determination.

'It is more and more common' - conceded Afanasii Alexeyevich - 'There may even be something to be said for it in terms of agricultural innovation... But how do you intend to arrange such a thing?'

'Ah, my dear uncle' – replied Pechorin with a broad smile – 'I had thought I might leave that in your own extremely capable hands'.

When Afanasii Alexeyevich had left, Dmitrii asked for tea and cakes to be brought from the kitchen and settled down in the chair facing Pechorin, his features a battleground of reproach and wry admiration.

'You really mustn't provoke him like that, Pechorin' – said Dmitrii.

'My dear Dmitrii' – Pechorin replied – 'He takes such great pains not to provoke *me* that I almost feel obliged'.

The tea and cakes had the desired restorative effect. Pechorin began to feel the strange disposition of the morning and the previous day lift, just as the chill began gradually to leave his bones. Dmitrii, who had observed Pechorin's mood without a word, now silently acknowledged the mischievous warmth in his demeanour, without setting any great store against its permanence.

'Two letters came for you while you were out, Pechorin' – said Dmitrii, with a measured cheerfulness, designed to encourage the faint glimmer of enthusiasm he hesitantly perceived in Pechorin.

'Oh' – Pechorin replied, in an equally measured display of disinteres. – 'The post has become uncommonly efficient since my sojourn in the south'.

'Hand delivered' – said Dmitrii.

Pechorin once again gave no outward sign of interest in the content of the letters, or indeed in the matter of who might be their authors.

'Aren't you going to read them?' – continued Dmitrii, his eagerness contending with slight annoyance, not primarily at Pechorin's display of *sang-froid*, but at his own foolishness in expecting anything else.

'I'll read them later' – Pechorin replied, reaching for the last of the little *madeleines*, which sat like a desert island amid the ocean of the pale blue china plate.

Dmitrii watched as Pechorin chewed, once again searching for some clue to his nephew's intentions, once again reproaching himself for such misplaced hopes. Pechorin took a sip of tea to wash down the *madeleine*, scouring his mind for some memory that might prepare him for the vicissitudes of the future. He found nothing.

When alone in his room, Pechorin took out the two letters and read them one after the other. The first was written in a tiny, spider-like script, which Pechorin recognised even before he read the signature at the bottom.

My Dear Grigorii Alexandrovich,

I very much wish to thank you, first of all, for your forbearance of yesterday evening: I have no wish to impose myself upon you, particularly in circumstances where, I am sure, you will have many demands on your time and energies; at the same time, and with the greatest of respect, I feel compelled – indeed, I feel it to be a duty – to invite you to continue our conversation in such circumstances as I began to describe. To that end, it would be an honour if you

would accompany me, on Thursday of this week, to a modest gathering at the home of a gentleman I will not, for the moment, name, but whose company I feel certain will be of interest and benefit to you – and, indeed, the reverse. If you are agreeable, I will call for you at your esteemed uncle's at 6 o'clock; if on the other hand I have misread your desires in this regard, I apologise and respectfully ask that you appraise me of such in advance of Thursday.
I remain, as always, your respectful,
Oleg Abramovich Lazarev

No one, of course, was witness to Pechorin as he read Lazarev's letter, but no witness would have been able, all the same, to gauge the response from his implacable features. Such a witness would, however, have been unable to mistake the surprise on Pechorin's face occasioned not only by the contents of the second letter, but by the fact that it was printed or embossed into a rather ornate little card by some sort of writing machine, imported, he would later learn, from Italy and described as a *tachigrafo*.

Respected Grigorii Alexandrovich Pechorin

Count Ivan Illarionovich Vorontsov-Dashkov
and his esteemed wife
Countess Alexandra Kirillovna Vorontsova-Dashkova

Have the pleasure of requesting your presence at a New Year's Eve
Bal masqué at their home on the English Embankment

8.00 for 8.30
Dress: formal, masked

R.S.V.P.

By the time Pechorin had finished reading, however, a certain sense of relief had triumphed over his initial surprise, which in turn gave way to a rueful smile at the tantalising opportunity this latter invitation might present – if indeed he were minded to accept it.

The afternoon had barely progressed past its mid-point on the following Thursday, but the sun had already set. Pechorin had made no reply to Lazarev's fevered invitation. He sat sipping tea in the warmth of Dmitrii's drawing-room, reflecting that, even now, it was not too late to disabuse that strange creature of whatever illusions he might harbour; not, of course, in general, but with specific regard to the future actions of a retired officer in His Majesty's Nizhegorodsky Dragoons – and one who, moreover, still bore the mark of disgrace. Pechorin took a copy of *The Contemporary* from a side-table by the glowing fireside and settled back into the warmth of his armchair.

On the stroke of six, the bell rang. Pechorin listened as a muffled conversation took place on the doorstep, before Aglaya appeared and informed him there was a gentleman to see him.

'Ask him to wait in the vestibule, Aglaya' - said Pechorin - 'Tell him I'll be with him shortly'.

The dirty snow that had begun to melt during the few daylight hours now crunched under their feet as a deep frost took hold. Pechorin and Lazarev made their way in silence along the Fontanka canal, crossed the Simeonovsky Bridge, and turned left into Mokhovaya Street, whose wooden pavements had, thankfully, been cleared of snow.

'It's not far' - said Lazarev, sensing in Pechorin a mild but unspoken annoyance.

Lazarev eventually came to a halt in front of a ramshackle, three-storey wooden house, which, in the manner of all but the most prestigious addresses, had been divided into apartments of one or, sometimes, two rooms. Pechorin followed him as he made his way through the communal entrance and up the stairs to the first floor, where he paused before a smartly painted door with no nameplate or number. Lazarev knocked twice, discreetly, and stepped back from the door. After a few seconds, a single knock, just as discreet, could be heard from inside the door, to which Lazarev responded by again knocking twice. The door opened to reveal a tall, bearded man in an impeccably tailored but slightly distressed frock-coat, the wire-frames of his spectacles perched perilously on his full, lugubrious face. He glanced quickly at Pechorin, then back to Lazarev.

'Come in, gentlemen' - he said at last in a deep bass voice, ushering them into a tiny hallway, furnished only by a coat-stand that had been buried under frock-coats, overcoats, and even furs - 'I'm delighted you could join us'.

'The pleasure is all ours, Mikhail Vasilevich' - said Lazarev with a curt bow - 'May I introduce Grigorii Alexandrovich Pechorin? Grigorii Alexandrovich... Mikhail Vasilevich Petushevsky'.

'Delighted, I'm sure' - said Pechorin, offering Petushevsky his hand with a friendly but insistent gaze.

Petushevsky took Pechorin's hand with unexpected force and vigour.

'I am honoured to make your acquaintance' - he said, enthusiastically returning Pechorin's gaze and without relinquishing his grip, a slight tremor now in his *basso profundo* - 'Honoured indeed'.

Petushevsky, as Pechorin immediately understood, was the most unlikely fellow. His physical bulk and quietly sonorous voice concealed a delicacy, even timidity that had marked his temperament from early youth, but which had become all the more pronounced as a result of the peculiar circumstances of his existence. Petushevsky was a Collegiate Assessor in the Ministry of Foreign Affairs, who had gradually formed the habit of inviting friends, many of them former acquaintances from St Petersburg University, to his modest apartments in the evenings, chiefly for the purpose of discussing the latest foreign publications. One of Petushevsky's responsibilities in the Ministry was to assist notable visitors who had encountered difficulties in Russia, by means of which he had gradually acquired one of the most enviable private collections of French and German books in St Petersburg. He was never more animated, in his professional or private life, than in the company of French visitors, from whom he had managed to acquire the principal publications of Blanc, Saint-Simon, and, above all, Charles Fourier: even his most devoted friends would roll their eyes when, perhaps five seconds into a conversation that had begun with 'Good day!', he would begin to regale them with quotations from Fourier's *Le nouveau monde*. Petushevsky was in fact principally known beyond his own immediate circle for his disastrous attempt to realise Fourier's idea of the *Phalanstère* on his failing estate near Novgorod, constructing an ideal community in which, he fervently hoped, all would live and work on an equal footing, regardless of their status. When the spry new building was complete, the forty or so peasant families indentured to the estate left their poor huts and entered this strange new, egalitarian world; but when Petushevsky next returned from St Petersburg, he found the *Phalanstère* and all its amenities burned to the ground and the peasants returned to their old world.

The skills of diplomacy and tact Petushevsky had developed in the parallel worlds of the civil service and his landed estate were honed to perfection, however, in the private confines of the literary and political circle that had steadily grown around his accommodating personality, where every stripe of progressive – and inevitably competing – opinion had constantly to be maintained in some passable equilibrium of solidarity. He now, with practised ease and care, ushered Pechorin and Lazarev through into an inner room, dominated by a large oval table, at which were seated perhaps a dozen men. Pechorin was silently astonished to recognise among them the curious fellow he had seen leaving Sinyukhaev's cell at Petropavlovsk, whose name he could not recall. They exchanged reserved nods of recognition. The remainder of the company looked mutely past both Lazarev and Petushevsky at Pechorin's incongruous figure. Alongside the critic he had encountered at Petropavlovsk sat a thin, nervous young man, fair-haired with a sickly complexion and small grey eyes which darted uneasily from object to object, his colourless lips contorted in agitation. Pechorin acknowledged him with the same restrained nod, but the young man could only feverishly look away.

The conversation, which had subsided at the entrance of Pechorin and Lazarev, gradually resumed and was quickly dominated by the thin voice of a heavily-built, bearded man in his late forties, brimming with indignation at some recently published novel.

'Such opinions are more than worthy of being in fashion' – he insisted, drawing the entire company into his orbit – 'This is the same picture of repulsive, fanatical characters one encounters in contemporary foreign novels'.

'You're much too unkind, Nikolai Pavlovich' – said a young poet, perhaps no more than twenty-one or twenty-two.

'Kindness has nothing to do with it' – insisted the man who had been identified as Nikolai Pavlovich – 'Foreign or not, it is precisely such novels that are ruining our morals and character: even though we read these pitiful groans with distaste, they nonetheless leave us with a feeling of pain, because in the end they produce the habit of believing that the world consists entirely of such people...'.

'Come' – continued the young poet calmly, more encouraged than daunted by the older man's indignation – 'Surely our reading public are sophisticated enough to understand that life is not a novel? And, in any case, the author has provided no shortage of positive characters'.

'Aha!' – replied Nikolai Pavlovich, warming to his theme – 'That is precisely the problem! The better people in this fictional world, according to their actions, arouse only worthless and base responses! And what must be the result? Contempt or disgust for mankind. Is this the aim of our earthly existence? Everyone is already so inclined towards hypochondria and misanthropy; why then, by means of such representations, must we develop or encourage such feelings? And so, I repeat, in my opinion this pitiful talent reveals in the author great depravity of mind'.

'Perhaps the author might clear his mind among the more virtuous ranks of our Caucasian troops, where he might even find characters more worthy of description?' – said another voice – 'What do you think, Lazarev?'

Lazarev, now seated between Pechorin and Petrushevsky, looked down at the deep blue of the cloth covering the table, searching, Pechorin understood, for a response that would offend neither side of the discussion. He was interrupted – or, more properly, delivered from the horns of his dilemma – before he could speak.

'From what I have seen of the Caucasus' – said Pechorin in a calm, firm voice – 'our reading public would greatly benefit from such a thing. Whether anyone would trouble to read it, however, is another matter entirely'.

The conversation followed its course for an hour or so without digressing from its ostensibly literary subject matter. Pechorin gradually grew bored, much to Lazarev's consternation, until at last Petushevsky, who had disappeared from the room, returned to declare that supper was served. Pechorin was somewhat pleasantly surprised that supper turned out to be a passable hot buffet, accompanied even by a few bottles of Burgundy. When the company had satisfied its material needs, some began to drift away from the table into little groups forming around the room. Pechorin searched for some clue as to the principles by which each group accumulated, personal dislikes no doubt vying with advance knowledge of what would be discussed and by whom. He remained at the oval table, glass in hand. Lazarev, it seemed, was intent on not leaving his side, while Petushevsky himself had drifted back to join them.

'Literature does not appear to be your favoured topic of discussion, Grigorii Alexandrovich' - said Petushevsky in his low voice, now somehow softer than when surrounded by his fellows.

'I read for pleasure, Mikhail Vasilevich' - Pechorin replied.

'Why of course' - said Petushevsky - 'But is not literature a source of knowledge of our society, of our fellow men? You yourself have acknowledged that the reader might benefit from the reading'.

'Certainly' - continued Pechorin - 'But if I wish to know something of our society, I will observe it at first-hand. Why would I require the intercession of some fellow who is more concerned to paint himself in a favourable light than do justice to his subject?'

'And what is your opinion of our society?' - asked Lazarev suddenly.

Pechorin glanced at Petushevsky and took a sip of Burgundy without looking at Lazarev.

'I see a society incapable of action' - Pechorin replied - 'A society so accustomed to obedience that its inhabitants, while endlessly desiring to change, have come to accept that change is impossible and are therefore eternally dissatisfied with life, with themselves, with everything'.

Petushevsky studied Pechorin with an indulgent smile.

'You are quite right, Grigorii Alexandrovich' - he said gently - 'When a man is dissatisfied, when he is unable to express himself and reveal what is best in him - not out of vanity, but out of a quite natural desire to fulfill himself - he is destined to fall into moral degradation of one kind or another: one fellow, if I may be so bold, takes to the bottle; another becomes a gambler and a cardsharp; a third becomes a quarrelsome bully; yet another, finally, goes out of his mind from *ambition* - at the same time despising his own ambition and all that he has had to suffer because of it'.

'We Russians have little personal dignity' - said Lazarev, rhyming with the sentiments of Petushevsky - 'Very few among us have managed to retain the sense of self necessary for action, without becoming an egoist who acts only in his own personal interest'.

Pechorin felt again that strange curiosity Lazarev had provoked in him in Stavropol, now exacerbated by the unexpected thrust of his words.

'I had not taken you for an egoist, Oleg Abramovich' - he said, no trace of his incipient smile apparent on his lips.

Lazarev bowed meekly in acknowledgement of Pechorin's barb, then continued with renewed force.

'The Lord has protected me from such a fate' - said Lazarev, looking intently at Pechorin - 'But to eradicate egoism from the heart of a man entirely is to eradicate his vital principle, his leaven, the salt of his personality'.

Pechorin returned Lazarev's gaze, now oblivious to the presence of Petushevsky.

'A rational acknowledgement of self-will is the highest manifestation of human dignity' - Lazarev continued, staring now into some distant imaginary - 'All can aspire to it. Few can attain it'.

The young poet who had gently taken issue with the literary judgements of the pompous Nikolai Pavlovich now joined them at the table, attracted, or so it seemed to Pechorin, by the quiet fervour of Lazarev's disquisition.

'Grigorii Alexandrovich' - said Petushevsky affably, perhaps relieved at an opportunity to change the topic under discussion - 'May I introduce Alexei Nikolaevich Plescheyev?'

Pechorin bowed slightly in acknowledgement, but the young man eagerly thrust out his hand and Pechorin took it.

'Delighted, I'm sure' - said Plescheyev, before turning his gaze to Petushevsky - 'You will forgive me for interrupting, Mikhail Vasilevich, but I couldn't help overhearing that the conversation had turned once again to... well, to human dignity... How are things on your estate?'

Pechorin exchanged glances with Lazarev, seeking reassurance that this seeming impertinence was considered within the bounds of acceptability in these peculiar surroundings.

'Oh' - Petushevsky replied as cheerfully as he could muster - 'Much better than they were! We must be guided by the desires of the people, as much as by our own'.

Pechorin once again looked to Lazarev for some key to this oblique exchange.

'And what about you, Grigorii Alexandrovich?' - said Plescheyev, turning to Pechorin - 'What are your views on human dignity and agricultural slavery?'

Pechorin frowned and made as if to reply, but heard instead the voice of Lazarev before he could speak.

'Come, Alexei Nikolaevich' - said Lazarev quietly - 'Even the Tsar, if those close to His Majesty are to be believed, has determined that the bondage of serfdom must come to an end'.

Pechorin's steady gaze concealed his profound confusion.

'His Majesty has sought the assistance of the Nobility in the matter of converting the status of the peasants from serfs to tenants' - continued Lazarev, ostensibly addressing Plescheyev, but intending his words for Pechorin.

'Nonetheless' - said Plescheyev, maintaining a light, even cheerful tone - 'I'd be most interested to hear Grigorii Alexandrovich's views on the matter. What do you say, Grigorii Alexandrovich? What price human dignity?'

Pechorin paused for a moment, quelling once more the impulse to react to Plescheyev's apparently wilful impertinence.

'I see no great difficulty, Alexei Nikolaevich' - said Pechorin calmly - 'If human dignity can be served and I receive a price in rent in the process'.

Lazarev smiled through thin lips, his eyes gleaming amid the ruins of his emaciated features.

Lazarev's smile had not faded by the time he and Pechorin parted on the Simeonovsky bridge, the gleam in his eyes piercing the frozen air.

'Goodnight, Grigorii Alexandrovich' – he said in an exultant tone – 'I hope your time has not been wasted'.

'Not at all' – Pechorin replied – 'I have all the time in the world'.

'Will you come again?' – asked Lazarev.

'Let's see, shall we?' – said Pechorin, smiling gently at Lazarev's unabashed persistence – 'Who knows what fate has in store for us, after all?'

Pechorin pulled the collar of his overcoat up around his ears and set off along the bank of the Fontanka, his boots sinking softly into the layer of snow that now covered the ice below. Thick flakes of snow fell from the silent sky, lit by the yellow glare of phosphorescent street-lamps. Pechorin could barely hear the muffled sound of his own footsteps, but, when he halted for a moment to light a cigar, he became suddenly conscious of a faint echo, which continued for two or three steps after his own had ceased. He thrust both hands back into his pockets and walked on, drawing gently from the cigar and periodically allowing little puffs of smoke to escape from the corner of his mouth. On a sudden impulse, he stopped again; and heard once again the muffled echo of his steps in the snow. He walked steadily for a few more paces, then stepped through an archway on his right, extinguished his cigar, and concealed himself behind a pillar. For a few seconds, in the enveloping silence of the snow-filled night, he thought he must have imagined the now absent sound of footsteps. Then, suddenly, they resumed, quickening towards the archway, faint yet unmistakable. Pechorin peered out from his place of concealment as a tall figure in an overcoat and hat, his moustaches and sideburns in the German style adorned with crystals of ice and snow, flashed past, his muffled footsteps gradually receding into the silent night.

CHAPTER THIRTY-THREE

LE BEAU MONDE

THE BAL MASQUÉ at the home of the Countess Alexandra Vorontsova-Dashkova on the English Embankment had been underway for some time when Pechorin stepped in through the main entrance, which opened out onto a grand reception hall. The low hum of chatter contended with the sound of a piano and the loud murmur of a fountain. The hall and its great staircase were crowded with civil and military tunics with bright decorations, the identity of their owners concealed by masks of all kinds and colours. Pechorin took a glass of champagne from a passing tray and was suddenly aware of Dmitrii at his elbow, ushering him towards the little theatre Countess Vorontsova-Dashkova's father, after the example of Catherine the Great, had insisted no respectable home could be without.

'What on earth are you doing?' - Dmitrii whispered through clenched teeth.

'The same as you, I expect' - replied Pechorin, enjoying the moment.

'Well, there's nothing much of interest happening in the main hall' - continued Dmitrii, now dragging Pechorin towards the little theatre with grim determination - 'This is where you'll find something to amuse yourself'.

'But what about our hostess?' - objected Pechorin, now laughing - 'Shouldn't I at least introduce myself?'

Dmitrii paused at the door to the theatre, the full horror of the situation now beginning to dawn upon him.

'You were invited?'

'Why of course, my dear uncle!' - Pechorin replied - 'You don't think I'd come to a ball to which I had not been invited, do you?'

Dmitrii drained his glass and pushed Pechorin across the threshold.

The *baignoires* of the opulent little theatre were adorned with elegant ladies in berets or velvet hats with feathers in them. A row of generals holding Venetian masks leaned over the *baignoires*, entertaining and complimenting the young beauties. As Pechorin and Dmitrii performed a silent mime-play by the stage, Dmitrii refusing to accept that futility was any reason not to persist in persuading Pechorin to leave, they were approached by an impeccably dressed young woman in a black dress trimmed with white and embroidered with lace, a bouquet of real flowers in her hand.

'Do you recognise me?' - the young woman asked with a smile, her dark eyes smouldering beneath her mask.

'I'm afraid I do not' - Pechorin replied with a curt bow - 'Although I'm not sure I would know you, even without the mask'.

'I know you, Lieutenant Pechorin' - she replied.

Pechorin glanced at Dmitrii, seeking a moment to disguise his surprise at the young woman's boldness. Dmitrii, for his part, abandoned the last scrap of hope that Pechorin's mask might somehow prevent his identification.

'It's no longer Lieutenant Pechorin, I'm glad to say' - he replied calmly - 'But tell me, how do you know me?'

'That is my business, Monsieur Pechorin' - the stranger replied.

'I'm flattered' - said Pechorin with a smile - 'I'm relieved only that there is very little to know'.

The young woman returned his smile, the dimples creasing at the corners of her mouth somehow giving the impression that she perhaps did know more than she felt the need to say.

'May I give you some advice, Monsieur Pechorin?' - she asked, still smiling.

'If you must' - said Pechorin, once again concealing his surprise.

'Don't stay too long' - said the young woman in a tone that belied the knowing smile still playing on her lips.

'Oh really?' - Pechoin replied evenly - 'And why is that?'

The young woman fixed him with her dark eyes from beneath her mask.

'Apart from the obvious?' - she said, still smiling - 'Well, perhaps you should think for a moment of that long blond hair and those deep brown eyes'.

The mysterious young woman turned and disappeared into the crowd, laughing as she went.

'Astonishing!' - said Pechorin, turning to Dmitrii - 'Who is that? Do you know her?'

'I have no idea' - replied Dmitrii, again taking Pechorin by the elbow and glancing towards the clutch of generals and young ladies in the *baignoires*, who had now arranged themselves into couples.

'Perhaps we should leave these gentlemen and their young ladies to it' - said Pechorin, glancing in the direction of the main hall, into which the mysterious stranger had vanished - 'I really must pay my respects to our hostess'.

Dmitrii hesitated for a moment, looking back into the hall like a man peering out from a precipice at the edge of the world.

'I suppose you're right' - said Dmitrii - 'But keep your mask on, whatever you do'.

The almost exclusively masculine gathering in the main hall was now relieved in places by the presence of the occasional elegantly attired lady of a more venerable generation than those who had gathered in the theatre. Pechorin caught sight of Countess Vorontsova-Dashkova in the midst of a clutch of silver-haired civil servants by the fountain, which murmured gently in affable competition with the constant hum of conversation. The Countess was not yet thirty years old, some twenty-five years younger than her esteemed husband. Pechorin had seen women more beautiful; he had known women more intelligent; but he was convinced in that moment that he had never known a woman in whom such qualities were more favourably combined. Her fine features, perfect skin, and refined bearing she quite purposefully framed by allowing her natural curls to fall unfettered to her shoulders, even in formal dress. Her social standing had not, moreover, diminished her capacity for empathy, her elegance had not occluded her simplicity, nor her capacity for a gaiety that all who came into contact with her immediately understood to be quite authentic. When she spoke – and especially when she laughed – she could be mistaken in such company for a girl of eighteen. She turned as Pechorin approached, recognising him immediately beneath his mask, and beamed in a manner entirely at odds with the words that sprang mellifluously from her lips.

'My dear Grigorii Alexandrovich! We were so very sorry to hear of the passing of your grandmother; please accept my condolences'.

'You are very kind, Countess' – Pechorin replied with a low, somewhat theatrical bow, which allowed him a moment to register the looks of consternation only partially concealed by the masks surrounding the Countess.

The Countess made her apologies to the admiring but now concerned gentlemen who had gathered around her, took Pechorin by the arm, and led him to a *chaise* by the wall on the far side of the fountain.

'I am most grateful for the invitation, Countess' – Pechorin began when they were seated – 'But I hope it would not be too impolite to inquire as to why you were so keen on my attendance?'

'Oh, I don't know' – said the Countess, her elegant features now overlain with an expression more suggestive of a mischievous schoolboy – 'Perhaps I wanted to see if you would come?'

'And why wouldn't I?' – replied Pechorin.

The Countess bowed her head slightly in order to contain the overly satisfied smile which came involuntarily to her lips.

'We are well aware of your situation, Grigorii Alexandrovich' – continued the Countess – 'Quite unfair!'

Pechorin composed himself once more and fixed the Countess with an indulgent stare.

'I wouldn't concern yourself about that, Countess' – he said softly, attempting at one and the same time to emphasize his lack of concern and downplay his inclination to express it – 'What is the worst that could happen?'

The Countess returned his gaze, a now openly mischievous smile playing on the corner of her lips.

'Oh, I don't know' – she said airily – 'Your mask might fall off and some miserable creature might report you'.

Pechorin smiled in return, content to allow the Countess her enjoyment of the game she had set in motion.

'Or perhaps a member of the Royal household might attend' – she continued, her eyes glistening – 'One never knows'.

Pechorin found Dmitrii engaged in a rather heated conversation with a writer, who Dmitrii had apparently accused of attending such gatherings for no reason other than to gather scabrous material for his uninspired little stories. The poor fellow seemed relieved, if somewhat confused, to be rescued by an insistent Pechorin, who discreetly pulled his uncle away from any casually intrusive ear.

'Did you know?' - said Pechorin, with almost no trace of reproach in his voice.

'Rumours had been circulating since yesterday' - Dmitrii replied - 'But, well... you know how rumours are'.

'Quite' - said Pechorin, the wryness in his smile intended to depose any trace of bitterness.

'Listen, Pechorin' - said Dmitrii - 'it is quite bad enough for you to be here; you know very well that news of that will make its way back to those who are interested - if in fact it hasn't already. But to remain in the presence of the Grand-Duke Mikhail...'.

Pechorin's calm expression belied the unashamed thrill that rose within him.

'Well' - Dmitrii continued - 'I think it would be better if you left'.

Pechorin studied his uncle with outward calm, while internally acknowledging - and even exulting in! - the anger that began to jostle with the thrill of anticipation.

'I'll do no such thing' - he said calmly, reaching for a glass of champagne from a passing tray.

Shortly before ten o'clock, the faint tinkling of the piano gave way to the triumphant surge of a string octet as couples took to the floor for a waltz. In the commotion that accompanied the stirring of music, few among the company remarked the entrance of the Grand-Duke Mikhail, who picked Countess Vorontsova-Dashkova out in the crowd and set off in her direction to pay his respects to the house. Pechorin watched from the doorway to the theatre as the Grand-Duke was surrounded by well-wishers, some in the frock-coat of the civil service, others in military uniform. After a few moments of seemingly affable conversation, the Grand-Duke began to look around the main hall, his demeanour suddenly changed. His gaze returned again and again to the doorway of the theatre, interspersed on each occasion by expressions of apparent indignation addressed to his companions. At length, amid whispered communications passed from one reveller to another around the perimeter of the dancefloor, the Grand-Duke set off towards the theatre.

'They'll arrest him!' - cried a voice after the Grand-Duke had passed out of earshot.

'Not in my house they won't!' - replied Count Vorontsov-Dashkov, setting off in pursuit.

The music stopped and the waltz came to an end, dance partners blocking the path of the Grand-Duke as they came and went from the floor. When he had come to within a few paces of where Pechorin stood, unmoved by Dmitrii's imprecations to avoid a public scandal, the music once again struck up. As if from nowhere, the Countess seized Pechorin's hand and launched him in a swirling waltz deep into the crowd. Every so often, between the carousel of faces, they caught a glimpse of the furious Grand-Duke, once again surrounded by grey-haired Generals, gesticulating in a manner whose significance could not be misinterpreted.

'Where do we go from here?' – asked Pechorin as they twirled away to the far side of the hall.

'Aren't you enjoying the dance, Monsieur Pechorin?' – replied the Countess, who gave the sincere impression that she had never, in fact, enjoyed herself quite so much.

'Immensely' – replied Pechorin – 'But I daresay you are not available for the next dance and the one after that'.

'Alas!' – the Countess replied – 'That is unfortunately so. There is a little sitting room to the left of the staircase' – she continued – 'I'll give you the signal when we come to it on the next circuit. Wait for me there'.

Pechorin caught one last glimpse of the Grand-Duke amid the sea of bobbing, twirling heads as they flew once more towards the main staircase.

'*Adieu*, Monsieur Pechorin' – cried the Countess.

Pechorin slipped deftly from the Countess's embrace and, without breaking stride, ducked behind a crowd of young officers and stepped through a door into a dimly lit sitting room. He felt a strange surge of energy in the air as he closed the door behind him, almost as if he had stepped into a magnetic field. There in the half-light, sitting in an armchair, he could make out a dress adorned with black lace, the mask still in place above it. Every detail of the attire of the mysterious stranger he had encountered briefly in the theatre exuded ostentatious charm. Her little hand was now clasped to her head in a gesture of enchanting fatigue, an inexpressible harmony in the manner in which she leaned back into the chair, in the charming ease of her entire being.

'Are you alone?' – Pechorin asked quietly.

'Yes' – she replied – 'I'm tired. Terribly tired'.

They were silent for a moment.

'Are you angry with me?' – she asked.

'Not at all' – replied Pechorin.

'It's terribly hot in here. Hot and stuffy. The air presses in on me; these people press in on me!'

Pechorin made no reply.

'My life is unbearable. I'm suffocating. Always the same faces, the same conversations. One day is just like the next. We poor women are the most pitiful creatures on earth. We have to conceal our better feelings; we do not dare display our best intentions; we give everything to society, to the significance society bestows upon us'.

Pechorin remained silent.

'We have to live with hateful people, listening to their words without feeling or thought. Oh, if only you knew how tired I am of all these ladies, all these gentlemen! The men are so base, the women painted, the entire gaudy chaos dull and suffocating! And what do they say about us? That we have no feelings, that we are incapable of love? How can one have feelings, how can one love someone where everyone thinks only of themselves?'

'That is true' – said Pechorin – 'It's impossible to love while thinking only of oneself'.

'Then why go on?' – the young woman asked in a trembling whisper – 'If genuine love is impossible, we have we gone even against God's will. What is there to live for?'

Pechorin paused for a moment, then resolved to utter something he had never before said, judging for some reason that in this half-light, to this masked and unknown young woman in a state of distress which rivalled her apparently disdainful self-confidence earlier in the evening, the bare truth might be told.

'A woman' – he said quietly – 'What is there that is better than a woman?'

'A woman' – the stranger replied – 'is all very well for as long as she is young and attractive to men. A woman is lauded for as long as her beauty affords her a certain value in society. But beauty fades... and the heroine falls, ridiculed by those who were once her suitors. And what remains? Nothing, except reproach; nothing at all, except for their insistence that we are incapable of feeling, incapable of love...'.

'And is that true?' – said Pechorin – 'Do you really love no one?'

'You don't know me, so I can speak openly' – she replied – 'I don't think so... although many have tried to love me. But I somehow don't believe them. Everyone has their own reasons, their own motives. I'm married, of course. My husband loves me, because I'm of use to him in society. A certain Adjutant loves me, because he hopes, through me, to make connections. A diplomat loves me, because it gives him a certain status in society. And there are a few more who love me because they've nothing better to do and because they're unbearable!'

Pechorin remained silent, seeing that there was nothing he could do or say to relieve the profound sadness which had engulfed this beautiful stranger.

'But what is to be done?' – she continued in a voice now calm, to which some trace of life had returned – 'I can speak so freely only from beneath this mask. But tomorrow, I will wear a different mask; and that mask I am fated never to remove'.

Pechorin took her by the hand and pressed it warmly in his own.

'I must leave' – he said – 'They will come for me soon, no doubt. But tell me, why did you warn me earlier not to stay too long?'

The stranger gazed out from beneath her mask, a bitter smile once again creasing into dimples at the corners of her mouth.

'You have already found out' – she replied – 'Did you really think they would allow you to live as you once did?'

Pechorin's own mask, he was sure, could not conceal his astonishment at these words. Who was this melancholic stranger and how could she know so much of his circumstance? Before he could reply, however, the question that had tormented him since their first encounter in the little theatre once more floated to the surface of his consciousness.

'And what about the long blond hair and the deep brown eyes?' – he asked, still folding her hand in his own.

'You'll find out soon enough...'.

Suddenly, before Pechorin could press his strange confessor, the door through which he had entered flew open to reveal Countess Vorontsova-Dashkova framed against the light of the main hall.

'Come!' – she said in a loud whisper – 'You can leave through the kitchens, but you must come right away!'

Pechorin raised the hand of the unknown stranger, kissed it softly, and hurried towards the door.

As he made his way through the kitchens, weaving between the startled staff who were preparing the late supper, Pechorin felt a faint, even absurd regret that he had not encountered these surroundings in the blue light of the dead of night, dashing in concealment from an assignation with the delightful Countess. Such thoughts were, however, vanquished by the sudden rush of frozen air as he emerged into the cloudless evening. Pechorin ignored the line of expectant cab-drivers, each wrapped in blankets over his overcoat against the biting cold, and made his way along the Embankment of the Nevá towards Senate Square, the river tossing like a man sick with fever, dreaming, perhaps, of the wounded and dying who had been driven beneath the breaking ice in December 1825. He turned towards the Admiralty building, its gilded spire dull against the dark sky, failing to spark some mute communication with the golden dome of St Isaac's Cathedral. He felt upon him the gaze of Peter the Great, mounted on his bronze steed, which reared atop an enormous granite monolith, dragged eight miles to this place by bonded serfs, terrible against the surrounding gloom, in his enormous mind enormous thoughts. Pechorin strode through the square towards the Lobanov-Rostotsky House, guarded by two great stone lions, where Tsar Nikolai had given the order to fire on the Decembrist rebels. He imagined for a moment the sound of hooves clattering on the cobblestones behind him, then realised, as he had in the silent snow-covered night returning from Petushevsky's, that his mind was not playing tricks upon him: persistent footsteps followed his own.

Pechorin at first quickened his pace, then suddenly slowed to a gentle stroll more appropriate for a warm day in the Summer Gardens. Nevsky Prospekt was still crowded with revellers, hurrying to the warm locations in which they would welcome the New Year. Any prospect of identifying his pursuers was lost among the milling crowds; he resolved instead to evade them. Pechorin now strode more purposefully through the streams of people until he came alongside the Stroganov Palace. Suddenly, he stepped into the filthy road, skipped between the startled drivers of cabs and the odd carriage, and disappeared along the bank of the Moika Canal, casting no more than a cursory glance towards the General Staff HQ on his left. As he turned right into a narrow lane, Pechorin once again slowed his pace without for a moment averting his gaze. He paused amid the steady stream of worshippers filing in through the doorway of the Finnish Lutheran church, where he was able to turn back towards the lane without, he hoped, revealing the suspicion that he was being pursued. Sure enough, two figures bundled up in dark overcoats and hats hurried through the snow towards the church, then, conscious of the little crowd forming in its doorway, stopped abruptly on the corner and gave the appearance of considering whether to attend the midnight service. On a sudden whim, Pechorin abandoned his intention of returning to Dmitrii's house, where, he fully expected, he would already find his agitated uncle. He slipped through the crowd behind the church into an unlit courtyard, which eventually opened out onto the Yekaterina Canal. He set off along the canal as quickly as the treacherous pavement would allow, then turned back on himself into Konyushennaya Square. Some strange intuition compelled him to the view that the Kuragin house might not only provide a more amenable environment in which to welcome the New Year; and, if he could not elude the shadowy figures pursuing him through the St Petersburg night, a more appropriate environment in which to confront them.

'Lord above us!' - exclaimed Anatolii Kuragin as Pechorin glided through the eternally open front door - 'I wasn't sure you were still alive!'

'I quite often share your uncertainty' - replied Pechorin, slipping out of his overcoat and depositing it in the entrance hall.

Pechorin had never laid eyes upon Kuragin when that gentleman did not have at least some quantity of wine flowing through his veins, although, on this occasion, that process did not appear to have progressed too far. Kuragin good-naturedly handed Pechorin a glass of Burgundy and fixed him with a gaze of mock severity.

'Now look here, Pechorin' - said Kuragin, visibly enjoying himself - 'The last occasion on which you graced my house with your presence, if I recall, set in motion a rather unfortunate sequence of events. I hope you're not planning a repeat'.

'Oh, I'm not planning anything at all, my dear Kuragin' - Pechorin replied airily - 'It's just that I was obliged, entirely unavoidably, to change my plans for the evening. I hope you don't mind?'

'Not at all!' - cried Kuragin in a great expansive roar, which gave way in turn to a more reflective, but no less ironic demeanour - 'From what I've heard, you have kept only the most impeccable company since your return to our northern capital'.

Pechorin merely raised his glass in acknowledgement of Kuragin's hospitality and made his way without a word through into an inner room, where in fifteen minutes or so the characteristically diverse company that had drifted into the harbour of the Kuragin house would welcome the New Year.

Pechorin nodded to two officers he recognised from the military academy, each of whom had abandoned uniform for New Year's Eve. A supernaturally thin violinist sat dolefully in the corner in evening dress, his violin, for now, exchanged for a wide-brimmed champagne glass. In normal circumstances, Kuragin's would have been entirely devoid of the female of our species, but on this very particular occasion a number of gentlemen present had elected to be accompanied by their wives, or at least by other women of their acquaintance. Pechorin positioned himself in a little company of civil servants, perhaps in their thirties, two of whom were deep in conversation with appealingly dressed ladies. He introduced himself with a curt nod, registering that none of these gentlemen knew who he was. For a moment, he thought of draining his glass, excusing himself, and pressing on to the redoubt of Dmitrii's house, but hesitated on the boundary between thought and action, restrained by the same obscure intuition that had gripped him on the bank of the Yekaterina Canal. Before some countervailing force could propel him once again into motion, Kuragin appeared in the doorway, all trace of the playful irony with which he had greeted Pechorin now absent from his saturnine features.

'It's almost time' – said Kuragin as he approached, gesturing as he did so to the violinist, who drained his glass and reached for his violin.

'Ladies and gentlemen!' – continued Kuragin, addressing the company, but with one eye angled firmly in Pechorin's direction – 'It's almost midnight! I invite you – in fact, I command you! – to charge your glasses'.

People came shuffling in from the other rooms, some from the upper floor, as two servants in impeccable evening dress circulated to fill the glasses of the gathered throng. Kuragin positioned himself by the great clock which stood against the wall by the fireplace, its minute-hand invisibly progressing towards the vertical. Pechorin nodded to one of the servants and obligingly tipped his glass, his gaze drawn over the servant's shoulder to a tall figure squeezing himself into the now congested room, his elaborate moustaches and sideburns immaculately tonsured in the German style. As he searched for some association for this slightly incongruous figure, another man stepped into the room behind him, taller and broad-shouldered, his tanned, lithe face unmistakeable beneath his glistening beard, his dark hair thrown back as if in a gesture of perpetual confrontation.

Just at that moment, the clock struck twelve and the company let out a great 'hurrah!', before each man – and occasional woman – turned to their fellows with lusty handshakes or warm embraces. These intimate congratulations complete, Kuragin gestured once again to the little violinist, who positioned himself in the corner of the room, his violin wedged beneath his chin, his bow theatrically raised above it in preparation.

'Ladies and gentlemen!' - Kuragin's voice rang out once more. - 'Join hands for "Auld Lang Syne"!'

Pechorin bowed in turn to the two ladies perched on the edge of the company of civil servants and took the hand of each in his own. The old Scots melody was as familiar as his own childhood. He hummed the words silently to himself as he looked across the great rough oval at his old acquaintance Martynov, who returned Pechorin's gaze with a barely perceptible nod and, Pechorin was certain, a suppressed smile of immense satisfaction.

When what passed for the formal element of the festivities had come to an end and the company began to disperse once again into every corner of Kuragin's house, Pechorin took his host by the elbow and led him up the stairs to the room on the first floor with high windows. Kuragin gestured to one of the servants as he passed, who duly followed with a bottle of Burgundy and two glasses.

'Tell me, Kuragin' - Pechorin began, when they were seated at an empty card-table - 'have you seen much of my old friend Martynov recently?'

'Not at all' - Kuragain replied - 'I knew that he had been discharged from service - people tell me things, you understand? - but I haven't seen him since he returned to St Petersburg'.

'And have any of these kind people had anything to say about how he makes a living?' - continued Pechorin.

'There have been one or two... oblique references' - said Kuragin - 'But I'm certain you will understand if I leave that matter to your own advising'.

'Very well' - Pechorin replied with a smile of acknowledgement - 'Tell me, however, do you know the gentleman he is with?'

Kuragin gazed evenly at Pechorin's open, expectant features, rolling his glass in his hand.

'von Müffling?' - he replied at last - 'That gentleman's occupation is known to half of St Petersburg, although not one among them would admit to possessing such knowledge'.

'Including you?' - Pechorin asked quietly.

'Including me' - replied Kuragin, taking a long draught from his glass.

Kuragin reached for the bottle to refill his emtpy glass, shaking his head in mock admonition as Pechorin placed a hand over his own.

'May I join you, gentlemen?' - said Martynov, appearing as if from nowhere and placing a glass on the green baize between them.

'Why of course' - Kuragin replied immediately in a rather stiff display of welcome - 'Unless of course you have any objection, Pechorin?'

Pechorin studied Martynov with his customary cool gaze, just a hint of a smile playing at the corner of his lips.

'I can hardly think of anyone I'd rather see' - he said, gesturing to Martynov to be seated.

'May I first of all offer my condolences, Pechorin' - said Martynov - 'My mother also sends her condolences; she saw you at the funeral'.

Pechorin searched his mind for some recollection of a woman who might have been Martynov's mother amid the crowd at the Smolny Convent, but could find none.

'I thank you' - Pechorin replied with a little bow - 'I know my grandmother held your mother in the greatest esteem'.

Martynov now drained his glass, throwing back his great mane of dark hair, before smoothing it into place with his other hand.

'Your health, gentlemen!' - cried Martynov - 'But please, you must forgive me, I have another engagement. It's good to see you, Pechorin'.

'Indeed' - Pechorin replied - 'No doubt we'll be seeing much more of each other'.

Martynov lifted his great bulk onto his feet without replying, bowed to Pechorin, then to Kuragin, and turned towards the door.

'Oh, Martynov' - said Pechorin.

Martynov turned once more towards his host and his former comrade-at-arms.

'Yes?' - he replied, just a hint of annoyance in his voice.

'Give my regards to Monsieur von Müffling, won't you?'

Martynov clenched his jaw, turned quickly on his heels, and disappeared down the stairs.

CHAPTER THIRTY-FOUR

SADOVAYA STREET

Pechorin saw himself in a veiled dream, surrounded by a most vivid company, his thoughts drowned out by the hum of music and dancing and the wild whispering of speeches learnt by heart. Soulless images of people now unmasked flickered at the edge of his consciousness. He dreamt of his cold hands brushing with careless daring against the long unafraid hands of society beauties, appearing to submit to their gleaming vanity, while his soul cherished an ancient dream, the sacred sounds of years long past. He wished for a moment to lose himself in memory, to fly in his mind to the past, as free as a bird.

He saw himself as a child, surrounded by familiar places, the old manor house so tall, the garden with its broken greenhouse. A net of green moss covered the sleeping pond, beyond it smoke rose through the flickering lights of the poor little village, haymakers homeward bound looming out of the fog which covered the fields in the distance. He dreamed he was walking through a dark alley, the evening light peering through the bushes, the yellowing leaves rustling beneath his hesitant footsteps. Suddenly, he felt a strange longing in his breast. He thought of her and, in dreams, wept for this creation of his heart, for those eyes burning with russet fire, for that smile as pink as the first glow of morning light in the glade. Suddenly, he saw before him the omnipotent master of some marvellous kingdom, sitting alone for days on end, assailed by burdensome doubts and passions, like a newly formed island serene amid the stormy seas, a bloom in the watery desert. As he began to drift up to the surface of consciousness, the illusion vanished, like an uninvited guest at a ball, driven away by the noise of the crowd. He awoke with both fists clenched in bitterness and rage.

The house was empty but for Aglaya the cook. Dmitrii had left before first light, propping a note and a larger envelope from Afanasii Alexeyevich on the breakfast table where he knew they would not escape Pechorin's attention. Aglaya placed a plate of eggs and leftover *kolbasá* on the table in front of Pechorin as he reluctantly unsealed the note, which invited him to sign the papers contained in the envelope, authorising the sale of some thirty percent of the peasants from the estate at Kropotovo. Aglaya watched unobtrusively in silent consternation as Pechorin tore the note in two, before throwing it, along with the still unsealed envelope, into the flames of the stove.

By the time Dmitrii returned at mid-morning, Pechorin's mood had improved to the point where he was able, not without some effort, to satisfy his uncle's curiosity about the events of the previous evening.

'She is quite a woman, don't you think?' - said Dmitrii with unconcealed enthusiasm - 'And, for all Count Vorontsov-Dashkov's undoubted qualities... well...'.

'Perhaps you should have an affair with her?' - replied Pechorin, determined at once to provoke and to conceal his own feelings.

'Me?' - exclaimed Dmitrii - 'I would remind you, Pechorin, that the honourable Countess chose to play out her little drama before all of St Petersburg society, not with me, but with you'.

Pechorin banished from his mind the all too brief, bitter-sweet reverie that had assailed him in the chaos of the Vorontsov-Dashkov kitchens and turned to Dmitrii with a look of feigned confusion.

'I'm sure she intended no harm' - he said - 'But tell me, did you discover the identity of the delightful creature we encountered in the theatre?'

'I have no idea' - Dmitrii replied with simple candour.

Pechorin did not pursue the point, preferring not to reveal how troubled he was by the lady's apparently detailed knowledge of his affairs, in part because he did not himself quite understand the reasons for his disquiet.

'I also still have no idea' - Dmitrii continued - 'how you managed to leave the ball before me, but arrive home after me'.

'Oh' - Pechorin replied - 'I ran into an old acquaintance'.

'Anyone I know?' - said Dmitrii, mimicking Pechorin's casual tone.

'As a matter of fact, yes'.

Dmitrii waited calmly for Pechorin to continue, but Pechorin gave the impression that pouring himself another cup of tea was at this precise moment the sum total of his earthly cares.

'Well?' - Dmitrii persisted.

'I welcomed the New Year in the company of the always engaging Kuragin' - Pechorin replied - 'And the not always so amusing Martynov'.

'Martynov!' - exclaimed Dmitrii, his surprise contending with resentment in the face of Pechorin's apparent ability, strange and at once familiar, to secure for himself a surplus of knowledge - 'I'd heard he had left the service; but I had no idea he was back in St Petersburg. Was he alone?'

Pechorin paused once more, now indeed probing for some indication of what Dmitrii might know before volunteering anything further.

'He was not, as it happens' - Pechorin replied calmly - 'He came in with a rather curious fellow, not someone I've come across before - at least, as far as I'm aware'.

'And do you know what this fellow is called?' - asked Dmitrii.

'His name is von Müffling' - replied Pechorin, registering with profound satisfaction the jolt of recognition on Dmitrii's desolate face.

Pechorin reacted to Dmitrii's sudden disappearance from the room with nonchalance, which survived even his reappearance with a bottle of cognac in one hand and two bowl-shaped glasses in the other.

'It's a bit early for that, don't you think?' - said Pechorin in a spirit of comic indulgence, as Dmitrii set down the glasses and poured each of them a generous measure.

'Drink it' - barked Dmitrii in a percussive monotone, before throwing back his glass and allowing it to come to rest with a loud and satisfied sigh.

Pechorin obeyed his uncle's uncommon command, noting as he did how exquisitely subtle was the fluid now slipping smoothly down his throat.

'Do you have something to tell me, my dear uncle?' - he asked.

'Did Kuragin know this von Müffling was in his house?' - Dmitrii replied, refilling his glass.

'He did'.

'And did he enlighten you as to this gentleman's occupation?'

'He didn't have to' - Pechorin replied calmly.

'What do you mean?'

'Well, he told me that half of St Petersburg knew what Monsieur von Müffling did for a living' - Pechorin continued, taking another sip and regarding his glass with warm admiration - 'But that not one among them would admit to the fact'.

'And?' - said Dmitrii, his exasperation now rising.

'And' - echoed Pechorin with icy calm, still staring into the bowl of his glass - 'I concluded therefore that Monsieur von Müffling is an agent of the Third Department'.

Dmitrii could muster in response only a wild, defeated stare, which Pechorin greeted by raising his glass towards his silent uncle and draining the contents.

'This really is fine cognac' - he said, his voice full of sincerity - 'You must tell me where you got it'.

Dmitrii could not be persuaded that von Müffling's presence was no more than might be expected in circumstances where an exiled officer had been permitted to return to St Petersburg on strict and specific conditions. Pechorin's protestations that he had barely given a thought to his surveillance, which he affected to assume would be a fixture in his life for more than the stipulated six months, Dmitrii regarded as no more than the latest conspicuous - and quite unnecessary - display of Pechorin's wilful disregard for his own best interests.

'Then why accept Countess Voronstsova-Dashkova's invitation?' - said Dmitrii, his exasperation shading into anger.

'Perhaps I wanted to confirm what I already knew' - Pechorin replied cheerfully - 'You know, put a name and a face to a shadowy figure?'

'von Müffling's identity is neither here nor there' - Dmitrii insisted - 'Martynov, on the other hand, is quite a different matter. You do realise what this means?'

'A man has to make a living, my dear uncle' - said Pechorin, now actively seeking to provoke - 'I somehow can't see Martynov in the civil service, can you?'

Dmitrii clenched his jaw in an attempt not to respond, anger now the master of his exasperation.

'Be careful, Pechorin' - he said at last - 'Martynov may be a fool, but a fool with the Third Department at his back is no laughing matter'.

Pechorin adjusted his demeanour from brazen provocation to mock offence.

'You disappoint me, my dear uncle' - he said gravely - 'I'm perfectly capable of dealing with Monsieur Martynov'.

Pechorin felt a sudden desire to walk in the open air. He threw on his overcoat and a hat, bid Dmitrii good day, and stepped out into the faint mid-day sunshine. His first thought was to head north along the Fontanka and make his way to the Imperial Stables, but, on a whim, he turned instead onto Nevsky Prospekt, past the Alexandrinsky Theatre, and turned left into Sadovaya Street. He came to a halt at last at the front door of the apartment in which Sasha Vereschagina and her mother still lived, hesitated for a moment before ringing the bell, then pressed it decisively into life, its faint trill drifting down from the upper floor. In a former life, Pechorin would have pushed open the door and entered, confident that he was both expected and welcome, but on this occasion he hesitated once again, until he could hear footsteps on the stairs. At last, the door opened to reveal Sasha, her mouth a little open in mute surprise at the identity of her unexpected guest, her fair hair longer than Pechorin recalled. Her soft, intelligent eyes, however, had lost none of their purposeful charm.

'I hope I'm not intruding' - said Pechorin with a warm and unaffected smile - 'I was passing and felt it would be remiss of me not to drop in'.

Sasha's lips moved together then broke into a smile as generous as Pechorin's own.

When they were seated in facing armchairs in the room with the piano, Pechorin was struck, in the most pleasant manner, by how different was this Sasha to the intense and much less assured girl she had been a year and half ago. There was undoubtedly something not just in her manner, but also in her features, which spoke of some new sense of self - or, perhaps more accurate, of an entirely reconstructed understanding of how she appeared to others. As Sasha talked - of mutual acquaintances, of the travails of her poor mother - Pechorin asked himself why he had failed to remark upon this transformation at the funeral; perhaps it had been concealed by the garb of mourning; or perhaps, he acknowledged silently to himself, he had been in no condition to notice.

'It is all very sad' - said Sasha - 'My poor mother, your poor grandmother'.

'My grandmother's cares are now behind her' - Pechorin replied - 'As for your mother, although I have perhaps never said this before in explicit terms, if there is anything I or Dmitrii can do, you must not hesitate to ask'.

'You are very kind' - said Sasha, her head slightly bowed - 'But tell me, how are you? I've heard one or two things from Dmitrii, although I feel certain he has protected me from the worst'.

'And why would you assume, if I may, that the worst was any part of it?' - Pechorin asked with a half-smile, which confirmed to Sasha that the man who had returned was after all the same as the man who had left.

Sasha replied with a gentle shake of the head, accepting that she would learn nothing of any importance from Pechorin, with regard equally to his sojourn in the south or his return to St Petersburg.

'And what about you?' - Pechorin continued, seizing the opportunity to redirect the conversation - 'What is your news?'

Sasha once again bowed her head very slightly, before looking up to meet Pechorin's gaze, her features now flushed pink, shaded by a beauty he had never previously suspected.

'I am to be married' - she said at last.

Pechorin was struck by recollection of his confusion at Sasha's earlier endeavours on his behalf and now confessed inwardly that his judgement had been occluded by an all-too-familiar, if decidedly unwelcome trait: he had, he now realised with some amusement, overestimated his own significance in Sasha's machinations around the fair Katya. And that could mean only one thing.

'Alexei?' - he said softly before Sasha could continue.

It was now Sasha's turn, in unconscious mimicry of Pechorin, to conceal her surprise, but not the love and gratitude etched into her suddenly beautiful features. She nodded in confirmation, but no words escaped her trembling lips.

When Sasha had recovered her poise, under Pechorin's unremitting but beneficent gaze, she explained that Alexei Lopatkin, on hearing of Katya Yessentukhova's departure to her grandmother's estate, had himself retreated to the estate near Pskov he still thought of as his father's, but was now in fact his own. Some three months later, news came that Katya was to be married to a diplomat twenty years her senior. That gentleman was initially assigned to the role of Consul to the United States of America, but, on confirmation of his marriage, he managed to secure a position instead in Tiflis. Alexei, accepting that Katya was forever lost to him, and reassured that she would not soon reappear in St Petersburg, emerged from his self-imposed exile - and fell into the arms of Sasha, who had demonstrated after all that a young woman with a mind might turn even the most unprepossessing circumstance to her advantage.

'I am delighted for you' - said Pechorin quietly, the sincerity in his voice undercut somewhat by a desire to commend Sasha for the ingenuity he had only just now managed to decipher - 'You were right, it would seem, that Katya was quite the wrong choice for Alexei'.

Pechorin surveyed Sasha's beaming expression, searching for some hint that she may have guessed at his own role in Katya's sudden withdrawal from society; but there was, he concluded with inward relief, none.

'And you were of course right' - Sasha countered - 'that Katya was quite the wrong choice for you...'.

Pechorin met this frank provocation to say more with a relaxed, amiable smile.

'Ah, my dear Sasha' – he said after a brief pause – 'I take no pleasure in being right in such matters. Perhaps one of these days I'll be wrong... Then what will become of me?'

Sasha smiled indulgently, torn between admiration for Pechorin's playful subtlety and a plaintive sadness that his intrigues, in all their sophisticated ambivalence, had not led to the same happy outcome as her own.

'I saw Vera' – said Sasha at last.

'Oh' – Pechorin replied with outward calm – 'How is she?'

'Perhaps you should ask her yourself' – said Sasha – 'She will be here tomorrow afternoon'.

Pechorin spent the last of the failing light among the bare trees of the Summer Gardens, wrestling with what tomorrow might bring. He had sincerely believed, bereft on the deserted road between Kislovodsk and Pyatigorsk, that he would never again lay eyes on Vera. Her absence from his grandmother's funeral had only confirmed in his mind that her marriage, despite the drama to which it had been exposed, had survived. Now, in the gathering dusk, he resolved once again not to resist what fate had decreed.

Dmitrii's house was deserted but for Aglaya the cook when Pechorin slipped into the warm, dimly lit drawing-room. He declined Aglaya's offer of tea and settled down into the armchair by the fire. Within moments, he was asleep, on this occasion undisturbed by the intrusion of dreams.

When he awoke, the hour-hand of the clock above the fireplace crept towards ten and the fire had dwindled almost to nothing. He rummaged in the empty kitchen for something to eat, then slipped on his overcoat and turned towards the door. Before he reached it, however, it opened to reveal Dmitrii, shivering in the damp, frozen evening, taken aback to find Pechorin in the dark hallway.

'Where are you going?' – asked Dmitrii, certain for some reason that Pechorin had not arrived moments before him.

'Oh, I thought I might seek entertainment of some sort' – Pechorin replied, brightening.

'Mind if I join you?' – asked Dmitrii with calm insistence.

'Not at all, my dear uncle' – said Pechorin with a smile – 'The more the merrier'.

Dmitrii managed for a few minutes to conceal his annoyance at Pechorin's leisurely gait, which, he bitterly told himself, was more suited to a June day than a freezing, fog-bound January night. On each occasion when he attempted to quicken the pace, he was forced to relent as he realised that Pechorin was only too happy to fall some way behind him. Pechorin sensed Dmitrii's displeasure even in the thick, frozen fog, but elected not to confront it directly.

'Where are we going?' – Pechorin asked suddenly, in an ostensibly serious tone.

'How on earth would I know?' - Dmitrii replied, now openly displaying his exasperation.

'Well, it's just that you keep pressing on ahead' - said Pechorin - 'I assumed you know where you're going'.

It was Dmitrii's turn now to arrest their progress. He came to a halt on the treacherous, unswept pavement, the cold gripping his lungs, his concern for Pechorin battling with frustration and despair at his nephew's studied disregard for his own situation.

'Of course I know where we're going!' - said Dmitrii, now almost shouting - 'But why must it take us so long to get there?'

Pechorin paused for a moment, not a little surprised by the authenticity of Dmitrii's anger.

'I'm terribly sorry' - he began - 'It's just that I wanted the gentlemen who will no doubt join us there to enjoy the evening air as much as you clearly are'.

Dmitrii, his stock of words exhausted, stamped his foot on the dirty and unevenly frozen ice, turned abruptly on his heels, and set off without a further thought for Pechorin or his perverse designs.

The Kuragin house was still quiet when at last they arrived, but lights twinkled gently from the lower and upper floors. Pechorin almost didn't recognise it at first, because, he quickly realised, he had never before seen it with its front door closed; even Kuragin's warm hospitality had been forced to find compromise with fifteen degrees of frost. Dmitrii was about to knock, but Pechorin slid past him without a word and gently pushed the door open. A wave of warm air rushed over them as they stepped inside.

'Leave the door, Dmitrii' - said Pechorin with a backward glance - 'Our friends will close it behind them'.

Kuragin welcomed them with no more than a hollow display of his customary *bonhomie*, a look of tension etched on his still sober features.

'My dear Pechorin' - he said with only faint enthusiasm - 'My dear Stolypin. To what do I owe this pleasure? And what can I do for you?'

Pechorin replied with an enveloping smile, frankly intended to dispel the tension on Kuragin's face and the awkwardness in his voice and movements.

'That's very kind of you, Kuragin' - he replied - 'A couple of bottles of Burgundy would be most welcome'.

As Kuragin bowed theatrically in confirmation of his request, Pechorin stepped onto the staircase to the upper floor, Dmitrii at his rear, before pausing and turning once again to the host.

'Four glasses, old man, if you would be so kind' - he said cheerfully, before disappearing up the stairs.

Pechorin registered a strange nostalgia for the otherwise deserted room on the first floor, its windows, designed for long, warm summer evenings, now black against the frozen night. He brushed his fingers against the green baize of the little card-table, before sitting down with his back against the windows, facing the door. Dmitrii, who knew from long experience that remonstration and censure would have no effect upon Pechorin – and had very recently been reminded that exasperation would certainly become an occasion for comic improvisation – now turned to the conspiratorial in an attempt to elicit at least some indication of the particular set of motivating forces currently impelling Pechorin's actions.

'What do you intend to do?' – asked Dmitrii.

Pechorin consented at least to modify his tone and manner, without conceding anything at all in the substance of his reply.

'I intend to have a glass of Burgundy and a chat with a former comrade-at-arms. Beyond that, I have no idea'.

Dmitrii weighed the neutrality of Pechorin's response, but, before he could formulate a reply, he became aware that they were no longer alone.

'Good evening, Martynov' – said Pechorin warmly – 'Good evening, Monsieur von Müffling. Please, join us. We've been expecting you'.

Martynov took the chair directly across from Pechorin, while von Müffling sat down facing Dmitrii. Pechorin poured each a glass of Burgundy, smiling as he did so.

'It's a dreadful evening to be out' – he said with just the slightest hint of mockery – 'Did you come with anything particular in mind? A game of cards, perhaps?'

'I don't play cards' – replied von Müffling in a neutral tone.

'And it's none of your damned business, Pechorin' – added Martynov, his customary irritation at Pechorin's oblique manner of speech rising immediately to the surface – 'A gentleman can go where he pleases without asking anyone's permission'.

Pechorin drew his features into an expression of faintly bewildered curiosity.

'I only wish that were true, my dear Martynov' – he replied, taking a sip of wine.

Martynov and von Müffling exchanged a glance, which neither sought to conceal.

'Ah' – said Pechorin. – 'I see. You wish to say that a *gentleman* may go where he pleases; but that a... well, a person who has attracted the displeasure of His Imperial Majesty may not'.

Dmitrii cast Pechorin a look of open admonition, his heart sinking at this immediate and explicit mention of the circumstances that had brought him into the orbit of von Müffling.

'Very well' – Pechorin continued, without looking at Dmitrii – 'I concede. But tell me, gentlemen, what are your views on how a gentleman makes his living?'

Both Martynov and von Müffling shifted in their chairs, Martynov letting out a little grunt of indignation, but neither was able to speak before Dmitrii took it upon himself to interrupt.

'Tell me, Martynov, how are your esteemed mother and your delightful sisters?' - he said cheerfully - 'We haven't had the pleasure of their company for some time now'.

'Oh, they're well' - Martynov replied, annoyed that Dmitrii had deflected from Pechorin's deliberate barb - 'They much prefer to spend winter in the countryside'.

'Very wise' - said Pechorin - 'Give my regards to your esteemed mother the next time you see her'.

Martynov glared back at Pechorin, mute in his fury.

The conversation meandered for a few minutes, carried in the main by Dmitrii's energy and diligence, Pechorin largely restricting himself to replenishing the glasses as Martynov and von Müffling worked steadily through whatever he placed in front of them. Dmitrii's skill in managing the course of the discussion was occasionally challenged by Martynov's insistence, quite naked in its intent, upon enquiring after the health of mutual acquaintances, which Pechorin studiously ignored.

'And how is Blagodatsky?' - Martynov asked artlessly - 'A terrible shame about Sinyukhaev'.

Dmitrii made once again to fashion a reply that might direct this line of enquiry into calmer waters, but was interrupted before he could speak.

'What do you care about Sinyukhaev?' - said Pechorin, his voice outwardly calm, but marked by an anger Dmitrii alone could identify.

Martynov took a long draught from his glass.

'I was merely expressing regret at the unfortunate fate of a former comrade-at-arms' - he said evenly, fixing Pechorin with a determined gaze.

'Regret?' - said Pechorin - 'I sincerely hope you never have any regrets on account of me'.

'I very much doubt that, Pechorin' - replied Martynov, now refilling his own glass - 'I'm sure you'll manage to engineer your own end without any help from me'.

Pechorin now paused in a state of concealed fury, which vied for mastery of his consciousness with a different form of rage, all the more insistent because it was provoked by the realisation that Martynov, contrary to all prior experience, quite clearly felt that the upper-hand in their jousting was no longer beyond his reach. Pechorin glanced for a moment towards von Müffling, as if seeking some clue to the source of Martynov's impertinence.

'I'm not sure I understand, my dear Martynov' - he managed to say calmly.

Martynov glanced at von Müffling, who replied with the faintest of smiles.

'How is the Countess Vorontsova-Dashkova?' - asked Martynov.

Dmitrii once again attempted to intervene, but Pechorin had replied before he could speak.

'I will warn you only once, Martynov' - he said quietly.

'Come, Monsieur Pechorin' - said von Müffling, as if performing a script that had been composed in advance - 'Monsieur Martynov was merely alluding to the fact that you made a rather unwise public appearance the other night. Nothing more'.

'Indeed, Pechorin' - said Dmitrii, with a cautionary glance - 'And perhaps we might bring this evening to a close. It's late'.

'It may very well be later than you think, my dear uncle' - Pechorin replied, although rising to his feet in apparent acquiescence.

Pechorin made his way to the staircase in silence, Dmitrii at his back, while Martynov and von Müffling assuaged their faint disappointment by pouring what remained of the wine. As Pechorin reached the doorway, he turned and put a hand on Dmitrii's shoulder, some vague compulsion struggling to fight its way up from the depths of his unconscious reason. Kuragin, hearing footsteps from below and no longer able to contain his anxious curiosity, appeared suddenly at the top of the stairs as Pechorin began to speak.

'Enjoy the rest of your evening, gentlemen' - he said with a slight bow, first to Martynov, then to von Müffling - 'But tell me, Martynov, before we go: why did you inquire after the health of the Countess Vorontsova-Dashkova, rather than question the wisdom of my presence? Have you no regard for the reputation of a respectable married lady?'

Martynov took a moment to calculate the intent of Pechorin's question, resolved that attack was much more enjoyable - and effective! - than the defence he had previously been obliged to adopt, and allowed a smile of brutish confidence to spread beneath his glistening moustaches.

'The Countess?' - he replied - 'I have no interest in the Countess. And I defer to you in all matters concerning married ladies, respectable or otherwise'.

Pechorin ignored Dmitrii's imploring gaze, met Kuragin's ashen expression with a smile, and swiftly resisted the temptation to inquire any further into the depths of Martynov's knowledge of what had befallen him at Pyatigorsk and Kislovodsk.

'That's enough, Martynov' - he said in an even tone - 'You will receive my seconds in the morning'.

Pechorin nodded curtly in the direction of Kuragin, before easing himself past and down the stairs, out into the frozen, fog-bound night. Dmitrii remained where he was for all of thirty seconds, his desolate, accusatory gaze fixed on the still smiling features of Martynov.

Just as the little drama at the Kuragin house was drawing to its close, in his private office on the upper floor of the Winter Palace, little more than a hundred yards away through the frozen fog, the Tsar was diligently working his way through the sheaf of decrees he routinely allowed to accumulate over the course of the day, or sometimes two. Nikolai much preferred the solitude and quiet of the evening to the bustle and endless intrusions of the day and had acquired the habit of sending his Ministers away, rather than allowing them to loiter in expectation of a signature or - God forbid! - an audience.

As a younger man, he had followed the example of despotic routine, obliging Ministers and entire Departments to wait until he was ready to indulge them, placing himself at the heart of a constantly expectant organism, every motion and reflex of which was an embodiment and performance of deference; now, absolutely assured of the obedience of every living and inanimate element in this complex system, he experienced their expectant obsequiousness as a constant irritation, an endless churn of miniature oppressions. The system worked much more to his satisfaction when no element – inanimate or living – remained visible in any one part of it for long enough to impinge on his consciousness.

Nikolai signed his name at the foot of a requisition from the Ministry of State Property and placed it face down on the gathering pile of documents he had already dealt with that evening. He turned then to the single document that had been submitted by Prince Chernyshev, the Minister for War, a list of recommendations for honours from regiments currently deployed in the Caucasus, provisionally approved by Count von Kleinmikhel, who currently occupied the position of Commander-in-Chief at the General Staff HQ on the far side of Palace Square. Nikolai reviewed the eight pages of closely spaced lines in the stately script of one of the Ministry's many scribes, organised into twelve separate lists from varying divisions, scattered according to some impenetrable logic from the Black Sea to the Caspian. He began to read more slowly when he came to the list organised under the name of General Grabbe. Then, encountering the entry 'Lieutenant Pechorin. Order of St Stanislav. Third Grade', he put down his quill and sat back from his desk. After a few moments of unsmiling reflection, he leaned forward once more, dipped his quill in the ornate ink-pot of solid gold Louis XIV had gifted to Catherine the Great, and inscribed a thick, dark line through Pechorin's name.

CHAPTER THIRTY-FIVE

A VISION

DMITRII STOLYPIN BOWED his head into the wet snow swirling in the howling wind. The rooms Martynov rented on Spasskaya Street were still some way off in the icy distance, tucked in behind the gilded domes of the Cathedral of the Transfiguration. Pechorin's instructions had been precise and unequivocal, but, nonetheless, before stipulating that they would fight with pistols, at ten paces, half an hour before dawn on the following morning on the Pargolovo road, Dmitrii would do what Pechorin had expressly forbidden: he would appeal to Martynov, as a former comrade-at-arms, to withdraw and bring this madness to an end.

What served as Martynov's reception room was in a state of disarray when Dmitrii stepped tentatively into the depths of its dimly lit interior. Martynov disguised his reluctance to meet Dmitrii's gaze by clearing a pair of breeches from the back of an upright armchair and inviting him to be seated, before himself crouching down on a low stool on the other side of the room. There was, Dmitrii told himself, at least some sliver of hope in Martynov's clear discomfort, his all-too-apparent desire to blend into the darker corners of his dishevelled abode.

'I'm sorry you find yourself in this position, Stolypin' – Martynov began, as if rousing himself to an outward appearance of conviction – 'I expect you've come to agree terms?'

'I have' – Dmitrii replied quietly – 'Although I should say from the outset that I am more than sorry with regard to your own circumstances. I wonder if what they're paying you is worth it?'

Martynov paused, but Dmitrii could not make out the expression on his face in the weak light.

'I'm not sure I understand you' – Martynov said at last – 'What circumstances? And who is paying me?'

Dmitrii calmly surveyed the chaos of the room, the shutters still closed and the curtains drawn, a lone lamp casting its light barely further than the corner in which it stood.

'Come, Martynov' – Dmitrii replied – 'We can be frank with one another. Monsieur von Müffling's profession is hardly a secret'.

'Indeed' – said Martynov, his great bulk leaning perilously forward on his little stool, his expression brightening – 'But let's survey the situation without prejudice, laying to one side all considerations that do not bear directly on the matter at hand. I have been challenged to a duel. I have accepted. What else is there to discuss, beyond the details of how we will fight?'

'Very well' – said Dmitrii – 'Tell me, frankly, why you were determined to deliver an insult you knew very well Pechorin could not let pass?'

'Insult?' - replied Martynov, his indignation vying with a rising amusement - 'You know as well as anyone that Pechorin has insulted me on more than one occasion. What's so insulting about a remark among men about a very public display with a conspicuously married woman?'

It was Dmitrii's turn to pause for a moment.

'I thought we had agreed to be frank, Martynov' - he continued - 'We both know you weren't referring to the Countess'.

Martynov lived without servants, although there was no doubt in Dmitrii's mind that this was more a consequence of choice than necessity. He disappeared into the other room without asking if Dmitrii would like some tea, although the sound of a kettle and the clinking of glasses confirmed that hospitality, of a sort, would be forthcoming. Dmitrii searched once again for some basis for the hope with which he had arrived, now quelled by Martynov's stubborn insistence that Pechorin alone was responsible for the course events had taken. When he had returned with tea and both men were once again seated, Martynov turned to Dmitrii with a more conciliatory expression, which for a fleeting moment revived the faint hope still flickering in his heart.

'Look here, Stolypin' - said Martynov - 'What would you have me do? You know very well that, were I to decline to fight, Pechorin would ensure that no man in St Petersburg would remain ignorant of that fact. You may not approve of me or my actions; but you can't expect to make a coward of me'.

'Very well' - Dmitrii replied, inwardly conceding defeat - 'But I will make one request: Pechorin asked me to stipulate that, in the event the matter was not concluded with pistols, you will then fight with swords' - said Dmitrii,

'And?' - Martynov said quietly.

'I ask you, as a former comrade-at-arms, and if you will not withdraw, to decline at least this request' - replied Dmitrii.

Martynov gave the impression of absorbing and reflecting upon the implications of Dmitrii's request with all seriousness, acknowledging to himself that, once again, he was obliged not only to calculate the intent of the man now before him, but also to divine how such intent related to the unknowable designs that lurked beneath the mask Pechorin presented to the world, which had always been particularly impenetrable when turned towards Martynov.

'And do you ask this more out of concern for me?' - asked Martynov, a wry smile now forming under his moustaches - 'Or for Pechorin?'

'What does it matter?' - Dmitrii replied - 'For both of you. For all of us'.

'Very well. Pistols it is' - said Martynov, still smiling - 'À demain'.

Dmitrii returned home to find Pechorin lying back on a chaise in the drawing room, puffing on a little French cigar, while Blagodatsky paced around the room, exasperation and fatigue etched into his every feature.

'Ah, Dmitrii!' - Pechorin exclaimed, with a cheerfulness that might have been mistaken for deception by anyone who did not know him, but which Dmitrii understood was only too genuine - 'I was just explaining to Blagodatsky here that there really is nothing to be done: I can hardly withdraw the challenge, after all – what would people say about me?'

Dmitrii exchanged glances with the desolate Blagodatsky, whose fate it seemed to be to watch in ashen despair while those he admired most rushed headlong into dangers from which he could not persuade them.

'And I don't suppose Martynov has agreed to withdraw?' – Pechorin continued, not looking at Dmitrii.

Dmitrii again said nothing, but bowed his head in anticipation of what he knew was to come.

'Don't worry, old man' – said Pechorin, a faint edge now detectable in his expansive cheerfulness – 'You had every right to ask; he will know that such a request has been made on your own behalf and not on mine'.

Dmitrii acknowledged the truth of Pechorin's words with a curt bow, which also served to conceal his inward relief that Pechorin had not thought to guess at any further unauthorised requests on his part.

'It's murder' – said Blagodatsky suddenly in a voice drained of all hope and life – 'You are consenting to your own murder'.

'I'm doing nothing of the sort, my dear Blagodatsky' – Pechorin replied, his voice warm with generous solicitation, as if it was Blagodatsky whose life was in danger – 'But you must forgive me, gentlemen: I have an appointment'.

Pechorin pressed briskly on the bell of the Vereschagin house, pushed open the door without on this occasion waiting for an answer, and skipped lightly up the stairs. Sasha met him in the hallway, smiling nervously.

'She's not here yet' – said Sasha – 'Perhaps you could say hello to my mother? I'll come for you when she arrives'.

Pechorin managed somehow to sublate his anticipation – and sudden disappointment – into nothing more than a curt nod of assent.

If Pechorin had not seen Yelizaveta Vereschagina, however briefly, at his grandmother's funeral, he might have imagined that she had not moved from the chair in which she sat two summers ago, her spinning wheel at her elbow, the room lit only by the same small table lamp, even in the middle of the afternoon. He might have imagined, too, that the tears now welling in her faded eyes had been suspended there for all time, never quite falling, but never again to recede. She seemed to be possessed by some desperate struggle of the soul as she looked up to greet Pechorin, who instinctively relieved her of the burden of speech.

'I am delighted, as ever, to see you, Yelizaveta Ivanovna' – he said quietly – 'And in more pleasant circumstances'.

Yelizaveta Ivanovna nodded her agreement, but for a moment seemed unable to speak in response.

'You are very kind' – she said at last – 'And it is very good of you to call'.

Pechorin was momentarily gripped by a pang of guilt and self-loathing, as if his desire to be sitting now in quite different company was entirely transparent before the mournful gaze of Madame Vereschagina.

'But tell me' – Yelizaveta Ivanovna continued before Pechorin could reply, seeming to gather her strength – 'What are your plans? Where are you living?'

'I'm living with Dmitrii Stolypin in his father's old house by the Anichkov Bridge' – Pechorin replied, relieved that the conversation had progressed to the everyday.

Yelizaveta Ivanovna seemed struck by these words in a manner which took Pechorin entirely by surprise. Her gaze drifted towards the weak light bleeding in through the window, then returned to Pechorin, her expression now marked by a renewed anguish.

'Did you know Dmitrii's father?' – she asked.

'I knew my great-uncle Arkadii when I was a child, of course' – Pechorin replied – 'Although I must confess I have very little recollection of him'.

'He was a remarkable man' – continued Yelizaveta Ivanovna in a hushed tone – 'And a great friend to my late husband. When the poet Ryleyev died, those of his friends who remained in St Petersburg were, perhaps understandably, reluctant to be publicly associated with him. The Commission on December had completed its work, but the arrests had not ceased. Your great-uncle Arkadii insisted on reading the elegy at Ryleyev's funeral, regardless of the consequences. By the time I returned to St Petersburg, he too had passed; and perhaps that was for the best'.

'I am glad you remember him with such respect and affection' – said Pechorin in an even tone – 'He no doubt conducted himself admirably in those difficult times'.

Yelizaveta Ivanovna paused for only a moment, some unknown power coursing through her being, her expression miraculously taking on the aspect of a woman twenty years younger.

'These times are no less difficult' – she said in a firm, clear voice – 'But they will pass. We must be assured of that'.

Pechorin was about to reply when Sasha suddenly appeared in the doorway.

'You are expected, Grigorii' – she said softly, her gaze turned towards her mother.

Pechorin rose, bowed to Yelizaveta Ivanovna, and turned to leave.

'Grigorii Alexandrovich?' – said Yelizaveta Ivanovna.

'Yes?' – Pechorin replied, turning once more to face her.

'I hope it won't be too long before we see you again'.

Pechorin nodded his assent and stepped out into the hallway without another word.

As he approached the entrance to the room with the piano, Pechorin suddenly became aware that the unexpected turn of his conversation with Yelizaveta Vereschagina had entirely displaced his anticipation – and anxiety – regarding the encounter that now awaited him. The image of Vera as he had left her on that fateful night in Kislovodsk now came flooding back, to be succeeded in turn by an image of his former self, weeping like a child in the wet grass by the deserted, open road. He cast this from his mind like a memory from childhood, conjured instead a canvas mounted upon an artist's easel, blank and expectantly awaiting the daub of paint, and stepped into the room, strange in its insistent familiarity.

Vera sat with her back to the piano, facing the door, her fair hair collected in a black *bandeau*, her complexion, although pale, replete once again with the bloom of health it had lost when they last met. Her features had also acquired a lean determination, the mark not so much of age, but of a certain maturity forged through responsibility. She was, he conceded silently to himself, as beautiful as he recalled, her deep brown eyes glistening in perfect counterpoint to the beauty spot poised delicately by the dimple on her right cheek. By her side sat a young woman in conspicuously plain dress, her hair drawn back rather severely above a pinafore buttoned almost to her throat. The young woman did not look up as Pechorin approached, her attention entirely consumed by the infant child perched amiably in her lap. Pechorin managed to tear his gaze from Vera, first to the silent young woman, then to the child. He opened his mouth as if to speak, but heard instead the gentle voice of Vera.

'Grigorii Alexandrovich' - she said in a soft, calm voice - 'How very good of you to come. Please, take a seat'.

Pechorin managed to utter a few words of greeting and sat down facing Vera, his gaze seeking to rest unobtrusively upon the young woman by her side, but on each occasion falling to the child in her lap, whose smiles were interrupted by the occasional gurgle of pleasure.

'Avdotya, my dear' - said Vera, turning to the girl - 'Could you please take Michel to see M-elle Vereschagina? Monsieur Pechorin and I won't be long'.

She turned once again to Pechorin as the girl rose, child in arms, and quietly left the room.

Pechorin moved his lips to speak, his gaze now compelled by Vera's solitary figure, but he once again heard the sound of her voice before his own.

'Do not ask me' - she said softly - 'If you ask, or make any reference to Michel, I will leave and we will never speak again'.

Pechorin's struggle to process the meaning of these words was exceeded only by his struggle to maintain for Vera an illusion of comprehension.

'Give me your word' - Vera insisted - 'I have never asked you for anything. You owe me this, at least'.

Pechorin could make no reply, only lowering his head in recognition that the conflicts raging within him had resolved themselves into meek acquiescence. He looked up after a few seconds and saw on Vera's face the signs of her own struggles, now and in the past. She had never looked more beautiful.

'You have my word' - he said at last, in a voice that seemed to emanate from some mysterious location beyond his conscious mind - 'But tell me: why then did you wish to see me?'

Vera gazed into Pechorin's eyes with a look of complete assurance, the look of a woman who had understood that, in order to compel the actions of others, she must first conquer her own fears.

'There is one more thing I must ask of you' - said Vera, in a voice Pechorin once again struggled to recognise.

'Oh, and what is that?' - Pechorin replied gently.

'I know all about your difficulties since returning to St Petersburg' - said Vera.

Her gaze drifted towards the windows onto the street below, her expression unchanged.

'You must withdraw from your dispute with Martynov' - she continued - 'They will kill you. And you must live...'.

Pechorin abandoned the habit of concealing his surprise and looked back at Vera with frank astonishment.

'How did you know?' - he asked, almost in a whisper, his mind drifting for reasons he could not decipher to the masked stranger at Countess Vorontsova-Dashkova's New Year's Ball.

'It doesn't matter how I know' - Vera replied without faltering - 'What matters is that you also know; and to go through with the whole affair in possession of that knowledge would be to commit a sin for which... for which you could never be forgiven'.

'So I am to make of myself a coward?' - said Pechorin, a trace of mocking self-assurance returning to his voice.

Vera's face now took on an expression Pechorin had never before observed, her eyes moving dismissively as she suppressed what might have become laughter.

'Don't you understand that your pride is a weakness?' - she said with renewed purpose - 'That your enemies will seek to exploit it until they have done with you? Let them call you a coward; your friends and... and those who love you will know that you have acted with the utmost courage'.

Pechorin made no reply.

'I have, until a few moments ago, never asked anything of you' - continued Vera - 'And I will never ask anything more. For your own sake, for the sake of... us all, do not sacrifice the possibilities of the future on the altar of your pride'.

Pechorin sat in silence as Vera rose and stepped towards the door. He remained quite still as he heard her voice, now once again transformed, call for Avdotya. After a few moments, the girl returned to the room with the child in her arms and passed him to Vera, who had remained standing.

'Monsieur Pechorin is leaving' - said Vera - 'Please see him to the door'.

Pechorin rose suddenly as if waking from slumber.

'I know the way' - he said quietly, gazing into Vera's deep brown eyes, her fair hair in repose under its black *bandeau*, the faintest trace of a dimple framing the beauty spot on her cheek, the little boy smiling peaceably in her arms.

The first hint of the oncoming dusk lay upon the city as Pechorin stumbled out onto Sadovaya Street, which bustled still with passers-by going about their business, the occasional lamp-lighter perched above their heads in pursuance of his own. He headed towards Nevsky Prospekt without a discernible thought in his mind, glided through the trickle of cabs and carriages without registering the startled, disgruntled frowns of their drivers, and disappeared into the streets beyond it. After a few minutes, he found himself in the little square in front of the Mikhailovsky Palace, where he looked around feverishly in a manner that would have disturbed any observer, although there were none, then hurried on towards the Yekaterina Canal. He soon found himself at the gates to the Imperial Stables and was about to step inside when he was suddenly halted by a voice from behind.

'Grigorii Alexandrovich' – said the voice.

Pechorin turned to see the emaciated features of Lazarev, his sunken eyes gleaming out of the dusk.

'I thought I might find you here' – said Lazarev – 'I called at your esteemed uncle's house, but to no avail'.

Pechorin surveyed Lazarev in a state of profound confusion, dimly conscious that the facility with which he customarily drew together the threads of sensation and information had for some reason deserted him.

'Oleg Abramovich' – he said weakly, in an attempt to preserve for Lazarev the illusion of control – 'How can I help you?'

'Please forgive the intrusion' – Lazarev replied – 'But when I received no response to my invitations to once again join our company at Mikhail Vasilevich's, I became somewhat concerned'.

Pechorin fought to register the meaning of Lazarev's words, imagined for a moment that he had somehow successfully understood them, then fell back into a state of resigned quiescence.

'Oleg Abramovich...' – he said in a voice Lazarev barely recognised – 'I fear that you are mistaken'.

Pechorin looked into the depths of the Imperial Stables, thought of Parader comfortable in his stall, then thought suddenly of Dmitrii, Blagodatsky, and his great-uncle Afanasii sitting by the fireside in the drawing-room of Dmitrii's house. He searched for the image of Vera, but could not find it. He turned away from the gates of the Imperial Stables and headed towards the river, leaving Lazarev standing alone and silent, his ghostly features gradually receding into the evening gloom.

When Pechorin reached the Embankment of the Nevá, he stopped for a moment and cast a penetrating glance along the river into the smoky distance, dimmed by frost, which suddenly turned crimson in the last purple light of a blood-red sunset as it faded beneath the hazy line of the horizon. Night fell on the city and the immeasurable plain of the Nevá, swollen with frozen snow, shone in the last gleam of the sun, strewn with endless myriads of sparkling, prickly hoar-frost. It was twenty degrees below zero. Frozen steam rose up from the horses, driven half to death, and from the people as they ran. The taut air quivered at the slightest sound. On both banks of the river, like giants, great columns of smoke rose up into the frozen sky from the roofs of the buildings, twining and untwining as they rose, so that it seemed new buildings were rising above the old ones, a new city was forming in the air... Finally, it seemed as though this entire world, with all its inhabitants, the strong and the weak, in the hovels of the poor and in gilded palaces – the comfort of the strong – resembled at this twilight hour some fantastical, magical vision, a dream that might itself suddenly disappear and rise like steam into the dark blue sky. A strange thought stirred in Pechorin's outcast soul. He shuddered and his heart seemed to fill with a sudden rush of blood, which flowed in a rising tide of some powerful and hitherto unknown sensation. It was as if he suddenly understood something that, until that moment, had only slumbered within him, unknown and uninvited; it was as if his eyes were suddenly open to a new and different world, until then glimpsed only through obscure sounds and certain mysterious signs. Pechorin's lips trembled, his eyes aflame, his complexion as white as the all-enveloping frost and snow. In that moment, he was sure, he had looked through into another world.

Martynov rode at a gentle, uneven trot between the alley of elm trees on the Pargolovo road, the grey light of the morning only just beginning to gather. von Müffling rode to his right; to his left, an ancient doctor of Baltic-German stock, who had been paid handsomely for whatever services the business of the day might require. When they reached the appointed place, Martynov brought his mount to an awkward halt, dismounted, and tethered the beast to a tree on the left-hand side of the alley. The others followed his example. Martynov took a slim silver flask from his hip pocket, raised it to his lips, then offered it in turn to his companions. von Müffling declined with a casual wave of the hand; the good doctor accepted willingly, before taking a long draught of the cognac contained within.

After five minutes or so had passed, the doctor sat down with his back to a tree and pushed his hat back from his face.

'Quite irregular' – he said in a somewhat exaggerated tone – 'These matters must, above all, be concluded before respectable people – and policemen – have risen to greet the day'.

'I wouldn't have any concerns on that score' – Martynov replied, shooting a theatrical grin in the direction of von Müffling, who managed only a grisly smile in response.

Ten minutes later, the doctor rose without a word, untethered his horse, and set off towards the city. Martynov and von Müffling stood in the middle of the alley, watching as he slowly disappeared into the distance, their smiles now replaced by expressions of uncomprehending indignation.

CHAPTER THIRTY-SIX

AN OLD MAN'S FONDEST WISH

I HAD LEFT TIFLIS for the last time, bound for home, for service and, who knew, perhaps even for marriage. My days of travelling through the deathless South, amid wars and mountain gorges, scrabbling together material that might flatter the reading habits of the ladies of our capitals, had come to an end. The war, I felt sure, would continue for some time, but I would henceforth know of it only through the pages of the *St Petersburg News*.

We spent the first night in a shack on Gud-Gorá, the coachmen trying without success to rustle up something edible for dinner, while I mourned the end of my great adventure. On the second morning, we hurtled through the Terek valley and the Dariali gorge, had breakfast in the shade of Mount Kazbek, took tea in the little town of Lars, and reached Vladikavkaz in time for dinner. I'll spare you the descriptions of the mountains, those utterances that convey nothing and pictures that represent nothing for those who have never been there and, especially, the statistical commentary, which absolutely no one will read.

I stayed at the inn where all those passing through stay and where, incidentally, there is no one to order to roast a pheasant or make some soup, because the three invalid soldiers in charge are either so stupid or so drunk that you can't get a word of sense out of them. I was informed that I would have to spend three days here, because the detachment had not arrived from Yekaterinograd and therefore, it followed, could not accompany me on the return journey. I tried to view this circumstance with 'detachment'! A bad pun, no doubt, and a bad pun is no consolation for we Russians... To amuse myself, I decided to write down Maxim Maximych's story about Bela, not then realising that it would become the first link in a long chain of tales; thus can an insignificant incident sometimes give rise to the cruellest of consequences. Although perhaps you do not know what a 'detachment' actually is? A detachment is a military escort, composed of half an infantry brigade and a cannon, which accompanies convoys through the Kabarda between Vladikavkaz and Yekaterinograd.

The first day passed in tedium. Early on the second day a carriage pulled into the courtyard... containing none other than Maxim Maximych! We greeted one another like old friends and I offered him my room. He didn't stand on ceremony, slapping me on the back and twisting his mouth into something like a smile. What a strange fellow! Maxim Maximych did, however, possess a profound knowledge of the culinary arts: he was unbelievably skilled at roasting pheasant, which he garnished with pickled gherkins, and

I must confess that I would have been stuck on dry rations without him. A bottle of Kakheti helped us forget the meagre number of courses, one in all. After dinner we lit our pipes and settled in, me by the window and Maxim Maximych by the warm stove; it was a raw, cold day. We said nothing. What was there to say? He had already told me everything of interest about himself and I had no news whatsoever to recount. I looked out of the window. Beyond the trees I could see the low houses scattered along the banks of the Terek, which flowed ever wider and wider, and then the blue jagged wall of the mountains, above which Kazbek looked out in its white cardinal's cap. In my mind I bade them farewell and felt very sorry to do so...

We sat like this for a long time. The sun went down behind the cold peaks and a pale mist began to spread through the valleys when the sound of a carriage bell and the shouts of coachmen rang out in the street. A few carts filled with filthy Armenians rolled into the courtyard of the inn, followed by an empty carriage; its smooth movement, comfortable fittings, and somewhat glamorous appearance gave it a faintly foreign air. Behind it walked a man with a thick moustache in a braided jacket, fairly well dressed for a servant. The slightly rakish manner in which he shook the ash from his pipe and shouted at the coachman made it impossible to mistake his status in life: he was clearly the indulged servant of a lazy master, something like a Russian Figaro.

'Tell me, my good man' – I shouted from the window – 'has the detachment arrived?'

He gave me a somewhat insolent look, straightened his tie, and turned away. One of the Armenians, smiling as he walked alongside him, answered in his place: yes, the detachment had arrived and would be setting off on the return journey the next morning.

'Thank God!' – said Maxim Maximych, just at that moment coming to the window – 'But what about that for a carriage!' – he added – 'Probably an official on his way to an inquest in Tiflis. They clearly don't know these mountains! It's no laughing matter my friend, the mountains are no friends of ours; they would destroy even an English carriage'.

'Let's go and find out who it belongs to' – I said.

We went out into the corridor. At the far end a door opened into a side room, into which the servant and the coachman were dragging suitcases.

'Tell me, brother' – said Maxim Maximych – 'whose is that wonderful carriage? Eh? A beautiful carriage!'

The servant muttered something to himself without turning round and went on unfastening the suitcases. Maxim Maximych became angry, touching the discourteous fellow on the shoulder.

'I'm speaking to you, my good man...'.

'Whose carriage?' – said the servant – 'My master's...'.

'And who is your master?'

'Pechorin' – came the reply.

'What did you say? - exclaimed Maxim Maximych, grabbing me by the sleeve - 'What did you say? Pechorin? My God! Has your master ever served in the Caucasus?'

Maxim Maximych's eyes beamed with joy.

'He has, as far as I know... although I haven't been with him long' - replied the servant.

'It's him, it's him... Grigorii Alexandrovich, yes? Your master and I were friends' - Maxim Maximych continued, giving the servant a friendly slap on the back, which made him stagger a little.

'Excuse me, sir, but you're keeping me back' - the servant said with a frown.

'What's the matter with you, brother? Didn't you hear me... your master and I were the best of friends, we shared the same quarters... Where is he staying?'

The servant declared that Pechorin was having dinner and spending the night at the residence of Colonel Nikitin.

'And will he not be calling in here this evening?' - asked Maxim Maximych - 'Or perhaps you, my good man, will be going over there for something... If you do, tell him that Maxim Maximych is here, tell him... well, he'll know. There'll be a rouble in it for you'.

The servant gave a contemptuous look at the mention of such a miserable sum, but assured Maxim Maximych that he would deliver the message.

'He'll come straight over!' - Maxim Maximych told me with a triumphant look - 'I'll wait for him at the gate... What a pity I don't know this Colonel Nikitin'.

He sat down on a bench by the gates and I went to my room. I confess that I was also impatient for Pechorin to appear. I hadn't formed a terribly positive opinion of him from Maxim Maximych's description, although certain aspects of his character struck me as remarkable.

An hour later, one of the old soldiers who ran the inn brought in a boiling *samovar* and a teapot.

'Maxim Maximych' - I shouted from the window - 'Would you like some tea?'

'Thank you, but I don't feel like it' - he replied.

'Have some tea! It's getting late, it's cold'.

'No thank you'.

'As you wish'.

I began to drink my tea alone, but ten minutes later the old fellow came into the room.

'You're quite right, better to have some tea. His servant left a while ago and I've been waiting all that time... he must have got held up'.

He quickly drank his tea, declined a second cup, and went back out to the gates in a state of great agitation. The old fellow was clearly upset by Pechorin's indifference, all the more so because he had just told me about their friendship and, only an hour ago, had been convinced that Pechorin would hurry over the moment he heard Maxim Maximych's name.

It was already late and dark when I once more opened the window and called to Maxim Maximych that it was time to go to bed. He muttered something through his teeth. I repeated the invitation; he didn't reply. I lay down, wrapped in my greatcoat, and left a candle burning by the bed. I was soon dozing and would have slept through peacefully if Maxim Maximych, now very late, had not woken me coming into the room. He threw his pipe on the table, paced around the room, put some wood in the stove, before at last lying down, coughing and tossing and turning for a long time.

'Are the bedbugs biting?' – I asked.

'Yes' – he replied with a heavy sigh.

I woke early the next day, but Maxim Maximych was already up. I found him sitting on the bench by the gates.

'I have to see the Commandant' – he said – 'Please send for me if Pechorin arrives'.

I promised I would and he hurried off, as if his limbs had suddenly regained the vigour and flexibility of their youth. It was a beautiful, fresh morning. Golden clouds gathered on the mountain-tops, like a second range of ethereal peaks. A broad square stretched out beyond the gates and beyond it the bazar bustled with people, this being a Sunday. Barefoot Ossetian boys circled around me, baskets of honeycomb on their shoulders, but I sent them packing. I wasn't in the mood; I was beginning to share the concern of the good Captain.

Not ten minutes had passed when the very man we had been waiting for appeared at the far end of the square. He was walking beside Colonel Nikitin, who now, having accompanied him as far as the inn, bid him farewell and returned to the fortress. I immediately sent one of the old soldiers for Maxim Maximych.

Pechorin's servant came out to meet him, informed him that they were about to start loading up, handed him his cigar case, and, taking some instructions, left to sort out his belongings. His master lit a cigar, yawned a couple of times, and sat down on a bench on the other side of the gates. In the flesh, I am now compelled to admit, Pechorin did not entirely conform to the picture I had composed for myself on the basis of Maxim Maximych's tales. He was of medium height; his slender, but well-built figure and broad shoulders indicated a strong constitution, capable of withstanding all the trials of a nomadic life and changes in climate, one that had not succumbed either to the debauch of city life or to emotional turmoil. His dusty velvet coat, fastened only by the two lower buttons, revealed brilliant white linen beneath, indicative of a man of good habits; his stained gloves looked as though they had been custom made for his small aristocratic hands and when he took off one of his gloves I was astonished by the slenderness of his pale fingers. His gait was casual, almost lazy, although I noticed that he didn't swing his arms – a sure sign of a certain secretiveness of character. These are, however, my own personal impressions, based on my own observation, and I have no desire to compel you to trust in them blindly; indeed, I have no right to do so, given that my own preconceptions were now gradually succumbing to the merciless light of naked reality.

As he sat down on the bench, his erect figure bent as though there was not a single bone in his spine. His entire demeanour betokened a certain weakness of the nervous system; he sat like some thirty-year-old coquette out of Balzac, perched on her cushioned armchair, exhausted after the ball. At first glance I would have said he was no more than twenty-three, although later I might have said as much as thirty. There was something child-like in his smile. His skin had a certain feminine softness. His naturally curly fair hair perfectly framed his pale, noble brow; on closer inspection, however, there were traces of wrinkles criss-crossing his face, which no doubt became more pronounced in moments of anger or emotional distress. Despite his fair hair, his moustache and brows were dark, a sign of breeding in a man, like a white mane and tail on a black horse. To complete the portrait, I should say that he had a slightly upturned nose, brilliant white teeth, and hazel-brown eyes... although perhaps I should say a little more about his eyes.

First of all – although perhaps you have observed this strange characteristic in certain people? – they did not laugh when he laughed! This is a sign either of a malign disposition or of profound and persistent sorrow. His half-hooded eyes shone with a kind of phosphorescent brilliance, if I can put it like that: not a reflection of passionate emotion or a playful imagination, but more the gleam of smooth steel, brilliant but cold. His gaze was quick but penetratingly grave and left you with the uncomfortable feeling of an indiscreet question; it might have seemed insolent, had it not also been so indifferent and calm.

Perhaps Pechorin struck me in this way because the impression I had formed of him from the few details I then knew about his life now came under fierce attack from the forces of reality; perhaps he would have made quite a different impression on someone else. But as you will hear about him from no one else but me, you have no choice but to content yourself with this portrayal. I should say in conclusion that he was far from unattractive and possessed one of those quite unusual faces that are so admired by society ladies.

The horses were already harnessed; the bell under the arch rang a number of times. Pechorin's servant had twice already gone to inform him that everything was ready; but Maxim Maximych had still not appeared. Fortunately, Pechorin was lost in thought as he looked out over the jagged blue peaks of the Caucasus and, it seemed, in no hurry to be on the road. I approached him.

'If you would like to wait just a little longer' – I said – 'you'll have the pleasure of meeting an old friend'.

'Of course...' - he replied quickly - 'they told me yesterday; but where is he?'

I turned towards the square and saw Maxim Maximych running towards us as fast as his legs would carry him. He reached us after a couple of minutes, gasping for breath. Sweat poured like rain down his face; wet clumps of grey hair stuck out from under his hat, sticking to his brow; his knees shook. He was about to throw his arms around Pechorin, who instead, somewhat coldly but with a polite smile, extended his hand. Maxim Maximych froze for a second, but then avidly took Pechorin's hand with both of his own; he still couldn't speak.

'How glad I am to see you, dear Maxim Maximych' - Pechorin said, addressing him in the formal style - 'How have you been?'

'And... and you... ' - the old fellow muttered, tears welling in his eyes - 'It's been so long... where are you headed?'

'I'm going to Persia, and beyond'.

'Right away? Wait a moment, my dear fellow! Must we part right now? We haven't seen one another for so long...'.

'It's time, Maxim Maximych' - came the reply.

'My God... my God! Why the great hurry? There's so much that I want to tell you, so much I want to ask... Have you left the army? How... what have you been doing?'

'Being bored!' - Pechorin answered with a smile.

'Do you remember our life at the fortress? What a glorious place for hunting! You were mad for hunting... And Bela?'

Pechorin went slightly pale and turned away.

'Yes, I remember' - he said at last, with an affected yawn.

Maxim Maximych tried to persuade him to stay for a couple of hours.

'We'll have a splendid lunch' - he said - 'I have two pheasants and the Kakheti here is very good... not quite as good as in Georgia, of course, but good stuff nonetheless. We can talk; you can tell me about life in St Petersburg... how about it?'

'There's really nothing to tell, dear Maxim Maximych... Farewell, it's time for me to go, I must hurry... Thank you for not forgetting me...' - Pechorin added, taking the old man's hand.

Maxim Maximych frowned... he was both sad and angry, although he tried to hide it.

'Forget!' - he growled - '*I* haven't forgotten anything... God be with you... I didn't think we would meet like this'.

'Enough, enough' - said Pechorin, giving him a friendly hug - 'Have I changed so much? What can one do... Each of us must travel his own path... Heaven only knows if we'll meet again!'

Pechorin was already sitting in the carriage when he said this and the coachman took up the reins.

'Wait, wait!' - shouted Maxim Maximych, grabbing hold of the carriage door - 'I almost forgot... I still have your papers, Grigorii Alexandrovich;

I've been dragging them around with me... I thought I might find you in Georgia, but God brought us here instead... What should I do with them?'

'Whatever you like!' – Pechorin replied – 'Farewell!'

'So you're going to Persia?' – Maxim Maximych shouted after the carriage. – 'When will you return?'

The carriage was already some distance away, but Pechorin made a sign with his hand, which might be translated as follows: 'Probably never! What is there to return for?'

The sound of the carriage bell and the clatter of wheels on the rocky road had long ceased; the poor old fellow still stood in precisely the same spot, deep in thought.

'Yes' – he said at last, trying to look as if he didn't care, although from time to time tears of disappointment glistened in his eyes – 'We were friends, of course, but what is friendship these days! What am I to him? I'm not rich, I have no position, we're not even close in age... But what a dandy he's become since returning to Petersburg; what about that carriage! And that stuck-up servant!'

These words were spoken with an ironic smile.

'Tell me' – he continued, turning towards me – 'What did you think of all that? And why in the name of the devil is he going to Persia? Ridiculous, quite ridiculous, I tell you... I always knew he was a volatile fellow and that he couldn't be relied on... But it's still a pity that he will come to a bad end... there's no doubt about it! I've always said that nothing good will come of those who forget their friends...'.

He turned away in order to conceal how upset he was and began to walk around his cart in the courtyard, pretending to check the wheels, his eyes filling with tears.

'Maxim Maximych' – I said, approaching him – 'What are these papers Pechorin has left with you?'

'God only knows! Notes of some kind...' – he replied.

'And what are you going to do with them?'

'What? Perhaps I'll use them as wadding for my rifle cartidges...'.

'Better give them to me' – I said quietly.

He looked at me in astonishment, growled something through his teeth, and began to rummage in his case; he pulled out a notebook and contemptuously threw it on the ground, then another, a third, a tenth... all met the same fate. His anger was like that of a child, which I found both funny and pitiful.

'That's the lot; I congratulate you on your acquisition...'.

'And I can do with them as I wish?'

'You can publish them in the newspapers for all I care! What am I, his friend? A relative? It's true we lived for a long time under the same roof... but I've shared a roof with plenty of people in my time!'

I seized the papers and quickly took them away, fearing that Maxim Maximych might change his mind. We were soon informed that the detachment would be leaving in three hours and I gave the order to begin loading.

Maxim Maximych came into the room just as I was putting on my hat, but he, it appeared, wasn't getting ready to leave; he had assumed a somewhat affected and cold manner.

'Are you not leaving, Maxim Maximych?' - I asked.

'No'.

'And why is that?'

'I still haven't seen the Commandant and I have some official papers for him'.

'I thought you'd already been over there?'

'Yes... I had' - he said haltingly - 'but he wasn't at home... and I didn't wait'.

I understood. The poor old fellow, perhaps for the first time in his life, had neglected his duties for his own personal ends (to put it a little formally)... and look how he had been rewarded.

'I'm very sorry, Maxim Maximych, I'm very sorry we must part so soon'.

'Well, we uneducated old men just can't keep up with you... you proud young society types; it's alright when you're down here among the flying Circassian bullets, but later you're ashamed even to offer a fellow your hand'.

'I don't deserve these reproaches, Maxim Maximych' - I protested.

'Yes, yes, I know... I was only speaking in general... I wish you all the best and a pleasant journey'.

We parted somewhat stiffly. Kind old Maxim Maximych had transformed into a stubborn, cantankerous old soldier. And why? Because Pechorin, thoughtlessly or for some other reason, had only offered him his hand, when Maxim Maximych had wanted to embrace! It is sad to see a young man's fondest hopes and dreams shattered as the rose-tinted lens through which he has viewed human affairs and feelings is suddenly removed. There remains, however, the hope that he will replace these former illusions with new ones, just as fleeting and no less sweet; but with what might they be replaced in a man of Maxim Maximych's age? The heart hardens and the soul selects her own society, whether we like it or not.

I departed alone.

CHAPTER THIRTY-SEVEN

A YOUNG MAN LOOKS TO THE PAST

My life in St Petersburg took the course I had imagined, with the exception that I did not, in the end, succumb to the pleasures of marriage. I entered the Civil Service as a Collegiate Assessor in the Ministry of Foreign Affairs, where I was fortunate - or, perhaps, unfortunate - enough to come into contact on rare occasions with Count Nesselrode, before the death of Tsar Nikolai and the humiliation of the Crimean War brought that gentleman's long and enduring influence over Russian political life to an end.

My stipend was sufficient for me to rent an apartment on Sadovaya Street, which eventuality brought me into the orbit of many of those who had known Pechorin, in circumstances of unequivocal good fortune. I made the acquaintance of the delightful Sasha Vereschagina, who now lived with her husband at the Lopatkin House on the Moika Canal, but had retained the apartments on Sadovaya Street for her mother, whose advancing years were belied by her sprightliness - reinvigorated, perhaps, by the prospect of a thaw in the political climate for which she had waited thirty years. Through Sasha, I was also fortunate enough to make the acquaintance of the estimable Sviatoslav Blagodatsky, who had risen to a position of modest respectability even before the death of the Tsar finally allowed him to lay the misfortunes of his youth entirely to rest. Beyond a casual acknowledgement that I had met Pechorin, fleetingly, on the open road, we never discussed him. For my part, I never raised the matter of Pechorin's papers, fearing that my limited acquaintance with each of his former friends was an insufficient basis for a matter so delicate and, potentially, dangerous. Neither Blagodatsky nor Sasha Vereschagina, I reluctantly concluded, and whatever they might know, were likely to resolve for me the mystery of what had befallen Pechorin after his return to the Caucasus.

By the time of the death of Nikolai, the succession of Alexander II, and the conclusion of the catastrophe in Crimea, I had not quite forgotten about Pechorin's papers and the notes I myself had made after my encounters with Maxim Maximych, but had at least dispensed with any hope of publishing them. The event that restored them to the centre of my attention - and would eventually lead to the completion of this tale - was indeed a curious one.

Count Ivan Vorontsov-Dashkov, who had once behaved so splendidly in shielding Pechorin from the public attentions of the Grand-Duke Mikhail - himself long since released from the mercies of his wife and five daughters - had died in 1854. A little over a year later, his widow, the Countess Alexandra, who had on that same evening mischievously exposed Pechorin to danger in order then to play the heroine in his rescue, now still impressive in her forties, married the eminent French surgeon, the Baron de Pouillet, and moved with him to

Paris. That unfortunate lady became fatally ill within a few months of settling in France, whereupon persistent rumours returned to St Petersburg to the effect that her husband had poisoned her for her money and jewellry, leaving her to perish in a hospital for the poor. No less a figure than Nikolai Nekrasov, persuaded that such rumours were true, published a sketch in *The Contemporary* in 1856, describing how an unfortunate 'Princess', recently departed for France, had been tyrannized and left for dead by her unscrupulous French husband. de Pouillet returned to St Petersburg that same year and, on learning of Nekrasov's scandalous tale, had burst in on the unsuspecting author and challenged him to a duel. The affair, thankfully, had ended peaceably: first, a Russian acquaintance of de Pouillet had explained that the story's title, 'The Princess', could not possibly refer to his late wife, who bore the title Countess; second, and more decisively, Alexandre Dumas *père*, then perhaps the most famous writer in France, was at that time travelling through Russia and, after visiting Nekrasov in St Petersburg, was able to convince de Pouillet that Nekrasov had not only been misled, but, consistent with the testimony of de Pouillet's Russian acquaintance, had not intended the Countess as his model. Countess Vorontsova-Dashkova, Dumas would later write in his memoirs, was a charming and intelligent woman, looked after until her last days by a husband not only devoted to her, but also a very rich man – who therefore stood to gain nothing from her passing.

The Vorontsova-Dashkova affair did, however, serve to revive my thoughts of Pechorin, eventually to the point where I was emboldened to raise the matter with Blagodatsky. I took advantage of our slight acquaintance and the occasion of a memorandum that was to be conveyed to his Department, offering, in all appearance of disinterested kindness to a young clerk in my office, to deliver it myself.

Blagodatsky was no doubt surprised by my sudden appearance in the middle of a Tuesday afternoon, but was possessed of such delicacy and tact that he gave no impression other than delight.

'Why, Anton Lavrentevich!' – he exclaimed – 'How very nice it is to see you. But tell me, to what do I owe the pleasure?'

'I have a memorandum from the Deputy Minister' – I replied, cheerfully concealing my embarrassment at having behaved in such an unorthodox manner – 'We would have sent it with one of the clerks, you understand, but I was glad of an excuse to step out of the office for a moment. And we have not seen one another for quite some time'.

Blagodatsky smiled amiably in response, his still handsome features framed by wisps of grey at the temples, his air of dependable modesty prevailing over the melancholy that had settled upon him as a much younger man, and which, he had no illusions, would now never leave him.

'You're quite right' – he replied, mimicking my rather forced enthusiasm – 'I make a point of having a stroll along the Embankment at lunchtime, whenever the weather is fair. These corridors are like a tomb sometimes, especially, I would imagine, for fellows like yourself. I never wore the tunic of an officer, which is just as well, for I do not therefore have to imagine what it must have felt like to exchange it for the frock-coat of our Civil Service'.

'Oh, I have long since become accustomed to our more sedentary and peaceful life' - I replied - 'Although, as it happens, I was reminded of my years in the South just recently, on account of a most curious affair'.

'Oh really?' - Blagodatsky replied with scrupulous courtesy - 'And what was that?'

'The terrible scandal of the Countess Vorontsova-Dashkova' - I replied as neutrally as I could manage.

Blagodatsky's amiable smile now turned involuntarily to a frown, more, I hoped, of confusion than displeasure.

'You must forgive me' - he said at last - 'In what way is the passing of Countess Vorontsova-Dashkova related to your service in the Caucasus?'

I paused for only a second or two, momentarily reluctant to proceed along the path I had opened, then suddenly convinced that retreat was impossible.

'Oh' - I began casually, before continuing with greater purpose - 'It's just that the news of her passing reminded me of Pechorin'.

Blagodatsky fell silent, sat back into the stiff brown leather of his office chair, and bid me take a seat on the other side of the desk facing him. His expression was now mournful, bereft of any trace of his polished amiability. He made as if to speak without turning his gaze towards me, then once again fell silent.

'Forgive me, Sviatoslav Afanasyevich' - I said quietly - 'I did not mean to cause you discomfort'.

'Not at all' - replied Blagodatsky - 'You caused me no discomfort other than surprise. But tell me, why would the death of Countess Vorontsova-Dashkova make you think of Pechorin? You met him only once, if I recall? Were you acquainted with the Countess?'

Here I struggled to maintain an outward appearance of measured calm. How could I have been so foolish? Only in that moment did I realise that not a soul on earth, with the exception of Maxim Maximych, had any inkling of my familiarity with the events of Pechorin's life. I had lived with them so long, it seemed, that I had forgotten they were not yet - at least not all of them - common knowledge.

'Pardon me, Sviatoslav Afanasyevich' - I continued in a halting voice - 'I did not know the Countess, but I became aware, through a mutual acquaintance, that she had been a... confidante of Pechorin in the weeks before his final departure from St Petersburg'.

Blagodatsky now studied me in a state of genuine perplexity, his brow riven with deep furrows, his smile a distant memory.

'I'm not sure I quite understand' - he said, somewhat more sharply.

'Well' - I continued - 'It occurred to me that the Countess, or indeed your good self, might have received some news of Pechorin after his departure'.

Blagodatsky's complexion now turned to alabaster, his head bowed, his entire being wracked with the pain of melancholy. He raised his head slowly, the effort of movement lesser only than the impossibility, it seemed, of speech.

'He was in Tiflis' - he said, almost in a whisper - 'He may have gone to Persia. That is all I know'.

I apologised to Blagodatsky for the intrusion, thanked him for his time, and stepped out into the dark corridor of the Ministry of War, resigned to the fact that the story of Pechorin had ended where I first and last saw him, waving from the window of a carriage as it trundled out of Vladikavkaz. I had taken a few steps along the corridor, when a voice called out from behind me.

'Anton Lavrentevich' - said Blagodatsky, his face still ashen - 'There is nothing else I can tell you' - He paused for a moment, then continued - 'But there is someone who can'.

A few days later, on a gloriously warm summer evening in June, I took a cab across the Palace Bridge onto Vasilevsky Island. The cab driver drove his single horse steadily towards the address I had given him on Bolshoi Prospekt, before coming to a gentle halt in front of a grand, but somewhat dilapidated building, the curtains in each of its windows drawn against the evening light. I paid and thanked the driver and stepped along the overgrown path to the front door, where, seeing no bell, I gave two firm knocks and waited. I was about to knock again, but was halted by the sound of a window opening from above. I looked up towards the source of the sound, but could see no one.

'It's open' - came a voice - 'Come up'.

The room in which Mungo sat was more akin to a cave than the kind of dwelling inhabited by retired members of the Russian gentry. The French wallpaper was a deep shade of blue, which recalled to my mind, for reasons I did not trouble to discern, the Dutch paintings I had once seen on a trip to Paris. There was a single dim lamp on a table against the far wall. To the left, away from the curtained window, Mungo reclined on a *chaise*, his back supported by numerous cushions covered in ornate Persian cloth. His hair fell in thick curls to his shoulders, still in the main a deep chestnut colour, but betraying little flecks of silver, which, I reasoned, may have appeared more prominent in natural light. His features were soft and handsome and might have been mistaken still for those of a boy, were it not for the weariness with which his eyes stared out into the gloom. Most striking of all - although it struck me last of all - was his attire, a long silken *kaftan* woven in intricate patterns I could only associate, once again, with Persia. As I approached, it seemed impossible to establish quite where the body of the man I was about to engage in conversation ended and where the luxuriant fabric in which he was ensconced began.

'Please' - he said in a drawl - 'Be seated'.

I surveyed the room for a moment, established that there was only a single wooden chair, and obeyed his laconic command.

I became suddenly aware that I had not the faintest idea of how to begin, comforted only by the fact that Mungo, through the interventions of Blagodatsky, had agreed to meet me; and, therefore, that he must not only be aware that I was enquiring after Pechorin - but was also willing, in principle, to shed light on his fate. I searched my mind for some pleasantry that might lead unobtrusively to the object of my inquiry, but was interrupted before I could speak.

'Who are you?' - Mungo asked suddenly, any trace of a drawl having left his voice - 'Some kind of writer, I expect?'

I took a moment to absorb this unexpected blow before replying.

'I confess' - I began hesitantly - 'that I harboured some such pretensions in my youth. I fancied myself a writer of travelogue, which I suppose in retrospect may have been no more than an attempt to make sense of the environment in which I found myself'.

'What environment?' - he asked curtly.

'The Caucasus' - I replied - 'I served for five years in the Grodnensky Regiment; I volunteered, in fact. But the environment I encountered did not correspond to the world of my youthful imagination; and so, I suppose, I invented for myself a different purpose for being there'.

I paused for a moment to gauge Mungo's response, but could discern nothing in the set of his soft features in the half-light.

'I have long since cast aside any such pretensions' - I continued - 'I am a Collegiate Assessor in the Ministry of Foreign Affairs'.

'Please accept my condolences' - said Mungo, with no trace of irony.

'Did you know him?' - he asked suddenly after a long silence.

'I met him once' - I replied - 'Very briefly, at Vladikavkaz, in the company of an admirable old Captain from the time of Yermolov'.

'And what was your impression of him?' - he continued.

'I learned nothing from my brief encounter with him' - I said with simple frankness - 'But I have acquired a certain picture from a number of sources'.

'So what then is your interest in him?' - he asked, somewhat more abruptly.

'If I'm entirely honest' - I replied without acknowledging his change of tone - 'I had forgotten all about Pechorin, just as my time in the Caucasus had receded to the margins of my memory. But a certain recent event recalled him to my mind and... well, I realised that, even after all these years, I did not know what had become of him'.

'And you think I do?' - Mungo replied with a smile of gleaming irony.

I had arrived convinced that I would have to proceed with a rare combination of diligence and ingenuity if I were to persuade Mungo to tell me what he knew about Pechorin's fate; now, in the faint glare of the smile emanating from the gloom, I saw such reasoned preparations for the foolish pretension they were and all but abandoned hope. I managed to hold Mungo's gaze for a few moments, before eventually turning away.

'He arrived with a boy' - said Mungo quietly after a minute or so had passed.

If anything, this unexpectedly forthright overture induced in me an even greater consternation. My mind raced in all directions in search of a suitable response, one that might not staunch the sudden and unexpected flow of his recollection. Where I ought to have been exultant that the ice had been so dramatically shattered, I was instead speechless, bereft of any means of encouraging him to further revelation. I was once again rescued by Mungo's unexpected but apparently unreserved willingness to speak: no doubt aware of my discomfort, he rewarded it only with the smile that had once raised his features above the realms of the merely handsome and made him the envy of St Petersburg society.

'He rescued the boy from a monastery' - he said, searching in my expression for some response - 'I'm sure I don't need to explain to you what is meant by that?'

I replied with a nod that signalled greater certainty than I in fact possessed.

'The boy had been taken from his tribe as an infant' - Mungo continued - 'They're made to live as servants until they're old enough to be prepared for the life of a Novice; it would appear that the Church in those parts has few other means of recruitment. He was no more than eleven years old when Pechorin arrived en route to Tiflis. Pechorin later told us how he had listened to the boy's despairing stories of how he had tried to escape and find his way back to his home village, on each occasion being captured and returned to his place of captivity. Pechorin replied that he could not restore the boy to his homeland, for he did not know where it was; but that he could restore his freedom. "Then" - Pechorin had told him - "You can go where you please". He agreed a price with the Deacon. The boy at first prepared to embark once again into the deserts and mountains that had provided the backdrop to his anguished attempts to escape, but after some reflection - and not a word from Pechorin - he resolved to remain with his liberator'.

'What was his name?' - I asked suddenly, gripped by an inexplicable curiosity for detail.

'I have no idea what name the boy was born with' - Mungo replied - 'We knew him only as Mikha'.

'I'm afraid I can't offer you any kind of hospitality' - Mungo continued after a few moments of silence.

'That's quite all right' - I replied, before continuing in somewhat emboldened fashion - 'But tell me, was he in Tiflis for long?'

Mungo surveyed me with an ironic curiosity with which I was quickly becoming familiar, then continued in his characteristic drawl.

'He stayed for almost three months, renting rooms in the house in which I lived on Bebutovskaya Street. Do you know Tiflis?'

I replied that I did.

'I must confess that I had fallen into a somewhat dissolute way of life' - he said with a faint smile - 'I imagined that Pechorin might accompany me, but nothing of the sort. I never saw him in the daytime without the boy, and only very rarely in the evenings. Remarkable, don't you think?'

I made only a slight movement of my head in reply.

'The boy held some strange power over him, no doubt' - he said - 'Although I barely heard him speak a word to Pechorin in public'.

'How do you mean?' - I asked, anxious to encourage him.

'Well, on one occasion we were at the writer Ladashvili's, eating and drinking the usual interminable round of toasts; Pechorin usually drank very little, or at least was skilled in concealing its effects upon him. But in those parts, as you will no doubt understand, it is very difficult to refuse to drink to the health of the elders, or of the host, or of the children, and so on'.

I smiled in recognition of this fact, which I had myself learned in somewhat troubling circumstances.

'We had reached the sixth or seventh toast' – Mungo continued – 'when the host invited Pechorin himself to make a toast. Pechorin rose to his feet with a curiously blank expression on his face, his gaze wandering somewhere above the heads of the gathered company, and began to speak: "I propose that we drink to His Imperial Majesty" – he said in a flat voice – "To the Empire". Well, you can imagine that not everyone among that company was disposed to raise their glass. Curiously enough, the greatest offence was taken not by any of our Georgian brethren, but by a young Russian officer by the name of Shidlovsky, who may have known something of Pechorin's past, and was thus convinced that his words were nothing more than a graceless provocation. Within moments, Shidlovsky was on his feet, insisting that Pechorin withdraw his remarks. Ladashvili shot me a glance designed to invite my own intervention, but I knew Pechorin far too well to imagine that there was any value in such a course of action. But just as Pechorin was about to get to his feet, to the astonishment of the entire company, and not least myself, little Mikha put a hand on his shoulder and whispered something in his ear, most likely in Tatar. Pechorin remained where he sat, a beneficent smile flowering upon his features. "You must excuse me, gentlemen" – he said, as if nothing at all had happened – "I sometimes forget that my little jokes are not to everyone's taste. Let us drink instead... to the future!" With that, he paid no further attention to the bemused Shidlovsky for the remainder of the evening and in fact appeared to everyone to be in the highest of spirits'.

Mungo let out a long, satisfied yawn and rearranged himself upon his mountain of pillows and cushions. I began to fear that he might soon draw our audience to a close and, in an attempt to maintain the flow of his reminiscence, I asked hurriedly if such events were common during Pechorin's stay in Tiflis.

'Not at first' – Mungo replied, stifling another yawn – 'As I said, the boy held some mysterious power over him, which I had never previously imagined possible. He spent his days reading or, if he ventured out in the heat of the afternoon, you would sometimes see him heading for the market square, with little Mikha trotting along at his side, resplendent in his *kaftan* and *kalpak*. I learned from one of my acquaintances that Pechorin had begun to inquire of an ancient Imeretian bookseller about the possibility of acquiring the *Complete Works* of Shakespeare, in English or French. Can you imagine! The old fellow at first waved Pechorin away with an incredulous smile, insisting that an individual volume might occasionally show up... but a complete set? Only Pechorin could conceive of such a thing. I once saw them in quite animated conversation, in the heat of the day, Pechorin comparatively serene in his short velvet jacket, breeches, and wide-brimmed hat, the old man in a long *kaftan*, waving his arms around and laughing. But in the end he got them! Where they had come from and how the old bookseller acquired them, God alone knows'.

I smiled encouragingly in response to Mungo's little anecdote, partly from genuine amusement at the scene, but partly also to confirm in his mind that I would happily listen to whatever he had to tell me, whether or not it had any bearing on the course of events.

'You paint quite a picture' - I replied.

'Indeed' - he said - 'I regret only that I did not in fact trouble to make a picture of that and many another scene'.

I conjured for myself a domestic portrait in oil on canvas, Pechorin in his reserved finery, staring out implacably at the artist, the native child in his *kaftan* and *kalpak* poised proudly at his right hand. My reverie was suddenly interrupted by the words I had feared.

'You must forgive me, Anton Lavrentevich' - said Mungo - 'I am tired'.

'Quite so' - I replied quickly in a tone of acquiescence - 'I have disturbed you for long enough. But perhaps we might speak again?'

Mungo gazed back at me from out of the gloom, a look of uncertainty only faintly discernible on his face.

'Perhaps' - he drawled - 'Perhaps'.

'But tell me' - I immediately replied - 'before I go: was he happy?'

Mungo's face now wore an expression of unmistakable confusion.

'Happy?' - he said quietly - 'Yes, I suppose he was. And I suppose also that he might have remained so, were it not for two things'.

'Oh' - I replied in as casual a tone as I could muster - 'And what were they?'

'Well, first of all' - he said - 'If Pechorin hadn't made the acquaintance of Madame de Hell'.

It was my turn now to wear an expression of bewilderment.

'The wife of the French Consul in Odessa' - Mungo replied - 'She was an ethnographer of some kind, as was her husband. They spent most of their time between Tiflis and the Crimea, more interested it would seem, in the customs and practices of the many tribes of the Caucasus than in diplomatic service'.

He paused once again and I could not tell whether it was done out of uncertainty, or quite deliberately for effect.

'Until she met Pechorin, of course' - he said at last.

'And the second thing?' - I asked, quickly recovering my poise.

Mungo now sat up on his *chaise* and looked directly at me for the first time since I had arrived. I could now see the marks of time and, no doubt, disappointment on his handsome face, the last shadow of its youth dissolving in the faint light. There was no question now that his manner might be contrived in pursuit of effect; he seemed, on the contrary, entirely consumed by a great and authentic sadness.

'The second thing?' - he replied in a voice that was no longer his own, before pausing for what seemed like an eternity - 'Well, if Martynov had not showed up'.

CHAPTER THIRTY-EIGHT

MADAME DE HELL

NOT LONG AFTER my visit to Mungo, I received a message from Blagodatsky containing news I had begun to suspect almost before I had left the curious house on Bolshoi Prospekt, which had been built only a few years previously, but had already taken on the appearance and air of a crumbling, dilapidated mansion house. The brief note informed me that, although Mungo was of course glad to have made my acquaintance, he had nonetheless come to the conclusion that further conversation was unnecessary: he had shared with me as much of what he knew of Pechorin's time in Tiflis as he wished. There would be no further opportunities to prise anything more from him.

My dismay did not prevent me from pursuing other potential sources of information, one chief among them: I spent two weeks in the attempt to discover the whereabouts of the very same Martynov who appeared to have played some role in bringing Mungo's incomplete tale to its premature conclusion. That endeavour reached its own unsatisfactory end with my discovery, through a distant relative of an officer with whom I had served in the south, that Martynov had disappeared from sight not long after Pechorin's departure from St Petersburg and, curiously, had not attended the funeral of his mother in 1851, when the estate passed into the hands of his fair sisters in the absence of the family's only son and heir. I was obliged to accept once again, as I had done somewhat less decisively some ten years previously, that the trail had gone cold: just as circumstance had entrusted me with a knowledge of Pechorin's life I could never have anticipated, its remaining mysteries would forever elude me.

Two months later, at that point in the movement of the seasons where the splendid, although unfortunately short-lived St Petersburg summer had given way to autumn, I was walking alone along the Nevsky Prospekt. The early September evening was full of light, if not warmth, and I had left the Department as early as was decent, intending to call into the confectioner *Wolff et Béranget* on my leisurely stroll home; contrary to my recent custom, I had an appointment later that evening for which a gift of confectionary was, if not quite a requirement, than at least a matter to be taken under advisement. Suddenly, when I was perhaps no more than fifty paces from the confectioner's shop, as so often happens in St Petersburg at that time of year, a shadow fell across the defenceless sun. All around, the colours of the buildings, carriages, even people became duller, then great drops of rain began to drum down on the pavement, throwing up the dust and setting passers-by into panicked motion. I raced between the exclamations and incongruous laughter, the sound of hooves and carriage wheels, between the umbrellas that suddenly sprouted above heads, but the rain became heavier and people began to abandon the pavements for the shelter of archways and doorways to shops and coffee-houses. By the time I reached *Wolff et Béranget*, my top-coat already soaked, the rain fell in torrents and the sound of thunder could be heard in the distance.

I stood in the confectioner's shop, surrounded by cakes and *patisserie*, looking out on the drenched Prospekt as the last few brave souls found their way to salvation. Nevsky was deserted, entirely abandoned to the elements. A great peal of thunder resounded in the sky. A flash of white lightning licked at the windows. Outside, a heavy carriage appeared beneath the downpour, in hand-to-hand combat with the raging elements, four grey horses at its head beating their hooves on the flooded road, their eyes wild with fear, the mouth of the postillion agape, as if intent on sucking in the rain. When it had passed, I suddenly caught sight of a lone figure walking slowly through the rain, oblivious to the elements, his overcoat soaked through, rain coursing from the long hair on his hatless head. I recognised him in an instant and rushed through the door of the confectioner's out into the downpour in pursuit. The rest of the world remained crouched in archways and doorways, curious but excluded from the scene. I weaved from side to side on the empty pavement as I followed him, blown by the wind and rain, incredulous that he was somehow able to maintain a steady course. I watched with relief as he stepped through the door of a tavern and I followed him, suddenly conscious of the warm rain that had now seeped into my underclothes.

Inside, the corridor led to a small sitting room with a bar, in which sat the owner, like a great balloon on a stick, his face a strange combination of impertinence and obsequiousness. His consumptive wife stood behind the bar, curlers still in her hair, alongside his daughter, who was the very image of the father, stout beyond her years, in a pale-blue apron and with a tray in her hands. At a table by the fire, still in his drenched overcoat and with his wet hair flat against his temples and cheeks, sat Mungo, a glass of vodka in his hand. Alongside him, already drunk and now animated by this new opportunity for manly conversation, sat a tall, heavy-set gentleman with sideburns and moustaches in the German style. Mungo drained the contents of his glass and waved it towards the benighted female figures behind the bar.

'Madame hostess!' - he cried, a trace of belligerence already discernible in his voice - 'Monsieur von Müffling and I would very much like another!'

I hesitated for a second in the doorway, but the figure I now recognised as von Müffling, as if he had suddenly stepped out from the pages of a novel, had noticed my presence even through his drunkenness. Mungo caught the direction of von Müffling's glance and followed it with his own, fixing it upon me with what seemed at first confusion, then devolving into ironic resignation.

'Well!' - he exclaimed - 'If it isn't our mysterious seeker after truth! Please, join us!'

I glanced once again at the ruined features of von Müffling, melting under a veneer of sweat, and took my place at their table.

Whatever the reasons for Mungo's reluctance to repeat our meeting of two months ago, he now seemed quite untroubled by my presence; on the contrary, the coincidence appeared to amuse him greatly, as he revealed in intermittent gleeful glances in the direction of von Müffling.

'What brings you to our humble tavern, my dear fellow?' – he asked with amiable irony, before continuing in a voice that might have been that of another man altogether – 'Or perhaps you're following me, is that it?'

'Not at all' – I replied immediately, discomfited by the sudden shift in tone – 'I was intending to purchase some confectionery when the rain suddenly burst upon us. I couldn't help notice you walking alone through the deserted street'.

'Confectionery, eh?' – said Mungo, now once again visibly enjoying himself – 'For anyone nice?'

'I didn't manage to make the purchase' – I said in a halting voice.

'More important things to do with your time, eh?' – he went on, before turning to von Müffling – 'What do you say, old man? Would you rather be here with a glass of vodka in your hand? Or paying a visit to some nice young lady, armed with a pretty gift-wrapped box bearing the legend *Wolff et Béranget?*'

von Müffling's expression of blank astonishment was as eloquent as any reply the befuddled creature could muster.

Mungo surveyed the empty glasses on the table before him, noting as he did that I was not yet even in possession of a full one. He ordered a round for the three of us, raised his glass, and gave all outward signs of a man about to propose a toast.

'To the future!' – he suddenly roared, before throwing back his head and draining the glass.

von Müffling immediately followed his example without pausing to register what he was toasting. I looked down with some trepidation at the glass before me, before raising it to my lips and taking a chaste sip.

'To the future' – I said quietly, holding Mungo's amused gaze – 'And to futures past'.

I took another sip as von Müffling began to slouch in his chair, then leaned forward to rest his arms on the table, cradling his great beard and moustaches between them. Mungo ordered another glass of vodka for himself and turned to me with a look of almost cheerful resignation.

'So what do you want to know, my dear fellow?' – he said.

'Tell me about Madame de Hell' – I replied, taking another sip from my glass.

He began to tell me how he had first made the acquaintance of Madame Adèle Hommaire de Hell, wife of Monsieur Xavier Hommaire de Hell, who was not only French Consul at Odessa, but a distinguished geographer and engineer, who counted among his many achievements the discovery of rich deposits of iron-ore near Kherson and a path-breaking volume of travelogue, ethnography, and geography entitled *Les steppes de la mer caspienne, la Crimée et la Russie méridionale*, published in three volumes in Paris. Madame de Hell was herself an aspiring writer of travelogue, who would later publish not only an account of her own travels in the Caucasus, but also edit her husband's posthumous book on Turkey and Persia after his death from a fever in the latter of those great lands, on a trip he had undertaken without his wife. Madame de Hell's literary gifts did not, however, play any significant role in Mungo's description of her.

'I must confess' - he said, in a voice clearly struggling with the force of the recollection - 'I had never met a woman like her. It was not just that she was strikingly beautiful, with long dark curls she did not trouble to conceal, even on formal occasions; she wore her age - she was at least thirty, perhaps more - with an ease we normally associate with the male of the species; and she spoke and acted in public settings with the confidence and assurance of even the most intelligent men. And not only that'.

'How do you mean?' - I asked, anxious to encourage his train of thought.

He shot me a glance charged with a quite different irony than that to which I had already become accustomed, but also with a sense of something like awe.

'She was described quite openly in that society as a "woman of easy habits"' - he said, as if unable to believe what he nonetheless felt compelled to report.

I made no reply.

'Social death for a woman of any standing whatsoever' - he continued - 'Even in the Caucasus. But Madame de Hell somehow bore the rumours - of which she cannot have been unaware - like the garland of victors. The aura and intrigue seemed somehow to enhance both her standing and her allure'.

'And, if I may ask' - I said - 'was her husband aware of such rumours?'

Mungo laughed and continued his recollection, now warming to the tale.

'I first met her at a reception at our Consulate' - he said - 'In the company of her distinguished husband... although that is not quite right, for she spent most of the evening in conversation with Monsieur Tetbu de Marigny, the Flemish Consul. I observed towards the end of the evening a word or two pass between husband and wife, after which I was introduced to her by our Consul - who was married to none other than Princess Yekaterina Yessentukhova; do you know her?'

'No' - I replied quietly - 'I have not had that pleasure'.

'Anyway' - Mungo continued - 'I had no sooner made Madame de Hell's acquaintance when she noticed that I was looking across the room in the direction of her husband. She took me discreetly by the arm and whispered conspiratorially: "Yes, he does take the role of husband far too seriously". As I stood in stunned silence, quite unaware of how to continue the conversation, she gestured with her beautiful head, its dark curls falling around her bare shoulders, in the direction of de Marigny: "Whereas this one I have played for a fool for some two years now; he has perhaps another year left in him". With that, she said how delightful it had been to make my acquaintance and left'.

I was suddenly conscious of the effort it had cost me to conceal my reaction to Mungo's characterisation of Madame de Hell, as I searched for a response that might encourage him to continue.

'And how did she meet Pechorin?' - I asked, perhaps too precipitately.

'They met at the summer house of Prince Orbeliani' - he continued, oblivious to my discomfort - 'A group of us were walking in the shade of the forest before lunch, when I noticed that both Pechorin and Madame de Hell were absent. I kept silent for as long as I could, waiting to see if Monsieur de Hell was also aware, which of course he very soon was'.

I gave him a look that must have betrayed something like fear, but said nothing.

'And where do you think we found them?' - he said with a sudden snort of laughter.

I shook my head but once again remained silent.

'We found them playing billiards in a little pavilion by the lake' - he continued - 'Madame de Hell, it seemed, had persuaded Pechorin to play by the English rules, as opposed to the Russian, and had not only won, but relieved him in the process of what must have been a fairly significant sum, because he later refused to tell me how much it was.

'I suppose the die was cast. The next time I saw them in one another's company was at the house of the dear Nina Griboyedova. I imagine there is no need to remind you of that fair lady's sufferings, which she has borne with such grace and fortitude since the unfortunate death of her husband'.

'1829' - I said quietly - 'A lifetime ago, if not in fact a different world'.

'Indeed. Pechorin had for some reason conceived of what I would only hesitate very slightly to call an obsession with Griboyedov and sought at the first opportunity to make the acquaintance of his widow. He had called on Madame Griboyedova on a number of occasions before that night, drawn perhaps by the mystery of what had compelled Griboyedov to accept his fate fifteen years before and travel to Tehran against all the advices of those closest to him, not least his young and uncomprehending wife. I have no idea what, if anything, he learned in their exchanges. But I do know that, on this night, in the presence of Madame de Hell, something had changed'.

'What do you mean?' - I asked, now myself in a state of genuine incomprehension - 'In general? Or in his relations with Madame de Hell?'

He paused for a moment, as if trying to solve a mystery that had eluded him at the time and in the long years since.

'I don't know' - he continued - 'Nina Griboyedova was herself still no more than thirty, still very beautiful, and possessed of a grace and charm that would never desert her. She still lived in the Akhverdev house, where Praskovia Nikolaevna Akhverdeva had been no less than a second mother to her as a child. Praskovia Nikolaevna was a second-cousin to Pechorin's mother and was close to his late grandmother when she moved to St Petersburg. I often wondered whether the old women had discussed the fate of their respective charges... stranger things have happened, you know.

'Pechorin was certainly enchanted by Nina Griboyedova, who provoked a mixture of sympathy and respect in him, notwithstanding her beauty. We never saw her father, Alexander Chavchavadze, who spent most of his time at his estate near Tsinandali'.

I nodded in recognition of the remarkable Chavchavadze, soldier-poet and translator of Pushkin into Georgian, who had exerted his influence as both soldier and statesman in the service of relations between Russia and Georgia with greater distinction than any man of his time.

'A great man' – I said sincerely – 'But why do you mention him in this connection?'

'There were rumours that he was displeased by Pechorin's attentions to his daughter and, while he had not quite forbidden her to see him, she knew that news of any public encounter would certainly get back to her father'.

I nodded again, this time in wry acknowledgement of his words, although he neither noticed the expression on my face, nor, if he had, could he have understood its meaning.

'Pechorin was talking to Nina Griboyedova and another lady whose name I don't recall... the wife of some general or other. His manner was polite and attentive, restricting himself to the most subtle of witticisms. Suddenly, Madame de Hell came into the room with her husband and made straight for the hostess. It transpired that they had not yet met and that French manners would not countenance accepting hospitality without a formal introduction.

"Nina Alexandrovna" – I heard Pechorin begin – "May I present His Honour Monsieur Xavier Hommaire de Hell, French Consul at Odessa. And his charming wife Madame Adèle Hommaire de Hell".

Monsieur de Hell gave a low, almost theatrical bow, and, to Madame Griboyedova's evident surprise, took her hand and placed upon it a kiss. Madame de Hell made only a short, barely perceptible motion with her head, then grasped Nina's hand and shook it firmly as if they were two generals meeting at Staff HQ.

"Monsieur and Madame de Hell are making a study of the Caucasus and the Caspian littoral" – Pechorin continued, as if nothing at all had happened.

"How fascinating" – Nina replied, with all the appearance of sincerity – "I hope you will paint our land and customs in a favourable light".

Monsieur de Hell's face was possessed by some faint trepidation, offset by the knowledge of years of consistent experience, as he briefly caught the gaze of Madame Griboyedova, before turning his eyes meekly to the floor. Madame de Hell opened her mouth to reply, but was interrupted by the calm, clear voice of Pechorin.

"The fruits of their labours will be published in a volume in Paris next year" – he said – "I'm sure Madame de Hell will be so kind as to send you a copy".

Nina Griboyedova smiled a thin smile as Madame de Hell nodded her consent.

'As the evening drew to a close, I began to take my leave. Pechorin told me he would follow very soon, but it was almost an hour after I had got back to the apartments before I heard him come in. The house fell silent and I assumed he had gone to bed for the night. A few minutes later, however, there came a light knock at my door. I rose and opened it, to find Pechorin in a silk *kaftan* and night-cap, a troubled smile on his pale lips.

"Come in" - I said wearily - "if you're coming".

He slipped past me without a word.

"What in the devil is going on?" - I asked insistently once he was seated - "What took you so long? And do you really think it's fair on the charming Madame Griboyedova to make such a display? Do what you want to do, by all means: but I would at least expect from you some measure of discretion".

Pechorin brightened at this, enjoying, as I was about to learn, my misreading - understandable though it may have been - of the situation.

"It's not what you think, my dear Mungo" - he said, with a curious glint in his eye.

"Then what the devil is it?" - I asked, my weariness now giving way to exasperation.

"Shall I tell you what happened after you left?" - he replied, still smiling.

"Oh, for God's sake, Pechorin!" - I exclaimed, before lowering my voice through fear that we might wake Mikha and continuing in a rasping whisper - "Please do get on with it!"

Pechorin smiled once more and began to recount the events of the later part of the evening.

"I'm not quite sure where to begin, old man" - he said, clearly enjoying himself - "I had just taken my leave of the delightful hostess, no more than five minutes after you had left, and was making my way down into the little vestibule at the front of the house, when I heard a voice from one of the rooms to the side. I followed it and, no sooner than I had stepped inside, Madame de Hell pushed the door closed behind me".

"What did she want?" - I asked blankly.

"She wanted, would you believe, to talk about Madame Griboyedova" - said Pechorin - "She told me - although I had not of course asked - that the charms of Madame Griboyedova were not for me: that she was beautiful, educated, intelligent, but that there was a certain severity in her, no doubt caused, or at least exacerbated, by the tragic death of her husband and the loss of their child when she was so young. She told me that the fair Nina was more likely to end her days in a Convent than in the drawing-rooms of high society. And that - can you believe the impertinence of the woman! - I was in any case more interested in the aura of the late husband than I was in the lady herself".

"And do you have any idea" - I interrupted - "why Madame de Hell was so keen to share with you these... these impressions?"

"Yes, I do". - Pechorin replied - "I most certainly do".

I was long accustomed to this infuriating habit of Pechorin and, determined that he not I would speak the next word, merely fixed him with as neutral a gaze as I could manage.

"She asked me to run away with her" - he said at last.

"What on earth?" - I replied, my determination to give him no particular encouragement vanquished by this quite unexpected turn of events.

"She told me to be ready to leave for Sokhumi at dawn two days hence" - he said, faintly incredulous at his own tale - "From there, we would sail to Odessa by private yacht".

"And from there?" - I asked, my voice now rising once again through the still of the night - "And what about her husband?"

"From there?" - Pechorin replied - "I have no idea, my dear Mungo, although I can't imagine France plays any role in the fair Madame's thoughts. Oh, and by the way" - he continued - "I'm not at all concerned about the husband".

Here I became more than exasperated, angry even at the lack of subtlety with which Pechorin sought to play down the seriousness of the situation, to aggrandize his own casual fatalism, which I did not think befitted him, even at his most evasive and cavalier.

"Why on earth would you say such a thing, Pechorin?" - I said coldly - "You can't expect me to believe that you regard the matter with such carelessness".

"Carelessness has nothing to do with" - he replied with an air of feigned perplexity - "It's just that I'm more concerned about Monsieur de Marigny than I am about Monsieur de Hell".

"And what does that gentleman have to do with it?" - I exclaimed, my patience now at an end.

"Well" - Pechorin continued - "when I had at last freed myself from the clutches of Madame de Hell, her imprecations to sail away with her ringing in my ears, I ran into Monsieur de Marigny as I was about to leave the house. I can only imagine from the way in which he had stationed himself by the front door and approached me as soon as I appeared that he knew of my whereabouts... and, perhaps, knew something of the topic of conversation".

I surveyed Pechorin with a familiar combination of admiration and exasperation.

"And what did Monsieur de Marigny have to say for himself?" - I asked.

Pechorin paused, although I would swear more out of genuine bemusement than from any desire to create an effect.

"He challenged me to a duel, my dear uncle" - he replied with his characteristic half-smile'.

Mungo looked away from me towards his glass, as if astonished that it was once again empty. He picked up the glass and waved it in the direction of the bar, where the landlord's wife and daughter still stood, listening to Mungo's strange tale with a fascination that was in no way diminished by their total incomprehension. He turned once more towards me and broke into a laugh, in which I could determine quite clearly the traces of grief and incredulity.

CHAPTER THIRTY-NINE

THE READINESS IS ALL

I TUMBLED OUT INTO the still wet streets of St Petersburg, Mungo at my side, a full moon rising in the deep blue sky. Not a trace of cloud remained. The air was strangely warm, our damp overcoats somehow a comfort. Mungo had insisted on leaving von Müffling in the care of the landlord and his wife and now stepped into the filthy road, waving his arms around in an attempt to hail a cab. A pair of black mares, their coats glistening in the moonlight, came to a halt in front of us and Mungo leapt up into the coach behind them.

'Well, what are you waiting for?' – he asked, leaning out of the window.
'Where are we going?' – I replied.
'Would you like me to continue my tale, or not?' – he said.
I made no reply and climbed up into the cab alongside him.

As the driver made his way along Bolshaya Konyushennaya, Mungo slipped into a peaceful sleep, a calm smile settling upon his once again youthful face. The cab stopped outside a three-storey building near the Imperial Stables on Konyushennaya Square, with tall windows on the upper floors shrouded in darkness; only a faint light glimmered from a window on the ground floor. Mungo was awakened by the sudden absence of motion, shivered as if to shake off the damp, and stepped down from the cab. I followed.

The front door to the house, which had perhaps once been grand, but was now showing signs of neglect and disrepair, fell open as Mungo pushed. There was no light in the hallway, so we made our way carefully through the darkness towards a faint strip of light at the foot of a door, presumably to the room we had seen lit from the outside. Mungo once again pushed it open without knocking, to reveal a tall figure with features as dilapidated as the house, stretched out in an armchair, coddling a glass of wine. The stranger looked up at me and I realised, with a sudden shock of impossible but certain recognition, where I was: Mungo had brought me to the Kuragin house in order to finish his tale.

'Would you oblige us with a bottle, old man?' – said Mungo in a cheerful slur.

The stranger who was Anatolii Kuragin surveyed me without any particular sign of interest and began to stir from his chair.

'Why of course, my dear Stolypin' – he replied – 'After all, what else is left to us?'

'Nothing at all, my dear Kuragin' – Mungo replied – 'Nothing at all'.

As Kuragin left the room, Mungo gestured to me to be seated and made himself comfortable on a low divan against the far wall, where the light of the little lamp barely penetrated. There was no other chair in the room but the one Kuragin himself had occupied. I hesitated for a moment, then perched myself at its edge. Kuragin duly returned with a bottle of Burgundy and two glasses, which he placed on the table alongside me. He poured, handed a glass to Mungo, then turned once again to leave.

'I'll leave you two gentlemen alone' – he said in the doorway – 'I expect you have much to talk about'.

'A fine fellow, Kuragin' – said Mungo as soon as Kuragain had closed the door beyond him – 'Do you know him?'

'I haven't had that pleasure' – I replied.

'Of course' – Mungo continued, taking a sip of Burgundy – 'his house is not what it once was: the stories I could tell…'.

I turned my eyes to the floor.

'I would be more than happy to hear them' – I replied – 'But I would much rather you completed the story you have already begun'.

I paused for a moment before continuing.

'Did Pechorin fight a duel?' – I asked in a whisper.

'He did' – Mungo replied – 'But not with Monsieur de Marigny. I suspect Madame de Hell may have intervened with that gentleman, because, the very next morning, he sent a note of apology, imploring Pechorin to disregard his behaviour of the night before. Pechorin later told me that Madame de Hell hoped – indeed expected – that Monsieur de Marigny, on learning of her plans, would follow the fugitive lovers; that she herself had almost certainly told de Marigny of her intentions, but had misjudged the vehemence of his response'.

I gave Mungo a confounded, defeated look.

'I called on Pechorin the following morning' – he continued – 'but he had left early with Mikha. The old woman who cooked and cleaned for him told me he had gone to the bookseller's in the market square. I set off at once, with no clear sense of what impelled me to speak to him; only a burning certainty that speak to him I must. I can barely convey to you the sight that awaited me on the fringes of the old market square. Pechorin was standing idly beneath a parasol, cigar in hand, chatting amiably with the old bookseller, who was expansive in his delight at the sale he had just made, which would by itself see him through the winter and beyond. Little Mikha, in his long flowing *kaftan* and bright blue *kalpak*, which shielded his head from the burning sun, was gravely conveying heavy bound volumes, three at a time, into a carriage Pechorin had hired for the purpose. The legend embossed into their spines confirmed that the old bookseller had somehow managed to fulfil Pechorin's fantastical request, and in the English original.

"What madness is this?" – I exclaimed as I approached, not quite sure if I was addressing Pechorin or the bookseller.

"Though this be madness, yet there is method in 't" – Pechorin replied with a beaming smile, winking at the bemused old bookseller.

When Mikha had finished loading the carriage, Pechorin paid the driver and sent the boy homewards with precise instructions to decant the newly acquired volumes and arrange them on the shelves in the inner of the two rooms he had rented. He bid the bookseller farewell and gestured to me to join him as he set off towards the sulphur baths at the foot of the Abanotubani gorge. He was indeed in a strange mood; the ironic reserve to which I had long become accustomed had given way to something more fervent, as if he was possessed of some secret at which the rest of us could only guess – and which amused him greatly.

"What are we going to do?" – I asked in some confusion.

"We're going to bathe, my dear uncle" – he replied with a manic cheerfulness.

'We soon arrived before an imposing building with Turkic archways and exquisite mosaic inlays, topped by a shimmering golden cupola. An ancient, gaunt figure in a turban stood at the entrance.

"*Hamardshoba, mekise*" – said Pechorin in a low voice.

"*Hamardshoba, tawadi*" – the old man replied, bowing in welcome as he opened the door.

We stepped into a great, warm hall, its walls covered in the same style of mosaic as the exterior, around which stood wooden benches, some of them adorned by a naked body. Pechorin began to remove his clothes and gestured to me to do the same, before leading me into a little room on the right-hand side, with marble benches set into the walls and a long rectangular hole in the floor, filled with steaming hot sulphurous water. I screwed up my nose at the smell of the sulphur, but Pechorin laughed dismissively.

"You do know that Tiflis exists only because of these waters, my dear uncle?" – he said in a tone of mock admonition – "King Vakhtang Gorgasali sent out his falcon some fourteen hundred years ago and could not understand why it had not returned, until he came upon the springs at which it had come to rest; thus was born a great city at the crossroads of Europe and Asia. Think of all the warriors and victors who have conquered this place – Jamal al-Din, Timur the Lame, Chagatai Khan, second son of Genghis Khan – all drunk and heavy with the blood they had shed, before stepping into the sulphur to become light and agile once again".

'Just then, the old man who had greeted us at the entrance came into the room. Pechorin stepped out of the bath, covered in soapsuds, and lay face down on one of the marble benches. The old *mekise* at first scrubbed Pechorin's skin with a mitten made of hemp, working up a lather to remove layers of dead skin as he moved steadily from the soles of his feet all the way to his face and scalp. When he had finished, he washed the curls of Pechorin's hair before rinsing him with two great buckets of warm water. I watched in astonishment as the *mekise* sprang up onto Pechorin's back, trampling with his bare feet, as light as a dancer on a ceremonial rug. The old man, still in his turban, then skipped back down to the floor and began to knead Pechorin's arms and shoulders with his fingers, before finally cradling his head in both arms and jerking it suddenly to one side with a great crack. Pechorin lifted himself carefully from the bench and disappeared into an adjoining room, which contained a raised plunge-pool filled with ice-cold water. The old *mekise* gestured to me to take Pechorin's place on the marble bench. I obeyed, albeit with a trepidation I did not scruple to conceal. Pechorin came back into the room draped in a sheet, sat down on one of the marble benches with a look of simple delight on his face, and lit a cigar.

"Relax, my dear uncle" - he said, beaming - "You'll soon feel like a new man".

'When my ordeal was over, we sat wrapped in our sheets, entirely shorn of the dust and cares of the outside world, smoking the little French cigars Pechorin had somehow managed to maintain in constant supply. An old woman brought in a tray of cold watermelon, cheese, walnuts, and the bread Georgians call *shoti*, along with two glasses of tea. Pechorin seemed like a man restored and, I must say, I myself felt better than I had done since I arrived in Tiflis.

"What did I tell you?" - Pechorin began, wiping the juice of the watermelon from his lips - "If I hadn't known you all my life, I swear I wouldn't recognise you!"

"I can hardly credit it" - I replied sincerely - "We must do this more often".

"Indeed" - he said, with a smile tinged with only the faintest trace of guilt - "I've been coming here every morning since I arrived".

My slight resentment that Pechorin hadn't previously asked me to accompany him was offset by anticipation of further such visits; but neither resentment nor anticipation could quell the familiar sense that Pechorin knew something I didn't.

"You're very cheerful, my dear nephew" - I said - "Aren't you at all concerned by this business with Madame de Hell? Or Monsieur de Marigny?"

Pechorin fixed me with his characteristic half-smile.

"What is there to be concerned about, my dear uncle?" - he replied.

"Do you know what you're going to do?" - I asked quickly, hopeful he might at least cast some light on his intentions for the following morning.

"Yes" - he replied curtly, still smiling.

"But you're not going to tell me?"

"Why, my dear Mungo, I would have thought you would be able to work that out for yourself. And besides, I have other things to be concerned about".

I felt once again a rising exasperation at Pechorin's uniquely irritating blend of nonchalance and mystery.

"And what might they be?" - I asked - "Will you tell me that, at least?"

"I'll do better than that, my dear uncle" - he replied, tossing a walnut into his open mouth - "I'll show you. Come on, drink up your tea. Let's take a stroll down to the post-station".

I did as I was instructed and we stepped out into the caress of the afternoon sun, as light and agile as the sulphur baths had promised.

'We crossed the Metekhi Bridge under the shadow of the twin minarets of the Abbas Shah Mosque and headed left along the banks of the Kura. I had not initially questioned why he might wish to visit the post-station, perhaps under the influence of the warm sulphurous water, or perhaps due to a barely conscious assumption that Pechorin would soon be leaving Tiflis, with or without Madame de Hell. When we arrived at what was no more than a dusty yard enclosed by an uneven wooden fence, with only a single, low wooden building, a pair of carriages, and a number of presentable horses gathered together under a rough shade, I began to sense that Pechorin had something quite different in mind; and I knew well enough by now that to enquire was pointless. We sat down on a bench in the shade alongside the horses. Pechorin lit a cigar and offered me one, which I gladly accepted. And there we sat, for what must have been the best part of an hour.

"Pechorin" - I said at last - "I'm sure this is a very pleasant way to spend an afternoon... but I wonder if you might tell me how much longer you're planning to stay?"

"Well, I would love to, my dear Mungo" - he said - "But I really don't know".

"What do you mean you don't know?" - I replied.

He turned to me as he lit another cigar, then adopted the expression of a patient tutor, indulgent of the incomprehension of his young charge.

"If I knew how long we'd have to wait" - he began - "I'd have to know also when the coach will arrive. And you know as well as I do that, in these parts, we may know with some certainty that, on any given day, a coach will arrive; but we may never know with any degree of certainty at all precisely when it will do so".

I declined his offer of another cigar and pulled my hat down over my eyes.

'When I awoke, the sun was arcing towards the low ridge of the hills to the west. I shivered, my light summer clothing suddenly inadequate now that the enervating glow of the bathhouse had diminished along with the warmth of the sun. Pechorin was nuzzling one of the horses tethered behind us and hadn't noticed that I was now awake. I listened as he murmured something in Tatar to the docile beast. Then, suddenly, his murmuring stopped and his bearing became more stiff. I now heard the distant rumble of coach wheels and wondered at the preternatural heightening of the senses that had allowed Pechorin to discern their presence seconds before me. He looked in my direction, a calm smile playing on his lips, and we listened together as the sound of the coach wheels came closer and closer, until at last the dusty and battered coach appeared above a little ridge, ploughing its steady course towards the yard.

"Are you going to tell me?" - I asked, already anticipating the reply.

"Why spoil the tension, my dear uncle?" - he replied - "You'll see for yourself soon enough".

'The coach at last came to rest in the near deserted yard. The station-master and a boy of no more than fourteen rushed out to greet it. Pechorin sat down on the bench alongside me, facing directly onto the right-hand side of the coach, which seemed to have come to a halt from exhaustion as much as any sense of having reached its destination.

"I do hope he gets out on this side" - said Pechorin in a steely, almost manic tone - "It would be quite distastefully comical if, after you have waited so long and so patiently, he should alight from the other side".

I gave him a look of confounded awe.

"For if Mungo like not the comedy..." - he continued.

Suddenly, the door of the coach swung open and a heavy leather bag fell crashing into the dust beneath it. It was followed by the figure of a man, so tall that it appeared for a moment he would be unable to squeeze through the door. The figure stood to its full height, a great mane of dark hair pushed back from the taut, sunburned face, rising like Mount Kazbek itself above a pair of broad, muscular shoulders, which even the finely tailored coat of English wool could not entirely conceal. I peered out from the shade into the gentle evening sunshine, but, before I could get a good look at the gentleman's features, Pechorin's clear, calm voice halted him in his stride.

"My dear Martynov" - he said. - "We've been expecting you for some time".

The figure, which I now recognised in astonishment was indeed that of Martynov, peered back into the shade from where the voice had emerged, as if he had convinced himself on the long journey south that hearing it would be the most natural thing in the world, only to be overwhelmed by its strange and unexpected quality in reality. He placed a hand above his brows, straining to penetrate the glare of the setting sun, but made no reply'.

Mungo was beginning to show signs of fatigue, which I feared might once again lead to the curtailment of his tale.

'Wait a moment' - I said suddenly, before getting to my feet and leaving the room.

I returned with another bottle of Burgundy, refilled both our glasses, and raised my own glass in amiable salute.

'How on earth did Pechorin know that Martynov was on his way south?' - I asked, anxious for him to resume his tale.

Mungo took an admiring sip from his glass and let out a curious little laugh.

'I never found out' - he said - 'Whenever I asked, he just laughed and shook his head. He was that kind of fellow: you never knew how much he knew and sometimes, in the later years, I suspected he had mastered the art of convincing people he knew more than he did... But then, as in the case of Martynov's sudden reappearance, he'd conjure some inexplicable, mysterious feat of knowledge... and of course never let on how he did it'.

'And did he also know why Martynov had come?' - I asked.

'He did, although at first he concealed that fact' - said Mungo.

'How do you mean?' - I insisted.

'Well' – he replied – 'he greeted Martynov most amiably, performing the role of the comrade reunited to the letter, which of course bemused and infuriated Martynov in equal measure. As I sat there on that bench, trying to make sense of what was unfolding, Pechorin gave no sign of concern.

"We must get you to your apartments, Martynov" – Pechorin told him, approaching with a warm smile and a handshake.

"Why the great rush" – Martynov replied.

"I hope you will forgive me' – Pechorin continued – "but I have taken the liberty of securing for you an invitation this evening at the Consulate of the French Republic. I was becoming quite concerned that your coach would arrive too late".

Martynov glared back in silence, grappling with the familiar sense that Pechorin was playing with him, despite his outward warmth.

"You're expected at eight" – said Pechorin, turning to leave – "Try not to be late, there's a good fellow".

'And did he come?' – I asked, gripped by anticipation.

'Oh yes, he came alright' – said Mungo – 'Although he didn't quite make it for eight... and I suspect that wine may have been consumed in the intervening period'.

He paused for a second, the shadow of a wry smile barely perceptible on his face.

'Not that that's any great deficiency in a man, you understand?' – he continued, taking another sip from his glass – 'Pechorin greeted him like a long-lost brother and introduced him with great ceremony to the hosts'.

"Monsieur and Madame Hommaire de Hell" – Pechorin said with a low bow – "My former comrade-at-arms, Lieutenant Martynov, retired".

Martynov bowed towards Monsieur de Hell, then took Madame de Hell's hand, bowed once again, and kissed it.

"Delighted and enchanted" – he said, struggling with the effort to conceal his immediate fascination with Madame de Hell – "I'm very grateful for the invitation... and indebted to Pechorin for his forethought".

A strange veil fell upon the expression of Madame de Hell, who turned inquisitively to her husband.

"Xavier, my dear" – she began – "I can't recall inviting Monsieur Martynov, can you?"

Monsieur de Hell managed to rouse only a brief shrug from his frozen shoulders.

"No matter" – continued Madame de Hell – "We are also delighted to make your acquaintance. Please, make yourself at home".

Martynov turned to where Pechorin had stood moments before, but Pechorin had disappeared...

'Martynov spent the next half hour furiously searching out Pechorin among the guests, pausing only to exchange pleasantries with one or two fellows he knew from active service. I don't know where Pechorin had gone

– he wouldn't tell me afterwards – but he reappeared, as if by magic, at the side of Madame de Hell, when Martynov was on the other side of the room. I watched as he began to make his way towards them, setting off discreetly from my own location with the intention of arriving at the same time. Martynov got there slightly in advance of me and, as I approached, I heard him once again greet Madame de Hell in the most loquacious of terms.

"Madame de Hell" – he began, once again taking her hand – "I must apologise for the circumstances in which we became acquainted; I hope you won't hold Pechorin's little joke against me".

"Not at all, Monsieur Martynov" – she replied – "Any friend of Monsieur Pechorin's is a friend of ours".

Pechorin flashed a self-satisfied smile in my direction.

"But tell me, Monsieur Martynov" – continued Madame de Hell – "What brings you to Tiflis?"

Martynov smiled awkwardly, but was nonetheless anxious to reward the beautiful Madame de Hell's inquiry with an engaging reply.

"Oh, I was here many times while on active service" – he began – "And, now that I am free of those obligations, I can think of no better place to spend the late summer months".

"What about your other obligations?" – Pechorin interrupted – "Can they also be discharged only in Tiflis?"

Martynov stood in furious silence.

"How fascinating!" – exclaimed Madame de Hell – "Please, Monsieur Martynov, I would be most interested to hear of your other obligations".

Martynov managed only a bitter smile in reply, before turning his gaze to Pechorin.

"I'm not sure this is quite the place for such a conversation" – said Martynov, recovering his poise – "Perhaps you would do me the honour of a word in private, Pechorin?"

"Why certainly" – Pechorin replied cheerfully – "But I must first conclude a small matter with our hostess".

Pechorin took his silver cigar-case from a front pocket, offered one to Martynov, and lit it for him.

"I'll join you outside in just a moment" – said Pechorin, before turning to me and offering me a cigar – "Mungo, perhaps you'd like to accompany Monsieur Martynov?"

As we turned to leave, Madame de Hell leaned into Pechorin and said in a just discernible whisper:

"If I was a man, I wouldn't challenge you to a duel; I'd shoot you point blank from undercover".

"In that case, as indeed for a number of other reasons" – Pechorin replied – "I am very glad you're not a man. But please, if you will excuse me...".

"Have you nothing else to say before leaving?" – she asked with a smile.

"What else is there to say?" – said Pechorin, returning her smile before turning towards the door.

"À *demain*" - I could just hear Madame de Hell say, her soft eyes glimmering'.

Mungo reached for the bottle of Burgundy, poured himself another glass, and gestured towards my own glass with the neck of the bottle.

'I don't know what else, if anything, passed between them' - he continued - 'But it was some time before he joined us on the veranda. I could not find words for Martynov and restricted myself to staring intently at him in a show of silent interrogation. At first, he affected not to notice, occasionally taking a long draw from his cigar, which he cradled in his nonchalantly cocked fingers. After some time, however, he became uneasy under my unrelenting gaze, his movements more mechanical, the effort of maintaining the appearance of ease more pronounced.

"What?" - he barked at last - "If you have something to say, please say it".

"Why are you here, Martynov?" - I asked in a voice unable to bear the weight of my anger.

"He's here to provoke me into a duel" - came the voice of Pechorin as he stepped out onto the veranda - "Isn't that right, Martynov?"

Martynov dropped the butt of his cigar and trod it into the painted wood of the veranda, searching for a response to Pechorin's sudden accusation.

"I'm not sure what you mean, Pechorin" - he replied at last - "After all, how could I be sure you would show up?"

Pechorin smiled a smile of genuine warmth and amusement.

"You can be assured" - he replied - "that on this occasion I will not disappoint you".

"Pechorin!" - I interrupted - "Why on earth would you give him the satisfaction? What if you are killed".

Pechorin maintained his gaze on Martynov, his smile undimmed.

"My dear uncle" - he said - "You do understand that this will never end until one of us is killed? Isn't that right, Martynov?"

Martynov said nothing.

"In any case" - Pechorin continued - "I intend to save my old comrade-at-arms the trouble".

"What do you mean?" - said Martynov, his smile now vanished, unable to conceal his incomprehension.

"Tomorrow morning at six, by St David's church on Mtatsminda" - said Pechorin calmly - "Pistols at twelve paces".

Martynov's mouth fell open in silent astonishment.

"If one of us is killed, that will be an end to it" - Pechorin went on - "But if neither of us is killed... let that also be an end to it. Do you agree?"

Martynov again said nothing.

"Come, my dear Martynov... you shoot from a pistol with a little more skill than you ride a horse. Surely you won't fail to kill me from twelve paces?" - continued Pechorin.

Martynov brought his lower jaw once more into contact with the upper, stiffened his neck and shoulders, and thrust out his chin in a show of resolve.

"Very well, Pechorin" - he said, before turning to me - "Stolypin, I have no doubt that, whatever the outcome, you will bear witness to the fact that Pechorin has challenged me to a duel, and that I had no option but to accept".

"He will" - Pechorin replied before I could speak, gesturing towards the stairway at the far end of the veranda with his head, then turning to leave.

As we reached the top of the stairs, Pechorin turned once again towards Martynov, who stood quite still by the rail of the veranda, the remains of his cigar still smouldering by his feet.

"Oh, and Martynov" - Pechorin continued, with a cheerfulness in his voice that turned my blood quite cold - "I am sure you will be able to find among your acquaintances in Tiflis two honest men who will act as your seconds. No doctor".

Martynov nodded his dumbfounded assent and we left.

CHAPTER FORTY

THE MEN OF HONOUR III

'My questions and loud objections rained down on Pechorin as we made our way back to our apartments' - Mungo continued, as if now in a fever - 'But he refused every one and merely advised me to get some sleep. I have no idea how much sleep he himself managed; I know only that he was up before me, because I awoke to the sound of a whispered conversation between him and Mikha in the hallway. Mikha had departed into the half-light by the time I had dressed and appeared in Pechorin's room, but he once again refused to share with me any detail of where the boy had gone and why. Only afterwards did I learn from Madame de Hell that a note had been delivered that morning before dawn at the French Consulate, which she later entrusted to my keeping.

> My Dearest Adéle,
> One should only meet three times with the object of one's adoration: the first time for oneself, the second time for the satisfaction of one's beloved, and the third time for the sake of society. We have already tempted fate far beyond these strictures and you must know in your heart that society, having no use for us, will never allow us the solace of one another's company. Si mon heure est venue, elle n'est pas à venir; so I bid you farewell and wish you - and your esteemed husband - every good fortune on your travels and, indeed, on your return to France.
> Yours, for one last moment,
> Grigorii

Mungo's voice faltered as he uttered Pechorin's name then trailed off into silence. I had little choice on this occasion but to abandon for a time my efforts to encourage him to continue his tale.

When he had at last brightened and even accepted my offer of some more wine, I ransacked my exhausted mind for a question that might impel him forward, rather than bring up the drawbridge of memory.

'I imagine it was Pechorin's way of concealing from the boy that he was about to fight a duel?' - I said quietly.

Mungo furrowed his brows in confusion, before breaking into a weak, ironic smile.

'Then you imagine quite wrong' - he replied - 'It was Pechorin's idea of honour! I don't believe he ever had any intention of running away with Madame de Hell; but, when fate had made that decision for him, he was determined that she should learn this from him alone, and not from grisly circumstance'.

'I'm not sure I understand' - I said, frowning.

'When I suggested that it was time for us to make our way up Mtatsminda' - said Mungo - 'Pechorin simply smiled and said that we would be on our way just as soon as Mikha returned'.

"What do you mean?" - I asked him - "Wouldn't it be better to leave before he comes back - if, that is, you intend to go through with this madness..."

"Oh, don't worry on that account, my dear uncle" - said Pechorin - "But aren't you rather overlooking something?"

I looked at him blankly.

"You will recall my stipulation that we would each be attended by two seconds?" - he said - "And where do you imagine I will find another second at this hour of the morning?"

My mind lurched from one state of incomprehension into another, yet more perplexing.

"You cannot seriously intend to take an innocent boy to the scene of a murder!" - I exclaimed at last - "If you do, you will do so without me".

"I'm not sure I understand you, my dear Mungo" - Pechorin replied - "What if I am killed? You cannot seriously intend to allow an innocent boy to deal with that eventuality alone? And besides, that innocent boy has seen things at which you and I can only wonder...".

Just at that moment, we heard the sound of the front door opening and closing, followed by light footsteps on the stairs. Mikha stepped through the door to Pechorin's quarters and confirmed with a curt bow that his task had been completed.

"Come" - said Pechorin, looking intently at the boy, but addressing his words to me - "It's time. We must hurry".

'We made our way to the foot of Mtatsminda just as the morning sun rose above the low hills to the east on the other bank of the Kura. The church of St David sat above our heads, framed by the solid mass behind it, as if the building and its modest dome had been carved into the hillside. I could hear the sound of my own breathing as the slope began to steepen, but Pechorin seemed unaffected, striding out ahead of me, Mikha trotting along at his rear. I wondered for the first time what, if anything, Pechorin had told the boy: had he prepared him for the possibility of his death? Or was Mikha so accustomed to obedience that the purpose of this early-morning expedition was of as little concern to him as any other? I felt a sudden rage towards Pechorin, occasioned by the thought that he would not only expose an innocent boy, one way or another, to the spectacle of death - but that he might leave us both to bury him. Such thoughts were dispelled only by the realisation that I was falling behind. I quickened my pace and eventually caught up with Pechorin and Mikha as they stepped out onto the plateau of St David's church.

'Martynov already stood in the doorway of the church in the full light of the sun, accompanied by two fellows in uniform, neither of whom I recognised. All three looked out in growing astonishment as we approached, shading their eyes against the low sun, each trying to convince himself that what he saw before him was no more than a trick of the light.

"What is the meaning of this?" – demanded one of the uniformed officers as we approached – "Is this your idea of a joke?"

"Not at all, Lieutenant Smertin" – Pechorin replied instantly, although neither of the two strangers had had the opportunity to introduce himself – "You will be aware that I specified two seconds. I see that you and Lieutenant Kulebakov have been kind enough to accompany Monsieur Martynov" – he continued, nodding to the other officer – "These are my seconds... Gentlemen, introduce yourselves!"

"We certainly will not!" – said the officer Pechorin had identified as Kulebakov, turning indignantly to Martynov, who remained motionless, rage and disbelief contending for mastery of his expression.

"Pechorin" – Martynov said at last in as calm a voice as he could manage – "This really is too far. You'll get us all arrested, whatever the outcome".

"Why so?" – Pechorin replied – "I trust in the loyalty and discretion of Mikha no less than that of my dear uncle. And I have raised no questions as to the integrity of your own seconds" – he continued, his gaze still fixed upon Martynov.

"That is quite enough!" – said Smertin – "I will have no part in this! In fact, Monsieur Pechorin, if you continue to insist, you and I will fight if Martynov doesn't put you out of your misery!"

"He is right" – said Martynov quickly – "You can't expect these gentlemen – or indeed myself – to go through with this in the presence of a child".

"Whyever not?" – said Pechorin, the trace of a smile fighting for expression around the corner of his lips – "Those are the terms on which we agreed. You will of course do as you please, but know this: I will not fight on any other terms".

Pechorin turned to Mikha with a warm smile. The boy's expression gave no clue as to whether he understood the conversation that had just taken place.

'I managed to rouse myself from the waking slumber that had gripped me and made as if to speak, but Pechorin silenced me with a brief motion of his jaw. Lieutenant Smertin drew Martynov and Kulebakov into a huddled, animated congress, from which only the occasional strained whisper emerged. Pechorin stepped away to the edge of the little plateau, where Mikha and I followed him. After some minutes, Smertin and Kulebakov stood erect and placed their hats on their indignant heads.

"You're a fool!" – spat out Smertin in the direction of Martynov, before turning to Pechorin as he left – "And if this fool does not deliver the fate you so richly deserve, you will hear from my second before nightfall".

Kulebakov gave a nervous grimace as he followed Smertin to the path back down the hill.

"I look forward to it, gentlemen!" – Pechorin called after them, removing his cap and giving a low, theatrical bow, before turning once again to Martynov, who remained alone in the door to the church – "I see your judgement has not improved with age, Martynov; I hope for your sake that your aim has...".

"But Pechorin" - I interrupted - "Martynov no longer has a second".

"Are you offering your services, my dear uncle?" - Pechorin replied with an indulgent smile - "Splendid. I knew I could count on you".

'Pechorin remained at the edge of the plateau with Mikha, the sun and the slumbering rooftops of the city below at his back. He then removed his light summer jacket and laid it carefully on the ground. Mikha offered him a lacquered wooden box, which Pechorin opened to reveal a short pistol with pleasing ornate inlays of silver.

"Are you quite intent on going through with this, Pechorin?" - I asked in a voice laden with resignation.

"I am" - he replied cheerfully - "Now would you be so good as to inspect my pistol and satisfy yourself that it is properly loaded? Your man will no doubt seek such reassurances before we engage".

I studied the expressionless features of Mikha, who remained quite still, thrusting the lacquered box out in front of him, his thin brown arms emerging like reeds from the sleeves of his *kaftan*. I lifted the pistol, satisfied myself that a ball had been loaded into its chamber and powder sprinkled in its plate. I nodded mechanically, entirely unsure of what my gesture might signify.

"I hope you know what you're doing, Pechorin" - I managed to say in a voice I no longer recognised - "And I hope also, should you live, that you are able to live with yourself".

I turned and made my way towards Martynov.

'I must confess I could barely look Martynov in the eye, but felt it nonetheless my duty to make one last attempt to avert the unfolding catastrophe.

"Are you so in thrall to your masters that you would kill - or be killed - in the presence of a child?" - I asked, still avoiding his gaze.

"I don't know what you're talking about, Stolypin" - Martynov replied - "And I would remind you that it is Pechorin, not me, who has authored this particular nonsense. He no doubt expected that I would refuse to fight in such circumstances; but I have had quite enough of his sly manipulations".

"Nonetheless" - I persisted - "If you are to shoot second, there are ways in which honour might be satisfied without one of you perishing".

"And if I am to shoot first?" - he said with just a trace of a smile - "Do you, as my second, advise me to place myself at the mercy of a fellow like Pechorin?"

I looked down at my boots, framed against the meticulous detail of dust and sand.

"Very well" - I said quietly - "But, in the event that you are to shoot second, will you at least consider my suggestion... Or would that not be enough for those who have sent you here?"

Martynov looked at me from under his dark brows with an expression of barely controlled fury.

"You have agreed to act for me" - he barked - "If you persist with these ridiculous accusations, I assure you, Stolypin, that you and I will fight if God grants me the capacity to do so".

'As I stood in mute confusion, searching desperately for a way out of the dead-end into which my too precipitate accusation had taken us, we were disturbed by the faint sound of approaching footsteps. We turned to behold the solemn face of Mikha, who bowed as he came to a halt before us. Martynov now seemed struck by the same helplessness that had overcome me just a moment before and could only stare at the boy in anticipation of some sudden emancipatory revelation.

"Pistol" – said Mikha at last.

I stared at the boy as if he had revealed to us the secrets of the universe, slow to realise that he was simply attending to his duties as second. Before I could speak, Martynov withdrew a short pistol from beneath his coat and handed it silently to the boy. Mikha peered down the barrel with the manner of expertise, before cocking and releasing the hammer. He returned the pistol to Martynov, his expression unchanged, bowed, and turned once more towards Pechorin.

'Pechorin began to move towards the middle of the little plateau, the silver inlay of his pistol glinting in the morning sun, Mikha following quietly at his side. Martynov and I set off to meet them without a word. As we approached, I was struck above all by the broad smile on Pechorin's face, which he directed towards Martynov as if he were greeting an old and dear friend he had not seen for many years. In response, Martynov gave no sign of the indignation or confusion he had once been unable to suppress; he had at last become accustomed to the vagaries of Pechorin's behaviour, which he now regarded, perhaps in some inward gymnastic of self-justification, as no more than wilful perversity.

"Gentlemen" – I said quickly, unconsciously determined to prevent either of them from speaking before I had performed all due formalities – "I wish to remind you that, having appeared this morning and thereby confirmed your willingness to fight, you have both satisfied your obligations in full. Will you agree to withdraw?"

My words had barely emerged into the peaceful morning air before Pechorin replied.

"If it be, 'tis not to come" – he said firmly, still smiling – "If it be not to come it will be now. If it be not now, yet it will come".

I turned hopelessly towards Martynov.

"You have had your answer" – he replied, anger coursing somewhere just beneath the surface of his still calm exterior.

"Very well" – I continued, now detached from the sound of my own voice.

I fumbled for a coin in my pocket but could not find one. Pechorin's hand appeared before me with a silver rouble in it, which I took without a word and turned towards Martynov.

"You have been the recipient of a challenge" – I somehow managed to say, barely able to comprehend my own words – "You will have the honour of calling to determine who will shoot first: heads or tails?"

"Heads" – said Martynov without a moment's hesitation.

I flipped the coin into the air and watched as it spun in a shimmering arc, throwing off tiny shards of reflected sunlight, before coming to rest in the dust. Pechorin leaned forward over the motionless coin. The face of the Tsar in half-profile peered crookedly back at him.

"Heads it is" – Pechorin whispered gently – "Lucky for you".

'I traced a line in the sand with my boot. I sought the gaze of Mikha for a moment before continuing and, not for the first time, was stunned by the quiet solemnity of his expression.

"Gentlemen" – I managed to say, my voice breaking at the foolish attempt I had made to speak loudly and decisively – "You will each withdraw six paces. Martynov will shoot first. Do you understand?"

Both men nodded in silent assent and turned away from one another, Martynov once more towards the door of the church, Pechorin towards the ancient city lying sleeping below. Mikha withdrew to one side as if compelled by Pechorin's silent will. I joined him. Pechorin turned once again to face Martynov, the rising sun at his back, his pistol clasped to the side of his right thigh. He undid the second button of his loose white shirt and pushed out his chest very slightly towards his opponent, turned his head momentarily towards the still figure of Mikha, and smiled.

'Martynov paused for a few seconds. I cannot say to this day whether he had to overcome one last struggle with conscience, or whether, like Pechorin, he had resigned himself to whatever fate might bring; I can say only that he gave no outward sign of disquiet. He slowly raised his pistol and pointed squarely at Pechorin's heart. His lips twitched as if he was about to speak, but no words came out. The barrel of Martynov's pistol then twitched as if in mimicry of his lips as it let out a sudden crack. I shuddered and shifted my gaze to the right, where Pechorin had fallen to his knees, the blood from a gaping wound between his left shoulder and breast-bone flowing steadily down his loose shirt. He leaned forward, the knuckles of his right hand still grasping his pistol as he steadied himself on the ground. I took a step towards him, but suddenly felt the thin grip of Mikha's hand on my forearm. I looked down into the calm, stern face of this veteran child and remained where I stood. When I looked once again in Pechorin's direction, I was astounded to see that he had half raised himself on one leg and was straining with both hands to stand erect, his blood now mingling with the dust and sand. Martynov watched in suspended horror as Pechorin slowly stood almost to full height, only his left shoulder stooped by the seemingly dead weight of his arm, which hung motionlessly against his side.

"Not bad, Martynov" – said Pechorin, as if at the card table, his soft voice belying the bloodied ravages of the left-hand side of his body – "A little more practice, and you'll be able to put fellows like me away without a second thought".

Martynov's frozen astonishment had now given way to unbridled fury, the blood rising in his face, his great jaw clenched as tightly as his fists.

"Not another word!" – bellowed Martynov – "I'd rather die than hear another word from your mouth. Shoot!"

"All in good time" – said Pechorin – "But I would like you to understand something before you die".

Martynov's fury turned to laughter, which rang out in great peals from his convulsed torso.

"Understand?" – he cried – "You want me to understand? If understanding could save me from death, I would still choose death. Shoot, damn you!"

Pechorin staggered slightly, his right arm still clutching the pistol by his side.

"I want you to understand" – Pechorin continued – "that I know that you are a hired assassin".

"Marvellous!" – exclaimed Martynov, his laughter wry and even warm – "You want me to understand what you know! How very decent of you! Very well. I understand that you know I am a hired assassin. Now shoot".

"And I want you to understand that I would not have killed you today, but for one thing".

"Oh" – said Martynov in a voice filled with bitter irony – "And what is that?"

Pechorin glanced towards Mikha, standing silent as the grave to his left.

"Look upon this child" – he said – "And contemplate the depths to which you have sunk".

Martynov refused to turn his head towards Mikha and gazed steadily into Pechorin's eyes. Pechorin staggered once more, steadying himself by shifting his weight onto his right leg as the blood seeped steadily down the left leg of his breeches. He looked briefly in my direction, with a faint smile more of sorrow than satisfaction, raised his pistol, and sank a bullet into the middle of Martynov's chest. I watched as Martynov's great frame collapsed and came to rest with a muffled thud in a heap in the dust.

'In my mind I had already taken a step towards him when I caught sight of Mikha flying out to my right towards Pechorin, who had once again sunk to his knees, his head resting on his bloodied chest. I turned and followed. Mikha wedged his thin figure behind Pechorin's back, pressing his little palm against the stained and weeping shirt. Pechorin raised his head and opened his eyes for a moment, before I helped Mikha lay him on his back, Mikha now supporting his head and shoulders. Pechorin's head rolled gently onto Mikha's neck as he lost consciousness. The boy struggled under the weight as the life drained from Pechorin's body, but managed to extricate himself in the same motion as he laid Pechorin's head upon the ground, still pressing on the wound with his little palm. I took off my shirt and began to tear it into strips, before binding them as tightly as I could over the wounded shoulder and down across his chest. The flow of blood began to ease and Mikha once more raised Pechorin's head, before administering tiny droplets of water from a calf-skin flask. After what seemed like an eternity, Pechorin opened his eyes and smiled.

"Don't speak" – I heard myself say – "You must save your energy".

"Come, my dear uncle" – said Pechorin – "Save my energy for what?"

The warmth of his smile was nothing less than miraculous, counterposed to the look of dread he must have seen on my face.

"Is that your voice I hear?" - he said, his own voice seeming to have travelled from somewhere beyond the horizon - "We should be grateful... There were moments when I thought we might not get the chance to say farewell".

"Farewell?" - I replied, straining my every nerve in the attempt to keep the dread from my countenance - "What nonsense... Would you leave a brother alone in this world".

Pechorin smiled once more, then reached out and took my hand in his.

"My time has come" - he said evenly - "I am ready to begin another life".

He closed his eyes and his chin dropped for one last time onto his chest. Mikha pressed Pechorin's wrist to his ear, then placed the palm of his hand over his mouth.

"*Inna lillahi wa inna ilayhi raji'un*" - he said gravely, looking up with burning eyes, still unsullied by tears - "He is dead".

We sat for a time in silence in the dim light of Kuragin's drawing-room. Had I been seated alongside Mungo, I might have placed my hand upon his own in a weak attempt to banish the ravages of the irrevocable past. Yet I remained in my place, silent and impotent in the face of his grief. Mungo raised his glass and drained the last of its contents, his gaze fixed on some imaginary point in space and time that was now entirely inaccessible to anyone but him.

'Did you bury him?' - I asked suddenly, for reasons I myself could not decipher.

Mungo at first appeared not to have heard these words, but at length released himself from the grip of whatever it was that had drawn him into that place between this world and another.

'We did' - he replied - 'We dragged Pechorin's body behind the church. I was astonished to find that two deep graves had already been dug, but the boy silenced me before I could speak with a quicksilver movement of his finger to his lips. We laid Pechorin in one of the graves. Before we began to shovel the dirt and sand on top of him, Mikha made some adjustment to Pechorin's mouth I could not quite discern and which I absently assumed might form some part of the scattered beliefs the boy had acquired over the course of his eleven or twelve years, his mind crammed with thoughts and events I could never hope to comprehend.

'When we had covered the body and levelled the ground as best we could, we returned to attend to the body of Martynov. We struggled with the great bulk, but eventually managed to deposit it in the second grave, before covering it over as we had done with Pechorin and once more levelling the ground. When we had completed our work, Mikha turned to me, his expression as still and solemn as it had been throughout.

"They will not find him" - he said - "Go".

I hesitated only for a moment, then rose to leave, impelled by some force in the boy's tone that I only later found the means to comprehend'.

'How do you mean?' - I asked, surprised by the sound of my own voice.

Mungo looked out at me once more through the gloom, oblivious to the first glimmer of the dawn light gathering around the edge of the curtained windows, his expression a mask of incomprehension and wonder.

'I wandered down the slope of Mtatsminda in a daze, shirtless beneath my summer jacket' – he continued – 'For some time, I could not remove from my mind the conviction that I must, above all else, ensure that the authorities learn nothing of what had occurred. I resolved to find Smertin and Kulebakov and secure from them promises that they would not divulge what they knew. Later, as I began to make inquiries as to their whereabouts, I realised, however, that my caution was in vain: neither Pechorin nor Martynov had survived to answer for their actions. There was little to conceal and no reason for doing so. I returned to my quarters, washed off the dust of the morning, and lay down to sleep.

'The sun had almost completed its arc towards the western horizon when I at last regained consciousness. I was suddenly struck by the realisation that I had left a child alone on Mtatsminda with only two graves for company. I dressed quickly and asked the cook if Mikha had returned. She told me she had not seen him since the day before and I had no reason to disbelieve her. I gulped down some tea, pulled on a jacket, and set off once more for St David's church.

'The slopes of Mtatsminda were barely recognisable from earlier that morning as I hurried alone towards the towering horizon. In the thin alleyways between the last of the poor houses which crowded into the lower slopes, children played merrily among the cattle, the sun throwing their long shadows back down towards the city. I froze momentarily under the gaze of a boy who could have been no older than Mikha, before he released me and turned once again to the babbling attentions of the younger boys who milled around him, pulling at his shirt and begging to be lifted up onto his shoulders.

'The church was in shadow when I crested the hill onto the plateau, protected from the rear by the Eocene majesty of the rock face. I hesitated for a moment, as I had done that same morning before leaving, then set off at a run past the shaded front door of the church towards the graves I now imagined I must have conjured in a dream. As I turned beyond the back wall, my mind seized only by a desperate fear that the signs of our earlier activity might remain visible, I came to an abrupt halt. The fear that had gripped my fevered consciousness now gave way to a blank, almost mystical astonishment. The ground where Martynov was buried remained undisturbed, conceding no possible clue to the eye of an observer who did not already know what lay beneath the soil. Alongside it, however, lay only a shallow pit, its soil heaped chaotically at its rear, the shovel that had dug it planted triumphantly upright. The grave I had myself covered over that very same morning was empty. Pechorin had vanished'.

The thin light of the morning now crept in around the edges of every window. I could see once again the expression on Mungo's face, almost beatific in its awe, shining through the ravages of age and dissolution the unforgiving morning light no longer troubled to conceal.

I smiled and turned away.

EPILOGUE

A HERD OF OXEN climbed majestically up the hillsides of the Dvalsky Pass. To the rear, the fortress of Gergera towered above the pass, naked as the mountainsides; ahead, there was a little bridge, shaped like a pan flute, which stretched over a fast-moving stream. A cart piled high with hay moved slowly across the bridge, before stopping at a turnpike on the far bank.

'Where have you come from?' - asked an ancient Armenian, his features as brown and gnarled as a walnut.

'From Tiflis' - came the reply.

'And where are you going?'

The man who had replied turned to the boy at his side and smiled.

'Who knows, eh?' - he asked softly - 'Who knows?'

The old Armenian at first made no reply, his gaze fixed upon the pair of fine chestnut mares which drew the cart. Who but a very rich man - or a fool - he thought to himself, would harness such fine horses to a hay-cart?

'And what are you carrying?' - asked the old man.

'Hay' - the driver of the cart replied - 'And some books'.

The old man looked at the boy sitting alongside, resplendent in his long *kaftan* and blue *kalpak*, his arms as thin as reeds, his skin several tones darker than that of his master. The boy tossed a coin towards the old man, who caught it deftly as it spun through the air. The pale-skinned man by his side then pulled gently on the reins and the cart trundled off towards the south. The old man's gaze followed it for a few minutes, before it disappeared at last below the far horizon.